TOM CLANCY'S NET FORCE®

*Don't miss any of these exciting adventures
starring the teens of Net Force . . .*

VIRTUAL VANDALS

The Net Force Explorers go head-to-head with a group of
teenage pranksters on-line—and find out firsthand that virtual bullets can kill you!

THE DEADLIEST GAME

The virtual Dominion of Sarxos is the most popular war
game on the Net. But someone is taking the game too seriously . . .

ONE IS THE LONELIEST NUMBER

The Net Force Explorers have exiled Roddy—who sabo-
taged one program too many. But Roddy's created a new
"playroom" to blow them away . . .

THE ULTIMATE ESCAPE

Net Force Explorer pilot Julio Cortez and his family are
being held hostage. And if the proper authorities refuse to
help, it'll be Net Force Explorers to the rescue!

THE GREAT RACE

A virtual space race against teams from other countries will
be a blast for the Net Force Explorers. But someone will go
to any extreme to sabotage the race—even murder . . .

END GAME

An exclusive resort is suffering Net thefts, and Net Force
Explorer Megan O'Malley is ready to take the thief
down. But the criminal has a plan to put her out of com-
mission—*permanently* . . .

(continued . . .)

CYBERSPY

A "wearable computer" permits a mysterious hacker access to a person's most private thoughts. It's up to Net Force Explorer David Gray to convince his friends of the danger—before secrets are revealed to unknown spies . . .

SHADOW OF HONOR

Was Net Force Explorer Andy Moore's deceased father a South African war hero or the perpetrator of a massacre? Andy's search for the truth puts every one of his fellow students at risk . . .

PRIVATE LIVES

The Net Force Explorers must delve into the secrets of their commander's life—to prove him innocent of murder . . .

SAFE HOUSE

To save a prominent scientist and his son, the Net Force Explorers embark on a terrifying virtual hunt for their enemies—before it's too late . . .

GAMEPREY

A gamer's convention turns deadly when virtual reality monsters escape their confines—and start tracking down the Net Force Explorers!

DUEL IDENTITY

A member of a fencing group lures the Net Force Explorers to his historical simulation site—where his dream of ruling a virtual nation is about to come true, but only at the cost of their lives . . .

TOM CLANCY'S NET FORCE®

DEATHWORLD

CREATED BY
Tom Clancy and **Steve Pieczenik**

Written by
Diane Duane

BERKLEY JAM BOOKS, NEW YORK

This is a work of fiction. Names, characters, places, and incidents are either the product of the author's imagination or are used fictitiously, and any resemblance to actual persons, living or dead, business establishments, events, or locales is entirely coincidental.

TOM CLANCY'S NET FORCE: DEATHWORLD

A Berkley Book / published by arrangement with
Netco Partners

PRINTING HISTORY
Berkley Jam edition / November 2000

The Penguin Putnam Inc. World Wide Web site address is
http://www.penguinputnam.com

ISBN: 0-425-17738-6

BERKLEY JAM BOOKS®
Berkley Jam Books are published by The Berkley Publishing Group,
a division of Penguin Putnam Inc.,
375 Hudson Street, New York, New York 10014.
BERKLEY JAM and its logo
are trademarks belonging to Penguin Putnam Inc.

PRINTED IN THE UNITED STATES OF AMERICA

10 9 8 7 6 5 4 3 2

We'd like to thank the following people, without whom this book would have not been possible: Martin H. Greenberg, Larry Segriff, Denise Little, and John Helfers at Tekno Books; Mitchell Rubenstein and Laurie Silvers at Hollywood.com; Tom Colgan of Penguin Putnam Inc.; Robert Youdelman, Esquire; and Tom Mallon, Esquire; and Robert Gottlieb of the William Morris Agency, agent and friend. We much appreciated the help.

I

Nick stood in front of the gateway, and looked up and up at the pillars of it, there in the dark and the silence.

The polished basalt pillars were very tall. There was no seeing the top of them. They seemed to stretch forever up into the darkness. But in the empty black air between them, words hung burning in red. They read:

ABANDON HOPE ALL YE WHO ENTER HERE™

Nick stood there in the silence for a few more moments, and then walked through the gates.

The first thing to assault him was the music, but then that was what he had come for, what had brought him here in the first place. Nick was finding it difficult to believe that there had ever been a time when he hadn't known about that particular bass beat, pounding and insistent. It was such a contrast to the voice singing above it, starting out so calm and scaling over the course of almost every song into a completely abandoned shriek of cheerful rage. That was what had gotten Nick's attention the first time he'd seen a Joey Bane virteo: the *cheerfulness*. This man was angry, and enjoyed it, and didn't care who knew. The song that met you at the gateway was that first one he'd heard, the most famous of Bane's songs, and the one Nick liked the best: "Too Jagged Off to Care."

Nick walked in through the darkness, and the music cycled up so that you could hardly hear the moans and wailing through or under it. The noise wasn't so bad up here, anyway. This was the Top Floor, a beginners' level, which, though it looked kind of impressive at first, was actually too dull and unshocking for any but the most hopeless types—mostly people who Nick thought must not get out a lot, or do anything much but answer their virtmail, too scared to venture out any further into virtuality. Nick had been just a little freaked by the concerted noise of human pain, the first time he had come in—but then the persistent welcoming beat of the Bane music had got him past that, and then after about fifteen or twenty minutes the landscape hadn't bothered Nick at all.

It was a wasteland. Gray lowering sky, stunted dead trees, shattered boulders, the temperature warm enough to be stifling, no wind. It was desolate, a place that looked the way he felt at the moment, and with the background noise, the howling and wailing, it sounded the way he felt, too. Nick shuffled along through the sterile gray dust, his hands stuffed down in the pockets of his coverall, and made a depressed face. He could just hear what his mother would be saying now, if she could see him: "Do you have to slump like that? Stand up straight. Look at you, you'd think you had nothing to live for—though, then again, with that last report from school—"

Nick frowned. He'd tried keeping his hands out of his pockets, as an experiment, for nearly a week. It didn't divert her from her usual themes in the slightest. School was her favorite subject right now. He was absolutely sick of hearing her go on and on about it. *As if there aren't lots of terrific things to do besides college,* Nick thought.

And I'm passing everything, even if I'm not acing it. But his mom wouldn't listen to anything of the kind, and as for his dad, he didn't seem to care. That by itself should have been a positive thing. "Let the boy alone, Miriam," he would mutter as he headed for the back of the house and the implant suite. "He has enough problems." And Nick certainly did. But whatever his father was interested in hearing, Nick's problems weren't it. Nick had started to wonder what he would have to do to cause a little interest.

Then he had found Deathworld.

Not that the people who used the virtual domain called it that, though, among themselves. "The Circles" was one of their private names for it, or "Bane's Place" or "The Bottom Floors"—though none of the people Nick had met here so far had ever *seen* the bottom floors, reputed to be truly terrifying regions of torment and fear, and desperately cool. Nick was eager to find out whether these rumors were true or just hype. You had to expect a certain amount of hype in conjunction with a place like this. After all, it was run by the biggest name in "shadow jazz," a man who had made his first million by the time he was only four years older than Nick. Nick sighed. *Now, there's a depressing thought. . . . I wonder what Dad would think of that if I reminded him?*

Then again, probably it would be smarter not to. Neither Nick, in his wildest dreams, or his dad was going to be a millionaire any time soon. That was something of a sore point with his dad. His dad's job at the vid studio wasn't terribly secure at the moment—there had just been another round of cutbacks, and everybody was nervous. Nick supposed he should feel sorry for his dad, but his dad hadn't done a whole lot of feeling sorry for Nick's troubles lately. Nick shrugged. Let his dad deal with it.

The old dry leafless tree that marked the near shore of the river was visible across the plain, and Nick made for it, kicking up the dust. If his dad was twitching over things at the moment, well, that was fine with Nick. When his dad had found out about Nick starting to spend time in Deathworld, when the bill for the household Net account came in last month, there had been trouble . . . more trouble than it merited, Nick had thought.

"I don't like you giving my hard-earned money to that man," his father had said while eating his dinner, as Nick passed through the kitchen. "The guy's a wacko. The domain is full of unwholesome stuff. I saw something about it on the news a few days ago. And Joey Bane has enough money already without dumping ours on the pile, too. You just cut it out."

Nick had muttered something noncommittal and escaped without making any statements about what he was going to do one way or another. But it was getting time for the new month's bill to come in, and his father would see the breakdown of the household's Net charges, and know where Nick had been.

Gonna be noise. . . .

Yet Nick was peculiarly satisfied at the prospect. Whatever ruckus his dad kicked up, in Nick's personal life there was too much advantage to be derived from being here, and he wasn't going to give it up. Nick was not an outstanding student, not great at sports, no huge success with the girls, but he was *in* here, and few enough kids at school or outside of it had been able to get in. There was a waiting list, and you could sit on it for weeks or months without result.

No one was sure what made the Bane computers pick you as one of the lucky ones to be let in. The assumption at school was that there was some kind of obscure "coolness" rating that no one understood. But being able to get access to the Circles at all, with a chance to see the dangerous stuff that was rumored to be down in those lowest levels, carried its own cachet. There were rumors about what had happened to people who had ventured down into those levels thinking they were tough enough . . . and discovering differently. There had been stories of some hos-

pitalizations . . . and everyone had heard about the suicides.

They didn't worry Nick. And as he thought about his
father's reaction to his access to Deathworld, they worried
him even less. His dad's annoyance pleased him somehow. *If Mom and I are supposed to make your life all
nice and smooth for you,* he thought, *well, it's not gonna
be that way. You haven't exactly made it that way for us.
Mom can do what she wants—but for me, I'm going to
enjoy myself a little. If it bothers you . . . tough. When I
do what you want, it doesn't make any difference. Let's
just see how it goes when I don't snap to attention every
time you open your mouth. Right!*

And Nick grinned. It felt good to even have a chance
to think such things, away from the little house where
everything was always the same, and nothing ever seemed
to change except for the worse, no matter what he did to
try to make things better.

The Tree was closer, and Nick thought he could hear
the cold sound of water flowing. Away across the dusty
plain, he could see various people moving around—some
of them in modern clothing, and real, or possibly so, many
more of them in clothes from other times and places, decades old, centuries or millennia old, wandering around
and lamenting their fates in a hundred languages and (as
the song said) "a hundred shades of scream." It was noisy,
but once you got past that, you noticed something. The
screams tended to repeat themselves after a while, up here.
Eventually you could start to work out, just by the sound,
without trying to have any conversations, which of these
figures were genuine people—other virtual visitors to
Deathworld, the "Guest Dead" who stopped in, as Nick
did, to make some noise of their own where it was safe
to do so, and to remind themselves how pointless life was.
Not that Nick was all that interested in the Guest Dead
up at this level, especially since he didn't need them anymore. There was much more exciting business farther
down, everybody said . . . people far more dangerous, more

interesting . . . and more isolated from the real world. Nick was so tired of the real world.

After he had beaten the first level, the screams and shrieks that went up on the smoky air from the tortured souls all around him stopped making much difference to Nick. Indeed, you got used to them after a while, and needed something a little more immediate, something newer and scarier, to shake you up. Though you couldn't just go and get it, for the system in Deathworld wouldn't let you down into the deeper circles until you had spent a certain amount of time in the upper ones, talking to the people you met there. When you met enough real people, and pooled with them what information you had about the level you were working on at the moment, your reward was to be allowed to progress deeper into the site, to the lower circles, where the virtual experiences got more vivid, more out-of-control.

Bane's voice sang through the darkness:

"The world gets more real,
and things just get worse:
run as fast as you like,
you can't outrun the hearse. . . ."

Nick kicked the dust up, approaching the Tree, and idly eyed the distant forms. In the beginning he had been surprised by the way the other people he saw had always seemed to be at a distance, no matter how long he walked toward them. Then he had discovered that this distancing was part of the domain's "idiom," and that it took an act of will to overcome it, not just the act of walking in a given direction. You had to go out of your way to actually talk to someone, had to strain against the fabric of this dark universe to break through. With some people you could strain against it all day and never get anywhere—they wouldn't hear you or see you. They stayed shut up in their own private little worlds. It was one of the games

Bane's Place played with you, either personally or at one remove, through the domain itself. For if the Circles had a motto other than the one hanging back there between the gates, it was "People stink. Life stinks. Everything stinks. Even this."

The music doesn't stink, though, Nick thought as he got closer to the Tree, noticing for the first time it not only had no leaves, but also no bark. Something seemed to have bitten it off. The music was one of the best things about this place, and Nick had no time for people who suggested it was all variations on the theme of "You're Going to Die Anyway, So You Might as Well Get Really Mad First."

There's a lot more to it than that. . . . Nick would know, for he had all the officially released song collections, and even a few of the "pirate" segments supposedly extracted from the depths of this very domain. Beyond getting far enough down to see if those pirate "lifts" were genuine, Nick's other great dream was to see one of the live Bane concerts some day. It wouldn't happen any time soon, for those concerts were much too expensive, the price of the tickets having to cover the (nowadays) extortionate price of actually taking a physical concert on the road. It was something few rock stars bothered to do anymore, in a time when the audience's experience could be arranged and controlled much more completely in a Net-based venue than anywhere in the real world. But Joey Bane did it, saying, "I'm just old-fashioned that way."

There was a hope that Nick might be able to afford one of the virtual concerts, this year or early next. *Assuming Dad doesn't blow his top when he sees the next Net access bill and ground me.* But Nick had been squirreling away his allowance for a long time now, even diverting what should have been lunch money at school, happy to go hungry when he considered the alternative. Soon he would have enough to see The Man Himself in concert, hear in a live performance that great legendary scream of rage and despair at the end of "Lady Macbeth," see for himself the onstage carnage as Bane destroyed yet another ten-thousand-dollar electric lute and the instruments of every-body else in his band at the end of "Cut the Strings." That would be worth any amount of grief from his dad and mom. *Just a couple of hours of freedom,* Nick thought. *In the company of someone who knows what the world's really like, who doesn't pull his punches, who tells the truth about how awful everything is. . . .* The dream had kept him going for a long while.

It wasn't so bad to hear that everything stank, after all. As long as you knew that there were lots of people who agreed with you that, painful though it might be, the truth was best. *Someday, when I move out, when I'm on my own, I'll spend as much time in Bane's Place as I want . . . and in other places, places on the edge, the scary stuff, the stuff my folks and all the deluded others don't want me to know about. They can wrap themselves up in their nicey-nice world if they like and pretend not to notice how awful things are. I'm going out where things are real. I'm strong enough to take it. . . .*

Nick was humming the first verse of "Nicey-Nice" as he came up to the Tree, and the air around him was be-ginning to mimic him with the backbeat of the song, and he could see the cold smoke coming up from the river, when he saw something that hadn't been there the last time he came. A rock. And sitting on the rock was a figure wearing the most tightly tailored black slicktite possible, with what at first glimpse looked like a big black egg cradled in his lap. As Nick got closer, he saw it better, and caught his breath; for even in this dreary light the "egg" shone and glinted as if it lay under an invisible spotlight. It was a smooth, rounded shape, not really black but a brown so dark as to be mistaken for black, with a short neck—an electric lute with an ebony body, all inlaid with a spidery platinum webwork—that most famous of instruments in dark jazz, Camiun. There were people who claimed that Camiun must be a little bit alive, or else haunted, since no mere man could make an instrument sound like that—like a soul in torment, or one just escaped from it. Joey Bane had said that on the day he discovered that the world was completely and irreversibly wicked, he would cut Camiun's strings, five minutes before he killed himself. . . .

He's only virtual, Nick thought, stopping by the stone. But the slender, muscular, dark-clad figure gazing down into the icy gray water flowing by now shook his longish hair back and glanced up at Nick sidewise . . . and Nick gulped. He had talked to people here who'd claimed to have met this particular apparition. Half the time he'd figured they'd been making it up. But here *he* was, or rather one of the virtual representations of him: Joey Bane himself—the singer in his guise as Dark Poet from his second song collection, *Discourse with Spirits,* looking out across the unrelieved darkness of the landscape behind him with an expression both morose and amused. The lute in his lap hummed softly to itself, because its master's fingers were presently motionless on the strings.

"Hey, Joey," Nick said.

That ironic smile curved itself up a little harder. *Hard* was the best word to describe it; it sat oddly on what would otherwise have been a young and innocent face.

"Nick," Joey said. "How goes the world?"

The domain's computer knew who Nick was, of course . . . but for a moment all he could do was shake his head. There were few enough places like this in the Net. Mostly big celebrities didn't bother going to the trouble to personalize their domains—there was usually just an introduction when you came in. In this case, whoever designed the domain had gone to some trouble to customize the output for the users. That was probably one of the reasons it was so popular. You got the chance to really talk to the star, or at least to the Net-encoded version of his personality.

"Badly. As usual," Nick said. That was the customary response, the answer that the audiences shouted back to The Man Himself at his concerts, live or visual, when he asked the question. The virtual Joey Bane smiled a little more grimly and put his hand over Camiun's strings to still the lute. It argued the point a little, fizzing and muttering under his touch.

"Yeah, yeah, everybody wants it their way," Joey growled at the lute, and then looked up again. "You just on your way in?" Bane's simulacrum said. "Can't see you hanging around this level after you've solved it. Unless it's the music." He looked bored at this possibility.

"No," Nick said, "I'm ready for something new."

"Bet you are," Bane said. "Been stuck on three for a couple of weeks now. Hit your level?"

It was, among Banies, a rude question, suggesting you were incapable of taking the hard stuff, the real world, the truth . . . or that you were just dim. Had someone Nick's age said something like this to him, the circumstances might have become violent. But this was Joey Bane, and that ironic look was dwelling on Nick, watching to see how he reacted.

"Don't know yet," Nick said, in a sudden burst of humility.

Bane looked at him darkly for a moment, and then laughed. "Nothing wrong with not knowing," he said. "You look pretty down, though."

"Aaah . . ." The implant had to be feeding the Bane-domain computer his EEG and other information that would have betrayed that fact. But the thin, hard face was also kindly, in a strange way, and Nick said, after a moment, "It's just my folks."

"Aha," Joey Bane said. He stroked a dark, dissonant spatter of notes out of Camiun. "The eternal problem. Can't choose 'em, can't get rid of 'em, can't do 'em without messing up the rug." He snickered softly. "We've still got a fair bunch of 'em down here, though. Fifth and sixth floor down, mostly."

" 'Still'? Why aren't all of them here permanently?"

"Oh, all of them spend a *little* time here," Bane said. "Mostly the part of their lives called 'your childhood.' "

Nick shot the virtstar a look.

Bane raised his eyebrows. "Anyway, the ones who stay," Bane said, "the really hard cases, are mostly down on six. With the other violent types. A few manage to get farther down . . . you ever get that far, you'll see." He shook his head, smiled again, touched Camiun's strings, and played a little minor-key imitation of an ambulance siren. "Gets tough down there," Bane said. "Don't know if you're really interested in going down that deep anyway, a nice kid like you. . . ."

"Won't be any time soon for me," Nick said, "at the rate I'm going." He thought he might as well tell the truth, even though it was embarrassing.

Bane looked at him. "Huh," he said. "Well, guess what, you've lucked into today's special offer. Every day we pick a few people for an upgrade. So come on down!"

To Nick's absolute astonishment, the earth started to rumble. Joey Bane got up, holding Camiun by the neck, and laid it over his shoulder, turning his back on the cold gray river. "You want to stand back, now," Bane said, stepping away from the rock. "You fall down the hole and land on your head, we won't be responsible. . . ."

The earth shuddered harder, and from the air all around them came an upscaling moan that turned into a screech, as if the ground itself was in torment. It split open before them, raggedly, with a terrible sound of ripping stone, and the chasm went stitching and stretching itself away for what looked like half a mile to either side before it stopped, and the rumbling settled back into silence. A fearsome red glow came boiling up out of it, as if light could be made liquid: a seething light, full of screams and howls of desperation and anguish.

"Hey, *spaz,*" Nick said softly, in complete admiration.

Bane stood there tapping his foot for a moment, then shook his head. "And am I supposed to *climb* down there?" he said to the air in extreme annoyance. "Hey! *Tech!!*"

An escalator appeared in front of them, leading down into the Pit.

"You can't get good help anymore," Bane muttered, heading for the escalator, "I'm telling you. Stinking road-ies, I should never have let them unionize. Come on."

The two of them got onto the escalator and started trun-dling down into the sulfur-smelling depths, past the thick layer of stone that made up the "floor" of the first level. Nick was glad to see it drop away behind him, for it really was rather boring, full of nothing but "screamers" and clueless Guest Dead wandering around trying to figure out what made this place so cool. This way of leaving the level was easier and less trouble than finding the rope ladder that was the usual way down onto the next level, the Second Floor.

They passed the last of the first rock floor, now a ceil-ing, and came down past that second level. The view was better from this clear space in the middle of everything than it would be on that level itself, for the weather in there was really foul. Right across that cratery, mud-colored landscape a terrible hurricane of a wind was end-lessly screaming, full of dirt and garbage, blowing wildly assorted junk past you all the time—drink cans and snack wrappers, torn, dirty paper and old shopping bags and small showers of gravel and stones, all borne along with a grimy near-horizontal rain. Various people were blown along there, too, or what remained of them. Until you saw their expressions, it was hard to tell whether they were chasing each other or actually fastened to each other somehow, so that where one went the other had to go, too. Their faces, though, when you caught a glimpse of them through the murk, were furious. They snatched and grasped at the person to whom they were bound, tearing flesh as they rolled and tumbled along around the great second-level circle, blown irresistibly by that wind.

"Ah, love," Bane said, "ain't it grand. . . ." He watched one particularly entangled couple go blowing by, clutch-ing and scratching at each other, shrieking in pain and rage. "You've been through here, of course. . . ."

"Didn't think much of it," Nick said, somewhat be-mused for the moment by the sight of someone else being blown by on that wind—a thin, middle-aged, hostile-looking woman, pedaling a bicycle. A faint yapping was coming from the bike's basket, but it was drowned by the howl of the wind almost instantly as the woman was swept away out of sight. Where had he seen that image before?

"Ah, you've never been in love, then," Joey Bane said. "Excuse me. Lust. Well, give it a few years. You'll be grabbing at some obscure object of desire and trying to pull all the best chunks out of it whether it wants you to or not, just like everybody else. And it'll stink. But then, doesn't everything?"

"Yeah," Nick said with some pleasure, though he tried to sound casual about it, as they dropped past the floor of that level and toward the next one. It was not a sentiment he would have gotten very far with at home. That was one of the things that made Deathworld such a trip.

"Intelligent young guy," said Joey Bane. "You'll go far. Well, down a few, anyway." And Nick had to grin. He knew this was all automatic, he wasn't as stupid as some of the people who insisted that all these virtreps of Bane were actually the man himself, "slumming" in his Net domain . . . though there were rumors that sometimes, down in the deepest levels, you might run across one that actually was Joey Bane, rewarding some unusually per-sistent or talented Banie with a personal audience. For his own part, while he was still up in these levels, Nick knew perfectly well that the master site computer had been re-cording his preferences since he started coming here—that it knew where he'd been and whom he'd talked to and what he'd said, and was tailoring his experience sec-ond by second to fit his needs and keep him coming back. It was probably reading Nick's body information through the implant chair right now, brainwaves and pulse and blood pressure and whatever, to make sure the things happening around him went in ways that he would like, that would make him keep coming back. But that was no big deal. Marketing computers all over the Net did that. And at the same time, it was fun. It was neat to talk to something that Bane himself had helped program to sound and react exactly the way he would.: . . .

They slid on past the level of the winds and the storm-borne couples. "Idiotic behavior, really," Joey was saying as he turned away from the view, "claiming they can't control themselves, that love made them do it. Poor excuse. So now they *really* can't control themselves." He gave Nick a narrow-eyed look that might have had a wink associated with it, but the light changed again as they plunged down past the next level of floor/ceiling and down into Floor Three, and Nick couldn't be sure what he had seen. "You wouldn't ever try a weak excuse like that, though. . . ."

"Uh, no," Nick said.

"Yeah, right," Joey Bane said, and didn't quite snicker. "Third floor, gluttony, excess, and general over-indulgence . . ."

If the weather had seemed bad on the level above, it was worse down here. Dirty sleet and freezing rain fell endlessly from blackness, and people both too fat and too thin ran along under it as if being scourged by whips, while behind them came a monstrous black-pelted shape, howling and snarling and grabbing them up in its jaws . . . grabbing them up and chewing on them like newly caught rats, times three. It had three sets of jaws, three heads—huge, ugly ones like those of pit bulls—and six burning eyes. At least Nick *thought* he counted six. This was an image he had been careful to keep his distance from, the couple times he'd been down here. If the Dog caught you, it could strip you of half your "time" credits in the domain and make you do the last couple of levels over again, which would get real boring real fast. Besides, it had been eating people when he had been here last, and the view had not been pretty. Nick's feeling at the time was that this was an aspect of "the truth" that it was going to take him a while to get used to.

The monster bounded to the edge of the floor of that circle and began barking and slavering furiously at the two of them as they passed. "Bad dog," Joey Bane yelled at it, "*bad* dog! Shut your mouths, it's *me!* The neighbors are gonna start complaining again!"

The monster kept right on barking as they passed. "Obedience school for *that* one was a waste of time," Joey muttered as the escalator took them by. "I tell you, this is the last time I let my sister pass off the runt of the litter on me. The poor guy's *damaged.* And he never gets enough to eat, either. He bolts his food and then he can't hold it down, and he . . . Oh, *look* at that." Bane turned his head and yelled over the railing of the escalator, "*Tech!* You better get somebody over here to clean that up! If he slips in that and hurts himself, the vet bills are coming out of your pay—"

Nick wasn't looking, and was trying not to look like he wasn't looking, as the hound went bounding off after another trio of running, shrieking prey. "The stomach acid eats the flooring," Joey Bane said. "Not the dog's fault, it's his diet. Fad dieters and runaway gourmets, what do you expect? They're so hung up on eating, or not eating, that they don't care what it does to them, or how many millions of people they starve in the process of feeding just a few a ton more than they need, or making special foods for themselves with no calories to speak of. . . ."

Nick gulped. He was hanging on to his control as best he could, trying to stay cool, to look cool, like none of this bothered him. *It may take me a while,* he thought, *I don't care how much time I'm going to have to spend in here, but I'm going to learn to cope with it whatever I do. I am not going to look stupid in front of—*

"Fourth floor down," Joey Bane said, looking over the rail of the escalator. "The Haves and the Throwaways. All gamblers, really, except some of them do it with stocks and bonds and margins and others do it at the gaming

tables or in factories where they burn up resources that
can't ever be replaced. . . ." He made a gentle *tsk, tsk*
noise as the two of them passed on by and downward.
"This is an awfully underrated area. Hardly anyone spends
more than the minimum time watching this bunch. It must
be the suits."

Or the screams, Nick thought, or these were truly ap-
palling. They came out of thick billowing darkness, and
there were terrible crashing and crushing noises coming
out of it as well, like a constant multicar accident being
continually enacted in the gloom. Nick swallowed as another crash produced a chorus of screams. They did not
sound like the kind of thing you would hear in a made-
for-Net drama. They sounded *real.*

"Accountants," Joey Bane said idly as they went past
one more thick rock floor/ceiling. "Not so quiet and colorless, are they? This is nothing, though. Wait till you see
what happens to the lawyers. Oh, not *all* of them, by any
means. Many of them are very nice people, but the ones
we get down here— Ah, here we are. Five . . ."

The music had been scaling up around them all the
while. Now, as they came out on the floor of the fifth
level, it crashed into the savage main chorus of "You Said
You Weren't Gonna Wait Up," and just as Nick was about
to start singing the next verse, the music started to fade
away into silence. This was not one of those dark circles,
and Nick swallowed when he saw what was there.

Huge cliffs reared up in the distance on all sides, and
beneath them strode and strutted gigantic parent-figures
dressed absurdly in clothes dating to before the turn of
the last century. Bizarre floppy sweats and backward hats,
and even stranger, the non-"smart" jeans of the previous
few decades, with T-shirts that hadn't yet learned the art
of molding themselves to the wearer's body. They stalked
around the dark rocky circle holding huge weapons in
their hands—though they hadn't started out as weapons,
actually, but as hammers and ax handles, kitchen knives
and rolled-up newspapers. Their eyes glowed with a ter-

rible light, and it wasn't until one or another of them had passed you that you saw the demons' wings, sinewed and fingered like those of bats, stunted and clawed. Among these awful figures, reaching no higher than their knees and running in all possible directions to get away from them, were adult figures in modern clothes, sliktites and leotites and new chitons, all terrified, all trying to get away . . . but they couldn't. There was nowhere for them to run, no way out, no way to climb the slick cliffs that bounded the circle here. The giant parent-demons pursued the helpless adults and attacked them with the household implements they carried. Nick wanted to look away, but an awful fascination kept him watching. The punishment was deadly and endless. Broken heads resealed themselves, packing the brains tracelessly back in: broken bones reknit themselves, and bruises spread just long enough to go black, then paled back out of lividity to normal flesh again as the demons with the clubs and ax handles chased after the abusing parents and gave them back what they had given their own children.

Next to Nick, Joey Bane was smiling slightly and singing what the lyric of the next verse would have been if the "outer" music had still been playing: "She hit it right on when she said it: 'They only hit you till you cry. . . .' " And the tormented ones were crying as they fled, yelling and howling as loudly as they could, but the demon-parents were all deaf, and couldn't hear them, and just kept hitting. Around and around they went, the demons beating their victims while intoning phrases like "This hurts me more than it hurts you" and "You'll thank me for this some day. . . ."

Nick had heard that one often enough lately, about college. Though no one had hit him while saying it, he had been bruised enough by the words, by Mother's absolute certainty that Nick would someday actually thank her for making him so miserable. *Does she even listen to herself say these things?* he wondered furiously, but she was suffering from the same syndrome as the demons here were. She didn't hear him. . . .

"Nasty neighborhood," Joey Bane said after a moment, lounging against a handy rock. "But these people should have known better. They started smacking their kids around to keep them in line . . . forgetting how they'd been smacked for the same reasons when they were kids, and it hadn't worked then, and it wasn't going to work now. . . ." His eyes blazed. "Or screaming at their kids day after day, telling them how stupid they are . . . until the kids finally begin to believe it. There are worse things than that, but not many. . . ."

Nick swallowed. "Do you think," he said slowly, "that . . . somewhere . . . this really happens to people like that?"

Joey Bane threw him a look. "I don't know about somewhere," he said. "But it sure happens *here* . . . and that's enough for me." He raised his eyebrows. "You?"

Nick swallowed. "Yeah," he said softly.

"Right," Joey said. "So listen . . . I've got places to be." Over his shoulder Camiun muttered a few notes under its breath. "Have fun while you're here . . . and take a good look around before you leave, so you can work out how to get down here on your own. The usual clues are here and there. Don't forget, it's not just child abusers who're down here. We've got all kinds of violence on this level."

He started off across the circle. Suddenly, in the direction Bane was heading, Nick could see something that hadn't been there before. Where there had only been tall cliffs, now he saw the towered and crenellated outlines of the ramparts and seven gateways of the Keep of the Dark Artificer. Nick was suddenly afire with excitement again. They said that once you got in there, you could hear music that had never been heard in concert . . . and with the music, said the rumors, went images of fury and violence and despair that were too wild and scary for anything of them ever to have been shown elsewhere in public. *Gotta see that!*

Nick started after Joey Bane, already just imagining what the other kids in school would say when they heard that not only was he a regular in Bane's Place, but that he'd gotten through the gates of the Keep and taken the Oath never to reveal what he had seen there. *This is gonna be spaz beyond belief....*

But Joey stopped and half-turned. "And where do you think *you're* going?"

"With you!"

"Not today, pally," Bane said.

"But you said it was an upgrade—"

"One-time," Joey Bane's virtual self said. "And did I say sixth floor? Didn't say a word about six. Two levels, that's what you get today."

Nick glared at him.

"What, you're complaining?" Bane said, and chuckled. "What a little ingrate. You ought to be careful... this kind of thing can go on your permanent record."

The good-natured mockery was somehow disarming. Nick's anger began to seep away. "Please," he said. "I just want to see inside the Keep...."

"What, for free? Half the Banies on the planet want in there," Bane said. "What makes you so special that you get it without working for it? Nobody gets in there until they solve all the higher levels and earn the points. You know the drill."

Nick frowned. "This whole thing has just been a come-on, hasn't it?" he said.

"Hey, all of life is marketing these days," Bane said. "Look... I'm in a good mood. You just spend the rest of the session walking around, getting to know some of these people. If *people* is the word we're looking for."

Nick looked behind him to where the vanished escalator had been. "But how am I supposed to get out? I haven't solved Four yet, I don't know where the entrance to this level is."

"Oh, well," Joey Bane said, "I guess that's fair. Look, you see those two over there—" He pointed off to one side, by the base of one of the huge cliffs, where a man with a lion's head and a woman with a tiger's were tearing at each other with terrible claws. "They might tell you the way out if you can get them to stop fighting for a moment." Bane looked at them and shook his head. "Songwriters," he said softly. "You can get too hung up on whose name comes first in the credits. . . ."

Nick looked at them dubiously. "Okay," he said. "Thanks."

"Polite," Joey said. "That's what I like to hear. Guess I don't have to cut the strings just yet." He turned away again and started walking once more toward the gates of the Dark Artificer's keep.

"You're gonna love Six!" he shouted over his shoulder. "Just wait'll you see who we've got in the Lake of Boiling Blood. Not to mention the lifts from the new *Wraiths of Wrath* collection—"

Nick could hardly bear the thought of not hearing that new music before everybody else did. "Why did you bring me just here and tell me all this stuff, and then just walk away?" he yelled. "Just to make me crazy, or what?"

"You figure it out!" Joey Bane yelled back, still walking away through the gathering darkness, as behind him a demon-giant in an old-fashioned Mets uniform chased a hapless mother and father across the circle with a baseball bat. Nick caught a glance at the back of the uniform shirt as the demon passed. The name was hard to make out, but its number was 666. Nice touch, that. "But haven't I been telling you life stinks?" Bane said. "Don't you even listen to the lyrics? Bye bye, stinker. . . ."

And he vanished into the darkness, laughing.

Nick stood there, heart pounding, not knowing whether to be delighted or furious. Finally he decided on furious . . . but it was a cheerful kind of fury, one that left him determined. "I'll be back!" he yelled at the darkness. "I'll do it, however much time it takes! I'll be back, and I'll meet you down on Six . . . and deeper than that!"

•   •   •

Only the faint sound of mocking laughter came floating back to him from the walls of the Keep, and a glint of silver and black as from away up high there, Camiun trilled once, amused.

It took a long while to get the lion man and the tiger woman to stop fighting and talk to him, but finally they showed him the way back up to Four, through a door, and up a stairway hidden in the stone of the cliffs, and the tiger woman dropped a line about a "golden key" that Nick was sure was a hint that had to do with how you were supposed to get into the Keep. Nick headed upward in a much improved mood, but there was still an edge of anger on his determination to come back here and show everybody that he hadn't hit his level, that he didn't need any more favors, that he was enough of a Banie to succeed down here no matter how the program tried to get under his skin, and no matter how long it took to do it. His dad was probably going to have a spasm when he saw the Net bill, but Nick was more certain than ever that he didn't care . . . this was worth it.

In the gateway the abandon-hope words were still burning red when he got back up there, but as Nick approached them, they twisted and curled in the air like burning red worms and formed themselves into new words. These said:

THE TIGER WOMAN IS A LIAR

He stopped and looked at that. *It's not completely true,* Nick thought. *She* did *tell me how to get back up to Four. . . .*

Then he paused just on the inside of the gateway, wondering. She and the lion man had interrupted each other constantly once he got them to stop ripping each other up, and now he wasn't at all sure just which of them had told him about the way back up to Four. But he definitely remembered her telling him about the key.

So is it a false lead? Or is this a lie itself?

Nick let out a long breath. He was going to have to come back as soon as he could and start working out how to get from Three to Four, so that he could test the situation and see what the real story was. *One thing you have to give this place,* Nick thought. *It keeps you coming back. . . .*

There was no point in lingering any longer, though. He had stuff to do at home. Nick passed through the gateway, and as usual, that big red asterisk appeared in the floor under his feet, burning like lava. Just for amusement, he stepped on it.

Instantly a vast carpet of glowing small print appeared beneath his feet, laid out and vanishing away into the virtual middle distance like the crawl in some old-fashioned space movie. It said:

© JOEY BANE ENTERPRISES 2018–2025. ALL RIGHTS RESERVED. THIS VIRTUAL DOMAIN IS A WORK OF FICTION. ANY RESEM-BLANCE OF ANY MANIFESTATION TO PER-SONS ALIVE OR DEAD IS COINCIDENTAL. THIS SITE IS TO BE USED FOR ENTERTAIN-MENT PURPOSES ONLY. YOU MUST BE SIX-TEEN YEARS OF AGE TO ENTER. BY ENTERING THIS VIRTUAL DOMAIN YOU STATE AND ACKNOWLEDGE THAT YOU HAVE READ AND UNDERSTAND THE TERMS AND CONDITIONS FOR USE OF THIS FACIL-ITY. YOU EXPRESSLY ACKNOWLEDGE THAT YOU INDEMNIFY AND HOLD BLAME-LESS JOEY BANE ENTERPRISES AND ITS AGENTS AND LICENSEES FOR ANY AD-VERSE AFFECT WHATSOEVER WHICH MAY BE INCURRED BY THE USE OF THIS FACIL-ITY, AND JOEY BANE ENTERPRISES AND ITS AGENTS AND LICENSEES ACCEPT NO RE-SPONSIBILITY FOR SUCH EFFECTS. . . .

Nick walked on down the carpet of words with his hands stuffed in his pockets, amused, half wishing his mom could see him, half dreading her reaction, now minutes away, when she found out where he'd been. *Well, it doesn't have to happen right this second. . . .*

YOU ALSO WAIVE IN PERPETUITY YOUR RIGHT AND THE RIGHT OF YOUR HEIRS OR AS-SIGNS OR ANY OTHER RESPONSIBLE PERSONS IN WHATEVER LEGAL RELATIONSHIP TO YOU TO MAKE ANY CLAIM WHATSOEVER AGAINST JOEY BANE ENTERPRISES AND ITS AGENTS AND LI-CENSEES IN ANY JURISDICTION NOW KNOWN OR ANY OTHER WHICH MAY HEREAFTER BE DIS-COVERED, IN PERPETUITY. THIS AGREEMENT IS BINDING IN THIS FORM IN ALL U.S. JURISDIC-TIONS EXCEPT THE FOLLOWING: MD, NY, ME, VT. MARYLAND LAW REQUIRES THE FOLLOW-ING DISCLAIMER: THIS FACILITY MAY CONTAIN CONTENT INTENDED TO SHOCK OR DISTURB. . . .

Nick snickered at that as he walked past it. *He* hadn't been all that shocked. Maybe people in Maryland were just too delicate to live. But he was made of sterner stuff. " 'Nicey-nice,' " he sang under his breath as he walked down the long strip of text, as if down a red carpet, "wast-ing your time, smiling at folks without reason or rhyme: life is too short as it is; it's a crime . . . only death's certain to call. . . ."

The music came up around him as he left, Joey Bane's voice singing, with Camiun providing the growling har-mony under the main line, and the pulse beat rhythm driv-ing it all. There was supposed to be a new version of "Nicey-Nice" out now. Nick resolved to break a little of his saved-up ticket money loose for it right away.

He turned off his implant, and vanished.

In the virtual realm Deathworld suddenly accrued an-other sixteen dollars and fifty-three cents of credit.

And in the real world, several hundred miles away, someone who had been in Deathworld only an hour before was found dead.

2

Charlie Davis was sitting in his virtual workspace, wondering how to get the steam engine to work. He could have cheated and called up the software company's help line, which would have sent him a helpful "ghost" of James Watt, but the prospect of doing so struck him as an admission of failure. So instead he sat on the floor of the workspace, staring at the pressure gauges all over the engine's shining brass outsides, and wondered what the heck to do next.

Charlie knew people whose workspaces were marvels of the "special effects" end of virtuality. One of his buddies in the Net Force Explorers kept her workspace on one of the moons of Saturn. Another one had built himself a perfect replica of Windsor Castle, which he had filled with expressions of his own hobby, model trains. Charlie had found that a little bizarre, especially the miniature train shed which Mikey had installed in St. George's Chapel. "You should talk," Mikey had retorted. "*Your* workspace used to be used for medical research the hard way—vivisection. . . ."

That hadn't been precisely true, but it wasn't the kind of discussion that Charlie much felt like having with someone pointlessly argumentative as Mikey, and he'd let it pass. Charlie had built his workspace into a duplicate of the eighteenth-century operating theater of the Royal College of Surgeons in London. It was a splendid if not very sterile space in which concentric circles of mahogany "bleachers" surrounded an oval area in which was set a scrubbed wood table on which some of the most important experiments in the medicine of that time had been done. The circulation of blood had been explored there, and the structure of human bone, and Pasteur had dropped by to lecture on germ theory. If the professors working there had occasionally gone a little loopy and tried things like transplanting the head of one dog onto the body of another, well, that was then, not now, and everybody was entitled to have a bad day, experimentally speaking. Meanwhile, Charlie loved the place, the warm wooden gleam and polished-brass shine of it. It was the birthplace of modern medicine, and Charlie was going to be a doctor one of these days . . . though he intended to become an operative for Net Force as well. The only question was which of these goals he was going to manage first.

Then Charlie sighed heavily. "Actually," he muttered, "the only question is how I'm going to get this stupid thing in front of me to work."

It was, of course, not a real steam engine, just a mathematical simulation of one. If it was built properly, it would look and run like a real steam engine in the virtual world. Now, any workspace software worth its purchase price, if you told it to create such a thing out of nothing, would do just that and not bother you with the sordid details. But Charlie was learning how to write simulations in the programming language Caldera II, the language which virtual environments used to create things out of nothing so that they would behave real. And Caldera was desperately complex, difficult to control, easy to screw up, and otherwise just a major pain.

Charlie was not particularly interested in steam engines. What he really wanted to use Caldera for was to model the activity of neurons in the living human brain. But to create such models in any programming language, even Caldera, was an immensely subtle and difficult business— if you were interested in building models that actually worked like their counterparts in the real world, anyway, and suggested reasons for the way they behaved as they did. The steam engine was one of the "sample" simulations which came with the most current Caldera software package, and a good place (the software company said) to start practicing before going on to the more involved simulations. The program which the tutorial coached you in writing was one that described in maddening detail the way the virtual environment running it was supposed to act, so that you would put out your hand and feel hard cold brass or polished wood instead of air or fog that just *looked* like brass or wood, and so that the article you created in virtuality would act like a real thing, obeying real rules of science, and reacting appropriately to whatever you did to it.

That was the theory, anyway. Unfortunately, Charlie had so far managed only a steam engine that looked like brass but felt like rubber, and which produced something that looked like steam, but was just cold vapor. He got up from the floor, walked around the engine, looked at it one more time.

"Okay," he said to the air. "Main program, routine five . . ."

A "window" opened in the air near him, showing the first of the lines and lines of code he had written so far, coached by the tutorial. Somewhere in here there was a statement that was wrong that the debugging routine hadn't found, and that the program thought was a genuine and valid instruction. *And it would be,* Charlie thought, annoyed, *if people built rubber steam engines.*

"Scroll down three," Charlie said. "Scroll down one. Scroll down one." He stared for several moments at that particular screenful of text, chewing his lip. After a moment he said, "Line sixty. Change statement. Old statement: 'vis 15 hardness 80 spong 12'. New statement: 'vis 15 hardness 120 spong 12.' "

"What the heck is a spong?" someone said out of the air behind him.

Charlie looked over his shoulder. Nick Melchior was there, one of his best friends from school, if not the best. There was something about Nick's sense of humor that meshed well with Charlie's, and besides, Nick seemed never to have seen anything even slightly funny about the idea that a kid from as painful and hopeless a background as Charlie's should be unswervingly set on becoming a doctor. Charlie, for his own part, was always amazed that anyone from as unsettled and insecure a background as Nick's should have been able to do as well at school and be as generally good-natured and good-tempered as he was, when at any moment his dad or the whole family might be uprooted and sent off to some distant foreign place to do virtcam work for one of the major news services.

Nick leaned against the mahogany railing around the "operating floor" and stared at the engine.

"I could try to explain what a spong is," Charlie said, "but I'd just confuse myself. I'm not sure *I* know all of what it is yet. It has to do with the way this thing reflects light . . . or at least, that's all I can make of it so far. . . ."

Nick pushed away from the railing and walked around the sim, eyeing it. He was fair-haired, green-eyed, biggish across the shoulders, though not one of the taller kids in Charlie's year—unusual when half the juniors in the class seemed to be shooting up like trees, having hit some weird kind of sympathetic growth spurt. Nick seemed stuck at about five four, and for Charlie, who was stuck at five two and was beginning to wonder morbidly whether he had some obscure glandular disorder, it was pleasant to have the company of someone who didn't look down at him as if from a great height and inquire sardonically as to why he didn't go out for basketball. "It looks good," Nick said.

"Yeah, well, if you put some chest rub in it, it'd make somebody a great cold vaporizer," Charlie muttered. "Go ahead, give it a kick."

"Huh?"

"Go on, kick it. Hard as you can."

The steam engine had four handsome brass-trimmed wheels with iron tires. Nick walked over to one of them, looked it over, and kicked it, hard. Then he started jumping around. *"Ow!* Sonofa—Wha'd you tell me to do *that* for?"

Charlie stared, dumbfounded. "Buddha on a bike," he said, "did I fix it?" He went over to the next wheel and kicked it too, quite hard, disbelieving—then joined Nick briefly in the dance. "Oh, *crud!"*

"Thanks loads, Charlie, like I don't have *enough* problems today, now I'm lamed for life, too!" Nick was now holding the injured foot and staring at it as if he could see through his boot to tell if something was broken.

"Ow, look, I'm sorry. I fixed it! I guess I must have fixed it, anyway. The train was soft, before, like rubber." Charlie leaned against the railing near Nick, rubbing his own foot and then bearing weight on it gingerly. "Sorry!" He stared at the engine. "What the frack did I fix? I wasn't working on the hardness. . . ."

"You're asking the wrong expert, expert. What you *can* do, O mighty medical talent, is tell me whether my foot's going to be this sore when I come out of virt."

"Dummy," Charlie said. "No. It won't hurt long here, either; you know pain can't be turned up even as high as in real life in here. Just as well. What's your problem, anyway?"

"My foot, clueless one, is—"

"Your *other* problem. Whatever you were yapping about when you came in."

"Oh. Just my dad."

"Are they sending him somewhere weird again?" Charlie boosted himself up to sit on the railing, morosely studying the steam engine.

"No. No, it's just Net stuff."

Charlie blinked. "What?"

"You remember Joey Bane's domain?"

"Oh, yeah. Death-o-rama or whatever."

"Deathworld."

"Yeah." Charlie had been through one of its upper levels briefly with Nick a couple of months back, but hadn't gone back. It was one of the more expensive domains to spend time in, and besides, he wasn't a big shadow jazz fan. His musical tastes ran more to hopflight, because of the rhythms, and terzia rizz, which was experiencing something of a comeback after four centuries of neglect. "So what's the problem?" Charlie said. "Bills getting too high?"

"Yeah, but that's not most of it. Mostly my mom and dad think it's corrupting me or something." Nick's good-natured face was twisted somewhat out of its usual placid shape, and as he hoisted himself up beside Charlie, the look lingered.

"You?" Charlie blew out an amused breath. "Nothing there to corrupt."

"Thanks loads, Dr. Genius. No, they're just freaked out by the news stories."

"I missed the news today," Charlie said. "It's Saturday. This is the day I take off from the world, theoretically."

"To spend time on really important things."

"James Watt thought so," Charlie said, he hoped not too sharply. "I like retrotech. So splash me. Meanwhile, what happened?"

"Somebody killed himself."

"Someone who'd been doing a lot of Deathworld?"

"Something like that." Nick rolled his eyes expressively, then paused, briefly distracted by the fresco on the ceiling, of the god Apollo receiving Aesculapius into heaven, while a lot of other gods in togas leaned in to observe, and possibly to pass private remarks on the new-

comer's snappy cane with the snakes wrapped around it.
"Who are all those people?"

"I'll tell you some other time, if I can ever get you to
stop interrupting yourself!"

Nick rolled his eyes again. "Some guy in Iowa," he
said. "A seventh-circler, apparently. He hanged himself.
At least that's what the police were saying."

"Did they say anything else about whether he'd been
depressed, or something like that?" Charlie said.

Nick shook his head. "Not that I heard. From the story
I heard, it sounded like they were in a hurry to get him
buried." He grimaced. "And as soon as my folks heard
about it, they went completely voidside. They don't want
me going in there, blah, blah, blah. . . ."

Charlie leaned back a little and looked over at his friend
with some concern. He had heard about the other suicides,
but he hadn't really thought of them as anything significant. Oh, obviously they were tragic for the people involved, and the people left behind, but a certain number
of people suicided every year due to misuse or overuse
of virtual services of one kind or another, and mostly the
psychiatrists figured that these were people who would
have found some other reason to do away with themselves
if the Net had not existed. Still . . . it was a little creepy.
"This is how many suicides of people associated with
Deathworld, now?"

"Six, I think they said."

Charlie looked at the steam engine thoughtfully.
"Seems like kind of a lot."

Nick plopped himself down on one of the front-row
benches and shrugged a don't-care kind of shrug. "Aw,
c'mon, Charlie, don't you side with them, too! You know
the world is full of idiots looking for a chance to pop
themselves off, and any excuse would do. It can't be
Deathworld's fault that they found their way down there
at one point or another. If it were, the government would
have found out about it and shut them down."

"Well . . ." Charlie got up with a sigh, walked around

the back of the steam engine and had a look at the coal box, which had somehow started to look a little transparent. He touched it. At least it was solid, which it hadn't been until just now. "Net Force *is* supposed to inspect and certify anything that looks like it might be dangerous to users," he said.

"So since they haven't shut it down, it must be okay," Nick said. He sighed. "Not that my dad is going to care one way or another. . . ."

Charlie kicked the coal box experimentally. It buckled under the kick, and he looked at the half-circle dent and moaned softly. "I am *never* gonna get the hang of this," he said, and went to sit down by Nick and stare at the steam engine. "Main program, routine six . . ."

Another window opened up, showing the beginning of the code that "built" the coal box. "Scroll down twenty," he said. "Repeat. Repeat. Scroll down one. Line ninety-three. Change statement. Old statement: 'vis 15 hardness 120 spong 12'. New statement: 'vis 15 hardness 90 spong 12.' "

The code readjusted itself. "I don't get it," Nick said. "You're going to go to medical school, do the doctor thing like your dad, you said."

"Yup." *And then go into Net Force,* Charlie added silently, but this was not something he discussed with anyone, not even with Nick. There was so much competition to get into that elite force, so many people who were also trying to get in . . . and it was not in Charlie's nature to want to have to say to anyone later, "I wanted to get in, but I couldn't make it." When he made it, when he started working for them in criminology or forensics after he got his MD and his specialty . . . that would be the time to discuss it, because he would have the ID in his wallet for anyone to see, his ticket to the cutting edge, to the most exciting work on Earth. Until that day came, though, Charlie had resolved to keep his intentions to himself. If his life had taught him anything up until now, it was caution.

"So what do you need this stuff for?"

"Modeling nervous systems," Charlie said. "And other things. Solid in-bone surgical prostheses, temporary replacement organs, stuff like that."

Nick gave him a wry look. "It looks like *this* system's making you nervous, all right," he said, "but that's about all. You should lose this stuff and get out and get yourself some fresh air."

Charlie sighed and leaned back on the bench, for the moment unwilling to go over and kick the coal box again, for fear of what he'd find. "Been listening to your folks too much, Nick? I bet they say the same thing."

"Yeah, well . . ." Nick gave him an amused look. "I can't help it. I can't get excited about baseball the way my dad can."

"Neither can I." The two of them laughed with approximately equal levels of irony. Once a week or so, all through the spring and summer, Charlie found himself wondering how his dad, a doctor of incredible intelligence and (usually) of good sense and taste, could go out, regular as clockwork, every Saturday when the weather was right and he wasn't on call, to play sandlot softball with the GWU med-surg team. Then, for the rest of the week, he would spend at least half an hour every morning mulling over the box scores of the most recent Braves games. He would periodically try to get Charlie interested in this as well, even try getting him interested in virtual Little League baseball . . . though Charlie's dad would then routinely talk himself out of this idea halfway through each new effort, muttering that the virtual form of the sport was a "poor second best." Charlie just nodded and put up with it, this being easier than arguing the point anew every week, or trying to explain one more time to his father that right now he was a whole lot more interested in modeling than in any sport yet invented.

"Seriously, though," Charlie said. "You consider taking a couple of weeks off from Deathworld, just to get your folks off your case? If they're really worried . . . it might be the kindest thing. Besides, once they were sure you weren't hooked on it or anything, or about to hang yourself from the shower-curtain rail as soon as they turn their backs, they might ease off a little."

Nick shook his head vigorously. "I've tried that before with other things," he said. "My mom doesn't even notice. My dad . . ." He sighed. "You let him win one, when it's something that matters, and he starts bearing down harder on everything else. Pretty soon I wouldn't have a life left, or at least no life that didn't look like what he thought it should look like. Besides, I'm finally getting somewhere down there. If I drop the momentum now, the system'll notice and stop fast-tracking me. I've been racking up enough points that I'm gonna get somewhere significant over the next month or so . . . finally get into the Dark Artificer's Keep and get a listen to the really good music." He shook his head. "My dad's just gonna have to lump it for the time being."

Charlie got up and went over to the coal box again, nudging it cautiously with one toe. The dent he had made in it abruptly sprang out . . . and the coal box went almost completely transparent, except for the coal, which "hung" there in midair as if sitting in some kind of wheeled plastic basket, like the ones in the "grocery stores" of old. "Frack," Charlie said, with feeling. "Frack, *frack*—"

"You oughta take a break from this," Nick said. "You're getting stressed out. Since when do you use language like that?"

Charlie looked with mild annoyance at Nick. But he had to admit that his friend had a point. "Program, quick save," Charlie said. "Then close program."

"Saved. Closing," said the computer, folding up the various open windows. The steam engine vanished, leaving them alone in the big wood-paneled hall, with squares of sunlight from the high windows now tracking themselves along the floor.

"Must be noontime. Probably I should get something to eat anyway," Charlie said. "Look, you wanna come over in the flesh later? We can make some burgers or something . . . nobody at home has anything planned for today." It was one of those moderately rare times when both his mother and his father had Saturday off.

"Thanks, but I'm busy this afternoon," Nick said. "They're offering a discount for Saturday Deathworld access between noon and six . . . apparently that's a slow time at the moment, with the summer coming on. Look, why don't you come with me? I can 'sub' you in on my account, and you can watch me get into the Keep." Nick grinned with excitement.

Charlie thought about it . . . then shook his head. "No, you go ahead . . . it's not my cuppa. But when you get out, drop by and let me know how it went. They let you make 'tapes'?"

"Nope . . . the content is all copyright. They control that pretty tightly. You try to copy an experience and show it outside of their protected routines, and there'll be lawyers on your doorstep five minutes later. But I can save the experience inside the 'realm,' and you can see it some other time."

"That sounds good. You do that, okay?"

"Okay." Nick headed for the stairs that led up to the door, then paused. "You *sure?* This is gonna be one for the ages."

"Nope . . . you go ahead. But thanks."

"Your loss," Nick said. "See you, Doc."

"Later, Mr. Nick," Charlie said.

His friend vanished. Charlie sat there a moment more, staring at where the steam engine had been, and then said to the computer, "Secure the space, please."

"Workspace secured," said the program that managed it, "all files confirmed saved; backup to SafeHouse remote facility accomplished."

Charlie closed his eyes and performed the specific slight muscle-twitch that deactivated his implant.

The world went dark. He opened his eyes, glanced around.

Sunshine was coming through the venetian blinds of the back window of the den. Charlie got up, stretched— no matter what claims the implant-chair people made, the built-in massage and muscle-toning programs never left you completely unstiff after a prolonged session on the Net. *I really should try to do something about that some-time,* he thought, shaking his arms to get the blood moving again as he climbed out of the chair. *Tweak the programming a little ...*

Then again, Charlie thought, *if I have as much luck with that programming as I'm having with Caldera at the moment, maybe I'd better leave well enough alone. I'd probably come out of a session with my arms and legs tied in knots.*

He walked over to the window and looked down. The back windows faced south. About twenty feet below him was their little pocket garden, a square of grass with a smaller square of paving slabs inside it, and various potted plants sitting around in it, mostly herbs for his mother's cooking. Behind the yard was another house's yard, and its windows, and to left and right the view was much the same.

Charlie yawned and went out of the den, heading down the stairs to the first floor and the kitchen level. The house was a two-century-old "brownstone" on 16 and W, a place which Charlie's father routinely referred to as "the Money Pit." The family had moved into it when it was only partly renovated. For their first year there, when Charlie had been eleven and then twelve, the place had been in a con-stant state of uproar involving inescapable plaster dust, thick paint-daubed plastic sheeting, piles of demolished brick being saved for recycling, and endless crews of workmen barging in and out at unpredictable intervals. Finally, sick of the delays and the expense, Charlie's fa-ther had thrown the workmen out (having first allowed them to finish the second floor and the basement) and had announced his intention to finish the third floor and the attic himself, in his spare time.

Charlie still snickered every time he heard the phrase, since his father, like any other doctor, had a tendency to come home from the hospital and spend what little spare time he had snoring. When his dad *did* get it together to work on "the upstairs," Charlie and his mom inevitably got dragooned into the act as well. Charlie could now mix plaster with the best of them, and his dad had announced that he was ready to be taught how to lay a hardwood floor. This had not happened yet—the new semester had begun, and in a teaching hospital like the one at George Washington University, that meant a lot less spare time for the doctors of middle seniority, like Charlie's dad. But Charlie didn't waste much time worrying about it. The house was comfortable enough as it was at present: three bedrooms and an office where one of the implant chairs lived, a kitchen and two bathrooms, and a den that housed the other implant chair, the main Net server, and a busy, messy library. The new master bedroom and private living area which his father was planning for the upstairs would happen someday, but for the moment, Charlie tended to treat it like anything else safely distant in the realm of myth.

Now Charlie headed down the stairs and made for the kitchen, which was in the back of the building, with doors opening out onto the little garden. He got himself a cup of coffee from the coffeemaker, which was always full night and day, and stood there for a moment, getting used to reality again, gazing out into the sunlight on the paving and the grass.

There were still times when Charlie woke up, very early in the morning, and felt bizarrely dislocated, as if his mind was comparing the shining new surroundings, the polished floor and pastel or stripped-brick walls, with some other reality, older, grittier, more basic. Floors that were not polished wood, but cracked linoleum, worn and dirty, scattered with garbage; walls that were not newly plastered and painted and hung with prints, but grimy, peeling, splotched with damp, holed where someone had punched them. The memory of someone shouting incomprehensible words of rage, someone else weeping: the memory of a face that should have been beautiful but was instead swollen and vague, blue with bruising. The smell of unwashed bodies, the smell of something burning; the too-clear image of a match under a spoon, a spray injector, a syringe—

"Hey, son, what's new in the world today?"

Charlie turned, swallowed, and the proper world came back, and with it his dad, lumbering into the kitchen, a big broad-shouldered, dark-skinned man in a polo shirt and jeans, high-cheekboned, with thoughtful eyes and a mouth that spent most of its time grinning. Now those dark eyes were unusually thoughtful as they took in the look on Charlie's face.

"Nothing much," Charlie said.

"How's that steam engine?"

"Malfunctioning," Charlie said, moving aside to let his dad at the coffee. His father tossed the morning paper onto the big table in the middle of the kitchen and went rooting in the cupboard for the gigantic coffee cup that read YOU DON'T HAVE TO BE CRAZY TO WORK HERE, BUT IT HELPS.

"Never trust retrotech," his father murmured, emptying what seemed to be about half the contents of the coffeemaker into that cup, and then going over to the fridge and opening the door. He reached in, then started rooting around. "Kenmore, where the heck's the milk?"

"No milk today," said the fridge.

"Well, I can *see* that, you dumb contraption, why didn't you order any?"

"Error 3033 Server Busy," said the refrigerator, somehow managing to sound a little sullen.

"Well, you just keep trying, Kenny, or we'll trade you in for a better model before you can say 'two percent low-fat'. See that?" his father said, shutting the refrigerator with a wounded air and heading back to the cupboard for dry coffee creamer. "I told you, never trust modern technology."

"You said never trust retrotech," Charlie said as his father sat down and grabbed the *Washington Post*. It started unfolding and unfolding itself across the flowered tablecloth to the default display size.

"That, either," Charlie's father said. "Now I'll have to go out and get milk before the game, or your mother'll be on my case."

"I can go get it, Dad."

"Would you?" His father looked up as if astonished by his son's kindness. It was a look Charlie had gotten used to over time, the expression of a man who has almost forgotten what free time is like, and is astonished to find that other people have any.

"No problem." *In fact, if I get out right now, I can escape before he asks me to—*

"You know, son," his father said, as the main sports page resolved itself in color and motion in front of him, showing a batter swinging and missing very conclusively at a 3–2 pitch, "a nice day like this, a boy your age should be out getting some fresh air with other kids. Now, if you felt like coming down to the park with me, after the game's over some of the other dads and I—"

"Y'know," Charlie said, "I just realized what I'm doing wrong with that steam engine." *Not working on it, among other things!* He headed out of the kitchen and down the hallway toward the "airlock" front hall where his bike sat. "Later, Dad. I'll get that milk first—"

His father was chuckling softly behind him. As Charlie pushed the front door open, wheeled the bike out it, closed the door again and spoke it locked, he began to wonder if he had been manipulated into getting the milk a touch more quickly than he would have done otherwise.

Nonetheless Charlie grinned a little as he got up on his bike. His mother and father—his foster mother and foster father, actually, though they were working to adopt him formally, really—were the world's best. A little manipulation, in the greater scheme of things, didn't matter in the slightest. He looked up at the stripped brick of the

outside of the building and saw, as if overlaying it faintly
even in the bright Saturday morning sunlight, that older,
darker memory: dimly lit hallways, echoing with laughter
bitter or abandoned, the sounds of pain, abuse, and loss.
That was all gone now. Nick and Adelie Davis had come
and taken him away from all that, into a world where life
had purpose besides getting high, and meaning besides
bare survival, and hope as opposed to none. When those
old memories came hunting Charlie, they never caused
him anything but pain. But he knew it would be stupid to
deny them, or try to escape them. If he was ever going to
be fully himself, they were going to have to be part of
the equation.

   But right now that could wait. Sunlight dissolved the
shadows, and Charlie pedaled off down to the nearby con-
venience store to get some milk, while turning over in his
mind the problem of a rubbery steam engine. *Shame I
can't get Nick interested in this. He'd be a help.* But Nick
plainly had other things on his mind. . . . *Guess that
means I'd better get busy.*

3

Nick stood by the Lake of Boiling Blood, gazing idly across its blooping, heaving depths, and decided that it looked a lot like spaghetti sauce.

He sighed. All around him the scalded screeches of various media figures of past and present—movie stars, singers, reporters, producers, directors—could be heard as they noisily repented their various overindulgences and infractions against taste, style, and veracity, while various demons pushed the Damned back into the boiling blood as they tried to escape, or pulled them out again (to give them a chance to recover, so that throwing them in again later would hurt more). The lake in which all the Violent-Against-Truth were imprisoned had numerous little fjords, pools, and lakelets winding up among the towering dark cliffs that embraced it on all sides, and from these could be heard particularly piercing shrieks and howls of anger and pain. Nick had stopped reacting to these now, having made the rounds of all the "specialty" areas in his search for clues about the way down to the Seventh Circle. He had seen and spent hours in the worst of them all, the giant boiling-magma Jacuzzi in which former talk-show hosts and literary critics held one another under, tearing at each other whenever anyone managed to struggle to the surface, and from even that awful scene he had come away more or less unscathed. The other, lesser torments on this level held no more terrors for Nick now. Even the stink of the lake that boiled but never burned was beginning to become a commonplace, and he was busily trying to work out the details of where he should be heading next. The Seventh Circle was beckoning.

Over everything ran the savage rhythms of the new "unpublished" tracks from *Forlorn Voices*; right now it was "Slasher's Surprise" playing, with Joey Bane's voice unusually soft in the leadup to the second verse, almost as if enticing you to lean in close and have your brain fried when the chorus began screaming in your ears.

"It never seems to have occurred to you
that if I cut you *you* would bleed. . . .
but then it also never seems to have occurred
that I might follow your own nasty lead:
Might get the strop out, might hone the edge down,
might put the blade in deep:
maybe tonight's little pain will teach you
to look before you leap!"

And then the shriek of sound, Camiun singing out like both tormented and tormentor alternately, and Joey Bane's sardonic scream:

"Surprise, surprise, see the blood flow,
Mister Do-unto-others-and-run!
Hey, what's the hurry, don't leave, don't go,
I'm up for more of your kind of fun—"

"Surprise, surprise," Nick sang softly to himself as he wandered along the lakeshore, looking casually for any spot he might have missed. He was getting ready to move on shortly, though, for he thought he had all the clues he needed. And Six was getting old, anyway. At first Six had seemed "seriously cool," to use his dad's ancient and hoary term. But now it had palled. In fact, at first Nick had been surprised to see how soon he had gotten used to it, how very *soon* it had all seemed slightly passé. . . . and more, things had not happened in the order he had expected. He had thought that once he hit Six, the Keep of the Dark Artificer would be waiting for him. But when he reached the spot in the Ashen Plain where rumor said it was supposed to stand, he had found nothing but a big rough sign spray-painted on permanently smoldering plywood, and stuck in the ground: GONE FISHING ON LEVEL 8. SUCKER!

At first Nick had been absolutely outraged at this, and had turned to leave, infuriated at the waste of time and money. But then he thought again, distracted for the moment by the initial sight of the lake, and the smell of it— horrifying enough, to a nose not used to it, to strike almost anyone still, or sick. He had controlled his heaves, and his initial reaction, and then it occurred to him: *Of course. It's a test. If everything stinks, why shouldn't everything stink here, too? Joey never said it would be otherwise.*

So Nick had sighed, and coughed, and started hiking around the shallow lake, looking for clues as to what was the best way down to Eight. This took him a long while, since the only source of clues was those people trapped in the blood, being pushed into it or scrambling out again. You had to talk to them, find out who they were and what they were doing here, and try to draw them out on the subject . . . not that they would necessarily cooperate. Not all of them would stand near the edge of the lake and talk to you, either. There were big gaggles and parties of them out in the hotter part of the lake, and they would stand or float there, alternately screaming and looking back toward shore, scornfully, like people at a cocktail party who're in with the crowd that really matters and have no inclination to move around and meet anyone less important.

Nick had spent a long time wandering around the edges of the lake, trying to overhear something that would be useful to him. This had made him pretty annoyed after a little while. *It feels like my life,* he had thought. *I'm supposed to be here escaping from reality, not getting stuck with more of the same!*

But there was no choice, for the only other sources of clues were the other players—and they were a close-mouthed bunch. None of them that Nick approached would talk to him, and finally he gave up trying. *Probably they figure they've spent good money to find out what they know so far,* Nick thought, *and they're not going to give it away to anyone for free.* Realizing this didn't make Nick feel any better, though, and eventually, after he had spent something like eight hours of "peak time" without any result, he had sat down with his back against a sullenly hot boulder and taken what he considered would be his last long look at the place.

Then—when he was off his guard, lost in his fury and unfocused—he saw the answer. He saw one of the game-players, not a demon, look over her shoulder as if concerned that she was being watched, and then after a moment of apparently seeing no one nearby, actually wade into the boiling blood and head out toward one particular group. And Nick's mouth dropped right open.

If she can do that, I *can do that!*

Nick got up and made for the edge of the lake. There for a moment he hesitated, for the stuff looked deadly. *But she did it!*

Gingerly he put a foot in. He didn't feel anything. Confused, Nick bent down and held his hand over the boiling blood. He could feel the heat, and it felt bad. But after a moment's hesitation he stuck his finger in—

To his astonishment, it didn't particularly hurt. The "boiling blood" was only about as hot as a really hot bath. And he alternately laughed and cursed himself all the way across the lake as he got right in and waded or swam toward one of the big "get-togethers" in the middle of the lava, a whole bunch of scalded, burnt people—or former people, all of whom looked as if they had been guests at a particularly interactive barbecue—who were standing around and laughing more than they were screaming. Nick felt dumb, in retrospect. He knew perfectly well that you couldn't suffer pain in a Net-based experience, or at least not pain bad enough to hurt you. The implant embedded in you was designed specifically to filter that kind of thing out. And it didn't necessarily follow that what hurt the Damned would necessarily hurt you. After all, they were supposed to suffer here. It struck Nick as likely enough that even in a real Hell, the torments wouldn't hurt someone who wasn't entitled to them.

Possibly there's a message there somewhere. In any case, Nick had learned to stop taking the physical images of things here at face value, as he would have in the real world. *Maybe that's the message, too. That nothing is what it seems. That nothing can really be trusted.*

It was a message that sank in deep. Nick put it aside for that moment, though, and got busy talking to the people out in the lake. In between torments he found them a voluble enough bunch. In fact it was hard to get them to *stop* talking, especially about their favorite topic, themselves. What was harder still was to get them to say anything about Deathworld itself, its structure and the way around it. Not that they seemed to be inhibited against this, specifically. They were just so utterly self-centered that even the torment of the boiling blood served only as a momentary distraction from their recitations of the important things they'd done, all the books they'd written and the money they'd made, the millions of people they'd influenced, the trends they'd set. Nick started to find this very choice when he paired their endless effusions against the fact that he only knew who a few of them were, out of hundreds he talked to. That week he did get a very thorough grounding in the faded pop culture of the last

fifty years, and an increasingly clear sense of how very
little of human endeavor lasts for any real length of time,
whether it's worthwhile or not.

Finally, though, Nick learned by observation that if you
asked questions while the demons were actually torturing
the Damned, or when they'd just been splashed by the
boiling blood, you could get straight answers for a few
seconds. The pain, it seemed, cleared their minds and
turned them away from themselves, however briefly. Nick
quickly established a short list of questions to fire at them
while it wasn't in their power to give him anything but a
straight answer. And after many hours of this, and a lot
of slogging around, now Nick had the information he
needed. The exit to Seven was actually down in that lake
of blood itself, right down at the bottom of it—that being
how the Power that ran this place kept the Damned from
escaping it. For while wholly immersed in the lava-blood,
then and only then were their minds cleared to the truth
of how little difference they had made in the world when
they were still breathing, and how in the present time, so
soon after their deaths, they were either completely forgotten or about to be so. Indeed, it was an irony which
hadn't escaped Nick's notice that only here, in this virtual
torment, were any of these people still even slightly famous anymore. Only the users of Deathworld, working
their way down through this level, were impelled to say,
"Just who was that guy?" . . . and go check the history
sources on the Net to find out. One of the very few ex-
ceptions to this rule, and a deeper irony still, was the
image of the old, old newscaster who had been alive until
very recently, but while still alive had as a joke privately
given the Deathworld designers permission to place him
here among so many of his lesser contemporaries. He did
not deserve to be here, and as a result he sat in something
of a place of honor, off in his own little hot tub full of
the burning lava of Truth, looking like a wrinkled old
Buddha with his mustache on fire, and refusing to say

anything to anyone except, with a grin, "That's the way it is. . . ."

Nick had been lost in admiration when he got the joke. *This is a great place,* Nick thought. *Better than anyplace else on the Net. I don't care how long it takes, or how much it costs. I'm going to solve it.* And indeed he had been in here every day, for every waking hour he could, for days now. It was a lot of use, he knew, a lot of time when he should have been doing other things, maybe. Schoolwork, or stuff around the house . . . But those images seemed to have less power than usual to bother him, which suited Nick fine. *Because they're not important. They can wait. This matters more. And if anyone doesn't like it, well, the world stinks, doesn't it? Let them just get used to it. . . .*

From where Nick stood now, looking out over the lake and up at the cliffs, he saw something which he had missed in earlier visits, but which he had now learned to enjoy, since it never happened the same way twice. One of the demons, a little batwinged guy who reminded him strangely of his science teacher from seventh grade—a round, small, jolly man—materialized up at the top of the highest of the cliffs around the lake. It had a long, long projection of stone sticking out of it over the lake, that cliff, and sometimes this narrow fingerlike projection was almost completely hidden in the miasma of brown-black smoke that rose from the lake. For the moment it was clear, though, and the little dumpy figure walked out to the very end of that narrow pier of stone, held its arms out in front of it, yelled "Geronimooooooo!" and jumped off. It twisted and turned any number of times as it fell through what seemed about a mile of air from that high promontory, tumbling, straightening again, spinning, finally tucking itself into a cannonball shape, then straightening out and hitting the surface in a perfect dive, striking into it like a spear and vanishing in a tremendous splash that threw burning, smoking liquid in every direction. All around, the Damned who were hit by the splash screamed

in anguish. From the side of the lake a group of six demons who had been sitting and watching the dive now
stood up and held up little pairs of cards with numbers
on them, one card in each claw: 5.4, 5.2, 5.1, 5.2, 4.8,
5.9. Then five out of six of them dropped their cards to
the ground and started whapping the demon who had
given the diver a 4.8 over his head.

I really have to find out who the heck "Geronimo" is,
Nick thought. *It might be a clue.*

He stood there for a moment more, and then thought,
*Okay. No use putting it off any longer. Let's put this to
the test, and see if I'm right.*

He looked over his shoulder to see if anyone real, any
of the gameplayers, were nearby to see what he was doing. It was a relatively quiet time. Nobody was nearby.
Nick stepped off the edge of the lakeshore and started
wading through the lake.

The Damned drew away from Nick a little, and some
of them stopped laughing, as they saw where he was
headed—that deepest part, where none of them went by
choice. "Surprise, surprise," he sang softly in chorus with
the great cry of rage filling the air above him,

"Never thought it'd happen,
Never thought you'd be the one!
"Surprise, surprise,
'Cause here comes the moment,
I'll shave you to the bone 'fore we're done!
Surprise, surprise—"

Nick knew he was on the verge of the deepest place.
He ducked under the lava—

And everything went black.

And in the darkness there burned nothing but two great
words written in blazing red fire:

SERVICE SUSPENDED

"WHAT?!" Nick screamed.

He blinked, blinked hard. There was light again, now, but it was just daylight, easing out of afternoon toward evening. It was the light that came through the translucence of the shades in the spare bedroom of the apartment where he lived with his folks, the room where the implant chair sat.

And his father standing there with the hand commlink in his hand. "Yes," he was saying to someone at the other end. "Thanks, it just went on. Yeah. Thanks."

His father folded up the hand phone and looked at Nick with an expression too flat and controlled to bode well for anyone.

"Well?" he said.

"What's the matter?" Nick cried. "What happened? Call the provider, something's wrong with the Net link!"

"I've just been talking with the provider," Nick's father said, in a voice carefully kept as expressionless as his face, "and there's nothing wrong with the link . . . not that hasn't just been fixed, anyway."

"But it went off while I was in the middle of—" *Uh-oh.* "—something important—"

His father held out an envelope for him to look at. It had their Net service provider's logo on it. In the spare room doorway his mother suddenly materialized, looking grim.

"I thought I told you," his father said, "to stay out of that Deathworld place."

Nick realized that this was not a time to attempt explanations. He said nothing.

"I thought we discussed it rationally," his father said. "You agreed to do as I said. Didn't you?"

"Dad, I—"

"Or I thought you had. I see now that I was mistaken. Eight hundred dollars"—the hand with the envelope in it was shaking now—"eight hundred *dollars* in prime-service charges in the last two weeks alone. Son, are you *nuts*? Did you seriously think I wouldn't find out about this? Did you think it was just going to go away, or that it didn't matter? Do you know what this is going to do to household finances for the next month, while we pay this off out of money that was intended for other things? Like spending money for our summer vacation?"

Nick gulped and looked at the floor.

His father stopped, too angry to say anything else for the moment. "Nicky, half your spending money is going to be docked weekly until you pay back this last bill," Nick's mother said. "It would be real smart for you to see about getting yourself some kind of part-time job for the summer, so you can get it paid off in less time. As regards any further Net access, you're grounded. If you want it, you can go down to the Square and rent a booth out of your own money, since you've proved you can't be trusted to use the Net responsibly at home. After the bill's paid off, we'll look at whether you're ready to have your own service restored."

Nick said nothing, just stood there with his ears burning.

"And assuming we give you your service back some day, if you ever pull a stunt like this again, we're going to have the thing pulled out," his father said. "I don't care if you think you need it for school, or because all your friends have it, or whatever. You can get up off your butt and walk to the library to do your research, the way I did when dinosaurs walked the earth. It didn't kill me. It won't kill you, either. And what your friends think isn't important compared to pulling your weight in this family and behaving like the money we work hard for actually means something, instead of you throwing it out the window in handfuls."

His father handed him the envelope and turned and went out. His mother stood there and looked at him for a moment, her expression not softening in the slightest.

"I left you some supper in the 'vector,' " she said. "Dad and I have to go out and run a couple of errands. Have your dinner and then get your homework done on the laptop. I had the provider copy all your school files to it before they blocked your workspace."

"Mom—"

"Now's not the time, Nicky," she said, the anger showing in her voice for the first time. "You have a lot of apologies to make, but not now. It sounds too easy now. Maybe in the next couple of days your dad and I can take what you have to say more seriously."

She went out. A moment later Nick heard the apartment door shut.

He stood there with the envelope in his hands, trembling, first with embarrassment—*Oh God, what will everybody say? What will they think? This is the end!*— and then, with something more familiar, something peculiarly more bearable, more acceptable: rage.

This stinks.

But then everything *stinks!*

He was right. Joey was absolutely right!

The only question is—am I going to take this lying down . . . or am I going to let them see that I'm not going to just take what they dish out?

There was only one possible answer to the question, for someone who had been down as far as Seven in Deathworld . . . only one possibly answer for a Banie.

" 'Surprise, surprise . . .' " Nick sang softly, and headed out of the room to have his supper, and start laying his plans.

Charlie came down the stairs from his bedroom early that Friday morning, still rubbing his eyes a little despite having been showered and dressed for half an hour now. He'd been up late putting final touches on a physics paper that was due today, and he was pleased with his efforts, even if he did feel like he wanted to turn right around and go straight back up the stairs to bed.

Charlie headed for the coffeemaker and was astounded to find it empty. He opened the cupboard above it, got out another drip-pak, slapped it into the holder, filled the brewing reservoir again, and got the brew cycle started. The coffeemaker promptly began making the noise which both his father and mother referred to as "Cheyne-Stokes respirations," a horrific gurgling gasp followed by a long "breath" outward that sounded more like a death rattle than anything else.

"Urgh," Charlie said to the coffeemaker, "you sound like I feel."

He went back to the table and glanced at the paper, which his dad had left there still folded. Charlie hit the "go" corner and it started to unfold itself in the usual manner, and at that point his dad came down the stairs with his white doctor's overcoat on and his stethoscope doubled up around his neck. "Did you start the coffee?"

"Yup. *Somebody* drank it all."

"Speak to your mother." Charlie's dad sat down and looked the paper over, regarding the front page with his usual mild interest, then started paging through to the part that really mattered. Charlie watched this process, secretly amused that his dad was managing to stay away from the sports pages for even this long—and then paused, catching sight of a headline on the first of the local news pages.

DOUBLE SUICIDE STUNS VA, MD PARENTS

Charlie leaned in closer over his dad's shoulder.

Arlington, May 7, 2025—Two families in the Arlington and Fairfax areas were grieving today for a son and a daughter who were found dead early Tuesday in what appeared to be a bizarre suicide pact. The bodies of Jeannine Metz, 18, and Malcolm Dwyer, 17, were discovered in a room in a hotel in Arlington, Virginia, last night, after relatives received timed e-mail messages from both teens. The messages contained slightly different versions of the same suicide note.

Police were called to the scene at 1:03 A.M. on

Tuesday by hotel management at the Arlington Radisson-Hilton Towers, who opened the room after being alerted by Net messages from the pair's concerned parents. Shortly thereafter the police on scene notified staff from the county coroner's office and secured the room for investigation as a possible crime scene, but by morning the coroner said that there was no initial indication of murder or other "foul play" as a factor. Further statements, he said, would have to await the processing of initial tissue sample tests and a full autopsy. The coroner's office declined to comment on details of the suicide method.

Dwyer and Metz were taken to Arlington Hospital, where they were identified by their parents. "I can't understand it," Metz's mother, Quinne Ryan Metz said when interviewed Monday morning by local media. "She was such a normal girl, she did well at school, there weren't any family problems, we were very close. . . ." Relatives of Malcolm Dwyer declined to speak to reporters.

Police investigating the suicides had no initial comment. They would not confirm or deny the suggestion that both teens had been regular users of the controversial "Deathworld" Net environment run by morbo-jazz star Joey Bane. Calls to Joey Bane Enterprises were not immediately returned Tuesday, but a Netted template press release from the firm's public relations department, issued to the media on Tuesday evening, stated that the managers of the Deathworld environment, because of privacy issues, do not comment on user information unless specifically required to by subpoena or other court order according to the guidelines established by the Protection of Personal Data Bill—

Charlie's dad looked up at him, momentarily distracted by his son's interest. "What?" he said.

Charlie gulped. "Nothing," he said. "I gotta go get ready for school. . . ."

He headed out, but not upstairs, where his books and the take-to-school computer were. He headed for the den and swung into the implant chair. He closed his eyes, twitched the implant awake. It lined up with the Net server and activated. Things went dark—

A moment later Charlie was in his workspace, down by the big worktable in the shining wooden-benched operating theater. The sun was already high there, pouring in the windows. It was noon in London.

"Nick?"

No answer. Charlie was a little surprised by that. He and Nick had for a long time maintained a "live shout" link between their two workspaces: when one of them said just the other's name by itself, while working, the computer would open up a portal between the two spaces without further fuss. *If he was going to change that, he would have told me. . . .*

"Main routine," Charlie said.

"Here."

"Link to Nick Melchior's main Net address."

"Linking now."

Suddenly the air around him went bright, and a sign appeared in it, hanging in front of him: SERVICE SUSPENDED. *Now, that's weird*—Charlie thought, until abruptly that sign flickered, to be replaced by another: FORWARDING.

Has the family changed its master Net address or something? Charlie wondered. It did happen. People changed providers from time to time if they didn't like the service they were getting, but Nick hadn't mentioned anything like that—

There was another flicker, and then Charlie found himself looking at Nick, who was sitting in a bare, white space, in an Eames chair, reading his mail in the form of the usual various floating icons, little colored or flashing cubes and spheres and pyramids and other isometric three-dimensional solids hovering around him in the air. "Nick?" Charlie said.

Nick looked up. "Oh, hi. Come on in."

"What's the blast?" Charlie looked around him with some bemusement. "Where's your workspace? You get tired of Castle Dracula?"

Nick grinned. "Mr. Tact. Nope, my folks pulled the plug on me. Sorry if it's a little bare in here. . . . I haven't had time to refurnish yet. I was mostly occupied with getting the forwarding routine installed around the service block my folks had the provider put in."

Charlie's eyes went wide. "Well, at least you're still online."

"Yeah. It's just a public-terminal account at the twenty-four-hour printing and mailbox place down in the Square, though. I can't spend as much time as I would usually. I have to sneak out to use it. Listen," Nick said as Charlie opened his mouth to say something. "I can't be with you long, I have to get back into Deathworld soonest. I'm on the verge of going seventh-circle, but my last save didn't take and I'm having to re-create a lot of stuff in off-peak."

"I won't keep you," Charlie said. "But listen, did you hear about those two new suicides?"

"Yeah." Nick actually shrugged. "The usual. They got tired of it all. The world stank, and they ditched it. And who could blame them? Anyway, they got a little media exposure on the way out. And they're probably better off. I mean, they couldn't be worse off than to be alive in this world. . . ."

This was so astonishing an assessment, and so utterly unlike anything Nick would normally say, that Charlie's mouth simply hung open for a moment. Finally he managed to say, "What about your folks? What happened to make them yank your boards?"

"My dad got the last Net bill a couple of days ago and pitched a real extinction-level fit," Nick said, and shrugged again. "You know me, though, I can't let it get me down. Got too much to do in the real world. I'm working my way down through the dark, down to the real stuff." He grinned. "You should hear some of the lifts I found down there! The best Bane stuff isn't out on open release, not by a long shot. He's been saving the best for his own people, for us Banies. You really should come down with me and have a listen for yourself."

"Uh, maybe over the weekend. Look, I gotta head out, it's school in an hour. Wanna have lunch?"

"Can't today . . . I've got to get off-campus and make the most of that access time—it's the only time of day when my folks don't really have a clue what I'm up to. Mornings and evenings, they may have their suspicions, but at lunch I'm free. Look, I gotta go, the system's ready for me."

"Yeah, okay, I—"

Nick's image vanished.

Charlie stood there for a moment and hardly knew what to think. *It's like the pod people came to visit and took my buddy Nick. Who the heck was* that??

For a moment more he stood there, irresolute. "Seven A.M." said the clock in the corner.

"Thanks," Charlie said. He was distracted, though. *This is just too weird. But . . . Deathworld. And then . . . these two kids.*

He started to worry.

After a moment he tried to be reasonable, to talk himself out of it. Nick was sensible, Nick was perfectly sane, Nick would never try anything like killing himself—

The normal Nick wouldn't, Charlie thought.

He stood there and sweated. Unlike most of his classmates at Bradford, Charlie knew what death looked like. There were some awful memories from his very early childhood that were not shadows. They were all too solid, and he did not access them willingly. But they were stirring now. And he didn't like the idea of possibly having that kind of memory about one of his best friends.

He's not suicidal, though!

Yet, said the skeptical part of his mind, the part that

his Mom said was capable of "Olympic-level worrying."

But what the frack can I do?

Charlie thought about that for a moment.

Then something occurred to him, an idea which he rejected, and then considered again.

"What time is it again?" he said.

"Seven oh two."

"Thanks." *And now the question is . . . would he be in the office this early?*

Well, I could always leave a message. Either way, it's worth a try. . . .

"Main routine," Charlie said. "Address book."

"What address, please?"

"James Winters, Net Force."

"Trying that commcode for you now."

Charlie swallowed. All Net Force Explorers had a comm-code for Winters, as their "head honcho" and liaison to the main organization. But relatively few of them ever used it—mostly because it was understood that, except in an emergency or a situation involving the safety or security of people using the Net, if anyone misused it, he or she would shortly be out of the Net Force Explorers on his or her ear. Charlie had been contacted by Winters once before, with no bad results. And he'd contacted Winters once before on his own recognizance, and hadn't gotten in trouble—but those calls had involved much more important business. Now, even as he waited, Charlie was beginning to have major reservations over whether Winters would consider this situation anywhere near as important. *If he starts thinking I'm taking advantage or something—*

Nonetheless, Charlie stood still and waited.

"Winters," said the voice almost before the virtuality settled in around Charlie. Winters's office, as it revealed itself a blink later, was relentlessly plain—a metal desk with neat piles of papers, printouts, and datascrips, a pen stand with a U.S. Marine insignia on it, a couple of file cabinets, one of which at least, Charlie suspected, was actually a Net data storage facility in disguise, dusty venetian blinds, and outside of them, a not-overly-inspiring view of a parking lot. The only soft touch about the place was the see-through bird feeder on the outside of the window, which was full of peanuts even though theoretically you were supposed to stop feeding birds after the first of April. The window, the walls, and the filing cabinets, maybe, were real. Everything else Charlie was seeing, he knew, was virtual, an expression of Winters's own workspace, or as much of it as he wanted you to see. Behind the desk sat the man himself: tall, lean, and hard-faced, with his trademark buzz cut looking even buzzier and shorter than usual. Winters must just have had a haircut. He did not look like someone whose time it would be smart to waste. But all the same, his gray eyes were friendly and interested, even at this hour of the morning.

"Charlie," said James Winters, and looked him up and down. "Been a while since we touched base. You're up early."

"Uh, so are you."

Winters shrugged. "Occupational hazard," he said. "One of the few times of the day when the link doesn't go off every five minutes."

"I wanted to catch you before I had to go out to class, if you have a few minutes," Charlie said.

"No problem at all. Come in, take a seat."

Charlie walked "in," sat down.

"How're your mother and father doing?" Winters said.

"Uh, they're fine. Dad's getting ready for some kind of in-service presentation on spinal surgery. Mom's doing a continuing education unit, something about the new nurse practitioner requirements."

"And you? You're coming up on end-of-term time," Winters said, leaning back in his chair. "How's the accelerated program coming along? Any problems?"

"Nothing serious," Charlie said. He did not feel this was the time to mention his personal feelings about calculus, or the fact that his accelerated program required that he take it, or the fact that he had never heard of any doctor needing it.

"That's not what your calc instructor says," Winters said, casting an eye over a glowing-outlined "text window" hanging in the air near his desk. That window looked transparent to Charlie, but he was certain it didn't look that way to Winters.

"I passed the test the second time," Charlie said, instantly breaking out in a sweat.

"I see that. Aced it, too," Winters said, and produced a small smile. "Better than I did the second time. Or the third, or the fourth. Relax . . . you're doing okay." That window vanished. "But this doesn't have anything to do with school, I take it."

"Not exactly," Charlie said. "I'm following up on something I'm curious about."

"Oh?"

"Deathworld."

Winters's eyebrows went up, and he folded his arms. "Saw that in the news, did you."

"That last double suicide, yes," Charlie said.

"No connection has been established," Winters said, "between the suicides and the virtual operation."

"Net Force checked it out, I guess."

"Very completely, after the first two." His eyes rested thoughtfully on Charlie for a moment. "No reason for you not to be given a few details, I suppose. Computer? Insight investigations. Deathworld." Another window opened, and Winters glanced at it. Text scrolled down and through it, and though Charlie could see it this time, it was reversed.

"The first one was in April of 2023," he said. "A young man, aged eighteen, then a young woman aged sixteen, about three weeks later, in early May. While little notice was taken of the first suicide, the second one began to raise concerns that something untoward might be happening. So an investigation was started. At about the same time the two sets of parents began to demand that Deathworld be shut down and Joey Bane be taken to court for reckless endangerment, corruption of youth, you name it. They felt sure that the site was feeding its users subliminal content of some kind, concealed messages that caused their children to kill themselves."

Winters raised his eyebrows. "Anyway, the investigation went forward. Six Net Force undercover operatives were dispatched to check out the Deathworld operation from the inside. Another four-overt agents examined the company's books, programming, and physical plant, and did a guided analysis of the virtual operation's code with the 'SysWatch' code sifter." He scanned down a little more of the text, shook his head, sat back again.

"And they didn't find anything," Charlie said.

"Nothing whatsoever. Clean bill of health," Winters said. "The place may look dysfunctional or even amoral to some people, but it's clean. Queasy-making, but clean."

"What did the kids' parents do?" Charlie said.

Winters sighed. "They continued to agitate for something to be done about the site—preferably to get it shut down. One of them, the mother of the first suicide, the boy, tried to get her senator and local congressman to put special bills through the House and Senate to that effect. That didn't come to anything, which is no surprise . . . the congressional calendar doesn't have time for all the things on it to start with. The other parents did the talk show circuit, gave a lot of interviews to the tabloid press, and they still send out periodic press releases to the various Netcasters and news agencies." He shook his head again. "Not that it's had much effect on Deathworld, or Joey Bane. If anything, it's publicity that increases usage. And truly, without any evidence to suggest that the site really is doing anything to unbalance people. . . ."

Winters turned to look out for a moment at the morning sun beginning to come in through his blinds. Then he glanced back at Charlie. "What brings this up right now?" he said.

"I've got a friend who's all of a sudden interested in

the place," Charlie said. "*Real* interested. In fact, lately he doesn't seem able to talk about much else."

"I take it this isn't normal for him."

"No," Charlie said. "And with these new suicides . . ."

Winters leaned forward with his elbows on his desk. "When you have the volume of people using Net-based facilities that we routinely have these days," he said, "the trouble is that almost any death, no matter how it looks, can genuinely be random." He touched a spot on his desk, and another window, a smaller one, opened itself in the air. It had nothing in it, as far as Charlie could see, but one long string of digits. "Here's today's bonus question," Winters said. "How many people are on the Net right now?"

Charlie tried to catch a glimpse of that long row of digits, but the problem was that almost all the numbers were changing so fast they were a blur. "Worldwide, or just nationally?"

Winters grinned. "Always the right question, with you. Worldwide."

Charlie tried to remember the last set of figures he'd heard. "A quarter of a billion?"

"Try five times that," Winters said, and flicked a finger at the window he'd been watching. It spun so that Charlie could read it. Most of the numbers were still bright blurs, but Charlie could see the numbers 1,263 . . . and then two more sets of three digits each after that, all impossible to read.

"One point two billion and change," Winters said, "just at the moment. It's a function of the time of day. Australia's having its after-dinner entertainment, but most of Greater Asia is still at work. Europe and Africa and Russia are on their lunch breaks, mostly, but they'll be back to work shortly. And the East Coast is up checking the news before it heads in to the office."

He leaned back and looked at the numbers. "The 'tide' ebbs and flows as the Earth turns and the terminator moves," he said, "but the number where the wave 'crests,' at the time of greatest usage, rarely drops below nine hundred million anymore. And it grows all the time as the Netted-in population grows. So, with this information in hand . . . a question. How many of those people are dying right now, while they're on the Net?"

Charlie opened his mouth and then closed it.

"You see the problem?" Winters said. "Let me whittle it down a little, since our viewpoint at the moment should probably stay strictly jurisdictional." The number in the window changed, grew smaller. "On this continent alone, there are a hundred and eighty million people using the Net right this moment. So, consider the statistics. Do you know how often someone dies in North America? Whether they're on the Net or not? From all causes."

"I'm not sure."

"Nineteen per minute," Winters said. "That's an average, of course. You get statistical clusters when there are a lot more deaths than that, and statistical 'dry spots' when there are many fewer. On the same average about fifteen children are born per minute . . . with the same kind of 'real-time' variation on the average. But considering that at peak times maybe half the total population might be on the Net, when their particular moment to die comes along—" He raised his eyebrows. "You can see how we get small clusters of numbers that seem to mean something, but don't necessarily. It tends to make us cautious about chasing patterns that almost inevitably turn out not to be patterns at all. And when you extend the statistical sampling to include the rest of the planet—you see how deceptive the numbers can become."

Charlie nodded.

Winters sighed and leaned back again. "We only have so big a budget," he said. "And there are a lot of people who watch very carefully how we use it. So Net Force has to be very careful of how we chase after data. Granted, we provide an important service. But no one likes a government agency that starts thinking itself too important to use its budget wisely. The day we stop producing results to match our output of funds..." He shrugged. "That day we, and the whole Net environment in our jurisdiction, are in big trouble."

"I see," Charlie said.

Winters paused as a small knocking sound came from the window, specifically, from the peanut feeder, where a small brown bird had just alighted. This in itself was nothing unusual, but the bird immediately picked up a peanut from the feeder, dropped it four stories, then picked up another one, and dropped that, and picked up another one, and dropped that...

"Now, stop that," Winters said. He turned, pulled up the venetian blinds, and tapped sharply on the window. "These guys, you give them all the food they can use, and what happens? They start to get picky. You! Yeah, it's you I'm talking to! Cut it out!"

He tapped on the window a few more times. The bird pointedly picked out two more peanuts, dropped them, and finally selected a third and flew away with it.

"I swear," Winters muttered, "they think I'm a charity." He sighed and turned back to Charlie.

"All right," he said. "If you find anything worth our attention, you'll let me know, of course. But you really should examine the possibility that your friend has something else going on in his life at this point which is making Deathworld look like an attractive alternative to physical reality. There are enough things on the Net that people find useful for that kind of purpose."

Charlie nodded. "I'm looking into it," he said. "But I really don't think that's it."

Winters regarded him with an expression that was hard for Charlie to understand, until he spoke. "Certainty," he said, and the tone was approving... in a way. "It's a wonderful thing to be so sure of your results that you'll discuss them with a superior before you produce the goods."

Charlie swallowed, and hoped it didn't show. "I'm pretty sure," Charlie said.

Winters sat quiet for a moment. "Good," he said. "Then go do some discovery, and report to me when you think you've found out everything you're going to find. If nothing else, what you turn up, if it's anything germane, can be appended to our master file. Data is always good, even if it's just deep background."

"All right," Charlie said. He got up.

Winters stopped him in his tracks with a dark look. "And Charlie—one thing. Any evidence you find that suggests *anything* like conspiracy, or anything else obviously illegal—I want to hear about it pronto. Don't get in over your head."

"Right, Mr. Winters," Charlie said, sweating again.

"Right. So get out of here and get to class."

Charlie started to get.

"Oh, and Charlie—"

He stopped and looked over his shoulder. Winters was half turned to bang on the window glass again, for the brown bird was back, chucking peanuts out of it, four stories down, at about a peanut per second. "One of the better uses for calculus, I'm told, is in the design of custom in-bone surgical prostheses. Check it out."

Charlie grinned. *Does that man read minds? Or just faces?*

He headed back to his workspace in a hurry to get ready for school . . . though school was now the last thing on his mind.

4

That afternoon at Bradford Academy, Charlie saw Nick at lunch, long enough to sit down next to him and spend twenty minutes or so there, but not long enough to have any decent conversation with him, for Nick was surrounded at his table by other kids who knew him, all of them plying him with questions about Deathworld and the Seventh Circle. Nick was positively smirking with glee, telling them about it in hints and riddles, mostly, and pausing to play the occasional scrap of a legally "lifted" audio track from the virtual experience on his pocket HardBard.

Charlie wasn't all that interested in the music. It sounded too much like unadulterated screaming to him, the vocals shrieking so relentlessly that it was hard even to make out the instrumentals, mostly blaring stuff in electrohorn and amplified lute so riddled with feedback that you could hardly tell what key it was in. What did concern him was Nick. His buddy was absolutely holding center court, and plainly enjoying it. A lot of the other students had heard about the suicides, and many of their parents had told them to stay out of Deathworld. A few, whose parents hadn't been concerned, had ventured in and then become seriously frustrated by the challenges of just the first level. All of them were pumping Nick for information about level one, or asking him if he knew any of the kids who'd killed themselves, or if he wasn't worried about getting in more trouble—but Nick was laughing it all off as if it was minor stuff.

Finally the crowd thinned briefly, and Charlie, who had actually had to stand and wait with his lunch tray until a seat opened up a few spaces down the table, was finally able to lean over and say, "Nick, you okay?"

"Huh?" Nick looked at him strangely. "Why wouldn't I be?"

"Your folks just yanked your circuitry," Charlie said. "Most of us might find that a little annoying."

Nick frowned. "It won't last forever," he said. "Besides, I'm getting a job lined up for over the summer. . . . I'll be able to pay for my own access time, and they won't be able to stand over me and say what I should do and what I shouldn't."

This made Charlie blink slightly. Nick was not exactly someone he would have categorized as the rebellious type . . . but all of a sudden all kinds of personality quirks that Charlie hadn't noticed before seemed to be popping out. *Could it just be some developmental thing?* Charlie wondered. *Kind of a stage? People get those. . . .*

"Besides," Nick said to him, looking a little ways across the room, "there's no point in assuming my folks are going to just let this drop, even after I've paid the bill off." And abruptly he looked depressed. His whole face sagged out of shape. "They stink, just like everything else, and if they don't give me trouble about this, they'll find something else pretty quick. About time I started pulling back a little, letting them realize that they don't get to say what kinds of things I enjoy, or get to run my whole life until there's none of it that feels worth living. Soon enough they won't be able to run any of my life, anyhow."

Charlie opened his mouth to start to say that whatever Nick's folks did, they didn't particularly stink. They were certainly no worse than his. And there was something slightly unnerving about the phrasing of that last line, when it came out of somebody wearing that profoundly depressed expression. But then Nick's face brightened up again, just as if someone had thrown a switch, and he said, "Anyway, did you hear the lifts I got?"

"Uh, it was hard not to hear them. The guy's voice is, uh—"

"Staggering, isn't it? Wait till you hear the stuff I bring back later in the week. I'm gonna make Seventh in a matter of hours, and there's a whole bunch of new stuff down there, really hard-edged." Nick grinned, a rather feral look. "And I already got a hint about some of it." He nudged Charlie conspiratorially with one elbow. "You know what the theme is down there?"

"No."

" 'Strung Out.' "

"Oh."

Nick laughed, a laugh that almost sounded like his usual self. "Charlie, you're so deadpan sometimes, they could make coffins out of you. 'Strung—' get it?" And he made a gesture above his head like someone pulling a noose tight, and crossed his eyes and stuck his tongue out, and made a "gack" noise.

Charlie blinked.

"Hey, Nicky," one of the other kids said from the group gathered around his HardBard, "the thing's stopped playing."

"Huh? Oh, that's the copy-defeat, it wants me touching it every so often—"

He scrambled up from the table and went over to them, leaving Charlie staring, somewhat bemused, at a cold cheeseburger. Then the "tone" sounded, a siren-bleat that was a five-minute warning of the approach of the next class period, and soon Nick had vanished, with everyone else. Charlie got up and ditched his tray in the recycler, and went off to his physics class. He got 97 percent on the physics paper he had turned in that morning, an occurrence that normally would have caused him either to do handstands or call the media. But by then, and even several hours later as he waited for the light-rail tram home from school, Charlie was feeling rather grim.

There was no sign of Nick at the school tram stop, at the time they usually met there to share the first part of their respective rides home. *He might have caught an earlier one,* Charlie thought. *Or else he's gone a different way. Maybe caught the bus around the corner, up to the Square, where his new access is.*

Doesn't mean anything's really wrong.

But Charlie was finding that hard to believe.

And what if the problem's actually at my end? Charlie thought, as the tram swung around the corner toward the little plaza that was nearest his house. It wasn't a pleasant idea. *Could it be that I just don't know my best friend as well as I thought I did?*

Charlie got off the tram at his stop and plodded down the street, for once completely unmoved by the scents drifting out of the neighborhood pizzeria, and turned the corner into his street. *And maybe I'm overreacting. Maybe it's nothing. He's been stressed. I've been real busy. . . .*

But that sudden look of depression that had taken possession of Nick's face was like nothing Charlie had seen before. He couldn't get it out of his head, nor could he stop thinking about the way it had come and gone like something turned on and off with a switch. As Charlie went up the front steps and let himself in, he realized he was more worried now than he had been before he talked to Winters.

His folks were out, as he'd known they would be. His mom was going to be coming in later than usual because of her in-service, and his dad was still at the slipped-disk seminar. Charlie rooted around in the freezer for a burrito, put it in the oven, waited thirty seconds for the "ding," put the thing on a plate, and ingested it at high speed, thinking. *You need to get a handle on this,* he told himself sternly. *You need to put Nick aside and concentrate on your research.*

Yeah, sure.

Nonetheless, Charlie sat down at the table, where the "newspaper" still sat, and pulled over a pencil and a scratchpad. "Whether you're going to crack someone's chest or paint a wall," his father always said—the last time, ruefully scraping the last teaspoonful out of a container of spackle—"always make a plan. It saves you time, it breeds more useful ideas, and it keeps you from looking stupid later."

Charlie scribbled on the pad for a few minutes. Having filled one page of it, Charlie paused, wondering one more time if all this was overreaction. *Might be able to get through to him now—*

He dropped his pencil and trotted upstairs to the den, sat down in the implant chair, lined up his implant with the server, and closed his eyes. A little shiver down the nerves, like a shiver of cold, but without having anything to do with temperature, and Charlie was standing in his workspace. Gaslights were lit around the walls of the oval room, producing the usual faint smoky/chemical smell. It was ten in the evening in London, and outside he could hear people making their way to the opera through the crowded eighteenth-century streets.

Charlie stood there looking around him. There were e-mails hanging there in the air over the worktable, bobbing gently up and down, but none of them were vibrating or bouncing around in the way Charlie had programmed his system to use when a message was urgent. He went over to the worktable, touched one of the e-mails. The air lit with its transmission information and source. MAJ GREEN—Nice to hear from her, but it could wait. He touched another of the little spheres floating there, and it lit from within with a blue glow. Next to it a man appeared, saying, "Tired of fast food? Looking for something better in regional cuisine? Come to Georgetown's newest—"

Charlie grimaced, grabbed the spammy little mail-sphere out of the air, dropped it on the floor, and stepped on it. It vanished with a satisfying crunch, and the man vanished as well, making a digitally strangled noise.

He sighed, looked around him. "Nick?" Charlie said.

"Making that connection for you now," Charlie's system said. "Access is open."

"All right—" He went over to the doorway that he used for access, and stuck his head through. But on the other side was nothing but the plain glowing whiteness he had seen before. There, sitting in the midst of it, was the Eames chair, and some mail-solids spinning unanswered in the air, but no sign of Nick.

He went back into his own space and said to his work-space, "Conditional instruction."

"Ready," the workspace maintenance program said. "State the conditions."

"If Nick Melchior calls, e-mails, or shouts for me," Charlie said, "call the house comms number until 2300 hours. Implement immediately."

"Conditional instruction saved. Implementing now."

"Thanks."

Charlie closed his eyes and told his link through the implant to undo itself. With that slight shiver, he was back in afternoon light, in the den again.

With a frown, Charlie went downstairs, sat down at the table, and once more started making notes on the scratch-pad. Soon he'd filled a page, and then another. He was more worried about Nick than he had been on the way home. Afternoon was shading toward dusk when he looked up again at a sound from down the hall.

"Charlie?"

"Down here, Mom," he said, looking with surprise at the pages of notes. His mom—small and dark and petite in her "formal" whites, which she didn't normally wear at work when doing psych—came strolling in, dropped some textbooks and her computer/workpad on the table, and draped her pink sweater over the chair at the table's other end. "You have anything to eat, sweetheart?" she said.

"Uh, yeah."

She opened the fridge and rooted around for a moment, coming up with a jug of iced tea. "I wish," his mother said, sloshing it thoughtfully, "that someone would explain to me why this always goes cloudy in here."

He thought about that. "Microparticulate matter?" Charlie said. "Tea's not really an infusion when you make it out of tea bags. It's a suspension. The characteristics of the suspension change when you chill it."

His mom shut the fridge and went to the cupboard for a glass, then came back to get some ice out of the freezer. "Sounds good to me."

"It's a theory," Charlie said. "I'll ask my physics teacher tomorrow."

"Why? Sounds like you're on the right track." She sat down at the table on his right, glancing idly at the newspaper.

As she did, her eye fell on the headline about the two suicides. Charlie saw her look, and he sighed and pushed away the notes he was making. "Mom—" He glanced up, trying to find a way to begin to explain it all to her.

"Charlie," she said, "what is it? You look like you've lost your best friend."

"Uh, not quite." And he found himself wondering whether the phrase, as she was using it, was intended simply as a cliché. It could be a slightly unnerving experience, having a psychiatric nurse as a mother. Not that she could read your mind or anything—in fact, her normal disclaimer was "I don't *have* to read minds. Faces are more than enough." *Maybe in my case,* Charlie thought, *it's more than usually true. She sees my face every day.* "Suicide—" Charlie said.

"Hmm," she said. "Are we coming at this as a general subject, or for a specific reason?"

He swallowed. "I'm worried about somebody."

"Who?"

Charlie shook his head. "Uh, I want to be clear about my facts first. How do you tell for sure if someone's going to kill themselves?"

"For sure?" his mother said, raising her eyebrows as she sat down. "You don't ever, for sure. I wish . . . Oh, there are various signs. Personality changes . . . changes in behavior, inability to concentrate or do business or schoolwork, for example . . . changes in the way someone sleeps or eats, feelings of worthlessness or hopelessness. Also, a lot of talk about suicide coming up suddenly can be significant. Or gestures like suddenly giving prized possessions away. . . ." She turned her glass around on the table. "You have to look to see how many of these signs are there at once, how serious they seem . . . and look hard to make sure that the person isn't doing these things for some other reason."

Charlie sat back in his chair. "Did you hear about these suicides in the Deathworld virtual environment?"

She raised her eyebrows. "Matter of fact, I have. There was a mention of them in an article in one of the psychiatric journals last month."

"Did the article say anything about what might have caused them?"

His mother thought for a moment. "Nothing concrete," she said. "The authors talked briefly about the details of the people who had suicided, but the article didn't go into a lot of depth. Mostly it was investigating the possibility that this was an 'artefactual suicide cluster,' a situation in which there are an unusually high number of suicides in a given area or set of circumstances, but none of the deaths exhibit any affiliation to the others—any identifiable common cause. A statistical fluke, in other words."

"You mean the article couldn't find any linkage among the suicides, except for the fact that they had all been in Deathworld."

"That's right." His mother shifted in her chair. "But

bear in mind, honey, that this was just a short article, and it was thin on detail."

Charlie thought about that for a moment. "Okay," he said. "Then tell me something else. Have you ever heard of someone committing suicide because of some kind of implanted suggestion?"

She looked thoughtfully at him for several seconds before replying. "While such things can be done," his mom said, "they take a lot of doing. A whole lot. The human mind is committed to keeping itself going, at any cost, even under what looks like intolerable pressure to the outside world. Sometimes it copes by going crazy. Even though that may not seem like a particularly wonderful option to you or me, it satisfies the mind's basic need—to keep on going. It takes a considerable intervention, a very noticeable level of interference, to subvert a mind sufficiently to make it completely give up that commitment to survive."

"Like they used to say that you couldn't be hypnotized into doing something you wouldn't normally do."

"Nothing important, no." His mother leaned back in the chair again. "Let's put it this way. Your whole life is a series of conditioning experiences. Your early life, for example, is about teaching you how to behave in human society, everything from 'Thou shalt not put thy feet up on the furniture' to 'Thou shalt not kill.' " Charlie hurriedly took his feet off the chair nearest to him. His mother smiled. "And your training, the conditioning you get from your parents, your teachers, your friends, slowly slots everything more or less into 'order of importance' in your unconscious, your ID, whatever you want to call the part of your brain that reacts before you really have time to think about it. You learn, ideally, which instructions are really important and which ones aren't. So someone who hypnotized you might not have too much trouble getting you to put your feet up on a chair. On the scale of 'important,' that's pretty low. But if they tried to tell you to kill yourself?" She shook her head. "You wouldn't do it. Not unless you had been conditioned all your life to believe your own survival wasn't particularly important . . . or unless you were deranged already."

"What about subliminal stuff, then?"

She stretched. "That has some effect, yes . . . but they've been arguing about it for a century now, and no one's sure how much. Again, the question has to be taken case by case. Some people are more susceptible to subliminals than others . . . and not necessarily people who are stressed or have psychiatric problems, either. Some environments are more conducive to the administration of subliminals than others, and suggestions which produce strong results in one format or medium will fail completely in another." She shrugged. "Use of subliminals in public communications is illegal, of course. Not to say there's not ongoing suspicion that they're occasionally used. But as for making someone kill themselves?" She shook her head. "I very much doubt it."

"What if someone found a new way to do it . . . more strongly, or in some way that couldn't be detected?"

"New things are happening all the time, honey," Charlie's mother said. "But what can't be changed is the principle on which such a technique would have to operate. To be subliminal, a command has to affect a mind without that mind noticing . . . and a healthy mind tends to notice when something tries to tell it to stop its own function."

Charlie sighed. "Okay."

"Now are you going to tell me what this is about?" she said. "Somehow I don't think this is for some report for school. Are you concerned about one of your friends?"

He hesitated. "Yeah," he said. "But, Mom, I can't tell you any more about it yet. I'm not sure I'm not completely off course."

She gave him a long, considering look. "Funny," she said. "Part of me wants to jump on the table and demand that you tell me everything right now. But part of me reminds that other part that if you're being careful about your conclusions, that's probably something you picked up from your dad and me over time." She smiled, and the expression was rather rueful.

Charlie's mother put the iced-tea glass down. "Okay," she said. "You tell me when you're ready. But, Charlie, if this starts to look like real trouble with your friend, whether you're ready or not, I want you to tell me then. Right?"

"Right," he said.

She got up and took her glass over to the sink, rinsed it out, and stuck it in the dishwasher. Charlie got up and stretched, too. "I feel silly," he said.

"Why, honey?"

"I feel like I should have known all this stuff. When it's explained, it sounds like common sense."

His mother chuckled. "Your father said the same kind of thing," she said, "when he and I first started talking about the human mind, all those years ago. No matter how medical schools swear they're going to pay more attention to the psych side of things, it never really happens. So I married your dad to make sure we would both have plenty of time for me to educate him."

Then she grinned. "Of course," she added, "he thinks the same about *me*. So I suppose we're even." Her smile got more wicked. "But then, doctors always do think they can teach nurses things. Far be it from us to dissuade them. Speaking of which, let me get changed out of this uniform before he gets home. . . ."

She headed out of the kitchen.

Charlie looked at his notes, then gathered them together and went up the stairs to go back online.

He spent the next three hours or so in his workspace, pulling off the Net every reference to the suicides that he could find. Shortly his space was full of scraps of virtual paper floating in the air, both those copied from his original notes and those sourced elsewhere on the Net. He had little windows screening video clips of police statements, too, and local Net and live-media reporters, and scraps of text burning in the air by themselves; stories chained together by little associational lines of light, and here and there a virtual report or reporter, with a genuine piece of landscape, or a person or persons talking. It was very crowded in Charlie's workspace, more so even than the time he called in Sir Isaac Newton and the whole Royal Academy to find out why it took them so long to get the Longitude Problem straightened out.

The images of the suicides were, by and large, not much use to him, and the stories routinely gave him information on everything except what he wanted to know. *What* caused *them . . . ?* No one seemed to have the slightest idea.

About *how* they happened, there was more information. One suicide had been in the kid's own bedroom, another had been in the living room of a kid's house while the parents were away. The third had been like the most recent one, in a hotel room not so far from the suicide's home. A fourth had been in a park. A fifth had been in a car in a public parking garage. Maine, New York City, the D.C. area, a suburb of Atlanta . . . *All East Coast,* Charlie thought, *except this one, in the garage. Colorado. Fort Collins—a college town.*

All of them, actually, were in or near college towns, even the suicide in Maine, in a suburb of Bangor. *But that would be Deathworld's target age, anyway,* Charlie thought. *Eighteen to twenty-five . . .* And the age spread of the victims varied: nineteen, several eighteen-year-olds, a twenty-one-year-old, another who was sixteen.

But that matches the stats, Charlie thought. After talking to his mother, one of the first things he had done online was to pull up stuff on suicide. The age spread of all these suicides generally matched the stats, too. There seemed to be a tendency toward suicide-proneness in the late teens and early twenties, for reasons that none of the authorities seemed able to agree on.

Charlie walked among the scraps of information hanging in the air around him, peering at them, trying to find a pattern. None was obvious, except for one or two mentions of how the suicides had happened. *And maybe there really isn't a pattern, no matter what I'd like to believe,* Charlie thought. *The cops must have looked at all this stuff and decided there was no connection.*

But for whatever reason, Charlie couldn't bring himself to believe this. There was something about all these deaths that bothered him.

Partly it had to do with what had been said in the two news accounts which were even slightly specific about methods . . . and what they implied matched uncomfortably to something Nick had mentioned. *"Strung out . . ."* From what Charlie could find out from random mentions in the chat groups dedicated to Bane and the Banies, there was a lot of this kind of hanging symbolism in the "lower circles." Mostly it was seen there as a good way to punish criminals, especially murderers.

Charlie turned to look at one of the displays, a virtual "snap" taken with a digital handheld sampler—a tabloid picture, obviously taken from a distance, against the law enforcement agency's wishes, using a heat-assisted imager and looking through a window that had carelessly been left open for a moment. It still raised the small hairs on the back of Charlie's neck. It looked, at first glance, like someone hadn't really thought things through. You wouldn't normally think that trying to do yourself in from a coat hook would be all that effective. But in this case it had worked entirely too well. And the face . . .

Charlie was not willing to spend too much time looking at it. The face told him very little. But the awkwardly splayed-out body troubled him more. The sight of it made him gulp, and then he was ashamed of himself, embarrassed, even though there was no one to know about his reaction. But it was going to take a long time to get rid of that initial wash of nervousness at seeing someone lying in that position . . . because when he had been tiny, he remembered seeing people like that in his first home, the home he preferred not to think about anymore. When those scenes surfaced from memory later in his life, when he was old enough to understand, Charlie had realized that those people had all either been stoned, or dead.

He gulped again. He was going to have to come to terms with the worst of those memories eventually, he knew. But it was hard.

For the moment Charlie went back to studying the news story that went with the image. It told him little about the cause of death that he didn't already know. Hanging, obviously. But nothing about the details surrounding the death. No autopsy information. None of the follow-up stories had given anything like that, especially not this virtual tabloid. It was the horror of the death itself that the tab was interested in selling.

I wonder, though. Are the police purposely having the news services withhold information? Charlie thought. It made sense. They might be waiting for someone to reveal information about the crime that only they knew, that they didn't want the general public to have access to.

Good for them. But it doesn't help me any. And he kept flashing on Nick saying, with glee, "Strung out—"

Charlie shook his head and looked back at the "window" in which he had the salient details of the deaths set out. There was something that had briefly attracted his attention earlier, and to which he now returned: the dates. The first suicides were in May and July of the year before last. The third and fourth had been in May and October of 2024 . . . and now here were the fifth and sixth, both in May as well. He remembered Winters's caution about the accidental aspects of this kind of thing. *But at the same time—could May mean something in particular to Deathworld people?* "What's Joey Bane's birthday?" he said to the computer.

"August 8, 1996."

Charlie sighed. "So much for that theory," he muttered. "Have we got the *Encyclopedia Retica* capsule on Bane?"

"Displaying it now."

It spilled out in front of Charlie in two different windows: the text version, with a discography of the man's

music and various analyses of his style by various critics—
most of them surprisingly supportive. Clearly Bane was
thought by his peers to genuinely be a talent, even if Charlie wasn't impressed. The other window had a sound-and-
motion record consisting of snippets of various concert
performances and interviews.

One of these, which appeared in the capsule only as a
soundbyte over some stills—Bane's voice saying, "My
goal is to get Hell to pay me royalties"—caught Charlie's
attention, if only because it was a quote he had heard
several times recently, in the brief flow of news following
the most recent double suicide, and never in context. He
got up, went over to the window, and poked the still then
showing with his finger. The computer said, "Holding.
What would you like me to do?"

"Expand that audio clip. Is there imagery to go with
it?"

"Yes. Expanding—"

Shortly Charlie found himself looking at a full-virtual
version of the infamous Josh Billings interview on CCNet.
There Joey Bane sat, at ease and dressed all in black, in
the well-known and instantly recognizable minimalist set,
looking relaxed and amused as the famous interviewer
tried, unsuccessfully, to get him to say something self-
incriminating. Charlie stood a few feet away, his arms
folded, and watched it.

"Look," Bane was saying to Billings's shocked face,
"you should stop being so hypocritical about it. There's
not a being on this planet who hasn't reflected on the
cruelty and pain of life, the unfairness of it. Some of the
greatest literature of every age has dwelt on the problem.
But nowadays, if we give any consideration to it at all,
we're so terrified of confronting the issue directly that we
do it in secret. There's no consensus that it's all right to
think these kind of thoughts anymore. In fact, nowadays
if you talk about death or pain, people almost immediately
start to think you're morbid, and if you talk about it *fre-
quently,* they're likely to try to have you hospitalized. Is

that fair? Is that sensible? These days we raise our kids
on fairy tales from two centuries ago, for pity's sake, and
suggest to them during the most impressionable part of
their lives that the most they're going to have to worry
about in life is wolves trying to steal their picnic baskets.
When they come to you with their real concerns—that
people suffer and die unfairly, and that the whole *world*
is essentially cruel and unfair, and living in its hurts, we
try to pretend it isn't so, we get uncomfortable, we turn
away and do anything we can to avoid the subject. We
don't have answers. Neither do our kids. If they're lucky
they'll grow up and find some answers that we haven't
seen . . . but *not* telling them the truth about the world, the
Bad News, in my opinion predisposes them to the kind
of despair that causes people to check out early. In my
site, at least, kids get told the truth. *Yes,* the world stinks!
What you do about it, that's *your* business. But at least
there's a place for them to express their anger, which is
a luxury a lot of them don't have anymore in our increasingly nicey-nice culture, where expressing an antisocial
idea 'inappropriately,' or in front of the wrong people,
can get you taken away from your parents indefinitely by
some meddling social worker. In my place kids can *see*
the truth, see the pain, and also see what happens to those
who don't handle that anger right, who seal it over until
it breaks out. You think I condone violence or crime or
hatred? No way. But there's a lot of all those things out
there, and pretending they're not isn't going to make them
go away. I think we help kids by at least *preparing* them
for the idea that the world stinks, so that when their folks
finally let them out of the overprotected hothouse environment that the modern home has become, they're ready
for what they're going to see when they're on their own
when Mommy and Daddy aren't holding their hands anymore. And that's where a lot of the resistance to our site
is coming from, from outraged mommies and daddies
who're ticked because we're telling their little darlings the

truth they never had the nerve or the brains to tell them
themselves. . . ."

It went on like that, nearly half an hour during which
poor Billings barely had room to get a word in edgewise.
Perhaps when he offered Bane the interview time, he
hadn't thought through what it would mean to offer virt-
time to a man with the aerobic advantages produced by
spending hours every night screaming and singing non-
stop on stages real or virtual all around the planet. Only
once did Bane pause, when Billings managed to say, "And
over your gates, where it says 'Abandon hope . . .' . . .
isn't *that* crime? Plagiarism?"

"Nope," Bane said cheerfully. "It was lying around in
the public domain, and no one was using it. I trademarked
it. My goal is to make Hell pay me royalties."

Having come to the soundbyte itself, the image froze
on the confident, arrogant face, and Charlie sat there looking at it for a while, thinking.

The folks accusing this guy of being evil, he thought,
*are wrong. He's not, really. Or at least I don't think he
is.*

*But still . . . something's going on at his site to cause it
to act as a 'core' for these suicides.*

Now all I want to know is: what?

Charlie stood there and brooded for a moment. The
man himself might not mean anyone any harm, but there
was always the possibility that someone in his organization did. That someone was either trying to sabotage
Deathworld by causing these suicides . . . or was running
some other agenda, something a lot more obscure.

After a moment Charlie sighed. If that was the case,
the odds of him ever finding out about it were minuscule.
Besides, he thought, *remember 'Occam's Razor.' Don't
go introducing possibilities into the equation out of nowhere. Deal with the ones you have evidence for, before
starting to make things up.*

Charlie turned away from Joey Bane, frozen there in
his chair, and frowned at the polished wood floor of the

old operating theater as he walked among the "exhibits." *And evidence is the problem. I don't have enough to come to any conclusions. For a good diagnosis, you need data—clinical data—on what happened to these people.*

I could ask Captain Winters. . . . But the information Charlie needed was medical. If it was in the Net Force files at all—which it might not be—it was almost certainly inaccessible under seal of confidentiality.

If there were some other way to get at it . . .

He thought about that. *Violating confidentiality . . . But that's not what I would be doing if I just* looked *at data like that illegally,* Charlie thought. *If I told anyone else about what I found, yes, then it would be. But this isn't about spreading the information around. It's about finding out what really happened. Because I don't think anyone else has yet.* . . .

Charlie sat down on one of the "ringside" benches and looked across at the frozen image of Joey Bane. *And if someone doesn't find out what did happen, it leaves us wide open for it to happen all over again.* . . .

He swallowed, thinking of Nick. Granted, Nick wasn't showing any signs of being suicidal that Charlie could detect. . . .

But then neither were these other kids, he thought. He got up and walked over to the various windows showing the excerpted stories of the earlier suicides, hanging there in the air. He poked a finger into one window, then another, starting their text scrolling by. The second one had a history of depression. But all the rest of them seemed to take everybody by surprise. . . .

"News alert."

Charlie glanced up at that. "Whatcha got?" he said to the workspace management system.

"You asked to be alerted of any news story containing the following term: Deathworld."

"Got something new? Yeah, play it."

Off to one side, in the few open spaces of floor left down in the "pit" at the moment, a newsman sitting behind a desk appeared, with his mouth open, frozen. "Playing content," the program said. "Source: FTNet nightly Net-business news bulletin, today, 1810 GMT—"

The clip started moving. "—ther news, Net host provider SourceStream today published weekly stats which are good news for shareholders, if a little on the macabre side," said the newsman. "Net access and revenue figures for the controversial Net environment 'Deathworld,' which hosts at SourceStream, are up nearly twenty percent from the last half-month reporting period. SourceStream spokesperson Wik Nellis declined to speculate on the sudden leap in the site's popularity, but other industry sources suspect that the cause is the spate of recent suicides which have attracted unwelcome attention from Net-content watchdog groups and law-enforcement agencies in various jurisdictions. Walk-throughs at the 'morbo-jazz' site are up sharply, with SourceStream again declining to confirm the exact numbers, but industry rivals suggest that the publicity may have attracted as many as five million new users to the site, with a potential revenue injection of as much as twenty million dollars in the past two weeks. Meanwhile, the merger of BBC with WOLTime has been—"

The clip froze again. Charlie stood there looking at it, slightly disgusted. "Sick," he said softly. *That these people should be making more money off the fact that their users had been killing themselves—*

Charlie made a face. Then he sighed. It probably wasn't their fault. But it annoyed him nonetheless.

"Save that," he said to the computer.

"Done," it said as he turned his back on the clip and looked at the other pieces of information littering the place, and strolled among them, trying to think. But a most paranoid idea occurred to Charlie suddenly, so awful that it stopped him dead in his tracks. Supposing that people at Deathworld were causing people to kill themselves in order to drive the user stats and revenue up?

He shivered. *Oh, that's a sick idea. This is making me morbid.*

Besides, you would need evidence that they were able to make people do something like that . . . and you don't have any.

Charlie sighed. *Just paranoia,* he thought, and walked among the "exhibits" for a few moments more. *Too many clues . . . not enough hard data for a real theory. For any kind of theory.*

I need harder data. I need those autopsy reports.

He sat down on one of the benches and looked out across the Pit.

But how am I going to get them?

He sat there thinking for a long time, while outside, eighteenth-century London started (finally) to go to bed, and the sky showing high up in the Royal Society's windows started to pale toward dawn.

And suddenly Charlie sat up straight. *Mark!*

"Time check," Charlie said.

"Twenty twenty-nine."

"I want to make a virtcall," he said. "Mark Gridley."

"Trying that connection for you now . . ."

In another part of the virtual realm entirely, it was raining fire, and Nick was standing under an asbestos golf umbrella and wondering just where to go from here.

The patter of ash and live cinder on the umbrella over his head would have been strangely soothing had it not been for the brimstone smell in the air and the shrieks and wails of those in torment. All the cries were wordless, here. The Damned in this circle had been deprived of the only thing that had marked them as human while they lived on earth, the gift of speech. In all other ways that mattered they were judged to have abandoned their humanity, and so they ran forever under the fiery rain, with demons scourging them through the black, blasted, ash-strewn landscape. In the distance, on the lowering horizon, a volcano was erupting, belching ash and fumes and fountains of lava into the air, and the ground rumbled constantly, crevasses always ready to open up and swallow the Damned as they ran.

Nick started forward cautiously. It was difficult to see where you were going, and those crevasses were very much on his mind—naturally you couldn't really get hurt down here, but until you knew what the crevasses entailed in terms of gameplay, it was wise to be cautious.

"Going somewhere?" someone said from behind him.

Nick turned and saw a shadow of someone about his height standing there and watching him, with folded arms. At least he thought they were folded. She was more a silhouette against the deeper darkness than anything else, apparently wearing a long dark "shellcoat" with its three draped layers—though the hood was pushed back to show a head with shoulder-length hair, held at what looked like a somewhat arrogant angle. She was eyeing him, finding him amusing.

"Are you real?" Nick said. Down here, it was a fair question.

"I'm another Banie, if that's what you mean," she said, tossing her hair out of her eyes, flicking away a couple of burning ashes. "You just get here?"

"Uh, yeah."

"Come on, then, and I'll get you oriented. You know where you're going?"

Nick pointed toward the only light he could see, the volcano.

"Mount Glede," she said, "that's the spot. Come on . . . it's a bit of a walk."

She set out, and Nick went after her. "Not used to doing this with a friendly guide," he said.

"Don't mistake me for anything friendly," said the dark shape next to him, sounding annoyed. "I'd as soon leave you to your own devices. But that's not how this circle works. We have to help each other." The expression in the girl's eyes was sullen and bored, as if she thought Nick was a waste of her time.

The opinion was mutual, but Nick had come far enough by now, and spent enough time and money in Deathworld, that he wasn't going to let mere bad temper, hers or his, interfere with his conquest of this environment. "You never did tell me what to call you," he said.

She didn't quite grit her teeth, and Nick could just hear her thinking, *I didn't intend to.* But finally, "Call me Shade," she said.

He smiled slightly, though he turned away so she wouldn't see it. Every Banie knew that Joey himself, or the surrogates of him which were part of the program, sometimes walked the circles in disguise, pretending to be just another Banie, and if you mistreated someone else who was working their way down, or went against the House Rules, the House could very well use it against you. Chances that might otherwise have been offered to you would be withheld; luck wouldn't go your way.

"So what do we do now?" he said.

"You didn't tell me your name, either," Shade said, eyeing him.

"Nick," he said. It was how the system knew him. He didn't see any point in establishing a handle just now.

"Well, Nick, mostly we head for the Mountain, and try to keep from getting distracted, or falling into any crevasses. That's gonna be a full-time job, so stay close and don't go running off after the inmates."

He followed her as she set off. It was difficult going until your eyes got used to it. The constant fall of ash produced an effect like black snow, a dead, soft, soot black with no highlights, no features—you put your feet down without any real sense of when they would hit anything solid. The only light was that dim red glow from the volcano, the swift-fading glimmer of the flakes of burning ash as they fell, and the burning whips of the demons that chased the Damned across the plain through the shin-high, fluffy blackness.

"Look," Nick said as he struggled to keep up with her,

"Shade, aren't we supposed to ask these guys here anything?"

She laughed at him. "Not much point in that," Shade said. "They can't do anything but scream. They could speak once, but it was taken away from them after they became murderers and wound up down here. According to Joey, they're no better than animals."

Nick opened his mouth, but she flung her hand out to stop him. "There," she said, and pointed right down in front of them. Slowly, softly, and silently, the earth was yawning open. He would have missed it until it was too late, and would already have been falling down into what he could just now make out as a dim, red, angry glare.

"Uh," Nick said, swallowing.

"Yeah, 'uh,' " Shade said, scornful. "Game over, if you fall into one of those. Big waste of time. No recall from that, either. No 'save' from a crevasse. So watch yourself."

Together they sidetracked a long way to their left to get to the point where the crevasse narrowed enough to be stepped over. "I was going to say," Nick said, "if they can't talk—what's the point of them being here?"

Shade looked at him with amusement. "It's not like seeing the guilty get punished for murder isn't worth something by itself. Wouldn't you say?"

Far away across the dark landscape, Nick thought he could hear something like an electrolute tuning up. His heart leaped. "That's a new 'lift'—"

Shade sighed. "Yeah, it's the warm-up for 'Strange Fruit.' Not a bad cut, that one."

" 'Strange Fruit'—"

"It's a cover," Shade said. "Joey doesn't do many covers. A lot of people down here think it's a tribute to the Angels of the Pit."

Nick shook his head, confused.

"You really haven't *talked* to a lot of people down here, have you," Shade said.

"Uh, no."

There was another long sigh. "I guess it's understand-able," she said, rather more softly, as they went forward. "The upper circles aren't much about talking to real peo-ple. The 'Angels of the Pit'—those are the kids who died after being down here."

"The ones who committed suicide—"

"We don't usually put it that way," Shade said, pausing again as another crevasse started to open up in front of them, and leading Nick off to the right this time. " 'Death wears many faces. . . .' That's what the song says. They left us before they were finished. Whatever made them do it, they're gone now, but we remember them. . . ."

This was so unlike what Nick had been thinking about the suicides that he was startled. "Didn't any of them make it . . . you know . . . all the way down?"

Shade shook her head. "No way. No one who's ever made it down into the heart of the Ninth has done any-thing like that. There are things that happen down on Nine. . . ." Her voice trailed off.

"Like what?" Nick was eager. He had almost never heard even a scrap of rumor about Nine before.

Shade laughed at him then. "You're asking me?" she said. "You think I've been down there? As if I'd still be slumming around up here if I had. . . ." She sounded scornful again. "No, some of them just come back and help a few newbies before they go on. I've got a ways to go yet."

They went on in silence for a while, following the faint tune-up notes of Camiun across the darkling plain. It was hard to judge distances, but Nick thought it would have been something like a mile in the "real" world. A Damned person ran by them, howling, in battle fatigues, and be-hind him came a couple of winged demons, their whips aflame, every stroke burning a white-hot slit through the big burly man's combat jacket as he fled from them. Nick slowed down to watch him go.

"Some gangster," Shade said, bored. "We get a lot of them down here. Little tin-pot dictators and their paramilitary hangers-on. While they're in power they think they're invulnerable, that they can kill anybody they like. But sooner or later it catches up with them. Their henchmen learn their bosses' lesson too well, that you don't have to treat anybody with pity, or compassion . . . and eventually the henchmen turn right around, shoot their bosses, and take their jobs. Not that they last long." She chuckled.

Ahead of them, the volcano seemed to be getting closer, and Nick squinted at it. There was something odd about the shadows at its base. He was distracted, though. The darkness, the ash and the screams, they all seemed to press in strangely, and Camiun's tinkly tuning cadences seemed unusually distant. "Kind of depressing down here," Nick said.

Shade looked at him thoughtfully as she jumped over a small narrow crevasse that opened up in front of them. "You feel that way?" she said.

Nick nodded. "Sometimes. But it's worse up at home . . . a whole 'nother story."

"Problems?"

Nick made a face. "The usual. My folks think I'm wasting money down here. Even some of my friends think I'm wasting time. None of them seem to think I'm capable of figuring out what I really want. 'You're too young to really know.' 'You'll get over this, it's just a fad. . . .' " He sighed, glanced up at her. "What about you?"

Shade laughed. "Yeah, I've heard the same kind of thing. I ignore it. And my folks and my friends don't know anything about down here . . . so I ignore them, too. They're all so concerned, like it's going to affect my mind somehow. But, I mean, what's down here that could possibly be more depressing than real life?" And she gave Nick a look that, even in this dim light, was extremely ironic. "Not enough money to do the things you want to, not enough time to do them if you had the money, not enough life to do everything you'd like to even if you had the time—what could be worse than that? This is just

dark. And for us, not even painful . . . not as painful as
the Real World." She pronounced the words with profound disdain. "A day job you can never afford to give
up until you're too old to remember what you would have
done with your days, if they'd been yours to spend, when
you were young. What's a little fire and brimstone to
that?"

She looked closely at Nick as they walked, almost as
if there was some response she was expecting.

"I don't know," Nick said. "Life stinks, yeah, but I
don't know if it stinks *that* much—"

"You *are* young yet," Shade said. "Just wait awhile.
You probably have all these great ideas about how wonderful it'll be when you get out on your own, how you'll
have all this terrific freedom. Wait till you do it, and see
how hard you have to work just to keep a roof over your
head and enough food inside you to keep your stomach
from waltzing with your backbone every night . . . while
the people you're interested in take themselves out of your
life, one by one." She laughed. "After too much life spent
that way . . . I can understand why some people might
want to . . . you know. Do what *they* did. The Pit Angels . . ."

Nick had no immediate answer to that, for what Shade
was saying had abruptly struck him with surprising force.
It had never occurred to him that he *wouldn't* find life better after he finally left home, that there might be a *bad*
side to freedom. But now, hearing it from someone down
here, the possibility occurred to him that he might be making a mistake. *Yet at the same time, if I don't make that
mistake, I'm trapped.* . . . Trapped with an angry mom and
dad, in an apartment that was too small and where they
watched his every move to see whether they would approve of it. And if he kept going the way he had been going, before this most recent blowup, what would follow?
College, but if he didn't manage to get a scholarship to
someplace far enough away that he would have to live on
campus, it would just be the same thing all over again . . .

but even more intolerable, because he would be *college-age* and still having to obey his parents' dumb rules. Everyone would laugh at him, and the whole point of college, getting away and exercising some independence, would be lost.

Yet Nick was pretty sure that he wasn't going to be in line for any scholarships. His grades hadn't been perfect. He was holding his own at Bradford, not in danger of failing . . . but the grades he had at the moment weren't going to get him into anything but the state college or one of the community colleges in the area. He could just hear his folks. *Why spend money on boarding at someplace that's only twenty miles away? You'll stay here with us.*

. . . *Where they can keep me under their thumb.*

Suddenly it all seemed very hopeless, and Nick just stopped where he was and gazed ahead in the blackness as Shade kept going. Suddenly he could understand it. Not wanting to go on, not seeing the point. Past college, what would there be for him? He wasn't even particularly sure what he wanted to do in the world. Or that there *was* anything for him to do in the world. For the past couple years now he had been surrounded by kids working hard, full of plans and goals, and he had laughed at them— busting their guts as if they were adults working at something that really counted. Now here he was, without any plans or goals, and suddenly Nick suspected that the other kids had, all along, known something he hadn't. Now they were heading toward lives, busy lives full of interesting things to do, even if the work was hard. *And here I am,* Nick thought, *with nothing. Nothing.*

And parents who're going to remind me of it every chance they get, for the foreseeable future.

Suddenly Nick could understand how nice it might be for it all just to stop. *Like going to sleep and not waking up.* The sudden desire for it to be that way, just quiet, just no more trouble, came down on him, darker and stranger than the surroundings . . . and Nick shivered.

Shade stopped, looked back at him. "Nick. Come on, what's the matter?"

"Uh, nothing."

That feeling was gone now, but it had been . . . weird. Nick went after her, shaking the umbrella a little to get the excess ash off it. The dark shape up ahead of them, in the shadow of the mountain, was a little better defined now, starting to look like a building. "Uh-oh, watch out for this one," Shade said, stopping very suddenly.

Nick stopped and looked down, stepping back hurriedly as the growing crevasse shot out arms in several directions, one of them stitching along right in front of his feet, the ash in front of him tipping down into it, faint flakes of darkness against the quickly revealed dull-red glow of the flow of lava, away down there. In the air above them, Camiun's tuning-up paused and then segued into a low quiet minor-key strumming. "So strange," Joey Bane's voice sang, "so strange . . ."

They made their way around the new crevasse, and kept walking. A shadow reared out of the air near them as they walked. Nick stopped and stared at what was swinging there. Two shapes. It wasn't a tree of any kind. It was some sort of metal framework, and a man and a woman were hanging upside down from it. "Mussolini," Shade said. "You know—Italy . . . last century. They caught up with him, eventually." She raised her eyebrows, just visible in the light of the nearby volcano. "There are plenty more like that around here if you care to investigate. . . ."

"Thanks, no." Nick gulped, sickened by the image swinging gently in front of him. Then he looked past Shade, still unnerved by that odd feeling that had come down on him, and saw something more to the point. Past the tall metal frame, at the foot of the volcano, was something that interested him a whole lot more. A faint shimmer of light, something genuinely reflective in all that dead matte black—a wide, dark sheet of water. It was the Lake of Tears, and beyond it, reflecting darkly, rose the Keep of the Dark Artificer at last, all gleaming black tow-

ers and walkways, and high up in one tower, a single
light.

"That's really it," Nick whispered. "Finally . . ."

"Yup," Shade said, looking at the Keep. To Nick's eye
she looked astonishingly blasé about something which, in
its way, was the heart of Deathworld. "Bigger than it
looks," she said. "Don't be fooled by it."

He nodded, then turned back to Shade. There was
something about her voice, something sad. . . . "Are you
okay?" Nick said.

She looked at him in surprise. "Why wouldn't I be?"
The answer was defensive, flip, a little sarcastic. . . .

Why wouldn't I be? he'd said to Charlie, and laughed
at him. And Charlie had genuinely been concerned. Nick
bit his lip. "Just asking," he said.

"Yeah, well, thanks." She tossed her hair back, a
shadow in her greater shadow. "So what are you waiting
for? You pass . . . you might as well go on in and see
what's waiting."

"Pass?" Nick was bemused. "But I didn't do anything."

Shade gave him that scornful look again. "You asked
the right question," she said, and began to fade away in
the volcano's feverish light.

"But which one?"

She grinned. "If you have to ask," Shade said, "I can't
explain it. Go on, go ahead and see if you get anywhere
in the Keep. The way to Nine is through the Keep, they
say . . . if you can figure it out. But I wouldn't hold out a
lot of hope."

She vanished completely.

Nick turned to look at the huge doors of the Keep.
Slowly, hauled open by troops of demons singing *yo-yo-
heave-ho*, and pulling on giant bronze ropes, the massive
doors swung open before him. Nick stood there feeling a
great flush of triumph as Camiun's voice cried out in
feedback-fuzzed ecstatic arpeggios all up and down the
scale.

The demons stood waiting, standing at attention.

Nick, though, stood still there, thinking.

The way to Nine is through the Keep, they say . . . if you can figure it out.

Nick stood there, considering, for a while . . . then deliberately turned his back on the Keep and started to kick his way back through the downfalling ash, back the way he had come.

"Hey," yelled one of the demons down by the door, "where ya goin'?"

"Back to help some people," Nick said, and scuffed off into the darkness, toward the edge of the Eighth Circle again.

From the shadow of the doors, a tall dark form, not a demon, faded back into existence, watching him go . . . and smiled.

5

Mark Gridley's workspace this week looked like the old Vehicle Assembly Building down at Cape Canaveral. This was a new one on Charlie, though it didn't exactly surprise him. On earlier visits he had seen it looking like an underground cave full of stalactites and stalagmites, like a single gigantic floor of an office building towering over the Singapore skyline, like the entrance hall of the Museum of Natural History in New York, like the salt flats outside Bonneville, Utah, and like the surface of the Moon—an area not far from the Lunar Appennines, where some astronauts had left their moon buggy. In his own version of that empty, arid place, Mark had constructed a garage for the buggy, one which had also quizzically sheltered a beat-up lawn mower and a folded-up Ping-Pong table. Charlie had come to believe, both at the sight of those workspaces and during some of the events later associated with his visits to them, that it was entirely possible Mark Gridley might have a hinge loose somewhere.

But whether he did or not, there was no ignoring the

fact that Mark was possibly the single most dangerous person on the planet, at least as far as the Net was concerned. Whether heredity had anything to do with it, Charlie wasn't sure. Having the head of Net Force for your father and a talented computer tech/heavy-duty philosopher for your mother could certainly predispose you to think more about the Net than a lot of people did. But just thinking about it a lot couldn't possibly endow anybody with the kind of talents Mark had with computers in general and the Net in particular. He was a genius at getting into any kind of computer system, and exploiting it while there. Maj Green had remarked once to Charlie that the Net Fairy had plainly been present at Mark's christening. Charlie wasn't so sure about that, but there was no keeping Mark out of any system he was interested in . . . and he was interested in everything.

At least, he always had been before. Today Charlie was banking on the idea that nothing had changed.

Charlie headed across the vast concrete floor of the VAB, looking for signs of life. He didn't see any. The huge space, thirty stories tall, was empty. This by itself wasn't so odd: in the real world it had been a long time since spacecraft had been built there, and mostly the building was kept for its history as the assembly area for the first rockets to take man to the Moon, and because demolishing the VAB would have upset the colonies of pygmy Cape buzzards that nested there and worked the little "pocket" weather system inside the building.

Off in one corner, though, about a quarter mile away, Charlie saw where a beam of sunlight came in through the movable cowling in the roof, and shone down on what looked like a conversation area—various chairs arranged in something like a circle, with a big low hardwood desk off to one side. Charlie made his way toward this, listening to the creaks and cheeps of the buzzards above him as they circled in a mini-updraft near the roof.

"WHO DISTURBS THE GREAT AND POWERFUL OZ?" thundered a huge voice all through the VAB. The buzzards squeaked in protest and flapped over to the sides of the building, perching and shaking their heads at the noise.

"It is I," Charlie said, rolling his eyes. "I mean, it's me, Squirt. Lay off the 'great and powerful' trip before I choke myself laughing."

"I don't think you take me seriously enough," said a much more normal voice, that of a thirteen-year-old kid again. It echoed in the huge space, but didn't roar as it had a moment before. Mark came into sight now from somewhere behind the "conversation circle," his arms full of e-mail images. He was wearing swim trunks and a MoldToYou T-shirt which was presently showing, one phrase at a time, in bold white letters on black, the message SPACE IS BIG / SPACE IS DARK / IT'S HARD TO FIND / A PLACE TO PARK / BURMA SHAVE.

Charlie blinked at that. Mark was part Thai, but he wasn't sure what Burma had to do with anything. "How is it possible to take you anything *but* seriously," he said. "You busy?"

"Nothing important," Mark said, dumping the load of e-mails onto his desk of the moment. They scrambled around on the surface of the desk, putting themselves in some prearranged order, and then ascended gently into the air and hovered there, like well-trained bubbles. "Just trying to get down to the bottom of the In-box before the end of the week."

"Why? What's the end of the week?"

Mark snickered and brushed his dark hair out of his eyes. He was due for a haircut, or maybe this was just some new style he was trying out. "My dad's been threatening to take me surf-fishing for about the last year. Well, the stars or whatever must be propitious, because we're going away for the weekend, up to some place on the Jersey shore. Or so he claims." Mark gave Charlie a knowing grin. "I'm betting you something'll come up Saturday morning and it'll all be off. But I can't absolutely count on it, so . . ."

"WAAAH," said something nearby, a raspy upscaling voice that vaguely suggested a soul in torment.

Mark looked over his shoulder. "Yeah, yeah, it'll be dinnertime soon," he said to someone Charlie couldn't see.

"What was that?" Charlie said, looking around. It didn't sound like a buzzard.

"The cat. Theo," Mark said. "Or, as we call him, The Gut Who Walks." Another piercing Siamese-cat shout filled the air, suggesting either that Theo didn't appreciate the characterization, or that this conversation wasn't producing food, or that he was testing the acoustics. "So look, what brings you by? Not that I don't think it's entirely social."

Charlie grinned. Mark had taken some ribbing from the older Net Force Explorers about his age, and his size— he was short and light even for a thirteen-year-old—until they started to discover that the area in which Mark was decidedly no lightweight was his brain, and that he could outthink, and sometimes outmove, any of them. Those who had christened him the Squirt as a joke had since turned it into a title of honor, and kids five or six years older than he was had soon learned not to treat Mark as if he were too young to be taken seriously. Charlie had never been one of these. He knew entirely too much about what it was like to have people decide because of your background that you weren't worth their time.

"Got a problem, Squirt," Charlie said.

Mark looked surprised, and eyed him curiously. "Yeah, you do, don't you?"

"Does it show?"

"You look bothered. What's the matter? Trouble with your folks?"

"Me? No." Charlie laughed, but he wasn't surprised that the sound didn't come out sounding particularly humorous. "Look, I have to ask you something."

"Blaze away."

"I'm not sure it's not illegal."

Mark put up his eyebrows. "Oh? Not your usual mode of operation, Mr. Straight Arrow."

"Don't remind me. I need to get at some information."

"You interest me strangely."

Mark's suddenly delighted expression made Charlie laugh. "Nothing real involved. I need to get at some medical records."

Mark looked bemused. "Thought you'd usually ask your dad about that kind of thing."

"Not just general information. I need to get at some county coroner's files."

"Aha," Mark said, and leaned back in his chair. "Not public files, then."

"Nope. Autopsies."

"Wow, truly disgusting," Mark said, not sounding disgusted in the slightest. "I wanna see, too."

"Not sure it would be good for you to see this stuff," Charlie said, uneasy. "Heck, I don't really even want to see it."

"You're gonna have a hard time getting at it in the first place without me," Mark said, sounding all too matter-of-fact. "Come on, Charlie, I'm not going to look over your shoulder if you're really worried. But it'd make me feel a lot better if you'd tell me what was going on."

Charlie didn't see that he had any choice. He sat down on one of the chairs pulled into the circle and told Mark the basics of his problem, without mentioning any names.

When he was finished, Mark sat down across the circle from him and folded his arms, thinking. "Been a lot of attention on Deathworld, hasn't there?" he said. "Since the last couple of suicides . . ."

"Yeah."

"But you don't need me to break in there, I take it."

"Nope. It's just this medical stuff I'm after."

Mark sighed. "Pity," he said. "Deathworld would have been a challenge. . . . But as for this other stuff, we can do it this evening, if you like."

"Really?"

"Shoot, we can do it now."

Mark opened a drawer in his desk, looked at the e-mail "solids" floating around above the desk. "Okay, everybody in. . . ."

One after another the icons dropped into the drawer, all but one, a recalcitrant sphere that hung bobbing in the air over the desk and wouldn't budge. "Yes, you, too, get in there!"

"You promised you would deal with this today," said the e-mail, in Jay Gridley's voice.

Charlie's eyebrows went up. Mark flushed pink and grabbed the mail out of the air, stuffing it in his pocket. "No rest for the weary," he said. "Never mind."

Mark dusted his hands off, knocked the drawer shut with his hip. "Okay," he said, "let's see what you've got."

Charlie fished around in his own pocket and came up with a notepad, the icon for a little file full of bureau names that he was carrying with him. He handed it to Mark. Mark tossed it onto the desk, and a window appeared in the air in front of them and displayed the list.

"Mmm," Mark said. "Bangor County Coroner's Office, Collins County Police Coroner, Arlington City Coroner's Department . . ." There were six offices matched with six victims—the paired suicide, the most recent one, was being handled by two different coroner's offices, as the kids had lived in two different jurisdictions.

Mark stood there with his arms folded, thinking for a moment. "Let's do the county systems first," he said. "Then the police ones. The cops are likely to have better security, and they might take us a little longer."

"You don't think they're likely to alert each other that someone's going after data on the suicides?" Charlie said, beginning to get nervous. He was feeling guilty already.

"I doubt it," said Mark. "There isn't nearly as much cooperation between police forces as there should be if they really want to make their systems secure. Especially regionally. Too much rivalry . . ." He grinned slightly. "Old habits die hard. Besides, these people don't seem to have been comparing notes in the first place, do they? I mean, just from what you told me now, the fact that all the suicides seem to involve a hanging of one kind or another—no one seems to have picked up on that. At least nothing's been mentioned about it on the news."

"They might be hiding that information," Charlie said, uncertain.

"If they were coordinating, yeah. But we don't have any proof that they are. So let's stir around a little and see what we find. If any of the data you're interested in is trip-wired, or has associational links to similar data in some other police department's network, then that might indicate that they're talking to each other privately about this stuff. Meanwhile"—he looked at the list—"Let's start with Bangor."

Mark looked around him. "Okay," he said to his workspace, "strike the set."

The VAB, the sunlight, the little flickery shadows of the buzzards away up high—it all vanished away in a blink, leaving them in a peculiar sort of darkness in which the two of them were illuminated, but nothing else was. The only other thing visible was the window with the names of the agencies Charlie wanted to raid for information. "Bring up the advanced-level penetration utility," Mark said.

And the floor of Mark's workspace suddenly became visible. More than visible. It was transparent, so that Charlie could see down into it, for what looked like maybe a thousand meters. The space below their feet was full of light, light of every color, columns and lines and pillars of it, some horizontal but mostly vertical, interwoven, sometimes even interpenetrating. This was an expression of a program that Mark had designed for getting into other programs. "What language did you write *this* in?" Charlie said, very impressed.

"Digamma, it's called. Nasty stuff."

"I believe you." Charlie knew in a general sort of way that every line of the light he saw reaching down to limitless depths beneath him was a statement in computer code of some kind, but there his knowledge stopped. "Man, I'm just getting the hang of Caldera. I thought *that* was complicated—!"

"Yeah, you wouldn't want to mess with Digamma unless you were seriously unbalanced," Mark said. He looked down into the abysses of light, and the whole deep panorama began moving with great speed underneath him, slipping sideways. Then it was as if the floor on which they stood plunged downward like an elevator, though they weren't actually moving at all—rather, the graphic expression of the "penetration" program was pouring itself up past the two of them into the air around them as ghosts of structures of light. It paused, then pouring sideways again as the program sorted for some specific spot that Mark had in mind. After a moment it stopped, which was a good thing, because Charlie's stomach was bouncing around inside him as if he was on a roller coaster.

" 'Unbalanced,' " Charlie said, trying to get control of himself. "This suggests certain possibilities about you, Mr. Gridley."

"Don't it just," Mark said, sounding distracted for a moment. "Necessary, though. A lot of the Net Force master computers' routines are running in Digamma . . . you want to work with those, you have to learn it eventually. My dad started teaching it to me when I was seven. I'm just now really getting the hang of it." He interlaced his fingers, cracked his knuckles. "Okay, now watch this."

He beckoned over the window in which Charlie's "addresses" were written, and poked the first one with his finger. "Identify," he said to his program, "and locate."

They stood there in the bright silence for a moment, and suddenly a string of letters and numbers which meant nothing whatsoever to Charlie strung themselves out in the air in front of him and Mark in a blaze of crimson. Around them, the colors of the penetration program went mostly to blues and greens.

"Good," Mark said. "That's the raw Net address. It tells

me a little about their security . . . which frankly, needs to be looked at. These guys must think they're safe from intrusion." He smiled slightly. "Well . . ."

"Can you get in?" Charlie said.

"In? We're in already." Mark glanced around him. "At least, we're in their system. Now we have to crack their security, preferably without them noticing, and go hunting. Look, the information you want, it'd probably be easier for you to identify as images, yeah?"

"That's the best way for me."

"Okay. Home system. Go graphic."

Everything went dark, then filled with light again, and the two of them found themselves looking at a wall. It reared up as high above them as they could see, and ran off to what seemed infinity in both directions. It appeared to be made of red brick, and some wit had posted up on it a neatly lettered sign that said: FIREWALL.

"Everybody's a comedian," Mark said, walking alongside the wall for a little way, examining it. "Let's see what we've got here. C³? Caldera? Levolor?" He patted the wall, felt one of the bricks. "Nope, it's Fomalhaut. One of the lousiest programming languages of the decade. *Why* in the world did they use Fomalhaut for this?"

Charlie stood watching Mark kick the wall once or twice in an experimental kind of way. "What's the matter with the language?"

"Terrible structure," Mark muttered. "You have to really like doing things over and over to use Fomalhaut. Look at this—" He glanced up and down the length of the wall. "In any normal virtual programming language, a wall like this would be set up with one command that you then told to repeat itself however many times, and then you would tell it where to stop, or to seal itself up. In Fomalhaut, you have to do every single command separately." Mark shook his head. "Each of these"—he kicked another brick—"represents a separate command. Really dumb."

"So why would they have used it, then?"

Mark shrugged. "Oh, some people might think it was better for security. More trouble, they would think, to have to disassemble a 'wall' brick by brick, you couldn't just subvert one. But plainly it didn't occur to them that sooner or later a more sophisticated way to deal with this protocol might come along. Or that someone else who knew the language really, really well—"

Mark reached out behind him, plucked something out of the empty air. It was a crowbar.

Charlie had to laugh. " 'More sophisticated'?"

"Yeah, don't laugh. You'll see. Meanwhile—" Mark stood there and touched one brick. It lit from within, revealing what looked like a little churning square of boiling alphabet soup, all letters and numbers. "Right." Mark said. "And this one—" He touched another brick, farther down the wall. It revealed another oblong full of soup. "Uh-huh. One more—"

The third brick revealed the same contents. Mark stood there for a moment. "Someone here," he said with satisfaction, "got real sloppy. These aren't all separately written instructions. They've been cloned from a single one. Jeez, a *lazy* Fomalhaut programmer. What's the point? Why use an obsessive-compulsive language, and then not obsess?"

Mark shouldered the crowbar and grinned at Charlie. "Never mind," he said, "we're in business."

He put two fingers in his mouth and whistled.

From some distance away came a tiny sound, like a faraway screech of surprise. "Aha," Mark said, cheerful. "Come on, that's what we're after."

He started to jog to their left, down the wall. Charlie followed him. "Look," he said, "what are our chances of getting caught in here?"

Mark grinned as he trotted along. "No better than one in a hundred at the moment." Charlie instantly broke out in a sweat. He preferred *much* longer odds. "I mean, think about it, Charlie! Programmers are a spoiled bunch these days. They work what they used to call 'banker's hours.'

Nobody in the coroner's office in some little county building in Maine is going to be hanging over their terminal at eight-thirty in the evening waiting to see if someone breaks in or not! If the system is even housed in the same building, which isn't necessarily the case. And their automatic system security is junk. I know, because I broke through it five minutes ago. I pretended to be its system administrator, and my penetration manager gave it a nice set of circular instructions to play with, based on its own check cycle . . . so right now it's doing the machine equivalent of staring in the mirror and telling itself that everything is fine. And here we are."

Mark stopped and pointed at a brick high up in the wall. "See that?"

That particular "brick" was glowing red hot. "Kind of hard to miss," Charlie said.

"That's the instruction all these other ones were cloned from. Now then." Mark started to walk up the air as if there were stairs there. With the crowbar he pried out that particular brick and caught it in one hand as it fell.

The wall started to crumble. Charlie jumped back, out of reflex, but as the wall tottered outward toward him, the bricks began to fade: By the time they reached the "floor," they were vanishing like fog in sunlight. A moment later he and Mark were looking out across a vast hall full of thousands of beige filing cabinets.

"Wow, imaginative," Mark said, sounding unusually dry. "Somebody in the data-processing department here really gets off on their work."

He walked down out of the air again, tossing the single glowing red brick in his hand as he did. "We'll hang on to this," Mark said. "We'll want it to put things back the way we found them when we're ready to go." He shoved the brick into the air between them. It vanished.

Charlie started walking among the lines and lines of filing cabinets. "This is the visual paradigm the people who work here have been using?" he said.

"The default, yeah," Mark said. "It may make it easier

for you to search. The clerking staff'll probably have left some markers for themselves, to make it easier to find things. But boy, oh, boy," and Mark chuckled, "at times like this, do I ever get seized with the desire to redecorate."

"Please *don't*," Charlie said, walking among the filing cabinets and looking at the little cards inserted in their drawer-fronts.

"Oh, come on, Charlie. Let me just leave a potted palm in here somewhere. I'll even tie a big red ribbon around it."

"No!" 2004–2005, read one cabinet: 2005–2006 . . . Charlie walked along the line of cabinets, looking for 2024.

"Just kidding," Mark said. Charlie wondered about that. "Aha," he said, and grinned at himself. Mark's turn of phrase was catching. "2020 . . ."

The 2024 cabinet was the fourth one down. Charlie pulled its top drawer open, and suddenly there were five other cabinets standing next to that one. "January through May," he said.

He headed for May, opened that cabinet up, and started riffling through the files there. *Delano,* he thought. *Richard Delano. May third* . . .

The file was there, a plain manila folder. Charlie pulled it out.

Instantly the air around him and Mark was full of windows. One of them showed a file structure "tree," full of files all of whose names began with DELANO. Another few windows showed pictures: crime scene shots, pictures of someone's house, probably Delano's. Then one more window said STATE PATHOLOGIST'S REPORT.

"Yes, indeed," Charlie said softly. "Mark, can I copy these into your workspace?"

"You can copy them right back to yours, if you like. I've still got a link open."

"Both, then. I want to make sure the data's safe."

"Consider it done." A big bright gold hoop appeared in

the air and set itself on fire. "Chuck anything you want copied through that: It'll make copies both places and then refile itself."

"Good." Charlie glanced at the ring, amused, then reached out and, with one finger, poked the window with the pathologist's report. It opened out into a series of still more windows, with screenfuls and screenfuls of text, and in one window, images of the body at autopsy. Charlie looked at this somberly, then turned his attention to the text.

"He looked real young," Mark said, from behind him, softly.

"Yeah. This was the sixteen-year-old," Charlie said as he read hurriedly down through the report, skimming it, and finding the words he had suspected he would find: *Strangulation. Self-inflicted—*

"Right," Charlie said, and folded the window down small, and chucked it through the ring. The ring flared. The window vanished. Charlie gathered all the information together again which had come out of the original file, and threw it, too, through the ring. Then he closed the file drawer.

"That it?" Mark said. "You sure you don't need anything else?"

"Not from here. But we've got five other places to hit, still."

"Gonna be a short, dull night for me at this rate," Mark said, sounding disappointed. "Never mind." They walked away from the filing cabinets again to the point where they had first entered, and Mark plucked that red brick out of its hiding place in the air. "Be fruitful and multiply," he told it, and dropped it on the floor.

A moment later there were two of it, and then four, and eight, sixteen, thirty-two, sixty-four . . . Within about thirty seconds the wall had completely rebuilt itself, even to the sign that read FIREWALL. "Mark—" Charlie said warningly, for the sign was now upside down.

"Oh, come on, Charlie! I was real good. I didn't even leave them a potted palm."

"Mark!"

"Oh, all right. Spoilsport."

The sign righted itself. A moment later they were back in Mark's space, where a stack of what appeared to be manila files was floating in midair, and Mark was referencing the "list" window again. "Next—"

The lines and columns and pillars of light dived and swooped around them again, and Charlie closed his eyes after a few seconds of it, since his stomach really did *not* like this. "Here we are," Mark said, and they found themselves in another walled area, but this time they were inside the painted concrete walls, not outside them.

"Hmm," Mark said. Charlie gulped, wanting to say a lot more than that, for the walls were moving in on them, like something out of an ancient 2-D horror flick . . . except that these walls were in 3-D, and, as they watched, were slowly sprouting long, cruel, inward-pointing iron spikes.

"Interesting," Mark said. "Those would pin us here, and ID us to the local system administrator, and lock a trace onto my system and any other one affiliated with this search. *If* we let them." He snapped his fingers, and the pale tracery of his own Digamma routines became more visible around the two of them inside the rapidly shrinking space.

"And we're not gonna let them do that," Charlie said, sweating harder, "are we . . . ?"

"Not a chance. Hush up now, I have to think."

Charlie started to sweat harder and closed his eyes again as once more the Digamma framework around them did its zoom-and-swoosh roller-coaster number.

"They're a little paranoid here," Mark said matter-of-factly. "I wonder if they've had a break-in recently?"

Charlie opened his eyes again. The disorienting slide and swoop of colors had stopped, and Mark was holding in his arms what appeared to be a wide pipe of pure glow-

ing yellow, as thick as the trunk of a tree. He was wedging
one end of it against the inward-pushing wall on the left-
hand side, and as Charlie watched Mark picked up the
other end of the branchless yellow "tree trunk" and began
to pull on it. It lengthened as he pulled, until it came right
up against the wall on the right-hand side. The walls
pushed against it, pushed. The "tree trunk" glowed briefly
brighter, bent a little—then braced itself still, bending no
more.

"There," Mark said. He watched the walls keep trying
to push, but they were making no headway. "Automatic
system," Mark said. "No one's watching it—banker's
hours, as I said. Or else someone's gone for coffee."

"Any way to tell which?" Charlie said, looking around
them for a way out.

"Not without taking a chance that they might notice,"
said Mark. "Come on, let's find you what you need—"
He walked over to the wall, brushed his fingers along it
in the same testing sort of gesture he had used with the
last one. "Huh," he said. "Thought so. Just Caldera, this
time. Here, watch this."

Charlie went over to him, looked over his shoulder.
"See this?" Mark said, and pushed his hand right into the
"wall." "You can manipulate the programming directly
without separate instructions, if you know where to grab
each line. And you can exploit the holographic nature of
the program—"

Charlie didn't know whether or not he should be relieved that he didn't have the slightest idea what Mark
was talking about. A second after Mark thrust his hand
into the wall, he pulled it out again, holding a doorknob.
"And as I thought," Mark said, "the programmer left herself a nice tidy way back into the main programming
space for when she was finished testing this." A door outlined itself in the wall: Mark used the doorknob to open
it and stepped through. "Mind your step, here—"

" 'She'?" Charlie asked, stepping through after him.
They appeared to be in a dimly lit office that stretched

for miles in all directions. "You sure about that?"

"Ninety percent," Mark said, walking through the office and looking around him. "Just something about the feel of it— Uh-oh. Somebody's in here. No, don't panic!"

Charlie froze and looked around him. Far off to his right, at what looked like about a mile's distance across this absurdly huge spread of carpeting and desks and office furniture and dividers, he could see a light shining over a desk.

"Just somebody looking at a file, somewhere else in the system," Mark said. "Possibly halfway across the city from where this facility is based. The odds of whoever it is being able to see us, or even being authorized to see us, are minuscule. Don't sweat it, just come on and let's see what the paradigm is—"

It took them only a few minutes to find it. Some of the desks had old-fashioned computer terminals on them, and Mark stopped by one of these and poked at it, a rounded eggy-looking thing done partly in a rather retro turquoise, partly in a translucent white plastic. "Somebody here has a sense of humor," Mark said, "or nice taste in antiques." He bent over to tap at the keyboard. "What's your victim's name in Colorado?"

"Velasquez."

"First initial?"

"J. Jaime."

"Which year?"

"Twenty-three."

"Right—" A moment later a large pile of square virtual datascrips appeared on the desk in front of them, and Mark glanced at them. "Copy again?"

Charlie looked through them. Each scrip, as he picked it up, showed him on its surface what it contained. AUTOPSY SYNOPSIS, Charlie read, RAW DATA, ORGAN ANALYSES, TOXICOLOGY—"Yeah."

Mark tapped at the console again. The datascrips vanished out of Charlie's hands. "Done. Let's beat it and hit the next one—"

They got out of there, Mark carefully removing his "tree trunk" and allowing the squashing walls to start coming together again, while at the same time wiping out any evidence of his and Charlie's intrusion. Then they hit the third facility, the coroner's office in Arlington. It had rather more effective security than the first two, so that Mark had to spend five minutes or so breaking in and making sure they wouldn't leave any trace of their entry behind, but the result was the same as in Bangor and Fort Collins.

The fourth Net-based system, at the coroner's offices in DeKalb County just east of Atlanta, to the astonishment of both of them had no security precautions installed around it whatsoever. Mark was practically dancing with frustration at such carelessness while Charlie raided it for the information he needed, and it was with the greatest of difficulty that Charlie kept Mark from building a security barrier around that system and then locking the DeKalb County staff out of it. Nothing Charlie could do, however, could keep Mark from putting up a big virtual billboard that said KILROY WAS HERE in front of the space.

"Somebody I should know?" Charlie said as he made sure the files were copied back to his space.

"Probably not," Mark said, disgusted, "and probably they won't, either."

"There won't be any trace that it was *you* doing that, will there?" Charlie said, nervous.

"Are you kidding? Of course not. You think I want my dad to—" Mark gave Charlie a look. "Never mind. Come on. Two more—"

They next hit the data storage system for the coroner's office in Queens. The City of New York system was surrounded with a set of nested security barriers so arcane that they actually kept Mark and Charlie away from the target data for a whole hour. Mark spent the whole time sweating and swearing—first in English, in language that Charlie wouldn't have thought Mark knew, and then in Thai, with great vehemence—as he dealt with the barriers, which in this implementation looked like layer after layer of barbed-wire fences, with long stretches of bare ground between them. But finally they fell, and the two of them found themselves making their way into a virtual domain that exactly duplicated the coroner's clerk's offices, right down to the potted plants and the baby pictures. The records Charlie found there were more complete than they had been anywhere else they had raided, and Charlie began thinking that they could have saved time by just raiding this one. *But how would we have known? And I need all that other data to make sure the case is watertight. . . .*

Charlie was taking a moment to look more closely at one of the files he was carrying while Mark chucked other records one by one through his ring-of-fire "copying" routine. He turned a page, and a great spill of organic-chemistry imaging and visualizations poured out into the air around them, long-chain molecules and imaging of translucent platelets and ribbony blood fractions. "Just *look* at this toxicology report," Charlie said, overcome with admiration. "Somebody here is a real professional."

"Yeah, well, so are their DP people," Mark said, sounding actively nervous for the first time. "Let's make it quick, huh?"

Charlie started to fold the file up preparatory to tossing it into the ring. This particular file was going to be useful for him. Most of the other coroners' blood and tox results had had rather minimal information about the dead person's blood chemistry. This one listed blood fractions that Charlie had only heard of in his most recent study. Whoever was working tox here was seriously interested in genetic microfractions, as well as—

Charlie stopped and looked curiously at one molecule that was hanging in the air off to one side. It looked familiar. He put the main file aside and went over to it, plucked it out of the air, turned it several different ways, looking at it. "Mark, hang on a minute."

"Okay, but no more than that. Whatcha got?"

"This looks familiar."

"It looks like Tinkertoys," Mark said. "Thought you were a little old for this kind of thing."

Charlie upended the molecule, tried looking at it from another angle. It didn't help. "Squirt, don't push your luck. Home system—"

"Online."

"Let me see this as golf balls."

"Processing."

The construct in his hands changed, got bulkier, and the "sticks" between the colored balls vanished, the chemical bonds now expressing themselves as spots where the balls squashed together. This was the method that his physics teacher had trained him to prefer, almost against Charlie's will, but it did work better than sticks and Ping-Pong balls for him. He turned the molecule over in his hands again, trying to find the best way to hold it. The benzene ring at one end suddenly triggered a memory, and so did the bromate structure sticking out of the middle of it.

"Charlie," Mark said, "you should save this for later . . . we really oughta get out of here."

Mark, getting nervous? It was worth seeing, though Charlie wasn't willing to linger under the circumstances. Nonetheless, he grinned to himself briefly. "Right. But one thing first. Home system—"

"Ready."

"Orthodox name for the compound."

"Scorbutal cohydrobromate."

Charlie's eyes narrowed. *Oh, no.* Oh, *no.* "I hate this," he growled.

Mark looked up at him. Charlie refused to repeat himself. "Come on," he said, folding up the file and chucking it through Mark's copying ring. It vanished, and the ring as well. "Let's get the heck out of here."

They hurriedly backtracked the way they had come, through a shortcut Mark had "wire-cut" to the outer security perimeter. He had to stop to reweave the wire, patching his cuts, but it didn't take him too long . . . which was as well, for far away, inside the "blockhouse" away inside the wire, Charlie thought he could hear sirens wailing. "Company?" he said.

"No kidding. Their security program woke up. Took it long enough—" The implementation was getting louder, as if closing in on them, and Charlie had no desire to see what form it was going to take when it finally appeared in their neighborhood. The last hole chopped into the outermost fence rewove itself. "Kill it!" Mark said to his penetration program, and then he and Charlie were once more standing in the darkness of his own workspace, surrounded by the light-forest of the Digamma penetration program.

Mark let out a long breath, and suddenly looked very thirteen. "These guys had it a little more on the ball than the others," he said.

Charlie grinned. "Not necessarily a bad thing. But Mark, you're not afraid of getting *caught,* are you?"

"Not much. I mean, no, of course not. It's just that, you know . . ."

"That that one was closer than you like to get." Charlie looked at him. "You want to call it quits?"

"No. Let's finish."

"Good," Charlie said, because they were shy only one set of information now, and it would be a shame to have to stop without it. There would always be that nagging doubt that some single important thing had been missed, the one piece of data which would have clinched the case. . . .

But Charlie rather thought it was clinched already. It would only be a matter of taking all this information home, sitting down with it and comparing everything very carefully. All he needed was the data from their last stop, the coroner's clerk's office in Forestville, Maryland. There the security was almost as nonexistent as it had been in Atlanta, and there Charlie picked up and copied the set of records belonging to the second kid involved in the recent "double" suicide. They were nowhere near as complete as the New York records had been, but they would have to do. The final raid took them fifteen minutes. At fifteen minutes and ten seconds they were standing in Mark's workspace again, with the forest of light sinking into the virtual floor under their feet. Mark let out a long breath of relief.

"Mark," Charlie said, "you're a hero."

"I'm modest, too," Mark said, wiping his forehead. "Ask me about it sometime." He plopped down in one of the chairs. "Lights!" he said to his workspace, and the VAB reasserted itself, the angle of the sun having changed slightly, but everything else as it had been before. From high up in the air, the creaky voices of buzzards could be heard, and beside Charlie, piled up on the floor, was a stack of manila files nearly as tall as he was. "It's all there," Mark said. "I'll keep copies secure for you, if you like."

"I'd appreciate it," Charlie said.

"No problem. But just what was that you found back in New York?"

Charlie shook his head. "Bad stuff," he said softly. "Ask me later."

"Mark?" a man's voice said from out of the air around them.

"Ohmigosh, get out of here, it's my dad," Mark said hurriedly. "Probably with a brain full of bait." He leaped for the pile of files, scooped them up and started stuffing them into one of his desk drawers. "These are encrypting. But I need to wipe my logs of these, and you, before he comes in. Go on, blast out of here!"

Charlie hurriedly headed for his doorway into Mark's space, which appeared a few feet away. "Mark—thanks!"

"Yeah, yeah, thank me later. When I get back, gimme a shout and tell me what you find!"

"I will!"

Mark vanished. Charlie was left standing in his workspace with a pile of files.

"Son," he heard his father say from outside in the real world. "You've been in there for an elephant's age. Want a sandwich?"

"Absolutely," Charlie muttered. He checked to make sure that the files were saved, and then closed down his workspace and returned to the real world, where his stomach was growling fiercely . . . but not so much so that it drowned out the nervous muttering in his head.

Scorbutal hydrobromate.

Were these really suicides . . . ?

Late the next afternoon Nick stood out in the softly falling ash, and held very still, listening for something beside the screams of the Damned. He didn't immediately hear the sound he was waiting for, but he was willing to wait for a good while. If there was anything he had been learning in the last couple of days, it was patience.

He was in no hurry to get back to the spot he had finally reached during the session before last, the first "sub-basement" of the Dark Artificer's Keep . . . even though his money was getting close to running out, even though his folks were getting increasingly interested in "sitting down and having a talk" with him. Nick had the secrets of the Eighth Circle seriously on his mind, for he was beginning to suspect that there was more to play for, a lot more, than just lifts of new songs and the possibility that you might meet one of the clone-Banes down here.

Nick had decided to follow a hunch. He had gone back to do what Shade told him she'd been doing: to talk to others he found wandering around the ashy wilderness on the far side of the Lake of Tears, and guide them through. At first he wondered whether this had been such a great idea, for the environment responded badly to it. It was as if the crevasses started to target Nick, going out of their way to stitch themselves straight at him as he made his way through the knee-deep ash. He had had a couple of extremely close calls over the first few hours, as the ground stubbornly, even maliciously, opened again and again under his feet. Once, if this had been reality, he would have left the skin of the palms of both hands on the jagged outcropping of rock that was all that kept him from plunging into the lava-filled abyss below. But Nick kept doing what he had decided to do. It was sheer stubbornness, at first. If the environment was going to target him, he was going to outlast it.

After five or six hours of this, things got a little better. The environment started getting less dangerous . . . or maybe Nick just got better at anticipating it. But he also stopped noticing quite so acutely what it was doing, for he started getting interested in the conversations he was having with the people he was guiding through. Their responses to the situation in which they suddenly found themselves varied from complete confusion to annoyance that they were no longer in control of their path through the darkness. But one way or another, they were all glad of the help, though some of them plainly would have choked rather than admit it. Some of them were wearing virtual "seemings" that were meant to make them look very impressive and self-sufficient indeed—tall shapes cowled in darkness, like the image of Joey Bane in the "front door" to the *Orpheus, Don't Look Back!* virteo collection, or barbarian heroes, or statuesque women wearing space-babe slicktights and toting projectile weapons the size of their upper bodies, or giant snarling beasts slinking along through the fiery night and trying to look independently deadly. Some of them protested at being saved from falling into a hole in the ground by a skinny high school kid in neodenims and a beat-up Mets batting helmet. Most of them "forgot" to thank him. But none of them, Nick noticed, told him to go away while he was actually helping them out.

At the end of his last session Nick had gone home exhausted and collapsed into bed too weary to even be annoyed with his mother, who had been waiting up for him. He had taken care of his homework before he'd left, so he wasn't sure why she was waiting, and she gave him an odd look as he passed through the front room on his way to bed.

"Honey," she said, in an unusually neutral tone of voice for her, "your friend Charlie called earlier."

"Yeah?"

"He was asking about something called a 'walk-through.' Would you know what he wanted?"

"Huh? Oh, yeah, I'll take care of it tomorrow." That caught Nick a little by surprise. Charlie wasn't much of a gamer, preferring to do "solid construction" sims, the more concrete kind of virtual experience. *All the same, if he's getting interested . . .*

Nick looked for Charlie the next day at school, but didn't see him. Either he'd had to swap his lunch periods to take care of some study commitment, or something else had happened to throw their schedules out of synch. Nick went through the day more or less on automatic, as he had done for the last couple of days, since things started to get really interesting back in Deathworld. That afternoon he headed back into the WorldBooths public Net-access center down at the Square in an unusually good mood, despite the fact that his money was getting so short. At the end of the week he would have some more allowance coming, and be able to really get back into the swing of Deathworld over the weekend. Nick had spent the day getting ahead of schedule on his homework, which his folks had been checking with unusual care. They'd have no excuse to bother him for two whole days.

And after that, when the money does run out . . . For two full days of gameplay would exhaust what he had.

Nick sighed, paid at the cashier's booth in front, took his recharged cash card, and headed back to his usual booth right at the rear, locking himself in and settling into the implant chair and slapping the card into it. *Have to deal with that when it happens*, Nick thought, and blinked his workspace into being around him.

It was still bare. He hadn't felt like spending the time to get his redecorating done. But off to one side, standing there, was a simulacrum of Charlie, in end-of-the-day shinesweats, arms folded, smiling that wry smile he wore sometimes, an expression that suggested he was feeling foolish about something.

"Go," Nick said to the simulacrum.

"Sorry I missed you," it said immediately, in Charlie's voice. "I was up late last night doing some research.— Look, all work and no play, you know the drill. . . . I was wondering if you had any walk-throughs of Deathworld. I wanted to have a look through, but I don't want to spend six weeks dragging around in the upper levels. You have something that can get me about halfway down? Give me a yell, or leave me a message."

The image froze again. Nick was caught between two impulses—to catch Charlie "live" right now, if possible, and take him down into Deathworld himself, or to leave him a message. The second impulse won.

"System," Nick said, "record reply . . ."

"Ready," the system said in its plain-vanilla voice. Nick raised his eyebrows. He really should get some Bane audio in here, if nothing else.

"Charlie, sorry I missed you, too," he said, getting up out of the "chair" on the virtual side and going over to the doorway where his files were stored at the moment. He opened it and looked in. "File access. Deathworld," he said, "press material, walk-through . . . Yeah, that one. Transfer to Charlie Davis's machine."

He turned back to the simulacrum of Charlie. "Here," he said. "This one came out of the 'Last Train Out' review environment about a month and a half ago . . . the data for the first three levels is still good, as far as I know. The company's been swapping in new material from about Four down, to defeat the older walk-throughs that're out there, but this should still be a help. Let me know if you have any problems. I'll talk to you later. . . ."

The simulacrum, having been answered, vanished. Nick breathed out, then closed the door and opened the second one, his automated login gateway to Deathworld.

He had implemented a "shortcut" entry that let him in to pick up where he had left off. The Deathworld system still showed him the copyright statement burning crimson in the air for a few seconds—there was no getting away from that, no matter how many times a day you might come in here—and then Nick walked through into the darkness awaiting him on the other side.

Falling ash, the volcano in the distance . . . Nick reached up into the air and re-created the "asbestos" golf umbrella he normally carried, and then started making his way toward the keep, to see who he might meet along the way. As he looked around, he was a little surprised by how few players seemed to be around. This was an unusually quiet period for this time of day. Normally Deathworld started to get noticeably busier around the time that high school and college classes let out in North America, though obviously there would have been plenty of Europeans and Asians in over the earlier part of the day.

Nick shrugged and made his way along through the black ash "snow," keeping an eye open for crevasses. For the moment they seemed to be avoiding him, though he saw what looked like a huge one opening away across the plain, and faintly he thought he heard some yells of surprise from that direction. It was a little too far for him to do any good. By the time he got there, everybody involved would either have saved themselves and each other, or fallen in.

He kept going, making for the Keep of the Dark Artificer. Shade's warning about the size of the place had been a useful one. Its interior was, Nick thought, probably bigger than the whole gigantic plain that surrounded it. This posed problems of topology that he didn't bother his head about, for the attraction of the Keep lay in the music that was in there, and also in the exploration of the countless dark rooms, deep caverns, and hidden towers associated with it, and (most important, Nick thought) the solution of the great Maze at the Keep's heart. He couldn't get rid of the feeling that the access to the fabled Ninth Circle had to do with that maze. Probably nothing so simple as just getting to the middle of it. Nick was sure you needed to do more than that, or have some specific piece of information once you arrived.

Nick skirted around the lake and headed for the doors of the Keep. The demons on guard there—little black-leather-skinned, batwinged guys about five feet tall, wearing ornate doormen's costumes and affable gargoyle faces—saw him coming and started pulling on the giant braided bronze ropes that opened the doors. He waved at them, in what was beginning to be a ritual. "Hey, there, boys," Nick said to the two nearest demons, "how're things going?"

"They stink," said the demons nearest the doors, in the ritual answer. One of them, pausing from the work, wiped his forehead with a big smudgy hankie and added, "*And* the boss turned down the union's request for the pay raise."

Nick made *tsk, tsk* noises as he passed them by, walking in over the shiny dark pavement, which some beneficent agency kept clear of the ash that was always falling outside. "Keep working on it, fellas. . . ." he said.

The doors closed behind him, and Nick paused there in the huge "front hall," looking around to see who else might be there. The Keep's vast entryway, lit by a huge crystal and onyx chandelier shaped like one more stalactite hanging from the great dome of the ceiling, routinely held a surprise or two. You might hear a snatch of music here that you hadn't caught elsewhere, or meet someone who would do your quest some good. At the moment, though, it was nearly as quiet inside as it had been outside. The place was practically empty. *A slack period,* Nick thought. *Coincidence.*

He walked on in, looking around at the bizarre portraiture that hung on the walls of the entryway. They were supposed to be images of gameplayers who had passed on successfully to Nine, Nick knew, normal people living in his own time. But the portraits made them all look like crazed royalty of two or three centuries back, in rococo clothes and wigs that looked like they might come alive and crawl off their wearers' heads. He wondered what his own portrait would wind up looking like if—*When. When* they did it.

Nick smiled slightly and headed in toward the doorway on the far side of the entry hall. Past that door was where things got interesting. Six staircases apparently designed by Escher led off toward the roof, and six more toward the basement, though none of them felt particularly like "up" or "down" when you were climbing them. Somewhere in this vast pile, in which none of the normal directions mattered, the Maze was hidden—a huge tangle of paths and walkways, arched and open, covering all six of the walls of a great cube of space somewhere in the Keep. Nick had actually found it accidentally, once, when he was first in here and just wandering around in the place trying to get a feel for it. Then he'd lost the Maze again while trying to work out how he'd found it to begin with. *A whim of the system,* he thought. *Never mind. Over the weekend there'll be time to start doing some proper searching—*

"Hey, Nick . . ."

He turned quickly at the sound of a slightly familiar voice. It was Shade again. In here she looked a little less like her name, but only a little less—just a young girl of maybe fifteen, in a long black outer coat, a short dark purple skirt, and a black sweater, dark purple hair, and eyes that shaded from violet to almost black depending on how much light there was. Those big dark eyes, and the somber set of her mouth, suggested some old sorrow hanging over her. She was pale. In this light, almost right under the great chandelier, Nick could see much better how frail she looked, how fragile. Not that Nick was so foolish as to be misled by appearances down here. As in most virtual environments, anyone could look like anything they pleased. For all he knew, up in the Real World, Shade was a six-foot-six, two hundred-and-eighty-pound football player. Somehow, though, Nick doubted it. There was a brittle feel to conversations with her that made him wonder if she was either a plant from Joey Bane Enterprises, someone used to see how players treated each other, or someone who wasn't really cut out for this particular virtual experience, but was just too stubborn to give it up.

"Hey, Shade," he said. "You doing okay?"

She sighed. Most of her conversations seemed to start with a sigh, or contain several of them. "I guess so," she said. "It's quiet today . . . you'd almost think everybody was scared off by something. . . ."

Nick shrugged. "Not me." The whole business with the Angels of the Pit had rolled off his back pretty quickly once he got into the Keep and started working on the business of solving it.

"I don't know. . . ." Shade said. "I wonder if maybe there's something to it."

"To what?"

She shrugged, gazing up and about her. "What they did . . ." She turned those violet eyes on him. "I keep wondering if it's really so terrible. When everything's going wrong . . ."

The way she trailed off, Nick had a feeling that she was about to tell him how everything was wrong for *her*, if he didn't stop her. He shook his head. "Some people might think it isn't," he said slowly. "I guess there are times when everything really does seem to stink. But that's not where I am at the moment."

"Things are better for you, then, at home?"

"I don't know about better," Nick said. "A little quieter, maybe." Certainly his father had been letting him alone . . . whether he was unwilling to restart their fight, or not, Nick wasn't sure. Just the news that Nick had a job lined up for the summer seemed to have quieted things down somewhat. For the rest of it, it was as if his mother and father had declared a truce for the moment. The lightening of the atmosphere in the house had been noticeable. "I'm not thinking about that right now, Shade. I'm on my way to the Maze. . . ."

"Aren't we all," Shade said, and laughed a little. "But I haven't finished exploring the Keep yet. There's still a lot of ground that I haven't covered yet. . . ."

Nick laughed. "You sound like you enjoy rummaging around in here for its own sake. Not me! I want the music."

"Oh, I do, too. . . ."

"Well, then, come on and help me find the Maze! That's the way down to Nine, and Nine's where the good music's supposed to be, the 'unknown' lifts. And Joey himself . . ."

Shade gave him an odd look, almost nervous. "Oh, I don't mind hanging around up here," she said. "Besides, they say that once you leave Eight for Nine, you can't come back."

That surprised him. "*Who* says?"

"Other people up here." Shade glanced around her, although those "other people" were not much in evidence right now. "All the time, in the Upper Circles, you see people from as far down as Eight wandering around. Slumming . . . helping the newbies, or torturing them with news of the lifts you can get down lower."

Nick nodded. He'd seen enough of this as he worked his way down. One and Two were particularly bad in this regard—a lot of the people from the circles between Three and Six seemed to enjoy coming up there and making the new Banies nuts. "But have you noticed," she said, "that you never see anyone from Nine?"

Nick nodded. This might have been why rumors about Nine were very few and far between. It left another question, of course: *If nobody from there comes back to tell us what's happening, then how are there any rumors at all?* But rumors didn't need reality to get started. That was one of the things this level was about, as he had been discovering.

"You hear anything else about how to get down there?" Nick said to Shade.

She shook her head. "Nothing that's done me any good," she said. "But I wish you luck."

"Yeah," Nick said, "thanks. Look, I'll see you on the way out, maybe?"

"Maybe you will."

She turned away.

"Hey, Shade—"

She glanced back at him.

"Thanks for helping, the other day."

"I didn't help," she said. "Not really." That faint air of sorrow seemed to come down on her again.

Shade headed for the doors, which swung back to let her out into the darkness. Nick watched her go, thinking, *Poor kid, I wonder what her problem is?* But then, if he asked her, he had the awful feeling he'd find out . . . and right now, he had enough problems of his own. Besides, tonight was about enjoyment . . . because he wasn't going to be able to afford much more of it.

Nick turned and made for the door at the back, the entry to the Stairwell of Doom, to pick a stair and see where it took him.

In the doorway a dark shape watched him for a few moments, then shrugged and turned away.

6

That evening Charlie was sitting once more in his work-space, with piles of files around him, in the blackest mood he'd been in for days. Part of it was because this session had been delayed. His sandwich with his father, last night, had segued into one of the more ferocious games of cut-throat "timed chess" they'd ever had, and his father had won—an unusual outcome. Charlie had chalked it up to the fact that he was slightly distracted by his evening out with Mark. Now, though, he was in the midst of analyzing the information that Mark had helped him bring back . . . and that was accounting for the rest of his dark mood.

Charlie sat leaning back on the bottom-most bench in his workspace, looking into the Pit. It was full of virtual information and exhibits again, so much so that he'd had to move the worktable out of the middle of it. Now the floor of the Pit was occupied by six different sets of in-formation, floating in the air . . . and what bothered Charlie the most was the similarities between four of them.

They had all been strangulations, of course. That was

bad enough. But in four of those suicides—the "double" suicide of just a few days ago, and the New York and Fort Collins ones—the toxicology reports had turned up something that would have immediately struck the authorities as suspicious, Charlie thought . . . if they had bothered comparing notes. But they hadn't.

He got up, strolled over to the New York suicide. This had been Renee Milford. Charlie had been through her autopsy, but he had no heart for looking at those pictures of her. He had found one that he preferred in one of the local New York virtual environments dedicated to news and current events—a family "virtshot" of Renee sitting at the beach in a one-piece bathing suit, with the tall brick water tower of Jones Beach State Park away behind her in the distance. She was blond, and pretty, and eighteen. Her smile was sunny, she had a slight sunburn on the tops of her shoulders, she was laughing at the camera, and she looked as if she didn't have a worry in the world. The picture had been taken in 2023, the year before she died.

Charlie looked down at the image of Renee sitting there, her hair a little tousled by the wind, blown sand glittering in the air. Next to her, hanging in the air like some kind of malevolent, multicolored, multilegged bug, was the image of the molecule the city toxicologist's analysis had found in her blood. It was scorbutal cohydrobromate.

The hydrobromates were not in the pharmacopeia, either the government's informal "N.P." or the official "U.S.P." list. They had no legitimate medical use. They were what an earlier generation had referred to as a "designer drug," a chemical built to get people high . . . and sometimes intended to perform other functions as well. In the case of the hydrobromates, the high was usually enough. But scorbutal hydrobromate, when it started to be produced in the 2010s, soon acquired a tarnished reputation, even for a recreational drug. It was a mind-dulling, inhibition-loosening drug, and was used by crooks who wanted their victims to be less than clear about what was happening to them. One form of it, delivered as an aerosol spray, had briefly been used on night trains in Europe in a real-life scenario of the old urban myth about people being "gassed" unconscious so they could be robbed in their sleeping compartments. The gangs who did this had been caught and put away, but not before the drug's reputation spread, and more of it started to be made all over the place, in Europe and then in North America. "Scobro" was popular, for it was cheap and relatively easy to make—it could be thrown together out of various readily available household chemicals and a well-known remedy for upset stomachs—and best of all, from the criminals' point of view, it tended to metabolize quickly. It was very short-acting. Having left the brain muddled and dozy, its molecule then came apart into its component bromides in the bloodstream itself, often before the liver even had a chance to start detoxifying it.

Charlie scowled at the molecular model hovering gently in the air by the image of Renee Milford, who appeared to have strangled herself in her parents' garage. The toxicologist in Queens—who knew what she had been thinking of, while she was working on this case, or what she might have suspected? But she had run a much more thorough and expensive blood series on Renee than had strictly been required . . . and the scorbutal had turned up in it. *Luck,* Charlie thought, *or just good timing.* The drug deconstructed itself even more quickly in the rapidly acidifying bloodstream of someone who was dying or dead than it did in the blood of a live person, and in a matter of minutes there might have been none of it left at all.

He sighed and moved on to the next set of "exhibits," the one for Malcolm Dwyer, who had been one of the two kids to die here in the D.C. area a few days ago. Malcolm had had a big dose of the drug, so much that even after the delay in finding his and Jeannine Metz's bodies, there had still been significant amounts of it in his bloodstream—enough, at least, to identify it by the bromide and bromate fractions pooled in the parts of his body already beginning to experience rigor. The coroner in Arlington had found it and recognized it immediately for what it was.

The problem was that, by itself, finding sco-bro in someone's bloodstream didn't mean that much. Yes, the drug was illegal, like almost all the other designer drugs. But lots of people took it anyway. And in a case like this, the nature of the crime scene would itself tend to minimize the role of any drug. After all, no drug could *make* you commit suicide . . . could it?

Charlie stood there, looking at Malcolm's image—another virtclip, a young black guy not that much older than Charlie, tall, good looking, cheerful. And dead now. Charlie's mother had been pretty certain that you couldn't cause anyone to suicide if they weren't already suicidal. But even she had been willing to admit that new ways of doing things were being invented every day. . . .

And how do I know this isn't a coincidence, anyway? Granted, it would have to be a huge one. . . .

Charlie walked around to the third set of data that had shown the drug. This was Jaime Velasquez, from Fort Collins. He was a little, dark-haired, dark-eyed boy built sort of like Mark Gridley, but older, and with a much more innocent face. The picture Charlie had of him was of a guy almost completely muffled up in ski clothes, grinning past a ski mask which a friend just out of shot in the same virtclip had just pulled down, waving his ski poles at the camera, then falling down in the snow as the same out-of-shot friend hooked a sky behind one of Jaime's knees and knocked him sprawling backward into the powder. In Jaime's bloodstream—either because he had had a very slight dose, or had lived long enough to detoxify it, or had been too long dead before they had found him—there had been almost none of the whole sco-bro molecule left at all. The toxicologist had either missed the bromide fragments in the postmortem blood samples, or had seen them and assumed they had come from some other source . . . or perhaps had dismissed them as unimportant. Either way, they hadn't been mentioned in his dictated text report.

But all the same, the drug had been there. Charlie heaved a big sigh of frustration. If the coroner in Colorado had known about the findings of his associates in New York and Maryland, he might have been able to get his own police force to examine the crime scene more carefully for signs that anyone else had been there. But it hadn't happened. There had been no comparison of data.

Charlie scowled as he walked around to the next set of exhibits. Some of it had to do with what Mark had described: separate states' failure to contribute information to a common pool, intrastate authorities' unwillingness to cooperate with one another. But there could have been other causes as well. *Coroners who saw what they wanted to see*, Charlie thought. *Or what they were convinced that they should be seeing. Just another suicide. Nothing unusual . . .*

But then each of them was looking at a separate case . . . not at one case as part of a group or set of cases. It's not their fault they didn't realize what they were looking at.

But here I am, Charlie thought, *and I think I know what I'm looking at.*

Murder.

The minute you find anything . . . said James Winters's voice in the back of his head.

Charlie opened his mouth to tell his system to place a call . . .

. . . then closed his mouth again, thinking.

You know what he's going to say, said something in the back of Charlie's mind.

He sat down on his bench again and looked out at the exhibits.

There were very few things that Charlie hated more than drugs. He had seen them ruin people's lives, had seen them ruin the life of his birth mother, the one person he had loved more than anyone else in the world. They'd killed her, slowly, by hours and inches. That memory was one that he didn't often examine closely. He was not up for looking very hard at it right this minute, either. But the moment he called James Winters and started to present this data to him, that painful old history was going to be held up in front of him by that careful and thorough man. Winters would say to him, *Are you sure this isn't clouding your judgment a little, Charlie? You know how you feel about drugs. I understand it completely. It makes perfect sense to me that you would want to keep other people from suffering the same kind of loss that you have.*

But you shouldn't let it make you see losses like that where there aren't any....

And he would remind Charlie once again about the huge numbers of people on the Net, and the incidence of accident and circumstance among those people, and the way they impacted on mortality statistics.

But it wouldn't matter. I know what I'm seeing here. These people did not commit suicide. They were "helped" to die.

Charlie looked over at the New York data again. Here, unfortunately, the investigation into Renee's death had been less wonderful. The coroner had been conscientious, but the police had not, and they had done very little work on the actual area where she had been found dead. Up in Maine, in Bangor, though, someone had been—suspicious? Or just not certain of what they were seeing. And there were some odd findings at the scene.

Charlie went around to Richard Delano's exhibit and looked at what was spread out there. There was a virtclip of Richard, a short, well-muscled guy, blond, gray-eyed, in baggies and a hot-weather vest, walloping someone's fastball in a softball game on some unnamed summer afternoon, then taking off around the bases, leaving a cloud of dust behind him. And there, spread out next to the clip, was the Bangor police department's own virtual version of the crime scene, the living room of the house where Richard had been found. They had gone right around the room and virtsnapped everything, in both macro and micro. They had come up with some odd fiber evidence: bits of cotton fluff that were found nowhere else in the house but in this one room, the living room. And they were on the "top" of the rug, not old, not trodden in as they might have been expected to be, but something new. And not native to any of the suicide's clothes. Charlie looked at the fibers, enlarged and hanging in the air like tangled white ropes.

A friend? Maybe. But a friend who had never been in the house before? Or in any part of it except the living room? That was a little weird. *Someone the person didn't know?* But there was no sign of forced entry. Whoever that person was, Richard Delano had let him or her in.

It was very odd, and Charlie didn't know what to make of it. Neither had the Bangor police. They had not been able to confirm any other person being in the apartment any time around the time of death—unfortunately the entrance to Delano's house had been hidden by shrubbery from the other houses in the street. The outside light had come on and gone off again within a minute or so as it might have no matter how many people were entering the house, and that was all anyone had noticed. Finally, after days of investigation, the police had listed their concerns about the crime scene as "inconclusive" and had moved on to other issues. If they had noticed scorbutal cohydrobromate in the body, they might have thought otherwise, but they hadn't.

Charlie looked over at the other two sets of evidence. They were inconclusive, too, lacking either any suggestion of other persons being in the area, or any detection of scobro in the victims. His case was not at all complete . . . and James Winters would not be convinced.

This'll all have been for nothing.

He put his head in his hands, depressed. Nick was still somewhere in the middle of Deathworld, and Charlie felt sure in his bones that someone else was still there, too, stalking the place, looking for another victim. *If I don't convince Winters that I'm right about what I've found, someone else is gonna get killed. Maybe not Nick... maybe someone else. But it doesn't matter in the slightest. Murder's going to happen.*

Especially since it's still May. Charlie could not get rid of the idea that this meant something specific.

Anyway, it's beyond coincidence at this point. What are the odds that all these suicides should just happen to be using this drug? ... And just happen to be in Deathworld, and just happen to kill themselves this way? Taken separately, there was always the chance. But this many coincidences, taken all together ... suddenly they weren't coincidences anymore.

Charlie breathed in, breathed out.

But it's still not proof of the kind that Winters is going to need. Everything I've got is circumstantial.

Now, if I had some proof that somebody was being targeted, being followed...

Yeah, like who? ... He was in no position to go through Deathworld and start asking questions of everybody he met. Word about nosy "strangers" and "newbies" traveled fast in these online demesnes. The Banies were probably no different than any other kind of fans defending their territory, in this regard. Anybody who showed up and started asking a lot of questions would be identified as a stooge, maybe a cop, and isolated, within hours. *Or else just get fed a lot of misinformation that would completely screw up any serious investigation.*

No, there has to be another way.

Charlie sat there for a long while, as it got lighter outside in the London of two centuries ago, and the sky started to turn a pale peach color up in the high windows.

Then he sat up straight.

All right, Charlie thought. *When investigation takes you as far as it can, when the data won't support the conclusions securely enough... then, if you're really sure you're right, you go find the information to* make *it support them.*

By catching somebody in the act....

• • •

Nick stood quiet between the dark stone walls, in the dripping darkness, with his eyes closed, and listened. It was the only way, down here, to tell truth from falsehood. Appearances were deceiving, as he had learned higher up in Deathworld, and there was no point in wasting your time on trying to work things out from the way they looked.

The inside of the Dark Artificer's Keep was the kingdom of fraud . . . all the different sorts of it: flattery and lies, hypocrisy and purposeful misdirection, rumors started to make trouble or destroy reputations. Counterfeiting and impersonation were punished there, and all the kinds of theft. Illegal copying was punished there, too, and theft of ideas . . . and since Joey Bane had suffered enough from that kind of thing in his early career, Nick was not entirely surprised to see the Thieves of Song hung up from the trees in the Black Arboretum, squawking out twisted fragments of song while the blackbirds picked at their tenderer bits. He had passed through there with some amusement, picking up in passing, from under a rock in the Arboretum, the clandestine lift of "Steal from Me . . ." with all the pirated versions of other Bane songs sampled and intercut into it, Joey Bane's own convoluted joke— the audio version of a trophy wall, one that grew and grew day by day, so that every new version was a collectors' item.

The punishments down here in the stony black tunnels and passageways were all variations on a single theme. Those who had stolen others' stories and lives and taken them for their own use were now bound forever in one place, immured in the black stones themselves, and forced to listen in silence to those who actually had lives of their own. It was the living who had the key to the secrets here. Their questions, asked of the darkness, were the answers to the Keep. As elsewhere in Deathworld, some of the people you met in the Keep were real players, but some were actors or "plants," part of the game, and to find out what they knew about the way down to the doorway into Nine, listening was the key.

At first it had seemed to Nick merely a frustration designed to weed out those who weren't really serious about finding the way down to Nine. But slowly he had begun to suspect the truth lay elsewhere. Whether he would find it in time to descend to Nine before his money ran out, and before his folks entirely lost patience, was now his main concern.

He sat down on one of the benches let into the wet black stone wall, underneath one of the occasional torches that were fitted into iron wall-brackets, and listened. It was damp down here. He was below the level of the lake, Nick guessed, and that warm saline body leaked and oozed through to most places on this level, trickling down walls, welling up as puddles in the narrow, close, dark stone passages. Listening was the whole art of finding your way around here, listening for the sound of water and the direction in which it ran, listening to other voices, finding your way to them, discovering what they had to say. It was not like Seven, where manipulation of the pain of the Damned was how you found out what you needed to know. Here, keeping your own mouth shut and your ears open was everything. Someone's story told in a long soft monologue, a phrase of music heard in silence and waited for, was what would make the difference. There was always a clue, something useful.

It's a shame that listening to people in the real world isn't always this useful, Nick thought. If it could be this way with other kids at school, or with parents, or other people you met, what a difference it would make. Unfortunately they were usually intent on forcing you to come around to their way of thinking, and any listening on their part was limited to checking to see whether you were agreeing with them.

Though who knows, he thought. *Maybe it would be possible to outlisten them, if you just had enough patience.*

He got up again, stretched. Last time Nick sat there for

nearly two hours before he caught that faint soft shimmer of music, far away in another passage, and after much feeling his way around in near-total darkness, he finally found his way to the little chest set into one of the stone walls, where the lift of "Down the Narrow Ways" had been hidden. But Nick didn't think there was any point in waiting here any longer, for a certain "feel" was missing to this tunnel/passage which the other one, where he'd found the lift, had had. So now Nick was trying to cover as much ground as possible in each session, trying to locate spots that had the same "feel," and which could also conceal doorways or hidden passages that might somehow lead to the Maze itself.

He turned right, then right again, down another low-ceilinged passageway, paused, and listened for sound, for that particular "feel." Nothing. Nick went on, trailing his hand along the wet, cold stone.

"Ow!" he said then, stopping and looking at the wall. Nothing but lumpy rock, and here and there something jutting out that might have been an elbow, a knee, frozen in the stone. Except where his hand had been—there was someone's mouth, there were teeth, and half-buried in the stone, the glint of an eye, watching him.

"Sorry," Nick said, making a resolution to watch where he put his hands in the future, and went on walking. *This could take me a long time,* Nick thought. Some of the walk-throughs claimed that the so-called "anteroom chambers," the approaches to the Maze itself, regenerated themselves in new and random patterns every few days, so that you would think you had learned them and then return to find them completely different. Others said that no such thing happened at all, and that the people making the claim were confused. Nick wasn't sure what to think. In his cynical moods, it struck him that randomly regenerating the pattern would be a great way to make some extra money. But somehow he didn't think Joey Bane was quite that desperate for funds. . . .

Nick came to a dark opening on his right and paused,

looked in. It was just a little cavelet, not much bigger than
a walk-in closet, with a stone bench built into the black
stone wall and going right around from one side to the
other. The light from the burning cresset out in the main
"hallway" reached it only dimly. Nick had run into these
in other parts of the "anteroom chambers" over the past
few hours, and often enough they were in places where
you might hear something if you stayed there long
enough. So he went in, and sat down, and spent a little
while more just listening.

His head turned as, down the corridor, in the direction
from which he had come, he heard voices, and the sound
of soft footsteps approaching. At first Nick was torn, and
thought about leaving . . . *not sure I want to meet anybody
right now.* . . . But he was also feeling a little lazy, and a
little curious, especially as the voices got closer. One was
a guy, one a girl, though her voice was not that light—it
had a husky sound. So far he had tended to keep to himself in Deathworld, except for a few chance encounters
such as that with Shade, but maybe it would be better to
start putting aside that tendency down here.

Nick stayed where he was. "Look, forget it," said the
soft husky voice. "I'm not going to waste any more time
arguing about it with you, either. I'm just going to find
it, no matter how long it takes. . . ."

Two shapes passed by the doorway, silhouetted against
the cresset-light from the passage. One of them kept right
on going, but the other paused to peer in, taking a moment
about it, letting her eyes get used to the dark. She was
about Nick's height, maybe a little younger than he was.
It was hard to tell. He saw a long fall of blond hair, nearly
waist length, stirring a little in the cool air running down
the passageway behind her; she was dressed in light shorts
and an "infrablack" T-shirt that glowed slightly, even in
this shadowy place, with the intensity of its darkness. She
drew in breath sharply as she looked at him.

Nick blinked. "Uh, sorry," he said.

She looked at him for a moment more. Elsewhere it

would have been an invasive stare, but in Deathworld you got familiar with it fairly quickly—the expression of someone trying to work out whether you were part of the game or not, and whether it was worth their while to stop to talk to you. Nick had to chuckle a little. "I'm not local," he said, that being one of the code phrases meant to indicate that you weren't a plant or a generated feature.

The girl looked at him a little less intently, but the expression was still curious. A moment later she was joined in the doorway by her companion. At first glance he looked like a football player—tall, big across the shoulders, brawny. The effect was increased by the fact that he was wearing *a plaidh mhor,* the so-called "great kilt" which was just coming into style for guys at the moment. The kilt was patterned in infrablack and a very dark blue, the so-called "Armstrong Hunting" plaid, and everything else about the guy's clothes matched, from shoes to the tied-on headband. He looked like her brother, or maybe an extremely well-matched boyfriend. "Somebody you know?" he said.

"No," Nick said, and "No," the girl said, in the same breath. Then the girl laughed.

"You waiting for somebody?" she said.

"Besides Joey? Nope," said Nick. "Nobody here right now but us chickens."

The guy looked at him like he was from Mars. The girl looked oddly at him, too, but then she laughed. "I thought my mom was the only person on earth to say that anymore," she said. "Suddenly I don't feel quite so weird."

The two of them glanced around them. Nick knew why. "No booby traps in here," he said. "It's a quiet spot."

"We should go—" the guy said.

"Why?" said the girl, sounding annoyed. "We haven't found anything. And we're not going to, not today, not before our nickel runs out, anyway. . . ."

"You're looking for—?" Nick said.

"The Maze," said the guy. "Like everyone else down here."

"Among other things," the girl muttered. She sighed. "You mind if we sit down?"

Nick moved down on the bench a little. They came into the chamber and sat down, looking around the way people do when they're suddenly in a small space with someone they don't know.

"Thanks," the girl said. "Sometimes the quiet down here gets to me." She sighed. "Tires me out, a little. . . ." Then she gave him a slightly embarrassed look. "Sorry," she said. "I'm Khasm."

"Nick," he said, nodding to her.

"I'm Spile," said the guy.

"Pleased," Nick said. To Khasm he said, "I know what you mean, though. It's a lot quieter down here than up in the top levels. Not quite so much of the screams and yells of the tormented."

Khasm laughed, a very brief sound, not all that humorous. "No need," she said. "*We're* the torment, walking around, doing what we want, saying what we like . . . and there's nothing they can do about it." She glanced at the wall, out of which here and there a face looked, frozen in stone, the only thing alive about them their eyes, which watched, watched everything.

Nick thought about what Khasm had said. Somewhere, once, he had read someone's opinion about life: *Hell is other people.* Maybe this was the same principle. "I wouldn't bet on them not being able to do anything," he said. "One of them bit me a little while ago."

"Hope you got your shots," Spile said, and grinned, also a rather mirthless expression. "You find any lifts around here?"

"Not close," Nick said. "The last one was about, oh, half a mile back that way." He pointed off to his left and behind him. "Or up a little . . . or down a little. You know how this place twists."

"What was it you found?" said the guy, fiddling with his plaid as if he wanted to get going again.

"Uh, 'Down the Narrow Ways.' "

The girl's eyes went wide. Nick could see it clearly even in this light. "You did? *Where?*"

Her intensity, and the almost anguished sound of her voice, surprised him. Sure, there were a lot of people who got really worked up about Bane's music . . . but so far Nick hadn't met any of them. "Uh, if you're really looking for it, I can show you. It's not too far, unless the corridors have reconfigured themselves."

"It's not for me," Khasm said. Nick suddenly noticed how tightly her fingers were laced together. "I have . . . I had a friend who was looking for it."

The sudden "had" came down in the middle of the sentence like a boot stamping on something. The hair stood up on the back of Nick's neck. "You . . ." He stopped, unused to being so certain about something, and uncertain just how to proceed. After a moment he said, much more softly, "You knew one of them. One of the Angels of the Pit."

"I *hate* that name," growled Spile, staring at the floor.

"Two of them," said Khasm, sounding bleak. "Or anyway, I knew Jeannie Metz. She lived down the street from me. We went to the same school. We were buddies." She looked over at Spile. "He and Mal Dwyer played virtual football together."

Nick didn't know what to say. But at the same time he was shocked into a sudden alertness that surprised him. This was more than just some story that would help you find your way to the Maze. This was real.

He couldn't keep himself from asking. "What made them do it?" he said softly.

Spile turned his head away, wouldn't say anything. "I don't know," said Khasm, angry. "I know *this*, though. She *wasn't* suicidal."

Nick wasn't going to say anything.

"I know what you're thinking!" Khasm burst out. "That nobody knows anybody as well as they think they do, and all that crap. I've had it up to *here* with hearing that, the last week! From everybody. Even her mom. *She* of all people should know better . . . but she really doesn't know her, either, it turns out. Not if she seriously thinks Jeannie did any drugs."

Nick opened his mouth, closed it. "Oh, yeah," Khasm said, "it wasn't in the news. The cops said they were doing her family a favor by not letting it get out . . . said it was tragic enough." She scowled. "But they told her family that, all right. Some favor."

"They claim," said Spile, looking up at last, "that it was one of these 'amnesia' drugs. Real convenient." He shook his head fiercely. "And now both the families are blaming each other's kid for getting the other one to kill themselves. Real neat." He glared at Nick. "Mal was the most normal, geekly guy you ever saw. Terrified of doing anything illegal. He wouldn't *ever* have done drugs, just because it would have embarrassed his folks, and he would have hated that. Plus, he wouldn't have seen the point anyway. He used to say to me, 'Why do I need another level of consciousness when I like the one I have just fine?' " He lowered his head, looking suddenly stricken, like someone who had too accurately reproduced someone's tone of voice, and now was stricken to the heart by it. "And he sure would never have killed himself," Spile said. "He'd been having a hard time of it lately . . . but not that hard!"

"And Jeannie hated drugs more than anything," Khasm said. "Her dad died of an overdose a few years ago. She'd *never* have done drugs, no matter how depressed she was!"

"Uh," Nick said. He was a little shocked to find himself edging away from them both. "Look, I'm sorry, I didn't mean—"

They looked at him in some shock themselves. Then Khasm sagged. "Sorry," she said. "I'm sorry. It's just that—you know how it is, everybody here we knew has been going around not asking the question—but you know they're thinking about it—and then when somebody does actually ask it—"

"It's okay," Nick said. ". . . Look, I can take you to where that 'lift' is."

"That'd be nice of you," Khasm said, sounding subdued.

"Yeah," said Spile. "Once we've got it . . . we can get out of here. . . ."

They stood up. "Down this way," Nick said, and started retracing his steps through the low dark corridors, with the other two behind him.

Neither of them said much for a while. After some minutes Khasm said, "The last time I saw her . . . it was a couple of weeks ago, with Mal and Bitsy and a few other friends. Down here. They loved this place." She sniffed once, softly, like someone trying to hide it. "She and Mal would come down here and hang out with the rest of us when things weren't going right . . . when we couldn't hang out together elsewhere."

Nick thought for a moment about the best way to phrase this. "Was there some kind of problem?"

"Oh, yeah, Jeannie and Mal had a thing going . . . and her mom didn't approve. Neither did his folks. They all thought they were too young to be thinking about marriage." Another sniff. "Both of them were angry about that, yeah, and a little depressed . . . but not *that* depressed. They were going to wait their parents out for a couple of years, let them get used to the idea. Jeannie told me so. And she told me that Mal agreed."

Nick paused at a corner, trying to remember which way he was headed. There was something niggling at him, and he felt he had to ask. He turned to Khasm. "Look, uh . . ." There was no kindly way to ask. He gave up trying. "You're saying she didn't ever mention suicide . . . ?"

"Exactly once in all the time I knew her," said Khasm, and somewhat to Nick's surprise, she didn't sound angry this time, just tired. "What normal person doesn't think about it every now and then? It would be sick not to admit that it happens. And dumb, when life gets nasty, not to admit that it wouldn't be nice if all the pain just stopped!

But not that way. She never talked about it to *do* it. You know what I mean?"

Nick thought of that sudden rush of make-it-stop that he'd had the other day. Yet at the same time he hadn't had the slightest intention of taking the thought through to its logical conclusion.

"That was why the drug thing was so awful," Spile said as they turned a sharp corner, left, then right again. "But at least it didn't make the news. . . ."

Nick thought about that. Somehow it didn't seem either accidental to him, or an act of kindness. The newspeople were notorious for publishing anything they could get their hands on, the more scandalous the better. *I wonder . . . is that something the cops are keeping secret?*

But why?

It was weirding him out. Nick saw as much pain and death and unhappiness on the Net news as anyone else did, but coming up against it in terms of real people, real lives, was something else again. And there was something else going on inside him, too. His dad was a Netcam man, one of the best. That was why he kept getting sent all over the place, why they had had to keep moving around so much when Nick was younger. Reporters fought to be assigned with his father, for he had (one of them had said once, in Nick's hearing) "a gift for finding trouble and following up on it." Now, unnerved, Nick was beginning to wonder whether that gift was starting to reveal itself in the next generation.

"Here," he said, and turned the last corner. Fortunately the corridors hadn't been doing anything unusual. Right up until now everything had been where it was supposed to be, and now the wall at the far end of what otherwise looked like a featureless dead end was exactly where Nick had left it. "Your account open?"

"Yeah," Khasm said. Nick went down to that blank wall, bent close to it. The light wasn't great down here, and he had only found this lift's hiding place because of a stubborn tendency to touch everything. "Here," he said, getting down on one knee. "See that kind of dimple there? It just caught my eye. It doesn't belong. . . ."

"Yeah," Khasm said again. She leaned down to touch it.

The rock in front of them seemed to tear itself open. A moment later they were all looking at what Nick had found earlier: a small chest carved of what appeared to be a single emerald. Down in the bottom of it was what Nick had found there before, when he opened it himself: a single eighth note, glowing gold.

Khasm looked at it for a long moment before she reached in and touched it. The air filled with the sound of Camiun's strings being plucked slowly, one after another, more as their own small soft poem on the air rather than any accompaniment, and then came Joey Bane's voice, sorrowful and low:

"I never went the way you told me to,
I argued every word you said.
I never thought the way you would have liked,
I never walked the way you led.

And now he's gone with you where I would not,
There in the dark he holds your hand;
And how I simply let you go to be with him
I'll never understand.

So now I have them all to myself, at last,
All my sorry, empty days,
And now I walk alone and self-sufficient
Down the narrow ways. . . .

Nick stayed where he was, didn't move, as Khasm and Spile held still and listened to the second verse of the song. Finally the last few notes faded away, and Khasm lifted the eighth note out of the casket and closed her hand around it. When she opened her hand again, the note was gone.

She stood up and sighed, and sniffled again, and for a few moments she wouldn't say anything. "When they release the body and let her mom bury her," Khasm said at last, "I'll play it at the grave for her . . . after the funeral, when things quiet down."

They went out into the corridor. Nick, following her and Spile, was finding it hard to understand how he felt. Spile was a silent lowering presence in this darkness, but there was no feeling of threat about him, only pain, and Khasm, her eyes downcast, seemed to have gotten control of herself again, but that was even worse for Nick, in a way, than the sound of her fighting with her tears had been.

"Look," he said. "If there's anything else I can do—"

Khasm shook her head. "This," she said, holding up the closed hand that no longer had an eighth note in it, "this meant a lot. Uh . . . thanks."

She went off down the corridor, and Spile started to go after her. Nick astonished himself by putting a hand on that huge arm. Spile stopped and stared at him.

"I mean it," he said.

Spile looked at him in a kind of lowering silence, then said, "Yeah. Thanks. I—"

"Nick Melchior," Nick said. "I'm in the login lists."

"Okay," said Spile. "I— Maybe we'll get in touch."

He went after Khasm. Nick stood there, watching them go, and then headed out into the corridor himself, in the opposite direction, slowly making his way back toward where he had been when they'd found him.

It had never occurred to him that there might have been something odd about those suicides. But Khasm and Spile had been absolutely certain. And now Nick found himself remembering that Charlie had been a little concerned about Deathworld, himself, and all the time Nick was spending there.

Was he thinking about the suicides, too?

There was no telling. But he had certainly mentioned them once . . . and Nick had brushed him off. And then

Charlie had asked him for that walk-through.

Nick had been delighted about this earlier: the idea of ranging around Deathworld with Charlie in tow would have been fun. Part of that was that Charlie was so smart about a lot of stuff. Nick didn't grudge him that. His buddy had been through hell in his time, a real hell as opposed to this rather entertaining fake one. But this would have been one place where, for once, Nick was just a little smarter than Charlie . . . and he didn't think Charlie would grudge him that, either.

Now, though, the concept had acquired an entirely different slant, and Nick wasn't sure he liked it at all. There was something about these suicides and Deathworld that was bothering him, all of a sudden . . . something fishy. And now Charlie was going to be wandering around down there, new to the place, not knowing the ropes. Anybody could come along and tell him anything . . . possibly get him in some kind of trouble.

Oh, come on, said the "sensible" part of Nick's brain. *It's not like the environment's dangerous, or anything. If it were, Net Force would come in and shut it down. And Charlie's not dumb! Far from it.*

But all the same . . . these suicides. . . .

All of a sudden they gave him the creeps.

I've got to go see Charlie, he thought. *As soon as I finish here today. . . .*

Nick headed off into the darkness.

Charlie had been up late again, the night before, sitting sideways on the lowest of the benches in his workspace with his feet up, studying the Deathworld walkthrough. It was complex, but not as bad as some environments he'd played in at one time or another. A lot of the business of getting through the upper circles seemed to involve talking to the Damned. That, by itself, was interesting for Charlie. Later on, once you got down to Eight, it started to be about talking to other gameplayers. *It's as if the game designers are trying to teach people to talk to each other,* Charlie thought. *Easing them into it gradually. It starts out as sort of an entertainment, 'look at all the bad people getting what's coming to them. . . . ' Then it changes focus.*

Charlie wasn't quite sure what to make of that. *Is this the work of some benign behind-the-scenes environment designer? Or could this be something that Bane wanted put in?*

He paused for a little while to scan through the various virtclips and text interviews with Bane that he had gathered together. In none of them did Joey Bane say much about his actual input into the environment's design. If anything, he seemed to avoid the topic, or to try to suggest (in one or two of the interviews) that he was a nontechie who didn't know much about computers or the Net.

That Charlie found hard to believe, especially in the light of the way the professional music business was these days. It had become inextricably interwoven with the Net in terms of music distribution and marketing over the last twenty years, and if there was anything Charlie was certain of as far as Joey Bane was concerned, it was that the man was expert, even inspired, in terms of marketing. He suspected that Bane was as involved in this as in anything else to which his name might be attached. But proving it . . .

Then again, there wasn't any reason to worry much about that right now. The environment itself was going to present its own challenges. *Because after Eight, after you find the way into the Maze and down into the Ninth level . . . no details.* Even the walk-throughs, which were theoretically slightly illegal and usually went out of their way to reveal such details, suddenly went dry. *It's as if it all stops there . . . or some really powerful influence is keeping people from discussing what they find there. Weird.*

The threat of lawsuits, maybe?

But then you would think that was enough to keep people from talking about the first eight levels, too. And it's not.

Charlie brooded over that for a while. *What influence was powerful enough to keep something so secret?*

If I get down there, I may find out.

Meanwhile— He swung up and walked around his little gallery of exhibits again. Charlie had folded away all the autopsy results, and now was left with the kids themselves, sitting on front steps, lying on beaches, hitting a softball again and again . . . Jaime and Richard. Jeannine and Malcolm. Renee and Mitch. *They could have been anybody from Bradford,* Charlie thought. *Or from any school around here. They look perfectly normal.* Except that they had all committed suicide. That was the problem, of course. A suicide looks like anybody else, until the crucial moment hits during which taking one more breath becomes just too painful.

And then there are cases like these, Charlie thought, *when there's something else going on . . .*

. . . and only one way to find out what.

He sighed, glancing up at the windows. It was fully dark in London now, but it was still afternoon on the East Coast. He and headed off toward the doorway that led to Mark Gridley's workspace, opened it, and put his head through.

The heat and humidity hit him like a blow. *Well, it's Florida, isn't it,* Charlie thought, and stepped into the hot sunlight and close still air inside the VAB. *But you can have a little too much reality. Mark can be such a perfectionist sometimes. . . .* "Mark," Charlie shouted as he walked across the concrete, "you in here?"

"Yeah," Mark said, from somewhere right across that huge space, though out of sight. "Be with you in a minute."

Charlie made his way across to where the hardwood desk had been sitting last time. It was gone. There was one of the new Rolls-Skoda cars there, the sleek new armored number that everyone was talking about. Its hood was up, and Mark was peering in at the engine.

Charlie came up beside him after a couple of minutes

and looked in, too. The engine was clean enough to eat off, a complex welter of shining tubes and piping and a massive engine block which had probably been carved in one piece out of a solid cube of steel. "Considering a purchase?" Charlie said. "Or is your dad worried about somebody's security?"

"Huh?" Mark straightened up, dusted his hands off. "No, it's just a sim," he said. "Somebody I know let me borrow it. They're having trouble with the way it runs. Keeps going nonphysical at bad moments."

Charlie thought rather ruefully of his steam engine. "I've been having spong troubles myself," he said. "But that's not what I came over for."

"So tell me." Mark put the Rolls's hood down and boosted himself up to sit on it. "And what happened with all those files?"

"A lot," Charlie said. "But, Mark, would you for cripe-sake turn on the air-conditioning? It's like a sauna in here."

"Nope," Mark said. "I'm waiting for something." He glanced up. Charlie followed his glance, but didn't see anything but the pygmy buzzards, way up high by the huge slot in the ceiling, circling near it. "So tell me what's up."

Charlie shook his head in mild exasperation, but went ahead to briefly describe what he had found in going through the autopsy files. "There's something going on about all these deaths that just doesn't feel right," he said. "And there's no way to look into it except from the inside."

Mark gave him a thoughtful look. "Looking into death from the inside," he said, "would seem to preclude you doing much of anything else."

"Not that far inside," Charlie said, with only a little annoyance. "Mark, I need you to wire me."

Charlie had expected to have to explain to Mark what he meant. To his surprise, he didn't. But he was also surprised to see Mark sit down on one of his folding chairs and blow out his cheeks like someone with a big problem.

"Don't need much, do you," Mark said.

"You can do it, can't you?" Charlie said.

"*Will* I do it? Yeah, you know I'll do whatever you need done. Is it going to be easy? No, not like raiding those systems the other night."

Mark pulled his feet up under him to sit cross-legged on the Rolls's hood. "That was stealing-from-the-cookie-jar stuff compared to this," he said. "Deathworld's probably got more copy protection schemes built into it than any environment I can think of. Bane's really sensitive to having his stuff ripped off . . . and half his technical staff keep busy inventing new and interesting ways to stop people from piping information directly out. A whole lot of stuff to have to defeat, second by second. And naturally you don't want anybody noticing what you're doing."

"Uh, no."

Mark sat there and brooded for a little. "By the way, what happened to your fishing trip?" Charlie said after a moment. "I didn't think I'd find you here."

Mark snickered. "Oh, I would have won. Dad has to stay home and do some classified thing." He shrugged. "Maybe it's just as well. He'll be out of my way for the rest of the weekend, and maybe longer . . . which is going to be good, since this is gonna need a lot of concentration. . . ."

The two of them sat there quietly for a few moments more. Then Mark said, "Talk to me later tonight. I'll let you know if it can be done."

"Okay," Charlie said, getting up. "Mark—thanks."

"Yeah, yeah . . ." But then Mark looked up, blinking. "You hear something?"

Charlie looked around. "Uh, no."

"I did, though—" Mark slid down off the hood of the Rolls, and looked up. *"Hey . . ."*

Charlie followed his glance. The buzzards were suddenly crowding off to one side of the VAB's upper reaches, and all looking hurriedly for high spots on which to perch, as if on the top of a cliff. Charlie looked up and saw . . .

He opened his mouth, then closed it again, for he didn't know how to describe what he was seeing. His first thought was *The air is thickening.* The idea seemed silly. But that was exactly what it was doing—thickening, like steam, like a thick fog, thicker, like smoke—though through it the sun poured from above, untroubled. Charlie shook his head, astounded. Clouds were forming above them, right there inside the VAB, and as Charlie watched, what looked like a thin silvery smoke seemed to start drifting down from them. He walked out into the middle of that space, not hurrying too much, for that silvery drift was taking a little time to come down, and finally he stopped, with Mark behind him, and felt, on his upturned face, the first fine drops of rain.

"Will you look at that," Mark said, triumphant. "It does this sometimes, the real one. I knew that if I'd really got this simulation down right, sooner or later it would happen." He pounded Charlie on the back and laughed. "Congratulations, Charlie, you've witnessed history!"

"Yeah," Charlie said, "and it's wet. . . ." He brushed the rain off his shoulders and made for the door, smiling slightly . . . but still thinking about that gallery of smiling faces sitting inside his own workspace, and intent on finding out what had happened to them . . .

. . . without becoming one more smile.

7

Nick exited Deathworld into the bare white space of his public-access area. He looked around at those white walls with a faint feeling of guilt. Even if they did eventually look better, when he got his decorating done, it wasn't going to be the same as his own space on the family's server. He felt annoyed at himself for not having been more careful with his time, and was starting to be annoyed at himself for getting his mom and dad so angry. He was beginning, much to his annoyance, to be able to see their point.

Pretty soon I'm going to be starting to think I should go apologize to them some more, Nick thought, rebellious.

But would that be such a bad idea? It might do something to change the fact that his life seemed to be completely screwed up at the moment.

You're just freaked because of this stuff Khasm and Spile told you about. . . .

He swallowed. That was true.

And Charlie . . .

"Charlie Davis's space," he said to the white walls around him.

Nick was feeling a little ashamed of himself. He should have stopped by days ago. But he'd been busy. . . .

"Trying that workspace for you now."

That busyness had been shaken out of him, now, by his conversation with Khasm and Spile. Until now Nick had assumed that the suicides were genuine, just people who somehow couldn't cope. It had never occurred to him that something else might be going on . . . and he still wasn't sure what, but the idea gave him the creeps.

"The space you require is accessible," said his public space's management program.

Nick got up out of the virtual version of the implant chair and went over to the air, pulling on the doorknob sticking out of it. The door opened, and he looked through into the big, circular, wood-paneled space with its portraits of doctors in frock coats and wigs, the stadium benches, and the steam engine down in the low part in the middle.

The steam engine wasn't there, though. What was there was a group of 2-D and 3-D images of people . . . kids Nick didn't know. He walked down the stairs between two sets of bleachers, looking at them. There was no sign of Charlie. Either he was out in the real world somewhere, or working on something else. . . .

Or he's in Deathworld someplace.

Nick thought about that, then went back up the stairs and stepped back into his workspace, shutting the access to Charlie's space behind him. Then he opened the doorway he usually used to access Deathworld. Burning red, the copyright information hung there in front of him. "Yeah, yeah, get on with it," Nick said. "Front-door access, please."

The long copyright warning notice hung there a few moments more, and then showed him the great front gates. Nick walked in and said, "Deathworld utilities, please . . ."

In front of him appeared a huge dark-green onyx desk, piled high with ledgers, and behind the desk, a clerk-demon wearing a green eyeshade, and sleeve garters and a bow tie (though no shirt). It looked up at him with a blunt, only slightly wicked face, like that of a cartoon bulldog with the demise of some cartoon cat on its mind. "Yeah? Oh, it's you, Nick."

"Hi, Scorchtrap," Nick said, strolling over to the desk. "How's the union thing going?"

"Aah, the usual," said the demon. "Management says they can't budge on the last offer, we say fine, we'll strike, they say okay, they'll bring in cheaper labor. . . ." The demon leaned to one side and spat brimstone into an ornately carved spittoon by the desk. Sulfurous smoke rose from it. "Scabs, that's what they mean. It stinks more than usual, Nick. Our problem is, we got no rights."

"Well, just hang in there," Nick said. "You guys have personality . . . they'd be nuts to get rid of you."

"From your mouth to the Boss's ear," said Scorchtrap. "Cheapskate that he is. He promised us that this bargaining round, he'd give us a decent profit-sharing agreement. Now he won't even give us the time of day. It's enough to make you lose your faith in market forces." The demon grimaced. "But enough of my problems. What can I do for you?"

"Looking for a friend of mine," Nick said. "Charlie Davis."

The demon pulled up a thick scroll from behind this desk. This unrolled out across the floor and into the distance, where it vanished, like railroad tracks converging at the horizon. Scorchtrap made a disgusted face, tossing the scroll to the desk. "Retrotech," he said, and reached into the air, grabbing a little cord that hadn't been there a second before, and pulling down a text window. "This guy come in here recently?"

"The past day or so, I think."

Scorchtrap studied the text that was scrolling through

the window too fast for Nick to read, and finally came to the end of it. "Nobody by that name."

"He might be using a 'nym.' "

"Yeah, but if he is, we can't disclose it," Scorchtrap said, pulling on the cord again. The window rolled itself up like an old-fashioned window blind, with the same flapping noise, and vanished. "Privacy legislation, you know how it is, Nick . . . gotta keep the nosey-bodies at bay. Even when it's in a good cause."

"Yeah, I guess." Nick let out a long breath. "Listen, do this for me. Let me have a look at the login records for the last couple of days."

Scorchtrap raised his eyebrows. "You kidding?" he said. "You must feel like curling up by the fire with a good book. You know how many people we get in here every day?"

"Just the newbies, Scorchtrap. There can't be that many of them."

"You wanna bet?" The demon shook his head, and reached up to pull that cord. The window came down again. "Been busy around here the last week or so, Nick. Lotta trouble upstairs . . . you know what about."

"I know," Nick said, somber, and leaned on his elbows on the desk, looking at the window.

Scorchtrap hadn't been kidding. Deathworld had experienced between five and ten thousand new user logins per hour from all over the planet during the period in which Nick was interested. Even though Nick waded through it as best he could, there was no telling what 'nym' Charlie might have chosen . . . for he was not one of the dim types who pick an anagram of their name, or their mother's maiden name, for a pseudonym.

Finally he sighed and gave up. Scorchtrap made a sympathetic *tsk, tsk* noise and rolled the log window up again. "Sorry about that, buddy," the demon said. "Anything else I can do for you today? Got some new 'lifts' being released on Six. . . ."

"Naah," Nick said, "not for me, today. I've got business

on Eight." He turned, waving at the demon. "You take it easy," he said.

"Yeah, you too, Nick. . . . Hey, wait a minute!"

Nick looked back. "Yeah?"

"You check the message boards yet?"

"Uh, no! Not a bad idea. Thanks, Scorchtrap."

"Any time, kid." The demon opened a large ledger labeled DAMNED WITH EXTREME PREJUDICE and started leafing through it. "And you keep your feet dry down in the Maze! You don't wanna catch anything down there."

Nick grinned. The desk, and the demon, vanished. In Nick's opinion, the Deathworld programmers were using the demons to keep themselves amused, sometimes possibly even playing them "live." This amused him, too, and he wasn't above playing the game with them when the opportunity presented itself. *It might improve my game stats*, he thought, *but besides that, why shouldn't they have fun, too?*

He walked through the darkness a little way to where he knew there was a huge archway somewhat reminiscent of the main gate. This one, though, had engraved in the stones of the arch the words MARX WAS WRONG: THE OPIUM OF THE MASSES IS NEWS.

Nick headed in through the archway and found himself in a tremendous room modeled after the Beaux-Arts reading room of the 42nd Street branch of the New York Public Library, but all done in black and gray, with high, dark windows, where the original had been done in ivory, wood, and gold. He made his way past the pillared "calls" desk, behind which a huge white lion was standing on its hind legs and going through some card-catalog drawers on the desktop, and glanced down the length of the room. There were two lines of huge long dark-topped tables, each table with four shaded lamps down the middle of it.

Nick walked to the nearest of these and sat down in the subdued light of one of the lamps.

Moving and shifting beneath the surface of the table were hundreds and hundreds of text messages, images, and "flat" virtclips, scrolling by, never stopping, all messages from Banies to Banies, talking about Deathworld itself, or the music, or other Banies, or Joey, or any of the myriad other things that Deathworld fans could possibly think of to discuss when they weren't actually exploring the place. Nick placed a hand flat down on the table and said, "Start a search, pleases. . . ."

"Whatcha lookin' for, boss?" said the table in another demon-gruff but friendly voice.

"Uh, any message from Charlie to anybody else?"

The table emitted a sigh. "You know how many Charlies we got in here, Nick?" it said. "You wanna narrow that search down a little, or don't you have a life?"

Nick laughed. "Any message from a Charlie to me, or from any Charlie to any Nick."

"Nothing found on the first search," the table said. "Nothing on the second. Try something else?"

Nick thought for a moment. *If Charlie's been in here, at least he hasn't been trying to reach me.* That could be a good thing . . . or might not. "Any public message about suicide," Nick said after a moment.

"You really *don't* have a life, do you," said the table. "Eighteen thousand messages about that in the last two weeks. And another six thousand went into the bit bucket between then and now. I *told* them I needed more storage, but do they listen to me, *nooooooo. . . .*"

"Yeah, right," Nick said. He leaned his head on one hand for a moment, thinking. "Look," he said, "show me any message in which the words 'I want to kill myself' or 'I feel like killing myself' or 'I want to end it all' are used."

"You want me to be a dumb machine and sort just for those phrases," the table said, sounding slightly affronted, "or can I get a little bit heuristic about this and also look for sentences that mean the same thing?"

"Uh, feel free."

"Better sample," the table said. "Still pretty big. Four hundred eighty-six messages."

"Okay," Nick said. "Okay, display them."

"You want something to drink?" the table said.

"A cola."

A glass of it appeared next to Nick on the table. "Statutory regulations require us to inform you that the ingestion of virtual beverages does not provide any hydration, nutrition, or other dietary benefit to your physical body," said the table in an intensely bored tone of voice. "Then again, there aren't any calories, either. So drink up, and don't spill."

Nick raised an eyebrow, picked up the glass, and drank, while starting to read the messages. Every time he had read enough of one, he tapped on the table and it vanished, to be replaced by another.

Pretty soon his tapping finger was getting tired. A lot of the messages were facetious. A lot of them were deadpan, in terms of composition . . . but when there was no video to go with the text, as often happened, there was no way to tell how serious the person leaving the message had been, or if they were serious at all. One message Nick came across, which had been left only a few hours before, was typical. WHAT'S THE POINT? said its subject line.

I DON'T KNOW WHAT PEOPLE ARE YELLING ABOUT. ITS ONLY DEATH. DEATH ISNT SO BAD COMPARED TO SOME OTHER THINGS THAT CAN HAPPEN TO YOU AND WHEN IT JUST HURTS TOO MUCH YOU WANT TO SAY ALL RIGHT LET IT ALL BE OVER WITH. MAYBE JOEY IS RIGHT MAYBE THIS IS THE TIME TO CUT THE STRINGS AND HAVE SOME PEACE AND QUIET. NOBODY WOULD REALLY CARE IF I WASNT HERE AND IN FACT I THINK THEY WOULD PREFER IT, IT WOULD BE LESS TROUBLE FOR EVERY-BODY I KNOW, ONE LESS THING TO WORRY ABOUT LIKE MY MOM SAYS. I DON'T KNOW WHAT LIFE IS FOR ANYWAY, THERE'S

NOTHING THAT SEEMS TO BE THE THING
I'M SUPPOSED TO BE FOR AND EVERYONE
ELSE SEEMS TO KNOW, I'M THE ONLY ONE
WHO DOESN'T HAVE A CLUE. THE SOONER
ALL THIS POINTLESSNESS IS OVER FOR ME
THE BETTER I THINK.

There were various replies to this, some sympathetic,
some jeering, but no one seemed to be taking it very seriously, or actually dealing with the idea that this person
really seemed to want to "end it all." No one even just
came out and said "Don't!" *Because they're afraid of finding that he or she was kidding around, maybe, and they
don't want to take the chance of looking stupid? . . .* Nick
let out a breath and glanced at the sender's name.
"MANTA." Just another handle, behind which sat a real
person in who knew what state of mind. At first glance it
would be easy to think it was someone too depressed even
to look over the text and correct it where the context filter
in the Deathworld voice-to-text system had slipped up. *A
yell for help?* Nick thought, glancing down at the time
stamps and other system information, node locations and
so forth, saved at the bottom of the message. *If it was
one, how could you even find the person? This stuff is all
coded, it isn't meant to help you locate them easily.*
Though he had heard that there were ways to track back
an original user to his virtmail account, even to his posting
location, from this footer material, if you knew how to
read it. *By the time you did, though, would the person
who'd left the message even still be breathing? . . .* And
if you *did* find them, would they just laugh at you for
taking their joke seriously?

Nick shook his head and went back to his reading, but
after about twenty minutes more he stopped, exasperated
by his inability to be certain about whether the messages
were genuine. "Is there any way to tell which of these
people mean it?" he said. "Semantic analysis or something?"

"I'm a computer, not a doctor," said the table. "That starts getting into diagnosis. You think I want the AMA after me? Life's tough enough."

Nick had to laugh. "Okay," Nick said, "forget it. But listen—" He thought for a moment. "Are there any messages from any of the . . . you know. The Angels of the Pit . . ."

"Three remain in the database," said the table. "But they've been locked off, Nick. Confidentiality issues."

Nick sat back in his seat, thinking a little more. "Okay," he said. "Would you do me a favor?"

"Anything within reason," said the table.

"If any messages come for me while I'm in-environment from a Charlie—or never mind that . . . from anybody—route them to me right away."

"You're overriding your previously set no-bother instruction?"

"Yeah."

"Got it. Let us know if you want it changed back at some point."

"Right. Thanks, guy." Nick patted the table, then got up and headed out of the reading room again.

He made his way back to his access door, back into his plain white workspace, and stood there a moment, thinking. *Do I want to comm him at home?*

Maybe not . . . it might freak his folks somehow. Or it might freak mine, if he called me back at home and let them know what it was about.

Instead, Nick made his way back into Charlie's workspace. "Hello . . ." he said, hoping to wake up the system.

"Hi, Nick," said the soft woman's voice that represented Charlie's "system manager." "Charlie says, 'Make yourself at home and use whatever you have to.' "

"Uh, good. I need to leave him a message."

"I can record virtual voice, virtual image and voice, or text.

Tell me what you prefer."

"Virtual image and voice."

"Go ahead. Stop for five seconds and then say 'Finished' when you're done."

"Charlie . . ." Nick said. "I have to tell you about this. I ran into some people in Deathworld . . . they knew a couple of the people who committed suicide. But they think something's going on, something odd. . . ."

He went on to lay out everything Khasm and Spile had told him . . . especially the part about drugs being involved. Then he summed up what he'd found when he searched the message database. Nothing much . . . but it might make it clear to Charlie why he was feeling a little weird about what was going on.

Finally he trailed off, not knowing what else to add. "Just comm me at home, if you can," Nick said. "Not too late . . . Dad's been working weird hours the past week or so. The studio had to send him to California for something . . . don't ask me why he couldn't just go there virtually." He tried to think if there was something else he should mention. He had the feeling that he'd forgotten something. "Okay? Comm me. And listen . . . be careful."

Nick paused. "Finished," he said.

"Thank you, Nick," Charlie's system said. "I will pass this on to Charlie as soon as he checks in."

"You have any idea where he is?"

"Not at the moment. I'm sorry."

Nick nodded. "Thanks . . ."

He wandered back up the steps again, not without pausing to look back at those images of kids his age, or a little older or a little younger. Wondering, he turned and headed back to his own workspace, trying to figure out what to do next. . . .

In the VAB, dusk was drawing in, and the big sodium lights hanging from the cross-gantries in the ceiling were turned on, flooding the concrete with a harsh, bright glare. "Okay," Mark said to Charlie, coming across the floor to him. "Here you are."

He held up what he carried, white and shimmering in

that fierce light. Charlie looked at it in bemusement. "It's a jacket," he said.

Mark rolled his eyes. " 'It's a jacket,' he says. Do you know how much *programming* there is in this thing? This is not just any jacket!"

"Okay," Charlie said, "it's a *magic* jacket. Do I have to wear a bow tie with it? And does the tie have to be magic, too?"

"I swear," Mark muttered, "once we both get somewhere physical at the same time, I'm going to whack you a good one with something that can't just be deleted. Here, put it on."

He helped Charlie into the jacket, a rather formal-looking one of the kind a gentleman might wear to dinner. To Charlie, it felt completely normal. "Nice material," he said, patting it down.

Mark stood back from him. "It should be," he said, rather sourly, "considering what it would cost you per hour if someone, I should use the word loosely, 'professional' had built this for you."

"I feel like a waiter," Charlie said. "Probably I look like one, too. So where's the switch?"

Mark sat on the Rolls and shook his head. " 'Switch'?" he said. "*Please.* And if you look like anything, you look like a doctor. And you'll probably make a great one someday, as long as you don't try understanding anything more complicated than a stethoscope, okay? . . . Look, there *aren't* any switches. You just wear it into Deathworld. You wear it out again. Make sure you *don't* take it off—not only because you won't be able to record anything you're perceiving, but because it's set up to work only when it's in circuit with your own virtual account and your own implant. I haven't been able to implement a whole lot of fail-safes, partly because I still don't completely understand how to subvert all their systems. But there's a real good chance that if the jacket comes out of circuit with you, with your implant I mean, every alarm in that place will go off. This would be a *bad* thing, because immediately afterward, every security op associated with Joey Bane Enterprises, not to mention every lawyer they've got, thousands of them probably, will be chasing you down the labyrinthine ways. You're getting all this?"

"Uh, yes," Charlie said. He was also enjoying it. It was always fun to get Mark annoyed about something. "Had a bad time getting the details worked out?" he asked.

Mark glowered at him. "I spent the better part of five hours analyzing Deathworld's security systems," he said.

"Oh, well, five *hours*," Charlie said.

"And if you think I enjoyed it, you're—"

Charlie started laughing. He couldn't help it. "Of *course* you enjoyed it!" he said. "You're a pirate at heart, Gridley. That's why it drives you nuts to be your father's son." He laughed some more, unable to stop.

Mark gave him a crooked smile. "Yeah, yeah, Mr. Psychoanalyst," he said. "Well, you can't help it, I guess, it's your mom's side of the family. Look, never mind that. Just don't let this thing off your back, okay? You can wear a 'seeming' over it—in fact, probably it'd be smart if you did."

"Okay," Charlie said.

"I had to do some jury-rigging," Mark said. "The security systems in Deathworld are really complex, and to keep the flow of information moving out of there and into your space, I had to do spectrum-fission on it, scatter it up and down several different kinds of in-Net communication then reweave it to 'singleband' throughput on the outside."

"I hope that wasn't meant to make some kind of sense to me," Charlie said, checking the jacket to see if it had an inside pocket. It did.

"That's data storage, in there," Mark said. "Meanwhile, just think of the outbound signal as white light broken down to a spectrum, then 'welded' back to white again," Mark said. "The important thing is, it worked when I tested it." He raised his eyebrows. "Though the first couple of test cycles were interesting. What matters is that what you see and hear will go back to your site and store themselves there. One thing: When you're done with the jacket, don't leave it in your workspace. Leave it in mine."

"Oh? How come?"

Mark gave him another of those endearing it's-like-this-stupid expressions. "If something goes wrong," he said, "or on the other hand, if something goes *right*, and in the unlikely event that someone gets cranky afterward about what's been done—you want the Deathworld people to take *you* to court for theft of intellectual property and copyright violations, thus ruining your not-even-started-yet brilliant medical career for ever after? Or do you want them to come after *me* for it, and let me take the heat as the Brilliant But Slightly Unstable Genius Son of the Director of Net Force?"

Phrased that way, the answer more or less made itself obvious. "Uh," Charlie said.

"Exactly, 'uh,'" said Mark. "So I've left my space open for you, day and night. As soon as you're done with a run, leave the jacket here. Over the desk. When you've done that and left, the logs at my end will wipe, leaving no 'electron trail' to your workspace. That much I managed with no trouble. But the rest of it remains technically a little fragile, so as I said, don't lose that jacket, *don't take it off. . . .*"

"Right."

"As for the rest of it," Mark said, "per our discussion about what you think's going to start to happen later, I've 'trip wired' the outside of your own workspace. I think I can safely say that no one will be able to detect that trip wiring. The minute someone tries to hack into any of your accounts—either yours or your folks'—alarms will go off here in my space, and my system will start a traceback on whoever's trying to get at your files. When that happens, your own space will alert you, if you're in Death-world, through the links I've built into the jacket. For times when you're not virtual, you'll want to install some

other alert method, to your home comms or whatever—
I've left the 'hot ends' of the alert routines visible for
you, in your space. Hook them up whatever way you like,
then camouflage them. After that, we'll have the information we need to send Net Force after whoever it is.
And then you and I will be covered with glory."

Mark grinned. "Assuming," he added, "that *they* don't
pitch eight kinds of fit when they find out what we're
doing." He made a pointing-upward gesture that indicated
the entire adult world in general, but specifically his father, and his mother, and Charlie's mom and dad, and
James Winters. "Because you haven't told them . . ."

Charlie made an unhappy face. "How did you know?"

"The same way I know that I haven't exactly told my
dad about what we're up to," Mark said. "*You* know
you're being careful . . . I know you're being careful. But
they don't understand, do they?"

"I'm not sure they would," Charlie said, "no." The
thought of what his father's face would look like, if he
told him what he was planning to do, had been haunting
him the last day or so. *And as for Mom* . . . But haunting
him more assiduously were the faces of Renee, and Malcolm, and Jeannine, and the rest of them. No one else was
in the position to find out as much about what had happened to them as Charlie was. And more to the point,
time was running out. There was only so much of the
month left, at which time Charlie was sure that the person
who he was sure had been stalking the "suicides," and
was somehow complicit in their deaths, might well go
dormant again. A year would go by during which media
and police attention to the suicides would wane, and then,
Charlie was sure, there would be more of them.

No more, he had thought last night, as he'd been going
over his plans, and had started putting them into operation
while scanning through some of the bleak-sounding messages left in the Deathworld "bulletin board" system. *No
more deaths*. The image of the dim hallway, the peeling

paint, a huddled form lying across the room from him, intruded itself again. *No more.*

"Hey," Mark said.

Charlie looked up.

Mark leaned back a little, let out a breath, looked the jacket up and down one more time. "Not that it's not a good idea. But are you absolutely sure you want to go through with this?"

Charlie walked around slowly and waved his arms around a little in the jacket, getting the feel of it. There was a faint fizzing sensation associated with it, something like the sensation that came with a mouthful of soft drink before you swallowed it. "Yeah," he said. "It's partly that I know I can pull this off, solve this problem, without having to run to 'the grown-ups' for help. But there's also the time problem. If I waited to do this the way my folks or Winters would rather have me do it, it could get to be too late." He shook his head. "So I don't see that I have a choice. There are things more important than just 'being careful.' "

"Yeah." Mark let out a long breath.

Charlie sighed as he came back and leaned against the Rolls. "Besides, for Winters at least, I'm going to need more solid evidence than I've currently got. What I'm sitting on right now won't stand up."

"Well," Mark said, "you'll have some solid stuff pretty soon, if you're right." He leaned back on the Rolls's hood. "But if you insist that it's not going to be enough just to have proof that someone tried to hack into your work-space . . ."

"It's going to have to go a little further than that," Charlie said. *Meaning that I am going to have to stake myself out as bait, not just virtually . . . but physically.* The prospect still made him nervous enough, though, that he was unwilling to say it out loud, even to Mark.

"I could see where it might," Mark said. "But the implementation's gonna be tricky. How's your research been coming?"

"Oh, fine," Charlie said. "There's tons of stuff available on the subject on the Net." He smiled, but the expression was grim. Suicide, even in these affluent times, was not something that was showing any tendency to go away. "I get depressed sometimes just reading it."

"That might be a good thing, under the circumstances. If one of the people you're interested in finding actually comes across you, you'll look more like you're really likely to do something about it."

"Don't even joke about it." Charlie had spent the last couple of evenings, when he wasn't busy with other things, studying the symptoms of impending suicide as carefully as if he was about to have a test on them . . . which, in a way, he was. If there was anything he knew about himself at the moment, it was that he wasn't in the slightest suicidal, but the descriptions of the feelings of those who were filled Charlie with pity. And the idea of such people being ruthlessly taken advantage of by someone with another agenda besides pity, a deadly one, left him furious.

Mark's expression was somber. "I wasn't joking . . . not really. But look . . . the minute you decide it's enough, that you have the data you need . . ."

"I'll call."

"Call a minute early," Mark said, "just to be safe. I won't be far from my workspace anytime I'm not in school."

Charlie got up, dusted the jacket down again. "Cut it out!" Mark said. "It's not like it can get dirty, or wrinkled."

"One less thing to worry about," Charlie sighed. He looked up at the faraway ceiling of the VAB. A couple of buzzards peered down at him from the tops of their metal cliffs. "You get it to rain again?"

Mark shook his head. "You can't hurry nature," he said, with a wry look. "Besides, I'm still analyzing the phenomenon. . . . There are some weird things about the humidity that have to be resolved. . . . When are you going to go in and try that out?"

"Tonight," Charlie said. "My folks are going out. I won't be disturbed. And then again early in the morning, and late tomorrow night again, and early in the morning after that. . . ." He slid down off the hood of the Rolls. "Until we get a result."

"Assuming you do," Mark said. "Well, just be careful. I'll be keeping an eye on the jacket's link to my space tonight, and whenever I'm in from now on. Yell if you need anything."

"Believe me, I will." Charlie headed toward the door back into his workspace. "I'll call you as soon as I go in, so you can check the link. Let me know if you find out you're going to be elsewhere, though."

"No chance of that tonight," said Mark, "or in the next few. At least not till I can get this thing's armor to stop going away without warning. . . ." He tapped the Skoda's hood. It lifted itself smoothly up. A moment later Mark was half under it, nothing showing but his neodenimed legs. Charlie took in this view, smiled slightly, and headed back to his space.

No one looked twice at the lone kid, small, kind of young looking, dressed in worn slicktites and a floppy striped "sagdown" shirt several years out of style, as he wandered around in the ash and darkness of the Eighth Circle. Banies came in all ages and sizes, and could look any way they pleased if they felt like going to the trouble of adopting a seeming, or could show themselves "as they were"— though if this was how this kid really looked, there were doubtless those who would have found him a little strange. His sense of style needed work, and the weary look on his face alone was enough to suggest that he probably was as depressing as a Joey Bane lyric himself.

He had been here for a while now, looking around him like someone feeling slightly lost. Anyone interested enough to notice would have seen that he tended to avoid the other Banies in the area, by and large, though he spoke politely enough to them when they approached him. Almost always, after a little while, they went off and left him where he was, and he found himself alone again.

And soon enough—though perhaps not soon enough for him—someone noticed.

The boy was kicking through the ash of the outer reaches with his back to Mount Glede, while in the area through which he walked, nothing could be heard but one song, over and over again, repeating at his request to the environment: the final chorus from the Seattle concert version of "Cut the Strings," with the six-minute instrument destruction sequence ending in the demolition of the venerable old King Dome, scheduled to be blown up anyway that year after the Quake of '22. For about the fifteenth time in a two-hour period, that vast crash and shriek of destruction filled the air, but the images accompanying it were being suppressed, and only darkness surrounded the boy who was listening, standing there, staring at the ash around his feet, like a dark statue. . . .

When the girl approached him, seemingly melting out of the storm of black ash that was falling at the moment, the look he gave her was less than interested.

"Hi," she said.

"Hi," the boy said, looking her over dully. Long dark coat, short purple skirt, black vee-neck top, purple hair, pale skin—she was taller than he was, maybe a year older, and she looked faintly annoyed. "What?" he said then, for she was staring at him.

"Are you lost?" she said.

"No." He turned away.

"Well, you *look* lost," she said after a moment. "In fact, I don't think I've seen anyone more lost-looking than you in the last couple months."

"That's nice," he said, glowering. "I don't recall asking you for your opinion."

He walked away from her . . . then stopped suddenly,

staring down at the crevasse which had just opened up at his feet.

"There's a lot of that going around," the girl said, sounding slightly amused. "Get very far on your own?"

"Not really," the boy muttered. "This place is an exercise in frustration."

"Life stinks. . . ." she said.

"Tell me something I don't know."

"That you're not going to get very close to the Keep without a guide," she said. "Even the walk-throughs mention that. Unless you've got one of the newer ones. . . ."

He backed away from the crevasse, angling a little away from the girl. "Maybe I don't want a guide," he said.

"Maybe you should have brought a chair," she said, "because you're gonna be stuck here a good long while without someone to go 'pathfinder' for you."

He started away from her, and almost as if the environment had heard her, another crevasse came tearing along the ground and passed right in front of him. There it stopped, while black ash snowed down from the edges of it into the fiery depths, glittering in the hot light.

He stared down into the crevasse, and his shoulders slumped. "It's never gonna stop doing that, is it?" he said.

"Nope," she said. "But some of us get the hang of anticipating it."

She tilted her head a little to one side, watching him. After a moment he turned, slow and reluctant. "All right," he said. "What would you suggest?"

"Telling me your name, for one thing," she said.

"Ch—Manta," he said.

"Manta. I'm Shade," she said. "You're pretty new around here, huh?"

"Yeah. Well, no. I've been here awhile . . . but I don't know the place real well as yet. . . ." He breathed out, then, turning again to look past the crevasses, across the dark plain toward Mount Glede. "I don't know if I'm going to," he said.

"You got problems?" Shade said, sitting down beside him.

"Huh?" Manta said, looking shocked. "Oh, no . . . everything's fine."

"I'm not so sure," Shade said. "You look sad."

"How can I look sad?" Manta said. "See, I'm smiling." He produced a smile that even in the darkness was not terribly convincing.

Shade laughed softly. It managed, somehow, to be a sorrowful laugh. "Yeah," she said, "I see that. I know that smile . . . I've worn it, sometimes."

"Have you been here a long time?" Manta said.

"A couple of years," said Shade, "in and out. I know the place pretty well."

"What're you doing here, then?" Manta said, studying the ground. "If you've been here that long, you should have solved the place by now. . . ."

"Oh, there's more to Deathworld than just solving it," said Shade, pulling her feet up under her to sit cross-legged. "It's about people as much as anything else. . . ."

"Seeing them get punished," Manta said bitterly, "yeah. That's worth something."

"It'd be pretty dull around here without the Damned," said Shade, glancing around her as a few of them ran by a few hundred meters away, pursued by demons. A couple of the Damned pitched straight down into a crevasse that opened before them, and the demons stood on the air above them and peered down, watching them fall. "Sounds like you're enjoying it, though."

"Like to see it really happening," said Manta softly.

"How much more real does it have to get?" said Shade. She gave him a thoughtful look. "Or is there somebody you'd particularly like to see it happening to?" Her voice was almost playful.

"Wouldn't be much point in that," Manta said. "It wouldn't make any difference." He shuffled his feet in the ash. "Nothing will, really."

He turned. "Look, forget it. I gotta go."

"Manta, wait," Shade said, walking around in front of him. "Look, you can't just turn away from people when they're trying to help you."

"Watch me," Manta said, his voice bitter. "I'm not worth helping. Let me alone for long enough, and it won't be an issue."

Shade gave him a look. "You know," she said, "if you weren't such a Banie, you'd be a waste of time. Look, how'd you ever get down this far with an attitude like that?"

"When you hear it from all the people around you all the time," Manta said, "you learn to get things done anyway. But I'm tired of it now." He turned and looked at Mount Glede again. "I just want to do this one thing . . . and then it's going to be all over with. I'm going to cut the strings. . . ."

Shade looked at him in silence for a moment. "That's not something to joke about," she said.

"You think I'm joking, too, huh?" Manta said, giving her a cold look. "Get your laughing done now, then. A week or so and you won't have another chance to do it while I'm around."

The look Shade gave him was odd. "Manta," she said, "you wouldn't really—"

"I see what happened to the earlier ones," Manta said, sitting down on a rock and looking at Mount Glede. "Whatever else their families thought, down here they have some honor, anyway. They're the Angels of the Pit. Maybe people down here are a little crazy . . . but at least someone notices whether they're here or not. Not like others—" He broke off.

"You don't have a lot of friends, do you. . . ." Shade said.

"I don't have *any* friends," Manta said. "And I don't want any. They just pretend to care about what's happening to you, and then they dump you when they realize what you're really like. I don't need any more of that—" He choked off, as if holding back tears.

"It's not like that," Shade said. "We're Banies. We have to look after each other, because no one else will. . . . I want you to meet someone I know. . . . He's felt the same way you have."

"If you think you're going to talk me out of how I feel," Manta said, "you're wasting your time."

Shade glowered at him. "It's my time. I can waste it if I like. Right now, though, I want you to give me a virtmail address for you, so we can meet down here again, and you can talk to my friend Kalki. He's a Banie, too. In fact, he's a more serious Banie than almost anyone else you're likely to run into down here. He's got the biggest 'lift' collection I've ever seen. Thing is, he was about ready to cut the strings once, too. But it's a mistake to do that while there's still music in them, Manta. He was there. He knows. You need to talk to him."

Manta studied the ash falling around them, and into the nearest crevasse. After several long moments he said, "I don't see why not. It's not going to make any difference." He raised his head and gave Shade a long, cool look. "If I do decide to cut the strings . . . there's nothing you can do to stop me. You, or anyone else."

"Of course not," Shade said. "But you have to be sure, first . . . otherwise Joey wouldn't like it."

"Like he'd care."

"You'd be surprised," Shade said. "Manta . . . give yourself a break."

"Nobody else has," he said. But he watched her as he said it.

Shade shook her head and held out her hand. "I'm not everybody else," she said. "Let me have an address for you, and later on, in a day or two maybe, you can talk to Kalki."

Manta looked at her doubtfully. But at last he held out his hand to her, and there was a little white envelope in it, the icon for a virtmail address. Shade reached out and took it from him, and tucked it away in one of the pockets of her coat.

"Meantime," she said, "let's see if we can't at least get you in the front door of the Keep. Come on!" Shade looked right and left. "It's narrower over there," she said. She held out a hand.

Manta hesitated . . . then took it. Together they made their way down along the length of the crevasse, stepped across it, and vanished into the darkness.

Some hours later, just after six the next morning, Charlie blinked his implant off and got up, stiffly, to walk around the den. His muscles ached more than usual, and once more he resolved to have a look at the implant chair's muscle management routines. They weren't as effective as usual. *Or I'm spending a lot more time in "the great never-never" than usual. . . .*

Probably the latter. Charlie stretched, then wandered downstairs to the kitchen. He glanced around and saw nothing of his mother's on the table. She was already on her way to work, possibly having another in-service today and so having to do her change-of-shift report with the night nurses on her floor earlier than usual. Charlie sighed and rooted around in the fridge for the milk, poured himself a glass, and downed it. Then he poured another and glugged that straight down, too.

His father came in and headed for the coffeepot. "Morning," Charlie said as he went by

"Thank you for not saying 'good,' " his father muttered. He was already in his whites. He got busy pouring himself a cup of coffee the size of a small birdbath in a big brown cup Charlie's mother had brought back from a nursing conference in Germany.

"Early seminar this morning?" Charlie said.

"Yup. Backbones again," said his father, and slurped the coffee. "Ow, hot . . ." He took the milk carton that Charlie handed him and poured milk into his coffee until it turned a very unassertive shade of beige. "Better. . . . It's just today and tomorrow, anyway, then life goes more or less back to normal." His father sighed. "Though I wish the school wouldn't run all these fellowship-program events at the same time that the accreditation team comes through."

"Maybe they do it on purpose. To show how a good teaching hospital runs under pressure."

His father looked at him with resignation over the cup. "That thought's crossed my mind. Nasty idea. In any case, there's nothing I can do about it. Meanwhile, *you* were up late again. I passed you when I came in. Third night in a row now."

"I'm doing research for a project," Charlie said. *Let him think it's for school. . . .*

"What on?"

"Suicide."

His father sighed. "Still thinking about those kids, huh? Your mother mentioned. Sad situation."

"Yeah," Charlie said. "It's pretty depressing."

His father chugged the much-milked coffee straight down. "Tell me about it. Well, ask your Mom if you need any more help. . . . I've gotta get out of here." He rinsed out the coffee cup, upended it by the sink, and headed for the door, pausing only to hug Charlie in passing. "I feel guilty," he said. "The absentee parent."

"It's not a problem, Dad."

"I want a rematch on that chess game. You promised me best two out of three."

"You tell me when," Charlie said. "Gonna stomp you."

"Don't be so sure. See you later. . . ."

The front door shut. Charlie stood looking out into the back garden, where the first rays of sun were beginning to fall. *I have been spending too much time "down there,"* he thought. *Good old normal sunlight is beginning to look strange.*

But it was in a good cause, and Charlie thought he was beginning to make some headway. *Shade . . .* There was definitely something odd about her, a sense of her watching him closely for some reaction. *Just hope the one I've found is the right one. . . .*

He slowly made his way upstairs with one more glass of milk. The information which Nick had given him was turning out to be very useful, both the 'walk-through' and the other info, the stuff about the kids he'd run into, Khasm and Spile. The rumor, confirmed to the two most recent suicides' parents, that drugs had been involved— and the information that this news was possibly being suppressed—all fit in very neatly with Charlie's suspicions. Especially the idea that they weren't genuinely suicidal. *Someone met them, probably in Deathworld, managed to get close enough to them, physically, to get sco-bro into them—and then set up their suicides....*

Now all Charlie needed was to re-create the initial part of the setup, without becoming a statistic himself.

To this end, the walk-through which Nick had given him had been extremely comprehensive, not as errorridden as Nick had feared, and Nick himself had also appended some material to it as notes which Charlie had found very useful. He sat down on the sofa across from the implant chair in the den, finishing his glass of milk, and thinking about his next moves, the ones he would begin tonight after school. Charlie had been able to get down to Eight in fairly short order. *I wonder if the system notices things like that....* Charlie thought. But then lots of people must tell their friends how to get through it quickly, how to meet them places.... *It probably all averages out in the end.*

Either way, I have to follow up this contact with Shade, and keep looking to see whatever else turns up. No way I'm going to sit around and let this happen to someone else. It's still May....

Charlie sighed, put the milk glass aside, and sat down in the implant chair—he still had about half an hour before he had to leave for school, and this was the best time to catch people. He closed his eyes, triggered his implant on again, and glanced around the lowest level of his workspace, where the 3-D and 4-D images still stood. "Workspace management," he said.

"Here, Charlie."

"Is Nick Melchior available?"

"Checking that for you now. But this time does not match his usual online times for the past two weeks. —Not available."

"Okay, what about Mark?"

"Mark's workspace is available as usual, and he is in residence."

"Good." Charlie went over to the usual access door, opened it. The VAB's lights were on. It was early enough at the Cape that not much light was getting in. Charlie wandered across the floor, where he could see the Rolls-Skoda, its hood still up, and a pair of legs still visible.

"That thing giving you trouble?"

"Please," said Mark, sounding tired. "If you see the man who invented technology, send him up. I have something for him." He stood up from under the hood and made an eloquent fist. "I just can't get this thing's armor to stay solid when it should." He sighed, straightened up. "There's always the possibility that I've found a bug in the programming language itself . . . but I really don't want to believe that. It would be big trouble. . . ."

The desk wasn't too far away, and Charlie saw the Magic Jacket lying over it as he had left it much earlier. "Is it okay?" he said.

"It was fine," Mark said. "I 'looked' in on you five or six times, just to check on it. No problems." He looked at Charlie, with a rather challenging expression. "Except with you. You didn't seem terribly comfortable down there."

"I hate it, the whole fake-seeming business," Charlie said. "Skulking and acting . . . I don't like not being me. Being me is hard enough, without having to fake being someone else as well." He let out a long breath. "But I guess this is in a good cause."

"You'd better believe it is," Mark said, "because you've had a trip."

Charlie swallowed. "What? *Already?* When?"

"Yesterday. Yesterday afternoon, actually. Someone unauthorized was trying to get into your space. I tried to get hold of you, but you were offline."

"Whew," Charlie said. "I wasn't expecting anything that fast." He thought for a moment. "Mark, that means that whoever tripped the 'wire' has definitely been reading the message boards in Deathworld. I didn't actually talk to anybody until this morning, real early, before school."

"How many people have you talked to?"

"Uh, six or seven. A couple have seemed interested in me . . . but I'm not entirely sure yet that it's more than casual. I should get a better idea later."

"Okay. Well, you're recording everything. . . ."

"I never take off the magic jacket . . . no matter how much it itches."

"It doesn't itch!"

"It *does*. It fizzes. I feel like I'm wearing a can of soda."

"Must be feedback through the implant," Mark said, thoughtful.

"Can't you do something about it?"

"Not while you're wearing it," Mark said. "Let me play with it today if I have some time. I'll leave it in your space when I'm done with it."

"Yeah, fine. But Mark, *who tripped the wire?!*"

"I don't know."

"You don't *know?* I thought you put a trace on the trip wire routine!"

"I did," Mark said, sounding extremely annoyed now, "but unfortunately, your pigeon was using an anonymizer to conceal the server of origin. They're perfectly legal. I thought the routine I had running would beat it . . . but this 'anonner' is a new one, just opened up. Among the identification routines it's been built to defeat is the one I was using. Dammit."

"But can't you use something . . . you know . . . from Net Force?"

Mark's voice got, if possible, even more annoyed. "The 'industrial strength' identification routines at Net Force are locked down tight, Charlie . . . to get permission to use the 'Drano' utilities, you have to have a court order and ID as a senior Net Force supervisor. Which I am not . . . yet. And I can't exactly ask any of them, either. So I'm winging it, using routines that have a lot less oomph. If I want to upgrade one of those to industrial strength I'm going to have to do that myself. In fact that's what I'll have to do after school today—go check out this new anonymizer, find out which protocols it's using, figure out how to defeat them. Probably take me a day or so. You better sit the next couple dances out until I can sensitize the 'trip wire' to backtrack the next hit correctly."

Charlie was fuming. "You don't know anything about where the 'trip' came from?"

"Not a thing," Mark said, sounding just as annoyed. "Could have been next door to you, or in Ulan Bator."

Charlie sighed. "Okay," he said. "Let me know when you get the new routine up again."

"I will. But look, Charlie, just give it all a rest for the moment. A day or so won't make any difference."

"Yeah . . ." Charlie headed out of the VAB and back to his own space, beginning now to be actively nervous. *A day or so* . . . But no matter what Mark said, Charlie couldn't get rid of the idea that it *could* matter. *It most definitely could.* . . .

8

Nick looked for Charlie at school that day but missed him at lunch again, and wasn't able to track him down between classes. He had things on his mind, and he really wanted to talk to Charlie about them.

His last-period class had been canceled, so Nick stopped by the wing of the school where he knew Charlie sometimes had a late upper-level biology class. But it had been relocated or rescheduled—the room was locked and empty. Nick let out an exasperated breath and started to walk home.

His path took him by the NetAccess center as usual, and there Nick paused by the door and took out the last commcard he had left, the one he had fished out of his bottom drawer in his bedroom several days earlier, having forgotten that it was there in the first place. Nick looked at the card and sighed. He was woefully short of cash, now—there wouldn't be any more allowance money until Friday, and this was only Tuesday. Yet at the same time he wanted to give Charlie the opportunity to walk through

Deathworld with a friend at his side, not only for enjoyment, but now, after his conversation with Khasm and Spile, for security as well.

And there were other matters on his mind. A random thought, something about the various lifts he had brought back from Deathworld with him, had been obsessing Nick for the past couple of days. The Eighth Circle was proving difficult to crack—*and it's gonna be impossible, without some more money to spend some more time there,* Nick thought. But he was noticing that the hints and whispers he had been expecting from "plants" in the Circle had been very few. He had been wandering around in those stony tunnels and up and down the Escheresque stairways for days now and had come up against—he smiled wryly at the expression—a stone wall.

Yet there had been more lifts available than usual, so many that his pocket lift carrier couldn't handle them all anymore, and Nick had to load them in and out of the storage area in his public server. Most of them were different versions of songs Nick already had lifts of. Only a collector, an aficionado, or a raving completist would feel the need to have them all. But Nick certainly fitted into the last category, at least, and it was while he was listening to some of the "alternate" versions in bed a few nights ago that he had noticed some of the lifts were alternates in other ways as well. They had lyrics that other versions of the songs didn't have—

He shook his head and went into the access center. "Hey, Nick," the guy behind the front counter said. "Early today—"

"Yeah, well, you might not see me for a few days," Nick said. "Running out of green . . ." He slapped the commcard up onto the reader plate.

"You're okay," said Dilish, the guy behind the counter. "Got a couple of hours left on that one."

"That much? Super! My usual one open?"

"No, there's someone in there, take Eight . . . I'll reroute your server info over there."

Nick went back to the booth and closed himself in, locking the sliding door and sitting down in the implant chair. A moment later he was standing in the usual white space, and he got up and reached into his pocket, coming up with the key that "remembered" his location from the last visit.

"Deathworld access," Nick said. The door in the air opened, a black rectangle in all that whiteness, and the copyright notice began rolling by. *Is it an illusion,* he wondered, *or does that thing actually get longer every time?* Finally it vanished, and Nick went through into the dimness of the Dark Artificer's Keep, entering into the dark stone corridor where he had been standing when he last exited.

Nick needed somewhere with a little more room for what he had in mind, so he backtracked through the tunnels to where they widened out into a round cavern, something like fifty meters across, that Eighth-Circle Banies referred to as the Bubble. Only a few people were there at the moment, passing across the empty stone space on their way to somewhere else. When they were gone, Nick said, "Sound management system . . ."

"Ready."

"Access lift library."

"Got it."

"Play 'Strings5.' "

Music and image faded in, and suddenly Joey Bane was there some meters away, alone and spotlighted in the darkness, sitting on the four-legged bar stool he used for these performances—one of many. It, like every other inanimate object onstage but Camiun, always wound up getting broken at the end of "Cut the Strings." It was last summer's concert in Los Angeles, at the Hollywood Bowl, and Joey was sweating. Even the Bowl's slightly cooler position in the mountains was no defense against the heat wave the L.A. basin had been suffering that week. Joey was looking out at the crowd with half a smile, let-

ting them settle, and finally he touched Camiun's strings
and sang:

> "I ran into Astraea with her veil on,
> sneaking out the party's back door:
> I stopped her right there and I got her a chair,
> asking what she was leaving for:
> 'The party's just getting started, my lady;
> what's the rush to leave us today?'
> And the goddess she looked at me and she said,
> 'There's nowhere left for me to stay . . .' "

Quietly the rest of the band came in, in that deceptively
soft and easygoing introduction, as the Goddess of Virtue
explains that the day she's feared has come, the day when
the human race is at last entirely wicked, when she must
finally hide her face and leave the world to its fate forever,
and Joey responded to the news—

> ". . . Nothing left to live for, nothing left to give for,
> nothing left to care about:
> Nothing left to cherish, all hopes left to perish,
> Nowhere to go but out!
> No one left to bring to, no pure heart to sing to,
> What's the point of hanging on?
> When the reason in the rhyme's all been eaten by
> crime,
> when the last joy's finally gone?"

—and then the great chorus of rage and desperation,
crashing down in chord after chord as Camiun and Joey
Bane together, full-throated, shouted down the blasting
band behind them:

> "Then cut the strings—
> let's be done with it—
> If the last night's here,
> then let's be one with it—

If the songs all die, if the music's all gone,
If the night's come crashing on the last free dawn,
what possible point is there in carrying on?
Cut-the-strings!"

Nick stood listening for enjoyment's sake, but his mind
was on the lyrics, especially the very first verse, which he
was now sure was not the usual one. Joey would sometimes play with the middle verses, inserting something
cruelly topical that suited the venue or the world situation
of the day, but Nick had never heard him vary the first
verse. Now he glanced over his shoulder for a second,
thinking of the "front hall" upstairs, before you ever got
into the Maze, ever came close to the tunnels or the Stairways to Nowhere—and Nick started to wonder about a
faint noise that he'd heard from behind one of those doors
that led off the front hall. . . .

The sound of the audience's upscaling howl of excitement brought Nick around again. Bane had stood up at
the first chorus—no one could sing that sitting down, not
and do it justice—but now, two choruses further along,
he turned around, and as always, Camiun was gone. None
of the concert virteos, no matter how you studied them,
ever shed much light on how that happened. Maybe it
was an illusionist's brand of magic, maybe it was something more obscure. But speculation always got lost in the
wake of what always happened next, which was Joey
Bane snatching yet another of Wil Kersten's unfortunate
guitars out of his hands and smashing it to smithereens
on the floor, or on some other piece of equipment that
happened to be at hand. Off he went on his expected ram-
page, the crowd screaming noisy approval in the background, and the concert dissolved in a shriek of tortured
amplification equipment and other shattered impedimenta.

Nick let it play itself out, and when the clip finally
faded into darkness, he stood there a moment later in the
Bubble, with the torches flickering around him from their
iron grips in the wall, and considered what to do next.

Upstairs. I want to check that door. I don't want to stay too long . . . gotta save a little time on this commcard for later in the week.

But first let's see if I can find Charlie . . . !

Charlie made his way home to find the house empty again—his mom wasn't back from the hospital yet—and, waiting for him in his workspace, bobbing gently up and down in the air, was the virtmail message he'd been hoping for. He made his way down the stairs of the lecture hall to it, and looked the little glowing sphere's exterior shell over to see if it was "canned" or "live"—some mails, when touched, would link live to the person who had sent them if he or she was available online.

No use taking chances, Charlie thought, even though he couldn't see anything to suggest a live linkage. "Workspace management," he said.

"Here, Charlie."

"Implement stealth routine one."

The interior of the Royal Society's lecture room went away, to be replaced by a plain white plain with blue "sky," a mimicry of a public-access space. Charlie looked at his hands and arms and saw that his workspace had settled a copy of his "Manta" seeming about him. He could see it, thinly, over his skin, transparent.

Satisfied, he reached out and touched the mail. A moment later Shade was standing in front of him, surrounded by a little halo of darkness. The message had been sent from somewhere in Deathworld.

"Manta," she said, "I got in touch with Kalki. He'll be in the World tonight around ten eastern. He really wants to see you and talk to you. Let me know if you can make it."

The image paused, waiting for Charlie to activate the reply function. For a moment he stood there looking at her earnest face, and chewed his lip.

Mark did say to give it a rest for a day or two. . . .

Yet at the same time, the thought kept coming up in the back of his head: *It's May. Early in May . . . And* every day lost meant the chance that someone else might die. *If one of these people are involved with the "suicides," and I lose the chance to get close to them while Mark's playing with his programming . . .*

Still. He was pretty definite.

Charlie sighed. "Start reply."

"Ready."

"Shade, thanks, but listen, I—" He stopped himself in the middle of saying "I can't make it." *Do you dare* not *take the chance?* The risk was just too great. In his mind's eye Charlie could just see the blurred look on some innocent kid's face as the drug took them, left them defenseless—"I might be a little late," he said, "but I'll be there. Thanks for letting me know. End."

The workspace collapsed the message down into a smaller sphere. "Ready to send?" it said.

"Send."

It vanished. Charlie looked at the empty air where it had been. Then, "Restore normal environment," he said.

The lecture hall came back. Charlie glanced around it, and at the six sets of images which had been restored to their original locations, and then headed off for Mark's workspace to collect the Magic Jacket.

Some hours later he was standing by the front doors of the Dark Artificer's Keep, waiting. There was a fairly steady stream of Banies coming in and going out, and demons stood by the doors on either side, at attention, looking like doormen at some expensive apartment building. Manta stood there off to one side in his floppy shirt and old worn black slicktites, twitching slightly, looking nervously around him. None of the Banies paid him the slightest attention.

"Waiting long?"

He didn't have to fake being startled. Manta turned hurriedly and saw a tall shape looming over him, somewhat indistinct in the darkness.

"You Manta?" he said.

"Uh, yeah. I don't—"

"I'm Kalki," the guy said. "Come on. Who can see anything here? Let's get a little closer to the doors." He took Manta's shoulder in a friendly way and guided him over that way.

Manta shivered a little. Allowing people he didn't know well to touch him had always come hard to him. It was something left over from his distant childhood he didn't readily discuss. As they got closer to the doors, and the light of the great chandelier spilling out of them, he got a better sense of what Kalki looked like. He was slender, about eighteen, and not wearing a seeming—or at least not an unusual one. He wore street clothes, just neos, a slipshirt, and a "bomber" jacket. His face was unusually handsome, with high cheekbones and eyes that drooped down at the corners a little, a look that would have been humorous if it wasn't so sad. *A seeming after all?* Manta thought. *Or am I just unusually paranoid?*

"Shade couldn't make it," Kalki said. "Some family thing came up, she said. She told me about you. . . ."

"Not too much, I hope," Manta said.

Kalki looked at him thoughtfully. "Come on," he said, "we can go in here and talk."

They went in through the Front Hall, and Manta looked up at the great black and gray chandelier, casting its cold light. "It gives me the creeps," he said softly.

Kalki chuckled. "You want creepy, you should try Nine," he said. "That'll raise the hair on your head, all right."

"You've been down to Nine?"

They headed off to the side of the huge space, where there were some benches faired into the stone of the massive walls. "I've been through the gates," Kalki said, sounding bored. "It looked so much like the beginning of Eight, to me, that I decided not to bother. They've gone to so much trouble, hiding the lifts down there, I wonder whether they're worth it . . . after all, the stuff I've found on Eight so far hasn't been so great. Sometimes I think it's just a ploy by the management to get everyone real excited about substandard stuff."

"The more I see of down here," Manta muttered, "the less excited I am about it."

"Yeah?" They sat down on one of the carved benches, watching people come and go through the great doors. "Shade told me," Kalki said, "that you were pretty sad about things. I see she wasn't exaggerating. . . ."

"Yeah." Manta looked out into the darkness, and then after a moment said, "She said you'd felt this way. . . ."

Kalki nodded. "A while ago now," he said. "It can be pretty tough when you're right down in the middle of it."

"I left some messages in the 'board' area," Manta said softly. "Just to try to get someone to talk to me. No one answered."

"Hey," Kalki said, "life *does* stink, doesn't it? The trouble is that people bring the outside reality in here with them. Here, you can change things . . . but out there, no one does anything about the nature of reality, the way people interact with each other. Or don't. No one listens to anything Joey's saying. And why should they? To do that, they'd have to admit the world stinks, in the first place."

"I don't have any trouble admitting that," Manta said. "It's been a waste of my time since I first started noticing things. Now . . ." He shook his head. "It's like every breath hurts. I'm tired of breathing."

Kalki let out a long breath. "You have folks?" he said.

This was the painful part, the lying. "My mom," he said. "But she's a druggie. The guy she's seeing . . ." He shook his head. "We don't see eye to eye. And they're a long-term thing. I'm gonna be 'phased out.' I can see it coming. She's gonna farm me out to some cousin of hers." Manta bowed his head, unable, unwilling to look up to see how Kalki was taking this.

"Sounds rough," Kalki said. "Look, Manta . . . you've got to believe it. It can get better. Without warning, sometimes."

Manta's laugh was bitter. "Is that the best you can come up with? That just *maybe* things might get better? The only way that's going to happen to me is if all this stops, if the hurting, and the yelling, and the pushing around, if it all just *stops*. I've had it. I don't mind being worthless, being in everybody's way, no use for anything, I can deal with that if I'm just left alone. But when they *make* you that way, and then they yell at you for it, when they take everything away from you and then scream at you for not acting normal, for letting them down—" The words choked off. "I couldn't even give stuff away, gave some of my stuff to the kids at school, the few things I had. They even yelled at me for that." He laughed, that harsh sound again. "It doesn't matter. Those things are safe now."

"You gave stuff away?"

Manta was silent for a moment. "When I realized my mom was going to send me off to Philly or wherever it is her cousin lives," he said, "and I wasn't going to be able to see my friends anymore..." He trailed off. "I knew she was gonna just throw all my stuff away...."

He listened hard to Kalki's silence. His mom had been pretty clear that suicidal people sometimes gave personal possessions away to friends in anticipation of the act itself.

Kalki shifted, and as Manta glanced back at him, he thought Kalki looked uncomfortable. "Look, Manta," Kalki said at last, "this isn't the best place to be having this conversation. You're talking about the most real thing there is ... your own existence. But places like this are *instead* of reality. They can be really attractive, or interesting, but they're not *real* contact, with real people." He shook his head, glancing around them. "So much of the uncertainty in the world, the pain ... I think it comes of there not being enough genuine contact."

He looked down at Manta. "We should get together and have this out," Kalki said. "Not here. Contact between human beings shouldn't have to be mediated by electrons." His voice was suddenly pained. "Or snatched in the few minutes between online experiences and virtual appointments. . . ."

"For what?" Manta said. "This is real enough. You don't have anything to say that's going to convince me. If you did, you'd have said it already." He got up. "Thanks, but—the talking time's over. I know what I need to do."

He took off across the huge "front hall."

"Manta, wait!" Kalki yelled after him, and came after, but Manta broke his connection to Deathworld, and vanished into the darkness.

A moment later Charlie was standing in his workspace again, slightly out of breath, not from any exertion, but from nerves. He glanced over at the readout connected to Mark's "trip wire" routine: glowing letters and numbers hung in the air, zeroed out, showing no attempts to access his space in any way.

Okay, Charlie thought, *the trap's baited. Now let's see what happens. . . .*

The next morning he came down from the den, yawning, feeling somehow faintly disappointed. Despite the fact that people seemed to have been reading "Manta's" messages on the Deathworld message facility, there were no answers to any of them. And no follow-through from Shade or Kalki. *I wonder if I overreacted a little,* he thought. *Scared Kalki off . . .*

This time his mother was in the kitchen, pouring coffee from a freshly filled pot, and the sound of the front door shutting told him that he had just missed his father. "You're up early," she said, turning as Charlie yawned again.

"Yeah," he said.

"Want some?" his mom said.

"Uh, you don't think it'll stunt my growth?"

She gave him a look. "Nah. That's just a matter of time. I doubt much of anything could do that at this point."

From the cupboard she got down the mug with the double duck on it and the motto EIDER WAY UP, filled it and handed it to him.

"Thanks . . ." he said, and flopped into one of the kitchen chairs.

They both drank coffee in silence for a moment. Then, "A lot of late nights, the last week or so," his mom said.

"Yeah."

"Dad says you're still researching suicide."

Charlie nodded.

His mother looked slightly resigned. "It has a kind of horrible fascination, I'll admit," she said. "Especially when life seems good, and it's difficult to understand how anyone could want to end it."

"Yeah," Charlie said, thinking of the six sets of images in his workspace, people he was not convinced had unanimously intended to end anything. "What's your schedule like today?"

His mother raised her eyebrows at him, plainly noticing the change of subject, but declining for the moment to comment. "The usual day shift, barring emergencies." She looked slightly relieved. "Though you know how it is trying to predict those. You?"

"School as usual," Charlie said. "Nothing exciting."

"Sounds wonderful," his mom said, finishing her coffee. "Look, Dad picked up some ribs last night, I was thinking of doing that thing with the hot sauce again for dinner."

"Yes, please!"

She grinned at him, rinsing out the coffee cup and leaving it to drain, then picking up her work-satchel from where it sat on one of the kitchen chairs. "Okay. Dinner around six, then. See you later, sweetie. . . ."

School went uneventfully. Charlie had left a message with Nick's mom that he wanted to get together with him for lunch, but at lunchtime Nick was nowhere to be found. *The most highly developed communications sys-*

tem in history, Charlie thought ruefully as the afternoon
went by, *and we're still playing Net Tag with each other.
Oh, well . . . I could always drop by his place. It's not
that much out of my way home. . . .*

He finished his afternoon bio class and headed home
after hanging around a little while to see if Nick surfaced.
There was no sign of him, so Charlie strolled in an ab-
sentminded way through the sweet spring-afternoon, considering neurotransmitter chemistry and the prospect of
his mom's hot and spicy ribs. There had been some discussion a week or so ago into exactly why the capsiacin
molecule was able to fool mouth tissue into thinking it
was injured, and trigger the release of endorphins. Charlie's bio teacher had suggested that there might be some
fake neurotransmitter "key" involved. *Doesn't sound genuine to me*, Charlie thought. *If it were, there would be a—*

The sound of a car slowing down close to him when
all the rest of the traffic was doing forty or better made
Charlie turn his head. A big car had slid up beside him,
and just as his head was turning its door popped open and
someone lunged out, reached out toward him—

It was only the reflexes of the nascent street kid Charlie
had once been that now saved him, the thing that even
these days sometimes made it hard for him to hold still
and let his mom hug him. *Don't let them touch you!
Touch is control—*

He twisted away and plunged off down Morrison
Street, away from the car. Charlie heard the whine of the
sonic going off behind him, someone actually trying to
stun him into collapse—but he was just out of range, and
his legs were moving faster than his brain for once. They
remembered fear more clearly and immediately than he
did, and while the intellectual constituent of the fear was
still working its way down from his brain to his adrenals
Charlie was already running, running as if the Devil himself was after him, down the street, turn the corner, down
the side alley that served that block of Morrison, turn
another corner in the opposite direction, run, *run*—He

barely felt the concrete beneath his feet, he was running so hard, and though his body was panting with terror and exertion already, Charlie's brain was running ahead of him, planning his escape.

It's a one-way street. They can't get down here easily. And I know this area—

He ran. His lungs started burning, and he ignored them. *I thought they were in a hurry. I was right. Too right.* Charlie gulped for air as he ran. *If they're ready to try a snatch in broad daylight, they're really serious. Got to get online right away. Got to get help. The cops—or better still, Net Force—*For the cops didn't know him. Net Force did. He needed Mark Gridley, or James Winters, just as fast as he could get to one or the other of them.

Is it the killer himself, Charlie thought, *or an accomplice? Does it matter? They're right behind me—*For he could hear an engine, getting closer. He didn't bother looking behind him. He turned immediately right and plunged across a brownstone's front yard, down the driveway beside it, heading into its paved backyard. There was a Dumpster up against the brick back wall. Charlie blessed its name and that of District Recycling Company, whoever they were. He went up onto the top of it in a rush and from there jumped up to grab the top of the wall, having already seen as he was going up that there was no broken glass embedded in it. Charlie went over the wall into the yard of the brownstone on the other side, paused for just a second to take it in—blind dirty windows, all with security shutters or shades down, another Dumpster, a couple of parked cars— *I know where I am,* he thought as he plunged out of the yard, into the brownstone's driveway and down to the wall in front of the building and the driveway's open gate. He looked up and down the street. *I can't let them catch me out here, where they have the advantage—size, weapons, mobility. If there's going to be a chase, let it be where I have a chance. Not out here!*

He ran like a sprinter, terrified that as he got to the corner he would see that car in front of him. *Dark blue,*

*a glossy new Dodge sedan of some kind, one of those big
ones, they keep changing the names, recent model, Virginia plates—* But it didn't materialize. Some kindly fate
gave him the few seconds he needed to fly in the door
of the WorldGate public Net-access place on the corner.
He stood there panting at the front desk, and the guy
who manned it straightened up from taking something out
of the shelves behind the desk, looked Charlie up and
down with an expression of complete boredom, and said,
"Yeah?"

"I need a booth!" Charlie said.

The behind-the-counter guy looked at him with a total
lack of urgency. "Cash or credit?"

Charlie fumbled in his pocket and came up with, to his
shock, not one of the family commcards, but something
he had grabbed off the hall table that morning on his way
to school, thinking that he might as well use up a little of
whatever comm time was on it: a public access commcard. Gulping, Charlie slapped it down on the reading
plate on the counter. The guy behind the counter read
what the plate and the commcard had to say to each other,
and pushed Charlie's card back toward him. "Only got
fifty-five minutes on that," he said.

Charlie swallowed. "Which booth?" he said.

"Six—"

He ran down the hallway between the booths, found
Six, slid the curved booth door shut behind him, then
palmsealed it locked. There he stood for a moment,
breathing hard, and then flung himself into the implant
chair which was the room's only furnishing. He leaned
back, sweating, lined his implant up with the chair's
pickup, closed his eyes—

Charlie opened them again on whiteness, and jumped
up out of the chair. He was standing on an infinite white
plane with a featureless blue "sky" above it, empty of
everything except a voice that said, "Welcome to a
WorldGate public Net-access facility. Instructions,
please?"

The terrible thing about it all was that the one place where Charlie would have felt safe and at least slightly in control, his own workspace, was the one place he couldn't now go. There was a better than even chance that it had been tampered with somehow, that his accessing it would trigger some tracing facility that would betray his presence here. And that door would only be closed for fifty-five minutes. Charlie had almost no cash on him to buy more time. After that he would have to go out the door, and if they had been able to track him down, one way or another, the people hunting him would be waiting there with some plausible story—

Then it was all too plain what would happen to him, what had happened to the others. If not today, then some other time real soon, at an unguarded moment, he would be snatched. Someone would stuff him full of scorbutal cohydrobromate, either with a FasJect or even just out of a spray can, the aerosol method. And when the drug took, in a matter of a few minutes, when he could not resist, Charlie would be spirited away into some private spot, a hotel room, say, and his "suicide" would be set up. Possibly even with his own cooperation, but in any case, he certainly wouldn't be in any condition to resist. *And even bearing in mind what Mom said . . . in this case, the odds are better than fifty-fifty that they can make you do something you wouldn't normally do. Think of what Nick said about Jeannine and Malcolm. . . .*

Charlie swallowed. "Workspace access," he said. "Address 77356936678822–847722—"

He rattled the number off as fast as he could, having to stop once or twice, because it wasn't one he normally had to remember. The whiteness around him flickered—

Charlie found himself standing in the middle of Grand Central Terminal in New York. This was his father's desperate joke about the state of his own schedule, which he described as being like living in Grand Central, though without being able to go downstairs to the Oyster Bar whenever he liked. The terminal's great main concourse was gloriously lit, with sun pouring down in great diagonally striking rays from the tall windows on the Vanderbilt Avenue side. But there were no people in it . . . and more to the point, to Charlie's despair, his father wasn't in it, either. Normally he had a big desk, made of the same creamy polished terrazzo of the floor, standing just west of the circular information kiosk with its polished brass knob-clock, but the desk was missing.

"Damn," Charlie whispered to himself. There was no point in leaving a message, no time— "Home system," Charlie said. "Workspace, new access, address, 77356936678822–8472086633—"

Another flicker. A second later Charlie was standing in his mother's space, which for reasons she had not explained to him was currently a huge stretch of sand just east of the Pyramids. The view was spectacular, until you turned around and saw that the suburbs of Cairo were directly behind you, and in fact you were standing in someone's backyard, with a picnic table and a swingset off to one side, and a lawn that was scrubby not for lack of water, but because some kids and an overenthusiastic dog or two had dug or worn it nearly flat. Charlie looked at the picnic table and saw a scatter of his mother's paperwork all over the top of it, stuff from the hospital, her computer pad, a bunch of flowers stuck in a crude vase that Charlie had made her from clay a long time ago. "Mom?" he said softly.

Her simulacrum appeared immediately. "Hi, honey," she said, but Charlie let out a breath of pure desperation, for she was canned. "Guess what? The best-laid plans have ganged agley after all. I'm going to be late again tonight, sorry . . . they needed some more warm bodies down in ER, they were short of staff. When you get home, be a sweetie and put some more white wine in the marinade for the ribs, okay? Otherwise, if you need me for something, call the hospital and have them page me, they'll—"

Damn. "Home system," Charlie said, racking his memory, and then shaking his head in frustration, for he couldn't remember James Winters's commcode or the code for his office. "Emergency call. Net Force headquarters—"

Suddenly he found himself looking at a uniformed lady, a cool-looking blonde, sitting behind a desk. "Net Force. How can I help you?"

"This is an emergency," Charlie said. "My name is Charlie Davis. I am a member of the Net Force Explorers. I need to talk to James Winters immediately!"

She smiled at him, an understanding expression, and Charlie was instantly angry enough to spit, for the look was that of someone humoring a child. He then instantly felt guilty for his anger, for there were thousands of Explorers scattered all over the North American continent, and there was no reason for this woman to believe that he had anything important going on in his life at all. "I'm sorry, but he's not available right now—"

"Then let me leave a message for him," Charlie said. "Please tell him that I have the data he asked me to correlate for him, but if I don't hear from him shortly, the body count may have increased by one. Tell him he can reach me here for the next fifty minutes—" And he rattled off the address of the Net center and of the present workspace. "Thank you! Workspace, new access address, 8846396677336—"

This number he knew well enough from having to input it about thirty times two weeks ago, when his address-filing facility had developed a fault that it took him the better part of an afternoon to put right. Charlie gulped, and then let out a breath of pure relief as the sunlight spilling in through the roof of the VAB appeared all around him, but grayed out, as if through a veil. "You are entering a restricted space," a harsh robotic voice said. "Access is forbidden. Track and trace protocols are in operation."

"Mark, it's me, it's Charlie!"

The grayness vanished immediately. He rushed out into

the sunlight across the concrete, looked around him. The Rolls-Skoda was sitting in the middle of the floor. High above him, he heard the buzzards softly squeaking and cheeping to one another as they worked the in-building updraft. *"Mark?"* he shouted, and to his embarrassment his voice broke in mid-word.

"Jeez," Mark said, though Charlie couldn't see from where, "what's up with you? You sound like a chicken."

There were about ten possible answers to that. "Mark, where are you? *I'm up the creek!"*

Mark appeared immediately in the middle of the floor, over by the Rolls. "Sorry, I was doing some maintenance," he said, heading over to Charlie. "What's up?"

"I'm stuck in a public access near the Square," Charlie said, "and somebody just tried to grab me off the street!"

"I'll call the cops," Mark said.

"Don't!"

Mark looked at him as if he was nuts. Charlie could entirely understand why. "You do that," Charlie said, "the minute they turn up there, whoever tried to grab me will just play it innocent and vanish, and we'll be no better off than we have been—either they'll come after me again later, at a better time, or else some other poor kid's gonna get grabbed instead. And probably killed! We've got to do something *now.* But we've got to keep whoever's chasing me on the hook, until the Net Force people can catch up with him, with me—"

"I'll hit the panic button," Mark said. Immediately the whole space filled with an astounding howl of klaxons. He looked around him with intense satisfaction.

"It's not going to help," Charlie said, "Winters isn't available!"

"I bet my dad is, though," said Mark. "He'll call the cavalry." He looked around him, then, with some concern, because nothing but the klaxon seemed to be happening. "Or he would if he was in his office—" he muttered.

"Mark, we have to do something *now!"*

"That'll go through to his pager," Mark said. "No point in us sitting around waiting."

"The guy chasing me," Charlie said, "it's a fair bet he'll realize what I've done. If he has any brains at all, he'll be in some other Net access place right now, trying to find out where I am online. Then he'll try to trace *me*— and I'm on limited time, all I had was a valuecard. I only have about forty-five minutes now before the door of my booth opens up—"

"Then we'd better get where you're expected to be," Mark said, "and stall."

Charlie stared at Mark. "You mean Deathworld—"

"Where else? How else is he going to track you if you're in a public access except by your Deathworld ID? And you've got a hot-pursuit situation, haven't you? Well, you don't want to *lose* the guy, do you? You just said you didn't want him to go to ground! He will, if he loses you." Mark looked at him, a challenging kind of look. "You've got to keep him chasing you until the cavalry comes over the hill, Charlie!"

Charlie gulped.

"But you won't be alone," Mark said. "Come on, Charlie . . . the game's afoot. And it's *us*. But we won't be the ones who get caught. Let's go where you're expected to go when you panic."

"My workspace."

"From in here, not direct from your access." Mark picked up the Magic Jacket from where it had been draped over the chair behind his "desk" and threw it at Charlie. "He, she, or they won't expect that. My antitrace protocols outside this space will at least slow them down. And then we'll get into Deathworld. But on the way, you think we might pick up someone else who knows his way around there . . . ?"

Charlie gulped, and began to see how it could go. And slowly he started to smile. It was still dangerous, and he was still scared. But this was exactly what he had been working toward. And he now had someone on his side.

"Nick," he said. "Yeah. It's worth a try. Come on, Mark, let's go . . . !"

Charlie came out into the ashy darkness between the Lake of Tears and the Dark Artificer's Keep, and stood looking around him for a second with Mark. Here and there in the darkness beyond the lake, the Damned ran by, pursued by the usual demons. Banies made their way toward the Keep, or into and out of it. There was no sign of any pursuit, but then he wasn't sure what pursuit would necessarily look like. It could wear a seeming as easily as he could, and didn't have to look like anyone he would recognize at the moment. *And is it Kalki? Or Shade? Or someone else they've sent after me?*

"One thing you've going for you," Mark said, "they'll be looking for one kid, not two."

"Great. That means they'll either pass me by, or find me and also try to trace and grab whoever's with me," Charlie said. "Why leave witnesses?"

This thought made Mark widen his eyes briefly. Then he grinned. "I don't think so somehow," Mark said. "I don't care who they are. They're not going to get into *my* workspace from my ID here. It's too well protected for that." He looked around them, though, with some concern. "But I don't think we should just be standing around. Where do we go?"

"For the moment," Charlie said, "safety in numbers. There are more people in the Keep than there are out here. Let's get inside."

They headed in through the front door. There were a fair number of Banies who used this spot as a gateway "access" while working on solving the Eighth Circle, and most of them were heading past Charlie and Mark toward the entryway that led to the Stairways to Nowhere. "We could lose ourselves pretty well in there, from the look of it," Mark said.

"*Lose* would be the word," Charlie said, nervous. "I don't know my way around in there real well—"

"Doesn't matter. Whoever's chasing you," Mark said, "we've just got to keep them in here, and occupied, until the Net Force people can get in and identify them."

Charlie swallowed. "Will they be able to do that in forty minutes?"

"More like thirty-five now," Mark said, not even having the grace to sound scared. "They'd better."

"But how are they going to find us?"

Mark tugged at the virtual "fabric" of the Magic Jacket's sleeve. "I left full details about this in the message to my dad," he said. "The tracking routine it uses is piping direct into his space. Anything you see or hear, he and Net Force will, too . . . and it's all archiving, storing virtual locations and addresses second by second. All we can do now is leave the tracking to him and his people, and get ourselves deep inside here . . . deep enough that anyone who comes after us is plainly doing it on purpose and not just as some kind of accident."

Charlie looked around him, looked at the entry to the stairways. "Okay," he said. "I guess we'd better—"

"*Manta!*"

Charlie jumped. But it wasn't Kalki's voice, or Shade's.

Not that that *means anything!* He turned, half-furious, half terrified——to see Nick hurrying toward them through the great doors. "Ohmygosh," Charlie said, grabbing Nick by the shoulders as he got close, "I'm gonna kill you! *Do you know who I thought you were?"*

"I can imagine. But I didn't want to yell your real name in the middle of all this. Who knew what could happen? Hey, nice jacket."

"Never mind the jacket. How did you know my handle?"

"I've been reading the message boards," Nick said. "I put some things together. Your message timings, for example. Look, can this wait? I got the message you left me about the people who're after you. Had to be the hero, didn't you?"

Charlie opened his mouth to make some angry retort, and then stopped himself, for Nick's tone wasn't angry or mocking. It was a compliment. "Uh—"

"Yeah. Well, there's something I've been wanting to try, and we'd better try it now, before somebody grabs us." He looked over at Mark. "Who's your friend?"

"Nick, this is Mark. Mark Winters, Nick Melchior. Mark's a virtwrangler, Nick. He's figured a way to track our progress in here." Charlie displayed the jacket. "Look, we have to give the bad guys a target, but one that's too tough to actually catch. That means we've got to get in deep enough that the people looking for me won't be able to find me. Help's coming, but we've gotta stall."

"Great. Come this way," Nick said, heading off to their right. "Nine be deep enough for you?"

"Nine?" Charlie swallowed. "Nick, one of them, the one who called himself Kalki, he said he'd been *through* the gates of Nine. . . ."

"He's full of it," Nick said. "*No* one can come back after they get through the gates of Nine. There's a 'limited resume' in place after that. The designers implemented it to stop all the walk-throughs from blowing the final solution of the environment."

"When did you find that out?"

"Yesterday. From the Gate Guardian."

"You found the way down to *Nine*?"

Nick nodded. "But I put it off . . . I didn't want to go through until you were along. So now we'll give it a try."

"You don't know if it *works* or not?" Mark said, sounding alarmed.

"We're gonna find out real quick," said Nick. "Come on!"

There were nine tall gray doors opening out of the left-hand side of the huge entry hall, genuine old-fashioned doors with lever handles, looking like something out of the seventeenth century, with fancy scrollwork carved around the gray stone doorjambs. "Don't look like we're rushing or anything," Nick said, "just stroll." Charlie found this extremely difficult to do under the circumstances, but he forced himself to slow down and keep pace with Nick.

"A lot of people look at this at one point or another," Nick said softly, "but usually there isn't anything here. There's a trick to it, though. . . ."

He went to the first of the five doors and stood by it, idly, listening. Then he shook his head.

"Nothing," Nick said, "but this is gonna be easier with three of us. Each of you, quick, go up to a door and listen. If you hear anything, open it right away. Don't look obvious about it, though. You don't want anyone noticing if you can help it!"

Mark headed for the next door up, and Charlie took a long breath, trying to calm himself, and went to the door after that. He stood by it . . . and then his eyes widened. A soft rumor and murmur of voices, like a crowd—

He pulled the door open a crack and peered in.

The sound didn't change, but Charlie looked in and saw that the dimly lit room was completely full of people, pushing, murmuring, moving together. It was in fact a vast dance floor, absolutely crammed with people in every kind of clothes, ancient and modern, and they were dancing hard to Joey Bane's music. Hanging up high from an almost invisible ceiling was, of all things, a mirrored "disco ball," and it shot glitters and spots of light all around the room as it turned, picking out here a jeweled headdress, there a studded white Elvis jacket, over there a slowglass jumpsuit. Charlie looked back around the door, signaled unobtrusively to Nick and Mark. They came over, and as they did, Charlie slipped in through the door. They came after him, and Nick shut the door behind him.

The instant he did, the sound came blasting up to full: the "flap mix" of "Don't Look Back," banging away with its wild 11/4 beat. Mark looked around him with admiration at the dancers. "They may be the Damned," he said, "but they've got rhythm."

"They're not the Damned," Nick said, grinning. "They're us."

Charlie looked at him, bemused. "It's a party," Nick said. "*The* Party. One of the environment-programmers' jokes. Everybody who ever visited Deathworld wanders in and out of here eventually. Not the real them, of course; just a recording of them, a sim. . . ."

"You mean we're in here somewhere, too?" Mark said, sounding slightly amused. "Someone might find that confusing. . . ."

"Sorry," Nick said, "but I don't think it works that way. The one time your simulacrum can't be found here is when you're genuinely on-site. So the Guardian told me. But other people might see it and not know for sure, for a while anyway, whether it was really you they were interacting with. . . ." He grinned. "There are probably some funny scenes, every now and then, because some people do just come here to dance. . . ."

"Looks like a good place to get lost in, anyway," Charlie said.

"Better than that," said Nick. "This is *the Party*. And since it is, there's a side door . . . and a Lady sneaking out of it. We've got to catch her. Come on—"

Nick started to push his way through the crowd. The other two followed him. It was hard going, hot and difficult. The oblivious dancers were packed incredibly tightly together and the music was jarringly loud. Even Nick looked like he was wincing a little at the volume.

Mark was close behind Charlie. "Are you sure your dad's people are gonna get here before our time runs out?" Charlie yelled to Mark, that being the only way he could make himself heard.

Mark was beginning to look uncomfortable. "Look," he shouted back, "I did the best I could. My dad gets busy, too! I told you, I sent a 'most urgent' to his virtpager. He'd never ignore that unless some seriously important government thing—"

"Like happens every day!" Charlie yelled. But there was no point in fighting about it now. Charlie took another deep breath, went plowing through the crowd in Nick's wake.

It got harder as they got closer to the center of things. *There's this, anyway,* Charlie thought, *it's not gonna be easy for anyone to follow us*— For that moment he disobeyed the advice of the music, looked over his shoulder.

And saw one of those tall doors behind them open. A second later he got a glimpse of a long black drapecoat, violet skirt, violet hair, as Shade came slipping in—

Uh-oh. Fear and loathing both rose in him, and Charlie struggled to deal with the reaction rationally. It wasn't as if she was going to be able to spray him with sco-bro here and now. *If she's even directly involved.* Had Mark gotten any concrete evidence that she was? Had he even managed to track down exactly who had tripped the "trip wire" around his workspace? *And is Shade someone different from Kalki—or is she the same person? For I didn't see them together....* Charlie gulped. *No time to spend worrying about all this now. Just follow Nick and keep them in here, and pray that Net Force is on the job*—

Ahead of him, Nick was maybe two thirds of the way through the crowd, moving faster now, as if it was beginning to thin a little in patches near the far edge of the room. He was making his way toward the far left corner. Charlie could just see that the crowd was somewhat sparser there. And also a black blot, a shape, leaning near a door, a normal human-sized door, not like the ones they had come through, a door that was just closing . . .

Nick came out of the crowd, with Charlie behind him, and Mark bringing up the rear. The black blot-shape, hard to see in the disco-ball dimness, was a tall, potbellied demon, presently standing in front of the newly closed door. He had little stubby black-leather wings, and he was wearing a uniform like the ones movie-theater ushers or hotel-lobby bellboys had worn a century ago, right down to a rather ridiculous looking little pillbox hat pushed over to one side and partly resting on one of his big ears. Nick, coming up to him, paused and looked at him oddly.

"Hey," he shouted over the music, "you're not Melch-grind! You're Wringscalpel! I remember how you wear that hat."

The demon with the flaming sword blinked at him. "Nick?" it shouted back, squinting at him. "Why, how are you, fella? You back again? I didn't think you were going to linger."

"Change of plans," Nick said loudly. "This isn't *your* usual patch, either."

"No, we have to rotate through all the 'portal' jobs," Wringscalpel said, sounding resigned. "Sometimes whether we've been briefed on them fine detail or not. If I had a nickel for—"

"Neither of us is gonna be *worth* a plugged nickel if we don't hurry up here, Wringer! We're in big trouble at the moment. Someone's chasing us, and we really need not to get caught."

"Now, you know I can't let you go through without passing the test. . . ."

"There is no *time* for that!" Nick yelled. "Wringscalpel, in Joey's own name, will you let us through here before you have a bunch more fake suicides on your hands?!"

"Test?" said Mark. "What test?"

Wringscalpel's eyes went wide. "But I *can't*. It's not that I wouldn't do it for you, Nick, it's just that the machine's routines won't allow—"

"*What* test?" Charlie said.

"He's not going to ask you what's your favorite color, if that's what you were thinking," Nick said. "Hurry up and ask the damn questions, then, Wringscalpel! I'm answering for all three of us."

"You two agree to that?" Wringscalpel said.

"Yes," Mark said, and "Yeah, yeah, just do it!" Charlie said, for he could see Shade getting closer to them.

"All right. You understand the rules? If you miss a question, you're all bumped back up to One—"

"Fine!"

"And they're not the same questions as yesterday, Nick, they change every hour—"

"Come *on!*" they yelled at him in unison.

"All right," Wringscalpel said. "What is the purpose of life?"

"He doesn't want anything easy, does he?" Charlie moaned.

"Shaddup, Charlie. *Pain,* Wringscalpel! And learning how to deal with it."

"What is the dawn of the soul?"

"Which version?" Nick said.

Wringscalpel looked surprised, then smiled. "London 2024."

"The other side, / where the shadows hide, / and the dark no longer falls: the night of pain, / when the final chord / Comes breaking through the walls!"

"Hey, you're serious about this," Wringscalpel said. "Are you sure I can't ask you your favorite color?"

"*No!* Get on with it!"

"What is Joey's middle name?"

"The one on his birth certificate," Nick said, "or the one from the press release?"

Wringscalpel grinned. "The birth certificate."

Nick swallowed. "Illusion," he said.

"There you go," said Wringacalpel, and began to grow. The floor of the place shook. The disco ball hanging from the ceiling of the Party Room started to tremble, and stalactites of crystal and onyx began to fall from way above it, causing screams among the partying multitudes, who scattered in every direction, but then returned to the dance floor as if driven there with whips.

Wringscalpel, though, was paying all of this no attention. His uniform was tearing and shredding away, falling to the floor, as the demon grew, lost his potbelly, gained wings that lost the toy look they had worn earlier and now looked seriously functional, gigantic pinions, that spread above him and out to either side. He cried a great cry that shook down more stalactites.

"Is he angry?" Charlie shouted at Nick over the din of the music, the screaming dancers, the crash of falling crystal.

Wringscapel heard this and laughed. "Angry? You kidding?" he said. "I get a bonus for this." He held out his huge hands, and suddenly they were filled with a flaming sword that lit the whole place blindingly in actinic blue-white fire. "And now I get to leave this job to somebody else, while I go up to Seven and kick some—"

"Yeah, great, later!" Nick shouted, and dodged under his arm, past him, through the suddenly open door.

Charlie and Mark followed him in a hurry. Past Wringscapel, on the other side of the door, it was as dark as the inside of a dog, and involuntarily Charlie looked behind them, back toward the light.

"Whoever's behind us, they can't follow us in here unless they pass the test," Nick said.

"Yeah, and what if they know the answers, too?" Mark said, looking around him in the darkness with some concern.

"There's still one thing I don't think they'll do," said Nick. "Come on!"

He ran into the dark. More slowly they went after him,

but their eyes were getting used to the dimness now. They were in a huge, huge cave, the size of a sports stadium, its stony ceiling lost above them.

"What are we supposed to be doing?" Mark said.

"Looking for the Lady," said Nick.

Charlie looked at him as they ran. " 'She left the party early' . . ." he said. "Or something like that."

"Something like that. We have to find her. She's the key."

"Shouldn't be hard, there's nobody but us in . . . uh-oh."

There were eyes in the darkness. They glowed. The predatory eyes blinked slowly and looked thoughtfully at the three of them.

"Ignore them," Nick said. "Look for a single light by itself."

It was hard. They walked on through the darkness, and it got hot and stifling, and the eyes pressed in close around them, and they could all hear breathing. . . . Charlie shook his head at the oppressive quality of the illusion. And he stopped, then, hearing footsteps behind him.

"There," Nick said. He pointed. One light, distant—not horizontal like the lights around them, but vertical, not green, but a pure white.

"What's the rush?" said a soft voice from behind them.

Charlie turned, and there she was, Shade, looking at him with an expression that was almost sad . . . but not quite.

I can't have more than fifteen minutes left, Charlie thought. *I've lost track. All I can do now is stall, keep her talking. . . .*

"Kalki told me you ran off without a word," she said. "Without even looking at him! He didn't mean to frighten you, really . . . he was just going to give you a ride. . . ."

And she's got to do more than just talk. "Was he?" Charlie said. "And what would we have done then? He and I. Or the three of us. If there really *are* two of you . . ."

"Why, talk," Shade said. "What else would happen?"

"I have two words for you," Charlie said. "Scorbutal cohydrobromate."

She looked at Charlie, and her eyes widened.

Not enough. "And a white cotton sweater," Charlie said. "It must have been very new, one of those teased-cotton ones . . . because it shed all over Richard Delano's rug."

The look on her face went horrified for a moment, just for a flicker. Then she got hold of herself again and smiled very slowly, a knowing smile. "Scorbutal? Someone your age," she said, "shouldn't be messing around with drugs, Manta. Your folks would be shocked to find out about it. Maybe some responsible adult should tell them what she thinks you've been up to, hmm? How you tried to buy some from her?"

He went hot with fury.

"But it doesn't matter," Shade said. Charlie stared at her, kept his mouth shut. "There are always other people to work with, aren't there? It's not like suicide is going to go away. There are always mixed-up kids who stumble into nasty places like this." She looked around her with scorn, at the eyes pressing in close. "Or going to incredible trouble to work themselves deep down into them. Places full of sick images and soul-destroying music and ugly ideas. Who would be surprised when kids who spend a lot of time in a place come to grief? No one would be surprised at all."

She looked at Nick and Mark. "It's nice to see you've picked up a couple of friends here, finally," Shade said. "But there will always be people who need friends, and aren't so spiteful and suspicious. For them . . . I'll always be here. Until Deathworld shuts down, some day. Maybe some day very soon . . . because, if there's justice, nothing lasts forever."

That smile again: self-satisfied, controlling. Charlie would have loved to have an excuse to punch her in the nose. But then he realized he didn't need to . . . and he stood quite still, and smiled just a little himself. He couldn't help it.

And a second later he had the satisfaction, as hot as the fury had been a moment before, of seeing her eyes go wide, as she stared at the man and woman who suddenly caught hold of her "seeming" from both sides. "Net Force," said the woman. "We have some questions we need to ask you, please, so if you'd come this way—"

There were suddenly about six other Net Force operatives there as well, all in their usual dark suits and coverslicks, and they closed in on the group. "You kids all right?" one of them said.

In the background Shade was shouting, "What? Who are you? This is an outrage! I want a lawyer—"

"Uh, we're fine," Nick said, looking around at the ruckus with some surprise. He looked at Mark and Charlie. "But how'd they get in here without answering the questions?"

"Either a search warrant," Mark said, looking at them with relief, "Or a 'back door.' Does it matter?" He looked at Shade as the agents walked her away. "Looks like it's gonna be a real interesting debrief. Here, wait a minute. . . ." he said to the agent who had spoken to Charlie.

Mark reached up and helped Charlie out of the Magic Jacket.

"Thanks, Squirt," Charlie said as Mark handed the jacket to the operative.

"It's still live," Mark said. "The evidential trail is still hot, so you'll want to lock it down when you get it back into the examination space at HQ."

"Thank you," said the op.

"And," said another voice out of the darkness, "I would appreciate it if someone would give me an explanation of what's been going on here . . ."

Jay Gridley came striding out of the dark—a lithe, intent-looking Thai-American man, in a business suit and tie. Right now, though, the intentness was mostly concentrated on his son. Mark was looking a little sheepish. "Uh, hi, Dad," he said, "you see, Charlie came to me with a problem—"

"Excuse me," said a quiet voice from out of the darkness behind them, "but were you looking for me?"

They all turned. The Goddess of Virtue stood there looking at them, while lifting up a long pale veil that had covered her face and head. Astraea was astonishingly beautiful, a tall and slender woman all robed in Greek-classical white, and her expression was severe, intelligent, and a little sorrowful.

Jay Gridley smiled slightly. "Uh, yes, ma'am. Routinely."

"Yeah," Nick said. "Mostly to say, don't go. . . ."

"But there is nowhere for me to stay," she said sadly. "My only dwelling is in the hearts of men, and all of mankind is wicked. . . ."

They looked at one another. "If you wait about two seconds," Charlie said, "not *all* . . . because a baby'll be born somewhere."

She smiled at him. It was like the sun coming up.

"Thank you," Astraea said. "I think I'll stay."

They were all quiet a moment. "Which way to the Ninth Circle?" Nick said at last.

"There is none," Astraea said. "Or rather, this is it. This is Despair, after all. But after this . . . you go out the far side. That way." She pointed, and suddenly there was a little light away off in the darkness, like an open door.

"Uh, thanks," Mark said. He was a little bemused as he said it, for Astraea had draped her former veil around her neck like a scarf, and now she reached around behind her into the darkness and came out with a sword and a pair of scales.

"And now," she said cheerfully, "back to the day job. See you later. . . ."

She vanished.

Mark looked up at his father. "You know her, Dad?" he said.

"You kidding?" said Jay Gridley softly, but with some

amusement, as he looked at the distant light. "She's one of my bosses." Then he looked down at his son, and his face acquired a severity more like that of Justice's. "Meanwhile . . . you and I need to talk. Briefly, because I have to get back to work. But later on we are going to have a long discussion. . . ."

Mark and his father vanished. Mark's expression was mostly unrepentant, despite his father's sternness. All Charlie thought it was wise to do was nod and grin just a little. When they were gone, Charlie started to turn toward Nick . . .

. . . and everything dissolved in a mist of light, back to a white plain and blue sky. A great voice came from the heavens and said to Charlie,

"Thank you for using Net Access. You have come to the end of your purchased access time for this session. Please see the customer representative for more time . . . or inquire about one of our monthly billing accounts!"

And suddenly he was sitting in the implant chair again . . . and behind him, there was a little *cchk!* noise as the door of the suite unlocked itself and slid open.

Charlie was on his feet in about a second, and out into the hallway. There he stopped, openmouthed with surprise.

The place was full of uniformed police. Two of them, right then, along with a dark-suited woman in plain clothes wearing the inimitable Net Force ID, were escorting out someone in handbinders. She was of medium height, dark-haired with some gray sprinkled through it, a little pudgy, maybe about forty. She was a profoundly ordinary-looking person, one he would have passed in the street a hundred times and never noticed. She looked ordinary, like a mother . . . and she was wearing a soft, fuzzy white short-sleeved cotton sweater.

There he lost his train of thought, for two more Net Force ops, a man and a woman, came walking down the hall toward Charlie.

"Charlie Davis?" one of them said.

"Uh, yes."

"Your father wants to see you," said the woman op. "Right now."

Ooops.

He walked outside, past the shocked-looking counter guy, and saw his dad standing there. By a police car—his mother was just getting out of another. The street was full of people slowing down to rubberneck, or standing there watching and talking. It looked like a disaster area.

He was afraid the disaster was going to be his.

But Charlie couldn't say a word for the moment. The relief, and the fear, and a host of other emotions, had all come crashing down on him together as he walked out of that booth and saw her—the woman who was Shade, or Kalki, or both—being taken away from the next booth to the one he had been in. *The next booth—!* Charlie went over to his mother and father, and they closed in on him, and he grabbed them both and hugged them hard.

"We're going to talk about this later," his father said, very low. "A lot. But I want to hear all of your side first."

"Thanks, Dad," Charlie said.

"But I notice that someone *else* is wearing the handcuffs," his mother said, "so I guess we can assume that you've been doing something that's going to make us proud."

Boy, I hope so, Charlie thought as they walked him away.

It was a long, long talk they had, and one that was going to take more than one evening to resolve. Charlie realized that when he was in bed that night, suffering from near-terminal embarrassment and upset, and at the same time, great pride . . . for word came down on the late news that evening that the cases of all the Deathworld "suicides" were being reopened. Additionally, after a very belated session with his mother's hot and spicy ribs (most of the dressing-down he suffered had happened while they were all in the kitchen together, and she was cooking), the vidphone went off. His father went to get it and didn't come back for something like twenty minutes.

"Who was it, honey?" Charlie's mother said.

"Jay Gridley," said Charlie's dad. He sat down and began to toy with one last rib he hadn't touched during dinner.

Charlie didn't say anything, though he very much wanted to—every word he had said, earlier, had seemed to trigger some new and interesting strain of the basic argument. "He says," Charlie's dad said, turning to Charlie, "that you may have saved ten or twenty people's lives."

Charlie swallowed.

"He also says you're to see James Winters tomorrow morning at eight," said his dad. "I assume that won't interfere with school?"

"Uh . . . no."

"Good. Let us know what happens. . . ."

"Uh, I will."

And that had been all. Charlie had gone to bed in a very subdued mood. But he had not been able to avoid seeing the look his mother and father exchanged as he'd gone upstairs. It had been worried, frightened, relieved . . . but not angry.

The next morning, having left his workspace and taken his seat in Winters's office, he wondered if being spared last night had simply left him mostly intact for a more thorough reaming-out today. Mark Gridley was there when Charlie got there, and he, too, was looking rather pale.

For a minute or two Winters just sat behind his desk, looking over documentation that was scrolling through the virtual window hanging nearby. Finally he shook his head and sat back, and looked at the two of them.

"Well," he said. "It's taken me the better part of last night and this morning, but I've finally finished reviewing the forensic and other information that our fast-response team went out to act on yesterday." He sighed. "Mark has already finished his debrief, but since he acted as 'enabler' for you on this, Charlie, I thought it might be wise to have him here to sketch in any details that're necessary. Does that meet with your approval?"

"Uh, yes, sir."

"With one note," said Winters. "The wild, I would say profligate, illegality of a lot of Mark's 'enabling' needs to be stressed here. I would have thought," he said to Mark, "that after the last time, I wouldn't need to have this discussion with you again. But I see that no human agency can possibly predict your actions. You, I'm just going to have to refer back to your father. Again."

Mark didn't quite squirm.

"Don't bother trying to play to the stands quite so blatantly," Winters said. "There is no one in the stands but me, and I am not cheering."

He looked slowly over at Charlie. "Meanwhile," Winters said, "your mother is a very understanding woman."

"She is? I mean, yes, sir, she is. . . ."

"Because she has not herself assisted in having you committed," Winters said, "on finding out what you've been up to these past couple of weeks. I seem to remember you telling me that, as soon as you came across any information concrete enough to warrant action, that you would let me know."

The silence settled down heavy. "I didn't think it was concrete enough yet," Charlie said, his voice sounding even smaller than he was afraid it would. "It needed to be tested."

"Using yourself as bait," Winters said.

"When you're hunting polar bear," said Charlie, "that's the only bait that's any good."

Winters looked at him hard for a moment. Then he sat back and rocked a little in his chair. "This much I'm going to give you," he said. "You were right about one thing. The woman you caught was definitely getting ready to do it again. Immediately. Besides the stun gun, we found a big spray can of sco-bro in the front seat of her car. And all the ropes and ligatures you could have desired were in the trunk, ready to use."

Charlie shivered. "It's still May," he said.

"Yes," said Winters. "That much you're right about. But why?"

Charlie blinked. "Why is it May?"

"I mean," Winters said, "why was she attacking these kids in May?"

Charlie shook his head. "I never did figure that out," he said.

"Because," said Winters softly, "that's very close to when *her* son committed suicide."

Charlie's eyes widened. "Richard—"

"Exactly wrong," said Winters, annoyed. "Don't guess, Charlie. There's been too much guessing in this, not enough precise use of data. Fatal for a doctor."

Charlie swallowed.

"Mitch Welles," said Winters.

"He was the first one," Charlie said. "April of 2023—" He shook his head.

"April," Winters said. "Not May. Now, Maureen Welles had . . . well, not exactly a collapse after her son died. But she wasn't well. After she recovered, she went on a campaign to prove that her son had been induced to kill himself by something that had been done to him in Deathworld. She spent all her efforts trying to get the legislation that I told you about through Congress. It didn't get her anywhere. She was sure that there was a conspiracy against her, but as I said, the only conspirator against her that anyone can identify was the Congressional calendar. And her own single-mindedness." He let out a long breath. "Her marriage went to pieces in the middle of it all. She and her husband separated—*he* said, because chasing down her son's murderer had become her entire life."

Winters went on rocking in his chair for a few moments, scowling at his desk.

"Sounds like she was obsessed," said Mark very quietly.

"It sounds like it," said Winters. "Well, all her complaints and attempts to get Deathworld shut down got her nowhere, as you might imagine, since there was no evidence whatever to suggest that the environment, or Bane, were implicated in any way in her son's death." He sighed. "And then the second suicide happened. That's when we got involved. Once could be an accident. Twice could be a coincidence—"

"Three times is enemy action," Mark said.

"Well, even proverbs can be wrong," said Winters, lacing his fingers together. "But this time, as it happens, it was indeed enemy action. Because Mitch Welles's mother decided that if the government and Net Force weren't going to do the responsible thing and shut Deathworld down, then she would do it herself."

He breathed out. "Well, that's the simple way to describe it. Your mom would know," and Winters glanced up at Charlie, "that the ways a human mind gets itself into such a position are usually a lot more subtle than people suspect from outside, or after the fact. After all, she had managed to convince herself, over time, that her son couldn't have killed himself, that it *had* to be murder. Well, acknowledging that he had committed suicide would mean admitting that it might possibly have been due to something *she'd* done wrong . . . so that was a realization that her mind buried as soon as it could. From that it was just a step to believing that Joey Bane was personally responsible for his death. And from there, maybe not such a long step to believing that anyone who was in Deathworld willingly was somehow complicit in her son's 'murder.' "

"Maybe," Charlie whispered. "It would explain a lot."

Winters shook his head. "It may be something like that which was going on in her head. The process itself is obscure, and it's probably going to stay that way for a while, because she's not talking about much of anything now. But soon enough Maureen Welles got the idea that, if people had accused her son of being a suicide, then she was going to turn that back on them, get revenge on them for hurting her, for hurting him like that. They would be the suicides, not him. She started monitoring the new login information, and the message boards, as anyone could . . . but her purpose was to pick likely targets, to make sure that the ones she 'worked with' in her Shade and Kalki personas seemed genuinely suicidal, people who 'were going to do it anyway.' Their deaths would make her son's look like what she was sure it was: something done to him, to them, by the environment they'd been spending time in. That this would also hurt Joey Bane must have occurred to her. She may even have had some fantasy of killing him and turning him into a 'suicide' as well. More to the point, though, she was sane enough to realize that a string of suicides would affect the place adversely."

"But it didn't," Charlie said. "It went wrong. In a lot of ways. No one put it together that the suicides were connected. And Deathworld got even more popular."

Winters's look was grim. "You're right. It backfired on her. Her methods were too subtle. Not subtle enough to completely prevent the suspicion, here and there, that these suicides weren't uncomplicated. But distributed over so much time, and such a large physical area, they didn't attract the attention she wanted. And she wasn't completely nuts, not yet. Her first murder took a lot out of her, scared her—scared her briefly sane. She kept quiet for a while. The next suicide, the one in October, was genuine, and had nothing to do with her. But come the next year, around April, her pain started to unseat her reason again. By May she was more than ready to murder someone else, as revenge against Bane . . . or as a kind of sacrifice to her dead son." He frowned. "And she did . . . then scared herself sane again for a little while."

"But she couldn't stay that way," Charlie said. "Probably the knowledge of what she'd been doing was starting to prey on her. And her son was still dead. . . ."

"And Deathworld was still in operation," Winters said, sounding a little sad now. "It must have been intolerable for her. One part of her wanting to believe that her son had been exonerated, avenged . . . another part of her continually wanting revenge on whatever had taken him away from her."

"And so she kept on killing," Mark said. "And then did it again, this month. . . ."

"Twice," Winters said, somber. "But now she was getting into the pattern of serial killers. One murder isn't enough. The same kind of murder isn't enough. They have to get closer together, be more terrible, somehow, to provide the same level of catharsis. But they never do."

"It's a drug," Charlie said softly.

"Something like one," said Winters. "The addiction always getting worse, in her case, because the dose increases and increases and doesn't do any good. And then this last time, she was driven to commit *two* murders . . . and no sooner have they happened than Deathworld, her old enemy, suddenly is doing better than ever. It drove her to levels of rage she'd never experienced before. She decided to go straight out to try to kill again. And found you . . . using some pretty advanced 'hunting' routines. She tripped the 'wire' around your workspace, as you thought. Felt you out, to make sure you were suicidal enough. And then went for the kill."

Winters's eyes were resting on Charlie in a way that made him even more uncomfortable than the man's anger had.

But there was only one answer to that look. Charlie swallowed. "You remember *Helicobacter?*" he said.

Mark looked at Charlie as if he was from Mars. But Winters's expression shifted microscopically to something a little less uneasy than it had been.

"*Helicobacter pylorii,*" Charlie said. "Forty years ago everybody thought stomach ulcers were caused by stomach acid." He had to laugh, for at this end of time, it sounded silly. But back then, they hadn't had any other answer that made sense. "Then a scientist, a doctor, noticed that in all the cultures he took of his patients' stomach ulcers, they all had this one bacterium present. *Helicobacter,* they called it, because it was shaped like a little helix. He worked with that bug for something like five years, until he was convinced that it was the cause of stomach ulcers, and that it could be killed, and the ulcers wiped out, just by using the right kind of antibiotic for long enough. He published papers, tried to convince everybody. They laughed at him. They said that the proof wasn't conclusive, that the evidence was all circumstantial. They wouldn't approve even animal testing, let alone human." Charlie smiled a smile as grim as Winters's had been. "So finally the guy swallowed a pure culture of *Helicobacter* and gave himself the fastest, nastiest case of bleeding ulcers anybody ever saw. Then he put himself on a course of antibiotics, and cured them."

Winters just looked at him.

"A lot of doctors have done stuff like that," Charlie said. "Pasteur. Jenner. It's traditional." He gulped, for Winters's look was not getting any friendlier. "When you're sure you're right. But when it's a life-and-death thing . . . the only life you have a right to put on the line is your own."

Winters just looked at him, like something carved from stone. "Mark," he said at last, "would you excuse us?"

Mark threw Charlie one apologetic glance, and then removed himself from the room with a speed that suggested he had recently had ion drivers installed.

A moment's silence ensued. "Now what the *hell* am I supposed to do with you," Winters said at last, "when you play the moral card on me like that."

Charlie thought it wisest to keep his mouth shut for the moment.

Winters sighed and leaned back in his chair again. "Your mother and father," he said, rubbing his face, "are going to have my hide off my bones if I don't come down on you hard for this dumb stunt. Which it was." Charlie looked down. "The 'morality card' aside. Morality starts at home, Charlie. You have *not* treated your folks very well. If you and the irrepressible Mr. Gridley hadn't had God's own luck, not to mention a sense of timing developed well beyond what people of your tender years should have, you could very well have been 'suicide' number seven. And maybe Mark and Nick for eight and nine. And regardless of the fact that the work and the evidence you left us would have made your death murder rather than suicide, and that your murderer would have been behind bars very quickly indeed, it would have shattered your parents' lives."

Charlie sat there with the sweat bursting out all over him, because he knew it was true, and that one way or another, he was unlikely to hear the end of this for months.

The silence stretched out again for a long while.

"All right," Winters said. "We'll see what you work out with them. They've let me know that, after talking to Jay Gridley, they think you should be allowed to continue as a Net Force Explorer. You may have to get used to being, uh, monitored a little more closely. You threw quite a scare into them."

Charlie swallowed. "Yes, sir."

"But there is this." He gave Charlie a thoughtful look. "If you hadn't done what you did . . . heaven knows who she might have killed next. How many more murders it would have taken to quieten her ghosts . . . and of course they wouldn't have stayed quiet, not for long." He sat back, looking at his folded hands. "Unfortunately, among the various kinds of serial killers, there are a few who 'seal over' very effectively for prolonged periods between crimes. They're crazy as bedbugs, but either they're not crazy enough to let their symptoms show where people can see them, or there's no one to see. Living by herself, her son dead, her husband pretty much permanently out of the picture, with no one to see how weird she got every

April . . . this could have gone on for a long while. It could have caused Deathworld to be shut down, and left Bane fighting endless lawsuits that would not have been his responsibility. So an injustice has been prevented . . . though frankly, from what I've seen of the place, I wonder if—"

Then Winters stopped himself. "No," he said, sounding annoyed. "Injustice is injustice, dammit, and artistic opinions shouldn't enter into it. That way lies tyranny. Now would you mind explaining why you're looking at me like that?"

Charlie had begun to smile, just a little. He couldn't help it. "I think there's more to that place than meets the eye," he said. "And really, Mr. Winters, I think the media've overstated the case a little about Deathworld. It's not as kinky and cruel as they think. It's more a teaching exercise."

"Oh, is it?" Winters said. "Well." He glanced down at his desk, reading something that had been manifesting under its surface for a while now.

He sighed. "It was always forensics with you, wasn't it?" he said. " 'The noblest use of science,' I heard one of my people call it. Well, some good has come of this aspect of your riffling of the records, anyway. There really should have been more cooperation among the various police forces handling the suicides. There are mechanisms set up for that, but they don't get used enough. This outcome will enable us to put bugs under some people's rumps, and have them look more closely at how to coordinate deaths that have similarities. A 'smart' system can be coached by forensic people and profilers to start handling and correlating data like this . . . as long as the cops put it in. And that a kid beat them to a serial killer might just shame them into using it." He raised his eyebrows. "Fine. But at the end of the day I suppose I might have known you'd do what you did, once faced with the evidence. Regardless of how earnestly you promised me you wouldn't jump the gun."

Charlie blushed hot again. *This is all I need. A rep as an incorrigible gun-jumper. With one of the two men who'll determine whether I ever work in Net Force at all. . . .*

"Don't mistake my intent," said Winters. "I don't mindlessly push the 'team player' concept because some corporate-minded superior makes me do it. I do it because it is the *sine qua non* of this organization, the single thing that makes us effective. When you start working with other people in Net Force someday, assuming that you graduate medical school without incident and that you are somehow spared for that work by an overly kindly Universe which keeps you from getting your butt kidnapped or killed when you put it in harm's way"— Charlie began wondering whether it was possible to feel as hot and embarrassed as he presently did without actually running a clinical fever— "then you are going to have to do what you tell them you're going to do, for the simple reason that they're going to act on that information, and when they do, if you're *not* doing what you said you were going to do, you may get them killed. They will be depending on you to keep your word. If you can't . . . you are no good to anyone. So get the polar bears and the *Helicobacter* out of your system *now,* because there'll be no room for them later."

Winters looked at him.

"Uh," Charlie said, "yes, sir."

There was a long silence. "Good," Winters said. "Then we understand each other. Insofar as anyone my age can truly understand anyone yours." He shook his head. "Which is little enough. Especially after I just heard you defending Deathworld to me." He raised his eyebrows at Charlie. "I wouldn't have thought you'd care much for the music, for one thing. I thought you were all for technotrad."

"The context," Charlie said, "makes other readings possible."

Winters gave him a cockeyed look. "I hear the sound

of someone managing information on what he considers a 'need to know' basis." He sighed. "You should go away, now, because you're making my head hurt." He glanced at the bird feeder stuck to his window, where a small brown bird was taking out one nut at a time and dropping it to the ground. "Even more than *he* was," Winters added, "until I realized what he's doing. He's feeding two of his buddies on the ground. Possibly his kids. They're too big to tell."

He made a shooing gesture at Charlie. Charlie got up. ". . . So get out of here," he said.

In haste, Charlie got out.

School that day went by in something of a blur, mostly caused by Charlie having to refuse again and again to say anything about what had happened down at the public access place near the Square. The case was now officially *sub judice* and could not be discussed. By the end of the day he was thoroughly tired of not being able to say anything, and seriously relieved to see Nick.

"Are you okay?" Charlie said to him as they started to walk in the general direction of home.

"Uh, yeah." Nick chuckled a little. "I didn't realize whose son Mark was! James Winters called my dad."

"He did? Oh, no!"

"No, it was okay," Nick said, sounding completely unconcerned . . . but then he didn't have to answer to James Winters. "My dad was really impressed."

"Winters didn't . . . say anything awful, did he?"

"Not at all. He was nice, actually. From what my mom said, he made me come out sounding like some kind of hero." He gave Charlie an odd look. "They're probably gonna hand you the same kind of stuff."

"I wouldn't worry too much about that," Charlie said. "It hasn't been a problem so far."

They headed for Nick's apartment, if only because Charlie wasn't willing to go straight home to his own and find some new and interesting aspect of last night's argument waiting for him. When they got there, though, Charlie wondered whether this had been wise, for Nick's mother was putting down the receiver of the vidphone with an odd look on her face.

Nick froze when he saw it. Charlie, not knowing what that kind of expression might mean on someone else's mother, didn't bother panicking. On his own, though, he would have been cautiously optimistic about what was to follow. "Hi, Mrs. Melchior . . ."

"Hi, Charlie honey, how are you?" She sounded very abstracted.

"Uh, hi, Mom," Nick said.

"Nick," his mother said, "what have you been doing?"

Charlie saw the oh-no-what-now look cross his friend's face. "We came straight from school, Mrs. Melchior," he said, hoping it wouldn't make things worse. "Did we—"

"No, Charlie, it's all right," said Nick's mother, looking dubious. "I guess. Honey, that was someone from the service provider."

Nick instantly burst out in a sweat that Charlie could see from two feet away, and indeed could practically feel. "Mom, in three weeks I'll have enough to give them about two hundred—"

"I wouldn't worry about that," his mother said, "because they say that the last month's bill has been paid in full."

Nick's eyes widened. "Oh, no. If Dad went and—"

"Your dad didn't do anything, honey," said Nick's mother, sitting down at the small kitchen table and looking at him oddly. "It seems someone from Joey Bane Enterprises got hold of them and said that the company was paying your expenses for 'your efforts on their behalf.' Which they took to mean the last month's comm charges, with a cash reserve to cover another year's worth of use. And apparently they're reimbursing you for your public access in the last couple of weeks."

"Oh, *wow*," Nick said, looking almost weak with relief,

and collapsing into the chair opposite his mom at the table.

Charlie stood and watched all this with poorly concealed approval.

"Charlie," said Nick's mother to him, turning on him what would have been a fairly fierce expression except for the confusion still underlying it, "did you have something to do with this?"

"I don't think so," Charlie said. *Not directly, anyway. Or at least not the way you think. . . .*

He was spared having to go through any longer a list of mental reservations by Nick's mother sighing, raising her hands in the air, letting them fall again. "Honey," she said, "it's very nice of them to come in and get you off the hook like this—"

"Mom," said Nick, "I'm going to keep the summer job . . . if it's all the same to you."

She looked at him thoughtfully. "That's the best thing I've heard all day," she said, and got up, heading down the hall toward the rear of the apartment. "Meanwhile, I suppose we'd better see about getting your server reconnected. . . ."

Nick and Charlie looked at each other as she went down to the den. "It's a miracle," Nick said softly.

"Somehow I doubt it."

"I wonder how much of . . . you know, what we did . . . is going to come out."

"I don't think it'd be smart for us to discuss that here," Charlie said softly. "Not under the circumstances. You gonna be online again tonight?"

"One way or another," Nick said. "I meant it about the job. . . . I noticed that when I'm out of the apartment more, the tension level around here goes down somewhat. I would have thought it'd be the other way around. Could it be that they wanted me to get out more or something? Even if it's just to use a public booth?"

Charlie shrugged. "Who knows," he said, "what parents think?"

"I know what you mean." Nick grinned a little. "I like to think of dealing with them as practice for when we finally meet up with alien life-forms."

"You and me both, brother. Well, if you ever find out why it's working better, tell me. Meanwhile, let's do whatever needs doing here, and then get out before the situation deteriorates somehow. . . ."

Later that evening Nick and Charlie met in Deathworld again, near the Keep of the Dark Artificer. This time there was no agenda, nothing to worry about. This time they could walk and talk and simply relax, debriefing each other. "You know," Nick said, once or twice catching a betraying expression on Charlie's face, "if I didn't know better . . . I'd think you were beginning to like some of this music."

"Oh, I don't know. . . ." Charlie said as they went in the gates of the Keep, and the demons there snapped to attention and saluted them. "Some of the rhythms are more interesting than I thought originally. . . ." He grinned. "But the lyrics . . ."

"Oh, give me a break. So they're depressive."

"Morbid," Charlie said, "that's the word I would have used."

They strolled through the great "front hall," while Charlie looked around him, apparently fascinated by the architecture. Nick raised his eyebrows, mildly exasperated. "Just because some idiot critics call it morbo-jazz," Nick said, "isn't any reason to take them seriously. It's hardly even jazz. If you think about it, you'll see that the basic riff structure has been completely . . . uh . . ."

He trailed off, coming to a stop, slowly becoming aware that Charlie was staring at him. " 'Completely uh?' "

There was a dark form standing in their path, all in black leather, a shadow dressed in shadows. "Hey, Nick," said Joey Bane, dry-voiced and ironic. "How goes it?"

Nick couldn't find it in his heart to say "Badly, as always," for this was the man himself, no simulacrum, no clone generated by the machine. The look in his eyes was too feral, too amused, and too real, for any program to fake.

Camiun was over his shoulder, and for once its strings were still. "I asked the system to let me know when you two gents came through next," Joey Bane said. "I believe your last visit was, well, to put it politely, interrupted. . . ."

"Uh," Nick said. "Yeah. I mean, no, it—"

"Look, relax," Bane said. "Nobody's going to ream you out. You did me and mine a favor. I thought I'd try to return it, a little. Come on."

He gestured them toward the back of the entry hall. They walked with him. "Besides," Joey said, "I would have come to take a look at you eventually, anyway. You just hurried me a little."

Nick goggled. On the other side of Joey, Charlie was looking at Nick and plainly trying not to burst out laughing. Nick ignored him. "You wanted to look at *me?* Why me?"

Bane laughed. "Because you're the one who's always subverting my staff."

Nick blushed. "I never—"

"You *always!* The DP people who do their dialogue are always saying, 'There's this kid who talks to us all the time, and treats us like people—' "

"Scorchtrap!"

"And the others. Bluebelch and Wringscalpel and Twistlestomp and the others. Where do they *get* these names, anyway? Whatever . . . *they* say the Demons want you to sit in on their next collective bargaining session. As if I don't give them stock options, and as if we didn't just have a split? What do they want now? Do they think I'm *made* of money?" Joey gave the two of them an ironic look. "But, kid, even the *tables* here say nice things about you. Somebody who's as kind to inanimate objects and support staff as you are will go far in the world."

Nick grinned. He couldn't think of anything to say to that.

"So," Joey said, "make yourselves at home. No connect charges for you two anymore. Though I think we'll see more of you than of your friend here." He nodded courteously enough to Charlie.

"I don't know," Charlie said suddenly, acquiring a wicked look. "I heard some material borrowed from Hovannes in that last lift Nick played for me. Maybe we have common ground after all."

Bane grinned. "Maybe we do. Stop in sometimes and find out. Meanwhile, what's your pleasure, gentlemen?"

"We were going to do the Ninth Circle," Nick said, looking over toward the doors on the left-hand side.

"I wouldn't go that way."

Nick looked at him in surprise. "Why not?"

"There's a shortcut. Who wants to go through all that stuff again? The noise, the crowd—" He waved his hand, made an annoyed noise. "Nick, why go through all that again? You did it once. Once is enough. Suffering for a purpose—" He looked up, as it were, through the depth of Deathworld, somehow including in the glance all the screaming and horror of the upper levels, all the rage, and the acknowledgment of evil. "That's one thing. Purification, punishment with an object, to deter or teach you never to do it again, that's one thing. But prolonging it indefinitely, punishment for its own sake, for the mere love of cruelty—" He shook his head. "That's not how we do it in Des Moines. Come on."

He led them toward the back of the entry hall. The place was empty, for the moment, except for the three of them. "One word," said Joey. "You got to the very threshold, last time, before you left. We have an agreement, which one of my clones would have administered to you before passing that last doorway you saw off in the distance. We do not discuss with *anyone* but other people who've passed Nine, what lies beyond that portal. Anyone who does and is caught at it is banned for life." He shrugged. "Every now and then someone breaks the promise and tells . . . but you know what? No one believes them. Suits me. And as for the rest of us . . . sometimes it's fun to have a secret. Sometimes it's fun to make a promise and keep it forever. Can you cope with that?"

They both nodded.

"Right," Joey said.

He put two fingers in his mouth and whistled, piercingly.

Suddenly the air was full of music the likes of which Nick had never heard before—Camiun singing, for once, not in its usual dark fierce minor, but in a triumphant clarion major that was most uncharacteristic. Around them, like a mist, like a dream, the darkness and the stone and the night all began to melt away. Light came pouring in, and the view across a green landscape that scaled up and up through rolling hills. Farther up yet, to mountains stacked halfway up the sky, green at first, then blinding with snow, but snow that looked down on what seemed like an eternal spring.

The chords crashed around them as Nick looked at Joey Bane, the only dark thing in all that landscape, with astonishment.

"Okay, so life stinks," Joey said, ". . . but then you stop complaining, and get on with finding out how to make it work."

Through waves of triumphant music of lute and bass and jazz sax the three of them walked uphill, into the light, toward the crowd of Banies dancing under the second sun.

$\mathcal{P}$ARTING IS SUCH SWEET SORROW . . .

Jack put out his hand, touched her shoulder. "Merry, I—"

"Sssh," she said, then stood up on tiptoe and pressed her lips against his, the heat of her searing his mouth, exploding his brain. She pressed against him in uneducated passion, ripping his heart in two, hurting him with her unquestioning love.

He could give in, give up, succumb. It would be so easy. All his questions, all his fears—he could banish them. Never ask the questions, never face the fears. He could take her, make her his own. Forget what his father had told him that last night, forget the past. Destroy her options.

It would be so easy.

Instead, he stood very still, not responding. Dying inside, but not responding.

And then he walked away.

ずら ずら ずら ずら

"Kasey Michaels creates characters who stick with you long after her wonderful stories are told. Her books are always on my nightstand."

—Kay Hooper, bestselling author of
After Caroline

Please turn the page for more praise for Kasey Michaels and her irresistible romances . . .

RAVES FOR THE "MISTRESS OF THE INTELLIGENT AND SOPHISTICATED"* REGENCY ROMANCE

❧ ❧ ❧

"A writing style, voice, and sense of humor perfectly suited to the era and genre."

—*Publishers Weekly*

"Kasey Michaels never fails to entertain us! She has an amazing talent for creating realistic and memorable characters!"

—*Literary Times*

COME NEAR ME

❧

"FANTASTIC! . . . One of the best things Kasey Michaels has written. . . . Wonderful twists and turns, filled with fascinating characters, and a hero and heroine to care about. . . . Innovative and daring, it steals its way into your heart and doesn't let go."

—*Gail Link,
Belles and Beaux of Romance Newsletter*

INDISCREET
ஒ

"Kasey Michaels returns with all the hallmarks that have made her a Regency romance treasure: humor, unforgettable characters, and a take on the era few others possess. Sheer reading pleasure!"

—Kathe Robbins, *Romantic Times*

ESCAPADE
ஒ

"The perfect choice for those who enjoy madcap romantic comedy amid the grandeur of the Regency era."

—Deborah Roy for Bookbug on the Web

"An awesome book . . . a cast of unbelievably funny characters, a wonderful plot line."

—*Rendezvous*

"Each character, with their own personality, comes alive on each and every page. This novel is a true delight, which will give readers many hours of enjoyment."

—Yvonne Herring, Writers Club Romance Group

Other books by Kasey Michaels

Indiscreet
Escapade
Come Near Me

KASEY MICHAELS

WAITING FOR YOU

WARNER BOOKS

A Time Warner Company

WARNER BOOKS EDITION

Cover design by Andrew Newman

Warner Books, Inc.
1271 Avenue of the Americas
New York, NY 10020

Visit our Web site at
www.twbookmark.com

A Time Warner Company

Printed in the United States of America

First Printing: October 2000

10 9 8 7 6 5 4 3 2 1

To Jill Gregory, *a tender heart;*
To Karen Katz, *a loving heart;*
And to Kate Hoffmann, *a wise and noble spirit.*

Also to Viktor, *and to all who know and love him.* . . .

O! Call back yesterday, bid time return.

—William Shakespeare

WAITING
FOR YOU

Act One

Assembling the Players

> All the world's a stage,
> And all the men and women merely players . . .
>
> —William Shakespeare

Chapter One

Most of England had been transformed into a winter fairyland that year, and Coltrane House, a magnificent estate located in Lincolnshire, resembled a Christmas package wrapped up in new-fallen snow.

Deer slept safely, hidden in thickets beneath tree branches heavy with snow. Foxes trod nimbly across the moonlit fields, following rabbit tracks as they hunted out a midnight snack.

In the nearby village, the cottagers had hours earlier banked their fires and were tucked up in their beds, their children asleep in the lofts, dreaming their childhood dreams.

Only Coltrane House itself, in the very center of the large estate, was still awake. Light spilled from nearly every window on the first two floors of the house, and the sound of people at play filtered out into the otherwise quiet night.

A fox that had dared the deep ditch of the ha-ha and found a way through a broken piece of the submerged fence at the bottom of that ditch warily approached the house. Perhaps it had been intrigued by the light, or even drawn to the house by the sound of laughter. But the uninvited guest didn't linger. The sound of a single gunshot split the night and the fox was on its way again, its stubby legs flying across the snow.

The fox need not have worried. The gunshot had come from inside the Main Saloon and the target had been a crystal vase once belonging to August Coltrane's deceased and unlamented wife.

There followed a loud male curse, the crack of another shot, and finally the sound of shattering glass.

August Coltrane threw back his head and laughed aloud. "God's teeth! *Two* shots, Grimey? Losing your touch, man, losing your touch."

"Devil take you, Coltrane," Lord Geoffrey Grimes responded, picking up yet another pistol from the generous collection of weapons on the table beside him. He waved it about wildly even as he squinted at the partygoers littering the Main Saloon. Two dozen men and their painted women cursed or squealed, then quickly dropped to the floor or scurried to duck behind any conveniently located bit of furniture.

"Cowards all," Lord Grimes scolded, then slumped in his chair. And belched.

His companion of the moment sighed, stuffed her bosoms back inside her gown, and took the pistol from him. "I'm supposin', my lord Grimey—" she began facetiously, sliding from his lap and slapping his hands away as he tried to reach up under her gown. "Like I said, I'm supposin', my lord Grimey, that you're past havin' any use for me this evenin'. Drunken sot," she grumbled as she flounced off, giving a wide smile to Baron Buckley, who was still lying supine on the floor, his trousers at his knees, his most prized possession exposed and—gunshots or no—still at the ready. "Ooou, ducks, that'd be a lovely thing," the woman said, dropping down beside him. "You wouldn't be mindin' little Lotte havin' a bit of that, now would you?"

The baron was more than willing to be generous, but his female companion took immediate exception. Within moments, the two women were rolling about on the floor, their hands ripping at each other's hair and clothing. Several gentlemen came out of hiding and began laying bets on the winner.

August Coltrane retook his seat on one of the couches after prudently picking up a pistol for himself, smiling as he surveyed the scene unfolding in front of him. He was having a good night, if he didn't end by having to wing Grimey in order to get the fellow to behave.

August Coltrane had been an extremely handsome man in his youth, which was now behind him as forty stared him hard in his heavy-lidded, bloodshot eyes. But if his youth had been misspent, he had every intention of making sure his autumn years would make his youthful exploits pale in comparison.

He gambled high. He drank in low places. He bedded every woman who'd have him, and some who wouldn't. He didn't give a snap for his country, his king, or even his ancestral home. Just as long as the money kept rolling in. Just as long as he could pretend he'd live forever.

And he told himself, over and over again, that he was a happy man.

Let others have their boring Christmas house parties, with caroling and hot cider and hard church pews in the morning. *He* knew how to make Christmas merry, by damn. "Twenty pounds on the redhead!" he called out loudly, crossing his booted ankles on the table in front of him, then lifted a bottle to his mouth and drank deeply.

"Bah! The devil with women, Coltrane," Lord Grimes shouted above the raucous jumble of noise and laughter, "and the devil with you. You promised us real entertainment tonight. Those two Irishers, remember? They were here a minute ago. Where in blazes did they go? The thespians, Coltrane? Where are they? Get 'em up here, Coltrane, make 'em speak. Don't need them both neither, just the fat one." He picked up the pistol once more. "I'd get *him* in one shot, damme if I couldn't."

Cluny and Clancy, of Cluny and Clancy Traveling Shakespearean Players fame (or infamy), heard Lord Grimes's boast as they cowered together behind a chair.

"Are you hearing this, Clancy?" the short, pudgy one asked even as he tried, unsuccessfully, to suck in his prodigious belly. "We came here to perform, you said. A week's work of Shakespeare in exchange for a warm bed, a bit of good food, and a fat purse. Happy Christmas to all! And now they're shooting pistols, Clancy, and I'm to be the Christmas goose!"

Clancy disentangled himself from Cluny's painfully tight embrace and, while still hiding behind the chair, attempted to straighten his dark green velvet doublet. "Hedge-born, unmuzzled snipes," he grumbled, peeking around the chair, taking a good look at the assembled guests. Lotte and the redhead rolled by, their bodices ripped, Lotte's teeth locked around the redhead's forearm. "Whoops!" he exclaimed, pulling his head back quickly, then taking a large handkerchief from his sleeve and wiping his damp brow. "Three and forty, I am, Cluny, and not old enough to be seeing the likes of that. Nothing else for it, my boy, we'll just have to stay on our knees and creep away. And don't be telling me who got us here, because I won't be hearing it, you understand?"

Cluny nodded, for he did understand. It was lowering,

that's what it was, to be reduced to wasting their great talents on drunks and doxies. But so was starving in a gutter. Cluny and Clancy Shakespearean Players had been four months without a paying engagement when August Coltrane had approached them in London two weeks earlier. He'd tossed them a purse, and commanded that they adjourn to Lincolnshire. Clancy had agreed to entertain at Coltrane's Christmas house party because anything was preferable to sleeping under a blanket of snow.

They didn't belong here. They belonged on the London stage, that's where they belonged. But it didn't seem destined to be. Instead, and for the past quarter century, they'd traveled England and Ireland in their wagon, the last ten years with their dear mule, Portia, in the traces. They'd driven from village to village, performing the Bard's immortal words for farmers and shopkeepers, sleeping in their wagon, and dreaming of one day treading the boards in London.

Coltrane House was a long way from London, and although they had dodged enough thrown fruit in the past to provide them with many a meal as they raced out of town, nobody had ever before taken a shot at them. It was enough to make a man reconsider his line of work, it was. Cluny was going to have a talk with Clancy about that very thing—if they made it out of the Main Saloon alive.

"It's a big house, Cluny," Clancy whispered to him. "We'll hide in one of the rooms until morning. Everything looks better in the morning, my sainted mother used to say. Now, follow me."

Cluny watched as Clancy, all long limbs and skinny shanks, got to his knees and began crawling toward the doors leading, he believed, to the formal dining room. His head all but butting into Clancy's skinny backside, Cluny did his best to "tiptoe" on his knees, his eyes squeezed shut as he held on to Clancy's ankles.

And they almost made it. In fact, Clancy already had his hand on the handle of the door to the dining room when August Coltrane spotted them and put a bullet into the door an inch above the handle.

"There you go, Grimey," Coltrane said genially as Clancy once more found himself enfolded by a shivering, quivering Cluny. "Never say I don't give my guests what they want. You—Irishers—get up on the stage and start emoting. Give us something to make our hearts sing. Unless you think *you* can sing for us?"

Clancy had to all but peel Cluny from him before he stood up, lifted his pointed chin, and glared at August Coltrane. "We are Shakespearean players, sir. We do *not* sing."

Cluny opened his eyes at last and looked across the room at August Coltrane. Their employer was a tall man, a devil-dark man, with black eyes that could pierce an iron pot at ten paces. "I sing a little, Clancy," he offered nervously.

"We do *As You Like It* tonight, Cluny," Clancy said firmly. "One small speech should do it, before they forget us again. Now, follow me, and we'll get this over with, then find us a chicken leg or two and a warm bed."

The next thing Cluny knew, he was standing on the small, makeshift stage in front of the fireplace. Clancy was bowing to the audience, telling them that his partner was about to delight them with Shakespeare's seven ages of man.

Seven? Cluny all but swallowed his tongue. Couldn't he just do four, then take his bow and run away? "I—I can't, Clancy. I just can't."

"Cluny, old friend, think," Clancy whispered in his ear. "What would the Bard do?"

"Take to his heels like a rabbit?" Cluny suggested, then

winced as Clancy gave him a clip on the back of the head that sent him staggering forward to the edge of the stage.

He looked out over his audience and winced again. The "ladies" had stopped fighting, and were now sprawled on the floor just in front of the stage, their clothing hanging from them in tatters as they made lewd, suggestive gestures at him. The lordship called Grimey was holding a bowl of oranges in his lap, and looking very much like he desired nothing better than a reason to toss them at the stage. The rest of the audience was not an audience at all, but seemed to be putting on a show of their own—one that had a lot to do with bare buttocks and giggling women pretending the men were stallions and they were out for a lively ride.

And August Coltrane, the man with the dead black eyes, was sitting on the couch, a bottle in one hand, a pistol in the other. A pistol pointed straight at Cluny's head.

Cluny gulped, took a step back, and felt Clancy's hand grabbing onto his burgundy-velvet doublet. "Now, Cluny," his partner pleaded. "From your belly, Cluny—*emote!*"

" 'All . . . um . . . all the world's a . . . a stage,' " Cluny began, realizing he had somehow lost all the spit in his mouth. Lord Grimes picked up one of the oranges, hefted it in his hand. A bullet in the brain might kill him quickly and cleanly, Cluny decided, but pelted oranges *hurt*. He found his voice. " 'All the world's a stage!' " he repeated quickly, " 'and all the men and women merely players; they have their exits and their entrances—' "

"Can you hear him, Coltrane?" Lord Grimes asked, then launched an orange toward the stage. "I bloody can't hear him. Speak up, man!"

"Oh God and all Your saints preserve me, and I'll never do anything bad again," Cluny whimpered, as Clancy stepped forward and deftly snagged the orange out of the air, took a bow. It was then that Cluny remembered who he was. He was Cluny, of Cluny and Clancy Shakespearean Players, by God, and he and Clancy had a show to put on!

He breathed in deeply, drew himself up to his full, unimposing height. He spread his pudgy, mended hose-clad legs wide, clapped his hands to his pear-shaped belly, and began again, his voice loud, clear, and carrying to the very ceiling. " 'And one man in his time plays many parts, his acts being seven ages. At first the infant, mewling and puking in the nurse's arms . . .' "

August Coltrane put down his pistol in order to take hold of the redhead, who had decided to help him out of his breeches. Lotte, not to be outdone, sidled up to Lord Grimes once more, her hands on her hips, loudly asking him if he'd rather be watching a play or playing himself.

"Right!" Lord Grimes said, pulling her down on his lap. "Here, grab some of these," he said, holding out the bowl of oranges. "You take the fat one, and I'll get the skinny-shanks one with the parrot nose."

"Take your bow now, Cluny," Clancy whispered as an orange whizzed past, to smash against the fireplace behind them. "Take your bow and exit, stage left. I'm close behind you."

Cluny needed no additional prompting. He scuttled fast as he could toward the doorway leading to the formal dining room, Clancy close on his heels.

He stopped just at the open door, screwed up his courage one last time, and struck a pose. " 'Sweep on, you fat and greedy citizens!' " he proclaimed loudly before hastily and prudently backing through the doorway.

"Now where, Clancy?" he asked breathlessly, pressing his back against the quickly closed door. "I don't think I can outrun them, if they mean to be nasty."

Clancy shook his head. "They're too drunk to chase us, and much too interested in their women to remember us beyond our leave-taking. Come on, Cluny. It's as I said we'd do. We'll raid the kitchens for a late supper, then find some-place safe to eat. We can finish our performance another time, if ever they remember we're still in residence."

Cluny sighed, then followed after his partner, complain-ing all the way. "We should leave right now," he pronounced as they rummaged, unimpeded, through the larders. The skeleton staff of servants had all gone to ground, hiding themselves from the mayhem breaking loose all over the house. "Leave, exit, run away, whatever you want to call it."

"We can't leave yet," Clancy informed him as they climbed the servant stairs. "They haven't paid us the ma-jority of what we're owed yet, remember? On our own, we don't even have enough blunt to feed poor Portia beyond another day. She's a dear enough thing, but she won't agree to pull the wagon an inch without her daily measure of oats."

"We'll apply to that young Sherlock fellow in the morn-ing," Cluny suggested, then sighed as Clancy headed up an-other narrow flight of stairs, to the topmost floor. "He's Coltrane's solicitor or man of business or whatever, right?" he questioned, huffing and puffing as he followed along. "He can pay us, and then we can move on. South, I'd say. Back to London. We can always find a friend and a bed in London."

"It's the week we promised, and the week we have to play," Clancy declared, as they came to the hallway at the top of the stairs. "I have my scruples, I do, even if our audi-ence is none but a bunch of roynish, motley-minded snipes. Besides, there must be a foot of snow out there, if you haven't looked. Now come on, it's quiet enough up here. Let's find us a dark room and have our feast."

Clancy stepped off down the hallway and Cluny fol-lowed. It was his lot in life, to follow Clancy. Mostly, he didn't mind, as Clancy was ever so smart. Except that it had been Clancy who'd accepted the invitation to perform at Coltrane House. That hadn't been so smart, now had it?

"We'll go in here," Clancy announced a moment later, already pushing open a door to their right and stepping inside before Cluny could point out the faint light spilling from beneath the door. Someone else might already be inside. Someone who might not appreciate visitors.

Chapter Two

Jack had been fighting sleep all evening long, with only his bone-deep hunger to keep him awake. He'd checked on Merry an hour earlier, then locked the door behind him as he made one last attempt to creep down to the kitchens for something to eat.

He'd gotten as far as the second-floor landing of the servant stairs before the sound of gunshots sent him stumbling back up, abandoning all thoughts of some cheese and bread in his panic to get back to Merry. He'd dropped the key three times, his fingers cold and fumbling, before he'd been able to open the door and get back inside the safety of the nursery.

And then he'd cried. He was horribly ashamed of himself, but he did cry. Not that it mattered; there was no one to hear him. No one to scold him, or to care.

Now he was sitting cross-legged on the cold wooden floor—a pale-faced, knobby-kneed, skinny boy of seven with a mop of badly combed black hair, his clothing frayed and patched and too thin to keep out the winter's chill. He hadn't drawn a blanket around his shoulders to warm himself, believing that his discomfort would keep him awake, keep Merry safe.

He kept both hands locked around the hilt of the rusty old sword he'd discovered in the attics, swearing to himself he'd cut down the first person who dared to come into the room.

And yet, for all his determination, pure physical exhaustion had taken a toll on his mind and body. He was a tall boy for his age, but even a tall seven is small when compared to a grown man. Coltrane House was filled to the rafters with grown men this week—loud, drunken men and their loud, drunken women.

Jack had long ago learned to stay in the nursery when the slovenly, underpaid servants ran off, leaving him alone. He'd learned to hide himself away whenever his father came home as he had yesterday, dragging his collection of dangerous friends along with him.

Yesterday when the few servants who remained at Coltrane House had seen the carriages begin to arrive, they'd all deserted the house, deserted Jack. Those first carriages had been filled with servants from his father's house in London, and everyone knew what that meant. The man always had to bring staff with him from the city when he planned one of his wild parties. And that London staff was there to serve August Coltrane, not his young son.

Before Jack could do more than raid the kitchens, quickly filling a basket with some small bits of food to hide in the nursery, August Coltrane himself had driven up to the front door.

He hadn't come up to the nursery. He hadn't sent anyone to bring his son to him. He probably didn't remember that he had a son. He probably didn't remember Merry either.

Jack wanted to be grateful for that. He was grateful.

Really. But how could a man forget his own son? What had his son done that was so terrible that his own father could forget him, pretend he didn't exist?

Jack angrily wiped a tear from his cheek as he thought about how alone he was, how little anyone cared if he lived or died. The servants didn't care. His father certainly didn't care.

The last time his father had come home Jack had actually dared to enter his bedchamber, hoping his father would talk to him, and possibly take him back to London with him. But August had been in bed with a naked woman on either side of him, and all he'd done was to ask if Jack wanted to join them.

The women's high-pitched giggles had followed Jack all the way back up the stairs to the nursery.

He hadn't spoken to his father since, and had been avoiding him for the two days and single night August had already been in residence this time. With luck, he wouldn't have to see the man at all, and his father would ride away, not to return until the summer. Mr. Sherlock had promised him, promised him that August wouldn't return before the summer, after something called "the Season" was over in London. Then Mr. Sherlock had told Jack something he already knew: stay in the nursery, boy, and don't let anyone see you.

All Jack had was Merry. He could kill himself, if it weren't for Merry. Kill himself, or run away, run very far away. That's what he would tell himself as he cried himself to sleep every night when his father was in residence, and even on some nights when he wasn't.

But he couldn't run, and he'd known that even before Merry had come to Coltrane House just three months ago. He had nowhere to go. And he would never kill himself, not really, even if there had been times he'd wanted to die.

He would kill his father instead. Jack had made up his mind the last time his father drove away from Coltrane House, and he'd crept downstairs and seen the destruction his father and his friends had left behind. Even Mr. Sherlock had said August Coltrane should be punished for what he was doing to the estate, so that Jack decided that it was all right that he wished his father dead. Dead, or at least very, very sorry.

But it wasn't all so terrible, not anymore. Merry was here now. And somehow that made it all right. Jack knew he could stand anything now, now that there was Merry. Now that he had someone to love, someone to love him. His father might be in residence, and all of the misery of the world was going on in the Main Saloon, but this time, for the first time, Jack wasn't completely alone.

He flexed his numb fingers, gripped the sword once more, felt his chest swell as he redoubled his resolve. He'd kill for Merry. He'd die for her. He hoped he didn't have to do either, but he would. He loved her that much, needed her that much.

Jack's stomach rumbled and he rubbed at it, wishing away his hunger. Only six more days. Six more days of sneaking food up the stairs, of searching out coal for the fire, of being very, very quiet and very, very careful. In six days, his father would leave. In six days, the servants would feel it safe to come back, feed them, light a better fire than he could build on his own. In six days he could relax. He could sleep. Oh, how he longed to sleep.

Jack didn't know how long he sat there, sat on the cold floor praying for blessed quiet, praying for the long night to be over. It could have been minutes, hours. When dawn came he would sleep for a little while, until Merry needed him. That's when his father slept, he and his friends sleeping the entire day away, playing the whole night long. Why were the days so short, the nights so long? Jack's eyelids drooped as he stared at the latch, his muscles aching in protest at being still for so long.

Suddenly, he heard a sound. Several sounds. The sound of feet walking on the bare boards. The sound of voices. Outside, in the hallway. No one had ever climbed all the way up here before—no one. He'd told himself he was ready, that he could defend Merry. Now he hesitated, remembering that he was only a stupid boy with a stupid old sword, and he couldn't protect anybody.

Maybe it was his father? Jack's heart leapt hopefully, his hopes plummeting just as quickly. He knew that he'd been wise to give up that expectation a long time ago. In fact, if his father had come to the nursery with one of his drunken friends, Jack and Merry were probably in trouble.

He dragged himself to his feet, the heavy sword nearly as tall as he was, and almost impossible to lift. But it would be all right. It had to be all right. The door was locked. Nobody was going to come in. Nobody was going to hurt Merry.

And then he watched, dumbfounded, as the latch depressed and the door opened.

Jack bit back a sob. How could he have been so stupid? He'd been sitting on the cold floor, tired and hungry and near to tears ever since he'd heard the gunshots and run back up the stairs . . . and he'd been guarding an unlocked door.

The door swung completely open and Jack's jaw dropped. There were men, two men, walking into the room. Two very strange-looking men. One was very tall and thin, with his skinny legs wrapped in dark green hose. The other was short and quite fat, and he looked as if the top half of his body had been stuffed inside an enormous velvet pillow.

They didn't see him, as they were much too busy arguing with each other.

"I can't help it, Clancy. I must speak. And when I speak

I still must say that we eat, we sleep, and then we run away," the fat one complained, his arms waving like a windmill as he followed after the skinny one.

"And I say, faint-heart, that 'thus far into the bowels of the land have we march'd on without impediment.' We're safe here, Cluny, at least for the night. Look around you—do you see any dragons?"

The fat one, so directed, looked around the room. The man's eyes looked high at first, sweeping the ceiling, and then they looked low. Low enough to see a seven-year-old boy. The man's eyes widened, showing white all the way around them. Jack growled, bared his teeth, tried desperately to brandish his sword.

"Um . . . we're not alone, Clancy," the fat one said, pointing to Jack. "Look, my friend, and see for yourself, for it's a fine sight, a fine soldier. And yet, 'he wears the rose of youth upon him.' "

The skinny one, Clancy, who had been shutting the door behind them, turned and looked at Jack. He tilted his head to one side, rubbed a finger down his huge, beaky nose and said, "I see him, Cluny. 'A Corinthian, a lad of mettle, a good boy.' "

Jack looked from one man to the other. Who were these men? Certainly they weren't his father's usual sort of guest. Their words confused him, their grand gestures and exaggerated poses appeared both threatening and somehow silly, and their strange clothing reminded him of old portraits hung in the West Wing gallery.

"Yes, Clancy, a lad of mettle," Cluny responded quietly, even as he smiled, waggled his fingers at Jack in greeting. "A very frightened lad. A heartbreakingly brave lad. A lad with a scowl as dark as any pirate's. In short, Clancy, a lad with a man's sword, and a look in his eye that does not bode well for the likes of us."

Jack growled in reaction, then lifted the sword a little higher, although the effort took nearly all the rest of his small store of strength. "One word more, sirs, and I'll kill you. Leave now. Go away!"

Clancy took one step more into the room. Then two. "I think I'll risk it, son. 'A man can die but once; we owe God a death,' " he said pleasantly, holding out a chicken leg, waving it lazily as he raised his eyebrows, shrugged. "Or the brave soldier can put down his sword and we can all eat a good supper and live another day?"

Cluny sidled up to his friend, spoke out of the corner of his mouth. " 'Tempt not a desperate man,' " he warned, then confounded Jack all the more by grinning at him once more as he produced an apple from somewhere in his clothing and offered it to him.

"Go away!" Jack ordered again, even as the aroma of chicken assaulted his nose, actually threatened to turn his stomach. "You've been warned, sirs—leave! Leave now, or I'll skewer you just for talking so strange!"

"Skewer us for our strange talk?" Cluny exclaimed, pressing his hands to his chest. "Did you hear that, Clancy? The boy's a critic. I say, son," he went on, smiling at Jack yet again, "we're not such bad actors, are we? We know our lines, we use our props, and we've a great affection for the Bard. That would be Shakespeare, my boy, Will Shakespeare. And we're Cluny and Clancy, of Cluny and Clancy Traveling Shakespearean Players. We should have told you that straight off, shouldn't we? Clancy—why didn't you tell the boy that?"

"I had thought to, Cluny," the second man said, dragging off his silly velvet hat and exposing a fairly bald head with very long strands of graying blond hair hanging from it—like a broom that had lost most of its bristles. "But then I thought we could show the boy what else we can do. We're known for our fine orations, certainly, but we're just as handy with a bit of juggling and the like. Right, Cluny?"

"True enough, Clancy." Cluny pulled a second apple from inside his velvet cushion of a jacket, then a third. He threw them up in the air, one after the other, and then caught them as they came back down. Caught them, threw them again, caught them again. Round and round and round. As Jack watched, growing dizzy as he tried to understand how the man could keep three apples in the air when he had only two hands, the one called Clancy began to sing, putting his hands on his hips as he did a little dance to accompany his words.

Whether it was Cluny's and Clancy's outlandish costumes, their strange speech, their general silliness, or the chicken leg, Jack would never know. But he relaxed at last, lowered the heavy sword. He then sighed wearily and sat down on the floor, too tired to fight, too defeated to flee. "You're not with him, are you?" he asked quietly, rubbing a hand across his eyes. "No, you couldn't be, even if you do sound as drunk as the rest of them."

He looked up at the two actors. Sadly. Searchingly. His bottom lip began to tremble, and he lowered the heavy sword. "Six more days and nights of this. How am I to do it? I'm *so* tired."

"Good boy," Clancy said as he dropped to his haunches in front of Jack, removed the sword from the boy's nerveless fingers, gently patted his head. Jack flinched then, even though he wasn't all that much afraid anymore. It was just that nobody ever touched him unless it was to give him a cuff on the ear or a kick to the backside. Someone patting his head was . . . well, it was not something he understood.

"Cluny," he heard Clancy continue, "I believe we've

stumbled into the nursery. Is that it, son? I don't want to believe this, but I do have to ask. Do you, God forbid, belong to the Awful August?"

Awful August. That brought a small smile to Jack's lips, and he relaxed even more. He nodded a single time, then slowly got to his feet. "I'm Jack, sirs. Jack Coltrane. August Coltrane is my papa. I hate him, you understand. Very, very much. That is chicken, isn't it? I—I haven't been able to sneak downstairs today, and the servants have all run away. It has been hard to feed us, but I've managed. Still, sir, if you were to ask me if I should like a piece of chicken . . ."

"Us? There's more of you, then? How many more?" Clancy asked, holding out the chicken leg once more. "How many times has the Awful August pupped?"

Jack couldn't help himself. He grabbed at the offer of food, began gnawing on the chicken leg as if he hadn't eaten in days, speaking as he chewed. "There's only me here. I'm the only Coltrane except for Papa." He looked at Cluny, at the cherry-cheeked little man who could make apples dance. He looked at Clancy, who had given him the chicken leg. Swallowing down hard, he decided to trust these two men. Did he really have any other choice? "And then there's Merry, of course," he added quietly.

"Merry, is it? Your nursemaid?" Cluny looked beyond the boy, to another door that stood open at the end of the room. "She'd be in there?"

"Not my nursemaid," Jack corrected, walking toward the doorway. "I don't need one, you know, and neither does Merry. We're fine enough by ourselves, with the servants and Mr. Sherlock helping out when they can. When they remember us," he trailed off, shrugging. He picked up a candle and motioned for the two men to follow after him.

"This is Merry," Jack told them a moment later, as he stood protectively in front of the cot in the center of the sparsely furnished room. "She's my father's ward. That's what Mr. Sherlock says, but I pretend she's really my sister. It's all right if I call her my sister, isn't it? She's doing just fine, because I'm still able to sneak to the dairy to get her milk, and she's ever so good and quiet, never crying and bringing the house down on us. I don't much like keeping her clean, but I do it." He looked at Cluny and Clancy with narrowed eyelids. "I warn you, sirs, I've sworn to kill anyone who tries to hurt her."

"Ah, Clancy, and would you be looking at this," Cluny said, dropping to his knees beside the small cot. Merry was awake, although she hadn't cried, but just lay there on her back, gurgling and cooing. Fuzz the color of a fiery dawn covered her head. Eyes huge and round and brilliantly blue looked up at her three visitors. "I've lost my heart, Clancy, that's as true as we're here, in the presence of an angel. 'I must dance barefoot on her wedding day . . .'" he whispered in awe, touching the back of his index finger to one soft, pink cheek. Merry giggled.

Clancy clucked his tongue a time or two, then put a hand on Jack's thin shoulder. "You haven't slept a wink in days, have you, my brave warrior? No. How could you, what with the racket and bawdy doings going on all around you. For shame, that a man should bring riffraff under his own roof, into a house holding innocent babies. Cluny—we have us a mission now, you know. We are going to protect these two babes, these infants in arms, these—"

"I'm not a baby!" Jack protested hotly, pulling away from Clancy's comforting grasp.

"And never were allowed to be one, I'll wager," Clancy agreed solemnly. "Now, come, sit. Eat. We'll talk, and Cluny will watch the little one."

Chapter Three

A friendship had been born that night—had it only been a mere two days ago?—so that Cluny and Clancy had remained at Coltrane House. They hid with Jack and Merry during the day, reluctantly dragging themselves downstairs at night to once more perform for their supper. Not that they were needed, or even missed. They merely peeked into the Main Saloon each night, saw what was going on, and then crept back up to the nursery without so much as speaking one line of Shakespeare.

Tonight would be their first performance in days, not that either man had his heart in the prospect of declaiming to drunken sots and their rude females. Even now, at August Coltrane's express demand, as Cluny took up where he'd left off the other evening, his mind was filled with thoughts of the two children and their terrible predicament.

Coltrane House was a mass of contradictions. A great, beautiful creation ruled by an ugly master. A mean, cold, lout of a man. With a son so brave, so loyal, and a ward so beautiful, so sweet. Two perfect children, both so horribly neglected.

Fortunately neglected. Cluny could think of nothing worse than August parading his young son and ward downstairs for the edification of his drunken guests. Jack should never be exposed to such raw adventure. Merry, only six months old according to Jack, would be even more at risk with the drunken women who might think it a grand idea to play mother to the infant.

How could a man behave so reprehensibly? To bring his drunken cronies and his shameless doxies into his home, to parade them in front of infants? To allow his guests the run of the house, the *ruin* of the house?

It was all so sad. Cluny's gentle heart had broken as he'd thought of Jack stubbornly standing guard in front of the nursery door for long, frightening hours. The child had robbed himself of sleep in order that Merry might rest, deprived himself of food for fear of leaving the child alone a moment longer than necessary. Clancy, Cluny's friend for most of his life, had actually cried as he watched over Jack that first night, after they'd finally convinced the boy to sleep by promising to stand guard for him. In all the years they'd been together, Cluny couldn't remember ever seeing Clancy cry.

For all Cluny had wished to escape Coltrane House, he had leapt at Clancy's declaration that they had been brought there by some divine plan. His friend truly believed they had been placed in just that spot, at just that time, in order to protect and defend those two sweet innocents.

And protect them they would, for as long as it was possible. Cluny sang to Merry, feeding her the milk he'd fetched from the dairy himself. Clancy performed *Macbeth* for young Jack, who twice fell asleep where he sat, a small smile on his face as he held tight to Merry's chubby little hand.

In another few days Awful August and his menagerie would decamp for other climes, or so Jack had told them. His papa never stayed at Coltrane House much above a sennight, and never more than twice a year. The child reported this knowledge calmly, even coldly. Almost as coldly as he had pronounced that someday, when he was grown, he would kill his papa for what he was doing to Coltrane House.

Perhaps that was why Cluny felt at least a little pleased with Awful August's command to continue with the seven ages of man as cataloged by the Bard. For Jack was a child, a man-child, and he would grow. He would climb the ladder of these seven ages. He would climb them over the broken back of the foolish, selfish, unthinking father who did not know that his greatest treasure hid from him in the nursery, plotting his demise.

An apple whipped past Cluny's nose, as if to remind him he had been speaking, and he looked out over his drunken audience, despising each and every one of them. If it weren't for Jack, for little Merry, he and Clancy would be gone from this horrid place at first light.

First? Oh, yes. *First.* Cluny drew another deep breath and forged on with his recitation. " 'At first the infant, mewling and puking in the nurse's arms;' " he continued above the din, forming his arms into a cradle for emphasis. " 'Then the whining school-boy, with his satchel, and shining morning face, creeping like snail unwillingly to school.' " He went up on his toes and took three small creeping steps. " 'And then,' " he continued, hands dramatically pressed to his heart, " 'the lover, sighing like furnace, with a woeful ballad made to his mistress' eyebrow. Then a soldier—' "

"I say, August," a drunken bully declared from the row of

chairs that had been drawn up in front of the fireplace, "how many is that? Three? Five? He said seven, didn't he? No, no. Can't abide that, can we? Here now, fellow," the man with the red nose and the bare-breasted doxy on his lap shouted, "we stop at three, no more. Stop at the lover, eh, what? Loving's something we all know, don't we, darlin'?" he asked of the giggling whore.

While Clancy picked up their meager props, sure that their presence was no longer required, Cluny—who really should have known better, but never did—stepped forward. Unfortunately, he was still holding the spear he'd been ready to employ as he spoke about the age of soldiering. "How dare you!" he bellowed, hot with Shakespeare's words, forgetting that he was an actor and not a soldier; that he was, at heart, a very timid man who bruised easily. "Scoundrels! Scoundrels, all! And with a child in the house. And a babe! Fie! Fie and fie again on you all!"

Clancy sighed and stepped in front of him, trying to shield his friend from the slings and arrows of outraged fortune that were sure to come. And they did indeed arrive, in the form of assorted fruit and a small statue of some nameless Greek god. But instead of pulling Cluny away, Clancy showed himself equally enraged and joined in his partner's tirade, calling on the Bard for inspiration. " 'The devil damn thee black, thou cream-fac'd loon; where gott'st thou that goose look?' " he exclaimed in some heat, as Clancy had a real feel for *Macbeth.*

"Oh, that was good, Clancy. Very good," Cluny complimented, then gulped as he watched the man in the front row rise and dump his doxy onto the floor. The man rose like a great woolly bear, eyes red with rage, to advance toward the makeshift stage, his fellow rowdies close behind him.

"However," Cluny continued quickly, his voice little more than a strangled squeak, "perhaps a prudent silence is in order? Or a hasty exit back to the nursery? Yes, that's it. 'A horse! a horse! my kingdom for a horse!' "

But the woolly bear-man's anger didn't stop Clancy. Cluny's fears didn't stop Clancy. Nothing much did, when the fellow was in a rage, most especially any sort of common sense. He yanked the spear from Cluny's nerveless fingers and swung it at the drunken wave that had nearly overcome the stage. " 'Away, you scullion! you rampallion! you fustilarian! I'll tickle your catastrophe!' " he shouted in his most eloquent, and most dangerous tones.

Now August Coltrane himself stomped onto the stage, grabbed the spear from Clancy, and broke the useless prop over his hip before tossing the pieces aside and heading straight at Cluny.

Cluny closed his eyes. It wasn't always a good idea to keep them open, he'd learned. Especially once one was lying on the floor, with one's knees drawn up to protect one's most important parts.

A few days later, their wounds bound and their bruises turning quite wonderful colors, Cluny and Clancy stood with Jack and watched as the last carriage drove away from Coltrane House through the rapidly melting snow. Cluny was cheered enough by this exodus to even give a little wave and call out, "Ta-ta, good sirs, and a good journey to you. May your horses go lame and your wheels find a multitude of deep ditches."

Clancy laughed at his friend's silliness, and Cluny smiled, well pleased with himself. In fact, both Clancy and Cluny were feeling quite pleased today.

A deal had been struck just that morning between the actors and Mr. Henry Sherlock, August Coltrane's estate manager, solicitor, and general man of business.

The actors had taken an immediate liking to Henry Sherlock, a rather handsome lad of little more than twenty, quite young to carry such vast responsibility on his shoulders. But he was a sober young man, and he had quickly agreed that Cluny and Clancy were just what Jack and Merry needed. That alone endeared him to them.

The deal itself was fairly straightforward. In exchange for their services as entertainers, which they had not been able to provide, Cluny and Clancy were now engaged to earn their promised purse by taking charge of the children in the nursery until such time as they had earned their pay.

At least, that's what Henry Sherlock had told a drunken and generally uncaring August Coltrane. The man had told Cluny and Clancy quite a different story. He was actually hiring the two men as permanent caretakers to Jack and Merry, as they had done such an exemplary job during August's visit to Coltrane House. In exchange for a roof over their heads and food in their bellies, they were to be allowed to remain at Coltrane House, as had been their expressed wish, for as long as they both did live.

"Because you're right, you know," Sherlock had gone on. "I can't call myself a good Christian if I let this sorry mess with the children continue so much as another day. It was bad enough when it was just the boy, but now, with young Meredith here as well these past months? No, it can't continue," Sherlock had told the two actors when they'd limped into his presence to swear they'd go straight to the King himself, to tell that good man of the sorry plight of Jack and Merry.

Henry Sherlock had seemed to understand their upset, and agreed with their opinion of August Coltrane. "He hates Jack, you know. He hated his wife, Jack's mother, a coal merchant's daughter he only married for her fortune. I remember one night—Mr. Coltrane had been quite in his cups—when he told me the best thing Jack had ever done for him, the only good thing, was the happy accident of killing his mother in childbed. Other than that, I truly believe he hates his son, who he sees as waiting gleefully in the wings, waiting for his father to die. Mr. Coltrane, I do believe, has quite a fear of dying, and plays hard so as to forget that fear. Jack's presence reminds him that he is mortal, that there is already someone here, ready to step into his boots. Mr. Coltrane says he's going to make sure the little brat has nothing left to inherit, and my greatest task is to make sure he isn't proved right, not that it's an easy job. As a matter of fact, if it hadn't been for Merry's father naming Mr. Coltrane as her guardian, and guardian of her inheritance, the bailiffs would have been here this Christmas, to share Mr. Coltrane's pudding with him."

Sherlock then shook his head sadly, said yet again how happy he was that Cluny and Clancy had agreed to stay on, take care of the children. "You have relieved my mind greatly. Not that there's money enough to pay you more than a pittance, I'm sorry to say. Coltrane House is a flourishing estate, but Mr. Coltrane has . . . well, to be as kind as possible knowing what we know, he has expenses. As it is, I'll have to let two servants go in order to allow you to stay, not that losing any one of them is a great loss. It's the best I can do."

The best Henry Sherlock could do had been more than enough to satisfy Cluny and Clancy.

And now Awful August was gone, not to return until the summer, and Cluny and Clancy had to get to work. The boy couldn't read, for one thing. Not a word. To Clancy, this was Awful August's greatest sin against his unwanted son, for a child who could not read could never know the world.

So Clancy would take charge of Jack, which was fine with Cluny, who had truly lost his heart to little Merry, the

darling cherub with the halo of red hair and the laughing
blue eyes.

They had already pulled their wagons behind the stables
and turned Portia out to pasture for all time. Once their bodies didn't ache so much from their beating, they would bring
all the rest of their possessions into the house and permanently set themselves up in a room near the nursery. No
more would they travel the roadways. No more would they
sleep under haystacks or be pelted with fruit as they shared
their beloved Shakespeare with the simple folk. That in itself was a blessing. Simple folk had such exemplary aim,
and they often threw rocks, not oranges.

"Come on, Jack, my lad," Clancy said now as they all
turned away from the windows in the Main Saloon and surveyed the wreckage Awful August and his guests had left behind. "First we find us some brooms and begin to clean up
this unholy mess. That should take no more than a week,
less if the servants come straggling back. And then, my lad,
while Cluny here talks nonsense to the babe, you and I shall
begin your education."

Cluny followed after them, carefully stepping around bits
of broken glass and righting a small stool as he passed by it.
"I'd rather see you in the kitchens, Clancy," he said consideringly. "You're a good man there if the meal is simple, and
you look well enough in an apron. I don't see you teaching
the boy his sums, not when you can't add three numbers in
a row if it takes you more than your ten fingers. What we
ought to do," he continued, braving Clancy's heated stare,
"is to send a note to Aloysius. That's what we ought to do,
don't you know."

"Aloysius?" Clancy repeated. "Aloysius Bromley? The
Aloysius Bromley we met in Cambridge? The one who left
the stage to play tutor to rich young boys with more hair

than wit? Do you think he'd come? We can't pay him, Cluny. We can't pay ourselves."

"Oh, I think we can, Clancy," Cluny told him as they headed for the empty kitchens. "I think our Mr. Sherlock would be willing to find a way for us to pay Aloysius. And any servants we might want to hire on as well—servants that wouldn't run off when Awful August rides up the drive. The man's conscience is paining him dearly, don't you know. He's little more than a lad himself, but he knows these dear children need good and loving care. It was one thing when it was just Jack, but to have a babe in the house, alone and unprotected? The lad was sickened, I tell you. He's grateful to us for our help. Why else do you suppose he's letting us stay on?"

"I won't have a nurse," Jack protested, hitching himself up and onto the greasy wooden table in the center of the kitchens, his bare legs swinging free. "I'm too old for a nurse, don't you know."

"Don't you know? Did you hear that, Clancy? He said 'don't you know.' Marvelous young mimic, but he's picking up our Irish ways, much as we've tried to beat them down these long years. We need Aloysius, and we need him tomorrow." He spread his arms wide, as if to encompass the entire kitchen, all of Coltrane House. "And we need a few good servants *yesterday*."

"We can't hire servants, Cluny," Clancy protested. "We wouldn't know how, for one thing. And I don't know that Sherlock would approve."

"I can think of some he would approve, Clancy. There's the Maxwells for two," Cluny said, beginning to feel quite pleased with himself. It wasn't often that he could outthink Clancy, and even less often when he didn't earn himself a clap on the ear for his efforts. "They're tired of the stage, and want a better future for their young daughter. Honey, I think her name is. Told me so themselves, while we were in London. Why, I can think of a half dozen good actors and actresses who would like nothing more than to retire to a country estate for a Season or two, if not longer. A warm bed, a dry roof, a few chores in exchange for a full belly? Oh, yes, I can think of dozens who'd jump at the chance. Why, we'd barely have to pay them a penny. We'd be beating away replacements with a stick, once word gets out of what we're doing."

"Yes, it could work." Clancy picked up a dirty pot, wincing as he looked inside it. "In fact, what a truly *splendid* idea. You amaze me at times, my friend. I'll go speak with young Mr. Sherlock." He dropped the pot back onto the table and, his bony shoulders squared for yet another battle, walked out of the room.

"We'll come with you. Come on, lad, we're off to do battle," Cluny said, motioning for Jack to hop down from the table and follow him. The pudgy little man raised his arm in front of him as if carrying a flag and began to march, Jack hard on his heels as they headed for Sherlock's small office. " 'Once more unto the breach, dear friends,' " Cluny cried enthusiastically, " 'once more!' "

Jack giggled, carefree and happy as any child, then began to skip, trying to keep up with his new and very dear friends.

Chapter Four

Aloysius Bromley cleared his throat, then delivered a level look at Merry, who had been fidgeting in her chair for the past ten minutes, bored beyond politeness with his droning recitation of the royal succession.

Dear Meredith. Little Meredith Fairfax. A good girl at eight years old. A sweet girl. And a rare handful.

Aloysius had allowed her to join fifteen-year-old Master John in his lessons for two reasons. One, the girl was bright enough that he enjoyed tutoring her. Two, he hadn't been able to figure a way to keep the determined child out of the schoolroom.

She should have a nanny, and then, later, a governess. As it was, with August Coltrane being so indifferent to the child who had been left in his care, Aloysius believed the girl fortunate to have clothes on her back.

And then there was John. John Coltrane. Dearest, most dangerously headstrong Jack. Aloysius had been aghast to learn, thanks to village gossip, that the boy's father had allowed the midwife to name the child after his mother had died in childbed. The midwife, being a simple woman, had believed Johnnie to be a good, solid name. August had apparently considered this to be a rare joke, and allowed it. Mostly, he had been happy to have his unwanted wife underground, and really didn't care much for the idea of fatherhood. So he ignored it. And ignored John as well, as much as he could. Cluny and Clancy had told Aloysius how neglected John had been. They'd told him that, and so very much more, the day he'd been engaged to tutor and otherwise civilize young Jack.

August ignored Merry as well, and had done from the moment the child, then a squalling infant, had been thrust upon him in some legal way no one had ever quite explained to Aloysius. He only knew August had charge of the child's eventual inheritance, and Aloysius knew that was good enough for the man who was probably spending as much of Merry's money as he could steal. The child would be lucky to have a half dozen pounds to her name when she finally reached her majority.

Not that Merry knew any of this. Not that an eight-year-old would even care about such things as an inheritance. Especially not a child like Merry. She was just happy to be alive, happy to be with her beloved Jack.

Aloysius didn't know why he stayed at Coltrane House. He was rarely ever paid, and often contributed some of his small personal income to the purchase of books and paper and ink. Not that he ever thought about going back on the stage; not now, as he entered the autumn of his life. But he certainly was more than qualified to teach in any of the universities rather than spending his declining years bearleading two wild young people who would otherwise grow up as complete savages.

Except that Aloysius had a soft heart. Or a soft head, as he had told himself more than once over the years. And so he stayed. Just as the Maxwells stayed, and so many others. Actors who were not out of work. Oh no, to hear them tell it, they were just "resting," and would soon go back on the road.

That none of them had left in eight years just showed how badly they'd needed the "rest." Mostly, Aloysius believed, he and his actor friends had all stayed because of John and Meredith. They were a family, that's what they were, joined together for the sake of these two children; caring for them, teaching them, watching over them—protecting them from August Coltrane.

Aloysius enjoyed watching Meredith and John together. They were like puppies, rolling and playing and sometimes nipping at each other, but always the best of good friends. John was the protective and sometimes teasing older brother, Meredith the adoring younger sister.

Which had been all well and good, with John being eleven to Meredith's four; and even now, with him a rough-and-ready fifteen to the girl's eight tender years. But what would happen when John was twenty-one, and Meredith fourteen? If John were still at Coltrane House—and the lad had sworn never to leave his beloved and beleaguered home to August's mercies—what then?

John, the tutor was sure, only saw Meredith as his father's ward, as his very good friend and companion. He teased with her, dragged her along on his exploits, treated her as a beloved and laughingly tolerated younger sister—sometimes as a person of no gender at all.

But Aloysius looked at Meredith and knew there was a beauty in the child that would someday mature, come to life with a vengeance. That red hair, those long, straight limbs. That wide, infectious smile. Those eyes, the color of a morning sky. She might be awkward and coltish now, probably would be for some time to come, but her mature beauty was not only a possibility, it was a certainty.

And unless Meredith changed her mind, which the stubborn child had never been wont to do, she planned to marry her beloved Jack once she was grown. Aloysius knew that because Meredith, in her childish honesty, had confided as much to him.

Yes, someday Meredith would grow, burst into the sweet flower of her young womanhood. What would John Coltrane do then? Would he still see her as his sister? Would Meredith allow him to dismiss her as nothing *more* than his sister?

Aloysius knew what Cluny dreamed of, what Clancy hoped for, what they both wanted with all their hearts. And it would be so simple, and rather wonderful, if John and Meredith were to one day look at each other and realize that there could be nothing more perfect than to marry and spend the rest of their lives together here at Coltrane House.

They both loved the estate, were united in their determination that August Coltrane should not be allowed to destroy it. They were both passionate about that, with John nearly obsessed with preserving the house, the land.

Yes, having John and Meredith discover each other as more than brother and sister would be quite a neat answer to a thorny problem. August was surely stealing all of Merry's money, so that she would be penniless, eventually dependent on John for the roof over her head. Meredith would never be offered a Season of her own, at least as long as August was alive, and would probably never leave the estate. Aloysius wanted more for Meredith than that. He also wanted John to put his passionate hatred for his father behind him and look forward to the life that stretched ahead of him.

It was what they all wanted. The Maxwells. Cluny and

Clancy. Honey. Gilda, and all the rest of the varied inhabitants of Coltrane House. Everyone wanted the best for both John and Meredith.

Cluny and Clancy, of course, were the most concerned of all. Like hens with just a single chick each, they protected, cosseted, amused, and generally had taken on the role of parents to Jack and Merry. Clancy had taken over Jack, and Cluny couldn't be pried loose from his adoration of Merry, even when she had put a frog in his bed.

Aloysius sighed, consigning his worries to the back of his brain. They had years to go before any of the problems he worried over could jump up and destroy the special affection these two children held for each other.

He closed the book he'd been holding, and placed it on the table in front of him. "All right, Miss Fairfax," he said, looking at the still-squirming child, "it's your turn, I suppose. I believe you've written a piece to recite?"

Merry grinned. It was a broad grin, in a small, narrow face. The child had a rare mouthful of brand-new, straight, white teeth—even if they were a bit large for her face at the moment—and when she grinned it was impossible not to grin along with her.

"Oh, yes, Mr. Bromley," she said now, hopping to her feet, a few sheets of bent and none-too-clean paper clutched in her hands. "I've found the grandest story." She turned to young John Coltrane. "You're going to love this story, Jack, I promise."

"Here we go," Jack said, rolling his eyes even as he leaned back in his hard chair, crossing one long leg over the other. "Are we up to it, do you suppose, Mr. Bromley? Another of Merry's *stories*?"

Merry shot him a look that warned him into silence. "Now," she said, standing beside her chair and shuffling importantly through the papers covered in her large, childish scrawl of misspelled and even made-up words, "if the *child* is done complaining, perhaps I shall be allowed to read?"

Aloysius covered his mouth with one fist, coughed. Old beyond her years, and much, much too intelligent. That was Meredith Fairfax. And John as well. No wonder he stayed on at Coltrane House with no thought of ever leaving. These were his children, his beloved children.

"Thank you," Merry said as, with a wave of his hand, Jack seemed to offer her the floor, if not his full attention. "Once upon a time," she began, hesitating only as Jack gave out with a theatrical groan, "there lived, quite near here, in Nottinghamshire to be exact, a most wonderful, courageous, intelligent, adventuresome—"

"That would be a paragon, Mr. Bromley, correct?" Jack interrupted, grinning. "It would also be boring."

"Robin Hood is *not* boring, Jack Coltrane," Merry exclaimed, giving him a hit on the shoulder with her rolled-up papers. "He was wonderful, and brave, and Maid Marian loved him and the people loved him, and he and his Merry Men took from the nasty rich and gave to the deserving poor, and . . . and, well it was wonderful! I can't think of anything more wonderful, and I only wish Robin Hood were here today, so I could ride with him and be one of his Merry Men."

"Merry, the Merry Man." Jack lifted his crossed hands over his head, to ward off her blows. "And you'd live in the forest and shoot the King's deer, and probably wear men's clothing along with it. Oh, what nonsense goes on inside your head, Merry. It's frightening, that's what it is."

Aloysius sighed, slowly got to his feet and clapped his hands so that they both came to attention, for at the heart of it they were good, obedient little savages. "Children, children. Enough. You're both dismissed for the day. Feel free to beat each other into flinders somewhere outside my schoolroom."

"Yes, Mr. Bromley," Merry said, dropping the tutor a curtsy. He'd tried to teach her how to be ladylike and feminine, but she was still all knees and elbows. He'd have to ask one of the others to take that part of her education in hand someday soon. Perhaps Lucy, the laundress? She'd once played Juliet, if he remembered correctly, although that had to have been a century ago.

"Come on, Merry," Jack prompted, yanking her unceremoniously to her feet and pulling her toward the door. "We're supposed to meet Kipp in the village at three."

"He's home, then?" Merry asked, skipping along beside Jack, not at all angry that he had made fun of her story. "I thought the term didn't end until next month. Was he sent down? Did he do something unforgivable? He told me at Christmas that he longed to be able to do something terrible enough to have himself sent down for a term. All the most ripping lads are sent down for at least one term, he said."

Jack shook his head. "His father's ill, Merry. His mother wrote that he must come home."

Merry stopped on the servant's stairs, sadly looking down at Jack, who had bounded ahead of her. "Oh, I didn't know. Is he very sick?"

Jack turned, looked up at her. "If you promise me you won't go running to Kipp and throwing yourself into his arms and—well, acting like a girl—I'll tell you."

Merry bit her bottom lip. "He's dying, then. Isn't he? Poor Kipp."

Jack ran a hand through his long, black hair, only idly wondering where the thin black ribbon that had held it in place had gotten to this time. "Yes, Merry. Kipp will be the new Viscount Willoughby within the month. Maybe less." His expression darkened. "There's Kipp, with a father he adores, and he's about to lose him. Me? I'm burdened with the worst father in the world, and the damned man will probably live forever."

She descended the steps until she was close enough to take Jack's hand, hold it to her cheek. "You can't wish your own father underground, Jack. That's a sin; Mr. Bromley says so. Wishing harm to somebody is as bad as doing harm to somebody. At least," she ended, smiling just a little, "that's what he said when I confided that I wished your father would break a leg and have to stay in London this summer. So I didn't wish it, and your father is here, even two months earlier than we'd expected. I hope you don't think his arrival was my fault."

Jack ruffled her already fairly tangled curls. "You're so simple, aren't you, Merry? Believing in fairy tales, not wishing bad to anyone, even my wretched father. If only I could be more like you."

She grabbed on to his arm, tripped along with him down the remainder of the stairs and out through the kitchens, to dance in front of him once they were outside. "But you can be, Jack," she exclaimed. "You don't have to be such a sourpuss. It isn't necessary, truly it isn't."

"Isn't it?" Jack asked, walking so quickly that Merry had to hike up her skirts and trot along, or else be left behind. There wasn't much she wouldn't do for Jack, and she certainly wouldn't be left behind simply because he was so caught up in one of his black moods that he didn't notice that he was running away from her. "He's destroying Coltrane House more and more each time he comes here. And now he comes in the spring, as well as in the summer. And always, always at Christmas. God, Merry, how I hate Christmas!"

Aloysius Bromley stood in front of an open window high above them, listening to Jack's anger exploding below him.

He watched as Merry ran alongside Jack through the long spring grass, trying to tease him out of his black humor. The tutor took a deep breath, letting it out slowly. Sadly. He wished there was something he could do. Something anyone could do.

But, in the end, all he and the others could do was to watch, and wait, until John Coltrane grew into his full manhood.

Because that's when the real trouble would start.

Chapter Five

It was autumn, one of the last warm days before the world
gently slipped into winter. Already the leaves were turning, some of them falling into the stream, swirling along,
caught in the mild current. The fourteen-year-old Merry's
world was pretty, as only Coltrane House could be, but it
would soon be very empty.

Jack would be leaving for his last year at school in a few
days. As happy as Merry was that Henry Sherlock had
somehow convinced Awful August that his son needed to be
sent away for his last bit of education, she already missed
him terribly. Not that Jack paid much attention to her when
he was home. Not that he had paid much attention to her at
all these past few years. At nearly twenty-one, he seemed to
have much more important things on his mind than spending time with her.

She bent, picked up a stone, skipped it once, twice, across
the top of the water, then watched it sink below the surface
several feet shy of the other shore. "Damn!"

"Mustn't swear, Merry. Your hair turns redder with every

naughty word." Jack reached out his hand, rubbing at her mop of tousled carroty curls, then he gave her head a playful push forward. "I figure it will all turn to fire any day now, and singe straight down to the roots. Better you should quote Shakespeare, as Cluny and Clancy have taught us. Let's see, what could you say about your prowess with a skipping stone? Oh, I know. A snippet of *Romeo and Juliet* seems right—'past hope, past cure, past help!' "

Merry turned to glare at Jack, a blistering retort on her lips, then smiled, her quick spurt of temper melting in the deep green pools of her beloved friend's eyes. He'd come to the stream, followed her, sought her out. How could she be angry with him? "Then show me how to do it, Jack," she pleaded, using her best wheedling voice and knowing that Jack never denied her anything, would never deny her anything.

"Again? I show you at least twice a year." He moved slightly behind her as she picked up another smooth, flat stone and held it in her right hand. "Oh, all right, Merry," he then agreed in mock fatigue, folding his hand over hers as their bodies came together, his taller, harder figure pressing against her slim back. "Position the stone just so—there, that's it. Now bend your wrist toward your belly, and thrust it out quickly, releasing the stone flatly—like this."

Merry watched as the stone hit the surface of the stream, dancing across it, once, twice, like a fashionable lady tiptoeing across a puddle-filled street and trying to keep her hem dry. She held her breath as the stone hit the third time, then released it in a rush as the stone skipped once more before landing safely on the other bank.

"We did it! We did it!" she exclaimed. She turned to all but leap into Jack's arms, her own thin ones clinging around his neck as she lifted her feet from the ground and allowed him to wheel her about in a full circle. "Ah, Jack, we can do *anything*."

His answering smile lit her world. Merry threw back her head and laughed, allowing him to swing her once more, and then again, until she was dizzy with the spinning, with the pleasure of being with her beloved Jack.

She slipped out of his arms and began picking up more stones, judging them for their worthiness as skipping stones. She began talking as fast as she could, keeping Jack by her side with her nonsense, trying to make him smile again. They talked of Cluny and Clancy, of the play their two good friends and the rest of the "company"—as the servants were called—would put on this very evening in honor of Jack's return to school. Merry kept talking and talking, lighting on any subject she could think of, anything at all she could say, anything that would keep him there with her.

And then she said too much.

She watched Jack's features grow hard as he sank down onto the bank, his elbows on his knees as he also seemed to be sinking into one of his black moods.

Merry sat down beside him, pressed her cheek against his shoulder, looked up into his face as she watched the darkness take him away from her. One moment they had been laughing, happy—purposely happy, doing their best to forget that Awful August was at Coltrane House. And the next Merry had done something young, and silly, and Jack's mood had plummeted. "I'm sorry, Jack," she said, wishing the slashing dimple back in his left cheek, knowing he'd have to smile for her to see it. "I shouldn't have said anything, even in jest."

He sliced her a look that showed that his eyes had turned to chips of cold green ice. "One of my father's guests pinched your . . . your—well, bloody hell! And you call telling me about it a *jest*?"

"If you'd let me finish my tale, yes," she said, sitting up and grabbing at his two hands, holding his so much larger ones between her own fairly dirty palms. "It was only that weasel-faced man, Jack. You know, the one who dresses all in black and spends his days snoring in the conservatory, too drunk to climb the stairs to his bedchamber? He pinched me, that's true enough—right on my bottom—as I was climbing up the stairs ahead of him this morning. He must have finally decided that his bed was more comfortable than the stone bench in the conservatory, I guess. And I didn't think, Jack. I didn't consider what Awful August might say. I simply kicked back my foot, and my heel landed firm on the fellow's nose. Poor Gilda is probably still scrubbing the weasel's blood from the stairs. Now, isn't that funny?"

Jack pulled his hands away from hers and clasped them tightly together in front of him, his knuckles turning white as he squeezed, probably imagining his father's guest's neck between his fingers. "I want to kill him. Kill my father. Kill them all." He turned to look at Merry and her heart skipped a beat, recognizing a new level of anger behind his eyes, tightening the skin across his cheekbones. "Why, Merry? Why do I spend my days hiding here at the stream, dreaming up revenges I'm not man enough to muster?"

Merry's bottom lip began to tremble, and she bit down on it for a moment, willing it still once more. "Because there is only one of you, Jack, and there are dozens of them. Awful August, his guests. What would you do, Jack, try to *muster* them all out of Coltrane House at the point of a single pistol or the lifting of a single fist? They'll be gone soon. They always are. You'll go off to school, and I'll sit and listen to Aloysius as he tells me about ancient Rome, and then Cluny will sneak me sugarplums as Clancy pushes vegetables at me, and the whole world will be as it was before your father's visit. We'll survive, Jack. We always have."

"It isn't enough!" Jack exploded to his feet, leaving Merry to scramble after him as he went walking straight into the stream, obviously in an attempt to cool his hot head. "You're his ward, Merry, and he doesn't even remember your existence, let alone think to protect you from those painted lechers he brings here with him. You're so young, so damnably innocent. You don't even know what could happen, do you? Well, I do. If one of them were to catch you alone, in one of the hallways—oh, bloody hell!"

He was knee-deep in the stream before his last explosive curse. He flung himself forward into the water, fully clothed, and fully hot, so hot Merry half expected to see steam rising from the water as his body made contact with it.

"I'd leave him here to drown," Merry told the birds and the trees as she kicked off her shoes and followed her friend into the water, "except that the water's no more than three feet deep, and even Jack Coltrane can't will himself to drown in a glass of water. Ah, well, if it's a cooling he wants, I suppose I can help him."

So saying, she threw her own slim body forward, closing her eyes as her body submerged. She stood up again quickly, gasping and gulping for air, the water being much colder than she'd first realized.

Pushing her long, wet hair from her eyes, she saw that Jack was now sitting on one of the rocks in the center of the stream, his own shoulder-length black hair gleaming ebony in the sunlight that filtered through the trees. He was laughing at her. "Look at you, Merry," he teased, shaking his head like a spaniel in an attempt to rid himself of water. "You look like a drowned fox. Not a rat, not with that hair. Whatever possessed you to jump in the water like that?"

She began walking toward him, hip-deep in the water that brushed past her in a slow, lazy current, feeling the drag of her too-short skirts against her calves. "I don't know, Jack. What possessed you to jump in the water?"

"I'm an idiot," he answered, grinning, so that she watched, enthralled, as the dimple showed in his left cheek. "I'm a bad-tempered, ill-favored, fast-acting, slow-thinking idiot."

She cocked her head to one side, shivering as a slight breeze kicked up and the air cooled her skin. "Fair enough. If you're an idiot, then I'm an idiot, too. As long as we can be idiots together. We always will be, won't we, Jack?"

"Be idiots?" he quipped, raising one dark eyebrow as he quite deliberately misunderstood her.

"Be together," she countered, leaning down to scoop up water with both hands, splashing at him so that he abandoned the rock and slipped into the water again, the better to splash back at her. "We must always be together, Jack," she said, her head turned to avoid the water flying at her head as he began advancing toward her. She kept up her own splashing, in self-defense. "I can't imagine life without you . . . you silly . . . wet . . . grumpypuss."

"Grumpypuss, is it?" Jack repeated, the strength and power of his splashes now reducing her to the point of covering her face in order not to drown while standing up. The years peeled back, to when they had been children together, and Merry believed she would never again be this happy.

And then, suddenly, Jack was right in front of her. He stopped splashing. Cursed low in his throat. She lowered her hands to her sides, looked at him curiously. He really was a grumpypuss. "*Now* what is the matter?" she asked, beginning to feel her own temper rise.

"Cover yourself," he said shortly, then walked past her, the current pulling against his legs. "Just for God's sake, cover yourself."

Merry didn't understand for a moment, then looked down

at herself, and saw what Jack had seen. Her stupid breasts, her stupid, stupid breasts which had begun to swell a year earlier, were plainly visible beneath her sopping-wet white dress. She hated what her body was doing to her, how it was changing her. Ever since she was twelve, when she'd begun to bleed and Mrs. Maxwell had explained that she was a woman now, Merry had noticed that Jack had begun avoiding her. And it wasn't fair. It wasn't her fault her body was doing this. Besides, what did Jack care about that? Surely these two stupid lumps on her chest couldn't change the way he felt about her?

"Jack?" she said, making her way back to the sloping bank, her arms crossed over her breasts. "Jack, please don't be mad."

He had his back to her, refused to turn around. "I'm not mad, Merry," he said, his voice kind, almost indulgent. "But there's something I have to do. You just stay here until your . . . until your dress dries, so that Mrs. Maxwell doesn't start clucking over you, all right?"

"But—"

"Merry, please," Jack said, cutting her off. "Just this once, do what I say."

"But you're not mad?" Merry was crying by then, stupid tears, but she had to ask the question.

"No, Merry, I'm not mad. I'll see you later, all right? And then, after you've bathed and changed, perhaps Kipp and I will show you how to shoot with a bow and arrow. Would you like to learn how to shoot, just like one of Robin Hood's Merry Men? I still remember how you admired that silly legend."

She nodded, unable to speak, then watched as he walked away, his fists clenched at his sides. Once he had disappeared into the trees, she sat down, put her head in her hands and cried.

She'd been wrong to tease him, wrong to tell him about the odious weasel, wrong to think she and Jack could be now as they once had been. She sniffled, wiping at her nose with the back of her hand. What was that quote Cluny had taught her just last week? Oh yes. It was a desperate cry from the Bard's *Richard II*: "O! call back yesterday, bid time return."

But Merry knew now that such a feat was impossible. No matter how you tried, the world moved forward. A boy grew into a man, and he left his childhood behind him. You could never call back yesterday.

"Well, that was interesting enough," Clancy said as he and Cluny tiptoed out of the trees, to watch as Jack all but ran across the lawns to the back of Coltrane House. " 'A Corinthian, a lad of mettle, a good boy.' That's my Jack, as I thought when first I saw him and will always say as we watch him grow into his manhood. But still a headstrong child in some ways, poor thing. He's off to think more black thoughts, I can feel it in my bones. It's because Awful August is in residence again, his boozy friends and painted women in tow. Jack's always at his darkest at times like these."

Cluny nodded enthusiastically. "It's Awful August's fault all right. Everything is his fault."

"Lewd, hasty-witted pignut," Clancy grumbled feelingly, enjoying the way the Bard's inspired curses combined in his mind. "Wenching, muddy-mettled moldwarp. Whoreson, sheep-biting clotpole. Ah, Cluny, didn't old Willie have a way with a good round of curses? Soothes a man no end, it does, to dance them off the tongue. Talk to me about the father some more, and I'll string a few more together. Liven up my day, you know."

"Later, Clancy," Cluny said, walking slowly, leaning

heavily on the cane he'd been forced to take up a year ago after a bad fall on the stairs. Clancy still had his health, if the rest of his hair had left him, but they were both feeling their years. Indeed, Clancy had even given up cooking the odd meal, handing that responsibility entirely over to Mrs. Maxwell. Which hadn't bothered Cluny, as the woman certainly did have a way with a joint of beef.

Now they spent their days resting, watching Jack and Merry grow, and worrying about the future. There were so many worries about the future.

The two of them had been sitting on the ground, unashamedly hiding, unashamedly eavesdropping. They'd followed Jack to the stream, hoping he would see Merry, hoping the two would talk, would learn to be easy with each other again. "It's always the same though, isn't it," Cluny said, sighing. "Jack will sulk and Merry will tease and, finally, Awful August and his band of drunkards will become bored with breaking the furniture and hie themselves back to London, leaving us all in peace again for a while."

Clancy bit his bottom lip, still watching Jack's long strides eating up the ground between the stream and the kitchen door. There was something about the angle of Jack's shoulders that set off warning bells in his brain. He began walking faster, wishing Cluny could move more quickly. "Do you really think so, Cluny? I don't know."

"We can only hope," Cluny said, then sighed again. "Did you see them, Clancy? A lovely sight, don't you think? The two of them, laughing and frolicking, just as they did years ago. As always for us, Clancy, dear Will said it best: 'It was a lover and his lass, with a hey, and a ho, and a hey non-ino.'"

"Hey and ho yourself, Cluny," Clancy replied, then absently cuffed his longtime friend's ear. "She's little more than a babe, and I saw him ogling the barmaid at the Hoop and Grapes just yesterday, his mind full of questions he's probably already had answered. Merry looks on him as a god, and he looks on her as she is. A child. We've years yet to wait for more than that, I fear. I only hope we live to see it."

Cluny sighed. "You heard what he said to her, how he reacted back there. No, Clancy, your Jack doesn't see Merry as a child. Not anymore, and not for some time. I think that's why he avoids her, don't you?"

Clancy rubbed at the end of his long, parrotlike beak of a nose. Then he shook his head. "No, you're wrong there, Cluny. He's not looking at her like *that*. She's only a child. Only fourteen, and much too young for him to think of her in that way."

"Exactly," Cluny said. "And the thought's as upsetting to your Jack as it is to you, I'll wager. Lord knows it's upsetting to me. I've asked Gilda to take her in hand, you know. Convince her to wash her face, cover her legs. Gilda knows a thing or two about walking, and talking, and dressing like a lady. Played Lady Macbeth three times, in Bath, even if that was twenty years ago. Yes, Clancy, it's time. Time my little angel grew up. Unless that scares your Jack even farther away, the poor confused boy."

Clancy opened his mouth, undoubtedly to defend Jack from Cluny's suggestion that he was little more than a boy, then promptly forgot what he was going to say as a loud crash echoed from the direction of Coltrane House. Clancy looked up at the house just in time to see two bodies land on the patio outside the Main Saloon as a hail of broken glass from the splintered and shattered French doors showered down on top of them.

"*Jack*! Damme, but I should have known it!" Clancy

cried, already breaking into a creaking run. "Come on, Cluny—Jack's in trouble!"

Trouble might have been too mild a word, as both men saw when they stepped onto the patio to see Jack straddling one of Awful August's guests. He was holding the man by the front of his shirt as he slammed his fist into his face, over and over again.

"It's the weasel," Clancy said, holding his side as he struggled to catch his breath, and looking down at the man who was dressed all in black, just as Merry had described him. "Jack, stop!"

But Jack wasn't listening. "Never . . . touch her," he was saying to the man, gritting the words out from between clenched teeth, punctuating his words with the rise and fall of his fist. "Never . . . never . . . never."

"Lor' 'ave mercy, 'e's killin' 'im!" one of the females crowded around the edge of the patio screamed. "Save my Bertie, somebody, save 'im!"

Clancy didn't know where he got the strength to pull Jack off the man he was beating so mercilessly. Between the two of them, he and Cluny dragged Jack away and led him to the stables.

"He *touched* her, Clancy," Jack told him, clearly as miserable and frustrated as he was angry. "God! How could I have let this happen? She's not safe, Clancy. Not anymore. Christ—you should have let me kill him!"

Cluny saddled a horse while Clancy spit on his handkerchief, then wiped at Jack's bloody lip. "And then what, Jack? Watch you hang? What happened to Merry wasn't your fault, but what will happen to you if you stay here would break this old man's heart, and Merry's as well. Listen to me. We can give you a purse, Jack. Enough to get you back to school. Mrs. Maxwell will send your bags after you.

But you have to go. You have to go now, before your father hears what you did."

"I can't, Clancy," Jack told him, his chest rising and falling rapidly as he tried to regain his breath. His clothes were still wet from the stream, and there were bits of broken glass stuck to him. Not that he seemed to notice. He looked back toward the house. "It's Merry. I—I can't leave her. Not like this. August will—"

"He'll do nothing, Jack," Cluny said, handing Jack a slim purse holding just enough coins to get him a meal or two on his way back to school. He'd have to sleep under the hedgerows, but if that was the only price he had to pay for his hotheaded behavior, the boy should count himself lucky. "Your father will yell and curse and drink himself blind, and then forget this ever happened. I promise you. Here, take this. I'm going to head off Merry before she comes back to the house, take her to Lady Willoughby for safekeeping until your father goes back to London. Your friend Kipp's mother will help us. I'm sure of it."

"No, I'm not going," Jack said, as Clancy brought up the horse Cluny had saddled, motioning for Jack to mount. "Don't you understand? He touched her, Clancy. That greasy son of a dog *touched* her. *Nobody* touches Merry! I had every right to hit him."

"Aye, boy, that you did, that you did," Clancy said soothingly, pushing a thick lock of wet hair back from Jack's sweat-slick brow. "And you did a fine job of it, too. But now cooler heads must rule, and it's time for you to go. Come back when you can, but not for Christmas, not when your papa's here. We'll be fine, Jack. We always are. And you'll write to us, and we'll write to you."

Clancy saw the tears in Jack's eyes, tears the boy would not allow to fall. Tears of anger, of frustration, wrung from the deepest regions of his heart. "Why, Clancy? Why is it always like this? Will it always be like this?"

"No, son," Clancy told him, pulling him into his embrace. Jack was nearly a half head taller than he now, but he was still his boy, his brave lad. "One day Coltrane House will be yours, and you can set it all to rights. You'll see. Now go. For the love I bear you, Jack, go now."

Chapter Six

Jack stood just outside the Coltrane House stables and remembered the day he'd beaten his father's guest into a jelly. That was before he had been persuaded to run away, to hide himself at school until his father forgot the incident.

He shouldn't have gone. He should have stayed. He should have finished with the man who'd dared to touch Merry, then gone hunting for his father while the fire of hate still raged in his belly. Finished it. Finished it all.

Instead, he had run. Run to school. Run to London with Kipp. Run away from Coltrane House.

Run away from Merry.

Instead, Henry Sherlock had written to him at school, laid out August's new rules for his son, and Jack had obeyed them. Henry had made sure that August had paid off Bertram Hager, the man Jack had beaten, and the incident was to be forgotten. Kipp's mother had agreed to shelter Merry at Willoughby Hall for as long as Henry thought advisable.

In return, Jack was to be banished from Coltrane House,

from Lincolnshire itself, for a full year, and kept to an allowance that barely fed and clothed him. If it hadn't been for Kipp's generosity, housing him in London between school terms, Jack would have been reduced to begging on the streets.

But he'd lasted out the year, somehow. It had been the longest year of his life. And yet, that year had taught him patience, which was not a bad lesson for the hotheaded young man to learn. He'd bided his time, done his penance, and he'd come home. He'd finished with school, if only because he'd promised Clancy and Mr. Bromley that he would. He was wiser to the ways of the world and more than ready to devote himself to his beloved Coltrane House. He was not quite twenty-two years old.

He'd walked in the front door, a year to the day since he'd left, to be personally greeted by his father. August had greeted Jack warmly, clapped an arm around his shoulders, then led him into the Main Saloon with the offer of a glass of wine. Jack hadn't been able to believe it, couldn't assimilate this change in his father. Had the man mellowed? Had he finally seen that he had a son, a son who still wanted to *be* a son, a son who had missed a father's love for all of his nearly two and twenty years?

And was it too late? Jack had wanted to hate his father, had hated his father. And yet, with this simple offer of friendship, of welcome, he had felt all his defenses crumbling. Difficult as it was to believe, he seemed now to be the Prodigal Son, and he was being welcomed home.

How pathetically stupid he had been, Jack thought now, remembering what had happened next.

August's welcome had lasted only until the doors to the Main Saloon shut behind him. He turned to his father questioningly as he heard the key being turned in the lock. A moment later, two hulking men Jack hadn't seen were holding tight to his arms, and his father's beefy fist had slammed into his stomach. His breath left him in a *whoosh*, and his knees buckled. He was powerless to defend himself.

"Bastard! Whoreson!" his father had screamed, hitting him again and again. "I've waited a year for this. Ungrateful whelp! Welcome you home, he said. I'll welcome you home! I should have strangled you at birth!"

They took turns hitting him, the three men, and when they'd tired of hitting him, they'd kicked him. Jack's nose had broken. He'd heard the crack of two ribs when he couldn't guard himself quickly enough from his father's boot, and he'd finally lost consciousness.

Jack had been confined to his bed for more than a month, locked away at August's orders, with only Clancy allowed to attend him. The old man had wept over him, tended his wounds, then finally explained what had happened, and why.

Merry, Clancy had reported—as Jack's first question had been about her—had once more been taken from Coltrane House. Cluny had dragged her, fighting and crying uncontrollably, all the way to Lady Willoughby's, where she would remain, under lock and key if necessary, until August left for London. And the blasted man was stubbornly remaining in residence, hosting a succession of wild parties that threatened to be the final fall of Coltrane House.

August Coltrane, Clancy had also reluctantly confided, had been soundly threatened the same day Jack had ridden away from Coltrane House, threatened by none other than Jack's rackety friend Kipp. It seemed bizarre, but Kipp *was* Viscount Willoughby, after all, for all his youth and apparent silliness. As viscount, he had ridden to Coltrane House the moment Cluny arrived at Willoughby Hall a year ago with a frightened Merry in tow. Kipp had warned August that he would destroy him in London society if he did not forgive his son, allow him to finish his schooling, then welcome him home.

August's reputation in London was not all that wonderful in the first place. It wouldn't have taken more than the viscount's condemnation of his Lincolnshire neighbor, a few stories about how he abused his son and neglected his ward, to have August Coltrane dropped from nearly every invitation list during the Season. Especially, Clancy had pointed out, since the Coltrane heir had been so openly welcomed into the viscount's London mansion.

Kipp had sworn Cluny and Clancy to secrecy, and never said a word to Jack himself, had never dropped so much as a hint about the steps he'd taken to help his friend. But even Kipp couldn't have foreseen what August had been planning by way of that "welcome" when Jack was finally allowed home once more.

Jack had recovered from the beating, at least physically, but vowed never to forget it. His reflection would always remind him, as his once straight nose now had a slight bend to it. But that had been a small price to pay for learning, for once and for all time, that his father would never accept him, never love him. He'd once believed that when he grew older, grew up, his father would have time for him. That hadn't been the case. Not when he was ten, not when he was fifteen, not when he'd turned twenty-one.

Now, at twenty-four, looking back at the years before and since his beating, Jack found it hard to believe he'd ever been so young or naive as to long for his father's approval. He could only be thankful that the man had seemed to forget him again entirely these past years.

Clancy had told him that was because August, never a fastidious man when it came to the women he chose to bed, had suffered once too often from the pox. The man's mind was going. What little remained of that mind was more often than not clouded with strong drink. In fact, the raucous house parties at Coltrane House had grown tamer, populated less by lowborn women and more by dedicated drinkers and gamblers. The candles in the Main Saloon burnt down to nubs each night Awful August was in residence, as the cards were dealt around the tables.

Jack and Henry Sherlock now ran Coltrane House between them. More and more, Henry took charge of the books, the finances, and Jack oversaw the estate by himself. He rode the fields every day, with Merry more often than not tagging along. At seventeen, she was still making a nuisance of herself, still refusing to see that it was time for her to grow up, begin wearing dresses and not his old breeches. It was time for her to pin up her hair, learn to be a lady, and to for God's sake leave him alone.

Lady Willoughby, good woman that she was, had thrown up her hands in defeat two years ago, declaring Merry a sweet girl, but a total loss when it came to gentle, feminine pursuits. All she wanted to do was to be with Jack, and Jack was always working on the estate. It was a large problem to Jack, and one he did not know how to solve.

"I don't see why Merry couldn't come along," Kipp said now, bringing Jack back to the moment. The moment, the stableyard, and the mission.

Jack gave his gelding's cinch a final check, then turned to his friend. "Oh, yes. I can see your point, Kipp. We're going out to do robbery, quite possibly stick our heads in a noose, and you think Merry might enjoy being one of our party. Of course. Tell you what. You stay here with the horses, and I'll go ask her. She always wanted to ride with Robin Hood, as I recall."

Kipp flushed as he ran a hand through his stylishly brushed blond locks. "You're right, Jack," he admitted, taking his horse's bridle and leading the bay mare out of the stables. "It's just that she's so convincing when she says she'll be a help and not a bother."

"Merry's seventeen, Kipp. The only thing she knows is how to be a bother. In fact, she's quite good at it."

"Only because she loves you, Jack," Kipp told him, grinning. "Not that you can see her worth spit, not when we've just come back from London and the fair Miss Wilkins is still very much on your mind. Does Merry know?"

Jack shook his head. "No, Kipp, she doesn't know. Not unless you've been running that tongue of yours on wheels again."

Kipp's laughter rang rich and deep. "You'd be referring, I suppose, to my quite innocent slip of the tongue last year. The one concerning you and the night you fell headfirst into that decanter of brandy?"

"Among others, yes. She all but broke down my door that night, Kipp. She even offered to hold my head as I leaned over the slop bucket, my stomach turning inside out."

"Because she loves you, you lucky dog. Or have you lost your ability to see real beauty when it's waved right in front of your nose? That hair, that face—those long, long legs. And so innocent with it all. A young bud, just bursting into bloom. I doubt she even knows how desirable she is."

Jack felt his temper rising, tried to tamp it down. "She's my sister, Kipp."

His friend looked at him levelly, all traces of humor gone from his handsome face. "No, Jack, she's not. And she knows it, even if you stubbornly refuse to admit that truth to yourself. Among other truths." Seeing by Jack's face that he was getting nowhere, Kipp tried another tack. "So, are you going to offer for Miss Wilkins?"

"Offer her what, Kipp?" Jack asked, the old bitterness always close to the surface. "I work on this land like any laborer. I travel to London once a year with you, shamefully sponging on your charity. I can't help Merry, I can't save Coltrane House, and I play stupid, dangerous games to keep from going mad. Is that what you want me to offer Elizabeth Wilkins, Kipp? Somehow I doubt she'd be flattered."

Jack swung gracefully into the saddle, not bothering to mention one more thing to his friend—that he didn't really even like Elizabeth Wilkins all that much. None of the women he'd met, none of the women he'd bedded, ever had been of that much interest to him. "Now, come on. I want us to be in position before it grows any darker."

"Oh, that wasn't kind, calling my Merry a bother," Cluny said, as he and Clancy stepped out from their hiding place between two stalls. He clutched both hands to his chest at the insult. " 'These words are razors to my wounded heart.' "

Clancy eyed his companion owlishly. "Jack only talks that way about Merry because he doesn't want Kipp to know how much he loves her. He does, you know. But she can be a bit of a pest. Admit it now, Cluny. She can."

Cluny hung his head. "She didn't set out to catch Jack kissing that flashy Molly Burns behind the stables. That's the last time we hire on a Covent Garden dancer for a season, and that's no lie."

"No, I suppose Merry didn't mean to see that. He didn't speak to her for a week, as I recall. Now, come on, Cluny. They've already got a good start on us, and we don't want to miss the fun. Or are you going to stay behind and watch over Merry's every move, like you usually do when Jack's father is here? As if she needs guarding, the little imp. Did you see her pull that pistol on Awful August's fat friend yesterday when he tried to kiss her? Ah, Jack wouldn't be happy if he could know that."

"She long ago learned not to carry those tales to his ears. Not after what happened the last time," Cluny reminded his friend as they retrieved two already-saddled horses from behind the stables. "Why, Awful August and those two louts might have killed the boy if we hadn't broken down the door and rescued him."

Clancy nodded, sighed. "I thought it was over then, Cluny. I thought Jack would leave for good, once he could walk again. But not my Jack, Cluny, not my Jack! Even then he didn't run. 'Fight till the last gasp.' That's my Jack, just like one of Old Will's best heroes. Now let's get to it, take ourselves off to our usual hiding place."

Cluny hobbled over to the mounting block and hauled himself into the saddle. His hip pained him when he walked, but hurt less when he was on horseback. Clancy, however, had never quite mastered riding, although he would have ridden to the edge of hell and beyond to watch over Jack. "I'm right behind you, Clancy," Cluny said, grinning as he watched Clancy's skinny rump begin to bump up and down, totally out of rhythm with that of his similarly saggy mount. " 'Over hill, over dale, thorough bush, thorough brier, over park, over pale, thorough—' "

Clancy turned his head, grimaced. "Oh, for God's sake man, just ride the bloody horse."

Chapter Seven

Jack sat with his back against a tree just at the edge of the road. Earlier on, he had settled on this vantage point to give a clear, unobstructed view of the roadway for a mile or more as it wended its way downhill, in the direction of Coltrane House.

"I'll miss this when it's finally over," Kipp said as he sat down beside him. He drew on a slim cheroot he secretly believed made him look more the Viscount Willoughby and less like a child playing at filling his beloved late father's boots. "Moonlight rides, the thrill of the thing. And the masks. I definitely enjoy the masks, even if you won't let me do more than watch your back from the bushes. The lone highwayman—so romantic to the ladies, and all of that. Who's our target? Who is silly enough to leave Coltrane House at dusk, rather than at midday? Not that I don't appreciate the romance of a moonlit robbery. And what did he take with him as payment for your father's gambling debt?"

Jack took the cheroot from his friend and stuck it between his own teeth. "Baron Hartley," he bit out, his eyes narrowing into slits. "He was too drunk to leave earlier. As to your other question, the good baron took a liking to the silver candlesticks in the morning room, among a few other things."

"Like what?"

"Honey Maxwell," Jack told him, grinning rather wickedly around the cheroot. "She doesn't, however, return his admiration. Nor do Honey's parents believe that their daughter is a Coltrane possession, and therefore to be bartered in exchange for a fistful of IOUs." The smile faded. "Which didn't keep the good baron from dragging her into his coach and setting a guard on her, awaiting his departure. Whether he's planning to take her all the way to London with him or just use her and discard her somewhere along the way—well, not that it matters. Not when the Forfeit Man rides."

"Bastard," Kipp said, shaking his head. "And your father allows it."

"My father *encourages* it, Kipp, as you well know." Jack handed the cheroot back to his friend as he stood up, stretched his long, lean frame. "It's the only way he can settle his gambling debts now that Henry has begun cleverly telling him that the estate is near bankruptcy and that the house cannot be mortgaged another time. The pity of it is, Henry's almost right. For all the income the estate generates, there's barely a penny left after my father's *expenses* are paid. The house is close to falling down around our ears."

"Maybe he'll die soon," Kipp said, shrugging. "He certainly doesn't look well, does he? Merry says his eyes are beginning to turn yellow, like egg yolks. It won't be long now, Jack."

"Yes, Kipp, it probably won't. And, damned as I am for wishing my own father underground, I can't wait. Henry's told me about August's will, and everything is to come to me. Not because August loves me. Oh, no. I'm sure he plans to laugh all the way to hell at the thought of leaving me as heir to a ruined house and his mountain of debt. And I'll have Merry's guardianship, of course. At least she'll gain the inheritance from her father once she's twenty-one."

"Do you really think there's anything left of Merry's money?" Kipp asked.

"There must be some monies he hasn't been legally able to touch. She'll have her rightful inheritance, Kipp," Jack said tightly, "if I have to mortgage my soul to get it for her. She'll have her money, a Season in London, the chance of a suitable marriage—everything I can give her. God knows she deserves no less."

"And that's what she wants?" Kipp shook his head. "I love you, Jack. I love you like a brother. But you're a blind ass."

Jack ignored his friend, not wanting to start an argument. He stood up, walked out of the trees and onto the roadway for a better look at his "inheritance" as it began to melt into the dark.

Coltrane House, with its seventy-five rooms and extensive gardens, was the most beautiful building in Lincolnshire. This Jack believed, had grown up believing. He loved his home, the house that had once been so grand, the lands that still were, thanks to Henry Sherlock's good management and Jack's own hard work.

There might have been no title attached to Coltrane House, but that hadn't kept its wellborn owners from creating one of the finest estates in the country. And one of the most profitable. That is until Jack's father had inherited the estate and immediately set about recklessly spending or gambling away every penny he could find or borrow.

Now, and for several years, there had been a new twist added to his father's reckless behavior. He had begun giving bits of Coltrane House away, exchanging them for payment of his ever-increasing gambling debts.

Now, after doing their best to destroy everything Jack loved, his father's guests took their leave—and more than that. They took away silver. They took away portraits. They carried off linen tablecloths and china figurines. They all but waddled out of the house under the weight of their treasures, with August laughing and helping them carry the bulk of the booty.

Rape. There was no other word for it. Several times a year, and for as long as Jack could remember, one way or the other his father had been raping Coltrane House. Stealing his heritage. Robbing the Coltrane name of everything but shame.

For too many years, Jack had been forced to look on. Watching. Helpless to do anything. Too young. Too weak. Powerless.

That had all changed the first day Jack had been able to hobble down the stairs after his beating, after August and his friends had returned once more to London. He'd walked through the house, stepping over broken bottles, surveying all the damage August had done to Coltrane House during Jack's yearlong absence.

Each room he entered bore testament to August's madness. Walls were stained or wallpaper ripped from them. Bullet holes riddled the woodwork. Furniture was missing, carpets had been rolled up, carried away. Even Jack's mother's portrait, that had hung in the music room, hadn't been spared. The frame was gone, probably hanging now in some London town house, but the portrait had been cut from the frame, nailed to the wall and used for target practice. The obscene placement of the bullet holes forced Jack to turn his head away. He had fallen to his knees, still weak from his injuries, and wept.

He could no longer excuse his father or deceive himself. He could no longer pretend that one day things would be better, that one day the man would wake up, realize the extent of his recklessness. By the time the old man died, there would be nothing left. Nothing. Not inside Coltrane House. Not inside Jack.

He had finally seen enough, suffered enough, gotten mad enough to strike back. He had been powerless far too long.

But no longer. By God, no longer!

First on his own, and then later with Kipp coming along to help, Jack had clothed himself in the black cape of a highwayman and gone out onto the roads. He waited for his father's guests as they drove back toward London, Coltrane booty stuffed in with their luggage. And he took back what was his.

The Forfeit Man. That was the silly, romantic name Kipp had given him, and the name that now was whispered in taverns. Stories of his exploits had taken on a dimension that was as untrue as it was flattering. Because Jack only took what was his—and his victims' purses, of course, just so that he wouldn't raise suspicion that he was anything more, or less, than a highwayman.

He'd robbed more than a dozen coaches so far, although local legend had it that he'd robbed twice that number. He hid away the Coltrane House booty in the attics and left the pilfered purses on the church steps. The whole adventure immensely tickled Kipp, who had a romantic flair, and nothing to lose. It wasn't his home that was being desecrated.

"I see dust. The coach will be climbing the hill in another two minutes," Jack said, shaking off his dark mood as he pulled a black mask down over his face. He touched his hands to the brace of pistols tucked into his trousers.

He'd picked this spot two miles from Coltrane House with care, because of the vantage point it gave him, and because the heavily loaded coaches had to slow considerably as they climbed the long hill to the sharp turn at the top. This made it easier for him to jump out from the trees and bellow the standard "Stand and deliver!" while brandishing his pistols. He'd do better with his gelding beneath him, he knew, but Macbeth was entirely too recognizable and Jack's personal funds, being close to nil, didn't run to buying a horse just for these odd moments of larceny.

Still, he'd been more than reasonably successful. Especially after his first, bumbling attempt, when the coachman had nearly laughed himself into a fit as he drove past, his passengers not in the least disturbed by the sight of a highwayman who could do no more than quickly dive into the trees or be run down by the coach.

Yes, now he was experienced. Much better at his craft. The costume helped, black capes, slouch hats, and full face masks being quite impressive by and large. And the pistols hadn't hurt, nor his rather singular height and commanding voice. Mostly, learning how to roll a log onto the roadway, blocking the coaches, had been his most successful idea.

All in all, he might even be said to enjoy himself on these daring excursions, except that he wouldn't admit that, even to himself.

He was on a mission. He was preserving Coltrane House. And he'd continue to do so until his father either dropped dead of an apoplexy, or he killed the man when the bastard went too far in one of his drunken sprees.

"One minute," Jack said, as Kipp took up his own position on the second branch of a nearby tree, his pistol at the ready even as he was hidden by the leaves.

They were ready.

Cluny and Clancy were also ready. They crouched low on the opposite side of the roadway, safely out of sight as they settled back to watch the Forfeit Man at work. They were equally prepared to step in and help if any assistance might be required—if their rheumatism let them, of course.

"Uh-oh," Cluny whispered suddenly, nudging Clancy in his skinny ribs. " 'But soft! what light through yonder window breaks? It is the east, and Juliet is the sun!' "

Clancy screwed up his long, thin face and gaped at his companion. "What the devil are you talking about?" he whispered back at the man. "What yonder? What window?"

"Over there," Cluny whispered, pointing to a tree some ten feet away. "Look up, into the branches. Can't you see her? It's Merry. Now, what do you suppose she thinks she's doing?"

"Merry? Where?" Clancy strained to see through the shadows. "Oh, wait, I see her. There she is. Well, isn't this above everything wonderful?" he spit sarcastically, still remembering to keep his voice low. "You should have stayed with her, Cluny. Locked the door. Thrown away the key. She's mischief, sure as we're sitting here. Jack's not going to like this." He turned to Cluny, giving him a push. "Well? Don't just sit there, your mouth hanging open. Go to the girl. Tie her to the tree. *Something*."

Cluny sighed deeply, knowing he had to do his duty. "All right, all right. I'm going." He put a hand to his breast, took a deep breath, and recited sorrowfully, " 'Good night, good night! parting is such sweet sorrow, that I shall say good night till it be morrow.' "

"No wonder they ran us out of Brighton," Clancy muttered under his breath. "That was pitiful." He watched as Cluny moved off, bent low over his paunch, leaning on his cane, but stepping carefully, quietly. They were getting too old for this, Clancy decided. Much too old for this.

Cluny made his way to the tree, then stood up, all but plastered himself to the back of the wide trunk, out of sight of the road, out of sight of Merry. Then he looked to Clancy, spread his hands, shook his head. "Now what do I do?" he mouthed silently.

Not that Merry probably would have heard him at any rate. Her concentration was obviously all directed toward Jack. Cluny edged around the tree trunk a few steps, looked up into the branches. Merry, he saw, had dressed herself in fairly dramatic black shirt and breeches. Her flaming hair was tucked under a toque cap, and the naughty child bore streaks of coal black on her cheeks, forehead, nose, and chin.

Definitely dressed for mischief, Cluny decided. Definitely, unlike Clancy and himself, planning to be more than an interested observer. Definitely on the hunt for Trouble, with a capital T.

And then he saw the worst of it. With one hand clamped over his mouth to stifle his gasp of alarm, he bent low once more, made his way back through the underbrush to Clancy's side. "She's got a pistol tucked into her waistband," he announced, his voice trembling. "That can't be good, can it?"

"A pistol?" Clancy blanched, so that his cheeks almost seemed to glow in the growing moonlight. "And she'll use it, sure as check, no thanks to Jack for teaching her how. 'That would hang us, every mother's son.' We have to stop her."

"How?"

Clancy winced as he heard the coach approaching. "I don't know. Gag her, tie her, pull her out of that tree and sit on her! Do *something*."

But it was already too late. And all Cluny and Clancy could do was to watch.

Good things happen seldom, usually one at a time, and spread over long years, so that the persons these good things happen to are of a mind to appreciate them. Bad things, however, Clancy had long ago decided, tend to occur in bunches, all but falling over themselves in their haste to pour cold water or hot oil on the poor souls who are the recipients of these tumbling catastrophes.

Such was the case as the coach appeared. The fallen log became obvious, and the coachman hauled on the reins. Jack stepped into the middle of the roadway while the horses were still plunging to an unexpected halt and called out loudly: "Stand and deliver!"

The coachman, not a timid sort, said something on the order of, "The divil, you say!" He raised up an evil-looking blunderbuss, prepared to blast Jack into his more heavenly incarnation.

At which point, having impatiently waited through far too many robberies to count, an eager Kipp gave out with a mighty yell and leapt from the tree branch even while firing one of his pistols. The ball whizzed close by the coachman's left ear.

Which caused Jack to momentarily forget himself enough to look in Kipp's direction.

Which gave the feisty coachman new heart, so that he lowered the blunderbuss once more, aiming straight at Jack's chest.

Which caused Merry to scream, then topple from her perch on the tree branch and fall hard to the ground. The scream, a prodigiously loud, piercing scream, begun while she was sitting on the branch, continued until she unceremoniously hit the ground with a bump, at which point all her wind was knocked out of her.

The bark of the pistol, Merry's scream, and perhaps even the loud "bump," caused the already-agitated horses to attempt to bolt.

Which caused the coachman, who had neglected to set

the brake, to tumble into the bottom of the foot box, the reins dragging between the traces.

The front coach wheels hit the log with some force and, unfortunately, not straight on. Things quickly coming to their inevitable conclusion, the coach performed as anyone could have predicted. It slowly toppled onto its side in the roadway even as Jack, ever brave if not always prudent, leapt to grab the off-leader's harness in an attempt to quiet the frantic horses.

The horse reared. Jack fell, his shoulder dealt a glancing blow by one flailing hoof. Merry, having regained her breath, screamed once more. Kipp leveled his second pistol at the large, roaring drunk, mad-as-fire Baron Hartley who was just then climbing up and out of the coach. Meanwhile, inside the coach, a vocal Honey was doing her best to outscream Merry.

Clancy, ever protective of his dearest Jack, broke from the trees and leapt in front of the off-leader, waving his hands, and warning, "Stubble yourself, you fly-bitten, guts-griping horn-beast!"

The horse, already nearly mad with fear, rolled its red-rimmed eyes and redoubled its efforts to be free of this terrible place and pounding off down the roadway.

"Oh, that wasn't wise, Clancy, was it?" Cluny said, as he helped Merry to her feet. She looked at him dumbly for a moment, then shook off his grip and ran to rescue Jack.

"Take the reins! Take the reins!" she shrieked.

Kipp shifted his wide-eyed gaze from Baron Hartley, to the panicked horses, to Jack, who was still lying on the ground, his bent arms protecting his head from flying hooves as he tried to roll himself out of danger.

Clancy bent to help Jack, and was struck on the back by the horse. He staggered a few steps, looked at Cluny, and then collapsed onto the ground.

The action became even more furious.

Kipp threw down his useless pistol and climbed up and over the coach wheel, then dropped between coach and horses without a thought to his own safety, doing his best to catch up the reins.

Honey's head appeared beside Baron Hartley's in the opened doorway. Resourceful as any country miss, she then bopped him neatly on his head with her wooden clog, sending his lordship to blinking and weaving. A second hit succeeded in rolling the man's eyes in his head, and he slowly sank back inside the coach.

Kipp got hold of the reins, shouting out his success just as Merry threw herself under the horse's hooves, obviously planning to protect Jack with her own body. She wasn't nonsensical, but she was young, and believed herself to be immortal, as most young people do.

Cluny, who had run fast as he could to help his friend, let go of the upright but staggering Clancy and ordered Merry to stand back, to get herself out of the way.

Clancy took two tottering steps before his long body folded up rather gracefully, and he sank to the ground once more.

The off-leader struck out yet again, Merry fell, and Jack grabbed at her, rolling the both of them clear.

"Merry!" Jack shouted, pulling the toque from her head so that her long red hair streamed out onto the ground. "For God's sake, Merry, open your eyes!"

Cluny was beside Jack, also bent low, looking at the rapidly purpling bruise near Merry's temple. He wrung his hands, then shouted in relief as his darling girl opened her eyes. "Her hair," he exclaimed. "God bless that thick mop—it's all that saved her."

Merry blinked a time or two, moaned only once as Jack

cradled her in his arms, cursing her and begging her to speak to him, tell him she was all right.

She lifted a hand to touch his face, smiled. "I'm fine, Jack," she told him. "Really." And then she lost consciousness.

Which, as the unimaginably unhappy end to this tumble of bad luck and worse fortune approached, might have been a good thing. Because that's when Awful August and a dozen of his cronies arrived on the scene . . . and all hell broke loose.

Chapter Eight

Merry closed her eyes as Honey pressed a cool, wet cloth against her temple, willing away the headache that had already served to turn her stomach a half dozen times.

"He hates me, I know it," she told the maid miserably, wishing there was only one Honey standing over her, and not two. "And he blames me for everything. I could see it in his eyes. And I don't blame him. If I hadn't screamed . . ." Her voice trailed off on a sigh.

The maid clucked her tongue and shook her head, removing the cloth and dipping it into the bowl of cold water once more. "It wasn't all your fault. You're just lucky you didn't break your brain, Missy. Break it clean in two. And it's a bleeding pity you didn't think to look at what I was about, because you didn't see me tap that awful baron on the head and send him sleeping. Did my heart a world of good, that did. Taking me to London, was he? I think not!"

Merry didn't bother explaining to Honey that the maid had been used as a pawn, an added incentive meant to flush the Forfeit Man out into the open. Honey was feeling more than a little heroic, and after her frightening experience in the coach with the baron, she deserved to feel good about what she'd done.

But Merry had been lying here on her bed for hours and hours, and if she wasn't yet seeing quite clearly, her mind had been tripping along at a furious rate. Awful August had planned the whole thing. He'd sent the baron and Honey out as bait and he'd come up with the Forfeit Man. He'd come up with Jack, his own son.

And, Merry remembered, shivering at the memory, Awful August had seemed quite pleased with himself as they'd arrived back at Coltrane House. No, he'd been beyond pleased. He'd appeared to be absolutely delighted. Perhaps even vindicated.

Honey had already told her that Cluny was busy caring for the injured Clancy, and that Jack and Kipp both were locked up in Jack's bedchamber, with two hulking guards posted outside the door so that nobody could get close to them. The men had been on guard all the night long while August and his friends drank and laughed in the Main Saloon, celebrating their victory over the Forfeit Man.

But now it was morning. Morning, and the time for reckoning. How would Awful August punish them? Merry bit her lip and took a deep breath, then forced herself to sit up as she heard the door to her bedchamber open.

Honey dropped a quick curtsy, mumbled, "Sir," and then all but flew toward the dressing room as Awful August entered the room. Merry wasn't surprised. Her guardian was three-parts drunk, reeling where he stood, but he still had the power in his large body to frighten more than just a young girl.

He glared at Honey with his black, dead eyes. "Come back here, girl," he bellowed, causing Merry's head to split in two just as Honey had predicted, so that her brains fell out onto the mattress. Or at least that's how it felt. He pointed an accusing finger at Merry. "I want this ungrateful child's face scrubbed and her body dressed in her best gown. Then I want her downstairs in the Main Saloon. In thirty minutes. Not a second more. Do you understand?"

"Yes, sir," Honey whimpered, twisting her hands in her apron. "But—but she doesn't exactly *have* a best gown, sir."

Merry looked at her guardian out of the corners of her eyes, watching as his normally sallow face turned an angry puce. "What concern of mine that is? Wrap her in a sheet. Roll her up in a rug, damn it! But have her downstairs in half an hour. My plan is going forward nicely, and I wish to be on the road to London by noon."

The door slammed shut behind his departing bulk, and Merry motioned that Honey should hand her the bowl— quickly. After being sick to her stomach yet again, she allowed Honey to wash her face free of the last traces of coal black. Then she stood as still as she could, swaying only slightly as the maid stripped her, then dressed her in the best gown of a badly fitting bunch. The gown was of heavy kerseymere and pulled across her breasts, the hem falling four inches short of her ankles.

"He's sending you to jail, that's what he's doing," Honey wailed, wiping her eyes between fits of misbuttoning Merry's gown. "Oh, he's a hard-hearted man, he is for sure. He'll probably horsewhip Master Jack before he sends him off to the hangman. Lord knows he could do that, horror that he is. And Cluny and Clancy are shut up in their room, with my da and the rest of the men locked up in the cellars. I didn't tell you that, but you should know it. Lord knows what'll happen to them. You should run, Missy, that's what you should do. Run away, run as fast as you can."

Merry lifted her hands to her temples and gently rubbed

her fingertips against her skin. "If any of that was meant to make me brave, Honey, I'm afraid you've failed." She gave the maid a kiss, then patted her cheek. "I can't run away, Honey. I've nowhere to go, for one thing. No money, no horse, no friends save Kipp, and I doubt his mama will let me in the front door once she finds out what he's been up to with Jack. Besides, I have to see Jack. I have to know he's all right."

"Ha! That one!" Honey said, sniffing. "Don't expect him to be greeting you with a shower of posies, Missy. Because I was fibbing to you, trying to be nice. He blames you, all right. I heard him when he was watching you being loaded onto the wagon for the ride back to Coltrane House, before you woke up and all. Cursing you every which way, that's what young Master Jack was doing, daring you not to die so's that he could murder you himself."

Merry felt her jaw set as she ground her teeth together. It was one thing for Merry to believe that Jack might blame her, but it was another thing entirely if Jack believed as much himself. "Oh, really? All my fault, is it? Well," she said, shrugging, "he's being like that, is he? Flying straight up to the boughs, his temper ruling his tongue and his brains always racing to catch up. Not that he really means any of it, Honey. I'm sure he was just worried about me, that's all."

Honey rolled her eyes.

Merry flushed to the roots of her fiery, badly tangled hair. "He does worry about me, you know. He just hasn't quite known how to show that worry these past years, ever since I started getting these ridiculous things," she insisted, raising her hands to cup her full breasts. "Before these he could pretend I was just like him, just like Kipp. Silly, isn't it? But I understand, and I can be generous."

"You can be foolish," Aloysius Bromley said as he stood in the doorway, his nightcap falling forward over one eye, the hem of his nightshirt tickling the tops of his bony bare feet. "You and Jack both. Foolish beyond any hope of salvation. Is this why I've stayed all these years? For this foolishness? Do you know what Coltrane has planned for the pair of you? What you and Jack, in your foolishness and penchants for mad starts have helped him to plan for the two of you? Do you have any idea?"

"No, sir." Merry answered respectfully. She tried to find her beloved onetime tutor ridiculous in his nightshirt, but was only able to see his faded gray eyes, and the very real worry in them. "It's to be very bad?"

"Come, infant, and take heart," Aloysius said gently, holding out his hand to her. "I've been let out of the cellars and sent to fetch you. We'll get through this, all of us. It won't be pretty, and you can't be too angry with Jack when he pouts and shouts wild things and makes a complete jackass out of himself. But it will all work out. Not today, not if I know Jack, and definitely not tomorrow. But it will be all right. In time, it will all be fine. I promise you."

Jack paced the prison of his bedchamber, pulling his left arm free of the sling Kipp had fashioned for him out of a torn bedsheet. He refused to wince at the pain that shot through his shoulder. "Idiot. I'm an idiot!"

"We're both idiots, Jack. And you'll wear a hole in that already-ragged carpet," Kipp offered conversationally as he lay on the mussed bed, his ankles crossed, his arms behind his head as he lazily contemplated the tattered overhead tester. "Besides, that wing could be broken, you know, not just bruised all to hell and back. In fact, all things considered, you really ought to sit down."

"Shut up, Kipp," Jack bit out angrily, crossing to the fireplace and giving one of the andirons a sharp kick, so that the meager fire shot out a few halfhearted sparks. "Just shut up, all right."

"Oh, yes, I can see how that would help. I shut up, you prowl, and we both wait for the roof to fall on us. It is going to fall on us, you know, courtesy of your father. He's been longing to pay me back for over three years now, for daring to interfere in his life. What do you think the bastard has planned? Those are some very large men he had with him. You might appear dashing with that crooked nose of yours, but I'm not looking forward to having this handsome face rearranged."

"Why not, Kipp? I always said you were too pretty by half." Jack lowered himself into a chair, favoring his bruised shoulder as he looked at his friend. "He won't turn us over to be jailed, or hanged, or transported, or whatever in hell happens to highwaymen. That would be too clean, too simple. Hell, he would have killed me years ago if he didn't so delight in torturing me. But he's definitely going to make us suffer, you can be sure of it. Still, I don't see him being satisfied with a simple beating. Not this time. God, if only I could have gotten a good swing at the bastard."

"You were otherwise occupied at the time, as I recall, holding on to Merry and begging her not to die. Poor infant. She'll be all right, won't she?"

Jack rubbed a hand over his eyes, trying to banish the vision of Merry's face as he'd last seen her. She'd begun to wake up by the time they'd all reached Coltrane House, although that bump on her head had looked very nasty. "Merry? She'll be fine. She's always fine. But what the devil she thought she was doing, following me, screaming like a stuck pig—damn! I hold her partly responsible for this mess, you know. Always on my heels, always following after me."

"She is a bit of an imp, isn't she? Such a bothersome infant, when she's not being endearing." Kipp sat up and swung his legs over the edge of the bed. "Well, this waiting about may be fine and enough for you, my friend, but the sun's up now and I'm not going to sit here any longer awaiting your father's pleasure. Penned up, like dogs in a cage. No, no, I can't allow it. I *am* the Viscount Willoughby, you know."

Jack felt a small smile tug at the corners of his mouth. "Oh, sit down, Kipp. You're not impressing me, God knows, not as a dog, and most certainly not as a viscount. Do you suppose he's sent for your mother?"

Kipp did sit down then, quite abruptly. "My mother? Damme, Jack, he wouldn't do that, would he? No man would do that to another, not even your father. Don't even think such a thing, if you please. I mean, hanging is hanging. But my mother? Crying over me, wringing her hands, lamenting how she'd nurtured a snake at her bosom. Good God!"

Jack rose, patted his friend on the back, then walked to the window and watched as the sun rose over the horizon. "I should have known I was becoming too predictable. Any fool would have known better. Always attacking from the same spot, only attacking coaches leaving Coltrane House. Even my drunken father could see that sending out the baron, with Honey along as bait, would be more than enough to put the Forfeit Man on the chase."

"I agree," Kipp said, physically shaking off the horrible mental mantle of expected maternal hysterics. "We were stupid. Brick stupid. August set a trap, and we neatly stepped into it."

"All that remains is our penalty for stupidity," Jack concluded, turning about as he heard the key turn in the lock. "And, in a minute, we'll know just what that is."

Kipp stood close beside Jack, pressing a bracing hand on his shoulder. "Here we go, my friend. Off to face our enemies; heading into the fire, as it were. As long as this punishment has nothing to do with my mother, I suppose I can swallow it."

A moment later, Kipp was swallowing a fist, and Jack was sprawled on top of a huge ruffian of a man, doing his best with his one good arm to shove the man's nose into his brain.

It was a short fight and a valiant one, but Jack and Kipp were no match for four strong men. Within minutes Jack was lying on the floor, his hands tied behind his back, his injured shoulder screaming with pain as his father stood over him, smiling.

"Now, *son*," August Coltrane said as he stuffed a cloth into Jack's mouth, "you and I are going to have us a small talk. Well, I'm going to talk. You, I'm afraid, are only going to listen. You are ready to listen to me now, Jack, aren't you?"

Merry sat on the couch in the Main Saloon, Aloysius beside her. She had a hand pressed against her head, wishing away the dull throbbing pain in her temple even as she prayed her stomach wouldn't betray her again. She wasn't cold, but for five minutes she'd been trying without success to stop her teeth from chattering.

The room was crowded with people she'd never seen before, or at least she'd always tried never to be so close to any of August's houseguests. There were four fairly well dressed men, including Baron Hartley, sitting at a table in the corner, telling jokes, drinking deep, and playing cards. A man in a yellow swallowtail coat was passed out on the couch across from her, snoring deeply as drool dribbled onto his chin. Five men dressed in rough clothes stood about the room as if on guard, their hands clasped behind their backs, their homely expressions bovine blank as they stared at her.

But what truly confused her was the presence of a man dressed all in black, a man holding a Bible in one hand and a bottle of wine in the other, and wearing the white collar of a clergyman.

She heard a commotion in the hallway, the slam of bodies hitting against the stairs, the walls. "Jack?" she cried out as the doors burst open, swinging back on their hinges. "Oh, God, Jack!" she cried out, trying to get to her feet, only to have Aloysius take her hand, quietly begging her to sit down and be very quiet.

August Coltrane walked into the room behind Jack, who had fallen to the floor after crashing through the doors, his hands cruelly tied behind his back, something stuffed in his mouth. Kipp was also there, his cheek bruised, one of his eyes beginning to swell and discolor. Kipp's hands were tied as well, and someone had also stuffed a piece of cloth in his mouth. As he hadn't fallen down, one of the men pushed him, helped him to the floor.

Merry looked at her guardian, the man she'd always avoided, the man whose pale face and cold, black eyes had haunted her nightmares for too many years. As he grew older, he only grew more menacing, more frightening. He was the devil, that's what Cluny said, and Merry believed it. Today especially, she believed it.

"What's going on? What's happening?" Merry asked Aloysius, her limbs trembling so badly she thought she might faint.

"I'm assuming," Aloysius told her, patting her hand, "that Jack has registered an objection to his father's plans, and that his father has decided to convince him to rethink that objection."

"His plans?" Merry asked blankly, watching as August Coltrane walked across the room, began conferring with the swaying, obviously drunken man wearing the collar of a— dear God! "He's going to kill them?" she asked, horrified. "He's going to have that man pray over them, and then kill them?"

"You—girl!" August bellowed before Aloysius could answer her, pointing to Merry and gesturing that she should stand up, come to him.

"Go, child," Aloysius said, giving her hand a last squeeze. "Don't say anything, don't argue. I wouldn't put it past the man to beat you as well. There is only one thing you and Jack can do, and that's to live through this."

Merry stood up, slowly, fearful that her legs might not support her, and then turned as she saw Jack get to his feet. He ran straight at August, his head lowered as if he meant to plow into the man like a battering ram.

"Jack!" she screamed, as Kipp tried to rise as well, only to be dealt a swift kick in the side by one of the guards. "Jack, don't!"

It was a daring assault, born of anger and frustration, Merry was sure, but an attack doomed to failure. Jack made it only a few yards before two of August's hired thugs tackled him, wrestled him to the floor.

"That's enough!" August commanded. "We want the boy to be able to say the words." He walked up to where Jack was now lying on his back, and pulled the cloth out of his mouth, untied his bound hands. Jack drew in several ragged breaths, his nose bloody, his chest rising and falling rapidly. "And you will say them, Jack, or else—wait a moment. I've just gotten an idea, now that you're proving stubborn yet again. I may just marry the pretty little piece myself, Jack, and then bed her right here, with you watching. Been a while since I had myself a virgin."

"Ha! That's a good one, August, you pox-ridden sot," one of the men at the card table called out. "You haven't been able to poke more than your own eye in years. Gentlemen, will anyone bet me that August here can do as he proposes? No? Didn't think so, August. You'll need a better threat than that."

"I could give her to you, Hartley," August said genially. "Except I heard you like poking your own mother."

"Insult me all you want, August," the baron responded just as cheerily. "Just get this over with, will you? I've still got a pounding head, no thanks to you. Ain't fun anymore, you know."

"You hear that, Jack? You're no longer amusing. And each moment you resist brings your friends closer to the hangman's noose," August said, giving Jack's legs a sharp kick. "Shall I send someone for the squire, and let Hartley here tell the fellow how he caught the Forfeit Man and his motley crew of cohorts? Hartley—we good English still hang women, don't we? I know we hang the Irish."

"Bastard." Jack gritted out, as Merry broke free of Aloysius's grasp and ran to him, threw her body over him in an attempt to protect him from further blows. "I'll send you to hell!"

"Oh, Jack, please be quiet," Merry begged. "Please don't make this worse."

"What's the matter, Jack?" August said, grabbing hold of Merry's arm, yanking her to her feet. He put his hand on the bodice of her gown and began to pull at it, so that Merry grabbed his hand in both of hers, trying to keep him from ripping the cloth straight down to her waist. "You do want to marry her, don't you? She wants to marry you. She wants it so badly she agreed to tell me where you'd be tonight. Led us straight to you, as a matter of fact. Didn't you, girl?"

"No!" Merry screamed. "No, I'd never do that. Never!"

"I know, Merry, I know," Jack told her, wiping at his bloody nose with the back of his hand. He looked up at his father. "Take your hands off her, old man, or I'll kill you now."

"Not until you can stand up by yourself, you won't. Now, what's it to be, boy? We do still have an agreement, don't we? Do you say the words, or do I? Do you say the words, or do your friends all hang? One way or another, we keep the little bitch and all her lovely money in the family, right? Can't let her reach her majority and just walk away with it, can we? And then there's the blunt I owe Hartley over there, and a few of the others. Too many London heads poking into my business for my own good, making noises about the funds I've been withdrawing. I need legal access to the rest of her inheritance now, Jack, and I'm going to get it with your help or without it. Your wife, Jack, but *my* money. But we've already discussed all of this, haven't we? We've already made our little bargain."

Merry lowered her head, bit August Coltrane's hand as hard as she could, hard enough to draw blood. He yowled in pain, then pulled his hand away and cuffed her across the cheek, sending her crashing to the floor beside Jack. She felt darkness closing around her and fought to remain conscious as she began to retch, her empty stomach turning violently again and again and again.

"Isn't that lovely? And quite a fitting touch, don't you think?" August drawled, holding his bleeding hand as he looked down on the two of them. "But I think our lovebirds are ready now, don't you, Vicar, if you're not too foxed to remember the words? Pull them to their feet, boys, and let's get on with it."

* * *

Merry roused slowly. She tried to open her eyes but the pain proved too much for her. She felt a pressure beside her and realized that she was lying on a bed, and that someone had just sat down beside her. "Jack?" she whispered, reaching out her hand.

"No, little one, it's only your own Cluny, who has been sitting by your bed these four days, waiting for you to wake up. But you're going to be fine, I promise you. Why, Clancy is up and around already, and Lord Willoughby is mending faster than his mama can cry over him. We're all going to be just fine."

Merry lay very still as Cluny held her hand, and she tried to remember. There was something she had to remember. Then, suddenly, she opened her eyes and tried to sit up. "Jack!"

"He's gone, sweetheart," Cluny told her as he took hold of her shoulders, gently pressed her back against the pillows. "But he's all right. Henry Sherlock found Maxwell and the others in the cellars and let them out. Fetched me out as well, and then we all took up arms and marched on the Main Saloon. Funny thing, how Awful August seems so afraid of our Sherlock, and I can't help but wonder why he is, but Clancy says a smart person doesn't question good luck. Ah, Merry, but it was a grand sight, I tell you. Rousted all the villains, had them running back to London, their tails between their legs. 'One for all or all for one we gage.'" He shook his head, smiled rather sadly. "I never did understand that one, Merry. What is a gage? I asked Clancy once, but he only cuffed my ear. Perhaps if I were to apply to Aloysius . . ."

Merry squeezed Cluny's hand. "Jack?" she asked again, wishing her mouth weren't so dry, wishing her head was clearer. She could remember some things now, remember the scene in the Main Saloon. She remembered Jack being beaten. She remembered him standing beside her, saying some words he was told to say, even as she recited them in her turn. But that's all she remembered. Perhaps she'd fainted? "Cluny, please . . . Jack?"

"I told you, my dear child. He's gone," Cluny said. "Safe enough, but gone. Gone from Coltrane House, gone from England itself."

"No," she moaned, as a single tear slipped down her cheek. "No."

"There was nothing else for it, Sherlock said, not with him being so broken and battered and all. Besides, Jack had already promised August he would go, in return for your safety. Yours, and the viscount's, and Clancy's and mine as well. It was a bad thing, Merry, but it could have been worse. He just as easily could have turned the five of us over to the hangman. As it is, no one will ever know what happened here, no one but us. And someday, someday soon, please God, Awful August will be burning in hell. At least we know Jack's father will never return to Coltrane House. Sherlock swore to go to the squire, tell him everything, unless he'd agree to keep his filthy self in London. I don't know what that everything is—something between him and Sherlock—but it must be very bad, seeing that Awful August quickly agreed to every condition. Good man, Sherlock, for all that he's such a cipher."

But Merry wasn't listening. "Gone? Gone where? Where has Jack gone?"

"We don't know," Clancy told her as he walked to the side of the bed, smiled down at her. "Sherlock took Jack to the docks himself, and put him on the first ship to sail with the tide. It was better that he go, Sherlock said, safer, for otherwise nobody would be able to stop him from hanging for killing Awful August. But he'll be back, my dearest girl.

He'll be back to claim his life, his inheritance, and most especially his wife."

"His . . . his wife?" The words. What were the words she and Jack had been told to say? *I, Meredith, take thee . . .* "I remember," she said, beginning to cry. "Oh, God, I remember. How he must hate me."

Act Two

Learning the Lines

> Wisely and slow.
> They stumble that run fast.
>
> —William Shakespeare

Chapter Nine

As London town houses went, this one went quite well. A good address. An impressive façade. High-ceilinged rooms filled with light and rather comfortable, yet stylish furniture. Renting a town house such as this for the Season would set a man back a good bit of blunt. Buying it outright could empty a lesser man's pockets.

The purchase hadn't made more than a minor impression on Jack Coltrane's fortune.

"Perceive me with jaw agape, impressed all hollow," Kipp Rutland, Viscount Willoughby, said as he and Jack strolled into the drawing room, the former heading unerringly for the well-stocked drinks table. "Makes the Willoughby Mansion seem almost shabby." He turned to Jack, smiled. "But not quite."

Kipp was as handsome as he'd ever been. Tall, blond, blue-eyed, and with the wide shoulders and narrow waist that flattered his clothes rather than the other way round. For all the beating he had taken from August's thugs, the man's face was still, as he had always been fond of saying, "so very damned pretty." Probably only Jack noticed the small lines around Kipp's mouth, a subtle new maturity that his friend seemed determined to hide.

Jack and Kipp had met earlier, on the street. They'd indulged themselves in the usual hail-fellow-well-met round of backslapping gentlemen who love each other and have not seen each other for years and years seem to find necessary in order to hide the fact that what they'd like to do best would be to fall into each other's arms and hold on for dear life.

Neither of them had yet mentioned the last time they'd seen each other. That last night. It was as if they'd made a tacit bargain never to speak of what had happened. That night, which had put a final period to both of their childhoods, had cruelly vaulted them out of any lingering dreams held by many a young man of four and twenty, had no part in their memories.

Yet they both remembered it. The events of that long-ago night hung between them now, so that they were both a little too casual, a little too cheerful.

And strangely competitive. Just as if each was saying to the other: "You see? I'm all right. That night didn't break me, didn't hurt me, didn't change me. Look how well I've done, how I've succeeded. How very ordinary, how very *normal* I am."

"I thought we might enjoy having a retreat here in town," Jack said, accepting a glass of wine from his friend, who seemed to be most comfortable in the role of host, even in someone else's house. "We were fortunate enough to find this place, complete with furnishings, servants, and a tolerable stable."

"And Lockhurst was fortunate to find you," Kipp said, seating himself comfortably. "The poor sot was all rolled-up, with bailiffs dining with the family three times a day, and moments from being tossed into the Fleet. Everyone knew it, except perhaps, for you. He's probably singing all the way back to Dorset, happy to still have someplace left to call home."

Jack smiled slightly, so that the crescent-shaped scar beside his left eye—one of his parting gifts from his father—served as a small, second dimple. "Are you telling me I'm a Johnny Raw, Kipp, and that you believe we actually paid down what this heap is worth? Ah, such a faint heart."

"You didn't?"

"No, dear friend, we did not. Lockhurst may have made a lucky escape from the Fleet, but he did it by being paid only pence on the pound. Or did you think I spent the last five years building an endearing belief in the goodness of my fellowman? We offered him less than half what our new domicile is worth, and the man grabbed at it with both hands. We'll sell it all if the whim strikes us, and pocket a tidy profit." He smiled again. "More than tidy."

"My congratulations, Jack," Kipp said, looking at Jack consideringly. "However, I might warn you that you're sounding much the shopkeeper, with all this talk of pence and pounds and profit. That's not done in Society, you know. Too crass by half, and all of that. We speak of horseflesh, and pretty women, and gaming. Oh, and, only three-fourths of the time, of gossip. I imagine you're being served up as the main conversational dish at several dozen dinner tables tonight, especially after you were seen driving in the Park yesterday, with that magnificent barbarian riding up beside you. Can he be part of the *we* you're talking about?"

Jack's dark features hardened. How much had five years changed Kipp? Enough so that Jack would momentarily find himself booting his childhood friend out of the house? "Wulitpallat? What of him?"

Kipp nearly choked on his sip of wine. "Wulit-*what*? And

Wulit-what of him, you ask? God's teeth, man, you drive through London with a wild Indian—a giant of a wild Indian, if I'm to believe all that I hear—sitting beside you, and you have to ask me *what of him*? You would have caused less of a stir if you'd entered the Park sporting a turban and riding on the back of a pink-spotted pachyderm. I hear that Lady Haliburton swooned dead away at the sight of your friend. Lord, that I could have been with you. So, may I borrow him? I'm already committed to dinner with the Haliburtons next week, you understand."

"I drove through the Park with Wulitpallat yesterday in order to get your attention, if you were in town. I could have come to Grosvenor Square I suppose, and left my card. But this was easier. I didn't think it would take you more than twenty-four hours to find me." Jack relaxed another notch, even as he lied. He'd already known Kipp was in town. He hadn't gone to him because he hadn't been sure of his reception. He had shown himself, then waited for Kipp's reaction, waited to see if he would seek him out or avoid him.

Now Jack knew that he needn't have worried. His friend was still, for the most part, the same silly, lighthearted Kipp. Had he really thought the man could have turned proper and judgmental, or that he hated him for what August had done? That he was disappointed in him for leaving the country, for staying away—and silent—for five long years? His head lowered to hide an unbidden smile, he said quietly, "And Walter is not only in business with me, Kipp, he's a friend. Much as I understand how you'd enjoy tweaking this Lady Haliburton, I must warn you, I'll not have him made into a joke."

"Walter, is it? Well, I suppose that's better than Wulit-whatever."

"Wulitpallat," Jack corrected. "The name means Good Fighter. And he is," he ended, now smiling openly. "I'd remember that, if I were you. Just in case you should someday think to harm so much as a hair on my head."

"I consider myself warned." Kipp stood, returned to the drinks table to refill his glass. He turned then, to look at his childhood friend. What he saw was a tall man, a leanly muscled man. A well-dressed man. A handsome man, dark and brooding, with his hair unfashionably long, severely combed off his forehead, and tied back in a black ribbon. A man with slashing cheeks, a years-deep tan, an aristocratic nose made more human by the bump on it. He had the look of a pirate about him. Or a wild Indian. The trappings of a gentleman did nothing but accentuate the fact that this was a deep, dark, dangerous man. The boy Jack once was had been dipped into the fire and come out as strong as Toledo steel. If he didn't know better, Kipp would have believed himself afraid of his old friend. At the very least, he was wary of him.

"So," he said, returning to his seat, "not being quite as ignorant as I pretend—so much easier that way, you know—I imagine it is safe to assume that you somehow ended up aboard a ship bound for America? Sherlock never would say, claiming he was protecting your privacy. Not that I mean to pry, but Walter's presence—good God, Jack, the magnificent beast of a man I heard described obviously looks nothing like a Walter—would tend to make one think that way."

"And what would a Walter look like?" Jack asked, prolonging the inevitable, as Kipp was suddenly beginning to show signs of digging himself in until he had a report of everything that had happened to his childhood chum over the past five years.

But Viscount Willoughby never approached anything in a straight line, and it didn't look as if he was about to make an exception. He pointed at Jack with his index finger. "Good question! What does a Walter look like? Not like you, that's for sure. Or me, for that matter. No. I see a thin man. Small. With spectacles that won't stay on his nose. And perhaps with a faint lisp? How does that sound?"

"It sounds like you're still making up characters to people those tall tales you used to spin when we were children. Do you still do that?"

"It's an old habit." Kipp flushed slightly, which surprised Jack, as he didn't know the man had a bone in his body capable of embarrassment. "I suppose I should just come out and ask you, shouldn't I? Very well. Tell me how you met Walter. How you made your fortune. How you landed back here in London, when you plan to drive to Coltrane House. Tell me everything."

"All in good time, Kipp, all in good time. You will be staying for the evening meal, won't you? I can introduce you to Walter then. I'll be interested in seeing your response to my business partner."

Kipp came within a whisker of stuttering. "So he truly is your business partner? You said *we* earlier, when you spoke of buying this place, but I didn't really believe—oh, Jack, you couldn't pry me out of here with a regiment of Walters herding me at the heads of their spears, or whatever it is Walters employ to maim and murder. He doesn't maim and murder, does he?"

"No. At least not recently," Jack answered with a smile, then shifted slightly in his seat, hating to ask the question that had been in the forefront of *his* mind for five long years. It was one thing to read the letters sent to him, try to read between the lines. It was another thing entirely to ask Kipp, who was her friend, who had actually been with her, talked with her as only a friend could. He knew he could count on Kipp to tell him the truth, the whole truth. He just didn't know if he was ready to hear it. "Tell me about Merry. Is she well? When did you last see her?"

Kipp pushed a hand through his thick blond hair, looking at Jack carefully, assessingly. "She's very well. I saw her just before coming up to town for a few weeks. Not precisely for the Season, but to see my tailor, you understand. I'm a slave to the man. Anyway, I begged her to accompany me, but she refuses to set foot off Coltrane land as long as she's mistress of the estate. She—" He broke off, spread his arms, drew his hands up into fists before allowing them to drop to his side, as if there was too much to say, so he'd say none of it. "She—she's fine, Jack. Just as you'd expect her to be."

Jack felt himself caught up in memories. Memories of the baby he'd held. The child he'd known. The pest he'd run from as his interests had outgrown hers. The young girl he'd run from even harder as he'd realized she'd begun weaving silly dreams about the two of them. For now, he would concentrate on the child, remembering her as he'd loved her best. Remembering her as he needed to think of her—as his sister. "Is her smile still so wide?"

Kipp sighed, nodded, and Jack felt his friend's sympathy stretching across the distance between them, touching him with compassion—and something else. Something he didn't believe he cared to recognize, because there was also censure in Kipp's sigh, and perhaps even resentment. And he felt a flush of anger. Jack remembered something Clancy had once said to him: "Ask the man wearing the shoe where it pinches." Kipp couldn't really know how Jack felt, no matter how he loved him, no matter how much they had shared. Only Jack knew where his shoe pinched, and why. And he would not be judged.

Then Kipp smiled, and Jack relaxed a little, although he remained on his guard.

"And that laugh of hers!" Kipp said, shaking his head. "Ah, Jack, it's still the same. That silly giggle, impossible to hear without feeling your heart lift, without wanting to laugh along with her. Not that I've heard it much, not in these last years."

"We all grow up, Kipp," Jack said shortly. "Life isn't quite as amusing when seen through more mature eyes. Unless Merry is still running amok, with Aloysius chasing after her, trying to keep her from mischief?"

"You counted on Aloysius quite a bit, didn't you, Jack? As you counted on Henry Sherlock—"

"Ah, Henry," Jack interrupted lazily, looking at his hands, turning them over, inspecting his fingernails, trying to hold onto his temper. He'd planned to be so cool, so composed. But it wasn't easy, and it was still early days. He'd have to keep a tighter rein on himself. Everything depended on finding the last pieces to the puzzle before he could act, before he could give Kipp the answers he clearly craved. He'd exposed Kipp to danger once, he wouldn't do it again. "And how is my good friend and protector, Kipp? Doing well, is he?"

"What?" Kipp asked, suddenly at attention. "I don't understand your tone. Are you saying he isn't your friend? God, Jack, you probably would have died that night if it hadn't been for Henry Sherlock. He's always been your friend."

"Yes, you'd think so, wouldn't you?" He looked at Kipp, saw the man's confusion.

"Yes, I *would* think so. Your father had gone mad, Jack. He could have turned us over to the Squire at any moment, even as you promised to do as he ordered. Henry saved your life, saved my life, saved *all* our lives."

Jack felt his muscles going tight. "Did he?"

Kipp ran a hand over his jaw, tipped his head as he stared at Jack. His eyelids narrowed. "Didn't he? What is it, Jack?

What do you know? Because you know something, don't you?"

Jack drew himself back, ignored the question. He'd said enough for now. More than enough. He was through having others help him, be hurt helping him. This battle was his, and his alone. Then he dared another question meant to tell him if he had become obsessed, or if his friend might feel at least something of what he felt—even if Kipp had not spent five long years examining those feelings. "Tell me something, Kipp. Tell me something about our good friend Henry. Our dear, quiet, all-but-invisible friend. Can you even describe him? Do you know the color of his eyes, how old he might be? Does he have any friends, any family? Or is he just another part of Coltrane House? As unnoticed as a door, or a chair that has sat in the same corner for decades. Are we just so used to him being there that no one questions *why* he stays?"

Kipp's eyes narrowed. "Damn it, Jack, why do I get the sudden feeling you don't trust me? I also have the feeling that you haven't just arrived in London, because I've just noticed something else. Something I missed in my initial joy at seeing you again. Your clothes, Jack. They have the cut of London about them. That can't be accomplished in a week. And there's something else. You haven't asked about my mother, Jack. You haven't asked about your father. You haven't even asked about Cluny and Clancy. You haven't asked because you already know. Don't you?"

Jack's features softened. "You have my deepest sympathies on your mother's passing, Kipp. Lady Willoughby was a brave, wonderful woman, and Merry and I owe her a debt that could never be repaid."

"Thank you," Kipp said, still eyeing him closely. "And your father?"

"What of him? He died two years ago in a drunken stumble down a flight of steps. Surely you don't expect to hear that I'm sorry, or fear that I'd want your condolences? As to Cluny and Clancy—yes, Kipp, I know that they're also dead," Jack ended quietly, feeling a tic begin to work at the side of his jaw. Dear God, how he'd mourned when word had come that Cluny and Clancy had died within days of each other, succumbing to a sickness that had taken a heavy toll as it cut through Lincolnshire.

When the letter bearing that news had arrived he'd known he'd run out of time, that he had to go home. Even if he wasn't quite ready, even if his plans weren't quite complete. He had always thought Cluny and Clancy would be there for him, as they'd always been there for Merry and him, that they would live forever. Even now, six months after reading the news, he didn't want to believe that they were gone. Not seeing them again before they'd died was just one more in a long list of regrets. And one more reason to want his revenge.

Kipp began to pace the carpet, looking at Jack, trying to look *through* him. "Yes, they're dead, and Aloysius is still alive. But you knew that, too, didn't you, as you mentioned him as if knowing he's still above ground? How, Jack? How do you know? Did it all come to you in a vision? Did you ever think of the cost Cluny and Clancy paid—paid gladly—to spend their lives with you and Merry, to protect you?"

"Careful, Kipp. I love you, but I won't have you question me. Not right now. I had reasons for what I did, what I plan to do."

Kipp went on as if Jack hadn't spoken. "And then, once you'd gone, we were all to guard Merry, protect her, help her, guide her. While you ran off to God knows where to lick your wounds and to do God knows what. All right, so you had to go. I agree, you had no choice. A year, Jack. Two at the most. I could have understood that. Merry could have understood that. But five years? My God, Jack, I don't want to talk about fortunes or Walters or even Cluny and Clancy. We thought you were *dead*."

"I'd assumed you might think that. It was better that way," Jack said tightly.

"Better for whom?" Kipp shook his head, looked at Jack closely. "No, don't tell me. I don't think I want to hear that sort of twisted logic. So let's talk about fortunes, shall we? How did you get so bloody rich, Jack? At least tell me that, as you say you love me. Privateering? Gambling? Or did you have more success as a highwayman in America than you did here? Whatever in hell it was you did, wherever in hell it was you went, there is nothing that can satisfactorily explain leaving your wife alone at Coltrane House for five long years. Nothing."

Jack steepled his fingers in front of his chin. When he spoke, his voice was low, and rather pleasant. "If that's so, then I won't explain. I owe you my thanks, Kipp, for every kind thing you and your mother did for Merry and me over the years. I owe you my deepest apologies for what happened that last night, for the beating you took because of me. But I repeat—I don't owe you an explanation for what I did when I left England, or what I plan to do now. Now, tell me about Merry, or don't tell me about her. I'm sure I can find out for myself when Walter and I adjourn to Coltrane House."

Kipp stood pacing, glared at the man he'd believed he loved as a brother. "I know he beat you, Jack. I know he beat you, and threatened you, and broke you—and then used you to secure Merry's inheritance in exchange for not delivering us to the hangman. I know you hate yourself for what you believe to be your weakness, and for the ruination of Merry's chance for a life outside of Coltrane House. But, damn it, it wasn't August who broke her heart. It was *you*. Tell you about Merry? I'll tell you, Jack. I'm more than happy to tell you. She detests you. Your wife *detests* you, Jack. And more power to her, by God, I say!"

Jack sat quietly, watching as his childhood friend stomped out of the room, out of the town house and, most probably, out of his life.

Then he stood, picked up his empty glass, and headed for the bellpull in the corner. He'd have to tell his new butler there'd be one less for supper.

Chapter Ten

Merry entered the Main Saloon with the long strides high riding boots and comfortable breeches afforded her. She nodded a greeting to Henry Sherlock, who immediately began to talk about nothing that interested her. She'd been out in the fields all morning and resented being summoned to meet with Henry, probably just to be told more bad news. Henry was so very good at bringing her bad news.

Rather than sit down, she walked across the room, heading in the direction of the highly polished mirror hanging above the shiny surface of a scarred and battered side table. Coltrane House might be falling down around their ears but at least Honey Maxwell and her parents kept the ruins tidy.

She ignored Henry Sherlock's droning recitation of Coltrane House finances as she lifted a hand to her faintly dirty cheek, pulling a face at her reflection before running careless fingers through her mussed curls. She'd always allowed her hair to grow to a length some inches below her shoulders, either wearing it loose or tied back with a strip of leather just to get the unruly mass out of her way. She frowned in the mirror, deciding that she'd made a mistake in not tying it back today. She'd have to spend hours after her bath, just setting this rat's nest to rights.

Merry leaned close to the mirror, retrieved a handkerchief from her pocket, and used a corner of it to ease an annoying bit of grit out of her eye. She then stood back, spit on the cloth, scrubbed at the smudge on her cheek. And frowned again. No wonder she usually avoided mirrors. Her eyes were too big, too blue, her mouth entirely too wide. Her complexion, that had always tended to freckle rather than turn brown like Jack's, was another great annoyance to her. She really ought to wear a hat when she was out in the sun, she supposed, but it was just too much bother.

Stuffing the handkerchief back into the pocket of her tight breeches, she noticed the way the white, flowing man's shirt she favored outlined her full breasts. That was unfortunate. Perhaps she should wear a vest, even on days as warm as this one, just to help cover her breasts. They were definitely more prominent now than when her budding body had first incited Jack's disgust. How old had she been then? Thirteen? Fourteen? It seemed so long ago. It seemed like yesterday.

She knew why she was looking at herself, assessing herself. Finding herself lacking, as she'd always found her physical self lacking. It was because she would soon be the ripe old age of twenty-two. In less than three months, difficult as it was for her to believe, she would be twenty-two years old. Actually, it could be in five months, or perhaps she was only a month away from her next birthday. She really didn't know.

Merry celebrated her birthday on July 31, and that was that. Cluny and Clancy had picked the date for her, as no one wanted to ask Awful August if he knew the correct date, and she had years of wonderful memories of the parties they'd had, the silly presents they'd given her. On her thirteenth birthday, the two men and all of the servants had performed *A Midsummer Night's Dream* especially for her, there in the Main Saloon. Jack had played the role of Puck. So many memories.

She blinked furiously, willing back the tears that still came too easily when she thought about Cluny and Clancy. Her dear, dear friends. The only family she'd ever known, had ever needed.

And then she smiled, hugged herself as she turned away from the mirror. Yes, her friends were dead. But they weren't gone. Not that she'd dare to say as much to anyone, for fear they'd think she'd become unhinged in her grief. Still, she knew. Cluny and Clancy were still there, still at Coltrane House, still watching over her. Still, just as she was, waiting for Jack to come home.

Waiting for Jack. All her life she'd been waiting for Jack. Her full mouth stretched into a taut line. Twenty-two. Was she really going to be that old? Twenty-two was a long way from five, from twelve, from seventeen. A long, often hard way. But travel those years she had, and she was not going back. Not for Jack. Not for anybody. That's what she told herself, ordered herself at night, when she fell into her lonely bed. And, still, she waited for Jack, thought about Jack, worried about Jack, missed him with all of her heart.

She looked at Henry Sherlock, at the man who also had always been in her life. The man who, like Kipp, had stayed, as opposed to the man who had gone away. Henry was sitting on one of the two facing couches that flanked a low round table. A large chandelier hung high above the small grouping of furniture. She really should move those couches—they weren't positioned properly, with the one Henry was sitting on being squarely under the chandelier. The chandelier should be hanging over the table, shouldn't

it? Ah, well. Once she'd overseen the repairs to the icehouse
and organized the harvest, then perhaps she'd have time to
rearrange furniture.

She commanded her wandering mind to come to attention and walked closer to Henry. He was talking, saying
something he surely believed to be important, but she hadn't
been listening to more than every third word.

Poor, sincere, dedicated, and deadly dull Henry. He must
be nearly fifty, his hair a thick mane of purest silver, his
body neat, compact and surprisingly muscular. He usually
smelled of lemon drops, and his head was full of more
knowledge about Coltrane House, both its land and its finances, than she could ever hope to learn.

She'd never seen him as a friend, not when she'd been
younger. He was and always had been Henry Sherlock; conveniently present when needed, conveniently absent when
he was not. She'd just accepted him as being a part of
Coltrane House, and a part of August Coltrane. Only in the
past two years had he become more noticeable to her, as
he'd begun to dress more like a London gentleman than a
country mouse or a quiet man of business.

Personally, she believed the man to be growing rather
silly now that he'd inherited all that money from his aunt,
now that he'd built his own house just over the boundary
from the Coltrane lands.

But she was grateful that, even with his newfound
wealth, he'd still retained his duties at Coltrane House. He
kept the ledgers, managed the payment of August Coltrane's
mountain of debts, advised her on questions about the every-
day running of the estate when she applied to him for his assistance. He even refused payment for helping her. And
she'd always be grateful to him for what he'd done for her,
for Jack. He'd saved them. Saved them more than once.

She supposed Henry believed that gave him some right to

tell her what was best for her, what was best for Coltrane House. Lord knew he was the sort of neat and tidy man who wanted everything orderly, in its proper place. But more and more often, she didn't want him telling her where *her* proper place was in the world as seen by Henry Sherlock. That must be a part of becoming an old lady of two and twenty. She was beginning to resent being told, for her own good, what *was* for her own good.

She sighed, pulled her attention back to the matter at hand, whatever that was. Probably another litany of debt Henry had discovered to recite to her, another lingering bill of August Coltrane's that still must be paid. Couldn't he simply pay the bill, without first telling her about it, dragging her in from the fields to worry her with it? Didn't she have enough on her mind? He had to know that she trusted him. After all, where would she be if she couldn't trust Henry?

But then, as Sherlock droned on, she caught a word she hadn't heard from him before today. "Just a moment, Henry, if you please. If I might interrupt? I believe I heard the word *annulment* mentioned, but I can't be sure. And I heard Jack's name mentioned in the same breath, too, didn't I?"

Henry Sherlock looked at her with those odd, colorless eyes of his, his full mouth turned down at the corners disapprovingly. She usually laughed when he tried to be stern with her, but she hadn't found his last words in the least amusing.

He cleared his throat, then spoke slowly, decisively. "We're discussing John in general, Meredith, and the problems he presents to your well-being. Which, as events would have it, has led me to broach the subject of an annulment of your marriage in particular. I've thoroughly researched the matter, and it can be done. But you're not listening to a word I'm saying, are you?"

Merry smiled, but it took all of her effort. She'd rather discuss old debts, or new problems on the estate. It was no secret to anybody that she never wanted to discuss Jack. "I'm sorry, Henry, and admit I was woolgathering. But I can't agree to an annulment, if that's what you were saying. That's impossible. If I did that, where would I go? Coltrane House is his, you know, and through him, mine. I'd lose Coltrane House. This is my home, Henry, and I will never leave it. Never. So, as much as you're probably put out with me now, may we speak of other things? The roof has sprung a new leak in the West Wing. I need to know how much we can spare to have it repaired."

The chandelier above Henry's head jingled gently, and Merry's nose tickled at the slight odor of camphor. She looked up at the chandelier. Sighed, relaxed. Allowed the comfort to reach inside her, calm her.

"You can spare twenty pounds for repairs this quarter, Meredith, no more."

"Thank you, Henry," she said politely. "I had hoped for more, but I'm sure you know best."

Henry frowned, and Merry knew he was going to return to the subject that appeared to interest him as much as it appalled her. "And, yes, Meredith, Coltrane House is John's. Everything is his. Not yours. That's my whole point."

Merry didn't see his point at all. He wasn't telling her anything she didn't already know. "Oh, have a cup of tea, Henry," she said, walking over to the facing couch and sitting down in front of the silver service Honey had brought in moments after Henry's arrival. "With plenty of sugar, to sweeten your mood. Or is something else bothering you?"

She lifted a cup in one hand and held it under the spout of the teapot. The piece sat inside its own cleverly designed holder, so that the pot could be tipped without ever having to hoist the heavy thing into the air. Jack had rescued the pot on his very first ride as the Forfeit Man.

Hot tea splashed into the bottom of the cup, swirling quite nicely as it climbed the sides . . . then spilled over onto the handmade lace doily lining the tray, turning the thing a deep brown.

"What did you say?" Merry asked hollowly, quickly letting go of the teapot once she realized what was happening. "Repeat that last little bit you just said, Henry, if you please."

"Ah," Sherlock purred, sitting at his ease on the facing couch, one leg crossed over the other. She suddenly, inexplicably, longed to hit him. "At last I have your full attention. Telling you that funds to sustain Coltrane House are low and dipping lower seems not to concern you. Warning you that your late father-in-law's major creditor is threatening dire consequences if you don't make a considerable payment to him before the end of the year means less than nothing to you. Pointing out that all our efforts to foolishly maintain the crumbling wreck we're sitting in have done little to save it from going to August's creditors—to your husband's creditors now—makes no impression. But mention John's name, and suddenly you are not only listening, you're begging that I should repeat myself."

Merry bowed her head, tried to collect herself. She hadn't meant to set Henry off on one of his lectures. "I'm sorry, Henry. I really hadn't been listening with more than half an ear. But did you just say that Jack's coming home? No, you couldn't have said that. Could you?"

Above their heads, the huge chandelier tinkled yet again, louder this time.

Henry quickly abandoned his seat, looked up at the chandelier. "Did you hear that? Meredith, this pile is falling apart. I wouldn't be surprised if that entire hulking monstrosity came crashing down on our heads one day."

"On yours, at least, Henry. I do believe I'm sitting well out of harm's way." Merry kept her head down as she used a linen napkin to dab at the spilled tea. Part of her wanted to scream, weep, gnash her teeth—whatever it was women did when in the throes of great emotion. Another part of her, the silly child inside her, longed to dance. Clearly Cluny and Clancy would have preferred to dance.

But could it be true? This time, could it be true? Was Jack coming home? She refused to believe it, didn't dare to believe it. "You could be right about the chandelier, Henry," she said, still attempting to compose herself. "Awful August and his guests often used it for target practice, remember? See the bullet holes in the ceiling? If you could look into those neat ledgers of yours, find a way for us to spare a few pounds to pay the price, I suppose I could engage someone to inspect and fix it?"

"A few pounds, is it? First the roof, and now the chandelier? You don't have a few *pence* to spare, Meredith. August mortgaged this heap to its rooftops, and I've been working like ten men these past years to hold off your creditors with piddling payments. I don't like to complain, Meredith, but it hasn't been easy, you know."

"And you've succeeded admirably, Henry. I'm so very grateful to you," Merry assured him, hoping to soothe his ruffled feathers. "Now, to get back to what you were saying. You've heard another rumor I suppose. We've heard a dozen rumors over the years. Two dozen. None of them have proved true yet. So why did you sound so sure just now, as you mentioned this one to me? It isn't like you to pass on silly gossip, Henry."

"Because this time it isn't just another rumor, Meredith." Henry patted the excruciatingly neat fall of lace bunched at his throat as he sat down once more, looked up at the chandelier. "Much to my own surprise, I've received a letter from London this morning. From John. He's back in England, and has announced his intention to arrive at Coltrane House in the next week to ten days."

"A letter? From Jack? Now you're lying to me outright, Henry," Merry said as a loud buzzing began in her ears. "If that were true, you would have told me the moment I entered the room."

"Everything in its own time, Merry," Henry told her smoothly. "An annulment would be clean, if not especially simple. But once John is back in residence? Ah, Meredith, he did not leave here happy with you, if you'll recall. I'm only trying to show you that you have options. One of those is to not be here at all when he comes home."

Merry struggled to control her breathing. She looked up at the chandelier. It simply hung there, silent. "I see." she said quietly, her lips numb. "Jack's coming home. He's really coming home, and you want me to run away because you feel he won't want to see me here? You might actually think that he'd try to *harm* me? I never knew, Henry, that you thought so little of Jack."

"I liked him well enough, Meredith. But we all remember Jack's foul moods, his hasty temper. I don't want you to suffer any more than you already have. You're wasting your youth here, taking care of Jack's property, not finding a life for yourself. You're young. You could marry again. I don't think I would be too far wrong if I mentioned to you that I believe Viscount Willoughby would be more than eager to—"

"I'm married," Merry said dully, not capable of saying more than that.

"I care for you, Meredith," Henry continued sincerely. "I always have. John wrote to me, Meredith, not to you. Doesn't that tell you anything? Doesn't that tell you that he is either hoping you're no longer at Coltrane House, or that, if you are, he wants nothing to do with you?"

"I'm his wife, Henry," Merry said, wishing she could hear at least a faint trace of confidence in her voice. "If Jack is coming home, I will, as his wife, most certainly be here to greet him."

"At which point you'd also be fully prepared to become his wife in every sense?" Henry sighed. "Do you really believe that he'll want that? You may love him, a schoolgirl's love that's more dream than reality, but do you honestly think he sees you the same way? If he loved you, do you believe he would have been able to stay away for five long years?"

"No, I don't," Merry admitted, rising slowly, like a very old woman, and walking toward the doorway. She had a great need to be shed of Henry's clumsy sympathy, to be alone someplace where she could think, she could cry, she could even scream.

Merry stopped just at the doorway, turned back to face Henry. She drew herself up straight and pronounced her next words slowly, carefully. "But you're wrong, Henry, wrong about how I feel. I'm waiting for Jack to come back, yes. So that I can murder him."

And then she ran out of the room.

Which didn't mean that other quarters weren't still to be heard from. High up in the chandelier, two ghostly figures, invisible to all but their own eyes, were having themselves a small celebration.

"We did hear him aright, we did!" Clancy shouted as, overcome with happiness, he grabbed on to the chain holding the chandelier aloft and swung around it three times, whirling like a top in his excitement. "Hie-ho, Hie-hee, my Jack is coming back to me!"

Cluny peered down from the chandelier to watch as Henry Sherlock gaped up at it, mumbled, "Falling apart. This whole ruin is falling apart," then quickly gathered himself together and left the room.

"It's true, Clancy," Cluny agreed, looking at his friend. "As sure as I'm dead, Jack is coming home. And, sure as I'm dead, Merry is going to murder him."

"But she loves him," Clancy chirped, his hands clasped to his breast. "Such a brilliant child, to love my Jack so."

"He doesn't deserve her," Cluny protested, but his heart wasn't really in the thing. Having Jack back would take so many of the worries off his dearest Merry's slim shoulders. And if Merry was happy, Cluny was happy. It had always been that simple.

"Cluny?" Clancy asked as he settled himself once more inside the branches of the chandelier. "Did you happen to notice that Sherlock *smiled* when Merry said she was going to kill Jack? Now, why do you suppose he smiled?"

Chapter Eleven

Jack reined in the huge black stallion at the crest of the hill, the exact place where, for good or bad, life as he'd known it had ended. This was the spot where he'd truly begun the long, hard journey into manhood. Deliberately leaving his heart behind. His humanity. And embracing cynicism with both hands, grabbing for it as a drowning man would a straw. Then holding on to it for five long, dark years.

Years when he'd refused to think. Refused to feel.

He'd turned away from friendship, from love. Even hate had been discarded in favor of the day-to-day quest for the one thing he believed he needed. Money.

When had the struggle become more important than life itself? When had he changed into the man he was now, the hollow shell he'd filled with banknotes and properties and the belief that money was the answer to any question? Every question. Money, which bought him information, which equaled power, which equaled . . . surely not happiness.

Happiness was a child, skipping stones across a stream.

Happiness was lying on your back in a freshly cut hay field, picking out faces in the clouds overhead. Happiness was watching a twelve-year-old Merry as Kipp taught her how to fence. Jack had laughed until his sides hurt as she'd distracted his friend by pointing up toward the sky, then stuck her button-tipped blade straight at his heart. Her aim had been off just enough that Kipp had found himself staring at the point as it pressed against the Willoughby family's hope for continued generations.

Happiness was Coltrane House, as he wanted to remember it, as he longed to remember it.

Happiness was Coltrane House as he, Jack Coltrane, would make it again, had worked so hard to make it again. Except that now Cluny and Clancy were dead, and could no longer be a part of Jack's tomorrows, as they had been such a large measure of his happiness in his yesterdays. They had left him, as surely as he had gone away from them, and he hadn't been there to say good-bye.

Too late, too late. He'd left his return too late. He'd been so caught up in his plans that he'd forgotten what was really important, *who* was really important. Yes, Coltrane House was important, saving the estate was important. But at what cost? At what sacrifice?

Had his promise to save Coltrane House been enough to justify leaving those he loved alone for five long years, only watching over them from a distance? Had he left his homecoming too late for any chance of happiness?

Jack sighed inwardly as he heard the curricle pull up beside him and waited while Walter set the brake. The man was about to make some profound comment, Jack was sure, and the least he could do would be to listen.

"From the topographical description you've given me," his friend said a moment later, "and taking into consideration the logistics of proper stagecoach robbery as contemplated by a green-as-grass lad with more hair than wit, I imagine I'm safe in assuming that this is the approximate location of the onset of your youthful disgrace?"

"Go to the devil, Walter," Jack said idly, shifting in the saddle. And then he smiled. A sad, yet faintly amused smile. "What a shambles we made of the thing. You should have seen us, friend. Everyone running, everyone screaming, shouting. Kipp trying to be in three places at once, and none of them the right one for more than a second. Honey screaming and crying and beating on the baron with her clog. Me, idiot that I was, believing I could stop a team of panicked horses. And then Merry, coming out of nowhere like that . . ." He bit his lip, lowered his head. "God. I thought she was dead."

"And when she wasn't," Walter said smoothly, "you wanted to kill her. Completely understandable."

"I talk too much when I'm drunk," Jack said, looking down at his companion. Walter was magnificent. There was no other description. Tall, broad, with dark skin, a high-bridged, noble nose, and hair as dark as midnight and faintly streaked with silver—hair he allowed to fall freely, to his shoulders. He wore his dark brown frock coat like a second skin over his wide shoulders. A simple cravat, a plain brown waistcoat, dark brown trousers whose seams strained under the pressure exerted by iron-hard thigh muscles. Walter appeared as a cross between a banker and a savage, a prize-fighter and a prime minister, a killer and a priest.

"That's true. You've said enough while in your cups that if your father were not already dead, I should have had to skin him slowly with a dull knife within an hour of stepping foot onto English soil," Walter said, sniffing appreciatively at his one affectation—the posy in his buttonhole. "As it is, I shall content myself with pissing on his grave." He smiled at Jack. "Would you care to join me?"

"I don't deserve you," Jack said with a slow smile. "In fact, friend, there are moments when you truly terrify me."

"It's my great mind," Walter said, inclining his head in a small, regal bow, accepting Jack's accolades. "Many are in awe of it, including myself, on occasion. That said, I believe it's time we part for an hour or more, as you must now gird your loins and ride down this hill. To Coltrane House, my friend, and to your bride." He jumped down from the curricle in one swift, graceful movement. "I shall remain here, rest the horses, and contemplate my place in this small, fateful dot in the universe."

"And who, then, shall guard my back? Kipp tells me Merry detests me," Jack said as he lifted his hat from his head, then replaced it at a more jaunty angle. "Remembering Merry, and knowing that Sherlock has undoubtedly told her of my arrival, I believe anything less than an accompanying regiment means I'm riding now to my death. Not that it appears you care what happens to me."

Walter, having settled the horses, sat himself down atop a rotting tree trunk—*the* rotting tree trunk, as a matter of fact, Jack had used so many years ago as the Forfeit Man—and smiled up at Jack. "The element of surprise still rides with you to some extent. She knows the attack is coming, but since you didn't give Sherlock a firm date for your arrival, she doesn't know when it is coming. She's on edge, frightened even as she prepares for you. Lacking sleep. Lacking comfort and peace. When the war whoop sounds, suddenly splits the air with its nerve-jangling terror, an opponent such as this does one of two things. She freezes to the ground, unable to react . . ."

"Yes?" Jack prompted as Walter bent to sniff the flower once more.

Walter smiled. "Or she blows a whacking great hole straight through you. In other words, my friend, do be careful, won't you? I've grown rather attached to you for one reason or another, none of which readily leaps to the forefront of my mind. Oh, wait, there is one. You've got a good heart, Jack. The only problem is that you misplaced it a few years ago. Perhaps you can ride down this hill now and find it?"

"I never took you for a romantic, Walter," Jack said, shifting uncomfortably in his saddle. "I'll see you in an hour or so?"

Walter nodded, then made shooing gestures with his hands, so that Jack knew he could delay his arrival at Coltrane House no longer.

He set his horse off at a slow walk, taking his time as he advanced down the hill, filling himself with his first sight of Coltrane House in five long, empty years.

As he rounded a turn in the roadway, he emerged from out of the trees and looked out upon the gentle, sweeping swells of lawn that led up to the house. A benevolent sun shone down brightly on the huge, rambling three-story structure, blinking brightly off the many-paned windows, warming the mellow pink brick, turning the ornate wooden trim a dazzling white. More than two dozen chimneys dotted the several roofs making up the original building and its many additions, the flat roofs all seemingly corralled by the white-stone balustrade that ran completely around their edges.

Many were the times Jack and Kipp had climbed out onto the roofs, to play hide-and-seek behind the tall chimneys, to frighten poor, beleaguered Aloysius Bromley into near apoplexies as they climbed up on the balustrades and ran along them, a good sixty feet above the ground. Even Merry had tried it, and Jack had finally known how Aloysius felt, being forced to watch helplessly such reckless disregard for personal safety.

"We all thought we were indestructible," Jack said, patting the stallion between its twitching ears. "Nothing could touch us, nothing could harm us."

He circled the building at a distance, taking in the sight of the glass-domed conservatory attached to the house, its sides made up of more than a dozen tall oriel windows. A person could lie on a bench inside the structure and watch the rain or the snow coming down out of the sky, safe from the elements while able to enjoy them at leisure.

He passed by the statuary garden, a half dozen fanciful creations erected by the same ancestor who'd ordered the landscaping of the grounds. He shook his head as he remembered the carnage his father and his firearm-wielding cronies had wreaked there over the years. The result could not have been worse if some mischievous god had used the statues as bowling pins. There wasn't a single statue not missing an arm, or a leg, or—most commonly—a head.

The evergreens making up the design of the garden were all woefully overgrown, their branches allowed to thicken and tangle so that they showed more brown than green. The lily pond, once filled with huge, golden fish, looked to have caved in on one side, and was choked with weeds.

The closer Jack rode, the more evidence of August's reign as master of Coltrane House came into focus. Two of the chimneys showed gaping holes in the brick. Part of the white-stone balustrade, in the area over the formal dining room, had loosened, a length of it tumbling to the ground where it still lay, smashed against the flagstones.

He could see the tall, thick columns lining the long covered walk that was one way to move from the center house to the East Wing—a pleasant area in which to stroll, or to sit under during rainy weather. None of the peeling, rotting columns had been painted in at least two decades, and a huge, raw wooden plank had been wedged against the third column, probably to keep it upright.

And yet the fields surrounding Coltrane House were already planted. The considerable number of livestock appeared well fed. The tenant cottages he'd seen earlier were freshly thatched, and the corn bins were still more than half-full. The sheep wandering the manor grounds beyond the overgrown ha-ha—how Merry had adored that silly name for a sunken fence—were fat and woolly.

"Sherlock's work," Jack breathed as he dismounted at the end of the circular stone drive in front of his childhood home. Like the lily pond, the drive was weed-choked, and it was also full of potholes, none of the drive having seen a rake or a fresh layer of stone in years. "I knew I could depend upon him to keep the estate profitable, just as he did when August was alive. But spend so much as a penny on the house? No, Henry Sherlock would never let Merry put out a penny that couldn't come back twice, even if the house collapsed around her. Keeping the estate, holding on to the land, that's what was and still is most important to Sherlock. Among other things," he ended, his jaw tight.

As he advanced toward the massive front doors of Coltrane House, Jack took one last assessment of the enormous building. The pair of wide, white-stone steps and the balustrade that matched those marching around the edges of the roof were stained and moldy. Three of the steps were cracked. The massive stone urns on either side of the door, once filled with artfully trimmed evergreens, were now just repositories for packed dirt and a few weeds.

Money. Coltrane House needed money. Vast amounts of it. And that was just on the outside. God only knew what he'd find on the inside.

Jack's leisurely ride around the house had taken away any element of surprise for anyone who might have chanced to spy him out one of the hundred or more windows. He therefore decided Walter's suggestion of a war whoop announcing his presence would probably be seen in the light of being slightly overdone. So thinking, he approached the doors and lifted a hand to raise the brightly shining brass knocker.

Which was as far as he got before one of the doors opened and he was staring down the barrel of a quite deadly-looking hunting rifle.

"You have five seconds to turn around and start running before I shoot you where you stand."

Jack refused to flinch. He raised one eyebrow, then slowly slid his gaze along the weapon until it collided with the figure of one very angry-looking young woman.

Who couldn't be Merry. Could she? Wait . . . yes. Yes, she could. There were the same huge sky-blue eyes. The same riot of curls, a darker red than he remembered, but just as wild, just as untamed. The freckles were still there, dancing across her nose and cheeks, although he saw no evidence of her wonderful, wide smile. And, unless he was mistaken, she was dressed in one of his old shirts, an outgrown pair of his breeches, and the riding boots he had worn at the age of twelve. God bless the child. She hadn't changed a bit.

But she had grown up, left the last of her childhood behind her. All her coltish awkwardness was gone, and she'd at last grown into her body, her long, once gangling limbs. She was beautiful. Unbelievably lovely. Tall, wonderfully formed, her posture graceful—or as graceful as one could be while wielding a rifle.

And she most definitely wasn't smiling. She wasn't laughing. She wasn't even throwing herself at him, doing her best to beat him into flinders for having deserted her.

She was simply staring at him. Looking at him without really seeing him, refusing to really see him.

Jack was just about to grab the barrel and pull the rifle from her hands when a voice from behind the door said, "Put it down, Merry. I've told you, shooting him won't do you any good at all. Poison, that's the ticket. It's slower, much more painful, and you're less likely to hang for it."

Merry's finger left the trigger just as Jack pushed the barrel out of the way and stepped past her, into the large foyer. "Mr. Bromley? Aloysius? Is that you?" he asked, holding out his hand to the gray-haired old man, who really hadn't changed a bit in five years. He still wore the same long scarf wrapped three times around his neck—be it summer or winter, the scarf remained. He still had the heavy-lidded look of a wise, slightly sad old sage, while maintaining a humor that could only be called wicked. Jack took the man's hand in both of his, squeezing it tightly. "God, it's good to see you!"

"And me you, Jack," the tutor said, his watery gray eyes twinkling. "I believe you still owe me a paper on Homer's *Odyssey*, however. Have it on my desk by tomorrow morning, if you please."

Jack grinned, feeling some of his tension easing away—at least as long as he kept his back to Merry, who still held the rifle even though it was now harmlessly pointed at the tiles. He knew what his former tutor was trying to say, and quickly agreed. "We'll split a bottle or two tonight as I tell you of my own odyssey instead, if that will suffice?"

"Done and done," Aloysius Bromley said, giving Jack a hearty slap on the back. "And then we will discuss the *Iliad*. You do remember, don't you, Jack? It's all about the siege of Troy. You might want to bring paper and pen, and take notes?"

"If we're all done being sloppy?"

Jack turned to look at Merry once more. Look at his wife once more. Dear Lord, his wife? No. It was still impossible to think of her that way. In fact, it was impossible to think of

her in any way at all. Because she was definitely no longer
the Merry he always tried so hard to remember. The Merry
he'd bounced on his knee, helped nurse through a bout of
measles, taught how to tie her bonnet strings, inadvertently
given a black eye when she'd failed to catch the ball he'd
thrown her.

No, she was none of those memories. She wasn't the
playmate he remembered. She wasn't the one who sat on the
sidelines, cheering his every exploit. She wasn't the silly infant who dogged his footsteps night and day, learning from
him, teasing him out of his dark moods, worshiping at his
feet.

Neither was she the Merry who had caught him out fumbling at a housemaid's breasts, the Merry who had then run
to Kipp to tell him that their good friend Jack was no better
than Awful August and his drunken guests.

And she most certainly wasn't the same injured innocent
his father had robbed of her inheritance, her freedom, by
forcing her into a marriage that had destroyed Jack's hopes
for her future.

"Merry?" Jack inquired, gesturing toward the Main Saloon. "If we might adjourn—minus this nasty piece, if you
don't mind," he added, removing the rifle from her nerveless
fingers and handing it over to the tutor, who took it gingerly.

Jack watched Merry's departing back as she whirled and
stormed toward the Main Saloon, leaving him to follow in
her wake if he dared. Good Lord, those old breeches of his
had never fit him so well. "Do I dare follow her?" he actually asked Aloysius, who only shrugged before turning to
pull his old body back up the stairs, to the safety of the
schoolroom.

Aloysius hesitated halfway up the first flight, turning to
look down at Jack. "She doesn't hate you, you know. She
hates herself because she can't hate you. Of course, she

doesn't know that, which is another way of saying that I believe you should watch your back, at least for a while. She's had five years to think up ways to make your life a living hell, and Merry has always been quite inventive, if you remember."

"But she was safe," Jack said, hating to hear the question in his own voice.

"Many would sacrifice safety for happiness, you know, Jack." Aloysius shook his head. "We gave Meredith what she needed, never what she wanted. You'll be amazed at how she's grown, Jack. Amazed, and surprised, and most probably impressed. But I doubt you'll enjoy yourself these next weeks and months. Be gentle with her, Jack, allow her to hate you for a while longer. In time, she'll make you an exemplary wife."

"I don't want a wife," Jack said flatly. "And, if I did, it certainly wouldn't be Merry. For God's sake, Aloysius, we grew up as brother and sister."

Aloysius lifted one end of his long scarf and fanned himself with it. "That may have been the way you felt ten years ago, Jack. But not by the time you left here, no matter how you might have still been lying to yourself, telling yourself that you knew what was best for her. So don't lie to me now, Jack, even if you need to delude yourself a while longer." He shook his head sadly. "You were always such an intelligent lad. I thought you might have learned something in the years since you rode away from here, your body bruised, your heart full of hate, of shame. Don't disappoint me, Jack. Don't disappoint me."

"Oh, that was cutting," Clancy said, looking down at Jack pityingly as Jack passed under the elaborate wooden arch he and Cluny were perched on, heading into the Main Saloon.

"Not cutting enough," Cluny responded hotly. "Doesn't want her? What makes him think she'll even have him? Still, did you see her? Did you see the pair of them, together again? Had you ever thought we'd live long enough to see such a sight? 'Eternity was in our lips and eyes, bliss in our brows' bent.'"

"'Ay, every inch a king!'" Clancy said feelingly, randomly grabbing at another of Shakespeare's lines, his clasped hands pressed to his breast. "But we didn't live long enough to see them, Cluny. When are you going to remember that we're dead?"

"It doesn't matter," Cluny said, wiping a nonexistent tear from his eye with the sleeve of his burgundy-velvet doublet. "They're together again, and our long wait is finally over. How many nights have I heard my sweet Merry crying for your naughty Jack? How many years did I watch her as she struggled on, alone, forgotten? She thought she was angry, believed she hated him. But she'll forgive him now, because she's a good girl at heart. She'll forgive him, and she'll love him, and we'll all be happy again. Although it might be prudent if I were to hide the rifle."

"Aloysius will take care to do that, I'm sure," Clancy said, sighing, then floated neatly down to the floor. "'Blessed are the peacemakers on earth.'"

Cluny nodded his agreement. "You want to see Jack again, Clancy? Oh, come on, I know you're longing to be close to him. Shall we join them then? Watch? Rattle the chandelier if they seem to be close to sword points?"

Clancy looked longingly toward the closed door. "So tall, so handsome, so immaculately turned-out. A gentleman of the world, Cluny, a gentleman of the world. He has become all that I've wanted for him, all that I've dreamed these more than twoscore years. I could watch him all day long."

"I thought so," Cluny said, holding his nose and slowly

floating down to the tile floor, where he landed with his feet a good two inches sunk into the tiles. Even after six months, landings remained a problem to him. "If Merry lets us in, of course. You know how she can get. Welcomes us like the flowers in May most times, but when she wants us out, we're out."

"She wouldn't dare. Not today of all days." Clancy turned to walk through the closed doors, into the Main Saloon. He stopped when his beaky nose collided with solid wood. "Saucy, stubborn baggage," he grumbled, then pressed his ear against the wood, frowned. "Can't hear a thing, Cluny. Come on, we'll go around outside, and peek in the windows."

"Can't," Cluny said, happy to share his knowledge with the man who had believed himself superior to him, the man who, basically, was mentally superior to him, both before their deaths and since. "Once Merry has said no, it's no, and we both know it. Don't go in her bedchamber unless I'm invited, don't get to tag along after her when she's riding the fields in a temper, don't get to listen when she don't want me to hear. That's the rules, Clancy, and we both have to obey them. We'll probably have more rules soon, too, once we introduce ourselves to Jack, and if he believes in us."

"If he believes in us? I never thought of that, Cluny," Clancy replied, slowly walking away, his steps dragging as he headed toward the kitchens. He always went to the kitchens when he was unhappy, to smell the aroma of good food being cooked up by Mrs. Maxwell. "What will I do, old friend, if he doesn't believe in me?"

"He will, Clancy, he will. Just give him time. He's barely even home, and has his hands quite full with Merry at the moment, I'm sure." Cluny gave one last, longing look toward the closed doors.

Loath to leave that spot, he lingered a moment more,

drawing on his love of Will Shakespeare, hoping to find the right words. " 'For aught that I could ever read, could ever hear by tale or history—' " he broke off, mid-quote, as the sound of shattering pottery escaped the Main Saloon, then finished quickly, " 'the course of true love never did run smooth.' Clancy!" he called out as he ran fast as he could to catch up with his friend. "Wait for me!"

Chapter Twelve

Merry glared at the broken bits of porcelain. "Well, that was bloody stupid! You used to be able to catch things, Jack."

"My apologies, Meredith," Jack said, gifting her with an elegant bow, which only made her want to pick up another figurine and toss it at his head. "Although I must say I'm gratified to see that there's still some furniture in here, and even a scattering of vases and the like. I would have thought August's greedy fingers had rid the place of every stick and bit of china."

"You know he never came here again, not after you'd gone. That was part of the bargain you made with the man, Jack, remember. Henry held him to it, I don't know how, and never cared enough to ask. What you see here are pieces the Forfeit Man retrieved, or those Mrs. Maxwell and I used to hide away when we thought Awful August might visit," Merry said, talking too much, wishing she could stop looking at him. Looking at him and drinking in the sight of him. Wanting to do nothing more than launch herself into his arms and welcome him home, tell him how much she'd missed him every single moment he'd been gone.

He looked so cool, so composed. So well dressed and presentable, while she stood here in her oldest clothes. Jack's oldest clothes, as she was sure he knew. Neither Merry nor the clothing she was wearing was all that clean, either, as she'd already ridden down to the stream, where she'd sat and thought—and cried—for almost an hour that morning.

Damn him for finding her looking like this. She should have shot him!

Instead, she decided to hurt him, and she knew just how to do it. "If you're meaning to go looking for Cluny and Clancy, you won't find them here. They're in the cemetery, and have been since two months before last Christmas. They died within days of each other, even though Clancy wasn't all that ill. I think he just didn't want to go on. Not with Cluny gone. Not with you gone."

She watched him closely, waiting for his reaction. For his look of shock, of pain, of shame.

"Yes, I know," Jack said without emotion, walking over to the drinks table and pouring himself a glass of wine. "Word came to me."

Merry had been about to sit down on one of the couches, but Jack's admission had her hopping to her feet once more. "Word—word *came* to you? What the devil does that mean, Jack? How did word *come* to you?"

"Ah," he said, coming to sit down on the facing couch, motioning for her to sit down as well. "Then Sherlock is to be believed. I had sworn him to secrecy, but until now I didn't know that he kept his word. So he never told you that he and I have kept up a correspondence these past five years?"

Merry did sit down. It was either that or she would have fallen down. "Henry—I don't believe it! He never said . . . never even hinted. . . . He even tried to convince me you could be dead . . ." She glared at Jack. "You bastard. Not a word, not a word in five years. You *could* have been dead, for all I knew, for all poor Cluny and Clancy knew. And I wish you *were* dead. I'd rather see you dead than see you the way you are now."

She turned her head, no longer able to look at him. Thank God she had willed Cluny and Clancy clear of the Main Saloon for now. They didn't deserve to hear how little Jack had cared for them. "Go away, Jack. Just go away. We don't want you here. We don't need you here."

"I'm afraid that isn't possible," Jack bit out, then downed the remainder of his wine as he stared at her levelly. "You see, Merry, I've come back to save you. You're looking at a very rich man, Merry, much as that must shock you. And I've returned home to claim my inheritance. This house, these lands. No more mortgages, Merry, no more debts. I'm here to settle them all."

"Really?" she said, turning to look at him once more, turning to glare at him once more. She didn't believe a word he was saying. "Isn't that interesting."

"Perhaps not interesting, Merry, but true nonetheless. I had hoped you might be at least marginally impressed."

"And your wife? Have you come home to claim her as well?" she asked, outwardly settling herself more comfortably into the couch, sitting at her ease, while inside she was flying in a dozen different directions.

"Our marriage? You're my sister, Merry, not my wife. Not in my heart, not in yours. Our marriage was a sham, and we both well know it. I stopped in London before coming down to Lincolnshire, bought a town house for you. A very good address I'm told, even Kipp says so. You can go there, take Honey and the Maxwells with you if you wish—take anyone you want. I'll hire a companion for you, begin work on gaining an annulment. I deserted you on your wedding day, and will admit to it, to that and the fact that the marriage was never consummated. By next spring you'll be having your Season, Merry. You can have everything your parents would have wanted for you, everything I've always planned for you."

She stood up, walked to a window overlooking the lawns, took herself as far from Jack as she could without leaving the room. "You're unbelievable, Jack. You have it all worked out, don't you? My whole life, *planned* for me. You go away, gather up a fortune, then come marching home with your full pockets and tell me to leave, take myself off. After I've spent the last five years holding *your* estate together. Not mine, Jack, right? Your estate, your home. Never mine. How very . . . convenient for you." She turned away from the window, to see him standing now, looking at her strangely. That had better not be pity she saw in his eyes, or she'd definitely have to kill him.

"Merry—sweetheart—the marriage has to be ended," he said, walking toward her. "We both know that. You were forced into it, I was beaten and threatened into it. We have to end it now, so that you can be free, so that you can get on with your life. I have the money now, the money that should have been yours the day you turned twenty-one. If August hadn't forced the marriage, taken every last penny for himself and called it your dowry."

"No." Merry backed up a step, held up a hand to warn him to stay where he was. "No, Jack. Absolutely not."

"No?" Jack halted where he was, looked at her narrowly. "No?" he repeated. He shook his head. "You don't want an annulment, Merry? You can't really want to stay married to me. Not if Kipp's right, and you hate me. Not if you have any sense in your head."

"Well, then, there you have it, don't you, Jack?" Merry asked sweetly. "I don't have any sense in my head. Not a ghost of sense. But don't believe I want to remain married to you, because I don't. I hate the very thought. But I like being Mrs. Coltrane, Jack. I very much like being mistress of Coltrane House, running the estate. I'm exceptionally good at it, you know. Extraordinarily good."

She walked toward him, confident once more, growing more confident as he backed up a single step, then two, knowing she had thrown him off his guard. "You used to ride as the Forfeit Man, Jack, remember?" she continued, her voice now hard, unyielding. "And then you rode out of my life, away from Coltrane House, the place you said you loved above everything. You just left, gave up. Quit. You've *forfeited* any right you might have to Coltrane House, Jack. Forfeited it to me. I deserve it. I earned it. And I love it every bit as much as you do. You're not going to send me away. Coltrane House is mine, Jack, and it will remain mine, even if I have to remain legally married to you in order to keep it."

She turned her back to him, then spun back with a hard glint in her eye. "Do you want heirs, Jack? I should think you might. Now, there's a dilemma your new fortune won't solve. What to do, what to do. Will you be able to touch your *sister*, do you think?"

She watched, her heart pounding in her chest, as Jack turned away from her, began to pace, obviously agitated, obviously longing to grab hold of her and shake her back to what he undoubtedly saw as sanity. *No more.* The words pounded inside her brain. No more would people tell her where she belonged, what she should do, how she was to be happy. Not Cluny, not Henry Sherlock, and not Jack Coltrane. No more!

"Are you mad, Merry?" Jack asked her. "You actually want this marriage to continue? A mutual dissolution of the marriage, a generous settlement, even the London town house I've bought for you . . . I'd never even considered that you'd—*Christ*." He ran a hand through his hair, dislodging a few locks from the neat queue at his nape so that they hung down around his face. "And I can't divorce you without ruining you and looking like the greatest cad in nature—and you know it. I don't believe this! Of all the stupidity—"

"You say you have plenty of money now, Jack. Money that seems very important to you. You could simply deed Coltrane House over to me, by way of a settlement, then take your annulment and go happily on your way. Buy yourself two estates, three. After all, Awful August has been in the ground for more than two years. Sherlock must have told you in his *letters* to you. If you waited those two years without coming back here, obviously Coltrane House doesn't mean that much to you," Merry suggested, dying inside, because one thing was true—he obviously did not want her. Had he only come back for Coltrane House? Was the estate all that meant anything to him? She had to know.

"Give you—give you Coltrane House?" Jack glared at her, seared her with his gaze, all but set her on fire with the heat of it as he answered her unspoken question. "Never!"

Merry nodded, walked past him on her way to the door. "Then we have nothing else to talk about, do we? We're married, we stay married, and we both stay at Coltrane House. I'll see that Maxwell takes your bags upstairs. You do have a coach following after you, don't you? And a valet, I suppose, as you were always all thumbs when it came to tying a cravat, and the one you're wearing bears the hall-mark of a master of the science. Kipp has educated me to understand these things. We dine at six, in the small dining room. Please be prompt."

She kept moving, knowing it was time to leave, before he exploded into a rage. Poor Jack, so very predictable. But he grabbed her upper arm as she went to breeze past him, drawing her up short, bending his head so that his face was a mere inch from hers. She could smell him, smell the animal heat of him. She was looking at Jack in the midst of one of his darkest rages. "Don't do this, Merry. You don't want me for a husband, you truly don't. Or haven't you considered the fullness of what you're proposing?"

Merry kept her eyes level with his, refusing to blink, refusing to look away. "I know you, Jack. I've known you all my life," she said quietly. "I know you even better than you know yourself. You don't frighten me. But I frighten you. Don't I? Because you don't know me at all. Not anymore." Then she shook off his grip and walked out of the room before the first tear slid down her cheek.

He was everything she remembered, everything she'd tried so hard to forget.

Merry sank down on the concrete bench inside the conservatory, not seeing the new blooms, not feeling the humidity in the air. All she could see was Jack.

He was still incredibly handsome, even more handsome than she remembered. Tall, strong, with long hair dark as midnight, dark as his blackest mood. His eyes were still that same startling green against whitest white, still intelligent and piercing and yet vulnerable, searching, full of questions.

He was the same Jack who had kissed her scraped knees. The same Jack who'd shared clandestine suppers with her in the nursery. The same Jack who used to sneak downstairs to get those delicious meals from Mrs. Maxwell, food that had supposedly been concocted for Awful August's guests, and not for the two hungry, hidden children. He was the same Jack who had taught her falconry, fishing, shooting, how to ride bareback across a fallow field and take a high fence without landing on her head. The same Jack who had promised always to love her, always to protect her, never to leave her.

The same Jack who had been beaten until he had broken, had agreed to stand beside Merry as a drunken vicar read them their vows so that August could rob the remainder of her inheritance without legal censure. The same Jack who had agreed to leave England in exchange for Merry's safety, in exchange for August's promise never to visit Coltrane House again.

He had gone away.

Without more than a few frantic words passing between them. He had gone without a single promise to return, without a backward glance. He hadn't left her a note, hadn't written a single letter to her or to Kipp in five long years.

He'd simply disappeared.

And left her alone.

Clancy had told her that he and Jack had managed to speak together for a few moments before Henry had driven away, Jack lying in the back of the farm wagon as it headed for the coast. Clancy had promised to look after Merry for him, to protect her, to enlist Cluny and Aloysius, Lady Willoughby and Kipp to stand along with the Maxwells as some sort of guardians until he could return to Coltrane House. For a while, Merry had believed, needed to believe Jack's thoughts were of her, that he would only be absent a little while, then return to her.

But the days had turned into weeks, and the weeks into

months, and Merry's hopes had begun to die. When the months slid into years she'd finally concluded that Clancy had only been kind, and had lied to her in an effort to protect Jack with a comforting untruth. Jack had probably wanted to leave. He'd hated and hated, and then he'd been humiliated, beaten. And he'd gone away. Not to recover and grow strong, but just to be gone.

And now he was back.

What had he done when he'd left Coltrane House? Where had he run to? What had he found waiting for him there? How had he survived, prospered? *Why had he come back?*

Did he look at her now and still see the child he'd always insisted remain a child to him, a sister to him, even as she had grown, become a girl of seventeen? Or had he, in their short, unhappy reunion in the Main Saloon, at last seen that she was a grown woman, her own woman? The rifle had been simple bravado, a silly throwback to the impetuous child she had been. But the woman who had faced him in the Main Saloon, the woman who had dared him, who had defied him, was a very different person indeed. Did he see that? Would he ever acknowledge that?

Did he even care?

"A very good afternoon to you, Mrs. Coltrane—no, please. Don't be startled. I didn't mean to frighten you, discommode you in any way. I'm Walter, Jack's friend, come here with him from America, and perfectly harmless although I've often been told I don't look the part. Can you imagine my shock upon hearing that? May I sit down?"

Merry looked up, a very long way up, and into the dark eyes of the man who'd just introduced himself. He looked oddly exotic, foreign and rather forbidding, but his expression was kind. And he'd said he was Jack's friend. She motioned for him to sit down beside her. "You've come from America with Jack? So that's where he's been? America?"

"Philadelphia, more exactly, and points west a time or two when we were purchasing land as investments." Walter turned to her, smiled. "And yes, I'm an Indian. Not a particularly savage one, but an Indian just the same. That was going to be your next question, wasn't it, Mrs. Coltrane?"

Merry felt herself blushing, for that had been exactly what she'd wanted to ask. She wiped at the tears that still lay on her cheeks, then gave the man her full attention, tried to smile. "I—I've seen engravings and the like. But there were feathers, and knives, and hatchets. And decidedly not frock coats. Are you sure you're an Indian? Perhaps if you were to raise one hand menacingly, then open your mouth really wide, pretending to give out a terrible yell before you relieved me of my hair?"

"Touché, Mrs. Coltrane." Walter sat down, smiled at her. "Well, since I haven't been able to send you screaming into the top of that small lemon tree over there, I suppose I shall just have to congratulate you on your own successful routing of my good friend, Jack. You know you couldn't have done anything more likely to have him considering a judicious retreat to the nearest inn than to have welcomed him home, the prodigal husband you can't—if you'll excuse me—wait to invite into your bed. After, of course, you made him feel so very comfortable by leveling a rifle at his heart."

"Jack told you all of that? My, you must be his very good friend. But it wasn't quite that way, Mister—um . . ."

"Just Walter, Mrs. Coltrane. I wouldn't expect anyone to get their tongue around more than that."

"All right. Walter. And it wasn't like that, really it wasn't. Well, perhaps half of it," she said, smiling slightly. "If Jack has already been so open with you, I suppose we two should also cry friends, just so that you don't think I'm always bloodthirsty. Jack certainly expected me to be angry with him, you see, perhaps even threaten to shoot him. I was merely behaving as he'd have wished—up until the moment when I behaved as I wished, that is."

She bent her head, laced her fingers together, feeling the hurt wash over her again. "As for the rest of it? That took me longer. I knew Jack was back, because Henry Sherlock told me." She looked at Walter. "You know about Henry Sherlock? Who he is?"

"I do," Walter said kindly, laying his hand on hers. "I tried to convince Jack to write to you personally, but he's a stubborn sort. He'd made his plan, and he would not deviate from it, not even for common sense."

Merry smiled sadly. "Oh, yes, you definitely are Jack's very good friend to know him that well. I know him well, too, Walter. And I knew what Jack would want when he came here. He would want to walk straight in and act as if he'd never been gone. As if there had been no marriage, no desertion. As if I was still a child, and hadn't been in charge of Coltrane House for several years. That's Jack, you see, master of all he surveys. Or so he thinks."

She raised her head, lifted her chin, looked into Walter's unreadable eyes. "Coltrane House is mine, by forfeit. Or at least it's half-mine. This is my home, the only home I've ever had. I love it with all my heart. And Jack Coltrane is not going to just stroll in here and take it away from me."

"So rather than try to keep him out, you invited him in, knowing he couldn't possibly accept your terms. Congratulations, Mrs. Coltrane. You've tied him up quite nicely. I couldn't have done better myself, and I pride myself on my ability to be as devious as possible." He folded his arms across his chest. "So, since we two have now cried friends, and since I hope that you will trust my discretion—what happens next?"

Merry looked at him, wide-eyed and genuinely startled. "Next? My God. I don't have the slightest idea."

Walter took the posy from his buttonhole, sniffed it appreciatively. "Ah, I see. Jack works from a carefully worked out but fatally flawed plan, and you simply go wherever your heart or your hurt leads you. This will be enjoyable, then, won't it? Definitely worth the sea voyage."

Chapter Thirteen

It had just gone six, and the second dinner gong had rung. Jack stood in the Main Saloon, remembering the conversation—argument—he and Merry had bumbled through earlier. He wondered if she was going to come down for dinner or just hide in the kitchens and dump poison into the green peas before Mrs. Maxwell brought them to the table.

He lifted the wineglass to his lips, then smiled ruefully. Little minx. He could always kill her, he supposed. Slip up behind her, throttle her, then stuff her body in a sack and toss it down a well. Hadn't that been one of Merry's favorite answers to the age-old question: "What shall we do about Awful August?"

Merry had always been full of outlandish solutions to insurmountable problems. Why, in a way, the Forfeit Man had been her idea, as she'd always been so enamored of Robin Hood and his Merry Men.

He frowned, remembering the Forfeit Man's last ride, remembering Merry's part in it. Remembering how she'd outtalked him—outthought him, actually—just a few hours earlier, there in the Main Saloon, and sent him crawling into a bottle in a way he hadn't done in nearly five years.

"Damned, interfering little monster," he grumbled to himself, downing the last of the wine he'd poured the moment he entered the Main Saloon. The wine would go well with the ale he'd been dedicatedly drinking most of the afternoon at The Hoop and Grapes in the village. "How could such a sweet baby have grown up into such a pain in my rump?" He collapsed into a chair, his legs splayed out in front of him. "And now she's grown into a woman. When did that happen? *How* did that happen? Sweet Jesus. What am I going to do with a grown woman?"

"Uh-oh. He's talking to himself, Clancy," Cluny said as he and his friend walked into the room. "That can't be good, can it?"

Clancy tipped his head, looked closely at Jack as he sipped his wine. "It might be. He's three-parts drunk, Cluny. It's what men do when women confound us. We dive head-first into a bottle. Poor Jack, although I am slightly encouraged. He'll be all right, at the end of it. Remember what the Bard said: 'Men have died from time to time, and worms have eaten them, but not for love.'"

"He loves her, then? I don't think so. I think he wants to strangle her. And here she comes now, the little dear, if my ears don't mistake me. To the chandelier, Clancy? It's best to be out of harm's way, don't you think?"

Cluny then tried to rise, boost himself off the floor and into a nice, slow, cross-legged float that would take him to the chandelier. He rose an inch, then fell back onto the carpet, unable to move. "Well, there's something I didn't expect." He furrowed his brow. "I'll just have to concentrate, won't I?"

What he did, however, was hiccup. And disappear.

"Cluny?" Clancy called out from the chandelier. "Where are you?"

Cluny peeked out of the top of the huge Chinese vase that sat beside the fireplace—the vase that was just now slightly rocking side to side thanks to the impact of one ghostly arrival. "How did that happen?" he asked.

"You hiccuped, you clay-brained giglet! You always do when you try to concentrate. Look, Jack's looking at you. Now get up here."

Cluny hastened to obey, all his ghostly skills deserting him, so that the vase rocked once more as he took his exit. Finally, on his third try, he managed to propel himself up and into the chandelier.

Jack looked at the vase, then looked at the empty wineglass in his hand, deciding that drunk was one thing, but hallucinating was quite another. He turned his back on the fireplace, dismissing whatever had happened as a trick of his ale- and wine-drugged mind.

He put the glass down just as Merry walked into the room, and he stood up, bowed to her as a gentleman should. Most gentlemen, he decided, would not have stopped at a bow. They'd be on their knees, worshiping her. She was glorious in pale green silk, her burnished curls piled high on her head, a modest string of garnets around her throat. If she were anyone but Merry, and he had first spied her out across a dance floor in London, Jack knew he'd probably be racing to her side, eager to add his name to her dance card.

As it was, however . . .

"Ah, sweet wife," he drawled, executing a rather handsome leg even as he pinned a smirk onto his face. "What? Unarmed?"

"Always the wit, weren't you?" Merry answered as she flounced herself down on one of the couches, much in the way she had as a child. "Maxwell tells me you've had your trunks deposited in your old chamber." Her grin was as near to evil as she could make her wide, sunny smile. "Are you having a new lock installed, or do you just plan to shove a chair under the handle to keep me out?"

Jack smiled at her words, then remembered that Merry had always been able to tease him out of his blackest moods. She had also, he likewise recalled as his smile disappeared, been responsible for nearly half of those dark moods in the first place.

He rubbed a hand across his forehead, trying to shake off the effects of a day of drinking, a badly planned bout of self-indulgence he already regretted. "Let's start over, shall we, Merry? I've enough on my plate at the moment, just being here again, without the two of us being at daggers-drawn."

Merry continued to glare at Jack for another moment, then spread her hands in her lap, looking down as if to inspect the state of her fingernails. "Very well," she said at last, looking up at him again. "Welcome home, Jack. So glad you're back. How nice of you to remember we exist." She lifted her head, the glare still intact. "There. Was that good enough? Or perhaps I should tell Mrs. Maxwell to forgo tonight's planned menu in favor of the fatted lamb I'll be running out to slay in honor of your return?"

Jack stifled a laugh. "Oh, if Aloysius could hear you you'd be writing an essay for him yet tonight. That's *calf*, Merry. Fatted calf."

"Is that so? Don't instruct me, Jack. We're past those days, long past," she grumbled. He watched as she fought to maintain her anger, then relaxed as a slow, wide grin claimed her features. God, she had the widest, most ingratiating smile. Always had. Even at six, when her front two teeth had gone missing. "Oh, Jack," she admitted, shaking her head. "I did miss you."

"I missed you too, infant. Very much." He thought she might jump up from her seat then, throw herself into his arms as she had been wont to do at the drop of a hint in days gone by. But she just sat there, no longer smiling. "What is it, Merry?"

"Infant, Jack?" she asked, cocking her head to one side. "I'm twenty-one years old, nearly twenty-two. And married. I've been married for five long years. To you. I'm scarcely an infant."

Maybe he'd been wrong. Maybe he hadn't had enough wine. Picking up his glass, he returned to the drinks table, poured himself another measure, then poured one for Merry as well. After all, as she'd said, she was a grown woman. Grown women were allowed a simple serving of wine, weren't they? Standing with his back to her, he picked up her glass, hesitated, then pulled the stopper from the cut-glass water decanter and poured two fingers of the liquid into Merry's wine.

He walked over to her, handed her the glass, watched as she took a sip, then glared at the glass as she pulled a face. "What's wrong?" he asked, all innocence.

"What's wrong?" she repeated as he sat down on the facing couch. "You've watered my wine, that's what's wrong. I'll thank you to remember that you are no longer in charge of me, Jack. Not what I do, and certainly not what I drink."

"On the contrary, Merry," he supplied silkily, crossing one leg over his knee as he relaxed against the cushions. "As you've also reminded me, I'm your husband. I am totally in charge of you. Just as I always was when you were running about the estate with your knees scratched and your nose dripping and your hair looking as if bats had taken up residence."

Merry pressed her hands together around the stem of the wineglass, which snapped, spilling wine all over her rather fetching gown. "Damn and blast!" She leapt to her feet, the two pieces of wineglass tumbling to the floor. "This is getting us nowhere, Jack. *Nowhere.*"

"Oh, I don't know," he said, smiling as she pulled out a handkerchief and began rubbing at the dark stain on the front of her gown. "I'm rather enjoying myself. Seeing you like this brings back many fond memories. Do you remember the day you tried to walk along the top of the fence outside the stables, and ended by falling headfirst into the rain barrel?"

The chandelier shivered above Jack's head.

He looked up at it curiously, then to Merry, who seemed to have somehow regained her good humor, sopping gown or not. "It's that bad? A shouted word is enough to make that thing tremble?"

Merry dismissed his concerns with a wave of her hand. "No, silly. The chandelier's firm. That's just Cluny or Clancy—or both of them, I suppose. The only other time they do that is when Henry Sherlock is visiting, upsetting me with all his dire predictions on how I'm soon to be living under a hedgerow, reduced to gnawing on pilfered turnips. I didn't tell you earlier because I wanted to punish you, but Cluny and Clancy are still here, Jack, still watching over us. They're here now, as a matter of fact. I can always tell, because I can smell the camphor on their costumes. Don't you smell it, Jack?"

Jack could feel his anger building yet again as he stood up, stepped away from the couches. His mood had taken more turns since Merry's entrance into the Main Saloon than a rabbit fighting its way out of a hedge maze. "Ghosts, Merry? You're standing there, happy as any village idiot, and telling me Cluny and Clancy are ghosts? That they're here now, in this room, dangling from the chandelier? Or doing a jig, perhaps? And you expect me to take you seriously when you tell me you're no longer the child I remember? That you're all grown up now? That you're my wife? Good God, and I thought I'd drunk enough today. I haven't, that's clear. I haven't drunk enough by half."

She let go of the skirt she was lightly fanning, trying to dry it, and took two steps in Jack's direction. Two very deliberate steps, so that he, incongruously, found himself backing up an equal distance. When she spoke, her voice was low and full of meaning, her hot gaze concentrated on his face.

"You listen to me, Jack Coltrane, and you listen to me very, very closely. No smirking, no jokes, and no black moods. This is my house. My estate. I only met you with that rifle because I wanted to put you off your stride, straight from the first moment you'd dared to show your face here after running away from Coltrane House, after running away from me. I said we were still married, that I wanted you to treat me as your wife, because I was sure that would give you pause, at least for a while. All that accomplished was to throw you into a bottle—several bottles, if my eyes and nose don't lie. And now you're lowering yourself to insults. You're refusing to see what's in front of your face—that I'm no longer a child, and no longer your damn responsibility. I am Mrs. Jack Coltrane, I am mistress of this estate, and you are nothing but an irritating interloper. I am in charge, Jack, not you. Not now, not ever. Do you understand?"

The chandelier tinkled again, and there was a sudden sound in the wide window embrasure, behind the curtains. The sound of something solid being given a good thump.

"What was that?" Jack asked, momentarily diverted, although his mind was already busy in trying to decide if he should point out a few obvious facts to Merry, or just turn her over his knee and spank her.

"Never mind that, it's just those ghosts you don't believe in," Merry said. "I'm asking you, Jack—do you understand? You're not welcome here."

"But I'm necessary," he said at last, suddenly realizing the full extent of Merry's dilemma, the real reason behind her anger. "I'm necessary because I am your husband. Because, and you must hate me for this, I've returned with full pockets, so that I can at last put Coltrane House to rights the way we've always dreamed of seeing it—not just the estate, but the house we both love. I'm also necessary as your husband, because you can't own this property in your own name. I have you to thank for pointing that out to me this morning. You live here as my wife, on my sufferance. In other words, and in short—you need me here, Merry. Or you need me dead."

"I'll settle for seeing you dead then, Jack. I don't need or want your money!" Merry shot at him, but she turned her back so that he couldn't see her eyes. Of course, he still knew she was about to lie to him. "I wanted to scare you off earlier, and that's why I said the debts were worse than they are. There are some small lingering debts, yes, but I'm paying them. I'm working hard, and I'm paying them. Henry says—"

"Sherlock," Jack interrupted, his voice edged with a distaste he didn't bother to hide. After all, he'd listened to the man when he'd written to him, told him it would be better for Merry if she were allowed to forget him, at least for a while, that Jack shouldn't contact her until she was not quite so angry with him. "Yes, you mentioned him earlier. How is the dear man?"

Jack watched as Merry turned back to him, the light of battle dying in her huge blue eyes. At last, at last, she seemed ready to tell him at least some of the truth. "Henry says a huge payment is due on our largest mortgage before the end of the year. No later, Jack, or there'll be the devil to pay. I work and I work, and there never seems to be an end to Awful August's debts. Do you really have enough money to save the estate? Do you really?"

Jack reached out, took Merry's hand, and felt his heart hitch momentarily as he ran his fingers over her palm, feeling the calluses he hadn't expected to find. She'd been telling the truth. She had been working the estate, probably even working in the fields. "Merry, I—"

She tugged her hand free as the dinner gong sounded again, giving a final warning that their evening meal would soon be served. "Henry's bound to have heard that you're back, considering that half the village drinks in the Hoop and Grapes. He'll be here tomorrow, I'm sure, ready to tell you what he delights in telling me—that Coltrane House is in danger of being signed over to our largest creditor."

Jack looked at Merry for long moments, moments during which he called himself almost every rotten name he could muster—and those were considerable. He thought of apologizing, yet again. But that wouldn't work. He thought about forcibly taking Merry into his arms, comforting her even if she didn't want comfort.

He settled for a brusquely businesslike tone as he said, "I'll meet with Sherlock tomorrow, at which time I'll ask that he prepare a full accounting of the estate's debts for me. I'm confident, Merry, that I will be able to satisfy all of August's lingering debts within the month."

Merry looked as if her next words would hurt her more than a tooth extraction performed by a trained ape. "Thank you," she said, her voice small, but then she rallied. "However, we have yet to settle the most important part of this, Jack, and you know it."

His temper, perhaps mellowed by drink, even temporarily muddled, hit him hot and fast. "Anyone would think you're longing to be bedded, Merry, for all you harp on this supposed marriage of ours. For the moment, however, I assure you that you're safe. I still want to see if we can solve this dilemma some other way."

Her chin came up defiantly. She looked at him through slitted eyelids, very much the grande dame, even if there was a wine stain on her gown and a tear in her eye. "Definitely, Jack. We'll sort it out some other way. As long as it ends with me as mistress of Coltrane House!" And then she turned on her heels and stomped out of the room, leaving him to stare after her, realizing that his temples had begun to pound, and his stomach didn't feel all that sound, either.

He sat down, looked up at the chandelier, looked toward the large vase that had earlier rattled on its base without anyone touching it. Ghosts, was it? Cluny and Clancy—still here, haunting the house? And Merry wanted him to treat her as a grown woman, a woman of sense?

If only Merry could be right. If only Cluny and Clancy were here, still in residence. Then, maybe, he could ease some of his guilt at not being here when they'd needed him most. He could tell them what he'd done, what he'd learned, what he planned to do. Tell them all the reasons why he'd stayed away so long, why he hadn't written to them, made sure they knew he hadn't forgotten them. Then, maybe, he could say good-bye.

He stared at the chandelier, considered what he would say, what he'd say first, after he'd said hello. How did one talk to ghosts? And what did one say if they talked back? Did he smell camphor? He didn't think he smelled camphor. And the chandelier was just hanging there, not moving at all.

Just hanging there . . . not moving . . .

"Oh, bloody hell! I must be out of my mind!" he exploded, then headed toward the doors leading to the gardens, hoping the early-evening air would clear his head.

Cluny stepped through the drapes hanging at the window embrasure and watched as Clancy floated down from the chandelier before joining him on one of the couches. "Don't know why I still must suffer the hiccups," he said, carefully easing himself against the cushions. "Shouldn't, being dead and all. Although I certainly gave Jack a start, didn't I? What a mess, don't you think? Ah, Clancy, 'We have seen better days.'"

Clancy sighed, nodded his agreement, watching as Jack disappeared beyond the French doors. "And we can't let him know we're here, Cluny, offer to help him. He's not ready to believe in us. He's not ready to believe in anything or anyone."

"He's certainly not ready to believe in my Merry. Or she in him. Did you see how they glared at each other? 'O! What a war of looks was then between them!' He couldn't even tell her how pretty she looked in that gown, with her hair all piled up, just like Gilda taught Honey to do it for her years ago. Gilda was ever so good with a brush, wasn't she? Not quite so good at playing Lady Macbeth though, poor thing, rest her soul."

"You know something, Cluny?" Clancy asked, tapping a finger against the side of his nose. "I've been thinking and thinking, and I am beginning to believe that Henry Sherlock may not be quite the friend we've all spent more than twenty years believing him to be. I don't know why. It's just a feeling I get, a look I see in Jack's eyes when the man's name is mentioned. Now why do you suppose I feel that way, Cluny? Cluny?" he repeated, looking around the room as he realized his friend was no longer sitting beside him.

And then he sighed, shook his head. There his friend was,

upside down atop the drinks table, looking wide-eyed and confused, his arms and legs flailing, his head completely stuck inside the brandy decanter. "Oh, Cluny—not another hiccup. Never you mind what I just said, all right? I'll do the concentrating for both of us."

Chapter Fourteen

Merry found Walter wandering the gardens before breakfast the next morning, looking for a perfect white rosebud to stick into his buttonhole. She knew that because he told her so at once, asking her permission before he snapped off a suitable bloom. He then apologized to the rosebud and thanked it for existing, for the pleasure its beauty gave the world, which made Merry like him even more than she had when they'd first met.

"The English countryside pleases me, I must say," Walter told her as he turned down the garden path, as if knowing she wanted to walk with him, talk with him. But he gave her time to marshal her thoughts, speaking of nature and weather and the prospect of at least a week's worth of sunny days ahead of them. He knew those things, he told her. He knew history, and complicated mathematics, but he also knew how to smell the air, interpret the breeze. He couldn't help that, he explained, for he was an Indian.

And that gave her the opening she had hoped for, an opening she immediately took. "Yes, you are, aren't you?

An Indian, that is. And most intelligent, I'm sure. I must introduce you to Mr. Aloysius Bromley, who will enjoy you very much. Just as I would enjoy hearing how you met Jack, how the two of you became friends—even dealt together in business?"

Walter's smile told her that he knew where she wanted to go, and that he was agreeable to taking her there. "Did you know, Mrs. Coltrane, that an Indian can do everything a white man can do? Oh, yes, we can. Except be accepted into society, of course. Except to be accepted in business, naturally. Except to be treated as an equal, even in America, this ancient Indian land that is now, supposedly, the brave new home of the free."

Merry shook her head. "I—I don't understand. I think what you're saying is terrible, but I don't understand it. You weren't a slave, were you?"

His smile was kind, almost indulgent, as was Aloysius Bromley's when that man was trying to impart something important to an uneducated yet eager child. "No, Mrs. Coltrane, we Indians are not slaves. One of the most important rules of owning slaves, as in owning any—forgive me—livestock, is to see that stock multiply. The Americans want us to go away, disappear—not to breed. We're too dangerous. Someday, they'll realize the same is true of the slaves they steal from Africa. Because, Mrs. Coltrane, someday these slaves will pick up books, as I picked up books. They will read, and they will learn. They will, in the eyes of their masters, become as dangerous as I am now."

"Oh," Merry said, feeling horribly ashamed of herself for not realizing that there was an entire world outside her own experience, a world full of miseries different from hers, but definitely no less important. "But—but you seem to be doing very well?"

"Yes, I am," Walter said matter-of-factly. "That's because

I'm brilliant. And because I was brilliant enough to find Jack."

"I don't understand."

"Oh, I think you do, Mrs. Coltrane. I found Jack—we found each other, actually—and Jack went into society for me, went into business for me. We bought land, in his name. We sold that land, bought more, sold more. Why, we even own a river nobody wanted—but they will, and we'll be ready for them. We bought buildings. There is a place in Philadelphia, a very desirable street—a block of very desirable streets—first proposed, years ago, by Benjamin Franklin. Jack and I own almost every parcel in those well-laid-out blocks."

"So he wasn't lying, scraping together every last penny for a good suit of clothes just to impress me? He *does* have money? How much?" Merry asked, then clamped a hand across her mouth, knowing she sounded quite mercenary indeed. "Oh, I'm so sorry! It's just that I'm so desperate . . . and much as I hate admitting it, Walter, I need money. I need it very badly. Not for me, but for Coltrane House."

Walter gave a slight inclination of his head, acknowledging her explanation. "Jack would spent his last penny, shed his final drop of blood, to save Coltrane House," he said, gesturing that they might turn around now, retrace their steps. "Fortunately, he won't have to do either. Ah—and who is this coming toward us?"

Loath to leave the subject of Jack's deep pockets, yet glad to be rescued from seeming to be such a moneygrubbing busybody, Merry turned to see her good friend and tutor advancing toward them along the path. Everyone except Jack had ended up taking their meals in their rooms last night—as no one seemed to want to share a table—so that introductions had not yet been made.

"Aloysius Bromley," she said moments later, "please

allow me to introduce you to Walter, Jack's friend from America. Walter, my tutor and companion, Mr. Bromley. Walter's an Indian, Aloysius. Do you have any books on Indians in the schoolroom? I'd like to read them, if I could?" She turned, smiled at Walter, adding, "I believe I'd like to read enough to be dangerous."

Aloysius looked at her through slitted eyelids, saying, "Yes, Meredith, there are books on Indians in the library, I believe. Most probably directly beside Mr. Samuel Johnson's Dictionary. I suggest, while you're so nearby it, you look up the word *incorrigible*." He then put out his hand, which Walter shook. "My apologies for my student, Walter. She mistakenly believes the whole world understands her, and loves her in spite of her failings."

"And she'd be absolutely correct, at least in my case, Mr. Bromley," Walter said, smiling at Merry, who could feel herself blushing to the roots of her hair. "Now, shall we continue our walk? I've already noticed some plants and bugs in this wild profusion that are foreign to me, and wish to learn their names, perhaps sketch them in my book. And, speaking of bugs, Mr. Bromley, perhaps you might someday find time to tell me more about August Coltrane? I have an interest, you understand."

Aloysius sniffed derisively, and Merry grinned at him. "Oh, go on, Aloysius, tell Walter about Awful August."

The old man fingered the fringe at the end of his long woolen scarf. "There's nothing much to tell, Walter, actually," he said. Then he smiled, took a deep breath, and announced: "Very well. August Coltrane was bovine-stupid. Loud. Crass. Prone to violence. Dedicatedly drunken, remarkably mean and petty, extraordinarily crude. And, praise God, he's also dead."

He let out a long breath, grinned. "Is that enough? I could toss in a few rather eloquent curses for good measure, but

Meredith here would only soak them up like a sea sponge and then squeeze them out later, most probably when the vicar comes to call."

"Probably," Merry agreed, stepping up on tiptoe to kiss the tutor's papery cheek, not at all bothered that Aloysius was talking about her as if she were still a child. "And now I will leave the two of you to become more fully acquainted. I'm off to the kitchens to be sure Mrs. Maxwell isn't overcome by the thought of three more mouths to feed. Jack's valet did arrive, didn't he?"

"Rhodes?" Walter said. "Yes, as a matter of fact, he and the luggage did arrive rather late last night, the driver having lost his way some ten miles from here. If I know Rhodes and, unfortunately, I do, I imagine he'll sleep in this morning, then request his breakfast served in his room."

Aloysius coughed into his hand. "Pardon me? Jack's valet will sleep in? Request his meal in his room?"

"Wait until you meet Rhodes, Mr. Bromley, and explanations will prove unnecessary, I assure you. If he ever leaves his rooms, that is," Walter said, taking the man's arm and heading toward a plant beside the path. "Now, as Mrs. Coltrane has business to attend to, perhaps you might be so kind as to help me with the name of this lovely plant?"

"Please, call me Aloysius. And, yes, Meredith, do run along," the tutor said, already adjusting his spectacles on his nose, the better to inspect the plant. "Well, now, Walter, I do believe what we're looking at here is a . . ."

Merry stood where she was for a moment, realizing that she had been dismissed. Dismissed by Walter, dismissed by Aloysius. She decided that she should most probably be insulted, but she couldn't find a bit of anger inside her. She was much too happy to see Aloysius happy. He'd been at such loose ends since Cluny and Clancy died. Walter seemed to provide enough interest to keep the old man nearly delirious with the curiosity he'd want satisfied.

Which would mean that Aloysius just might be too busy to give her the lectures he was otherwise bound to deliver concerning Jack, their marriage, and her intention to somehow accept Jack's money and then toss him out on his ear. Mostly, she'd be happy to avoid Aloysius because her beloved friend and tutor could always tell when she was not telling the truth. He'd gently nag and badger her until he made her face the real truth, which had a lot to do with Jack, but nothing to do with his leaving Coltrane House.

She sighed deeply, then turned down a side path that led to the kitchens, that real truth still weighing on her shoulders. There might or might not exist a way to get Jack out of Coltrane House. There definitely was no way to get him out of her heart.

If one were to sit in one spot long enough, Walter had told Jack, eventually the entire world would pass by on its way to somewhere else. In the case of Henry Sherlock, Jack was equally sure, "eventually" would take no longer than a day after hearing that he indeed was back in residence at Coltrane House.

When Maxwell announced Sherlock's arrival, Jack— who had been sitting at his ease in his late father's study— looked to the mantel and the clock that ticked there. "Twenty-two hours, twelve minutes," he said out loud, depositing the ancient ledger he'd been looking at into the top drawer of the desk. He steepled his hands in front of him, staring at the doorway.

Clancy, who had been lying on the leather couch in the corner, raised his head, the better to see Jack's face. "And now I'll see if I'm right," he said, not that there was anyone to hear him.

Henry Sherlock walked through the doorway with the air of a man who expected to find the same person he'd last seen five years ago. A broken youth, beaten and battered, grateful for any small service he, the munificent Henry Sherlock, could perform for him.

What he got was Jack Coltrane, all of him. The boy, the man. The youthful anger, the maturity necessary to keep that anger well hidden. The victim, the survivor.

"Hello, Sherlock. Do sit down," Jack said, not rising from his own seat, not offering his hand. Instead, he waved the man to the chair he'd earlier set in front of the desk. A small chair, straight-backed and reasonably uncomfortable. A chair without arms, a chair without consequence. The seat for a subservient, for a man come to pay his respects to the master of Coltrane House. Walter had taught him this small trick, and Jack waited now to see if it worked on Henry Sherlock as well as it had done on other men, in Philadelphia.

"John," Sherlock said, only slightly inclining his head as he split his coattails and sat down. My, but the man was dressing much better than the last time Jack had seen him. "I cannot tell you how gratified I am to see you looking so well. Your letters gave me no indication that I should expect you to appear so prosperous."

"Nor did yours tell me how well you've done for yourself, Sherlock," Jack answered smoothly. "Not quite so much the easily overlooked man now, are you? Why is that, do you suppose?"

Henry Sherlock didn't squirm in his uncomfortable chair. His face didn't go hot with embarrassed color. In fact, the man didn't so much as blink. "That's easily answered. My aunt—you do remember my aunt, don't you, John, the one I visited from time to time? The dear lady died, sadly, and as it turned out, left me with quite a comfortable fortune. I thought I had told you in one of my letters, but it appears I did not."

Jack looked at the man for long moments, then rose and stepped to the drinks table Maxwell had set up in the corner. "Claret?" he asked as he opened the decanter, turning his head to look over his shoulder at the man, who he caught out surreptitiously wiping his brow with a large white handkerchief.

Interesting.

"Merry has told me that, your fortunate circumstances to one side, you still maintain the estate books, as a gesture of your friendship," Jack said as he handed the man a glass, then returned to sit behind the desk once more. "I want to thank you for that, Sherlock, and for watching over Merry as she gained her footing, took on the role of estate manager. Determined little thing, isn't she? And I will say that I was mightily impressed by the condition of the estate as I rode through it on my way here. I'm not as pleased with the condition of Coltrane House itself, but as you told me in your letters, there were August's debts to pay."

"I've done my best, John, through my affection for you and Meredith. After all, I've been a part of Coltrane House since I was little more than a boy myself." He sat back, crossed his legs at the knee. "You're twenty-nine, John, isn't that right? And I've been here since I was twenty, since the year before you were born. I could hardly turn my back on you and Merry, not after all these years."

"How very loyal of you," Jack said, keeping his smile mild, his expression polite. "You've remained here, foregoing the chance to move in London Society—at least its fringes, which would be opened to you. You've purchased a house, Merry has told me, kept yourself within easy reach of Coltrane House. I'm in your debt, Sherlock. Truly I am."

He stood up once more, so that he looked down at the

seated man of business across the width of the desktop. "But I'm home now, and I shall take over the running of the estate. My partner in business, who has accompanied me here from Philadelphia, will take over the financial aspects, which means I'd like all of the records, journals, and ledgers brought here as soon as possible. I assume that you have them, as I've not been able to locate any ledgers less than twenty years old. You will bring them to me? Tomorrow, perhaps?"

Come on, Jack thought furiously as he maintained his smile. *Come on, Sherlock. Flinch. Blink. Do something that betrays you. You didn't expect ever to see me again, did you? And, if you did, you didn't expect what you're seeing now. You swallowed my lies that I was barely eking out an existence in Philadelphia, that I was too ashamed to return to England. Come on, Sherlock. Blink.*

"Of course, John," Sherlock said, getting to his feet. "I can understand why you'd wish to see the ledgers, and I'd be happy to supply them to you as well as explain the various accounts to your man. I'll have them brought to Coltrane House tomorrow morning. As for myself, I'll be unavailable for the next few days, as I've unfortunately found myself with commitments in Southwell. Would Friday be convenient for me to meet with your business partner? Now, with that behind us, once again—welcome home."

Henry Sherlock then extended his hand.

This time, almost automatically, yet very much against his own will, Jack took it.

Chapter Fifteen

Merry kicked at a stone with the tip of her half boot, then looked down to see that it was a perfect skipping stone. Most of the good ones resided on the opposite bank again, which meant she'd one day have to go across and start skipping stones back in this direction. But this one was here, she was here, and she certainly had nothing else to do.

Well, that wasn't exactly true. She had more than enough to do. If she were going to ride the estate, that is, which she'd most certainly refused to do earlier when Jack had asked her to accompany him on his inspection of the property. Not that she wasn't proud of the estate, proud of how well she managed the fields, the forestry, the sawmill, the animals, all of it. She simply couldn't ride with Jack, watch as he began asserting himself as owner once more, taking the reins from her hands even as she watched.

Merry bent down, picked up the skipping stone and two less well shaped specimens, and walked to the bank of the stream.

No, she hadn't wanted to ride along with Jack. Let him

ride out alone, see the planted fields, talk to the workers, inspect the mill, the dairy, the orchards. Let him listen while the tenants and day laborers told him about their mistress, about her, and what a wonderful job of work she'd been doing in his absence. Let him hear how she had worked side by side with them these past five years. Let them tell Jack how they never could have survived without her—how they *had* survived without him. And let him choke on the knowledge!

She skipped one of the stones across the stream, hitting once, twice—then sinking like, well, like a stone.

She glared at the ripples left by the misthrown stone. "Damn!"

Cluny sighed theatrically. "Poor dear. 'Sometimes hath the brightest day a cloud; and after summer evermore succeeds barren winter, with his wrathful nipping cold—' "

"Would you just shut up," Clancy said, giving his ghostly partner a jab in his well-padded ribs as the two of them sat on the large flat rock in the middle of the stream, watching Merry. "The child's in a mood, that's all. And before you say so, no, it's not Jack's fault. What did the child expect—all the flowers of May in one go?"

"I don't like to see her sad, that's all," Cluny said, sticking out his lower lip in a pout. It was amazing how sharp a ghostly elbow could be. "Look at her, Clancy. I know her so well. She's got a mind jammed full of worries this afternoon, poor angel."

And, in fact, Merry was just beginning a mental inventory of woes and worries. Coltrane House itself might be falling down around their ears, she knew, but every workable field was planted, every bit of livestock was fat and healthy, every fruit tree was pruned. Every cottage was thatched, the millstones were all in good repair. The estate was sound, and would produce a healthy profit if not for August Coltrane's massive debts.

What a crushing mass of debt the man had left to her. Debts of honor—as if gambling losses were in the least honorable—had been paid first, as Henry had sworn to her that this was the way of gentlemen. Tradesmen's bills, wages, necessary repairs and replacement purchases—all of those had to be dealt with, with many of those accounts in terrible arrears.

She skipped another stone, the best of the three, and watched it lightly dance across the surface of the water, landing safely on the other side. She smiled, both at her success, and as she remembered having paid so many bills with her hard work.

Because *she* had paid them. She had paid them all. In her role as wife to the absent owner, she had authorized each payment, agreed to each expense as Henry presented it to her for consideration. She had worked and worked, sometimes doing without sleep during the harvest, and she had paid them all.

Merry held the last stone, absently rubbing its flat surface with her thumb, knowing that even as much of her troubles were behind her the worst still lay in front of her.

Even after paying dozens and dozens of bills, the mortgages and private loans Awful August had accumulated with the thoroughness of a dedicated collector still hung over Coltrane House. Five years of scrimping, of saving, of both small and large economies, had not made more than a small dent in those loans and mortgages. She was paying the required interest, as Henry had explained, but all her hard work had not yet reduced the principal of those loans by so much as a bent penny.

As a result, part of Merry was secretly doing handsprings that Jack had returned. A solvent Jack. A man with coins enough in his pocket to begin paying off these last, horrendous debts before August's creditors swooped into Lincolnshire and legally took Coltrane House out from under them.

At the same time, she hated Jack. Hated him for leaving, hated him for staying away. Hated him for coming back and treating her as if she were still a child—telling her what she should do, even who she should be, *where* she should be.

It didn't matter if Jack was the richest man on the entire earth—or if he gave her a home of her own and a generous monetary settlement. None of it mattered if she couldn't be mistress of Coltrane House. She wanted to live here, where she had always lived, in the place she'd always loved. Where she'd always hoped to live with the man she loved.

Here, in this place, where her memories were so much happier than her realities or her hopes for the future.

And it was all Jack's fault.

Yes, she hated him. And she loved him. She hated him because she loved him, would always love him. If only he had come home sooner. If only he'd said he'd missed her with all his heart, that he couldn't be happy without her, that she was not just a part of his life, but his whole life, past, present, and future. His wife.

"His wife?" Merry spit out angrily. "Ha! I'd rather eat dirt!" She hefted the last stone in her hand, then launched it, overhand, into the stream. It hit with an unsatisfying plunk, and immediately sank.

"You'd do better with a rod and reel, Merry, my love. Stoning fish to death takes better aim, I believe. And a rather larger rock."

"Kipp!" Merry whirled around, nearly toppling into the stream in her haste before she ran headlong at her friend, all but vaulting into his arms. "Oh, Kipp—you're home! You're home!"

"And about to be choked to death," he said, disentangling her arms from around his neck, then giving her a kiss on the forehead as she slid down the front of his body until her toes once more touched the ground. "Well, now," he said, holding on to her as he looked down into her face, "how is my little pigeon? Still safe in her coop now that the fox has come home? I could be wrong, but her feathers appear to be at least slightly ruffled."

Merry screwed up her face comically at Kipp's words, then gave a flip of her head to show that she did not care in the least about what she was about to say. "If you mean is Jack here, yes, he is. You saw him in London, didn't you? Yes, I'm sure you did. Everyone knew he was back, except for me. And I, my friend, to answer your question, am still safe as houses." She pushed out of his arms, bending to pick up another stone—not a good skipping stone, but she needed to keep her hands busy. And her eyes averted. "Jack hasn't been the least trouble to me. Not the least."

"You've killed him, then? Good for you."

Merry threw the stone into the stream, not even bothering to watch where it landed. "No, Kipp, I haven't killed him," she said, sitting down on the grassy bank, bending her knees so that she could wrap her arms around her calves. She sighed, and said, "But now that you mention it . . ."

Kipp joined her on the bank, not seeming to care if his buckskin breeches might be ruined. Kipp was like that, she knew—as fine a dresser as Mr. Beau Brummell had been rumored to be in his time, and yet ready and willing to toss all of his consequence away when the spirit moved him.

"You can tell me the truth, Merry. I did see Jack in London, just as you guessed. All stiff-backed with pride, telling me how rich he is now, how smart he is now. Barely mentioning Coltrane House, only asking about you as if you were some sort of afterthought. Not offering more than a word of explanation for not writing to us over the years, for not coming home sooner. I had to leave, Merry, or else we'd have been rolling about on the floor like two schoolboys, beating at each other. I couldn't do that, you know," he ended, smiling. "I have my reputation as a devout coward to be considered."

Merry turned her head, resting her cheek against her knees as she grinned at her good friend. "Yes, Kipp, there is that, isn't there?" She'd known him forever, so that she accepted his startling handsomeness without thought, just the way she accepted his intelligent brown eyes, his sleekly combed blond hair, and the endearing cleft in his chin. Kipp enjoyed playing the fool, but she also knew he was deep, deeper than he'd like anyone to know, and she could see that he was hurting now. Hurting because his good friend, his best friend, had grown into a stranger. An unlikable stranger.

"He wants me to end the marriage, seek an annulment," she said, watching Kipp's face as she spoke, watching as a muscle in his jaw gave a single twitch. "He's even bought me a house in London."

"How gallant of him," Kipp bit out, looking at Merry intensely, "although he hid that truth from me with some faradiddle about the town house being some sort of business investment. I wonder if he gave one moment's thought to the fact that you love Coltrane House as much as he does. Doesn't he remember that this has been the only home you've ever known and you might not want to leave it? Hell, did he even thank you for preserving his bloody inheritance for him while he was gone?"

"Thank me?" Merry frowned, knowing that Jack hadn't thanked her, and that she hadn't wanted his thanks. She had done what she'd done for love of Coltrane House. But he could have praised her, told her she'd done her job well. He hadn't done any of that. "No, Kipp. He didn't. He's just come back and taken over. He's even given his man, Walter, the care of the books, relieving Henry of his obligations, which must please poor Sherlock no end."

Kipp reached out and ruffled Merry's breeze-tangled curls. "Ah, what a child you still are, my love, for all that you look and act so grown-up sometimes. Our quiet friend Henry has to be anything but pleased. You and Jack may love the estate, but Henry has been the one who has always seemed to almost worship it. Not that I'll ever be anything but thankful for the way he always seemed able to manage Jack's father, find ways to keep you and Jack safe. And me, of course. I think Henry, having no family of his own, saw you and Jack as his family. Coltrane House, and the people in it, have become his whole life."

"Perhaps," Merry said, flopping back so that she was lying on the ground, looking up at the blue sky through a canopy of leaves clinging to the branches above their heads. "And even with all of Henry's help, we almost lost everything. I didn't tell you, Kipp, but the largest creditor was about to foreclose, and would have done so the end of this year. Except that Jack says he'll be able to pay the man off, pay off all the loans, all the mortgages."

Kipp ground out a string of curses. When he calmed down, he touched Merry's arm, so that she gazed up at him as he shook his head, looking at her in concern generously mixed with outrage. "How many times, Merry? How many times have I told you to come to me if you needed money? You know I would have helped you, would still help you if Jack's wealth turns out to be more in his mind than in his pockets. You could even pay me back, if you insisted, and with no interest. Except perhaps," he added with a smile, "that I'd demand you promise to smile at me at least once a week for the rest of our natural lives."

Merry lifted a hand to cup Kipp's cheek. "Thank you," she said, her eyes filling with tears. "You're such a good, dear friend, Kipp. I don't deserve you."

"Is that a suggestion that perhaps I do? Nothing like having one's good, dear friend lying in the grass with one's good, dear wife to understand the value of friendship, is there?"

Kipp shot to his feet, giving Merry a clear sight of Jack as he approached along the bank of the stream, glaring at the pair of them.

"This isn't what you think, you idiot," Kipp said, putting himself fully between Jack and Merry. "And what if it is? It's not like you care anyway, is it, Jack?"

"How long, Kipp?" Jack demanded, his hands drawn up into fists. "How long have you wanted her?"

Merry had grown up around Jack's quick temper, and she was still able to gauge its depth when it gripped him. This one was bad. Very bad. And Kipp wasn't helping! She sighed, then reluctantly stood up, stepping in front of Kipp.

"Such a dog in the manger you are, Jack. You don't want me—just as I don't want you—but no one else is to have me, is that it? Or are you still playing at big brother, and just want Kipp to come to you and ask permission to flirt with me? Still, you're right, Jack," she said, giving his chest a good, solid poke with the tip of one finger. "Kipp and I *are* lovers. We're madly in love. Madly, deeply, passionately. That's why he was in London, where he's keeping an opera dancer named Crystal—silly name, but then what would an opera dancer call herself, if not Crystal? He gave her diamonds this past Christmas, gullible idiot that he is. And that's why I don't want a divorce. Because I'm so in love with our dearest, most brilliant Kipp. That makes perfect sense, too, doesn't it?"

She knew which part of her little speech would sink into Jack's brain, cut through all the anger to the fine sense of the ridiculous he was capable of when he wasn't feeling like such a thundercloud. She took a step back, watched while he digested every word, saw as his anger dissipated.

"You told her about some opera dancer?" Jack said at last, pushing Merry out of the way so that he could step closer to Kipp. "You actually told her? Of all the hair-witted, empty-skulled—my God, Kipp, how many times do I have to tell you the brat's ears are always open, always listening? How can you forget that, especially after the time she parroted to your father about the day she saw the two of us stripped to the buff, preparing to swim in this same damn stream we're standing next to now? Your father took a stick to you and me both for that one. She's a child, Kipp, a sweet, naughty, impressionable, big-mouthed child."

"Oh, now wait just a moment," Merry protested as Kipp and Jack fell against each other, laughing at memories that did nothing but embarrass her. It was one thing to have de-fused Jack's temper, to have shown him how silly he was to ever think that Kipp was in love with her. Goodness, in love with her? And why would Jack care, anyway, as *he* certainly wasn't? But it was another thing entirely for the two of them to be laughing at her!

And now they were ignoring her. Again. As they'd done too many times in the past.

"Forgive me, Kipp. I must have been out of my mind," Jack was saying, patting Kipp on the back. "I don't know what's wrong with me, but my head's so full of memories since I came back, so full of anger at old hurts, hurts both real and imagined."

"No, Jack," Kipp was saying, giving him a friendly hit on

the shoulder. "It's my fault. Entirely. I expected too much, forgot too much in your absence. You've been living in some sort of hell, haven't you?"

"Oh, if this isn't just so sweet! Treacle, running out of both your mouths. You should have bibs on, you know, to catch the drips." Merry wondered that the two men couldn't see the heat of her anger shimmering in the air. "First you hate each other, and now you're crying friends. Why don't you just kiss each other, and be done with it?" Merry jammed her fists on her hips and glared at the two of them. They, in turn, were continuing to ignore her and were already planning an evening together at Willoughby Hall so they could crack a few bottles and talk over old times. It was, of course, an invitation that didn't include her.

And then Merry noticed something else. Jack was standing halfway down the sloping bank, with his back to the stream, Kipp standing just in front of him, slightly off-balance as he still kept a hand clapped to his friend's shoulder.

Merry knew she shouldn't.

She really shouldn't.

She really, really shouldn't.

Yes, she *should*.

Clancy noticed something as well as he and Cluny perched on their rock in the middle of the stream. He saw the gleam of mischief in Merry's eyes. Recognized it. "Jack?" Clancy prompted, floating over to wave his hands in front of the oblivious man. "Oh, Jack . . . take a look at Merry, Jack, would you? Really, Jack. Over this way. Take a look at Merry. You really, *really* should look at her." Then he floated away, gesturing for Cluny to come forward. "Oh, the devil with it. He deserves it."

A moment later, after the short, sharp application of both Merry's hands to the small of Kipp's back, both men were lying prone in the stream; spitting, splashing, and very, very wet.

"That should finish cooling them off, eh, Clancy?" Cluny said brightly.

Meanwhile, Merry, feeling much better about almost everything, was halfway up the path before either Kipp or Jack could get to his feet.

Chapter Sixteen

Jack saw Merry as she and her mount galloped across a field left fallow for the season, her long hair flying free in the breeze, her tall, lithe body clad in what he already knew were an old shirt and breeches he'd long ago outgrown.

He'd taught her to ride astride, as he'd taught her so many things, and Merry had always been an apt pupil. Still, Jack's heart leapt up and lodged in his throat as she bent low over the mare's neck and pointed the animal straight at a five-barred gate.

"Damned brat," he grumbled through clenched teeth as horse and rider flew into the air, effortlessly clearing the obstacle and landing lightly on the other side. His heart, which had stopped in fear, began to beat again.

Was he ever to have a moment's peace, a moment's rest?

He'd been home for slightly less than forty-eight hours. He'd had a rifle pointed at him, been told ghosts resided in the Main Saloon chandelier. He'd confronted more than a few ghosts of his own, and done his best to pretend they didn't exist. He'd been both shouted at and royally snubbed.

He'd been condescended to and, for just the moment, out-maneuvered by Henry Sherlock. He'd made several wrong assumptions, made an ass of himself, actually—at least twice—and been pushed into a stream.

All in all, a fairly eventful two days.

But now, bathed and dressed in clean, dry clothing once more, and with the afternoon shadows growing longer and his temper more under control, he was going to attempt the most asinine achievement of all—chasing Merry down and talking calmly and rationally to her when she was feeling at least three shades less than rational.

Even if she frightened the hell out of him. Because she was a grown woman now. Not a chubby-cheeked infant. Not a silly, grubby, all-knees-and-elbows girl running after him, begging him to slow down so that she could catch up to him. Not the budding girl of the too-large smile and the unex-pectedly developing body he'd begun to back away from as he reached his own manhood and she remained a girl, a woman-child he had no idea how to deal with, talk to, han-dle. She wasn't even the Merry he had given in and wed in order to keep her safe. The Merry he'd ended only in saving for the moment, taking away any chances she might have had to see more of the world and make choices for herself.

He had been afraid of that half woman, half child of sev-enteen. He could admit that to himself now. He'd been too young to know what to do with her, how to keep her from worshiping him, how to keep himself from seeing her as more than a sister—hating himself for sometimes seeing her as more than a sister.

So, yes, he was very much afraid, even as he sought her out, even as he knew where to find her. Because, just as Merry knew how to infuriate him, how to placate him, how to annoy and tease him, he also knew her; how she was prone to think, to react. She always took to the fields when

her temper grabbed hold and reason became something
other people offered just to drive her to distraction. He even
believed he might know where she was heading.

And he'd been right. She was headed to the cemetery,
probably to Cluny's and Clancy's graves. To sit with them,
probably to talk with them. Jack only hoped she'd been unable to get them to answer her.

"I miss them, too, sweetheart," he said as he watched her
ride up the hill to the fenced-in cemetery that stood at the
top. Suddenly his mind formed a mental picture of Cluny
and Clancy, and how they'd looked the first night he'd met
them. What a silly, silly, mismatched pair they'd been, wearing outrageous clothes as they'd walked into the nursery,
and into his life and heart.

He smiled as he urged his horse into a walk, recalling
how Clancy had quoted him lines from Shakespeare as they
all sat cross-legged on the nursery-room floor, eating deli-
cacies filched from the kitchens.

He remembered how Cluny had fallen head over ears in
love with Merry, singing to her, cooing to her, watching over
her so Jack could get some much-needed sleep.

How they'd enlivened Jack's life, enriched it, broadened
it. Probably saved it. He smiled as he thought about Clancy,
who had given up the stage for Jack, but had never given up
his love of Shakespeare. How many times had Jack watched
him perform, never to tire of seeing him posture like a king
or simper like a lady as he spoke lines from *Macbeth* and
other plays. Jack decided with the fondness of memory, the
man had made an absolutely exemplary witch.

" 'Eye of newt and toe of frog, wool of bat and tongue of
dog,' " Jack quoted aloud now, the line coming to him easily, and serving to start another smile spreading on his face.
It was the first time since their deaths that he'd been able to

think of his two old friends, his protectors, and then smile. It felt good. It felt very, very good.

He maneuvered his mount so that he could bend down, unlatch the gate Merry and her mount had soared over so effortlessly. He could have cleared the barrier; the stallion was certainly up to it even if this was strange territory. But opening the gate and passing through safely and sanely seemed the proper thing to do. After all, Jack had already taken one tumble today at Merry's hands. He'd be damned if he'd let her goad him into another one.

By the time Jack had circled around the hill, staying out of Merry's sight as long as possible, she had dismounted, tying her horse's reins to a low-hanging branch. She was already kneeling on the ground in front of two small, still-new headstones that he was sure marked the final places of Cluny and Clancy Traveling Shakespearean Players.

A bunch of wildflowers was propped up at the base of each stone, and Merry seemed to be doing some rudimentary housekeeping of both sites. She was also talking, although Jack couldn't hear what she was saying. He considered that a small blessing.

Then her mount sensed the presence of the black stallion and gave out with a nervous whinny, causing Merry's head to jerk around to see who was invading her moment of private conversation.

"You!" she snapped out, all but jumping to her feet in anger. "Five years you're gone, Jack, and now you're stuck to my side like a burr caught in my clothing. Don't you know when you're not wanted?"

"I think I do, Merry," he responded lightly, walking over to stand beside the graves. "I received my first, slight hint when I knocked on the door of my childhood home and was met with a loaded rifle wielded by a monstrous little brat telling me to go away. But, then, once that monstrous little brat realized that I wasn't going to go, and that I had, in fact, brought a few buckets of money with me to throw at her problems, I was allowed to stay. In my own house."

"We've discussed that. It's over," Merry said, turning as if to leave him where he stood. But Jack was too fast for her, and caught her arm, keeping her beside him. "Oh, let go, Jack. Don't you know I can't stand the sight of you right now? I should have left you and Kipp to beat each other into flinders, except that Kipp hadn't done anything wrong. Only you, Jack. Always and forever, only you."

Her invective washed over him, leaving remarkably little impression. That surprised him, for he'd been more angry than he could say to have been greeted as if he'd come home bearing the Black Plague, and been just as unwelcome. "I know I was wrong, Merry. I wasn't wrong to leave. We both know my father left me no other choice except to send us all to the hangman." That wasn't the whole truth, but it was enough to go on with for now.

He glanced down at the headstones, let the sadness he felt penetrate his heart, his soul. Then he looked at Merry again, looked at her and allowed her to see the pain in his eyes. "But I was wrong to stay away so long. I won't ask your forgiveness because that's impossible. But I will ask you to put all of that behind us now, Merry, as it's important to Coltrane House that we do."

She stared at him for long moments, then tipped her head down, lowered her long, thick lashes, and looked up at him through them. Little minx. Did she have any idea how appealing she looked? Yes, she probably did. Definitely did. She'd done more than grow up in the past five years, done more than grow into the promise he'd begun to see before he left, had begun to fear. She'd learned to be a woman, for all her breeches and boots.

"I suppose you're right, Jack. Arguing about the past

can't change it. But you could at least have brought me a present," she ended. He watched her spectacular smile begin, growing wider and wider, turning her into the Merry he remembered, the same Merry who had always been able to twist him straight around her little finger, leaving him powerless to resist her charms.

"I did," he admitted, motioning for her to sit down, then joining her on the thick, sun-warmed grass. "I brought you a doll. Quite a present for one's wife, don't you think? It's amazing how a person can delude himself, if he really tries."

"A doll? Oh, Jack, how could you!" she exclaimed, then giggled. "I never played with dolls. I was much too busy chasing after you and Kipp, making your lives unbearable."

"Too true," he said, flicking at her cheek with one finger. "Do you remember the time we locked you in your room so that we could go hunting without you?"

"And I showed up just in time to run screaming into the field, scaring all the deer into hiding? Yes, I remember. You almost shot me by mistake."

"By mistake?" Jack teased. "Well, if that's the way you choose to remember the incident."

She tried to look stern, then laughed. "Kipp still asks me how I escaped my room, but I won't tell him. He likes to think that I tied all my bedclothes together and lowered myself out the window, which is ridiculous, because my window must be a good thirty feet above a very hard flagstone patio. A person could crack a head, doing anything that foolhardy."

"So, how did you escape? I've often wondered that myself. Honey let you out, didn't she?"

Merry trailed a hand across the grass in front of one of the headstones. "It was Cluny. Poor man. I used him shamelessly sometimes, much as I loved him. Still love him," she said quietly, her gaze shifting momentarily toward the two small stones.

"Cluny? And he swore to me that he hadn't been near your room that night. Shame on him," Jack said, smiling. "Of course, I used Clancy a time or two, to cover my tracks when Aloysius was searching for me and I wanted to go fishing with Kipp instead of reciting Latin verbs."

"So we should both be apologizing, shouldn't we? Do you want to go first, or should I?"

Jack looked at the headstones, then at Merry. "Are you saying they're here? I thought they were camping in the chandelier in the Main Saloon?"

Merry leaned closer to him, mischief dancing in her eyes. "Oh, they can be anywhere, Jack. In the house, in the stables, at the stream. Here. Anywhere at all on the estate. They can hear you, they can see you, they can do things to you. Nice things, if they like you, and if they don't? Well, Jack, do you really want to find out?"

"I don't smell camphor, Merry," he told her, willing to indulge her nonsense, as it seemed to make her happy. "Didn't you say the smell of camphor accompanies them when they, um, *visit*?"

She actually had the audacity to frown, appear disappointed. "You don't smell it? Really, Jack? Oh, they must be so disappointed. Couldn't you at least *try* to believe in them? I think perhaps they need you to believe in them before they let you know they're here. Maybe if you *talked* to them?"

Jack shook his head. "Talk to them? No, Merry. You believe in them, and that's enough. Just, when you speak to them again—and I'm convinced you will—would you kindly tell them to stay out of my rooms? I wouldn't want to think I have an audience when I'm cleaning my teeth."

"You're a stubborn man, Jack, but I'm not worried. You'll believe me someday. And now we'll leave the discussion of ghosts for a while, if you want to talk about something else," Merry said, tipping her head as she looked at him, openly tried to gauge his mood. "And you do, don't you? You want to talk about Kipp. Our good friend Kipp."

"Actually, Merry," Jack admitted honestly, "the last thing I want to talk about is our good friend Kipp. Because I do think he's half in love with you."

Without a word, Merry stood up and walked over to stand beside the wide trunk of an old tree, to stare down at the fields below them.

Jack looked at her, watched her slim figure as she walked away from him. He waited a little while, waited as Merry composed herself, then joined her in looking out over Coltrane land as it spread out in front of them. "How do you feel about him, Merry?" he asked, his voice quiet, hoping that she'd be willing to talk, and not take refuge in either a joke or a tirade. "He's a fine man. Do you want him? Do you want to be free to even think about wanting him?"

"Kipp has been here, Jack," Merry said at last. "He's always been here. His mother allowed me to stay with them each time your father was in residence. He helped teach me how to manage the estate, the cottagers. He made me laugh, kept me from being lonely, frightened. He . . . he held me when I cried."

"I see," Jack said. "Then of course you love him. Who would believe it—that our silly Kipp could turn out to be the man, and that I would turn craven and run away?"

"I know why you left, Jack. You had no choice. I had no choice but to stay here. I kept Coltrane House for you, and I waited for you. I waited so long that I began to hate you, wish you'd never come back." Her voice dropped to a near whisper. "Now you have, and we both have to deal with that, don't we? But you're wrong. I love Kipp, and always will. But I'm not in love with him, and he's not in love with me."

Jack didn't know what to say, so he said nothing. He simply stood there, watching as Merry mounted her horse without assistance and rode away.

Because Merry was right. Kipp was right. He had stayed away too long, no matter how sound his reasons had seemed at the time. He could have been home two years ago, when word came that his father had died. He'd had enough money then, not a fortune, but more than enough money. But he'd wanted more. He'd wanted to come home more than successful, more than simply the hero come to save the estate. He'd wanted to come home with *answers*.

At the same time he'd dragged his feet because he didn't know what to say to Merry, didn't know how to deal with her after so many years of absence. What did one say to a wife who is not a wife, a sister who is not a sister—a child who is no longer a child? How did he ever forget that she had witnessed his greatest humiliation?

He waited until Merry was out of sight, then mounted his stallion and rode off in the opposite direction . . . leaving the ghosts to consider all they'd heard and seen.

"You heard, Clancy? No more sitting on the footboard and sighing over the boy while he sleeps," Cluny said as each hovered above his own headstone.

Clancy was dressed all in mourning, as he thought suited the occasion, a huge black cape hanging on his thin shoulders. Cluny, however, was dressed less dramatically, in the costume of a serving wench. The wench was a device the two often employed. Cluny, in his bright yellow wig and striped dress, would step to the front of the stage and explain to their country-bumpkin audience just what "Birnam Wood to high Dunsinane Hill shall come" and other Shakespearean brilliance actually meant. It cut down on the number of tree branches they had to have at the ready, for one thing.

"He didn't really mean that," Clancy protested, sweeping one end of his cape up and over his shoulder. "He doesn't believe in us, so he can't mean that."

"I suppose. We're probably lucky they didn't kiss, you know," Cluny said consideringly. "Remember what happened the day Maxwell kissed Mrs. Maxwell in the kitchens? Blam! Next thing we knew we were both sitting rump sideways in the buttery. Worse than the hiccups, kissing is, for jumbling us about. Don't know where we'd end up if they decide to kiss someday."

"I don't think we have to worry about the two of them kissing each other, not for a while at least, more's the pity," Clancy answered, sighing. "I suppose it's enough that they're smiling at each other, teasing with each other a bit between arguments. Kissing will just have to wait a while longer. And it's all Awful August's fault, for forcing what you and I both know would have come along naturally enough without him. My poor, poor Jack. 'Was ever woman in this humour woo'd? Was ever woman in this humour won?' My heart is sore, watching the boy."

Cluny patted his friend's shoulder. "You're a good man, Clancy. Perhaps a great one. 'This earth, that bears thee dead, bears not alive so stout a gentleman.'"

"Thank you. I could do much worse, dear friend, than to spend my eternity with you and your good heart. But it's all so sad, Cluny. The whole of it. Us being dead and unable to help. It's as if we die a new death each day. All we seem able to do is watch ourselves rot."

Cluny looked down from his perch on his own tombstone, looked speculatively at the ground below him. "Not yet, we haven't. You want to go take a look, then, Clancy? We could, you know. Slip on down, take a peek, see how we're faring. But I don't think so." He pressed his hands to his chest, as he always did when about to give his most affecting speeches. " 'To what base uses we may return, Horatio! Why may not imagination trace the noble dust of Alexander, till he find it stopping a bung-hole?' "

Clancy found both Cluny's suggestion and unfortunate quote quite particularly distasteful to contemplate. He gave him a whacking-great swat, sending the pudgy ghost tumbling head over heels through the air until he landed half inside a tree, only his rump visible. "Get yourself out of there, you lumpish, mammering twit. It's time we were back at the house, watching to see Merry and Jack don't make things even worse by being so wretchedly honest while never saying a single thing that's in their hearts."

Cluny turned himself around inside the tree, poking his head out to stare at Clancy. "They won't do that, Clancy. They've made a shaky start of it, but it will all turn right in the end. Like me," he ended, pulling himself free of the tree, shaking himself all over as he readjusted his wig. He spread his arms wide, smiling, and inviting Clancy's inspection. "See?"

It was probably a good thing that the unbelieving Jack and his temperamental stallion were out of earshot, because Clancy stared at Cluny, then gave out a highly impressive ghostly moan and buried his head in his hands.

Act Three

The Play's the Thing

Thus the whirligig of time
brings in his revenges.

—William Shakespeare

Chapter Seventeen

"'To be or not to be—that is the question: whether 'tis nobler in the mind to suffer the slings and arrows of outrageous—'"

"Oh, shut up, why don't you!"

Cluny rubbed at his abused skull—Clancy was forever whacking him across the back of his head, and to great effect—and subsided into his allotted space behind the drapes in the window seat. "I was just putting forth a question, that's all. Jack must be wondering the same thing himself."

As Jack had just been slung the outrageous fortune of yet another of Merry's verbal slings and arrows—before she had flounced out of the room, that is—the question was perhaps not quite as misplaced as Clancy's reaction considered it. But, then, Clancy had been woefully out of sorts these past weeks, watching his dearest Jack meet with failure after failure, frustration after frustration.

First Jack had been stern with Merry, which had been as effective—as Cluny had so inelegantly pointed out—as spitting into the wind.

Then Jack had been kind. And as Clancy had remarked approvingly at the time, " 'This is a way to kill a wife with kindness.' "

Except that Merry didn't seem to do too well with kindness, either. She had, both ghosts had at last conceded, quite a nasty way of flinging kindness straight back in one's face. Twice as hard as it had been launched, in fact.

"He hasn't made a right step since he got back here, you know," Clancy said, sighing. "Your Merry has him all at sixes and sevens." He poked his head out through the draperies as a new sound disturbed him. "Uh-oh, here comes the savage. Perhaps we can gain some help from that quarter?"

Jack, oblivious to his audience, had just poured himself a glass of claret. He turned his head and nodded, silently acknowledging Walter's entrance into the Main Saloon. He was glad that his friend had left his arrival too late to see that he had, once again, done something entirely stupid and sent Merry off, steaming in anger. And yet, did he really require Walter's presence at the moment at all? Between the Indian and Aloysius, he'd had more advice this past fortnight than any three men should have to bear.

"I just passed Merry in the hallway, Jack," Walter said, seating himself on the couch placed directly below the chandelier. There was so little furniture left in the enormous cavern of a room, and all of it bunched together in the center of it, both for light and for its proximity to the oversize, central fireplace.

"Did you now, Walter?" Jack responded, pouring his friend a glass of water from the pitcher Maxwell always made sure to have handy for the man. "I hope you didn't get in her way. She'd probably have glared you into a puddle of pure terror, then walked straight over you."

Walter accepted the glass, smiling at Jack as he sat down

on the couch directly across from him. "You know, it's difficult for me to believe that you were so successful as my agent in America, endlessly polite and ingratiating to all those silly men with more money than wit. You walked among them, upright as any man, making friends and competently furthering our business until, with a lot of work and a few brilliant strokes of good luck, it became our most lovely empire. And yet you can't seem to say more than three words to Mrs. Coltrane without dropping to all fours and baying at the moon."

Jack stared into his glass. "I told her I'd ordered a tenant thrown off the estate," he said matter-of-factly. "She's off to tell the man to stop packing up his children and belongings, as only she has the right to say who stays at Coltrane House, and who goes."

"And is she right or wrong?"

Jack shook his head, trying to sort out his thoughts. "She was wrong and right, Walter. I, on the other hand, was just plain wrong. I'm getting very good at being very wrong, you know. It seems the man's wife died in childbed three months ago, leaving him with six small children. But I didn't ask if there was a problem. Simply didn't take the time. All I saw was that he wasn't in the fields, wasn't working. Merry, being Merry, saw much more."

He shrugged his shoulders, sighed. "And so I've dropped yet lower in my wife's estimation, which probably puts me on a level slightly below that of the worms crawling in the gardens."

"Ah, Jack. For all my efforts, taking the raw clay I found and carefully molding it, you have now succeeded in reverting overnight to doing your acting first and leaving your thinking until later. You apologized, of course? Agreed to go see this poor, unfortunate man and offer any assistance possible?"

"I would have, if Merry hadn't all but attacked me, poking her finger in my chest as she rattled off all the very good reasons I should be drawn and quartered, my entrails nibbled on by goats. I'll go see Jenkins later, see what I can do for him, perhaps hire some woman from the village to care for his children until he's better able to manage."

He got up, returned to the drinks table to pour himself another glass. "I literally jumped at the chance to make some sort of mark as owner of Coltrane House. I don't know how I could have been so blind, acted so hastily. But there's nothing for me to do here, Walter. It's as if I'm totally unnecessary, superfluous. Merry has the entire estate running smoothly. The land is productive, the outbuildings are sound, the tenants happy. You're working on the ledgers. I'm as useless as a fifth leg on a dog, and if I tell Merry to stop running the estate, she'll have reason to hate me even more than she does now."

"You're about to pay off all of Coltrane House's debts, Jack," Walter reminded him. "That ought to stand for something."

Jack's smile was rueful. "Yes, it should, shouldn't it?" He collapsed onto the couch once more, running a hand through his hair, dislodging one lock from its careful sleekness so that it fell forward, to hang unnoticed beside his cheek. "I truly thought that with enough money . . ."

"Money being the same as power," Walter said knowingly. "It's a common mistake, Jack. You were powerless here, before your father beat you and tossed you out. Youth has its merits and strengths, but not when being forced to deal with adult problems. So you went away, the whipped dog, and vowed to return the triumphant hero. You'd rescue Coltrane House, restore it to its former glory, and Merry would be so thankful for your help that she'd simply forget that you'd left her here, alone, for five long years. She'd

look up to you again, as she'd done all her life, and not remember how you'd looked the last time she saw you. It was
a good plan, and you worked hard to achieve it, Jack." Walter's sigh was eloquent. "Unfortunately, it wasn't the right
plan."

Jack's smile was wry. "Thank you, dear, great sage. Although I believe you may have left your so-astute observa-
tions a little late? Or did you—and do you still—enjoy
watching as I continually and most doggedly make an ass of
myself?"

"I've been amused to a point, yes. Aloysius and I both,"
Walter conceded, sniffing at the pale yellow rosebud in his
lapel. "There are many ways to stand tall, Jack, and quite a
few of them involve first repeatedly falling to your knees.
As long, that is, as you learn something from each stumble.
Tell me, have you considered involving your dear wife in
the restoration of this great pile? A lovely place, I assure
you, but it hurts my eyes to look at the disrepair, the empty
spaces where there should be furniture and paintings and
lovely draperies. If you were to offer to work with her on the
estate, even consulting with her until she can see that you're
not entirely incompetent or heartless, she might be persuaded to involve herself in some of the more aesthetic renovations your lovely, powerful money makes possible? If
you ask her nicely, of course."

"In that case—" Jack stood, motioning for Walter to follow him into the small drawing room. "You'll probably
sleep much better tonight, my friend," he said rather smugly,
"knowing that your dogged determination to make me into
something more than I was when first we met has not been
a total failure." He threw open the door, stood back, and motioned for his friend to step inside. "*Voilà*! I've always wondered when using *voilà* would be appropriate and not

overdone. Go on, Walter, take a look for yourself. I think this is one such instance, don't you?"

The room was a jumble of swatches and bolts of material, as well as a staggering array of pattern books. In the middle of these mountains sat Aloysius Bromley, making a charcoal sketch of something rather Ionic-looking, and explaining each new stroke of the charcoal to the small, furiously nodding man sitting beside him. Both were speaking Greek.

"Mr. Poppo—his name is prodigiously longer than that, but Aloysius says he insists on Mr. Poppo—arrived from London only this morning, at the request of my dear, childhood tutor," Jack explained as he followed Walter into the room. "Mr. Poppo, I understand, works with marble. And Mr. Poppo is only one of many tradesmen and assorted, variously talented persons either already arrived here or soon to take up residence in the West Wing. Experts all, Aloysius assures me."

"Indeed," Walter said, picking up a book of fabric swatches and beginning to leaf through it.

"Yes, Walter, indeed." Jack was feeling rather proud of himself, which was never a good thing when he was dealing with either Walter or Aloysius. But he'd had a difficult morning with Merry, and felt some small need to crow. "I've hired enough bodies and artistic spleens to keep Merry riding herd on them all the day long. There's enough work here for her to deal with without time to give a thought to what I might be doing elsewhere on the estate. Learning what the estate is about and then seamlessly slipping myself into the place of authority being my main objective, of course. This was all my idea, believe it or not, but Aloysius was kind enough to help me with the particulars. Isn't that right, Aloysius?"

The old man lifted his head from his work, squinting at Jack. "Go away, boy. We're working here. Oh—hullo, Walter. Care to join us? I value your opinion, and would ask it on the mantelpiece in this room. Sadly cracked, as you can see. Mr. Poppo vows it needs replacing, but my heart is in repairing it to its former glory."

"Will the cost be the same?" Walter asked, stepping between Jack and yet another pile of fabric samples. "Ask him, my friend, if the remuneration is to be the same for restoration as it is for replacement, as if you are willing to pay the same amount either way. I think then you will understand each other better, as well as knowing if restoration is at all possible."

Jack grinned at his old tutor. "You see, Aloysius? To learn what is possible, always ask the price as if you're willing to pay it. If your Mr. Poppo still says it is impossible to repair the mantelpiece, then you'll know it's true. If he says he can fix it for the same price as it would cost to replace it, you'll know he can fix it for less. Pay him what he asks this one time, and make up the loss in your next transaction, now that you know how to deal with him, what to believe and what to discount when the man opens his mouth to speak. That's what you taught me, Walter, right?"

"And it worked well, didn't it, Jack?" Walter said, smiling his broad smile. "Especially with that purchase from Adam Fowler, transparent fool that he was. Five hundred prime acres for the price of four hundred, wasn't it?"

"If you two are done congratulating yourselves on your brilliance," Aloysius said, fanning himself with the end of his scarf, "might I humbly point out that Mr. Poppo speaks English?"

Jack looked at Walter and Walter looked at Jack, and then they both looked at Mr. Poppo. A broadly smiling Mr. Poppo. "Fifty quid more ta repair the thing, good sirs," he said as Jack began laughing, laughing so hard he had to put a hand on Walter's shoulder to keep from falling down. "I am at heart an artist, but it's more trouble for me, yer know, ta fix than ta build," Mr. Poppo went on doggedly. "Does that help tell yer how ta deal with me?"

"That it does, Mr. Poppo, that it does," Jack said, wiping at his eyes. Walter stood stock-still, his dignity highly affronted, for the man prided himself on being, if not the most clever negotiator on earth, at least very close to the best. "And we'll see the mantelpiece repaired, if you please, for twenty-five more quid, not fifty. Is that agreeable?"

"You could have had him for ten," Walter grumbled a moment later, turning his back on the smiling Mr. Poppo and leaving the room in as close to a huff as the very proper gentleman could manage. "Clearly both our talents lie elsewhere than in such domestic renovations. You belong in the fields, running the estate and paying the bills. I belong with my head in a ledger, working with numbers, not with artisans and draperies and what are bound to be maddening arguments as to which shade of blue is the truest. Aloysius is a good sort, but he'll turn this place into another Parthenon if left to run free with his ideas, and beggar you into the bargain. Find your wife, Jack, and put that most sensible young woman in charge here before your pockets are empty and we're all living under the hedgerows."

Honey opened the door to the master's bedchamber at the sound of a sharp, imperative knock an hour before dinner was slated to be served, then stepped back in surprise, to allow Jack entry.

Merry, who had been sitting by the hearth, was brushing her unbound hair, still damp from her bath. She turned to watch him cross the room with his usual long strides, then sit himself down in one of the pair of leather chairs flanking the fireplace.

His face was a near thundercloud, although he tried to

hide that beneath a smile Merry could only see as woefully transparent. She'd known him all her life. When was he going to realize that his face betrayed his every emotion? Perhaps not to anyone else, but most certainly to her. Right now, she'd have to say that he seemed more frustrated than angry, and frustration had never set well on the Coltrane features.

"I'll finish this myself, Honey," she told the hovering maid. "Why don't you go downstairs and see if you can help your mother in the kitchens?"

"Are you sure, Missy?" Honey, poor thing, looked caught between delight that Mr. and Mrs. Coltrane were finally in the same bedchamber—where everyone knew they belonged—and fear that allowing Jack Coltrane into the room was her greatest mistake since she'd kissed Jimmy, the underfootman, without first checking on the whereabouts of her father.

"Now." That single word, followed by Jack's short, hard glance, served to make up Honey's mind and send her into a series of jerky curtsies as she hastily backed from the room.

"What a bugbear you are, Jack. Was it necessary to frighten her?" Merry asked, pulling the brush through her hair. She was still only in her underslip and dressing gown. But as the dressing gown had once been his, and was both as unrevealing and as unflattering as a shroud, she didn't see any reason to protest that he should leave until she could make herself presentable. Besides, she didn't care how she looked. Why should she, if he didn't?

"I've known Honey as long as you have, Merry, and she's known me. You don't really believe she thought I'd bite off her head, do you?"

"Probably not," Merry answered, shrugging. "You're much too busy throwing good tenants off the estate." As soon as the words were out of her mouth she longed to draw them back. She should be ashamed of herself. She already knew that Jack had ridden out to see Robbie Jenkins this afternoon, and had even apologized to the man. It was one of the things she loved about Jack, and always had. He admitted when he was wrong. He'd even admitted he had been wrong to delay his return to Coltrane House. So why couldn't she forgive him, welcome him home, turn over the reins of running the estate to him?

The answer to that was unfortunately simple. If Jack took over Coltrane House, it would leave her with nothing to do, nowhere to go. Even if the rest of the world were to be dished up to her on a platter, if the serving didn't include Jack and Coltrane House, she'd rather starve.

Her hands froze around the brush as she realized that she wasn't being absolutely honest with herself. She could live without Coltrane House, if she had to. She could live without *things*. But she could never live without Jack. Never be happy, without Jack. She'd worshiped him as a child. As a woman—God help her—she loved him. Loved him as a woman was meant to love a man. Had most probably been in love with him since she was fourteen. Not that she could let him know.

"I'm sorry, Jack," she said at last, resting the brush in her lap, trying not to look at him, let him see the truth she had always known but had finally accepted. "I shouldn't have said that. We'll talk about something else, all right? Honey tells me we've been overrun with simpering gentlemen in high heels and burly workmen hired from every village within ten miles of here. And I noticed someone poking around up on the roof as I walked up from the stables. What are you planning now, Jack?"

He came down out of the chair, picking up the brush and moving behind her. He began pulling the brush through her hair, just as he'd done a thousand times when she was a child. He worked slowly, carefully, making sure to be gentle with the knots in her damp curls. He took such good care of her. He'd always taken such good care of her.

She drew her breath in slowly, held it. Tried not to melt backwards, into his arms. Tried to think, listen, and not react in a way that would mostly probably send him screaming from the room.

"You know what I'm planning, Merry," Jack said as she sat there, her eyes closed, awash in sensations so alien, so frightening, that she almost forgot to breathe at all. "I vowed to put Coltrane House to rights, and that's just what I'm going to do. But I'd like your help, Merry, if you're willing."

"My—my help?" She hated herself at that moment, hated him. How could she not, when she suddenly felt as if the rug of the world had been somehow ripped out from beneath her, and she was in danger of falling into some deep, dark, unexplored place. "Aren't I doing enough as it is?"

He reached around her, picking up her right hand, rubbing his thumb across her palm, across the calluses on that palm. "You're doing too much, Merry. It's time, more than time, to be reasonable about this. It's time to share the heavy responsibility that is Coltrane House. Not that you aren't splendid, not that the estate isn't splendid as well. But I'm home now, and I know how to run the estate. In fact, Walter and I left two large holdings in Pennsylvania, in the hands of our managers, to travel to England."

Merry fought to regain her mental balance, taking refuge in insult. "Bragging, Jack? How unlike you. But, then, I really can't assume to know you anymore, can I? Even you must admit you're not the Jack we both remember."

"And you're hardly the Merry I remember," Jack said, finding a knot in her hair and carefully working through it with the brush. Yes, he had always and forever taken such good care of her. Such loving care of her. But that was different from being *in* love with her. A shaft of exquisite pain ripped through her, and she was glad she was sitting, for surely that pain would have sent her falling to her knees.

"The Merry I remember," she heard Jack saying, "worshiped me unconditionally, would have leapt through hoops to please me. I believe I rather miss that."

"We all grow up," Merry said shortly, dipping her head forward so that her hair fell across her face, hiding her expression. "We grow up, we put away our childhood days, our childish ways. We have to put away our yesterdays."

His touch was light as he pulled her hair behind her ear, ran a finger along the side of her cheek. "And our dreams? Do we put those away as well, Merry?"

When those dreams aren't shared? she thought. *Yes, yes you put those dreams away, hide them as best you can.*

He was killing her, killing her slowly, and he didn't even know it. She turned her head to look at him, knowing her eyes were brimming with tears, suddenly not caring if he could see her pain. And she lied. Made sure it was the most believable lie of her life. "We put them away, Jack, yes. Those that we can save. We tuck them away beside the careless promises that someone has either chosen to forget or has crushed beneath his boots. It's true, I still have dreams, Jack. But they're different dreams from those in my silly, oblivious childhood." She took a deep breath, let it out slowly, and deliberately lied to him. "And you're not in them anymore."

"No. I suppose I'm not."

"However," she went on doggedly, before she lost her nerve. She'd give him what he wanted from her, all that he wanted from her. She always had, she always would. But never before had she known such a terrible cost to that giving.

"However," she repeated, "that doesn't mean I don't

know what you want, or that I haven't been aware that I'm waging a losing battle these past two weeks, for these past five long years. I'll leave the running of the estate to you and bury myself in paints and wallpapers and fabrics, just as you wish. If I cannot be master of the estate, I shall be its mistress—at least until you've discovered some further way to usurp me."

"Usurp you? Jesus, Merry, that isn't what I want from you. I—"

"No," she interrupted. "Of course it isn't. Your visions were very different. You wanted me to agree to an annulment and then simply walk away. Didn't you?"

His eyes flashed with quick temper. "The marriage doesn't have anything to do with it. Not anymore, perhaps not ever. It's you, Merry. I'm worried about you. I'd planned and planned, but I never considered that you would want to stay at Coltrane House once I'd come back."

He ran a hand through his hair, ruthlessly pulling it loose from the tie that had captured it at his nape, and she watched as he turned into a younger Jack, the Jack she remembered, the Jack she had worshiped. She could hate him for being so blockheaded, for not seeing what was so clearly in front of his face, but that was impossible. Not when she loved him so, wanted his happiness above all things—above even her own happiness. "Why would I have wanted to leave, Jack?" she asked, taking his hand in hers. "This is my home, has always been my home."

"I know, I know," he said, sighing, squeezing her fingers. "But after everything that had happened, and the way I allowed my father to trap us into marriage—the way I ran off, the coward leaving you behind—I'd simply assumed you'd want to run away from here the moment that became possible. Run away from me. Start a new life, forget the past, forget all the ugliness."

He didn't understand. He truly didn't understand.

"Ugliness? I never knew any ugliness, Jack, much as you can't seem to comprehend that. Never. But, as you were making all these assumptions about me, Jack, you were also believing that I'd remain a biddable child forever, weren't you? That I'd never grow up, that I'd always be that same malleable, worshiping little sister who used to chase you, and pester you, and hang on your every word as if it were golden?"

He reached out, traced a trembling finger over her cheek. "My little sister? Is that how I see you now? When I look at you, Merry, after all these years, with all my memories of the infant, the child—is that really who I see?"

She watched as he looked at her for long moments, moments during which she suddenly found it necessary to grip the edges of her too-large dressing gown close together over her breasts. His face paled at her action, and he dropped his hand from her cheek, dropped his gaze, turned his head.

She retrieved the brush and faced the fireplace, returning to her homely chore as Jack rose to his feet and silently slipped out of the room. . . .

Chapter Eighteen

Jack was feeling much more relaxed. Merry had been as good as her word. She'd been waiting for him the next morning at the stables, and they had ridden out together. She'd introduced him to the workers he still didn't know, whispered the name of those he should remember from years ago so that he wouldn't put a foot wrong. And then she'd retired to Coltrane House and begun overseeing the renovations.

After two weeks of being an observer, he now rode the lands as their owner, their master. Merry had given him the gift of his own property. Now it was up to him to earn the respect of the people who worked it for him.

But first he would pay Henry Sherlock a small visit, see if the man was still so cool, so collected. Feeling so secure. Merry had pointed out the man's small property that bordered on the farthest reaches of the Coltrane House estate, and Jack had bristled as he belatedly realized that the house sat on Coltrane land.

"How?" was all he'd asked, sitting in the saddle, looking

at the house that, although not large, showed every sign of being built with a generous and perhaps even lavish purse.

"Your father's will," Merry had answered, knowing what he meant by his question. "He gave Henry the land in reward for his 'good and loyal service.' His inheritance from his aunt paid for the house itself, I suppose. Henry could have removed to London but he does so love Coltrane House. He said he couldn't imagine leaving it. I was surprised, as I never thought Henry to be sentimental. Kipp even says he thinks Henry worships the estate."

Jack remembered Merry's words as he rode up the circular drive in front of Henry Sherlock's three-story brick house. He had difficulty in seeing any man without his own estate as being content to molder in the country once he had the funds to set himself up permanently in town. He definitely couldn't quite believe his father to have ever been a sentimental creature, and wished he knew what sort of "good and loyal service" Sherlock had performed to earn this reward. Was doing August Coltrane's dirty work for two dozen years a rewardable service? Jack wasn't sure.

No, Jack didn't believe his father had left Henry Sherlock a shovelful of Coltrane land, at least not willingly. He did, however, believe in greed, even in blackmail, and this lavishly modest house screamed both at him.

Maybe he hadn't stayed away from Coltrane House too long. He'd left an angry, impotent youth, and returned a much wiser man. A man who had seen the world, both the good and the bad—and learned to know the difference. He would have been no match for Henry Sherlock five years ago, three years ago. But now? Now he felt ready to deal with the man. All he needed were a few remaining pieces, and the puzzle of Henry Sherlock would be solved. Not that he was in any hurry to apprise Sherlock of that fact.

A young boy in very good livery ran out to take Jack's

mount from him. An older man in even better livery opened the front door and escorted him into the main drawing room to "await the master, who has not been expecting any after-noon calls."

The foyer had been impressive, with a massive chandelier hanging in its center, but the drawing room was above impressive. Everywhere Jack looked, money looked back at him. Stuccoed walls painted in palest yellow, a domed, highly decorative ceiling holding its own blue sky and a goodly supply of cherubs. Masses of glass in nearly floor to ceiling windows, with three pair of French doors leading out onto a wide patio. Furniture in the best of taste, constructed by the finest of craftsmen. Mirrors, paintings, vases, sculptures in their carved niches on the walls. No fewer than three fine carpets under his feet.

Sherlock's dear, deceased aunt must have been more wealthy than anyone had supposed, to have left her nephew with enough money to construct and then fill such a show-place. How gratified Sherlock must have been, both by her thoughtfulness in remembering him, and in August's gift of land.

It all couldn't have worked out better for Sherlock, as a matter of fact. Unless August had left him Coltrane House, something even his reprobate father would never have done, because what was Coltrane remained Coltrane. There may have been no love between father and son, but there was blood.

Sherlock had to have known this, could never have hoped to take possession of Coltrane House. So why had he stayed, even after he'd had the wherewithal to leave? Why had he built his house here? What was it that kept him close to Coltrane House?

Jack believed he knew the *what*; but he had yet to learn the *how*. If he was right . . .

So close, so close. The puzzle was so close to being completed, the last pieces fixed in place. Jack and Walter were so close, now that they had the actual ledgers. Another few days, Walter had said, another week at the most.

He had to wait, hold on to his eagerness, his impulse to question Sherlock. If he and Walter were right, Jack would have his answers, or at least most of them. If Jack was wrong, he wouldn't have made a fool of himself and insulted a man who had twice saved his life.

Jack helped himself to a glass of claret, impressed with the quality of both the wine and the glass holding it, then seated himself on a chair near the fireplace and awaited his host. He arose slowly a few minutes later when Henry Sherlock finally appeared, and crossed the room to shake his host's hand.

"So sorry to intrude like this, Sherlock," he said, noticing that the man seemed rather flustered, and remembering that Sherlock liked everything neat, everything tidy. An unexpected visitor in the middle of the day, coming to interrupt him from whatever he was doing, wasn't tidy. "I was out riding, you understand, and stopped here purely on impulse. You have quite a lovely house, Sherlock. Very impressive."

"Why, thank you, John. It's not at all large, but it suits me," Sherlock said, waving Jack back to his seat. "And I'm glad you stopped. I've been meaning to ride over to Coltrane House, talk some more with that interesting friend of yours. Walter, is it? Yes, that's right. Very interesting fellow. Has he had any trouble reading the ledgers? I don't think he should. And how is dear Meredith? I confess I must wonder at the strangeness of the situation you both find yourselves in now that you've come home, you understand. After what your father told you that last night. But, no—we won't speak of that now, will we?"

Jack kept his expression hovering somewhere between bland and vaguely interested, even as he wondered when Henry Sherlock had decided that the two of them could actually converse as friends, perhaps even as intimates. And why, dear God, did he think he could bring up the subject of that last night without Jack breaking his nose for him? "Merry's doing very well, Sherlock," he said evenly. "We're overrun with workmen and the like, but she's a good girl, and a born manager. You and I already know that, don't we?"

He put down his glass and stood up once more, resting an arm against the marble mantelpiece. He felt more alert, standing. "As I've already said, you've got quite a fine home here, Sherlock. I doubt there's much that could outshine it, either in the country or in London. Did you gather all of this together yourself? Merry might want your opinion on some of the colors and fabrics she'll be choosing."

Sherlock tipped his head, looking up at Jack with question in his eyes. "You can afford all of this? There's still the mortgages, you know. Much as it pains me to say this, you'd only be decorating Coltrane House for its new owner if you can't pay them soon. This Walter person does understand that, doesn't he? He has informed you of the amounts of the mortgage payments, the total amount of your debt?"

"Yes, Sherlock, he has," Jack said, "And I'm ready to pay—once I know whom I'll be paying. You do have names and directions for me, don't you? You may have forgotten, but the ledgers only contain last names, along with dates and amounts paid. Walter is also compiling other figures for me as he works back through the ledgers. Other loans my father incurred over the years, thankfully smaller loans. A trifling thing, surely, but utterly fascinating to me."

Sherlock didn't react, didn't turn pale, didn't squirm in his chair, show any signs that Jack might possibly be calling his integrity into doubt. "The names, John? Why, you're right. I don't believe the full names are recorded in the ledgers. I'll provide you with a list, along with their directions. Let's see, there's MacDougal, the one owed the thirty thousand by the end of the year. He's in Scotland, nursing gout, I believe. Then there's Newbury—a coal merchant in Newcastle. Your father met him some few years ago, I believe. And a Mr. Gold, a moneylender in London. Although I believe he is bedridden these days, his sons carry on the business through correspondence with me. And now with you, won't they?"

He smiled, spreading his hands. "That's all that's left, John. The other debts have all been paid except, as you said, for those few small loans. Coltrane House has always been immensely profitable, and Meredith was agreeable to taking my advice and learning from my own experience as estate manager before I limited myself to handling your father's legal and monetary transactions."

"And both Merry and I are in your debt, Sherlock, as I've said before," Jack said, wondering just how true his words might be, and just how much he was considering without any facts to back up his suppositions.

Until he was entirely sure of his facts, he had to tread carefully, not frighten the man away before he could tighten the noose. It was time he opened his mouth once more, and said something totally naive, horribly stupid. "Only the payments are recorded in the ledgers, of course, not the total of the mortgages. Thirty thousand to MacDougal, you said a moment ago, right? That's not quite so stiff. And to Newbury and Gold? What do those two mortgages amount to, exactly?"

Sherlock coughed into his fist. "You misunderstood me, and misunderstood your man Walter as well, unless he's truly unfit to be interpreting the ledgers. Thirty thousand is the next yearly *payment* to MacDougal, John. But that's *only* the interest, not the amount of the debt. Wasn't that clear? That number is still so high as to be nearly unimaginable; four hundred thousand pounds, to be exact. And you still owe another twenty thousand in annual interest on top of that crushing amount on the other two, newer mortgages. Twelve to Newbury. Eight to Gold. In short, John, these three mortgages amount to more than a half million pounds of debt."

Jack kept his expression deliberately blank, bordering on the bovine. "I see. I guess you could say I hadn't quite understood you before now. I must have misunderstood Walter as well, I suppose."

"And how could you hope to take it all in, John, with the figures so high? But it's all there, everything is recorded in the ledgers. What you have to ask yourself, John, is why you would even pay the thirty, or the twenty, when there would still be three unpayable principals still owing? Yes, I've kept the estate running, paid the yearly interest all this time, but only because I could not convince your father to sell, convince you or Meredith to sell. Your father lived hard, John, and he lived high. It would be so much easier to allow MacDougal to take the estate, and the smaller mortgages, off your hands, wouldn't it?"

"Would it, Sherlock?"

"Yes. Yes it would. You're young, John. You say you're wealthy now in your own right, although no fortune could absorb a loss of nearly six hundred thousand pounds without feeling the pinch. Your man—Walter—told me about your estates in America, your businesses in America. I'm impressed, John. Truly I am. Leave this place, this unhappy place that must haunt you with terrible memories, and go back to where you will be happy. It only makes sense, John. Doesn't it?"

"I see," Jack said, stepping away from the mantel. "And Merry? What of her, Sherlock? What of my wife?"

"Your wife, John? Hardly that. I can be honest with you, can't I? My largest regret in this life is that I didn't arrive soon enough to stop that travesty from occurring. Neither of you wanted the marriage, neither of you consented. You were beaten into it, Meredith was bullied into it. But I know you'll provide for Meredith. You're a man of honor, John, and always were."

"Why, thank you, Sherlock," Jack said, more than ready to leave. "And thank you for the information you'll be sending over to Coltrane House tomorrow. I appreciate it, and everything you've done for Merry and me over the years." Then he simply bowed to the man and, caught between wondering if he were an idiot or simply a cad, he allowed Henry Sherlock to put a friendly arm around his shoulders and escort him out of the house.

It wasn't until he was riding back to Coltrane House that Jack shook his head in grudging admiration of Henry Sherlock, saying, "That inventive son of a bitch. And he almost pulled it off."

Jack was whistling. Merry, hiding out in the gardens, away from Mr. Poppo and a dozen more like him, didn't know whether to be happy or frustrated when she heard his tune.

If Jack was happy, she should be happy. And yet, what was making Jack so happy? Probably nothing that would also make her happy. Not when he'd been ignoring her so pointedly for two days.

She stayed down on her knees, ruthlessly tugging at weeds that had dared to grow up around the base of the rose-bushes lining the path, deciding that Jack would find her if he wanted to, but that she was not going out of her way to be discovered.

Nearby, Cluny and Clancy lay stretched out on cement benches flanking the walkway. Clancy was asleep. Snoring, actually. Cluny lay with his head propped against one bent arm, watching his dear Merry work. It was a lovely thing, it was, watching others work.

As the sound of whistling grew closer, and as he watched Merry seem to shrink closer to the ground, Cluny sat up and called to his friend. "Psst! Psst! Clancy—the boy's home. And by the sound of it, he's coming this way. Here's our chance."

"Jack? Jack's here?" Clancy opened his eyes, stretched, then floated up to sit on a tree branch that gave him a better view of the gardens. "Ah, there he is. And here he comes. We'll let them alone for a while, hope they do well enough on their own. But if they don't . . ."

"If they don't, I know what to do," Cluny said, grinning, because it had been his plan, and Clancy had actually termed it "brilliant." Wasn't often a man got a "brilliant" out of Clancy, no it was not.

The whistling got closer, although it was difficult to tell directions from a simple sound like a whistle. Merry pulled another weed, fighting its long roots for a bit, then flung it up and over her shoulder in a small gesture of triumph.

"Well, there's a greeting I won't soon forget," Jack said, and Merry turned around quickly, in time to see him examining the weed in his hand even as he wiped a smudge of mud from his cheek. "Some people simply say hello to each other, Merry, you know. Hello, good afternoon, how nice to see you. Easy words. Easy to say, easy to interpret. But I'm at a loss here, Merry. What does a weed smacked into one's face mean?"

Merry pushed herself to her feet, wiping her muddy

hands on the huge white apron she'd tied around her before coming out into the gardens. He was dressed just as casually, in riding breeches and a white-lawn shirt opened at the collar. Except he looked handsome, and she felt like a kitchen drudge.

"It means, I suppose," she ventured carefully, "that if you really want to join me, you may do so, but at your own peril." Then she smiled. "I really didn't mean to do that, you know. However . . ." She let her words die away, even as her smile grew wider. "You've got a bit of leaf stuck above your left ear, Jack. I hesitate to mention it, in case you're thinking of starting some new fashion, but you might want to remove it?"

"Is there now? Well, that takes me back. Aloysius always said birds could nest in my hair, as I was always coming home rolled in dirt and full of twigs. Do you remember, Merry?"

She watched as he reached up, located the leaf, and then brushed it away. He was right. His hair had always been full of grass, bits of hay. They had both romped the hills and meadows without regard for their clothing, their appearance, or what the world might think about them. Tumbling about in sweet grass, playing silly games, tickling each other. Jack was horribly ticklish. It may have been difficult to get him down, but once she'd done it, once she'd straddled him, she could have him begging for mercy in a matter of moments. He had this one spot, just above his waist, that—

Merry bent her head, feeling hot color rush into her cheeks.

"Merry? Is something wrong?"

She bit her bottom lip, shook her head. She'd sat on him! Yes, they had been children. She, at least, had been a child. But she'd persisted in such childish games even after Jack had warned her to stop. Even after Jack had begun to hide from her, slip away with Kipp to visit the village tavern, to walk out with country girls she'd hated with a deep and terrible passion.

"What a pest I must have been, Jack," she said now, looking up at him, tears standing in her eyes. "What a torture to you. I'm so sorry."

"You were incorrigible," he said, his smile teasing and light. And then he sobered. "Really, Merry, do you honestly believe I regret a moment of our lives, a single moment we were together? You were my friend, my sister, my entire family. You were also probably the only reason I stayed at Coltrane House, the only reason I didn't run off to join a band of gypsies or some such thing, ruining my life forever. A pest, Merry, a torture? I don't think I could have survived here, survived August, without you."

"Honestly?" she asked, wishing his words didn't mean so much to her, wishing he'd stop calling her his sister. She wasn't his sister, had never been his sister. She was what she'd always wanted to be—his wife. "You're not simply being kind?"

She took a step forward, longing to be closer to Jack, moving almost without conscious thought . . . and Clancy yelled "Now!"

Cluny, always an obedient sort, immediately stuck out the small branch he'd been holding as he crouched by the side of the pathway. It caught Merry's ankle in mid-stride, sending her hurtling straight into Jack's arms.

"Perfect!" Clancy pronounced, clapping his hands. He looked at Jack, at Merry, then sighed, pulling a large red-cotton square from his pocket and noisily blowing his nose. " 'Now join your hands, and with your hands your hearts.' Ah, Cluny, isn't this wonderful?"

"It's deceitful, that's what it is," Cluny said, having second thoughts as he sat back on his haunches and watched the pair as they stood close together, caught between surprise and embarrassment. "Unless we shortly find ourselves in the potting shed, up to our knee joints in compost, of course. Then we'll know our plan worked."

Merry stood with her palms pressed up against Jack's chest, feeling the strength of his hands as they gripped her waist, steadying her even as she held on to his shirt. She could feel his heart beating beneath her palms, felt that heart skip a beat, as hers had just done. "I—I must have tripped over something," she said at last, after wetting her suddenly dry lips with the tip of her tongue.

Really, she had never been clumsy before—had she meant to trip, meant to end up this way, in Jack's arms? Or had Cluny and Clancy been lending a little friendly help? Shame on them if they had—although, actually, it hadn't been all that shabby an idea. She bent her head, unable to look at Jack, who certainly would never understand her sudden smile, and who certainly wouldn't care for her explanation of that smile. "I'm sorry," she mumbled quietly.

"Sorry, Merry?" he said, and she heard his words through a strange buzzing in her ears. She should let go of him. She really should step back, walk away. Except that if she tried to move, she'd fall down. She was sure of it. And her near-to-buckling knees proved it when he said, "I don't know if I am."

She felt his knuckle under her chin and gasped as he gently raised her head so that she could see the question in his green eyes. He put his hands on her elbows, hinting that she should raise her arms to his shoulders, that she should return his embrace. She did so willingly, always and ever eager to follow Jack's lead. She held her breath as his head moved closer, his mouth moved closer, as she closed her eyes and waited . . . waited for the moment she'd been waiting for most of her life. . . .

"I say—Jack? Jack, where the devil are you? Maxwell said he thought he saw you on your way out here."

"Willoughby!" Clancy gritted out between clenched teeth. "Isn't this just like him, Cluny? Flap-mouthed, frothy wagtail! Go away! Go away!"

Merry jumped back as if she'd just been scalded, pressing her hands to her cheeks as Jack gave out with a string of curses she hadn't known even existed. They both turned to see Kipp, immaculately dressed as always, as if just returning from a stroll down Bond Street. He was loping down the path toward them, his hat in his hands.

"Ah, there you are. And you, too, Merry. Good, very good. I won't have to tell the story twice."

"Who said you had to tell it once?" Jack grumbled, and Merry bit her lip, trying not to laugh, or to be too pleased with Jack's reaction to the interruption. Although how he could speak at all remained beyond her, as she couldn't have formed a single word on her own, even called for help if her hair had caught on fire. "What story, Kipp? What has you in such a twist?"

Kipp stopped on the path, wiped at his forehead with a fine linen square, gave out with a deep, rather satisfied smile, and announced: "It's the Forfeit Man, Jack. I was just in the village and heard it all. He rode again last night. After all these years, Jack, the Forfeit Man is riding once more. Now, what do you have to say to that—or did you already know? Of course you did. Devilish unfair of you not to have included Merry and me in the fun, you know."

"Jack?" Merry asked, looking at him, trying to gauge his reaction to the news. "What do you know about this?"

But Jack didn't answer. And Merry couldn't read his expression. For the first time in her life, she believed herself to be no closer to Jack Coltrane than she would have been to a stranger she was just now encountering for the first time. His jaw set, his eyes hooded, he motioned for Merry and Kipp to precede him on the pathway leading back to the house.

"Now, see here, Jack," Kipp protested. "We're just supposed to tag after you like eager puppies? I mean, you could at least *ask* us."

"Yes, Jack—" Merry objected right along with him.

"We'll talk in my study, Merry," Jack said firmly, adult to child, and she had no choice but to obey him. It was amazing how quickly she could turn from thoughts of melting in his arms to plans for choking him into unconsciousness and then tying him up and feeding him to the hogs.

But, then, it had always been that way with Jack.

It was one of the many reasons she loved him, had always loved him, was cursed to forever love him. The idiot!

Chapter Nineteen

"I can't hear anything. Can you hear anything?"

Cluny pressed his own ear against the thick oak door, then stepped back and shook his head. "She wants us out, Clancy, and that's the way it has to be. Probably trying to protect Jack, dear little girl that she is. The fewer who know, the better, the less chance of word getting out. That sort of thing."

Clancy cuffed Cluny on the side of the head. "We're ghosts, you fool-born gudgeon. Who are we going to tell? She's just being mean, that's all. Females, they can be like that. As the Bard said—"

"Oh, shut up," Cluny responded wearily, rubbing his sore head. Merry had thoroughly disappointed him, but he couldn't be angry with her, he simply couldn't. So he'd be angry with Clancy instead. "There. I've said it. All these years, and I've finally said it. Just shut up, Clancy. I know when I'm not wanted, and Merry doesn't want me. And now I'm going to take a nap, especially if we're going to have to stay awake half the night at the stables. Tonight, and every night, waiting to see if the Forfeit Man rides out."

Clancy gaped at Cluny in surprise for a moment, then took one last look at the door and followed after his friend. "You're right. We'll have to be at the stables every night, there's nothing else for it. But it's high time those two children settled themselves and we were out of here, off to our heavenly reward. More than time. Let's just hope they don't bollix it up in there without our help, that's all I can say."

"All right, Kipp," Jack said on the other side of the thick oak door. He seated himself behind the desk in his study after pouring wine for his friend and lemonade for Merry, who'd thanked him with a blood-chilling glare. "Begin at the beginning, if you please, and tell me the whole of it. Just the whole of it, Kipp, without your imagination taking part in any of the description, if you please."

Kipp winked at Merry as he sat down in the chair beside hers. "Guess that leaves out the fire-breathing dragons and silver-wheeled chariots sweeping down out of the skies, don't it, Merry? No seven-foot-tall giant, red-eyed highwayman, no swordplay, no bloodshed, no swooning maidens. Pity."

Merry giggled, then looked to Jack and tried desperately and quite obviously to rearrange her features in some semblance of solemnity, showing him at least a small sign of a willingness to be serious as they discussed a very serious subject. Then she giggled again and he sighed audibly. "Oh, Jack, don't be so stiff," she scolded. "It's Kipp you're talking to, remember? You know he can't tell a story without dressing it up a bit to make it more interesting. It's what he does, for goodness sake."

"Merry . . ." Kipp began warningly, and Jack was happy enough to allow his friend to try silencing their less-than-helpful giggler. "No need to remind Jack of the fool I am, not when we've got serious business here."

"It is that," Jack said, shaking his head. "The Forfeit Man? God. Where did he strike, Kipp, and when?"

"About a mile from the usual spot, on the main road leading south. Last night. Is that succinct enough for you, Jack, or should I go on?" He crossed one leg over the other and sat back in his chair, steepling his fingers together as he looked at Jack. "Besides, I'm sure you can tell me the rest."

"Me?" Jack looked honestly disgusted. "Christ, Kipp— are you mad? Why on earth would I play at such a stupid, dangerous game?"

Kipp looked to Merry. "Oh, I don't know, Jack. To impress a lady?"

Jack fell back into his chair, glaring at Kipp. "You're an ass, Kipp," he said without heat, at last realizing what his friend was trying to do. At least he thought he did. "You've made this whole thing up, haven't you? Made it up just to see how the land lies here, between Merry and me? Why don't you just ask us? Ask us what's going on between us?"

Kipp's left eyebrow climbed toward his hairline. "And you'd tell me?"

"Never," Jack answered, grinning. "Merry? Do you want to tell him?"

Merry's grin was also wide, and only as innocent as Jack's, which wasn't innocent at all. It was an old game, keeping secrets from the always inquisitive Kipp, and one they obviously had not yet tired of playing. Even now, when the subject of Kipp's question was deadly serious—especially now, when the subject was deadly serious. "I'd rather stand on my head in front of Aloysius and recite the entire royal succession, backwards," she said, patting his arm. "Sorry, Kipp."

Kipp shook his head, laughed at his own gullibility, as if he'd truly believed, at least for a moment, that he'd be allowed inside that small, charmed circle that had been

Merry's and Jack's alone for all of their lives. "You'll never change. Either of you. Even when Merry's contemplating slicing up your guts for garters, and when you're complaining that she doesn't give you a moment's peace. So, you've decided to do what any person of sense can see should be done? Stay married?"

About halfway through Kipp's happy, damning speech, Jack had begun wondering how his friend would look with his own foot jammed down his gullet. He'd grab at his throat, his face would turn blue, his eyes begin to pop out. It was a lovely image, actually. "Go to hell, Kipp," was, however, all he said when that man turned to smile at a clearly incensed Merry.

"Yes, Kipp," she said. "Why don't you go to hell? You could probably give the devil a few suggestions as to how to run his life. In the meantime, I think it was perfectly horrid of you to make up that story about the Forfeit Man, just so that you could tease us, and pry into what is clearly none of your affair. You should be ashamed of yourself."

"I would be, pet, if I'd made the whole thing up. But I haven't. Jack, the Forfeit Man *did* ride last night. If you don't believe me, ask Squire Headley, who is minus a fat purse this morning. Ask his wife, who was put into strong hysterics. Ask their daughter, Anna, who is mooning about the place—as I hear it—talking about the fact that the Forfeit Man introduced himself, then made her *forfeit* a kiss to him in order to save her pearl necklace. It's a new twist to the game, the kiss as forfeit, but I rather like it, don't you? And then he left the squire's purse on the church steps this morning—not that our dear Headley will ever know that, of course."

He tipped his head as he looked at Jack, looked quite smugly at Jack. "But, then, I'm still not telling you anything you don't already know. Am I, friend?"

Jack brought both fists down hard on the desktop. "Christ on a crutch, Kipp," he exploded, "would you stop telling me that I'm the Forfeit Man?"

"You're not?" Kipp's skeptical tone set a fire raging in Jack's chest. If his own good friend didn't believe him, who would?

"Think about this, Kipp," Jack said, as Merry pulled her legs up under her on the chair, looking at him not in anger, or even in question, but only giving him her full attention, as if he were about to recite. "When I was here, the Forfeit Man rode. I left, and the Forfeit Man disappeared. Now I'm back—and the Forfeit Man is riding again? I doubt it will take too long before somebody realizes those facts. Do you think I have some grand wish to end up in gaol, or transported? Even hanged?"

Kipp raised his hand, offering his opinion. "But still, if you wished to remind someone of your hey-go-mad ways, dredge up memories of a carefree youth, impress a certain wife . . ."

Jack turned away from him in disgust. Was Kipp insane? Resurrect the Forfeit Man? Remind Merry of how low he had fallen, how his recklessness had ended with Merry injured, with him and Kipp beaten into a jelly? Oh, yes. That's just what he wanted to do.

"You're like a dog with a bone, Kipp," Merry jibed facetiously, and Jack turned to look at her as she spoke. "If you want to think that way, perhaps you should consider that *I* am the Forfeit Man this time, trying to do much the same thing you're accusing Jack of doing, even as he denies it."

Now Kipp laughed, deep in his throat. "You, Merry? You're probably tall enough, even hey-go-mad enough, but—" His smile faded. "My God, Merry. You aren't, are you?"

"No, Kipp, I'm not capable of such a thing," she told

him, leaning forward to look deep into his eyes. "Especially. that nonsense about kissing missish Anna Headley, even for the lark of listening to her shriek, then faint dead away. But *you* are."

Jack watched as Kipp pressed both spread hands to his chest, his eyes wide with horror as he repressed a shudder. "Me? *Me*? Donning a hood and cloak, hiding in a damp woods at midnight, leaping out to yell 'stand and deliver,' and taking the chance of ending my life with a huge, drafty hole in my heart? Or worse—kissing Anna Headley? 'E-gods, Merry," he said, picking a small bit of lint off the front of his jacket, "as if that should ever happen."

"That's true enough, Merry," Jack said, coming around to sit on the edge of the desk. "Kipp's the complete gentleman now, and the complete fop—don't frown, Kipp, you know full well what you are. He's outgrown any hint of adventure in favor of gambling hells, rout parties, and balls. Haven't you, Kipp? Seriously, Merry, could you see dearest Kipp in a simple black cape and mask, see him dressed in anything his London tailor hadn't fashioned expressly for him? As for poor Anna Headley, I must say I don't remember much about her, but I'm willing to take your word for her missishness."

Merry left her chair in order to sit up beside him on the desktop. "But, Jack, if it isn't you, and it isn't me," she glared at Kipp, "and it isn't Kipp, then who is it?"

"And just as important, Merry," Jack said, taking her hand, "why is he taking such care to let everyone know he's riding out as the Forfeit Man?"

Kipp tapped a finger against his lips. "As far as we know, Jack, no one has ever figured out that you were the original Forfeit Man. Which leaves those who always did know, right? Can't be Aloysius. He's too old. Can't be your Walter, as I certainly can't see him kissing Miss Headley." He pointed the finger at Jack. "Sherlock?"

"Henry?" Merry rolled her eyes. "Henry Sherlock? Have you been drinking, Kipp?"

"All right, I admit it probably isn't Sherlock. Unless—"

"Unless what, Kipp?" Jack asked quickly, as Kipp was suddenly looking much too serious. "Unless, employing your theory, he's trying to impress a lady?" he ended carefully, and Kipp gave him a slight nod, as if to say he understood that he was to remain silent. "Merry? Would you be impressed all hollow if Sherlock has been running about the countryside, playing at highwayman? Would it make your maidenly heart go pit-a-pat?"

She stuck her tongue out at him, which sent Kipp into mercilessly teasing her about her new admirer. Jack watched as the two began squabbling like children, leaving him time to consider what he'd thought of a moment earlier. Not that Kipp wouldn't come to him later to demand an explanation of the look he'd shot him, he was sure. And that was probably good, because it was time he told Kipp everything. The man was his oldest friend, and he deserved the truth. It was past time he began to trust again.

Still, as Kipp had said, there were only a few people who knew Jack had been the Forfeit Man. Cluny and Clancy. They were both dead. Aloysius. Kipp. Merry. And Henry Sherlock.

Damn! He must have slipped somewhere during his visit to Sherlock's house, let him see more than he wanted to show him. The man had to know he was suspicious of him. And he had to be feeling guilty, even fearful that he was about to be exposed. Riding out as the Forfeit Man was as good as a confession.

For Jack.

But Jack still had no real proof. Nothing solid, nothing he

could take to the courts. He would soon, if the gods were kind, if the ledgers gave up their secrets, if the men he'd hired in London found something as they searched through Sherlock's past. But there was nothing yet, nothing solid, nothing sure. Not yet.

Jack ran a hand through his hair as he thought about the ledgers. Nearly thirty years' worth of those damnable, neat and tidy ledgers. Henry Sherlock was a thief, and possibly much more than a thief. Jack knew it, he could feel it. Sherlock's greedy slip of the tongue two days ago proved it. But if Walter could find nothing suspicious in the ledgers, if they could find no hard evidence—what then?

Jack looked at Merry, who was accusing Kipp of being a silly, brainless popinjay—"always were, always will be"— and then to his friend, who was saying, singsong, "Henry loves Merry, Henry loves Merry" as he protectively covered his head with his arms.

Jack wearily rubbed at his forehead as Kipp and Merry continued to tease each other, pointing out past follies and childhood adventures that still had the power to embarrass the other person.

"At least Kipp's diverted her for the moment," Jack grumbled to himself as he walked over to look out a window, knowing he was being ridiculous. "Besides, it might not be Sherlock. Maybe it's Maxwell, or Honey. Or maybe Merry's ghosties have taken to moonlit rides across the countryside. Oh, God, why isn't anything simple?"

Merry stopped outside the windows to the study and peeked in at Jack as he stood hunched over the desk. He leaned down to see something Walter was pointing out to him in one of the dozen or so thick ledgers that were lying opened on the desktop.

It had already gone ten o'clock, and the study was filled

with candles, causing a glare against the glass that made it difficult for her to see him clearly, but she was sure Jack was frowning. She'd frowned herself, when she'd first read the ledgers, before she'd finally thrown up her hands and simply let Henry do the work for her.

Poor Jack. So many debts to be paid. How she'd cursed Jack's father when she learned that her hard work, her aching back, her worries and sleepless nights were all going to pay debts such as one thousand pounds to "Wild Jim Horsley, Wimbledon, Faro," and three thousand pounds to "L. Whitacker, Bath, Whist."

Dozens of gambling debts. A ledger stuffed with nothing but tradesmen's bills.

And those damnable mortgages.

Those were the worst of all.

Merry had spent the past two years working to pay old debts for August's longtime mistress, his casual doxies, his wasteful ways, his careless spending, his inept gambling. She'd paid for the wine he'd drunk six years earlier and the food he'd eaten the week before he died.

She'd even paid for the drunken vicar he'd promised ten pounds a year if he would close his eyes and perform the marriage between her and Jack without asking any questions. Like why the bride was weeping, or why the groom was so bruised and bloody that he had to be supported by two men in order to stand. If it took ten pounds a year to keep that man's silence, that was one bill she'd gladly pay.

Merry turned away from the window and began retracing her steps along the pathway she knew by heart, even in the dark. Jack was in the study. Safe. He wasn't out riding the roadways, robbing coaches as their occupants sought out a posting inn or traveled home from someone's dinner party.

She couldn't be sure he hadn't been lying, that he truly hadn't played at being the Forfeit Man last night. Except that he had everything to lose by pulling such a silly stunt, and absolutely nothing to gain. But, then, did she really know him anymore?

He said he'd made his fortune with Walter, buying land in America, then selling it again at a profit or renting it out for even more profit. Jack and an Indian?

The story hardly seemed plausible, except that Walter certainly presented himself as a man capable of doing whatever it was he set out to do. Walter also struck her as totally honest, forthright. So, if Jack wouldn't want Merry reminded of that terrible last night the Forfeit Man had ridden out, and if he wasn't in need of the money he could rob from unwary travelers . . .

"There's simply no reason for Jack to be the Forfeit Man," she said out loud as she sat down on a stone bench just outside the Main Saloon, the light from the chandelier inside spilling out onto the flagstones. "No reason at all."

She sighed, pulling her thin shawl more closely around her shoulders, feeling a headache beginning behind her eyes. "And it can't be Kipp. He's a romantic fool, but not so careless as to put Jack in danger."

"Willoughby? Must she talk about him?" Cluny asked, rolling his eyes as he and Clancy perched on a branch of the tree above Merry's head. " 'I dote on his very absence.' "

"He loves her, poor fool," Clancy said, worrying at his thumbnail with his teeth. "But Merry's right. Jack is in danger if the Forfeit Man is riding. Having Jack hang is one way of finally being rid of him, clearing the way as it were. Could Willoughby be putting a fine face of friendship on it, while secretly doing his possible to remove his rival once and for all?"

Cluny shook his head. "I think you're fair and far out there, Clancy. The viscount loves Merry too much to hurt her. Loves Jack, too, I'm positive of it. But at least my

Merry's here, trying to guess the identity of the Forfeit Man, so we know she's not the one behind the mask. And if the Forfeit Man strikes again tonight, that means it isn't Jack either, as he's knee-deep in those old ledgers once more. Now be quiet. She's talking to herself again."

"And it couldn't be Henry. That's simply too ridiculous. He's been a good friend. I could never have kept Coltrane House this long, not without his help."

"A good friend, is it? Hah! I don't think Jack thinks so. And if Jack doesn't think so, we don't think so, right? What say we give the silly girl a bit of a nudge, point out her error to her?" Clancy said, leaning down over the branch to wag a finger at the top of Merry's head. " 'A back-friend, a shoulder slapper!' That's what he is, missy, and don't you forget it!"

Merry retrieved one of the small shower of leaves that had fallen into her lap, spinning it between her fingers as she looked up into the night-dark branches. Strange. There was no wind, and the leaves were new, not nearly ready to fall.

And then she sniffed the night air, smiled. "Yes, you are here, aren't you? I can even feel your closeness, now that I'm paying attention. Oh, how I wish you could talk, that I could see you both just one more time. I'm sorry I wouldn't let you into the study with us today, but I know how you can be when you're excited. All those ghostly tinkles and bumps. You really must learn to control them better, you know. As well as learning not to trip me, as Jack and I will get where we're going in our own time, in our own way. Or not. Do we have an understanding?"

Merry believed in Cluny's and Clancy's presence so thoroughly, she didn't feel in the least silly as she spoke to them, or as she waited for them to reply in the only way they could.

The French doors in front of the bench opened, as if

inviting her inside the Main Saloon. Others would nervously vow a gust of wind had somehow opened them, even if there were no breeze. Jack, ever practical, would probably say that the catch was faulty and simply had come open by itself.

But Merry knew better.

"Oh, so I'm to be a good girl and go to bed, am I?" she asked, smiling. "All right, if you insist. It has been a rather long day, in many ways. But no more matchmaking, all right? Promise me."

She waited a full minute, but nothing happened. No more leaves fluttered down, no sounds were heard, and the French doors stayed open. "I see," she said, standing up, resting her hands on her hips. "So that's how it's going to be, hmm? Well, shame on you. Shame on you both!"

Merry walked to the opened doors, then turned around, looking out into the garden once more. "And thank you," she said, grinning, before she stepped inside and closed the doors behind her.

Clancy let go of Cluny, whom he'd been holding still, with one hand wrapped around his friend's portly body, the other clapped over the ghost's mouth.

"You see?" Clancy said smugly. "Isn't it a good thing I stopped you? There was no need to lie. She doesn't really want us to stop interfering."

Cluny straightened his blue-velvet doublet and rubbed at his mouth, trying to put his jaw back where he most liked having it. "Interfering?" he repeated, grinning at Clancy. "Why, we never interfere. Do we? In fact, I'd say it's time we made for bed ourselves, so that we can wake early and not interfere again tomorrow. Just as often as possible."

Chapter Twenty

Jack stormed into the Main Saloon, a man with a mission. And a temper. "Merry? Is there a single damned spot in this pile I can go to and not hear the sound of hammers and saws and bickering voices raised in righteous anger over the efficacy of striped satin over blue damask? Merry? Do you hear me?"

Above his head, rather draped inside the looping arms of the chandelier, two sleepy ghosts rubbed at their eyes and came to attention.

Jack watched in astonishment as Merry turned around rather inquisitively, smiled when she saw him, and then pulled small wads of cotton wool from both her ears. "I thought I heard something. You bellowed, Jack? What is it? I'm quite busy," she said, returning to her task, which seemed to have a lot to do with turning pages in a book filled with detailed drawings of chimneypieces.

He reached around her and pulled the book from her hands. "You've done this on purpose, haven't you? I asked you to take charge of the renovations, and you've decided to punish me with them. I go into my study, and there's a man in there, measuring the walls—as he sings. In Italian. Very loud Italian."

"The walls need to be repaired—the gunshot holes, and dents and gashes from thrown bits of furniture, you know—and then painted. We're considering a dark green, and perhaps some wainscoting. Would you like that, Jack? After all, I should ask your opinion."

Jack glared at her, refusing to see how lovely she looked in a yellow-and-white sprigged-muslin gown, her dark copper curls carelessly tied up on top of her head. She'd planned this confrontation, and he knew it. Planned the gown, the place, probably had calculated even the exact moment he would come after her, his temper flaring. He didn't know why, not yet, but he'd find out. Lord knew Merry would tell him. But, in the meantime, he supposed he just ought to play along. Besides, he really *was* angry.

"Don't interrupt while I'm complaining, Merry, if you please. Mrs. Maxwell says half her kitchens are in turmoil and we'll be eating cold food tonight unless certain people put her stove back where they found it. Maxwell is overseeing the installation of bellpulls, which is not a shabby idea, considering the magnitude of this old building. But now they're ripping out a wall in my bedchamber in order to install the damn thing, which they say they won't actually do for another three weeks. There are painters on ladders all over the front of the house and, from the sound of it, someone's ripping out half our chimneys. My valet is in tears—well, never mind that, there's nothing unusual there—but bits of plaster kept falling onto my plate at breakfast thanks to whatever madness is going on in the room above the breakfast room. My guess is that somebody is killing somebody else and the latter isn't going quietly."

Clancy giggled. "Mad as fire, isn't he? And you'll notice

how his words just *flow*, Cluny. Beat and meter, beat and meter. Boy has a bit of Shakespeare in his soul, thanks to us. But that's the way to be with contrary females. Forceful, but lyrical. Now she'll ask his forgiveness, and simper, and he'll soon be kissing her."

"You think so, Clancy?" Cluny said, wincing slightly as he looked down at Merry, knowing he'd never seen the dear girl simper. "Merry has a way with beat and meter herself, you know, and she can be just as forceful as Jack when she gets the bit between her teeth."

Merry waited until Jack had sat down on the couch across from hers, then smiled at him in a most condescending way. "You wanted me to be in charge, Jack. Remember? You took me away from the fields and put me down in front of buckets of paint, with a dozen voices asking me to choose which color should go where, which fabric would best suit which piece of furniture. On and on and on. It isn't easy, Jack, dealing with all these people you've sent me, each of them with his own opinions—none of which seem to match those of anyone else. Your valet isn't the only man in tears this morning, you know."

Jack looked at Merry and believed he finally recognized just what she was about. She wanted to drive him crazy, had set out to create chaos, and planned to make him demand she put someone else in charge of the repairs. More pointedly, she wanted him to step in, take over, and let her get back to the fields, where she felt appreciated.

"Yes, Merry, I did want you to be in charge. I do want you to be in charge. However, did you never hear of the word *organization*?"

Her large blue eyes became slitted. "And did you never hear of *cooperation*, Jack?"

"Told you. Hold on, Clancy, here we go!"

"Meaning?" Jack asked tightly.

"*Meaning*, Jack, that it seems to be all or nothing for you. You've always been that way. Meaning that everyone always has to do things the way you want. Because you're always right, aren't you, Jack? You always know what's best for everyone. Dear little Merry, such a sweet child, but a little headstrong, needing direction. But that's all right—because I know what's best for her, and she'll listen to me sooner or later."

"You see, Clancy? You see that? She got him—a flush hit. Look at your Jack, just sitting there. Poor boy. 'He dies, and makes no sigh.' "

Clancy worried at his bottom lip and made encouraging shoving motions with his hands, trying to coax Jack into speech as he would shove a boxer back into the ring after taking a blow to the chin that had knocked him to his knees.

Jack looked at Merry, saw the flush of anger in her cheeks, saw the quick tears she just as quickly tried to hide. "We aren't talking about playing games or building rafts to float down the stream, are we, Merry? We're not even talking about what's happening now. Once again, yet again, we're talking about how I left Coltrane House, why I left. Aren't we?"

"Possibly. Do you want to talk about that? About both the times you ran away from me?" She shrugged, looking toward the French doors, at the man who was standing just outside, chipping flaking paint from the wooden frames around the panes. He waved at her, and she sighed, smiled, and waved back. "For myself, I'm trying to talk about several things, Jack, perhaps including why you kept leaving Coltrane House. You tried to change what was happening here when your father was alive, and couldn't. I know how that hurt you. But now you're back yet again, and this time you're finally in charge. My goodness, you most certainly are in charge now, aren't you? In charge of everything, including me."

Jack scratched at a spot just in front of his ear, feeling an unpalatable truth turning over in his stomach as he tried hard not to digest it. "Surely you, of anyone, should know why I couldn't stay? That it was best for you that I go?"

"Best for me? Really." Merry's features set themselves into hard lines as she stared at Jack, as her hands drew up into tight fists in her lap. "Did you ever think to ask me what *I* thought was best for me? Did you ever ask me what *I* wanted, how *I* felt about being left behind? What if I had wanted to go with you? I was your wife, after all. I could have gone to America with you."

"You were only seventeen——"

"I was a *person*! Not your sister, not your friend. I was a person. And your wife."

"And a female," Jack pointed out, feeling as if he were suddenly standing on very thin ice, and about to plunge through it into freezing cold water.

"And a female, yes," Merry repeated dully. "I had to stay here, didn't I, Jack? I had no choice, you left me with no choice. Because females are not allowed to go haring off to exotic lands——"

"Philadelphia is hardly exotic, Merry," Jack interrupted, trying to smile. It didn't work.

"Any place is exotic, Jack, when measured against Coltrane House, especially with the chance Awful August could someday break his word and show up for another of his *parties*. Safer, too, even with wild Indians roaming about—and don't interrupt me to point out that Walter isn't exactly a wild Indian, because you know damn well what I mean."

"May I at least interrupt to point out that you shouldn't be saying 'damn' quite so much?" Jack knew he was being maddening, but he'd do anything not to hear what Merry had to say.

"No, *damnit*, you may not. I was here, Jack, because of you. Somebody had to stay. I didn't get to muck about, have adventures, have myself a ripping-great time, and all without a thought to old promises, old dreams. You kept the hurts all inside of you, Jack, didn't you? You kept them, and you nurtured them, and you probably succeeded because of them. But you forgot the dreams, you forgot the promises. You never even thought about me, except to remember that I'd seen you at your lowest point, that I'd seen you defeated. And you don't see me as I am now. I'm still a child to you. An embarrassment to you, actually. I don't know that I can ever forgive you for that."

"Is that it, Merry? Is that all?" Jack stood, walked around the low round table, and sat down beside her. "Because I want us to settle this now, and then never return to the subject again. Tell me everything that's on your mind, everything that you've wanted to say to me—yell at me—for the past five years and obviously more than that. Do you want to talk about that last day, our supposed wedding day?" He sent up a silent prayer that she'd say no. Because he wasn't ready to tell her everything. He didn't know if he'd ever be ready.

She shook her head. "I don't think so. And—and as I told you, I understand that you had to leave. I could murder you for staying away so long, but I do understand why you had to go. Truly. It's just—"

Jack gave a silent sigh of relief, knowing he'd just been handed a reprieve. "I think I'm beginning to understand now, Merry. It's just that I came back, expecting everything to be the way it was when I left. Minus Awful August, of course," he said, once more trying to smile, to lighten the mood that still could only be termed oppressive. "I trusted Henry Sherlock, I trusted Kipp and his mother. I trusted Cluny and Clancy, the Maxwells, Aloysius. I believed they'd care for you, keep you safe. And, because you deserve to know the truth, I'm now telling you that I've always been watching over Coltrane House from a distance, Merry, whether you believe that or not."

"Oh, really?" she asked, her hands moving nervously in her lap. "How?"

Jack took her hands in his, squeezed her fingers. He'd tell her this much. At the least, she deserved this much of the truth. "All right. I wasn't going to tell you this, but I guess I'm human enough to want you to like me again, at least a little. You've read the ledgers, Merry. Sherlock told me so. Do you remember the names of Newbury and Gold?"

She nodded, looking at him curiously. "Two of the mortgage-holders. Newbury is a coal merchant, I believe. And Mr. Gold is a moneylender in London. Why?"

"Because I'm Newbury, Merry, and Walter is Gold. I told you that Walter's my business partner, and he is. As a matter of fact, he owns half of the town house in London and a small part of Coltrane House. It's an agreement between gentlemen, Merry. Walter has an interest in everything that's mine, and I have an interest in everything that's his."

Merry looked at him for long moments, then shook her head. "I don't understand. Oh, I understand that you and Walter are partners. But not the rest of it. How can you and Walter be Newbury and Gold?"

Jack smiled, began to relax. "We're not really Newbury and Gold, Merry. Two gentlemen we hired are the actual Newbury and Gold, but the money they were so quick to lend my impecunious father was mine and Walter's. Thanks to Walter who originally put up the monies from Newbury and Gold, and thanks to me as well, once I'd learned at his knee, I've been able to keep a financial eye on this place almost since I met him, which was less than three months after I left England. Did you really think I'd allow Coltrane House to be sold out from under us through my father's stupidity? That I'd let you lose the only home you'd ever known?"

Above them, unnoticed in the daylight, the entire chandelier lit, every single last candle. The ghosts' happiness, however, may have been a tad premature.

Merry's cheeks paled, and her grip on his hands was tight enough to make him wince. "I don't believe it. You're holding the mortgages on your own property? I've been working day and night, worrying day and night ever since your father died—since before your father died—to pay *you*?"

Jack's slow smile was perhaps an unfortunate choice. "Well, damn it, Merry, I think you're right. How about that?"

"That's *not* funny! And I suppose now you're going to tell me you're that horrible MacDougal, too?" she asked, trying to pull her hands free of him, except that he wasn't stupid enough to allow her to free her hands just so that she could pummel him with her fists. He hadn't been gone that long. He spoke quickly, knowing his next words would go a long way toward defusing her anger.

"No. No, I'm not, sorry to say."

He watched Merry's anger fade. "Does Henry know? That you and Walter are the true holders of two of the mortgages, that is? He must be pleased to know the debts aren't quite as bad now as he's been telling us."

"He might be, if I told him," Jack said, choosing his words carefully. This was another reason he hadn't wanted to say anything to Merry quite yet. One wrong word, one wrong inflection, and she'd know what he was thinking, probably even what he was planning. "I've taken over the ledgers, all the finances now, and with Walter's help I see no reason to trouble Sherlock with any more of our business. In

other words, I'd rather we kept my small deception our little secret. Which is not to say that I'm not grateful for all of
Sherlock's good and faithful service to you and Coltrane
House. In fact, I'm thinking of asking him to invest some of
my funds for me. He certainly seems to have the head for it,
considering his own circumstances. That's a fine house the
man has, very definitely."

" 'You lie in your throat,' " Clancy said, leaning down to
wag a finger at Jack. "I know you, Jack Coltrane, and you're
handing Merry a faradiddle. Now why do you do that?"

Merry nodded, her eyes not quite meeting his, which
caused Jack some worry. "Henry would like that, Jack.
Much as he's happy to see you home, I believe he loves
Coltrane House with all his heart, and would be devastated
if he didn't feel welcome here anymore, feel needed." Then
she looked him straight in the eye and grinned. "Even if he
is the dullest stick in nature."

Jack threw back his head and laughed out loud, pulling
Merry against his chest and giving her a hug. "Oh, God,
Merry, but you're wonderful," he said, pressing a kiss
against the top of her head. "I'm sorry I left—twice, as
you've just reminded me—without even saying good-bye.
I'm sorry that I didn't write to you, that I made you believe
I'd cut you out of my life, my memory, forever." He looked
across the room, to where a smiling, china-faced doll in a
long lace gown stared back at him from a small chair. "And
I'm still sorry for that doll, not that you'll ever let me forget
it, will you?"

She snuggled against him. "Never," she said, rubbing a
hand on his chest, the way she had done as a child, drawing
warmth from him.

Except this time Jack didn't feel very brotherly, and
Merry's hand seemed to burn straight through his shirt and
into his skin, branding him. He carefully pushed her a little

bit away from him and looked into her eyes, trying to remember that these were the same eyes he'd wiped when she'd fallen down and skinned her six-year-old knees.

But remembering didn't do any good. All he could see was the Merry he held in his arms. The Merry who was his wife, his torment, his life.

"I hereby promise," he said solemnly, "that from this moment on you and I are partners in Coltrane House. *We* will ride the fields. *We* will discuss drainage and millstones." He hesitated, wincing slightly, as a true anvil chorus seemed to break out over their heads. "And we'll work together on the house itself. Starting with organizing some sort of plan to have the workmen present in only one wing at a time, so that we all don't go stark, staring mad within a week. Agreed?"

"Agreed," Merry said, then let out a small yelp and threw herself into his arms once more. "Blast them!" she exploded as Jack lifted a crystal prism from her lap and held it up, looking at it, then the chandelier, in curiosity.

"Blast whom, Merry?" he asked, thinking that perhaps the workmen should concentrate all their efforts on the central part of the house, starting with the chandelier in this room.

"Cluny and Clancy, of course," she said, shaking a fist in the general direction of the chandelier. "I told you—I'm in charge of me, not you."

Jack pushed Merry up against the back of the couch, holding on to her shoulders as he leaned over her. He was caught between anger and laughter, but anger seemed to be winning. "They're hammering up above us, Merry, remember? That's what brought that prism down. Not your ghosties. God, and you keep telling me to remember that you're no longer a child. How am I supposed to do that, if you insist in believing this place is haunted?"

"Not haunted, Jack. Cared for. Guarded. Protected."

Jack shook his head, knowing he should move away from Merry, stand up, walk out of the room. Knowing he wasn't going anywhere. "And you truly believe in all of this?"

"Yes, Jack, I truly believe in all of this. Cluny and Clancy may be dead, but they're still here. Watching over us. I used to think they wouldn't leave until you came home, but now I think they're staying until we're all happy, settled. Or until you believe in them and they can say good-bye. Don't you need to say good-bye to them?"

Jack didn't know what to say—a feeling that was becoming all too familiar to him. If he told Merry she was being silly, she'd hate him again. If he told her he believed in her ghosts, she'd know he was lying to her.

"I'm sorry you felt so alone when they died, Merry," he said at last, stroking her cheek with the back of his hand. "I'm sorry for every day you had to fight on alone, every day you believed yourself to be abandoned and forgotten."

She captured his hand in hers as it lay against her cheek, looked deeply into his eyes. Looked at him with love in her eyes.

"Merry, don't do this," Jack said, his breath coming hard as he felt himself falling forward into those huge, trusting blue eyes. "Please, sweetheart. Don't do this. We both need more time, more time to think, more time to talk . . . get out all the old hurts, the problems that still hang over us . . ."

It was ridiculous. He was leaning over her, not the other way round. She didn't have him trapped, unable to move. All he had to do was sit back, stand up. Leave.

As he'd left her before.

"Do you remember, Jack?" she was saying as she continued to look up at him, holding him to her by invisible threads that had the strength of iron bars. "Do you remember that day at the stream, the day you taught me how to skip stones?"

His mind was uncooperative, his memory nonexistent. He couldn't think of Merry the child. Not now. Not now, when he was looking at Merry the woman. Trying, oh, God, trying, to forget he'd ever known her any other way.

"I called you a grumpypuss, and you splashed me," she hinted quietly when he didn't answer her. She was leading him somewhere, and he wasn't sure he wanted to go.

"You did that often enough, I suppose—called me a grumpypuss," he said, suddenly realizing that his free hand had somehow come to be holding on to Merry's slim waist as he sat close against her. "Merry—"

"I did that often enough because you were so often in your dark moods, and I had to tease you out of them before you did something silly. Anyway, you splashed me, and then you told me to cover myself—and then you ran back to the house and beat one of Awful August's guests into a jelly. You do remember the day. You'd have to, because it was the day you first ran away from Coltrane House. I didn't see you for a full year after that."

Jack felt a tic beginning at the side of his chin. Yes, she was definitely taking him someplace. And he definitely did not want to go. "I remember. I thought we were done talking about the reasons I left Coltrane House."

"Not quite, Jack. Because, well, I have a confession of my own to make. I always believed that you'd hit that man because you couldn't hit *me*," Merry said, releasing his hand. He moved it away from her cheek—and then he spent long seconds wondering where in hell he could next put it that wouldn't damn him forever. "I believed that you were more than willing to leave for a year, because you couldn't stand to look at me."

"You thought that? God, Merry, that wasn't true, isn't true." Well, at least he had a place to put his hand now. He rubbed the side of his neck with it, wondering if it were possible for a man to strangle himself. "You were growing up, Merry, and I couldn't face it. Didn't want to face it, didn't know what to do about it. That probably *is* why I hit that bastard—because he saw that you were growing up."

"Ah, yes, and now we come to the very crux of the matter, don't we? I'm not a child anymore, Jack. I'm as old now as you were when you left Coltrane House for the first time, when you found a way to run away from me. And I'm your wife. You almost kissed me the other night. Kipp interrupted us in the gardens, and you've been avoiding me ever since, staying with Walter, looking at old ledgers, hiding on the estate. How long are you going to keep running away from me? Running away from yourself?"

"There are too many people about, Merry," Jack said shortly, looking to the French doors, and the workman who was lingering outside, occasionally glancing through the panes at them. "We'll talk later," he added, and closed his eyes to the quick shaft of pain in Merry's as he pushed himself to his feet.

"Of course, Jack. We'll do that. We'll talk later."

"You'll ride out with me this afternoon?"

She looked up at him, her expression blank. "If you want. And we'll work on a plan tonight, after dinner, for how the repairs are to proceed?"

Jack nodded his agreement, knowing that in his cowardice he had managed a reprieve, and knowing that Merry knew it as well. "Together, Merry. We'll work everything out together. Just the way you want, just the way it should have been all along. No more running away. I promise you." And then he turned and left the room, before he could say anything else, something like, "I love you, Merry."

Merry sat very still, only sighing a time or two before picking up the book once more and beginning to look through it. Cluny sighed himself, then peeked down from the chandelier, to see that Merry looked sad, but still rather satisfied.

He sat back down beside Clancy, and said, "Well, that didn't go so badly from the look of things. There was more than one problem settled in that little conversation, you know. She got him to agree to stick close as plaster to her, so she'll know if he's the Forfeit Man, and she's gotten him to agree to let her do what she likes best, ride the estate. And they're going to talk some more. That's best of all, isn't it, Clancy? 'What though the mast be now blown overboard, the cable broke, the holding-anchor lost, and half our sailors swallow'd in the flood. Yet lives our pilot still.' "

"And you call that a victory?" Clancy grumbled. "Bacon-brained, gorbellied mammot. Didn't you see? Couldn't you tell? You may know Merry, but I know my Jack. He loves her, but he's still fighting some devil we don't know, I'm sure of it. Something's still wrong here, Cluny. Something's still terribly, terribly wrong."

Chapter Twenty-one

Merry gazed into the mirror in the Main Saloon, remembering how Gilda had long ago said that a clean face and a pleasing smile were fine enough, but there was no harm in fiddling a bit with what the good Lord gave you, just applying a gentle nudge or two where one might be needed.

To that end, Gilda had taught Honey how to assist her young mistress in taming her riot of curls over the curling rod, and even how to use the rouge pots. Not that Merry would ever consider painting her cheeks or lips. She tipped her head to one side, inspected her reflection. Well, perhaps just a little. Just the lips.

"No," she declared at last, turning away from the mirror. "I'll not chase after the man more than I already have done. I just won't."

"Did you say something, Mrs. Coltrane?"

Merry shook her head, then walked back over to the couches where Walter and Aloysius had been chatting over glasses of lemonade while waiting for Jack and Kipp to join them for dinner. "No, Walter," she said, "I was just wondering something out loud. And, please, can't you call me Merry? Nobody calls me Mrs. Coltrane."

"They should, you know, for that's who you are. Isn't that right, Aloysius?"

The old man looked up at Merry and smiled. "She's a lot of things, our Meredith is, dear Walter. Right now, however, I don't see a wife. I see a little girl. A confused and unhappy little girl. A little girl with a head full of questions and, Lord help us, perhaps a plan or two. Am I correct, Meredith?"

Merry sat down on the couch beside Aloysius, plopped herself down actually, without a thought to how Honey had labored for an hour upstairs, arranging her hair, dressing her in one of her small wardrobe of gowns. She looked across the low table at Walter.

"Tell me, please. Tell me how you and Jack came to know each other, become partners. He has told me some things, but not nearly enough. I want to know, Walter, I really do. How did Jack live after leaving Coltrane House, after leaving England?"

She watched the two men exchange glances, and bit at her bottom lip as she waited for Aloysius to nod, give his approval. Cluny and Aloysius had been as close to fathers as Merry had ever known, and she honored her tutor's opinion. If Aloysius felt it was time she heard the truth, she would hear it.

"Very well, Merry," Walter said after a moment. "Shall I begin at the beginning?"

Merry grinned and sat up very straight on the couch, tucking one foot under her as she leaned forward, anxious to hear every single word.

Walter lifted his lapel, sniffed deeply at the white rosebud that resided there. "I was strolling the docks," he then began quietly, "inspecting the goods that had just arrived from England, goods I would purchase if at all possible. I could buy at the docks, you understand, even if I wasn't welcomed into the shops with open arms. A minor inconvenience, although there were—are—days I rather resent the notion that my money is good as long as I don't show my face in the wrong place at the wrong time."

"I'm very sorry, Walter," Merry said. "That's so unfair."

The man shrugged his wide shoulders. "It's life, Merry. Not all of it is pleasant. Now, as I was walking the dock, more than a little interested in a piece of fine furniture that was the property of one Mr. William Bates—a man with no great love of savages, as he called us—I happened to notice a young man walking down the gangplank, a single bag in his hand, an angry yet confused look on his face."

"Jack," Merry said quietly, edging forward on the couch even more. "How did he look? Was he rail-thin? I'm sure he couldn't have had a good voyage, as he left here so beaten, so ill."

"Shhh, Meredith," Aloysius said, putting a hand on her arm. "Let Walter tell the story."

"Thank you, Aloysius. And, to answer your question, Merry, Jack looked thin, yes, but quite well. So tall, his long black hair tied back very neatly, the scowl on his face telling me he wasn't sure what to do next and any hint of indecision was an anathema to him. I had been alone in my lifetime. I knew how it felt to be alone. I was intrigued, but I turned away, hopeful that Mr. Bates could be convinced to part with the object I wished to purchase."

He smiled. "But it was not to be. Dear Mr. Bates took one look at me, then turned his back, refusing to speak, to listen. And then Jack walked by. I could see that he was a gentleman, by the way he carried himself, by the way his clothes were cut, even though his cuffs were threadbare, his shirt collar frayed. I stepped in front of him, told him I had a business proposition for a man who might be looking to earn himself some money. Jack could have turned away, he could have cursed me, even hit me, I suppose—although I could have milled him down, of course. He was thin, as I said, and I am not a small man. But Jack listened, and then he smiled. And by nightfall I had a very lovely armoire sitting in my parlor."

"You gave Jack the money, pointed out the armoire and Mr. Bates, and had him buy it for you," Merry said, understanding quickly. "And that's how you and Jack came to go into business with each other. So Jack was never alone in Philadelphia, never had to walk the streets begging for crusts of bread?"

"Would you be happier if he had?"

Merry felt her cheeks growing hot at Aloysius's question. "Well, he could have suffered a *little*," she said honestly.

"Oh, my dear Merry," Walter said solemnly. "Jack did suffer. He suffered every day he wasn't here, at Coltrane House. He worked hard, very hard, every day, learning from me, acting for me. He paid back every penny he felt he owed to me for his 'education.' And he fell into bed each night, exhausted, only to wake many of those nights, crying out your name. For the longest time, I must admit, I rather detested you, Merry. I thought you had broken his young heart and he'd run away from England to escape the sight of you."

"He—he'd call out my name?" Merry slipped her hand into Aloysius's, her bottom lip trembling as she fought back tears. She'd been right to ask her questions. She'd really needed to hear this, hear all of it. "I didn't know."

"Good evening, everybody. Didn't know what, Merry?" Kipp asked as he strolled into the Main Saloon, a half-eaten apple in his hand. "You can't mean there's anything in this world that you don't know. At least not once you've decided you have to know it."

Merry adored Kipp, always had, but there were times she could cheerfully wish him in China. Especially when he was being inquisitive. "Oh, nothing much, Kipp, really. I was just saying that I didn't know that Walter didn't know you were Aramintha Zane."

Kipp, who had just taken another bite of apple, nearly choked on the thing before it shot halfway across the room, leaving him coughing and gasping for breath. "Merry!" he got out at last. "That was our secret. God—if Jack had heard you? I'd never live it down, Merry, and you know it."

Merry shot a quick look to Walter, who was very nicely keeping his mouth shut rather than saying something like "Who is Aramintha Zane and what are you talking about, Merry?" So she said, "Isn't that silly, Walter? As if Jack would find anything to laugh at in Kipp's little adventure as a novelist? In fact, I believe Jack would be extremely intrigued if he were to read *Love's Forfeit: Adventures of a Highwayman.* Don't you think so? As I have my very own copy in my room, all three volumes, I could probably lend it to him. Except you did sign those for me, didn't you, when you gave them to me for Christmas last year."

"How much, Merry?" Kipp asked, taking her hand and helping her to rise from her seat. "How much will it take for your vow of silence?"

Merry smiled up at him, ignoring the tsk-tsking coming from Aloysius. "Walk with me in the gardens before we're called in to dinner, Kipp, and I'll tell you, all right?"

They were just passing through the French doors when Merry looked back into the room, to see Aloysius speaking in low tones while Walter's eyes grew wide and his grin even wider. She might, as hostess, be seen as deserting her guests, but she certainly had not left them with nothing to talk about!

"Now," Kipp said, once they were walking along the

pathways in the gardens, "what was that nonsense in aid of, Merry? It's not like you to be mean, so I imagine you want something from me that I'm predisposed not to give. Am I right?"

Merry shook off the last of her shock—and her reluctant happiness—in hearing that a tormented Jack had called out her name in his nightmares, and smiled up at her lifelong friend. "How well you know me," she said, patting his arm. "The Forfeit Man didn't ride last night, Kipp," she said, getting directly to the point. "I know, because I sent someone into the village today to inquire if there were any robberies last night."

"Uh-oh," Kipp said, comically rolling his eyes. "Here we go."

"Kipp, be serious, if you please. Jack was here all night last night. I know that because I stayed awake half the night, watching out my windows at the stables. Which, you will agree, doesn't prove he's not the Forfeit Man because the Forfeit Man stayed home last night."

"You really believe Jack is playing the highwayman again?"

She shook her head. "It was you who thought that, Kipp, remember? And it was Jack who showed us both how dangerous it would be if anyone were to remember the last time the Forfeit Man rode, and who was absent for five years before the highwayman rode out again. Now, if it wasn't you, Kipp, having yourself a bit of a lark, and if it wasn't Jack— or me!—then someone is going out of his way to land Jack in trouble. You have figured that out by now, haven't you, Kipp?"

He pulled her down beside him on one of the stone benches. "And that would be terrible, wouldn't it, Merry? For Jack, for all of us. And most especially for you. You love him, don't you? I know you've worshiped him ever since you were a child. But you love him, too. Don't you? You really love him."

Merry turned away from him, looked out over the gardens that lay slightly muted in the gathering dusk. "We seem to speak of nonsense every time I see you lately, Kipp," she said quietly. "Why do you keep asking me this question?"

She felt his hand on hers, and she closed her eyes against sudden tears. "Because I need to know, sweetheart. I really, truly need to know."

She looked down, seeing Kipp's large hand covering hers, wishing she could feel something other than friendship, a friendship mingled with sadness because she couldn't be what he wanted of her. She had been Jack's all of her life. There had never been anyone else. She had never wanted anyone else. "I'm sorry, Kipp," she whispered at last. "Truly sorry."

His pat on her hand before he released it was a little too cheerful, his tone a little too bright as he stood up, looked down at her, and smiled his most endearing smile. "Very well, then, now I know, don't I? For once and for all time, I know. I've probably always known, but you know me, don't you—always weaving daydreams. So. What is it you want me to do?"

"You're still going to help me?" Merry stood, threw herself into his arms. "Oh, Kipp—I do love you! You're the best friend anyone could have!"

"Thank you, sweetheart. And if you ever repeat those two sentences to me, Merry, in that exact order, I believe I shall have no recourse except to go drown myself," he said, disentangling himself from her embrace. "Now, let me guess. You want me to spend my nights skulking up and down the roadways, probably catching my death of damp, searching out the miscreant who is impersonating our dear Jack, then haul the bastard to justice. Am I right?"

"You're as right as can be," she told him, taking his hand in hers as they walked back toward the house. "But you won't be skulking up and down the roadways alone, because I'll be with you. If Jack isn't going to do anything to help himself, we are. As his very best friends, we'll simply have to save him."

"So he can kill me for allowing you to put yourself in danger? Oh, I think not, sweetheart. I truly think not."

"Now, Kipp," Merry said encouragingly. "You know I'm not at all missish, and can ride as well as you. Shoot, too, if it becomes necessary. We should be on the road by ten, don't you think? All you have to do is bring along a mount from your stables, and wait for me at the bottom of the gardens . . ."

Jack watched Kipp and Merry until they were out of sight along the curving pathway. Then he stepped into a small clearing, and looked up at the sky. "He'll give in to her before they reenter the house," he told the stars just beginning to appear. "He always has, when Merry begs a favor, and the more ridiculous and foolhardy the plan, the more he's prone to agree to be a part of it."

Then he counted to ten before slowly walking toward the house himself, ready to watch Merry as she danced her way through dinner, preparing everyone for the "early night" she would undoubtedly announce even before the tea cart was brought into the Main Saloon.

"We'll be going along, of course," Clancy said from his perch in one of the trees overlooking the pathway.

"Highwayman hunting?" Cluny answered, walking straight through a rosebush as he looked up at his friend. "I think not. As the Bard said, Clancy, 'For you and I are past our dancing days.' I don't think I'd much care to go jostling about on the back of a horse."

"Nonsense! We're healthier as ghosts than we've been in thirty years," Clancy exclaimed, floating down from the tree to stand, arms akimbo, in front of his friend. "I think the green doublet, don't you? We'll dress and be ready and waiting at the bottom of the gardens at ten o'clock. Now buck up! 'Once more unto the breach, dear friends, once more . . .'"

Unaware of Cluny and Clancy's plans, Jack entered the Main Saloon, bowed and smiled to everyone just as Maxwell announced that dinner was served. Taking Merry's arm before Kipp could so much as move, he walked with her into the dining room, lavishly complimenting her on her hair, her gown, and on the fact that she had grown into such a fine, and refined, lady.

"Such a refreshing change from your hey-go-mad youth, Merry," he said, watching as hot color stained her cheeks, and enjoying himself very much. "With our new honesty with each other, I'll admit there were times I despaired of your ever growing up. But now you have and, I must tell you, I couldn't be more pleased. You wanted me to see you as a woman, Merry. Tonight I definitely do. Shall we talk later, do you think?"

"Thank you, Jack," she said—pronouncing each word through gritted teeth, actually, he noticed with an inward smile. He had handed her a dilemma, and she knew it, although she couldn't have known that he knew it as well. "I, as always, live only to have you proud of me. However, it *has* been a very long day, what with one thing or another, and very wearying. Perhaps we could talk tomorrow?"

Things only got better from that point, if one was to consider that having some small fun at Merry's expense could be considered a good thing. She was subtle at first, or as subtle as Merry knew how to be, speaking about her very busy day, her fears that tomorrow would prove to be even busier.

She yawned into her fist several times, and even once closed her eyes, sighed, and said, "Oh, I think I must be growing old, to be so tired."

Jack hid a smile behind his hand as he remembered a line from the Shakespeare Clancy had taught him: "Well said; that was laid on with a trowel."

"What a delicious meal. I've certainly missed good, plain English food," Jack said as the last course was removed. "You know, I've been longing for a game of chess for days. Merry, you still play, don't you? Perhaps you'll agree to play against me, while Walter takes on Kipp here, or Aloysius?"

Aloysius put down his glass, and said, "Much as I would enjoy playing, I enjoy watching even more. Except, perhaps, for tonight. I've had a long day with the esteemed Mr. Poppo, frankly, and crave my bed, so you'll have to excuse me."

"And me," Walter said, rising from his chair along with Aloysius. "I'm all but cross-eyed from looking at ledgers all day. Another time, perhaps, Lord Willoughby? But you will excuse me now, won't you? I don't believe I can even so much as face dessert."

"Definitely, definitely," Kipp said, just a smidgen too readily. "In fact, I'm rather tired myself. Long day with my solicitor and all of that. Signing papers, pretending to know what I'm signing—that sort of thing. Why, I'll probably be sound asleep by ten." To prove his point, he yawned most prodigiously, even scratched at his belly like an old man contemplating a nap.

"Really," Jack said, looking once more to Merry even as his friend and his tutor left the dining room together. The two men looked about as innocent as a pair of cats with canary feathers sticking out of the corners of their mouths. Could it be that everyone at Coltrane House planned to go Forfeit Man hunting tonight? "Well, sweetheart, I guess that leaves the two of us, doesn't it, once we toss tired old Kipp out of here before he falls forward into his plate."

"It would," she agreed, "if I wanted to play chess, which I don't. I've been bludgeoning my brain all day today, working out strategies that keep the painters clear of the carpenters, deciding if walls should be repaired first, or floors—that sort of thing. And then there was fighting with Jones; the fool who moved Mrs. Maxwell's stove without a thought to how we all were to eat while it sat in the middle of the kitchens. I simply can't imagine an evening of using my brain for anything more than filling the empty spot inside my skull so that my head doesn't rattle when I lay it on my pillow—which I shall do before ten tonight."

Rats deserting the sinking ship. That's what it looked like to Jack as he bid Kipp good night and watched Merry all but run up the stairs in a grand hurry to get herself to bed. He walked into the Main Saloon behind Maxwell, who was wheeling in the tea cart, and told him he could just wheel it back out again, perhaps to share its contents with Mrs. Maxwell and Honey—or Jones and Mr. Poppo, and whoever else was cluttering up the house.

Pouring himself a glass of port he really didn't want, Jack sat down beneath the chandelier, crossed his legs, and looked up at the glittering candles. "Well? Are you here, or do you have business elsewhere, too?" When there was no answer—not that he'd expected one—he stood up, put down his still-full glass, and headed for the butler's pantry. He was fairly sure there was a key to the master bedchamber hanging on a hook inside the door, keys to every door that led out of the master bedchamber.

The Forfeit Man might ride tonight. Kipp might ride tonight. Walter and Aloysius might do whatever it was they surely were planning to do tonight.

But Meredith Fairfax Coltrane was by damn going to spend the entire night in her rooms!

"I should have known he gave in too easily," Merry said, shaking the handle to the door leading from her dressing room to the hallway. "And I was too cowhanded with my excuses. A single game of chess. How long could it have taken to beat him? He always uses his queen too wildly. But no. I had to be so obvious that Jack had to know I had something planned for later tonight. How can I keep forgetting that he knows me so well?"

She shook the handle again, but it was no use. She'd checked the main door, the door from the master's dressing room, the small door that led to a back stairway leading down to the kitchens. They were locked. They were all locked.

"Asking me if I wanted to *talk* more tonight," she grumbled, giving the door a kick with her riding boot. "Hinting that we'd do more than talk, when we both know neither of us is ready for more than talk, not yet. I should have known!"

Merry stomped back into the main chamber and glared at the hole in the wall. The hole had been put there in anticipation of providing the master bedchamber with a bellpull she could use to summon Honey. The hole was there, but the bellpull was not. There were holes all over the walls throughout the house, but none of them was more than a hole at this point. Well, that would change! First thing tomorrow morning, she'd put every last workman to completing the job.

Which did her absolutely no good at the moment, especially when she'd told Honey to go off to bed, and Honey's bed was a full floor removed from the main bedchamber.

Merry was dressed, all in black, as befitted a person out

to skulk about in the dark, hunting imitation highwaymen. Kipp was probably already at the bottom of the gardens, holding the bridle of the horse he'd brought for her. The Forfeit Man was probably already in position somewhere alongside the roadway, ready to pounce.

And she was here, caged like an animal, totally powerless.

"*Pssst!* Over here, Merry," Cluny said, doing a small jig as he pointed to the key he'd slipped under the door just before he'd walked through it. He'd already unlocked the door, but Merry hadn't checked it a second time, so she didn't know that he was being helpful.

"She doesn't see it," Clancy said, looking at himself in the tall mirror in the corner. "Do I look all right? Menacing enough? Perhaps the addition of a small sword?"

"What difference does it make? Nobody can see you, anyway. Here, I'll put the key on this table. Surely she'll see it now."

Cluny peeked out the window, squinting as he looked out over the gardens washed in moonlight. "Willoughby's out there, I'm sure of it. But, as his heart isn't in this anyway, he'll not wait long." He turned away from the window and looked at Merry, who was busily pacing the carpet in front of the bed, even more busily calling Jack Coltrane some very nasty names.

"Such language! Shame on you, young lady," Clancy said, then looked at the mantel clock and frowned. It had gone eight minutes past ten. "Cluny, we already know the Indian is out there stumbling around in the dark, and Aloysius as well, for all the good it will do either of them. Jack escaped me a half hour ago, so I know he's also out and about. Merry is my only hope to get off Coltrane land and protect Jack. That said—" he concluded, walking over to the table and picking up the key, "—here you go, young lady. Catch it!"

Something hard hit Merry flat on her buttocks, then fell heavily to the floor. She whirled around, ready to face her attacker, then looked down to see a large key lying on the carpet. A smile split her face as she bent down and picked up the key, then grabbed her black toque and ran for the door. "Oh, thank you! I should have known you wouldn't let me down. Thank you. Thank you!"

Chapter Twenty-two

Walter might have been an Indian, a full-blooded member of the Lenni Lenape tribe. His skills, however, lent themselves more to numbers and business than they did stealth and any knowledge of how to move through the dark without being detected. And when one couldn't ride, and when one doggedly refused to walk anywhere, most any chance of getting from here to there undetected was rather slim.

Jack followed the tracks of the curricle until he ascertained that Walter and Aloysius were definitely heading in the direction of Henry Sherlock's small mansion.

"So, you think so, too, do you? Very well, gentlemen, I'll leave you to watch Sherlock, see if he's riding out tonight," he said out loud. He reined in his stallion and turned about, heading for the main roadway where the Forfeit Man had struck two nights previously.

He rode on for another three miles, then dismounted, tied the stallion's reins to a sturdy branch several yards away from the road, and set out through the trees on foot.

His eyes slitted against darkness the moon couldn't penetrate. He moved stealthily but quickly, fairly certain that Kipp would believe that the best place to wait would be at their old spot beside the fallen log. Kipp was many things, but he was also fairly consistent in how he thought. Jack was sure his friend would not think that traveling over unknown ground in the dark was a very smart decision. That is, if he'd come here at all and wasn't at home, already tucked into his bed, happy to have escaped Merry's plans for the evening.

But, no. There he was, just ahead of him. Kipp looked rather dashing, dressed all in black, his blond hair covered by a black silk scarf tied around his head like a pirate. Jack wondered if he should just watch, or sneak up behind his old friend and give him a good scare.

But Jack's smile left him as he saw Merry beside Kipp. Merry, who he had been sure was still at Coltrane House, locked up in her rooms. He should have known better. Merry only stayed where she was when she didn't want to be someplace else.

He looked at her, what he could see of her. She looked entirely too comfortable dressed in Jack's old black cape. She and Kipp were both on horseback as they waited behind a trio of conveniently placed oaks, holding their mounts in place and waiting for sounds in the darkness.

Jack went down on his haunches, also waiting, and wondering just what he thought they all would do if the new Forfeit Man appeared.

"I still say we should be farther down the road, Kipp," Jack heard Merry complain, probably not for the first time. Her voice came to him easily through the quiet night. "Now, remember. We can't shoot the man. I know it's not Jack, I just know it. But if it is—"

"If it is, I'm going to toss him to the ground and strangle him," Kipp said, then shivered. "I should have worn a cloak, you know. Dashed damp out here. You'd think highwaymen would operate in the daytime more often, wouldn't you? So much warmer, and fewer biting bugs out to eat us alive, too, I'll wager."

Kipp's heart clearly wasn't in this adventure of Merry's. Jack had to clamp his lips tightly shut to keep from laughing out loud as the man slapped at the side of his neck, obviously the unhappy victim of yet another biting bug.

And then Jack's senses came fully alert as, from behind him, the sound of a coach traveling at high speed reached his ears. It was still a faint sound, but he was sure of what he heard. At that speed, horses and coach would never be able safely to negotiate the turn leading to the steep downward slope of the hill.

"Dammit," he spit out, already racing back to where he'd tied his horse, and leaping into the saddle. The stallion reacted immediately, and Jack crashed through the trees, onto the roadway, waiting for the coach to appear.

He didn't have long to wait, only mere seconds. As the coach neared he turned the stallion and pushed it into a wild, instant gallop through the darkness.

Keeping to the very edge of the roadway, he looked back over his shoulder, watching as a wild-eyed team of four crazed horses advanced on him. The coach they were pulling along with them careened widely from side to side. There was no driver in the box.

As the leader came abreast of him, Jack kicked his feet free of the stirrups. He uttered a short, pithy curse, and flung himself onto the leader's back even as he reached frantically for the off-leader's halter.

It took seconds, minutes, hours, for the horses to react to him, to slow, to stop finally just at the beginning of the sharp turn that led to the downward slope of roadway, and certain disaster.

Jack slid off the leader's back, still holding tightly to the reins, and called out, "Is anyone in the coach? Are you all right?"

There was no answer from the coach, but Jack heard the approach of Kipp's and Merry's mounts. He yelled for Kipp to climb up to the box and throw the brake on the coach, knowing damn full well the scene was too familiar for comfort.

"Merry, you check inside the coach—no! Wait! I'll do that." Jack didn't know if anyone inside the coach was injured, perhaps even dead. He didn't want Merry to see that, not if he could help it.

"Jack?" Merry questioned, dismounting and tying her borrowed mare's reins to the back of the coach. "I can't believe it! You *are* doing it. Oh, Jack—how *could* you?"

Jack left the horses and trotted back to grab Merry by the arm, pulling her away from the coach door. "You think I was robbing this coach? Are you insane? I'm only out here because of you—and how the devil did you get out of your room?"

Merry glared at him, her mouth tightly shut.

"Uh-oh," Cluny said as he and Clancy arrived on the scene, huffing and puffing and still brushing dust off their clothes. They'd both been flung off the back of Kipp's and Merry's horses by their hosts' unexpected bolt onto the roadway. "If she tells him, he'll probably have an apoplexy right here, with us watching. Distract him, Clancy, or we'll be listening to a lecture none of us wants to hear. Dispiriting, that's what it is, to continually hear the boy telling us we don't exist."

Clancy, who'd had just about enough excitement for one evening, was happy to oblige. He yanked open the door to the coach, then watched as a rather large, overdressed man tumbled straight through him, and onto the ground. "There. That should do it."

"Lord Hardcastle!" Kipp exclaimed, lightly jumping down from the box, to the wheel, to the dirt roadway. He hastily pulled the scarf from his head, shoved it into his pocket. "Well, fancy meeting you here. I last saw you in London, wasn't it? Trying to rid yourself—er—popping off another beautiful daughter? Are you all right, sir?" He grabbed hold of the back of his lordship's rather expansive breeches and hauled the man upright. "Here, up we go—ah, that's better."

"Willoughby? By God it is—Willoughby!" Lord Hardcastle grabbed onto Kipp's shoulders and pulled him into a breath-robbing embrace. "I thought we were dead, truly I did. But you saved us, didn't you, boy? Who'd believe it, mincing fop that you are—ah, but I don't mean that, now do I?"

He released Kipp at last, just as Jack pulled Merry behind a wide oak tree and clamped a hand over her mouth to keep her silent. Lord Hardcastle then called out: "Susan? Susan, dearest, look who has saved us. Willoughby. You remember—that silly fool we saw chasing butterflies in the park last month. Would you believe it?"

Jack, still holding Merry's hand, led her through the trees alongside the road. He motioned for her to stand very still, and very quiet, while he rescued her mount from the back of the coach. It was too dark, and Lord Hardcastle was too befuddled to notice.

"Well, actually, to be truthful, it wasn't I who—" Kipp was casting his gaze around frantically, definitely not wishing to be featured in the role of hero. Definitely not, especially as Lady Susan was already out of the coach and looking very much like someone who might want to kiss someone who had saved her from A Horrid And Certain

Death. His explanation was cut short as Lady Susan, her father's daughter in so many ways—both in emotional spleen and anatomical size—launched herself into Kipp's arms, and then promptly fainted.

"Swoons quite well, don't she, Clancy?" Cluny asked, studying Lady Susan, then imitating her as he fell forward into Clancy's arms. "I should try that, next time we perform the Bard's—"

"Would you stubble it!" Clancy ordered, pushing Cluny away, so that the rotund ghost found himself sitting rump down in the middle of a briar bush.

As Kipp stared pleadingly into the dark woods, Jack raised a single finger to his lips, then pointed behind him, into the darkness, sure his friend would understand that it was imperative that Merry not been seen. Her presence, and her attire, were both not the sort of thing either Jack or Kipp would want to be the topic of discussion as Lord Hardcastle recounted this evening's adventure to his friends.

Kipp's nod was slight—most of his strength and concentration necessarily being put into supporting the unconscious Lady Susan—but Jack saw it, and melted back into the darkness.

It took several minutes, but Lady Susan was at last sufficiently roused to stand upright on her own. Lord Hardcastle explained how they had come to be barreling along the roadway sans driver, the very man who began moaning and kicking from his place stuffed in the boot, his hands and feet tightly tied together.

"We were lost. Coachie must have missed a turn somewhere, for we should have arrived at Lord Lasser's house party shortly after dark. I have no idea where our second coach is, with my valet and Susan's maid—and all our clothing, come to think of it. We were then set upon by a highwayman, of course, just as I feared, as no sane man travels the road this late in the evening, not with his child by his side," his lordship said, wiping his brow with a large white handkerchief he'd pulled from his pocket.

"Took my purse, took dearest Susan's ruby necklace and ring, then tied up Coachie and stuffed him in the boot. Next thing I knew, he'd turned the whip on the cattle and sent them haring off down the road, Susan and myself falling about inside the coach, unable to do more than pray. We were dead, Willoughby, until you rescued us."

"My dear goodness," Kipp said, pressing one hand against his hip as he took up a stance that, to Jack, seemed to be a mix of both boredom and gentlemanly shock. "But just one highwayman, my lord? Surely it would have taken an entire gang of thieves to subdue you as you defended dear Lady Susan."

Lord Hardcastle coughed a time or two, the sound rumbling up from his large belly. "Yes, yes. Of course, Willoughby. You would think that. But it was Coachie's fault, you know, stopping like that. Once the pistol had been stuffed in my face, I had no choice but to hand over my own. The girl, Willoughby. I couldn't risk violence, now could I?"

"Indeed not, my lord," Kipp said, turning toward Jack and rolling his eyes, so that Jack clapped a hand over Merry's mouth to keep her giggles from giving them away. "Tell me, my lord, did you by chance get a look at this terrible highwayman? Could you see his face, perhaps?"

"He was masked—from the top of his head to his nose," Lady Susan said, beginning to fan herself. "And he was big. Very tall."

"He was huge," Lord Hardcastle added, holding his hand up over his head, as if to indicate the highwayman's size. "Nearly a giant."

"Dressed in black. In black from head to toe. Um—like you, actually."

"He had pistols. Two of them."

"And the way of a gentleman about him, for the little he spoke. At least he said 'please,' when he motioned for me to remove my necklace."

"I see," Kipp went on, nodding. "I've heard of this man, and have been hunting him myself tonight. Hence my attire, Lady Susan. And—much as I detest such a personal question inquiry, Lady Susan, I fear I now must ask this—did he kiss you?"

"Did he *kiss* me?" Lady Susan's bottom lip pushed forward in a pout. "No," she pronounced rather wistfully, "he didn't."

"Kiss her? As if he'd dare!" Lord Hardcastle exclaimed, pulling a suddenly crestfallen Lady Susan close against him. "He said nothing more than to order us to hand over our valuables. To the Forfeit Man—that's what he said. Forfeit Man? What rot—bunch of romantic twaddle! Now Willoughby, if you're done asking inane questions, I think it's time you escorted us to your estate, where we will pass the remainder of the night as your guests. Perhaps a few days, actually, as I believe my daughter to be very overset by this night's work. She's a delicate child. Isn't that right, Susie?"

Lady Susan visibly wilted—quite a feat for a young lady who looked capable of picking up the entire coach and carrying it on her back to Kipp's estate. "Oh, yes, Papa. I fear I shall have a spell, if I'm not soon someplace warm and safe. How awfully kind of you, my lord, to offer your home to us."

"My pleasure, my lady, my lord," Kipp said, executing quite a tolerable leg, considering his head was turned toward the trees and his face bore an expression that told Jack he would owe him more than a small favor next time they met.

"Come on," Jack whispered to Merry, dragging her after him as the two of them, plus Merry's mare, tracked through the trees, on the lookout for Jack's stallion.

"Come on," Clancy said, calling Cluny to attention, as he was still studiously staring at Lady Susan, mimicking her every simpering movement. "We need to stay with Jack and Merry if we're to get back to Coltrane House. This should prove an interesting ride, don't you think?"

Almost as soon as the coach pulled away, Kipp leading the coachie on his bay gelding, Jack's stallion came walking through the woods, his reins dragging along on the ground. "Here, boy," Jack ordered, snapping his fingers.

"What's his name?" Merry asked as Jack quickly, and none too gently, lifted her onto her borrowed mare.

"He doesn't have one," Jack said shortly, his mind too occupied with what he'd seen, what he'd heard, to pay attention to his answer.

"He doesn't have one?" Merry shook her head. "Whyever not?"

"Does it matter?" Jack asked, leading the way to the roadway, then waiting for Merry to move her mount alongside his. He hadn't named the stallion he'd bought at Tattersall's in London because he hadn't known if he was going to be able to stay at Coltrane House, if he was even going to be able to remain in England. He hadn't wanted to make any new attachments, not even to a horse. He'd been that unsure of his welcome, of how well he'd be able to manage the old memories, the old hurts.

They rode in silence, each occupied with their own thoughts, until they reached the Coltrane stables. Jack helped Merry dismount before they both automatically began tending to their own mounts, making sure the horses were settled before heading back to the house.

"So it isn't you," Merry said at last. "I'm glad. I didn't think you were that hare-witted, but I couldn't be sure."

"Thank you," Jack said. "I think. And it isn't Kipp either. Frankly, I had wondered if he might have been behind the resurrection of the Forfeit Man. He's mad enough, in his own rather bizarre way."

Merry laughed, leaning against Jack companionably as they made their way through the darkness, heading for a side door to Coltrane House that they'd used many a night when they'd been out and about without anyone's knowledge. "Except—"

"Except what, Merry? You heard what Hardcastle said. The highwayman told him he was the Forfeit Man. Went out of his way to do it, I'd say," Jack said as they crept up the servant stairs. Fatigue numbed his legs even as he slowly became aware that he was probably going to be sore in the morning, and have his share of bruises as well, as he'd landed on more harness than horse when he'd jumped onto the leader.

"Except that the highwayman didn't kiss Lady Susan. I mean, if he kissed Anna Headley, he certainly could have pushed up his courage enough to kiss Lady Susan as well. Now, why do you suppose he didn't?"

"A fuller moon? A better look?" Jack said, grinning. And then he sobered. "You're not trying to say that there are two men out there impersonating the Forfeit Man. Are you?" He'd thought so himself, but hadn't considered that Merry would also.

Merry pulled the toque from her head, releasing a cascade of warm, living curls that fell to below her shoulders. "I don't know what I'm saying, Jack. Anna was kissed and Lady Susan was not. And Lady Susan wasn't allowed to keep her jewelry. The robberies occurred on the same road, but not at all in the same manner."

Merry's quick mind had settled on the same questions Jack already had wandering around inside his own head. "That's true. They're becoming more dangerous. The first robbery didn't include putting the occupants of the coach in danger. Hardcastle and his daughter could very well have been badly injured or killed if we hadn't been there. Everyone and his maiden aunt will be screaming for the Forfeit Man to be found and hanged now, even those who praised him five years ago."

"I know," Merry said, sighing. "Just as I know we have to catch him—them—before someone decides that you're him." She wrinkled up her nose, obviously trying to lighten the heavy mood that was descending on both of them. "Or is that he? Aloysius would know, not that I'm going to wake him up and ask him."

Merry's mention of their shared tutor brought Jack's mind around to the thought of Aloysius and Walter, and what the two of them might have discovered this evening. "You can ask him in the morning, sweetheart, at the same time you explain to me how you unlocked this door," he said, steering Merry to the door to the master bedchamber. He ran a hand over her hair, as he had done a thousand times in the treasured past. This time, it was a mistake. A big mistake. "Now," he said rather brusquely, to cover his sudden discomfort, "it's bed for you, all right?"

"Really?" she asked, smiling up at him. "You mean you're not going to first read me a lecture on how horribly stupid I was to go highwayman hunting tonight?"

"I'd lock you in your rooms for a fortnight if it weren't for the fact that I need your help with the nonsense we've got going on in every room of this pile. Besides which you'd probably find your way out within five minutes. But that doesn't mean I'm not angry with you. Kipp, too. Although," he ended, trying to smile even as he wished himself miles from the temptation he saw in Merry's eyes, "I do believe Kipp is probably going to do sufficient penance these next few days."

Merry opened the door to the master chamber and stepped through. She tipped her head to one side, looking up at Jack, who had just caught sight of the high, wide bed half-hidden in the dimness inside the room. "Penance? Oh—yes, I see what you mean. Lady Susan was looking at him rather fatuously, wasn't she? Oh, dear. Poor Kipp. Um—do you want to come inside? We could talk a little more? And we wouldn't scandalize anyone, you know, as we are married."

"What? Oh, yes, poor Kipp," Jack repeated, knowing he was looking at the marriage bed that was his by right, by law. And Merry—bless her, damn him—was looking at him as if she knew that he was hers by right, by law. "But not now, Merry. It's late. I think I'll just go to bed."

He watched as her smile faded, as her chin set so that it wouldn't wobble, so that the quick tears in her eyes wouldn't dare to spill down her suddenly white cheeks. "Oh. Yes, it is late, isn't it?"

Jack put out a hand, touched her shoulder. "Merry, I—"

"Sssh," she said, then stood up on tiptoe and pressed her lips against his, the heat of her searing his mouth, exploding his brain. She pressed against him in uneducated passion, ripping his heart in two, hurting him with her unquestioning love.

He could give in, give up, succumb. It would be so easy. All his questions, all his fears—he could banish them. Never ask the questions, never face the fears. He could take her, make her his own. Forget what his father had told him that last night, forget the past. Destroy her options.

It would be so easy.

Instead, he stood very still, not responding. Dying inside, but not responding.

And then he walked away.

Chapter Twenty-three

Mr. Poppo was taken from his work on the dining room fireplace and put onto working on the one in Jack's room. Other workers were set to work in Jack's chamber. If there was no work for them there, Merry told them to enter the adjoining chambers and do whatever they could—hopefully with hammers, and beginning at seven of the clock every morning.

Merry kept busy, and out of sight. Everyone seemed to have silently agreed to bide their time for a while, walk in place.

And the Forfeit Man struck three more times in as many days.

On the fourth day, just as Jack and Merry had walked into the Main Saloon before dinner, Squire Headley arrived at Coltrane House. Maxwell announced the man even as the squire brushed past him, into the room.

"Look at the nodcock in that horrid rigout, Cluny, would you? Strutting, fat-kidneyed minnow," Clancy said from their perch on the chandelier. "Or, as my sainted mother would have said—a hedgehog dressed in silk is still a hedgehog."

"That belly, Clancy! 'A very valiant trencherman.' And you see the nose?" Cluny pointed out as he watched the squire walk beneath him, heading for one of the couches. "Man's a drinker, mark my words. Would probably drink ink if there was nothing else to hand. But what do you suppose he wants here? None of the local gentry come here, never have. *Sssh,* he's saying something."

"Never knew you well," the squire said to Jack as he accepted a glass of wine. "Never took the time, actually. And that father of yours? M'wife wouldn't let me within miles of this place when he was in residence. Not that we didn't hear the talk, you understand, know what was going on. Shameful, that's what it was—and with children in the house. No, no. My Sarah wouldn't stand for me setting a foot on this property. The drinking, the—excuse me, missy—the whoring. Letting the two of you run wild, with no thought to the proprieties. Actors in the house as well? No, no. Sarah couldn't abide any of that. Good Christian woman, my wife."

Merry rolled her eyes as she took up a seat on one of the couches. Good Christian woman, indeed. The squire's wife knew there were two children in the house, and she did nothing? Never lifted a finger to help, never raised a voice in protest? "I'm sure she prayed for our souls, Squire," Merry said at last, when she could force open her tightly clenched teeth.

" 'A hit, a very palpable hit,' " Clancy chirped, applauding Merry's response.

Cluny threw Merry a half dozen kisses. " 'O tiger's heart wrapp'd in a woman's hide!' "

"What? Prayed for your souls? Oh. Oh, yes. Yes, of course." The squire ran a finger inside his starched collar as color ran into his jowls, his cheeks. "She did that. I'm sure she did that. Always praying, my Sarah. Drive a man to drink—all that praying, the sermons read after dinner. Um. *Harrumph!* Well, Coltrane, you're probably wondering what I'm doing here?"

"The thought had occurred, yes," Jack said, and Merry watched as he stood in front of the mantel, one arm draped against the marble, a glass of wine dangling from his fingertips. He was so handsome. So outwardly calm. So completely incensed. She was angry enough with him for having turned away from her the other night—again—to be a little glad that he was uncomfortable. But if Squire Headley didn't soon say something of sense, she'd leap to Jack's defense before her husband could murder the man.

The squire sat down on the facing couch, opened two buttons on his brocade vest. The man dressed as if he were to be presented at court and ended by looking like a hog squeezed into a sausage tube. He pulled a folded sheet of paper from somewhere inside his jacket. "I received this around two o'clock today. I don't know where it came from, if you're about to ask me, Coltrane, but it concerns you."

"In what way?" Jack asked.

"Not in a flattering one, that's for certain," Headley said, then cleared his throat and looked at Jack, seemed to inspect him for outward flaws.

"Is that so?" Jack commented, and Merry shot him a look that pleaded with him to be quiet, to wait, and to let events unfold without interruption.

"*Harrumph!* Yes. Well, to continue. As you know, I am mostly in charge of maintaining the law in this region, which is why the letter was directed to me, I'm sure. It—it contains a rather damning accusation, Coltrane, and I'm hoping you can assure me that it's nothing but a bit of nonsense."

Merry's stomach sank to her toes.

"That would be my hope as well, Squire," Jack said, pushing away from the mantel and walking over to sit down on the couch beside Merry. "If I might see the letter?"

"No need," the man said, already shoving the paper back inside his vest. "I believe I can tell you what it says, you can deny the accusation, and I can be home in time for dinner. All right?"

Jack inclined his head slightly. "By all means, Squire. As it is, who could depend upon the wild Jack Coltrane even to be able to read? Growing up here as I did, left to my reprobate father's devices—and your wife's prayers."

The chandelier tinkled slightly as Clancy stood up and cheered Jack's response.

"Now see here, young man!"

"My dear Squire," Merry said quickly, laying a hand on the man's arm, so that he didn't leap to his feet and storm out of the house in high dudgeon. "My husband sometimes speaks without thinking." She shot Jack a look that promised a dozen more workmen hammering at dawn if he didn't behave. "He didn't mean to be insulting—did you, dearest?"

"My apologies, sir," Jack said, his smile so suddenly sweet that Merry realized that he'd learned a few things during his time in Philadelphia. Not enough to keep his temper from flashing when the subject of his father came up, obviously, but at least he hadn't leapt across the low table and begun choking the squire with his own neckcloth.

"Apology accepted, Coltrane," the squire said magnanimously—and probably with a smidgen of self protection in mind. "Now, to make this as brief as possible, let me tell you that it has been brought to my attention that the Forfeit Man rode five years ago, and that the Forfeit Man rides again today. Within a few miles of this estate, each and every time.

Let me tell you that it also has been brought to my attention that you were here five years ago, Coltrane, and that you're here now."

Merry slipped her hand into Jack's, squeezed it warningly.

"Which, as the anonymous letter writer has undoubtedly deduced, means that I am the Forfeit Man. Is that what you're trying to say, Squire? The letter is unsigned, isn't it?"

"Oh, yes, yes. Definitely unsigned. Cowardly, I'd say. But impossible to ignore. My Sarah, she said—well, never mind about that," Headley amended quickly, as Jack leveled a marvelously daunting stare in the man's direction. "This is how it is, son. You left Coltrane House with little more than the clothes on your back, as my correspondent also points out, and returned rather wealthy. It has been suggested by my correspondent that you began your trade here, as a youth, perfected it during your absence, and have now come home to continue your . . . er . . . your work."

"Prove it."

"I—I beg your pardon?"

Merry rolled her eyes. "What my husband means, Squire," she said, attempting to freeze Jack to the couch with another stare, this one as frigid as a February morning, "is that your anonymous correspondent—so cowardly, don't you think, not signing one's name?—has no proof. Does he?"

The squire looked to Merry, then to Jack, and then down at his toes. "No. There's no proof. But—"

Merry stood up, which made it mandatory for any gentleman to do the same. "You know what I think, Squire?" she asked as she slipped her arm through his and turned him toward the foyer. "I think the real Forfeit Man penned that terrible letter, just to send you off chasing your tail. That's what I think. But you're much too intelligent to do that, aren't you?"

"Too—yes. Yes!" The squire was maneuvered into the foyer, where Maxwell waited with hat and gloves in hand. "That's exactly right, Mrs. Coltrane. I'm not going to be hoodwinked by such a shabby thing as an unsigned accusation, no matter what Sarah—that is . . . certainly not! Coltrane," he then said, shaking Jack's hand, as he had followed them into the foyer. "My apologies, young man."

"Accepted, of course," Jack said with remarkable restraint, and both he and Merry stood in the open doorway to wave the squire on his way. "His wife will send him back here again tomorrow, you know, his tail between his legs, at which point I'll probably be arrested. I remember seeing the dear squire's lady in the village years ago, and she swept past me, muttering something about Coltrane trash."

"Awful August made friends everywhere he went, didn't he?" Merry said, looking up at Jack, trying to coax that dimple into his cheek.

But it wasn't to be. Jack had been insulted, and he had been hurt. Again. "I think I'll ride over to see Kipp. The plan to capture the Forfeit Man suddenly holds much more appeal for me."

Another time—any other time—Merry would have protested at being left out of whatever conversation Jack and Kipp were about to have. But not this time. "Of course," she said, stepping away from him, stepping back, just as he wanted her to step back, keep her distance. "I imagine Kipp's cook can feed you just as well as Mrs. Maxwell."

"You're not going to leap down my throat, beg me to take you along?"

She kept her head high, her voice steady, even as her mind was doing cartwheels, sorting through names of everyone who knew that Jack had once ridden as the Forfeit Man.

Her conclusion surprised her, but was already beginning to make some strange sort of sense. "I wouldn't even think about it," she said sincerely. "You couldn't be more plain about not wanting my help."

"Merry—" he called after her as she turned on her heels, headed for the stairs. "Oh, the devil with it!" he said, leaving the house, slamming the door after him.

"Good, he's gone, and believing I can't see a truth that's as plain as the bump on Clancy's nose. Does the man think I've no brains at all?"

Twenty minutes later, her lovely yellow gown lying on a heap on the floor, and dressed in her shirt and breeches, Merry arrived at Henry Sherlock's small mansion.

She paced the drawing room as Henry's butler went in search of him, slapping her riding whip against her booted leg, going over the strategy she'd planned on the ride across the fields. A few tears, a bit of mild, feminine hysteria, a plea for help. And then watch Henry closely, watch him very closely. That should do it.

"Meredith? My gracious, dear, what brings you here just at dinnertime?"

She turned, looked at him, then ran across the room, flung herself into his arms. "Henry, Henry, forgive me! But it's just so terrible!"

"Terrible? How so? Is something wrong at Coltrane House? Yes, yes, of course something's wrong at Coltrane House. Why else would you be here?" He disentangled himself from her embrace and led her over to the couch, gently sat her down. "I'll just pour you a small glass of wine, and then, once you've composed yourself, you can tell me everything, all right?"

Merry pressed her lips together, nodded. And then she watched Henry as he went to the drinks table and poured them each a glass of wine. Was there a certain spring in his step? Did he show any signs of an enthusiasm to hear bad news? No. He didn't. He was behaving as he always did, the kind, helpful Henry.

"Thank you, Henry," she said, sniffling, as he handed her a partially filled glass. "I—I'm a little better now. But I didn't know who else to go to, Henry. Jack rode to see Kipp, but we all know Kipp can't help. So I thought of you. Always so helpful to us, Henry, whenever Jack and I are in trouble."

He sat down beside her, eyed her curiously. "You and John, Meredith? How are you and John in trouble? To hear John tell it, you're all doing just fine at Coltrane House, without a worry in the world."

She leaned forward, put her glass down on the table, then began twisting her hands in her lap. "Not anymore, Henry. It's the Forfeit Man. You do remember the Forfeit Man, don't you?"

"One of the servants told me a highwayman had robbed several coaches, endangered several lives. But I hadn't thought beyond that, hadn't thought that—the *Forfeit Man?* How?" Henry sat back against the cushions, looked up at the ceiling as if trying to read an answer written there. "Oh my," he breathed, then shook his head, looked at her with pity in his eyes. "You poor dear thing. I knew it, Meredith, I knew it. John told me he'd made his fortune in America, after five years of correspondence in which he'd never mentioned any such thing. I tried to believe him, I really did. I tried to take both John and that Indian of his seriously, believe he'd come by any monies he'd made honestly. But I knew it wasn't true. In my heart of hearts, I knew it."

He stood up, began to pace, his hands clasped behind his back. "A thief, Meredith. John left a thief, and he came back a worse thief. My dear, dear, girl, I'm so sorry."

"No!" Merry protested, hopping to her feet, impressed with Henry's sincerity, even if she didn't believe a word he was saying. "No, Henry, you're wrong. Jack isn't a thief. He isn't the Forfeit Man. Well," she amended, remembering to sniffle a time or two, "at least he isn't the Forfeit Man *this time*. Except that someone sent a horrible letter to the squire saying that he is, and the squire just left Coltrane House after all but arresting Jack."

"The squire, Meredith? And a letter?" He spread his hands as if to try to gather in all that Merry had told him. "But who would write such a letter? Was it signed? No, of course not. Cowards don't sign their names, do they? If you're going to accuse someone, you stand up and do it to his face. But, Meredith, nobody knows John once rode out as a highwayman. Just you, and me, and . . ." He rubbed his hands together, looked at her closely. "You say John has ridden over to Viscount Willoughby's? Tell me, Meredith, was he angry when he left?"

"Kipp?" Merry exclaimed, genuinely surprised, and now most definitely impressed. The man was attempting to make her believe Kipp had betrayed Jack. "Oh, no, Henry," she said, backing up a step. "That—that couldn't be! Could it?"

"The man is in love with you, you know," Henry said gently. "He has waited five long years for you to see what anyone else could see."

"No, Henry, you're wrong." Merry had come here to confront Henry, to see how he reacted to the news that Jack might soon be arrested. She hadn't come here to discuss Kipp. "He's always been fond of me, may have once thought—but no. He knows that Jack and I are married, and he knows that we're going to remain married. He knows that we—that we love each other."

Henry put a hand on her shoulder, looked at her kindly. "Yes, the viscount knows that you love John. We all know that, Meredith, have always known that. But the viscount doesn't know that John can't love you."

"Can't . . . *can't* love me?"

"Yes, Meredith, *can't.* You're saying that you are John's wife, and you're right, may August Coltrane burn in hell for all eternity. By law, you are John's wife."

"But . . . ?" Merry asked, feeling her blood run cold.

"I'd so wanted to protect you, Meredith. We both wanted to protect you, John and I, never tell you. John was more than willing to run away, leave the country, rather than to tell you."

"Tell me? Tell me what?"

Henry turned his head away from her, then slowly brought it back around, looked at her once more. "My dear child, don't hate me for asking this question. Have you and John begun to live together as man and wife? Please tell me John is only a thief, and not a monster. Tell me I haven't been wrong to trust that the boy has some semblance of honor, of decency. Let me believe I wasn't wrong to trust that he'd finally returned to England to set things right, to procure an annulment."

Merry began to tremble in real fear. She no longer had to feign being upset, close to hysteria. What had happened? She'd come here to bait Henry, to watch as he betrayed himself to her by either his expression or his word. And now it was all falling apart, and she didn't know what had happened.

She didn't want to hear whatever it was Henry was about to tell her. Not now. Not when she was only steps away from happiness. "What are you trying to say, Henry?" she asked again as he picked up her wine glass, handed it to her.

"Something I'd hoped never to have to say, my dear child," he told her, motioning for her to sit down once more. "Something John learned from his father, and in my hearing, the night he married you, the same night he very sensibly left England, promising me he'd never, never ever return.

You'd begun to believe that as well, and with time, I'd hoped to convince you to seek an annulment on your own, make a life for yourself without ever having to know the truth. But I've wronged you, my dear. Wronged you terribly by trying to protect you. It's the truth that will protect you, I can see that now. And it's the truth I have to tell you. Meredith, dear, dear wronged child, you're going to have to be brave . . ."

Chapter Twenty-four

Jack took his time returning from the Willoughby estate, having arrived there only to learn that Kipp and his guests—the encroaching Lord Hardcastle and his exceedingly available daughter—had gone out for the evening. Kipp was a social creature, and he probably was also seeking safety in numbers rather than to be the only eligible bachelor on Lady Susan's horizon. But he had picked a damnably bad time to be away from home.

Thinking to check on Merry before he went to his study for another long night with Walter and the ledgers, Jack climbed the stairs slowly, wondering when it was he had started feeling so old, so tired.

He could only hope she'd talk to him. He should have invited her along to visit Kipp, and would have, he supposed. But she'd seemed happy enough to stay here, at Coltrane House. She'd seemed understanding, almost biddable.

"Damn!" he exploded, running down the hallway as he realized what he'd been thinking. "If she's out hunting the Forfeit Man again . . . what a fool I am, thinking Merry could ever be something as easy as *biddable*." He squared himself in front of the doors to the main bedchamber, knocked on one sharply.

Only a few moments later, the double doors swung open to reveal a nearly wild-eyed Merry.

"Honey, I said I wasn't to be—*you*!"

She tried to slam the doors shut in his face, but Jack could see the panic in her eyes, the horror, and he pushed into the room, closing those same doors behind him. There were clothes everywhere. Tumbling from drawers, strewn across the bed, stuffed half-in, half-out of several small portmanteaux. "Going somewhere, Merry?" he asked, wincing as her expressive blue eyes filled with tears. He took hold of her shoulders.

She slapped at his hands, jumped back as if he'd somehow hurt her. "Don't touch me. How can you even *think* to touch me? How many times must I play the ignorant fool for you?"

Jack felt his temper rising, and ruthlessly beat it into submission. "Merry," he said quietly as she continued to back away from him, "tell me what's wrong, all right? I've only been gone a little more than an hour. What happened?" He indicated the scattered clothing with a wave of his hand. "And don't tell me you're running away because I went to see Kipp instead of talking to you about that damnable anonymous letter, because I won't believe it. You've done something, haven't you?" He ran a hand through his hair, ruthlessly tearing away the black ribbon holding it in place, throwing it to the floor. "Damn it, Merry, what did you do?"

"What did I do? What did *I* do? It's you, Jack. You're the one who knew, not me," she said, ignoring his question. She took a single step toward him, her eyelids narrowed, jabbing an accusing finger in his direction. "That's why. That's why you left the same night as our sham of a wedding. That's why you didn't want to come back. And that's why you won't touch me, won't come near me except for the times I did everything but *throw* myself at your head. And that's probably only because you'd once loved me—as a *child*."

She spun away from him, dropped her head into her hands for a moment, then whirled around to face him once more. All the agony in the world was in her eyes. "Why couldn't you have told me? Why did you let me make a damn fool of myself? Chasing after you . . . believing . . . wanting so very much to be with you, for us to be together. Loving you! You bastard—loving you!"

Jack's life as he knew it ended in that moment. She knew—how she knew he had yet to understand—and she would never forgive him. He'd begun to believe their love was enough to overcome what he had to tell her, but now he knew he'd been wrong. "Merry," he said softly, soothingly, "I'm sorry. I'm so sorry. I was a coward, I know it. But how could I tell you? Where does a person go to find the words? You're my whole life, Merry. It all could have been different. Better—so much better. Happier. Instead, August robbed you of your life, your inheritance, your chance for the childhood you should have known, the place in society you deserved. And for money. In the name of greed, and excess, and selfishness. All for the god-awful love of money!"

She stared at him, looking at him closely, listening to his every word, drinking in the sight of him as if, after tonight, she'd never see him again. And then she frowned, as if she didn't quite understand what he was saying.

"He did it on purpose," Jack continued, taking hold of Merry's ice-cold hands and leading her over to the bed, sitting down beside her. "He made it impossible for me to refuse to marry you, and then he told me the one thing that would keep any man of honor—even a raw, savage youth like me—from ever knowing a moment's happiness with that marriage."

He squeezed her fingers as he looked at her, saw all of his happy memories, all of his hopes for a life filled with something other than misery, loneliness. "If only we'd just met for the first time now, Merry. One look at you, one dance, and I'd have been your slave. You would have married me just so that I wouldn't keep following you around on my knees, begging you to love me. To, please God, love me."

She shrank away from him, and Jack felt his heart plummet to his toes. He'd left it too late. Always too late. Years and years too late. Would he never learn? "The first time . . ." he began slowly, his voice breaking as he lost the fight to keep his emotions in check. "The first time we met you weren't quite six months old. I remember someone bringing you into the nursery as I hid behind the doors, then leaving you alone in your cot.

"I stayed in my corner for a while, then slowly walked over to the cot and looked down at you lying there. You didn't see me right away. You were much too busy playing with your own fingers, cooing to them, talking to them." Jack smiled at the memory, smiled through the tears he didn't notice gathering in his eyes. "I remember bending down, peering into your little monkey face. And then you saw me.

"You looked up at me for a long time, Merry, a very long time. I thought you might cry, but you didn't. You just looked at me, as if trying to decide if I were friend or foe. And then you smiled. You smiled, and the sun came out right there, upstairs in the nursery. I leaned down, wanting to be closer to you, and you giggled, then reached up and caught hold of my nose. How you held on to me!"

Jack absently lifted a hand, stroked at the side of his nose. "I should have known then, Merry. I should have known right there and then. I'd never be free of you. I'd never want to be free of you." He stood up, walked away from her. Turned. Looked back at all he'd lost. "You're right to leave, Merry. You don't deserve to be stuck here at Coltrane House. You never did."

Merry looked at him for a long time, just as she had done the first time he'd seen her. But she wasn't smiling now. Huge tears rolled, unheeded, down her pale cheeks. "How could he do it, Jack?" she asked brokenly. "How could he be such a monster as to marry us to each other? His son to his bastard daughter? His own children . . ."

Jack sat down. He didn't bother to hunt out a chair, couldn't possibly navigate his way back over to the bed. He simply sat down on the floor and looked at Merry. "What in bloody hell are you talking about?"

"The . . . the . . . why, the same thing you're talking about," she answered, slipping to the floor, to sit with her back against the bedrail. "That—that . . . oh, God, Jack. You already know. I know you already know. That we're half brother and sister. I went to see Henry tonight, and he finally told me. He told me that's why he—"

Jack leapt to his feet. "I'll kill him! To hell with plans, to hell with answers! I'm going to *strangle* the bastard!"

He ran to the doors to the hallway, but they were locked, which gave Merry time to catch up to him, grab on to his arm, beg him to wait, to for God's sake wait until he was calmer, until he was thinking more clearly.

Jack shook her off as he tried, once more, to open the doors. "Where's the key, Merry? Where's the goddamn key!"

"I don't know," she said, dragging at him once more, urging him away from the doors. "Cluny and Clancy must have locked us in, taken the key. I know you don't believe that, Jack, but that must be what's happened. Now please, please—come over to the fire and sit down. You can't kill

Henry for trying to protect me all these years, or for telling the truth now."

The moment Merry had said they were brother and sister, Jack's brain had frozen into a cold hate that had no more than a nodding relationship with anything so mundane as common sense, even sanity. His anger had overwhelmed him, robbed him of reason, filled him with one desire and one only—to race to Henry Sherlock's elaborate house, pull him out of it by the roots of his silvery hair, and then hang parts of the bastard on every tree within three miles.

And yet here he was, still inside Coltrane House, locked inside Coltrane House, for God's sake—and with Merry telling him a pair of ghosts had hidden the key?

"I'm going out of my mind," he said, backing away from the door, from Merry. "I'm acting like an idiot, a complete fool—and I'm actually believing, just for this one moment, that two men who died over six months ago have just saved my life. Because I'd hang for what I want to do to Henry Sherlock, Merry. I swear to you—I'd hang."

"Oh, Jack . . ."

"And to leave you?" He pulled her into his arms, crushed her against him. "How could I hear what I've just heard, and then leave you here alone? Oh Christ. Christ, Christ, *Christ!*"

"It's all right, Jack," Merry said, rubbing at his back as she held him tightly. She was trying to absorb some of his pain, just as she'd always protected him from himself, from his own mad temper, his impulsiveness—his blockheaded stupidity. "It's all right, it's all right."

He let her soothe him for a few moments, moments during which he tried to collect his thoughts, lose some of the red haze of near madness that had swept over him when Merry had told him what Henry Sherlock had said. "We're not brother and sister, Merry," he whispered into her ear as he gently pushed back her riot of curls, pressed his lips against her soft white skin. "You've got to believe me in this, sweetheart. You were born Meredith Fairfax. We're not brother and sister."

He released her, slowly, unwilling to let her go if only for a moment, then led her over to sit on the rug in front of the fireplace. "My father—August. I feel cleaner calling him August. He told me something that last night, Merry, the night I agreed to marry you even after knowing I was ruining your future, even as I was perhaps saving your life, saving Kipp's life, Cluny and Clancy's lives. That was bad enough, that he'd threatened to turn us all over to the hangman. But his little story—and he told it with such drunken glee, Merry—made everything worse, ten times worse."

"But he didn't tell you that we're brother and sister?"

"No, Merry, he didn't, I swear it. And Sherlock knows the real story, damn him; he was there to hear all of it. I've had time, in these last years, to investigate the story August did tell me, and because of that I at least know that, thank God, we're *not* brother and sister. Even August wasn't monster enough to tell that lie."

He ran a hand through his hair, absently pushing it away from his face. "God, what I'm going to tell you almost sounds unimportant now, after the monstrous lie you've been told. But, at the time, it was enough to have me agreeing to leave England, perhaps forever. And that story, that truth, has kept me away from you since my return, coward that I am. I thought, believed, you'd hate me once you knew the truth, even as I knew I couldn't come to you, love you, without telling you that truth." He looked at her, shook his head. "Will I always be such an idiot?"

Merry wiped at her eyes, ran the back of her hand beneath her nose, just as she'd done as a child and had succumbed to tears over some small, childish tragedy. "Tell me the story August told you. I—I'm listening, Jack. Truly."

They were half kneeling on the rug, their knees touching, the small fire burning brightly in the grate, giving the large chamber its only illumination in the ever-increasing darkness. The world had narrowed to include only the two of them, and the story Jack had to tell.

"After—after I'd finally agreed to the marriage," he said, taking Merry's hands in his, "August told me something he had done seventeen years earlier. The year you came to Coltrane House, Merry, the year you became his ward. I never wanted you to know, but I couldn't be with you, be married to you, without first telling you the truth."

He paused, wishing he didn't have to tell her, even while knowing that there could be no more secrets between them. Not if they were ever to have any small chance at happiness.

"Your father, William Fairfax, lost his wife when you were born—just as August had lost his wife when I was born, not that August cared one way or the other. For some reason, however, this shared experience served to draw your father close to August when they met in London, until the point where he actually made August your guardian if anything should happen to him. I think August deliberately set out to gain your father's confidence—I'm sure of it. Because your father was a very wealthy man.

"You lived in Sussex, by the way, born to a baron's second daughter and an earl's nephew. You had a family, Merry, your mother's family, who tried, for some time, to take you away from your father and, later, from August. But your father's will prevailed in the end, and you lost your family. They're all dead now, Merry, and you never had the chance to meet them." He squeezed her fingers. "You lost so very much. The estate where you were born went to some distant male cousin on your father's death. Over the years you lost your inheritance, your dowry, your right to enter Society and make a brilliant match."

Merry's bottom lip began to quiver and Jack's heart plummeted to his toes, knowing that there was more to tell, worse to say. "Within a month of making August your guardian, the two men were hunting when there was an accident. One of the gun carriers tripped, the gun went off, and your father was shot in the back. Killed."

"An accident? Was it an accident, Jack?" Merry was being forced to take in a lot of information—and at the same time rid herself of Henry Sherlock's cruel misinformation. But she had a good mind, a clear-thinking mind. And everything had to be said, said immediately, that night.

"No, Merry, it wasn't an accident. August arranged the whole thing, hired the man who did the actual shooting—all of it." He closed his eyes, saw his father's leering face as he'd told him the truth. "You were brought here within days of your father's funeral, hidden away here while August began spending your money. Do you understand now, Merry? Your whole life changed because of my father. You're an orphan, because of him. You grew up in near poverty, thanks to him. You grew up wild, without a woman's touch, without a chance for anything except rape at the hands of one of August's drunken guests.

"Your whole life would have been different, happier, if it weren't for August Coltrane. That's why I fought the marriage, Merry, why I kept fighting it for five long years, even when, deep inside, I knew that I loved you. That I'd always love you. There's a whole world waiting beyond Coltrane House, a whole world you've yet to experience, that you *deserve* to see. I can't let August's greed trap you here, no matter how much I might want you to stay. I want you to have everything, Merry. Everything you deserve, everything August denied you. Everything *I* denied you by agreeing to our forced marriage."

Merry shook her head, sighed. "Oh, Jack," she said, moving closer to him. "You're right. You *are* an idiot. A sweet, wonderful idiot. But do you ever really listen to yourself? Do you ever really listen to *anyone*? A few minutes ago, I said I love you, even as I believed I was losing you forever. I believe you said you love me. Not as children. Not the way it was before. A newer love. A better love. A man and a woman, loving."

He made to push her away, even as he longed to draw her closer. "Merry," he said reasonably, "you need time to think about this, think about all of it. Until then, I cannot in good conscience—"

She pressed a hand against his mouth. "I'd like you to shut up now, if you don't mind. I have a few things to say to you."

When he reluctantly nodded his agreement, she removed her hand and smiled into his face. "You told me a sad story, Jack. A sad, terrible story about people I never knew, a world I can't even imagine. Coltrane House is my home, the only home I've ever known. *You're* the only family I've ever known, Jack, the only family I've ever wanted or needed. Don't you tell me I could have had a better life somewhere else. I couldn't. I couldn't give back a single day of the life I've had here and not miss that day with every fiber of my being. I kept Coltrane House for you, Jack, not me. I kept it, worked for it, cried over it, because it was a part of *you*. Even when I hated you, I loved you. First as a child loves and, later, as a woman loves. When Henry told me what he told me tonight . . ."

Her voice broke for a moment, then she recovered herself. "I wanted to die, Jack. Just go somewhere and die. I wanted to run, run as fast and as far as I could—just the way you did. I thought I understood why you'd left, the shame that forced you to leave. But I never experienced such shame for myself until tonight. I didn't want to face you, couldn't bear to see you even one more time."

Jack reached out his hand, stroked her cheek. "If you had gone—if you'd gone without a word, without explaining . . ."

"We could have lost another five years," she said, cupping her hand on his.

"Never," he said, drawing her closer, feeling his heart heal. "I would have chased you to the ends of the earth."

Her smile lit his world. "Yes, you can do that, being a man and all. We women, however, aren't allowed to go haring off to exotic places."

"Oh, all right. I suppose Philadelphia could be called at least a little bit exotic," he said, returning her smile even as he moved closer, closer, until their mouths were nearly touching.

"Perhaps one day you'll take me there, and I can see for myself," she whispered as her eyelids fluttered shut.

"Fine," he said, his mind and his heart fighting for supremacy. "Right after we strangle Henry Sherlock," he said, then let his heart win the battle as he captured Merry's mouth with his own.

He was gentle because this was his Merry, his treasure, his love. She was his, had always been his. He would protect her. Cherish her. Never hurt her. Never again. Never, never ever, hurt her.

He lifted her in his arms, carried her to the bed, laid her down amid piles of satin and lace, pushed aside ruffled slips and worn nightrails as he joined her, took her in his arms, kissed her hair, her cheeks, her throat.

Her mouth.

He could worship that mouth for a lifetime. He ran his

tongue over her top lip. Suckled at her full bottom lip, drawing it into his mouth until he could feel her smile, hear her soft giggle. Her arms lifted, encircled his neck, and he eased more fully against her, convinced her to open her mouth, allow him entry. He caught her sighed breath, drew it in deeply, made it his own.

He fumbled with the buttons on her shirt. Nervous, bumbling. Holding himself back, longing to move forward.

She was here. In his arms. Willingly, wonderfully in his arms. His best friend, his lover, his wife.

Somehow, their clothing disappeared. Somehow, her high, full breasts were exposed to his eyes, his touch, his worshiping mouth. Somehow, he was between her legs, legs she had curled around him, wrapped around him. She held on to him without fear, without hesitation, allowing him to guide them both, lead them both.

A lifetime ago he'd taught her to crawl, to walk.

Now he would teach her to fly.

"I don't want to hurt you." He whispered the words against her ear, even as she nipped at his throat with her teeth. "I don't ever want to hurt you. I don't want you to cry, not ever again, Merry, not in this lifetime."

She lifted herself against him, pushed against him, helped force the entry he'd been delaying, dreading, longing for, would have gladly died for. He felt her stiffen with momentary shock, felt a slight shudder skitter across her skin. "Now, Jack," she whispered against his sweat-slick skin as she pressed her head into his chest even as she pulled him closer, closer. "Show me. Teach me. Let me know you believe I'm a woman now."

"Oh, God." Jack tried to swallow, but couldn't. He tried to move, but his body wouldn't respond. He nipped at her throat, shaped her with his hands as, slowly, he came back into himself, traveling back through time, through space, through memory. This was Merry he held in his arms. His Merry. His life. His hope, his love, his very existence.

He had been alone before she'd come into his life, had been lost during those years he'd denied himself what he'd known he'd wanted since she was fourteen. A child, who longed to be a woman. He'd wanted her since he'd been a clumsy youth, who didn't know what to do with that earnest, open, loving child, so that he'd begun to push her away, then had run from her for good reasons as well as bad.

"You," he whispered as, at last, he began the age-old movements that were now so new, so fraught with tension, with longing, and yet with gentleness. "It was always you, Merry. Always. My love. My own sweet love. My only love . . ."

Time vanished into a void. The Coltrane marriage bed, that had seen so many loveless unions, floated into that nothingness, filling it, changing it, capturing a moment in time that would last for a lifetime.

Love became passion, passion turned to need, and the need was fed by more love. Always more love. Tender fury ripped through Jack, guided him, led him to the brink—then held him there as Merry cried out, shuddered in his arms.

Only then, with her holding on to him, sobbing his name, did he drive into her with all of himself, giving all of himself. As Jack's body arched, as his seed buried itself deep inside her, Merry cried out once more, her fingernails ripping into his back, branding him as hers for now, for forever.

He collapsed against her, trying to catch his breath, and he felt her stroking his hair, pushing it back from his face as she gifted his cheek with small kisses.

And then she laughed.

"What?" he said, raising himself up on his elbows, looking down at her face through the curtain of his own dark

hair. Her smile was wide and happy and very, very loving.
"What's so funny, Merry?"

She ran a finger over his forehead, then down the length
of his nose. "Oh, nothing," she said, then giggled. "It's just
that I've realized that I've finally found a much simpler way
to tease you out of your dark moods. I mean, do you still
really want to get up, go out, and strangle Henry Sherlock?"

Jack felt his temper rise again, but he was in control of it
now, in control of himself. With Merry by his side, loving
him, the largest heartache in his life was gone. With Merry
to love him, there could be no dark clouds. None that could
hurt him at least, or be more important to him than Merry.
Being with Merry. Loving Merry.

"Jack? Answer me. Do you still want to go strangle
Henry Sherlock?"

Yes. Yes, he did. But he had another way to destroy him.
If Walter was right, there was a better way.

Jack leaned down, kissed her. "Maybe tomorrow," he
said, sliding his hand up and onto her breast even as he
pulled her onto her side, into his arms. "Yes. Definitely tomorrow." He kissed her again. "I'll deal with Sherlock tomorrow. After breakfast. A very late breakfast."

Act Four

"Once more unto the breach, dear friends, once more . . ."

The wheel is come full circle.

—William Shakespeare

Chapter Twenty-five

" 'If we should fail—' "

" 'We fail? But screw your courage to the sticking-place and we'll not fail.' Jack and Merry still need us, to rout Sherlock, to capture the Forfeit Man."

"All right, if you say so, Clancy." Cluny looked at his good friend and ghostly companion. "Um . . . where is that, anyway?" he then asked. "The sticking-place, that is? I'm thinking we should probably know where it is, if we're going to be screwing our courage to it."

The next thing he knew, Cluny was feeling an open-hand cuff across the back of his head, which was Clancy's long-established way of answering unanswerable questions. And so, with his courage lurking about somewhere, looking for a place to screw itself to, the chubby little ghost sighed in resignation and followed after his friend as they both headed for the stables.

"Did you see her in the gardens this morning, Clancy?" he asked, for at least the tenth time. "Wasn't she lovely?

Wasn't she grand? So in love, so very happy. 'Sits as one new-risen from a dream.' "

"Did you see Jack, locking himself in his study with that Walter person all the day long, the two of them reading through ledger after ledger, even those old dusty ones they found in a cabinet? It's not like my Jack to be poking through old books—not when any fool knows he'll find his best answers by pointing a pistol under Henry Sherlock's chin and asking him politely."

"He's learning, Clancy. Learning to fight a new way, win a new way. He has to, what with Squire Headley to contend with and all."

"You see that. I see that. How I wish you could have whispered as much in Merry's ear, so that we wouldn't be heading out highwayman hunting again tonight. And while you're telling her all of this, Cluny, you might also want to mention to her that it isn't nice to tell whopping great fibs to her husband, making him think she's sitting in a tub when she's really running about, searching for this new Forfeit Man."

Cluny sighed, knowing Clancy was right. But he also knew that Merry had been shutting the pair of them out all day, not letting them close once she'd politely thanked them for locking the doors last night. It had been up to the ghosts to locate her, to follow her to the stables after dark, to watch as she saddled her horse and made ready to ride out alone.

"We have no choice but to follow after her, do we?" he said, surrendering the last of his misgivings. " 'One for all, or all for one we gage!' " And then he tugged on Clancy's sleeve. "You know, I've yet to find this sticking point, so perhaps there are no answers to some questions, and I dearly love the Bard, you know I do. But, Clancy? Could you at least tell me this, please? I've been wondering for ever so long. What's a gage? Or is it that you don't know, either?"

"Curse you, Cluny, am I supposed to know everything? Now come on." Clancy hopped up behind Merry as she walked her mount out of the stables, then held out a hand, urging Cluny to join him. A moment later, all three were on the roadway, heading off into the darkness, heading off into the unknown.

It was a pleasant enough trip, for as long as it lasted. Merry was moving fairly fast, as the moon was bright and the horse knew the route. Cluny might have voiced some concern earlier that Merry might not appreciate their company that night, as she hadn't seemed to want it all the day long, but Clancy had no such fears. Indeed, as they made their way to the roadway, he was so pleased as to turn to Cluny and announce: "Ah, just as it was for us long ago, good friend. Remember? 'Thus far into the bowels of the land have we march'd on without impediment.' "

Which was just about three seconds before the pair of ghosts hit what seemed to be an invisible wall, at which time they were knocked backward, head over heels, landing in the dirt as Merry and her mount passed over the border between Coltrane land and the rest of the world. She actually, Clancy saw, turned in her seat, and waved, cheeky brat that she was.

Clancy let his head drop back and lay flat on his back, staring up at the stars. " 'Give me another horse!' " he commanded, once he could catch his breath. " 'Bind up my wounds!' "

"Wounds?" Cluny, who had likewise been lying supine, gazing at stars—how close they seemed, as if dancing in a circle directly above his head—crawled over to minister to his friend. " 'Give me your hand, and let me feel your pulse,' " he quoted, grabbing for his friend's now wildly flailing arm. "Oh, no pulse. Of course. Forgot that. You don't have a pulse. Neither do I, come to think of it."

"Nor do you possess a brain," Clancy declared feelingly, getting to his feet and brushing imaginary dirt from the seat of his second-best costume, the royal blue velvet, and always a personal favorite. "Well, that's that, Cluny," he said, turning to start walking back to the house. "She's on her own now, God help us all."

The new Forfeit Man was a reliable sort. He always struck within a mile of Jack's own favorite spot for coach-robbing. It was the single best stretch of roadway for larceny, after all, with the sharp turn, the steep hill that made it imperative that a coach traveling the road in either direction slow to a near crawl.

It wouldn't be impossible that the highwayman could strike along some other roadway, but he'd been consistent so far, and Merry had no reason to believe he would change his tactics that night. Not that Squire Headley, a coward to his marrow, had so much as organized a small party of men to patrol the roadway, to seek out the robber and capture him. No, not Squire Headley. He was much too busy listening to his sermon-spouting, Jack-condemning Sarah, and reading anonymous notes.

Merry knew Jack would flay her alive if he knew what she was doing. She'd considered this fact from every possible angle all the day long. She'd then decided that, as she'd never really listened to him in the past when her mind told her to act differently, there was really no point in denying her own instincts now.

Besides, it was partially his fault.

He really shouldn't have left her alone so long, left her in charge of herself, left her to her own devices. A year, maybe two, and she would have been everything he remembered. But she'd been her own person, been forced to be her own person, for five long years. She loved Jack. Loved him with all her heart and soul. Loved him more, after the night they'd spent together, than she had believed it possible to love anyone, even Jack.

But she wasn't going to sit home and mind her embroidery hoop or whatever it was wives did, not while Henry Sherlock was out to destroy her husband. And most certainly not after Henry Sherlock had told her the most terrible lie a person could tell.

Aloysius had explained everything to her that afternoon. He'd explained that Jack believed Henry had been stealing from the estate, had probably been stealing from it for thirty years, ever since Awful August had stupidly, drunkenly, put the man in charge. Walter and Jack were convinced of this thievery even though they'd yet to confirm it, which was why they were locked in the study, poring over the ledgers. For no matter how clever the crook, Aloysius said, crooks always make a mistake.

Jack and Walter were out to find that mistake. The key to Henry Sherlock's downfall was to be found inside those ledgers. All they had to do was find it.

Which, Merry had agreed then and still agreed, was a commendable plan. A very civilized plan. Just the sort of plan a man like Walter would devise, and a man like Jack, who had come into his maturity under Walter's tutelage, would agree to follow.

To a point. That's what Merry worried about. That's what had Merry so nervous that she hadn't eaten all day, even as she'd allowed Honey to giggle and fuss and say that young lovers never did have much of an appetite for food. Other things, yes, but not food.

How long would Jack be content to find his justice in exposing Henry as a thief? How long before he broke the promise she'd extracted from him that morning after they'd made love, the promise not to confront Henry with his terrible lie nor beat him into a jelly for having frightened Merry?

Besides, this civilized plan of Walter's did not extend to exposing Henry as the new Forfeit Man. Squire Headley was an idiot, and one who probably wouldn't know one end of a ledger from another. But a trussed-up Henry Sherlock, clad in his highwayman clothes, stuffed inside the coach he'd been about to rob and delivered to the man's door—well, even Squire Headley could understand that sort of evidence.

She felt badly about leaving Cluny and Clancy behind, about having shut her mind to them as she'd learned to do, but this was a mission she planned to perform on her own, without interference. Cluny and Clancy were helpful sorts, good souls, both of them, but she might have to end up shooting somebody, and she really didn't want the ghosts to see that.

So she'd lied to her husband, she'd refused Cluny's and Clancy's company, and she'd ridden off into the night, bound and determined to rid Jack's life, her life, of the one man who stood between them and perfect happiness.

It wasn't until she'd tied up her mount and taken up position by the side of the road on the nearly rotted tree trunk, that Merry began to consider the uncomfortable notion that perhaps her escape from Coltrane House had been just a little too easy.

Jack knew her. He knew her very well—even better after last night, after an unforgettable night of loving, being loved. The realization had her blushing in the darkness, so she pushed that thought away and concentrated on the fact that he knew her. And yet, knowing her, he'd calmly said good night to her and gone back to that mountain of ledgers.

Why?

Merry sat very still, not making a sound, barely breathing, until she heard a twig snap somewhere behind her.

"You can come out now, Kipp," she said, sighing, then waited until Kipp levered one long leg, then the other, over the log and sat down beside her.

"Hello, sweetheart," he said affably enough. "Lovely night, isn't it? I brought some meat and cheese with me. Want some?"

Merry shook her head, tamped down her anger. "Jack sent you, didn't he?" she said, accepting a thick wedge of cheese. "He knew what I was going to do, and he sent you to watch over me."

"Actually," Kipp drawled, slipping the small knife back into his boot top, "we weren't quite sure where you'd go. You could have gone straight to Sherlock the moment Jack's back was turned, bent on having the man's liver on a spit. Not that I'd blame you. I'd like to do the same myself. I've been watching the stables all afternoon, in fact, waiting for you. Not my most pleasant afternoon, considering that the only concealed spot was downwind of the manure heap, but friends must endure these things, you know, when they're called upon. If you'd turned off the road, heading for Sherlock, I was to stop you by any means possible. I really appreciate not having to do that, sweetheart. So—we're here to capture the highwayman, right? We could go home now, I suppose. But, as long as we're already out and about?"

Merry didn't bother to answer him. "When did Jack see you, speak with you?" she asked instead. "He didn't leave me until almost noon and, as far as I know, he's been closeted with Walter for all of the day and evening. I imagine he sent you a note, telling you of Henry's horrible lie to me, and of how Jack is convinced he's somehow been stealing from the estate? Yes, that must have been it. A note."

Kipp nodded his agreement, his handsome face going

momentarily hard with anger at the mention of Sherlock and the inexcusable lie the man had told her. Then he smiled. "Not until noon? Really? Shame on our Jack, being such a slugabed, especially when there's a Sherlock to be punished. Marriage to you must have at last wrought a near miracle on our hotheaded friend's temper. My congratulations, sweetheart."

Merry felt heat creeping into her cheeks again, but quickly banished any thought of embarrassment. This was Kipp, after all. Her friend and confidant. "I think he's very happy," she said, leaning her head against Kipp's shoulder. "Happy enough not to want to do anything rash, or stupid, that might destroy that happiness."

Kipp laid an arm across her shoulders, giving her a slight squeeze. "While, for you, happiness has sent you out to attempt just about the most harebrained bit of ridiculousness you've ever conceived. And, remembering how you once took it into your head to hoist a pair of Awful August's breeches to the top of the flagpole—that's saying something."

Merry giggled, burrowing into Kipp's shoulder even as she put her arms around him, hugging him tightly. "Oh, Kipp—I'm so happy! Last night I thought my world was over, my life was over. And now?" She pushed herself away from him so that she could look up into his face. "You can't imagine it, Kipp. You just cannot imagine how wonderful it is to be in love. Totally and completely in love, and being loved in return."

He touched a finger to the tip of her nose, then ran it down over her lips, tapped lightly against her chin before pulling his finger away; before releasing her completely, before standing up, taking three deliberate steps away from her. "You're right, sweetheart. I can't imagine such a thing. You and Jack deserve every happiness."

Too late, Merry realized what she'd done, what she'd said. She got slowly to her feet, walked over to him, laid her cheek against his chest. "I'm sorry, Kipp," she said quietly, tears pricking at her eyes. "I'm so sorry. But I've thought about this. You don't love me. Not really. I want nothing more than to be here, at Coltrane House. You enjoy the country, I know, but you also couldn't survive without London. The parties, the excitement . . . Aramintha Zane?"

He laughed as he took hold of her shoulders, peered down into her face through the darkness. "I suppose you're right, Merry." He bent down, kissed her cheek. "You and Jack belong together, were always meant to be together. And," he added, smiling at her, coaxing a smile from her, "for better or worse, I do believe you even deserve each other."

"Oh, Kipp," Merry said, wiping at her eyes. "Jack and I are so lucky to have you in our lives. Thank you."

He waggled his eyebrows at her. "Well, now," he said lightly, "if it's thanks you want to offer—would you consider inviting Lady Susan to Coltrane House for tea? Anything—*anything*—that will get her out of my house? It's not that she's not a fine woman. She's even quite a devotee of Aramintha Zane's novels—but she's looking at me much too closely these past days. Almost hungrily. I've begun to wonder if perhaps I have a peach pastry tied around my neck that I've yet to notice."

"Oh, Kipp," Merry repeated, this time laughing at his silliness. "Let's go home. I must have been out of my mind to come out here in the first place. I'm a real wife now, and I've got to learn to depend on my husband to know best how to protect us. Especially when that husband sees straight through my plans and sends you out to watch over me. Besides, even the new Forfeit Man can't be expected to ride out every night. Come on. We'll ride to Coltrane House to-

gether, and pull Jack away from those damnable ledgers for
a—Wait? Did you hear that?"

Kipp quickly pulled her down beside him, drawing a pistol from his waistband even as he was motioning for her to
be silent.

The sound came again. The jingle of harness, the sounds
of voices raised in anger. Holding tight to Kipp's hand,
Merry followed him as they made their way through the
trees alongside the path, heading in the direction of the
noise.

Even with the moon no longer quite full, it was easy to
see the coach that had drawn to a halt not quite seventy-five
yards down the road. Coach lanterns lit the area well
enough, in fact, for Merry to get a tolerably good look at the
highwayman holding an evil-looking weapon on the coach
driver, who sat on the box, his hands pointed toward the
heavens.

The highwayman silently signaled for the driver to climb
down from the box and approach the horse. A moment later,
his head neatly rapped by the butt of a pistol, the coachman
lay on the ground, unconscious.

"Bastard," Kipp breathed. "Cowardly bastard."

"It's not Sherlock," Merry whispered, disappointed.
"He's too tall, too thin to be Henry, don't you think? Damn.
Damn and blast, Kipp—it *has* to be Henry."

"Not necessarily. Did you really think he'd do his own
dirty work, sweetheart?" Kipp asked her, even as they
moved closer, inch by inch, watching as the highwayman
dismounted, walked toward the coach door. "Now stay
here—I've got to help whoever is inside that coach. It's the
gentlemanly thing to do, you understand."

Merry narrowed her eyes, realizing that, if there had ever
been any romance in the notion of capturing the highway-

man, it had vanished the moment she'd seen the coach driver fall to the ground. "Couldn't you just shoot him?"

"I can't. The brake's not set, for one thing, and the driver is lying too close to the wheels. A gunshot could set the team racing off down the road. I won't risk that unless it looks as if the bastard means to harm the occupants of the coach. Now stay here, all right? Don't move an inch, put yourself anywhere close to danger, or else, even if I live through this, Jack will kill me."

"No. It's my fault you're here, and I'm going to help. Or were you just going to walk into the roadway and bid everyone a good evening, then politely ask the man to hand over his weapon?"

Kipp's smile was dazzling. "Something like that," he said. "You know me so well. Here—take this rock, and wait for my signal. Then throw it at the miscreant. Oh, and try not to hit the horses, all right?"

"Kipp—" Merry began, then rolled her eyes as he broke free of her grasp and stepped out onto the roadway, into the light of the carriage lamps. "Oh, Kipp," she moaned quietly, watching as he struck a pose, a lace handkerchief dangling from his left hand, his right held behind him, the pistol cocked and at the ready.

"Good evening! Lovely night for a robbery, what? Moon. Stars. A coach. Everything that is needed, and all right here, ripe for the picking, yes?"

"I don't believe it. That's a line from his stupid novel. He's out of his mind," Merry whispered, drawing her own pistol and aiming it directly at the highwayman, who had whirled about to glare, wide-eyed, at Kipp. Well, at least now she knew the plot, what was expected of her. She only hoped the highwayman knew he was about to be captured, and didn't attempt to rewrite the ending of the story.

"Now, now, my good man," Kipp warned as the highwayman leveled his pistol at him. "Think, if you will. Fire that nasty-looking pistol, and the horses will bolt, sending any hope of an evening's profit barreling down the road, out of reach. Much better, don't you think, simply to agree to split the takings?"

The highwayman, most of his face hidden behind black silk, pointed a finger at Kipp. "Split the takings? With *you*? Why should I?"

"Out of the goodness of your heart? No. I didn't think so. Perhaps if I told you that my cohort in crime is, even as we speak, aiming a pistol at your heart? Might that serve to convince you? Oh, cohort—now might be a good time to make yourself known."

Merry looked at the rock in her left hand, then at Kipp, who had stepped slightly to his right, giving her a clear sight of the highwayman. She could skip stones across a stream. She could hit a target with an arrow. She could shoot tolerably well. Certainly she could successfully toss a rock at something as big as a highwayman.

She laid down her pistol, then spit into her hands, just as Jack had always done. She stood up, and launched the rock as hard as she could, then ducked back down into the bushes even as her makeshift weapon collided with the target. She knew the rock had made a flush hit, because she heard the highwayman yelp in unexpected pain.

By the time she'd jumped back up again, the highwayman was lying on the ground beside the coach driver, the two of them both "asleep." Standing beside them, Kipp was inspecting the hilt of his pistol as if for cracks in the hand-carved ivory.

"We did it! We did it!" she shouted, running into the roadway and flinging herself at Kipp, nearly knocking him off his feet. "Oh, Aramintha, you darling fool, we caught the Forfeit Man!"

The sole occupant of the coach, a wealthy merchant from Dorset traveling to see his brother, alighted and stood wiping his forehead, still shivering in fear for his heavy purse if not his life. Kipp bent down and stripped the black silk from the highwayman's face.

Merry's smile faded, and her joy disappeared with it. She'd been right. The highwayman wasn't Henry Sherlock. He wasn't anyone she had ever seen before in her life.

"Everything would have been so much easier if it had been Henry," she said as Kipp pulled off his neckcloth to use in lieu of rope and began tying the man's hands together behind his back.

"Not easy to please, are you, sweetheart?" Kipp teased, even as he bowed to the merchant, who had recovered himself enough to begin thanking his rescuers, profusely. "Perhaps if I'd been shot? Maybe then you could join this dear man in his hallelujah and thank-you-good-sir chorus? Nothing too much, you understand, as I'm by nature a humble man. But you could offer me something? I did, after all, step straight into the path of certain death—and all while putting my life into your hands. I think, upon reflection, that I am either very brave—or very stupid."

"You're a wonderful idiot," Merry said, shaking her head, Kipp's levity making her smile for a moment. But only for a moment. "But it should have been Henry. Squire Headley could have had him hanged for robbery, and Jack wouldn't still be reading and plotting and probably finding something that makes him lose his temper entirely and go haring off to choke the man. Because that's what he'll do in the end, you know, Kipp. He might be trying his best not to, but Henry almost destroyed us with his lies and his thefts. And sooner or later, Walter and Aloysius aren't going to be able to convince Jack that putting the man in gaol is sufficient punishment. I know Jack, Kipp, and he's not behaving like Jack. But he will, sooner or later."

She sat down in the dirt and glared at the unknown highwayman. "Oh, why couldn't you have been Henry? I so needed you to be Henry."

Chapter Twenty-six

"Here. Here it is at last, Walter, the very first mention of MacDougal. Christ, I'd begun to think we'd never find it." Jack poked a fingertip at the name Henry Sherlock had written into a ledger twenty-seven years earlier. "Five hundred thousand pounds in return for a mortgage on Coltrane House. Now, why do we need to know this?"

"Simple curiosity, Jack, and the need to keep you occupied while I made my last calculations." Walter pulled the ledger closer, adjusted the spectacles that rode low on his nose. "Yes, yes, that's it, the first mention. We've already seen the yearly entries for the payments of interest owing on the loan. Thirty thousand pounds a year, and without a single deduction in the principal. Twenty-seven years, at thirty thousand pounds a year. Add blockhead to your list of condemnations of your father, Jack, for it certainly fits."

Jack ran a hand through his hair, absently cursing the loss of the narrow black ribbon he'd tied in it earlier in the day, now long since lost. "Nobody can spend or gamble away that much money, Walter, not even August. We already know he had over one hundred thousand from Merry in the space of seventeen years, with notations that these were all legal expenses necessary to her upkeep. This loan from MacDougal. The money you and I loaned the estate to keep it from falling to his creditors. Other mortgages that were paid off over the past twenty years. And the estate was always profitable, even in the worst years. Yet the expenses are all there, eating up all the money the estate produced."

He sat back in his chair, flung out his hands. "How in hell is Coltrane House still so in debt? I want to see some sign of cheating in these ledgers, Walter. I want to see where Sherlock has been dipping his fingers into the Coltrane pie. But I don't see it. I just don't see any evidence, anything we can prove."

Jack stood up, tossing the last ledger onto the desktop. "I'm going to see him. I'm going to see him, and I'm going to break him into very small pieces. Not because of Coltrane House or the way he's been stealing from us, but because of what he tried to do with Merry last night. Christ, if you could have seen her face! I never should have let you talk me out of it, Walter. Even if we could understand what he's done, we can't prove anything. The men I hired to look into Sherlock's background haven't found anything. I'm glad they were able to give me the information about Merry, so that I could tell her about her family. But they haven't found the last piece of the puzzle of Henry Sherlock, because there *is* no last piece of the puzzle." He lifted his hands, let them drop. "Nothing. We've got *nothing*."

Walter kept his head bent over the ledgers he had spread out in front of him, only lifting a hand in Jack's direction as he said, "Sit down, Jack, and stop acting like a hotheaded youth. I think I've got it. Yes . . . yes . . . I've got it. There's only one possible explanation." He sat back in his chair, his smile broad. "Henry Sherlock is James MacDougal."

"What?" Jack did as he was told, sitting down once more. "Where did Sherlock get five hundred thousand pounds to lend to August?"

Walter's smile grew even wider. "He didn't. Didn't lend him five hundred thousand pounds, that is. He only *said* he did." Obviously feeling quite pleased with himself, he stood up and began to pace back and forth behind the desk as Jack watched. Watched, and listened.

"I never could trap a hare worth a damn, Jack. If I'd had to spear a fish or starve, I'd have starved," Walter said, stopping to look out the window, into the darkness. "I could never see the point of running everywhere when I could ride. And I never considered deer hide to be my notion of either personal physical comfort or sartorial splendor. But, oh, how I adored numbers. From the moment the good Reverend found me after my parents died of the Englishman's measles, found me and took me in to live with him, I discovered my destiny in numbers. Figures. Neat columns, all adding up. Checks and balances. The lovely, exquisite science of it all."

"I know, Walter," Jack sad, trying to be patient as his friend told him a story he'd heard before, had enjoyed before, yet felt impatient with now. "Numbers never lie, never cheat. Numbers are pure. Better than women, to hear you tell it—not that I ever believed that part. Now, tell me what your pure, honest numbers said to you that told you Sherlock is also MacDougal."

Walter turned away from the window, gestured toward the ledgers. "It's all in there, if you look at it correctly. Sherlock must love numbers, too, because he felt the need to write out all the checks and balances, even those he'd made up out of whole cloth. He wrote down every real penny he stole, balancing it penny for fictitious penny with the loans he invented—without a cent of the supposed loans ever really hitting the Coltrane coffers. Nonexistent funds in, real funds out—mostly, real funds out. He didn't hide his thefts, he cataloged them. Very neatly, actually. That's probably why I didn't see it sooner, as I was looking for sloppy mistakes. But once I did . . . once I did . . ."

Jack raked both hands through his hair, then shook his head, shook off his frustration. "You're not going to tell me, are you? You're going to hold this all close to you, rejoicing in your brilliance, and slowly drive me insane."

Walter sat down once more, spread his hands out in front of him, the teacher about to explain a basic series of facts to his student. "Assume for a minute, Jack, that Coltrane House has always been self-sufficient. Assume that Henry Sherlock, for all his dishonesty, was actually a very fine manager, that even August's wild expenses were not enough to jeopardize the estate. And your lovely wife, the dear Merry, was also a competent manager, just as she said, just as you and I could both plainly see when we arrived here to find an estate that could not possibly be better run, better controlled."

"Then why the loans? The mortgages? And why, if the estate is so damned self-sufficient, is Coltrane House itself about to fall down around our ears?"

"Numbers, Jack," Walter said, indicating the ledgers once more. "Numbers, and a drunken, stupid, oblivious August. Numbers, and a young woman who believed what she saw, what she was told. This has been going on for more than two dozen years. It would take hours, days, to show you exactly what I mean, precisely what I found. Suffice it to say that you trust me, and that I've found what you're looking for, all right?"

Jack nodded, agreeing. It had been a long day. A very long, frustrating day that had come after many long, frustrating days of poring over these same damn ledgers. He wanted to find his wife, wanted to hold her, to love her. "Go on, good master," he said facetiously. "Your pupil is listening."

"Thank you, Jack. You're a fine student—when you choose to be. Now. To keep this as simple as possible, I'll tell you that Merry's money—her father's money—never saw anything except the insides of Henry Sherlock's pockets. The supposed five-hundred-thousand-pound mortgage never truly happened—although the yearly interest definitely was paid. To Henry Sherlock. The loans you and I made to the estate ended up in Henry Sherlock's pockets."

"If you say so, although the ledgers don't reflect that. At the least, we do know that the interest payments written in the ledgers are a lie, considering the fact that our Newbury and Gold have yet to receive a penny in repayment," Jack said, nodding his head. "Still, I was astounded to hear him say that those two mortgages amounted to nearly one hundred thousand pounds, when we both know they only totaled twenty-five thousand. I thought we had him that day, Walter, I truly did. But then I realized we'd have to find a way to *prove* what he'd done, and explaining to the squire that we were actually Newbury and Gold—well, you've seen the man. He'd never understand the half of it."

"I know, Jack, I know. But, to get back to what I've learned? Slowly, surely, and quite regularly, every penny the estate earned and he could somehow justify went directly into Henry Sherlock's pockets. It was only when August's wild expenditures outran the estate's earnings that things got, well, sticky. At those times, Henry actually had to cough up some of his own funds—his own stolen funds—to keep Coltrane House afloat. How that must have galled him. Truth to tell, Henry was probably the first to rejoice when August died, and the gambling debts and such finally stopped."

Walter picked up one ledger, turned it around so that Jack could read it. "Anyway, that's what I finally noticed, Jack. The regularity of the payments—except when August's real expenses got out of hand, at which time the payments were abated, just until more money could flow in from the natural income generated by the estate. These regular payments, Jack, were all made to a recurring set of names. Year after year after year."

Jack nodded, beginning to understand. For all that he was a creature who loved the earth, felt most at home when working the land, riding his estates, he still had a competent head for figures, for business. Walter had made sure of that.

"A creature of numbers, your Sherlock," Walter continued, "and an orderly man. MacDougal received thirty thousand pounds once a year. A Simon March has been paid five thousand pounds a quarter for the past twenty years, except for the times he paid monies into the estate, when the estate was in trouble. And there are three others—William Hollis, Edward Blacker, Richard Leeds. And they're all Henry Sherlock, Jack, I'm sure of it. It's the neatness of it, the orderliness of it all. Real loans tend to be much more haphazard."

He rummaged through the pile of ledgers on the desk, pulling out three of them, slowly dropping them one after the other into Jack's outstretched hands as he spoke. "Here are the years Henry had actually to pay into the estate in order to keep his greed afloat. Three times, Jack—twenty-one years ago . . . five years ago . . . and again only two years ago, when prices dropped so badly after the war. That's what proves it to me."

"Can we prove this to anyone else?" he asked, looking up at Walter. "Any of it?"

Walter took off his spectacles, laid them on the desktop. "That's the unfortunate part, Jack. I don't think we can. Any more than we can prove that all those gaming debts we've seen registered in the ledgers were real. Merry may have been working to put even more money in Sherlock's pockets. But I don't think I'd tell her that. You'll need more than Lord Willoughby watching over her to keep her from racing off to throttle the man. You'd probably need an entire regiment, poor girl. Not that she could have known. It took me weeks to figure it out, myself, and I'm very good at what I do. Henry had me pretty dazzled with details before I could see the larger picture."

Jack looked at the ledger pages a moment longer, then pushed the book away, sat back in his chair. "So, if we can't prove any of this, Walter—what's the sense of it? How have we helped ourselves?"

Walter lifted his lapel, sniffed at the pink rosebud that resided there. "Well, dear boy, for one thing, we won't be paying Sherlock that thirty thousand pounds anymore on a sham mortgage. I don't know about you, but I'm feeling rather gratified to know that. After all, if we can't produce proof, he also can't produce MacDougal."

He sat back, steepled his fingers. "You have to admire the man, his genius. August made a shambles of this house, and Sherlock let him. After all, why waste good money repairing what was soon to be broken again? And, having this house fall into disrepair bolstered the fact, in Merry's eyes, in ours, that the estate was in real trouble."

Jack listened with half an ear, his mind trying to wrap itself around the reasons for Henry Sherlock's thievery. "He was building himself a fortune," he mused aloud, rubbing at his chin. "But it was more than that. He stayed here, even after August was gone. Built his mansion here."

He looked at Walter, who was smiling a slow, wide smile, as if proud of his pupil. "It isn't just the money," Jack said, his eyelids narrowing. "He wants Coltrane House. He wants the whole thing. He's been planning, and waiting, for almost thirty years. And he came so close. So *close*."

Jack stood up, began to pace, even as Walter had done before him. "If I hadn't returned, if I hadn't come back here when I did, MacDougal—Sherlock—would have taken over the estate at the end of the year. God, Walter—how he must have loved seeing me. No wonder he kept writing to me, telling me to stay away a little longer, that Merry needed more time to stop hating me."

He stopped pacing, turned to glare at his friend. "But we can't prove any of this? Is that right, Walter? That is what you said, isn't it?"

Walter took off his spectacles, laid them on the desktop. "I think we can confront him with what we now know," he said carefully. "That would frighten him, perhaps, but it wouldn't do much more than that. His plan worked only when you were young, and then if you weren't here. I don't think Sherlock is a violent sort, not by inclination. But he needs you dead now, Jack. That much is also obvious, so much so that he's resurrected the Forfeit Man in hopes of seeing you hang, even pointed Squire Headley in your direction. And so, much as I have always believed in logical approaches to problems, it would seem that your dear wife has the right of it after all. We need to capture the Forfeit Man."

There was a knock at the door, and Maxwell entered, bowed to Jack. "You wished to know when Mrs. Coltrane returned, Master Jack. His lordship brought her back safe as houses a few minutes ago. She's in her dressing room now, and Honey has prepared a bath for her."

Jack looked to Walter, who was once more shuffling ledgers on the desktop. "We're done here?" he asked, torn between wanting to find a way to rid them of Henry Sherlock and an almost overwhelming desire to see his wife as she lazed in a hot tub, covered in bubbles. It wasn't, perhaps, the sort of logical thinking Walter so prided himself on, but each man had to have his own priorities.

He rubbed a hand across his chin, remembering that, with all that was going on in his life these past twenty-four hours, he hadn't made time for Rhodes to shave him today. "A bath seems like a good idea," he said, then asked Maxwell to please have a tub prepared for him as well, in his dressing room. "That is, Walter, if you don't mind?"

"Oh, go—go," Walter said, closing one of the ledgers with a snap. "We'll continue this in the morning."

Jack was already out of the door, before Walter had finished speaking.

The satin coverlet on the high, wide marriage bed was turned down, the sheets strewn with rose petals. Candles burned on every table, lined the mantel above the fire, stood in front of the mirror over one large chest, the candlelight reflected in the glass. A bottle of wine sat on the table beside the bed, two crystal goblets at the ready.

Clancy looked, sighed, touched a finger to one of the half dozen vases of freshly cut flowers, and pronounced the chamber ready, even as Cluny, his arms full of rose petals, danced about, spreading the fragrant blossoms over the carpets, flinging them hither and yon with what only could be called ghostly abandon.

"You think so?" Cluny asked, stopping to survey the handiwork the two had wrought in twenty happy minutes of ghostly concentration and only a few unfortunate hiccups. "Perhaps the kitchen cat—lying in front of the fire. That would be a nice touch, don't you think? But no. 'To gild refined gold, to paint the lily, to throw a perfume on the violet, to smooth the ice, or add another hue unto the rainbow—'"

"Enough! Enough!" Clancy protested. "Besides, I hear stirring in Merry's dressing room. It's time to go."

Cluny's bottom lip came out in a pout. "Go? But I thought—"

"We can't stay, Cluny. Merry will take one look at what we've done, thank us politely, Jack will join her—and the next thing you know we'll both be climbing out of the well. In other words, we can't stay."

"Can't? Not even for a minute? Just long enough for Merry to see what we've done?"

"No!"

"Oh . . . uh-oh! Too late, Clancy. Here they come."

Merry had her head buried against Jack's throat as he carried her into the room. He'd surprised her just as Honey had been helping her into her dressing gown—his old dressing gown—but any hint of embarrassment she might have felt disappeared into giggles as Honey had looked at Jack, had seen that he, too, was clad only in a dressing gown. The maid had blinked, screeched, bobbed a hasty curtsy, and run from the room.

Jack hadn't said a word. Words hadn't been necessary. He'd simply come to Merry, smiled at her, and lifted her into his arms. He smelled of soap, and she had slid her hand into his still-damp hair, which hung to his shoulders. He felt solid beneath the plush velvet of the dressing gown, and yet she wasn't at all frightened, at all nervous. This was Jack, and he loved her.

She heard the sound of the door to the dressing room being kicked closed behind them, and knew that she'd soon be lying on the bed, lost in Jack's arms, lost in the magic of love. There was really no reason for words. None at all.

"What in bloody hell happened in here?"

Merry sighed, lifted her head, looked at the room, then buried her face against Jack's body once more. "Cluny and

Clancy," she said, trying not to giggle. "It couldn't be any-one else. Aren't they sweet? I imagine this is their way of giving us their blessing."

The next thing she knew, Merry was standing on her own two feet, looking at one rather belligerent male.

"Merry," he said, his lips barely moving, "I understood when you were six, and insisted that you had a friend named Patricia who was truly responsible for every naughty thing you ever did—even if nobody else could see her. I humored you when you were twelve, and said that an-gels had sung you to sleep each night after you'd fallen from that tree and broken your arm and the pain kept you awake. I even kept myself from arguing with you when you said Cluny and Clancy had locked me in here last night. But do *not* tell me that they had anything to do with this."

Merry walked over to the bouquet of daisies that sat on her dressing table, bent down, sniffed their fragrance. "All right, Jack. I won't tell you that." She straightened, turned, and asked him directly: "So, who did do it? Honey? Mrs. Maxwell?" She leaned toward him, grinning. *"Aloysius?"*

"Christ," Jack said, walking over to the bed, sitting down on the edge—on the one place not entirely covered in rose petals. "All right, Merry. For the sake of argument—and only for the sake of argument—let's say that, just for this moment, I believe you. Are they still here?"

Cluny floated down from the ceiling, where he had been pulling faces at one of the cherubs painted there, and danced a short, lively jig in front of Jack, who paid him no notice at all.

Merry hugged herself, trying not to smile. Poor Jack. She closed her eyes, concentrated. "Yes," she said at last, giving in to the smile. "They're here. Take a deep breath, Jack, smell the camphor. It's there, hiding under the smell of all these flowers."

"She's always saying that." Clancy floated down from his own perch, sniffed at his sleeve, then at Cluny. "And she's right. Would you believe that, Cluny? She's right!"

"Camphor, of course," Jack said, rolling his eyes. "All right, Merry. They're here. And now they're gone. Because I've just wished them away. I can do that, can't I? Didn't you say they listen to you?"

Merry pulled one daisy from the vase, twirling it between her fingers. "They listen to me, Jack, because I believe in them. You, however, don't believe in them. No matter how much you might want to be kind, to humor me, you don't believe in them."

He moved over, made room for her to sit down on the edge of the bed. "So it's useless for me to tell them to go away, is that what you're saying?"

"Unless you believe, yes. Of course, I can't be sure, but something makes me *feel* as if I'm correct."

She watched as Jack thought about this for a moment, seemed to digest what she'd said. "I want them to be here, you know. With all my heart, I *want* them to be here. Oh, very well." Jack smiled, squeezed Merry's fingers, then stood up, spread his arms wide as if to encompass the entire room. "Thank you, gentlemen, for all of this," he said, sweeping his invisible audience an elegant bow.

And then he became deadly serious, his voice losing any trace of humor as he added, quite solemnly, "Thank you for everything you've done, for the way you've comforted Merry, protected her in my absence. Thank you for all you've taught me, all you've shown me, for the worlds you opened to me. And Clancy? Cluny? Thank you for being here when I needed you, for all the years you made a frightened little boy feel safe, even loved. I'll never, never forget you."

Cluny looked at Clancy, and they both smiled. "He

might not truly believe we're here, old friend, but he does love us. That's enough, isn't it?"

"It is, indeed, old friend," Clancy answered quietly. "It is indeed."

Merry blinked back tears as she tugged on Jack's sleeve to gain his attention. "I do love you, Jack Coltrane," she said as he smiled at her, looking young and rather sheepish. "Now, for pity's sake—tell them to go away for a little while."

"No need to ask twice," Clancy said, quickly pulling himself back to attention and leading Cluny across the floor, then pushing him straight through the window, hastening to follow after him. "Rather a nice, safe float to the ground, I say, than ending up in Maxwell's pantry, watching him pick at his nails with a kitchen knife."

"I still don't smell camphor," Jack said, standing in front of Merry, holding on to both her hands.

"Neither do I, not anymore," she said, scooting more fully onto the mattress, pulling him with her, and uncaring that her dressing gown had fallen open, revealing her thighs.

"Then they're gone? We're all alone?" Jack's smile was positively wicked as he left go of her hands, stripped off his dressing gown.

"All alone, Jack," she said, watching as he lay down beside her on the bed, his masculine body surrounded by pink, yellow, and red rose petals. "Alone enough that I can say that I've forgiven you for sending Kipp after me tonight, to watch over me like some nursemaid. Even as I'm sure you forgive me for wanting to be of some help to you. Now, should I tell you what Kipp and I did tonight, what we discovered? It's really important."

He leaned toward her, began nibbling at her earlobe. "I'd rather you didn't, sweetheart. Unless you'd like to listen while I tell you what Walter and I found after a day and half a night of paging through dusty ledgers yet again? It's important, too."

She wrinkled up her nose in distaste at the thought of anything quite so boring, even as a giggle escaped her. Jack's warm breath was in her ear, sending shivers down her spine, tickling her even as an only recently experienced yet already-welcome warmth spread in her belly. "You wouldn't *dare* tell me all of that tonight," she said, abruptly sitting up, only to turn to him, reach down, and unerringly find that certain, marvelously ticklish spot just above his waist.

They rolled back and forth across the bed like puppies tumbling together in a meadow, rose petals clinging to bare skin, hands moving to tickle, to tease . . . and then to caress. To reach. To find. To stroke.

Jack's breath was harsh in Merry's ears as he came to her, as she moved beneath him, as together, as a new, inseparable one, they explored a world of pleasure without pain, a universe devoid of plots or worries or enemies intent of robbing them of their happiness.

Merry held on to him, held on tightly so that she wouldn't be lost forever in a world of sensations that grew and grew, became more urgent. She held him, felt his muscles ripple beneath her fingertips, felt the strength of his thighs as he slipped between her legs. He rolled over, so that he was suddenly on his back, so that she was suddenly, unexpectedly, sitting above him. Still one with him. Still wildly, gloriously one with him.

Her eyes closed, her head thrown back, she felt his thumbs teasing at her nipples, his hands cupping the weight of her. Then they moved lower, slid down her belly, found their way to the heart of her, the heat of her.

"Jack—" she began nervously, but then wave after wave

of sensation claimed her, holding her to him even as she felt herself spin off into the unknown. "Oh, God—*Jack*."

He held her, held her tightly, allowed her to collapse against him. She was unable to catch her breath as her body continued to move without her direction, to pulse, to clench, to become so fluid she could no longer tell where her own body ended and Jack's began.

And then he moved inside her. Slowly. As if there was all the time in the world for pleasure, and he planned to make good use of every last minute of it. He pushed himself into her, deeply, then withdrew. Returned. Teased. Brought her body back to life even as she thought there was no more sensation possible.

"I love you, Merry," he whispered into her ear as his hips lifted, lifted again—moving faster, going deeper. "I love you, I love you, I love, love, love—"

Laughing, crying, she captured his mouth with her own.

Chapter Twenty-seven

Jack contentedly nibbled on Merry's ear, whispering nonsense to her as she lay on her back beneath the satin coverlet, trying very hard not to wake up. She halfheartedly slapped at his hand as he slid it over her naked body, hinted at his intentions. It was morning, and probably a lovely day beyond the room-darkening draperies, but she was obviously in no hurry to see it.

He was in no hurry either, as a matter of fact. The world could wait. Henry Sherlock could wait. He knew, with his mind, that he was being foolish, perhaps even dangerously foolish. But he had just discovered Merry, discovered love. And a man in love could always find an excuse for foolishness. He moved closer beneath the sheets, slid his hand across Merry's flat belly.

Merry grabbed his hand with both of hers, squeezed it tightly. "Jack?"

"Hmmm?" he murmured, stroking his tongue down the length of her slim throat.

"Jack!" Her fingers nearly crushed his. "Do you know this man?"

"Man?" Merry's question—and her strong grip—broke into his mood. "What man?" He raised his head, looked at Merry, saw her blue eyes wide with astonishment.

"I beg your pardon, sir, but this is the second day running that you have not been where you were supposed to be when I arrived to wake you, as I've been charged with waking you at seven each morning. As well you know, sir, for it was you who instructed me thusly. I never saw you yesterday, sir. Not to shave, not to bathe—although I understand you did finally indulge in some sort of slapdash ablutions late last night. Without summoning me, sir, which I consider an affront even if I should never have even considered rising from my bed at that hour. Not with all I do for you the whole day long. Pressing neckcloths. Polishing boots. Pulling those disgusting burrs from your jackets."

"Oh, God." Jack closed his eyes, rested his head on Merry's shoulder even as she dragged the covers more completely around her. Then he turned, looked across the room at the small, thin man who stood just inside the dressing-room door, wringing his hands, his bottom lip trembling with emotion.

"I cannot continue in this manner, sir," the man warned, his voice beginning to quaver. "I simply cannot. The upheaval of it all! I need an orderly existence. My nerves—well, they're overset, that's all. Overset. I shall require breakfast in my room, sir, and perhaps a day in bed as well. You do understand, don't you sir?"

"Yes, yes, I understand. Now go away, all right? I'll have someone else ready my bath, shave me. Or I'll do it myself. Lord knows I know how."

"Sir!" The word was a sob of despair. "Not ask me? Not use me? Oh, how could you, sir? Well, let me tell you, I shall be waiting for you in your dressing room at quarter past the hour. Shave yourself? I should perish of the shame, sir. Perish!"

By this time, Jack was holding a hand across Merry's mouth, to keep her giggles silent. He only released her after the door to the dressing room slammed shut, leaving them alone once more.

"Oh, Jack," Merry exclaimed, sitting up in the bed, so that her bare breasts were most immodestly and quite delightfully exposed to his sight. "Who on earth was that?"

"Rhodes," Jack said, admiring what he believed to be the loveliest view in nature. "My valet."

"I've never seen him. I remember that you've mentioned him, but I've never seen him. Well, with seventy-five rooms in this pile, I suppose that isn't quite as extraordinary as it could be. Does he really breakfast in his room? Who serves him?"

Jack began kissing Merry's arm, the side of her breast. "I have no idea. Somebody must, I suppose. Umm . . . you taste good. Slide back down here, sweetheart, I've decided to breakfast on you."

"Jack!" She slapped his hands away, pushed at him so that he fell onto his back with a frustrated groan. "Where on earth did you find him? Why did you keep him after you found him?"

He gave up, knowing that somehow Rhodes had become the morning's topic of conversation, and that Merry wouldn't let him alone until he explained. "Walter and I purchased a town house in London, remember," he said, sitting up, punching at the pillows before leaning against them. "Rhodes, it seems, came along with the house and the rest of the servants. Walter took the curricle in the stables for his own, and gave me Rhodes in return. I thought it a splendid bargain at the time," he ended, sighing as he raked a hand through his hair, "but now I'm rethinking my supposed brilliant negotiations, and Walter has yet to let me hear the end of it."

"A town house in London? Oh, yes, I remember now. You were going to give it to me. I think I'll forgive you for that, if you tell me about the place."

He grinned at her, delighting that she hadn't hit him for his cavalier idea of tossing a sum of money and a residence at her, then sending her away for her own good. "You'll like it, Merry. And quite a good address in Mayfair, to hear Kipp tell it. Would you like to go there, see it?"

Merry snuggled against him, reminding him of his earlier plans for this morning. "Do you know that I've never been more than five miles from Coltrane House, Jack, not in my entire life? Would I like to travel to London? Goodness, but you ask silly questions."

She kissed his chest, gave him a swift hug, then sighed theatrically. "But, first, I suppose we have to convince Henry it's time for him to tell us the truth. Unless we can convince the Forfeit Man to tell Squire Headley who hired him. Do you suppose spending a night in the Willoughby Hall cellars, trussed up like a Christmas goose, has made the man at all talkative?"

Jack was still having difficulty believing that Kipp and Merry had actually captured the highwayman. He had allowed Merry her small adventure, knowing that Kipp would be close behind, guarding her. But he had never, not in his wildest imaginings, supposed that Merry would do more than catch cold as she sat beside the roadway, awaiting the Forfeit Man.

By the time Jack had heard Merry's explanation of her night's work, and by the time he had all but leapt into a shirt and breeches—Rhodes was otherwise occupied, sipping tea in his bed——Kipp had sent a note telling him he'd taken the highwayman to see the squire.

This Jack learned from Walter, who, it seemed, had not bothered to go to bed at all, and was still ensconced in the study, reading through Coltrane House papers.

"I still can't believe it," Jack said, falling into the chair he'd left not all that many hours ago. "Kipp, single-handedly capturing the Forfeit Man. I could just as easily imagine you, Walter, riding up on the winning nag at the village's yearly fair."

"Yes, yes, that would be something to see, wouldn't it?" Walter agreed, throwing Jack a quelling look. "But I think you'd rather see this," he said, shuffling through stacks of papers until he came up with a sheaf of legal-looking documents. "Here you go, Jack. While Kipp is busy delivering the Forfeit Man to Squire Headley, why don't you amuse yourself with a bit of reading?"

"In a minute, Walter," Jack said, taking the papers, placing them on his lap without looking at them. "You're sure Kipp told you the man he captured said he'd been hired by Henry Sherlock?"

Walter sighed, sat back in his chair. "Actually, Jack, his lordship told me that the man had said he'd been paid by some white-haired cove what lived in a bloody damn mansion and who hadn't paid him half enough blunt to have him hang for him." He sniffed at the wilting rosebud in his lapel. "Or something like that. You do realize that it won't be long before Sherlock realizes something is amiss, when his henchman doesn't come home to roost this morning?"

"I do. And I also realize that the so astute Squire Headley isn't going to believe our highwayman over Henry Sherlock, a respected member of the community. Or believe me, for that matter. His so-Christian Sarah wouldn't let him. Even Kipp is known far and wide as a bit of a loose screw, so that

I doubt even his title will help us. I didn't have the heart to tell Merry any of that, of course, as she's happily believing that Henry will be on his way to prison before luncheon is announced."

"In which case, I suggest you read this copy of your late father's will. All in all, Jack, I've had an interesting night, as I roamed these rooms, unable to sleep. I stumbled across the papers earlier this morning, in the music room of all places, stuck in with a stack of music books. I can't imagine why we didn't ask to see it before, or why Sherlock would have left it lying about. I've decided, however, that August must have read this copy, stuffed it away in the first place he found, then went off to drink himself stupid yet again. Read it, Jack. I believe we've found that last missing piece of the puzzle."

Jack looked down at the papers, then at Walter. "You've already read it? Perhaps, then, you could tell me what I should know?"

"Oh, allow me, Walter, please," Aloysius Bromley said, walking into the room and taking up the chair beside Jack's. "It's quite interesting, John, reading the two of them."

Jack picked up the papers, began to read. "The two of them?"

The old tutor wrapped his long scarf more tightly around his thin throat, then smiled sadly. "I read the will Sherlock showed me years ago. Indeed, he had me witness your father's signature. The will was quite simple, deeding everything to you. I supposed that blood won out at the end, and August preferred keeping the property in the family. I'd like to say he did it because he loved you, John, but you're a grown man now, and beyond such pleasant fantasies."

"Then, last night—early this morning, actually, I found this copy, one for a more recent will," Walter said, taking up the story. "Dated, as a matter of fact, not five days after you left England. Our friend Aloysius, I probably do not have to point out to you, was not asked to witness this second will."

Jack rose, went to the drinks table to have a glass of wine. It was only eight o'clock, clearly too early for imbibing, but he suddenly felt the need to wet his dry throat. "Go on."

Walter sighed. "Always so impatient. I could read you the paragraphs that differ from the will Aloysius witnessed so many years ago—they're long and dusty and very legal-sounding. But what it comes down to is that, on top of the land given to Sherlock, if you were to die without issue, Jack, Henry Sherlock inherits the entire estate. Merry was to be given a small income for life and a cottage in the village."

Jack put down the wine decanter without opening it. "If I were to—why, that miserable son of a—" He broke off, rubbing a hand over his mouth, taking in the depth of Henry Sherlock's conspiracy to gain control of Coltrane House.

Jack returned to his chair, sat down. "For years, gentlemen. Sherlock must have been planning this for years. Telling me Merry was safe, but didn't want to see me. Telling me the best thing I could do for Merry would be to stay away, never come home. Knowing what August had told me, knowing how guilty I felt for all that happened to Merry's father, to her. I only wonder that he didn't kill me that night, and have done with it."

"I wondered the same thing myself, John," Aloysius said, sighing. "I finally decided, after Walter told me of the false loans and such, that it would have been too soon. August had just gained control of Meredith's inheritance, thanks to your marriage to her. Sherlock probably needed time. Time to raid those funds carefully, time in which to draw up the new will. Time for August to die."

"Yes, time for my father to die. And we couldn't both die at the same time; that wouldn't be neat, or orderly," Jack said, thinking out loud. "And I didn't die, although no one in England knew I was alive, except for Sherlock. But that was all right. He had his land when August died. He built his house, furnished it, even as this house fell deeper into disrepair. He slowly established himself as someone with enough money to eventually purchase Coltrane House. No one could suspect him of anything illegal, not when he'd fought for so long to help Merry. He could afford to move slowly, because even Merry's fine management couldn't produce enough money to pay this year's interest on the mortgage to MacDougal—to him. Another few months, gentlemen, and Coltrane House would have fallen into Sherlock's hands like a very fine, ripe plum."

"I'm sorry, John," Aloysius said sadly. "I should have seen something . . . I should have known. But Sherlock has always seemed so loyal, so trustworthy. And he did save your life that last night."

"Did he?" Jack sat slumped in his chair. "Consider this, Aloysius, if you will. Sherlock was always there to help, but it was always after the fact. Once he'd gotten what he wanted, and he definitely wanted Merry's dowry, definitely wanted me out of England."

"After the fact?" Aloysius repeated. "By God, John, you're right! He allowed Cluny and Clancy to stay, but only *after* Meredith was already here. He fought for you to be able to go away to school, but only *after* you'd grown old enough to take a hand in the running of the estate, only *after* you were old enough to possibly be in his way. He marshaled everyone to break down the doors that last night and save you from August, but not until *after* the ceremony had been completed. Well, he certainly established himself in the role of savior to Coltrane House, didn't he? And all the while, he was lining his own pockets, waiting for the time to be right."

Jack nodded his agreement, then stood up, threw down

the copy of the will. "Walter, Aloysius, pack a change of clothes and be ready to leave here in an hour. Merry will be going with you."

"Leave?" Walter asked. "To go where?"

"To London," Jack said shortly. "To our town house in London. An hour, gentlemen. No more." Then he got up, not bothering to excuse himself, and went in search of Merry. She had promised to be a very good, dutiful wife, and stay safely inside Coltrane House all day long, overseeing the workmen.

Because, whether Kipp was successful in convincing Squire Headley or not, Henry Sherlock had to know by now that his plan was in trouble, that his hired henchman would most probably talk, giving him away, and that his hopes of owning Coltrane House had just vanished.

After nearly thirty years of plotting, of patience and planning, Henry Sherlock was probably not going to react very well to that knowledge. He could run away, Jack supposed, but he couldn't see Sherlock leaving his fine mansion, leaving behind all he'd worked for, schemed for, for nearly thirty years.

He could deal with Sherlock, Jack was confident of that. He could and would deal with him. But, first, he had to get Merry safely away from Coltrane House. Away from what was certain to be a rapidly approaching danger.

Chapter Twenty-eight

Merry heard Jack's sharp, confident steps on the tiles outside the Main Saloon and sent up a silent prayer that they'd fade as he continued past the closed doors, on his way to somewhere else.

But it wasn't to be. The doors opened and Jack stepped through them, saying, "There you are, sweetheart. I'm afraid I'm going to have to ask you to—"

"Hello, John," Henry Sherlock said from his seat on the couch. "Good of you to join us."

"Don't, Jack," Merry warned quickly, as Jack showed every sign of lunging straight at Sherlock. She pointed across the large room, to the French doors leading outside to the gardens. The doors she had opened earlier, to catch a hint of breeze, only to have eased Sherlock's entry into the house. Two rather large, loutish-looking men, both holding pistols, stood just inside the doors, lounging against the wall. "He's not alone."

"Yes," Jack said, looking at the two men as they walked over to stand directly behind the couch where Sherlock sat, their pistols trained straight at Jack's heart. "I can see that. Are you all right, sweetheart?"

"I'm fine," Merry answered, then smiled. It was absurd. It was all so absurd. They were in their own house, for pity's sake. Nothing could happen to them in their own house. "How are you, darling? Do you think I should ring for Maxwell, perhaps ask him to bring our guests a tray?"

"Or a trough," Jack said, his tone light, his eyes hard. "Henry, you've eaten from the Coltrane trough before, haven't you? All but leapt in with both feet, to wallow there."

"Oh, please," Henry said, rising from his seat even as he motioned for Jack to join Merry on the facing couch. "You're not amusing, either of you. There, that's good. Sit down, John, and stay there, and we'll wait for Squire Headley together."

Merry reached out, took hold of Jack's hand, knowing her fingers were ice-cold, shaking. "Henry is here because he has somehow heard that Kipp captured the Forfeit Man. I can't imagine how he heard so quickly, can you? But to continue. He's convinced, Henry says, that you hired the man to rob coaches for you, and he wants to protect me from you until the squire comes to take you away, which he's equally convinced will happen very shortly. Isn't that kind of him? Even if he did feel it necessary to hold a pistol directed at me in order to keep me from warning you of his presence."

"Thus our two armed friends?" Jack nodded to each man in turn. "How interesting. But it won't work, Sherlock. Kipp persuaded the man to confess, and it was your name he sang out, not mine. He's undoubtedly singing that same name to the good squire right now. You probably should have paid him more, don't you think? Lord knows you had the where-withal, even if it came from someone else's pocket."

Jack stood up, and Merry stood with him, still holding tightly to his hand. "Now, before you rush off, Sherlock, let me tell you what else I know. I know about the lie you told Merry—and I'd kill you for it if I didn't already know that you're going to hang for your other crimes. I know about the will you had August sign five days after Merry and I were married. You remember that will, don't you, Henry? The will that names you as heir should I take ill and die, or meet with an unfortunate accident—or hang. Amusing isn't it, in a way. The noose is there, but it's now your neck and not mine that will be stuck into it."

Merry watched hot color run into Sherlock's normally pale cheeks, saw his usual air of confidence evaporate before her eyes. She felt Jack squeeze her fingers even as he took a step closer to her, wordlessly urged her to step to her left, moving away from the couches, closer to the fireplace, closer to the French doors.

Above them, high up at the ceiling, the chandelier shivered as if the prisms had been caught in a breeze.

"What to do, what to do?" Cluny was saying as he all but leapt into his friend's arms, quaking with fright. " 'I would give all my fame for a pot of ale and safety.' "

Clancy carefully disengaged himself from Cluny's tight grasp. "You've got no fame, you idiot."

"No fame?" Cluny looked crestfallen for a moment, then brightened. "Perhaps the ale at least? But, no. We've got to save these dear children. This is why we're still here, I'm sure of it. To save our Merry and Jack. But how, Clancy? How?"

Even with her mind full of questions and her heart clogged with fear, Merry felt it, felt Cluny's and Clancy's presence. She sent up a small prayer of thanks, squeezing Jack's hand one more time, so that he looked at her.

If ever there was a time for him to believe, truly to believe, it was now. She cast her gaze upward, toward the chandelier. Hoping he understood. Feeling her heart lighten, leap into her throat when he nodded slightly, showing her that he did.

"Did you see that, Cluny? They looked up here, the both of them. And Jack—Jack *winked* at me. You're right, they're counting on us." Clancy puffed out his thin chest, lifted his chin. "I always knew this day would come. This is our time, Cluny. Our time to shine!"

"Give it up, Sherlock," Jack said, easing Merry yet another step toward the French doors, and away from the chandelier. "You won't convince Squire Headley, and you won't convince a court, not once we've laid out thirty years of ledgers that prove your crime. Because I know, Sherlock, I know it all now. You're no longer dealing with drunken August, or a hotheaded youth, or a naive young girl."

Merry glared at her husband, although she knew this wasn't precisely the best time to point out to him that she rather resented being termed a naive young girl.

"I know about MacDougal—all the money you stole from the estate over the years. Now, why don't you just simply surrender," Jack suggested amicably, "send these two fellows away, and we can discuss things like civilized men? Perhaps there's more to it, more that I know, and I don't really want you punished. At the least, I don't want to have a direct hand in that punishment. Rather the way you've always operated, Henry, isn't it? At least until lately."

Civilized? Jack was being civilized. Her Jack? This wasn't like him. It wasn't like Jack at all. But it was nice. Merry actually began to relax, until Henry Sherlock spoke once more.

"Clever boy. Headley's an ass, you're right about that. I can't put my faith in having him coming here to arrest you, more's the pity. That was a miscalculation on my part. But you seem to forget, John, just who is holding the weapons. Now sit down, the pair of you."

Henry stood up, pulled a pistol from his waistband, leveled it at Jack. "You couldn't stay away, could you? You had to come back. You had to ruin everything. Just as I had it all in my grasp, just as I was about to have everything I've planned for, worked for. Well, you can't have it. *I* built Coltrane House into the most profitable estate in all of Lincolnshire. *I* kept the estate running even as August tried his damnedest to throw himself into bankruptcy. Drunken sot. Ungrateful bastard."

Merry couldn't take her eyes off the pistol Henry was waving about recklessly, knowing that Jack could be dead at any moment. And then Jack spoke, and she wanted to kill him herself. Did he have to antagonize Henry? Did he have to dare being angry with the man?

Because what Jack said was, "August wasn't half the bastard you are, Sherlock. Telling Merry that she and I are sister and brother? I didn't come after you when I heard that monumental lie. I listened to my friends, to my wife. I let them convince me that there was a better way to destroy you than with my bare hands, a more civilized approach to the matter. A few moments ago I even agreed to let you leave, walk away, because of something I've just figured out, a stunning burst of knowledge that turns my stomach."

Merry looked at Sherlock, saw his fingers tightening around the pistol. "Jack, stop. Please stop."

"It's all right, Merry. I have to tell Henry here something else now, even knowing what I now know. My wife is wrong. My friends are wrong. My way is the right one. And that's what I'm going to do, Henry. I'm going to drop you where you stand." He paused for a moment, then spoke again. "Although I wouldn't be averse to a ghost of assistance."

And then, as Merry closed her eyes, sure Jack had killed himself out of his own mouth, she heard the telltale tinkle of the chandelier. Realizing what Jack was trying to do, she opened her eyes, looked up at the chandelier that hung over the facing couch, watched as it began to tremble, to shake.

"Although you might be applauding my performance, gentlemen," Jack said, pushing Merry away from him, "might I suggest that now would be a good time to bring the curtain *down*?"

"Can we do it, Clancy?" Cluny asked, doing his best to jump on the chandelier even as he tugged on the chain holding it to the ceiling. "I don't think we can do it. I'm too nervous, and about to get the hiccups."

"No you won't, and yes we can." Clancy spoke quickly, furiously, as he laid a hand on Cluny's arm. "But not this way. We're not strong enough this way. We're going to have to *will* the chandelier to fall, the way we willed the flowers into the bedchamber last night. I know we've never done anything this important before, we've never done evil to do good. We may not be able to, I don't know. But we have to try, Cluny, we have to try. Take my hand, Cluny, take both my hands. Close your eyes—and for God's sake hold your breath! Now, for Jack . . . for Merry . . . for all the years, and all the love . . . concentrate, Cluny. *Concentrate*."

"What in bloody hell?" one of the two armed men asked, looking up at the chandelier as it began to tremble, to shake.

The second man, not even as articulate as his companion, merely stared, his mouth dropped open.

Sherlock also looked at the chandelier, then shifted his

arm, aiming his pistol at Merry even as he moved away from the couch. "Cursed damned house!"

It all happened in the space of three heartbeats. Just long enough for Jack to throw himself in front of Merry, trying to shield her. Just long enough for the chandelier to break loose from its moorings. Just long enough for the sound of a single pistol shot to be lost in the larger sound of a man's scream and the tremendous crash of heavy brass and three hundred crystal prisms hitting the floor.

Merry felt Jack flinch even as he grabbed her, threw her to the floor. But he was up again just as quickly, running after Sherlock, who had somehow escaped the falling chandelier. The two armed men had also evaded the danger, although both had somehow lost their pistols in the process. They were standing stock-still, looking at the chandelier, obviously too stunned to move.

"Jack—wait!" Merry screamed, trying to rise, getting tripped by her own skirts, cursing and sobbing as she struggled to her feet only in time to see Jack disappearing into the gardens.

"Merry, what happened? We heard a crash and—bloody hell, Aloysius, would you look at that!" Walter exclaimed.

"Those men, Walter," Merry said, feeling stupid, feeling frantic. She looked down at her hand, saw that there was blood on it, more blood on the carpet. Jack had been shot. The stupid man had let himself be shot. "Do something with them!"

"It would be my pleasure," she heard him say, even as she ran from the room, chasing after Jack. She raced through the overgrown gardens, her feet nearly flying as she ran down the path, broke out onto the wide, sweeping lawns beyond.

And then she saw them.

They were fighting. Not the sort of fight she'd seen in ink

drawings in August's study. Jack and Sherlock were brawl-
ing. Wrestling. Hitting each other, falling to the ground,
rolling over and over in the grass.

Sherlock kept standing up, dragging himself to his feet,
running a few steps before Jack would chase after him,
tackle him, bring him crashing to the ground once more.

It was a silent fight, a bloody fight, and it seemed to go
on forever. Walter and Aloysius joined her, watching along
with her.

And the fight went on.

"He's hurt," Merry said, as Walter slid an arm around her
shoulders, pulling her against him as she longed to give in to
impulse and launch herself into the fight, no matter how
much Jack would hate her for it. "It's his left arm, Walter—
do you see it? He's been shot. He can barely lift his arm anymore. We've got to stop this!"

"He won't thank us, Merry. This is Jack's fight, and we
must let him fight it," Walter said, and she bit back a sob,
flinching as Sherlock landed a blow to Jack's left shoulder,
sending him to his knees. He tried to hold on to Sherlock's
legs with his good arm, keep the man from running away,
but he obviously didn't have the strength.

"Now we have to stop him—he's running away!" Merry
shouted, breaking free of Walter's protective embrace.
"Oh," she then said, stupidly beginning to smile. "Never
mind." She lifted her skirts and began trotting in Jack's direction. "Come on, we'll help Jack."

"You help Jack," Walter said, stripping off his dark
brown jacket to reveal a pair of very muscular arms beneath
his neat white shirt. "I find that, unenamored as I am of such
physical exertion, I feel a great need to chase after Sherlock
and finish the job Jack started."

"No need, Walter," Aloysius said, even as he followed

after Merry. "Merry understands. Sherlock's heading straight for the ha-ha."

The trio reached Jack's side just as he was staggering to his feet, reeling about like a drunken sailor, watching Sherlock's progress as he held on to his injured left arm. Blood saturated his sleeve and was beginning to drip from his fingertips. "He's heading for the ha-ha, Merry," he said, then collapsed to his knees. "I only hope I don't pass out before I see this."

"What's a ha-ha?" Walter asked Merry, who was kneeling beside Jack, ripping a length of material from the bottom of her slip in order to tie it around her husband's arm.

"A rather ancient, remarkably simple bit of architecture, actually. A ha-ha, my friend, is a submerged fence," Aloysius explained, tossing the end of his scarf over his shoulder as he pointed in the same direction Sherlock was heading, his gait uneven, his head pushed forward, as if he couldn't remain upright in any other position. "In this case, a rather deep pit dug all the way around this side of Coltrane House, with a fence running along the base of the pit, and meant to keep the sheep and other animals from wandering too close to the buildings. It doesn't obstruct the view, as a real fence would, you understand. I don't think Sherlock, in his agitation, remembers that it's there. After all, it has been in a sad state for years, barely a ditch at all."

Merry tied the strip of material tightly around Jack's arm, even as she, along with the others, watched Henry Sherlock's progress. He kept looking back over his shoulder as if checking for pursuers even as he continued his mad flight. "He really isn't paying any attention, is he, Jack? And he couldn't know that we've repaired it, dug the trench deeper just last week. Should we warn him?"

"Warn him? We'll haul him out, sweetheart, but that's all we'll do."

"Good," she said, satisfied, then watched as Henry continued to run across the grass. She watched, smiling, until he abruptly disappeared, tumbling into the six-foot-deep ha-ha.

"So," Walter said after a moment, bending down to help Jack to his feet. "That's a ha-ha, is it? Well, all I can say to that, much as it pains me, is ha. *Ha-ha.*"

Chapter Twenty-nine

"**H**ow is he? Will he die? Weedy, hedge-born apple-john. Wouldn't bother me if he died."

Cluny floated over to check, looking down assessingly at Sherlock, who was sprawled on one of the couches—the one not smothered in chandelier—and appearing very much the worse for his tumble into the ha-ha. " 'With the help of a surgeon, he might yet recover, and prove an ass,' " Cluny said, not too unhappily. "Uh-oh, here comes the Indian. Do you think he'll scalp him? I could watch that. Yes, I could."

"You sent away a physically battered and heartbroken boy," Walter said as he stopped in front of the couch, looked down at Sherlock. "And he returned a man. Not at all what you expected. The son is not what his father was, and that was your mistake. But, then, it had all been so simple for you, hadn't it? For all those years. You couldn't imagine anything but one success neatly following after another."

Jack listened to his friend speak, even as he sprawled in a chair, allowing Merry to dab a cold, wet cloth against the cut on his lip, and his bruised and rapidly swelling eye.

She'd already bandaged his arm, which had been a bloody wound but not a serious one, the ball having passed straight through his flesh. "It's a pity Aloysius felt the need to lie down, or else he'd be here to listen to this. However, if you think Walter's praising me, sweetheart," he added quietly, "you'd be wrong. He's patting himself on the back for having taken up that broken youth and making a man of him." He smiled, then winced as his lip split open once more. "And he'd be right to take any credit there may be."

"*Shhh,*" she warned, dabbing at his lip again. "Don't talk. What will happen now?" she asked, then winced at her own question. "Well, you can talk, I suppose, as long as you try not to open your mouth. He'll hang, won't he?"

Jack nodded, his mood solemn. "Oh, yes, Merry. Henry is going to hang. Several times, if that were possible." He sat forward, taking the cloth from her hand. "Ah, here's Kipp, with the good squire in tow."

He nodded to Kipp, who gave him a faint, negative shake of his head. So, that's the way it was going to be? Perhaps it was for the best. There were still too many unanswered questions, one of them the most important of all. "I'm glad he's here," he said, keeping his voice deliberately light-hearted. "Now we can settle this."

"Settle this?" Merry took hold of his arm, tried to push him back down in the chair as he moved to stand up. "Are you out of your mind, Jack? You're not going to settle anything. Henry is a bad man, we know that. The squire knows that, and that's all that's needed. You're going upstairs, and you're going to bed. *Now.*"

"Isn't that sweet, Clancy? Hear how she loves him. Loves him enough to beat him over the head if she has to, just to take care of him. My mother was like that, you know."

"Hush, Cluny. Something's havey-cavey here. I don't know what, but Jack isn't happy. Why isn't he happy?"

Jack felt as if he'd been tossed down a flight of stairs—twice—but he carefully bent down, kissed Merry's cheek. "Later, sweetheart. I don't ever want to see Henry Sherlock again, so we're going to settle this now." He looked over at the couch, to where the man lay in an untidy heap, his right leg in a rude splint, his head wrapped in bloody bandages. "Besides, I need to know if I'm right about something, even as I hope I'm not."

Merry opened her mouth to protest, but was cut off by Kipp's enthusiastic greeting. Sighing, she stepped back, allowing Kipp to embrace Jack—at which point Jack did flinch in pain, not that he minded his friend's display of affection. It covered the fact that Kipp was also whispering something into his ear.

"Well, well, well," Kipp said, stepping back and looking around the room. "Quite a party I've missed, wasn't it? How nice of you to send someone to fetch the squire and myself, however belatedly. Would anyone care to tell me what happened here? We could start with the chandelier, I believe."

"Yes, yes! Tell him about the chandelier, Jack! Tell him what we did!"

"He can't do that, you idiot," Clancy said, cuffing the top of Cluny's oft-abused head. "Who'd believe him?"

"Only if Jack agrees to sit down," Merry said, glaring at her husband. "I mean it," she added, wagging her finger at him just like—Jack's smile split his lip open once more—well, just like a wife.

Jack returned to his chair, knowing his wife was not above pushing him into it. Besides, in his weakened state, he might just fall down, and then he'd never hear the end of it—not if he knew Merry.

"You look like you could use a drink, old sport," Kipp

said, and promptly went to the drinks table to pour out several glasses of wine, which he then offered to the company. "Not you, Sherlock," he said, "or those two trussed up over there. Who are they, anyway? They look as if they've been beaten with rather large clubs."

"They're two more of Sherlock's hirelings," Jack said, accepting a glass. "I believe there were three Forfeit Men, not one."

Kipp raised one well-defined brow. "Three? Well, that would explain the different methods of robbery, wouldn't it? Which one kissed the squire's daughter, do you think?" he asked, leaning down to half whisper in Jack's ear. "We should make sure the law goes lightly on him, yes?"

As Kipp walked toward the two men who sat on the floor in the far corner of the room, their hands and feet tied in stout ropes, Jack warned, "Don't do it, Kipp, don't ask. I need allies at the moment, not enemies. Not if we're going to sort this all out."

Merry followed after Kipp, standing beside him as they both looked at Sherlock's henchmen. "Walter beat them both into flinders, Kipp. In less than a moment, to hear Aloysius tell it, although I wasn't here to see. Isn't that remarkable?"

"Walter?" Kipp turned, bowed to the Indian, who returned the gesture, then faced the two captives once more. "Gentlemen, allow me to introduce you to a better man. His name, in case you missed it, is Wulli—what—yes, well, something like that—and it means good fighter. But, then," he ended, smiling as only Kipp could smile, "you probably already know that, don't you?"

"Good lad, his lordship, if a bit of a rascal," Clancy said. "If we were to stay here, we could probably help him."

"Help him do what?"

"Find a woman to love, of course. 'But, O, how bitter a

thing it is to look into happiness through another man's eyes.' "

"Oh," Cluny said, looking at Kipp, seeing the man's smile, the faint shadow in his eyes. "Yes, you're right. He needs someone to love, doesn't he?"

"If you're quite done?" Jack prompted as Merry began to giggle at Kipp's nonsense. "Squire Headley? I would appreciate it if you would be witness to what I most sincerely hope will now be Henry Sherlock's confession to murder. You do want to make a clean breast of things, don't you, Sherlock? After all, you were rather brilliant, in a decidedly evil way, and quite successful for a lot of years. Surely you want to talk about it—especially as you're going to hang for your other crimes, whether you confess to murder or not."

Sherlock tried to push himself up on the couch, but could only groan, then fall back against the cushions. "Go to the devil, Coltrane," he gritted out, glaring at Jack. "You can't prove anything."

"I don't have to prove anything, Sherlock, as the results are the same for you whether you confess or not," Jack reminded him. "Highwaymen hang. Isn't that correct, Squire?"

"Eh? What?" The squire quickly finished his drink, looked questioningly to Kipp, then nodded, even as he wiped his mouth with his sleeve. "Oh, yes. Yes. That's the law, all right. Scaring my Anna like that—oh, yes, Coltrane. Hanging. That's the law. But you said murder, Coltrane. Hang for that as well, of course. Who was killed?"

"My father, I believe, for one," Jack said, surprised to feel a pang of regret, of sorrow that he had never, not in his whole life, been able to look at that man with anything even vaguely resembling respect, or love. "And you killed him. Didn't you, Henry?"

"Oh, very well, as I'm going to hang anyway," Sherlock

said, sighing. "Yes, John. I killed him. Why not? All those years. All my work, my plans. And he kept trying to ruin them, ruin Coltrane House. I'd watched, twice before, while he almost lost the estate. *My* estate. My genius saved it every time, my ideas, my plans, not that he was ever grateful. I wasn't going to stand back and do nothing while he attempted to lose everything a third time. The only good thing that man ever did was to die."

"Jack?"

Jack smiled at Walter, who was looking at him in some confusion. "It's all right, Walter. I'm all right. I wasn't sure a moment ago, but now I am. It wasn't a drunken tumble down the stairs while my father was in London, as we'd heard. Henry killed August." He stood up, unable to remain still, even as he felt his reserves of strength slipping away. He really should be in bed, just as Merry said. Just a few minutes more—then it would be over.

"But how?" Kipp asked. "How did you guess?"

"It was something Walter pointed out to me last night. I don't know why, but it all has suddenly fallen into place for me, become logical, if ugly. Do you remember, Walter? Three times, you said. Three times during the past years Coltrane House was nearly lost, the estate was nearly bankrupted—by August's excesses. For Sherlock was always a good manager. Weren't you, Sherlock?"

"A good manager, and a bad, bad man." Clancy sniffed. " 'A rascally yea-forsooth man.' "

The man's features hardened. "You should be grateful to me, Coltrane, you know. I saved the estate. I worked so hard. And he'd gamble it all away, every penny we had, everything we didn't have."

"Yes, you did work hard. I'll grant you that. And for little appreciation. So you began taking a few pennies for yourself when times were good," Jack continued as Sherlock once more sank back against the cushion someone had placed behind his head. "More than a few pennies. August killed Merry's father the first time he needed money, and you probably knew about it, didn't you? God knows you may even have helped plan the crime. Her money kept you well and happy for a long, long time. And then, five years ago, you arranged for Merry and me to marry the second time the estate was in real trouble, which released even more of her inheritance for your use. What I couldn't understand until last night, until today, was why you didn't have me killed, why you were content with simply having me banished. That was generous of you, Henry, but stupid."

Sherlock did not react well to being called stupid. "You were as good as dead when I put you on that ship," he responded angrily. "Besides, who could have believed that you'd ever come back? Hotheaded young fool! By rights, you should be drunk in a gutter—or dead."

Jack smiled as Merry slipped her hand into his. "I suppose I should thank you for underestimating me. Tell me, when did you turn from simple greed to the notion that duping a drunken man and lining your own pockets wasn't enough? When did you decide you had to possess the estate yourself? Was it the day you finally found out the truth, or did you always know it?"

"I don't want to talk anymore," Sherlock said, turning his head toward the back of the couch. "You know so much— you tell me what I did, and when I did it."

"All right," Jack said, accepting another glass of wine from Kipp, then sitting down once more. "I'll tell you what I think happened. I think you were the one who convinced August to kill Merry's father. I think that you later convinced August that a marriage between Merry and me was the best way to get more money for the estate. After all, when the estate was in trouble you had to suspend your small incomes you'd come to depend upon. The payments to the fictitious William Hollis, Edward Blacker, Richard Leeds—all of them you. The supposed interest paid to the equally fictitious MacDougal—none of it could be yours, not if Coltrane House were to fall into bankruptcy. You also planned the rest of what happened that last night, didn't you?"

"What's the boy talking about?" Squire Headley asked. Kipp just waved away the man's question, handed him another full glass of wine. "But I don't understand what the boy is talking about. I've just come here to have somebody hang for what he did to my daughter."

"I *earned* that money," Sherlock said, glaring at Jack, speaking quickly, as if he'd been longing to say the words for thirty long years. "Every last penny. Fighting with that drunken sot, watching him destroy the estate. Riding horses through the planted fields—up the main staircase of this house. The gambling. The women. God—the women!"

He raised his hands, bunched them into fists. "You weren't on that ship for more than twenty minutes before I realized—before I understood that now, now I could have it all. For years I thought building my own private fortune was reward enough, revenge enough. But it wasn't. I didn't want this pile—it's ugly, ruined. But if I could have the land? That's what I needed, what I deserved. The land, the land I built and protected, the land I *knew*, loved. And my own house. *My* house. *My* land. Not yours, John. Mine."

Sherlock's eyes glittered dangerously, and Merry moved closer to Jack, sitting on the arm of the chair as if to protect him.

"I was patient," Sherlock continued, the center of everyone's attention, and seeming to enjoy that attention. For so long he had been a cipher, a shadow figure; needed, but unnoticed. "I'd been patient for a long time. What were a few more years? It didn't matter; I'd know when the time was right. I drew up a new will for August. I needed that will. I needed time to arrange things, plan. A measure of time between the will and August's death, so that no suspicion would arise, no questions would be asked. A measure of time between his death and my takeover of Coltrane House, time in which to establish that I had sufficient funds for such a large purchase. But that was all right. It had to be neat. It had to be orderly. And I wanted to be sure there would be enough money for my house. That was important. But it took me a long time to decide to actually do it, to know that I actually *could* kill him."

"It's numbers, not the actual money," Walter said, nodding. "Some of us simply need the numbers to be right. The checks, the balances—and the timing. I understand."

Sherlock shot Walter a murderous look. "I don't need you to understand. And you're wrong, Indian. You're so very, very wrong."

"Be nice, Sherlock," Jack warned tightly, even more sure now that he was soon going to hear what he didn't want to hear. "Nobody likes you very much. Now, we'll continue to proceed slowly, all right? What happened to ruin your fine plans? Your orderly progression, as it were?"

Sherlock rubbed a hand across his eyes, sighed. "He lost thirty thousand pounds in a single night of faro. He'd promised—no more gambling. Promised me! Thirty thousand pounds—in a single night. I never wanted his blood on my hands, but I knew I couldn't wait for him just to die. I couldn't wait for word to come to me that you'd died as well. Coltrane House was going to be lost—again. I couldn't allow that. There's an end to patience, you know."

He pointed a finger at Merry, who shrank back, pressed herself against Jack. "Still, I was prepared to be patient again with you. More than patient, while I built my house, while I bided my time. But you hung on, refused my advice to stop fighting and just sell the estate. And you," he continued, glaring at Jack. "More than her, you were my mistake. I was mere months from having everything I'd planned for—mere months! Why couldn't you at least have been your father's son?"

Jack leaned an elbow on the side of the chair, rested his chin on his fist. And said the words. "Why should I have been, Henry? You weren't."

Sherlock's face went so white Merry thought he was about to faint. "Jack?" she asked, turning to look at him questioningly. "What are you suggesting?"

"The same thing Henry suggested to you, sweetheart," he told her, putting a hand on her arm. "I wondered how he'd come up with such an insane story, that August could have cuckolded your father. And then it struck me—it was a story Henry found quite easy to believe. Shall we finish this now? How long, Henry? How long were you working here, working as August's trusted employee, before you found out you were his bastard son? How long before you decided that you deserved all the money you were stealing? How long before you convinced yourself that you were justified in killing your own father? Although I will thank you for shrinking from fratricide, at least until today."

"I don't kill children, I only take what's mine." Sherlock set his jaw, closed his eyes. "Our father littered the countryside with his bastards, never giving them a second thought. But not me, John. Not *me*. He knew who I was, at the end of it, just before I pushed him down those stairs. You should be thanking me, do you know that? And I'm not going to say another word, *brother*. It's over now, so what's the point?"

"I agree," Jack said, sighing. The last piece of the puzzle had slipped silently into place. "I think I've heard enough, that we've all heard enough."

"More than enough, I'd say," Kipp agreed, looking to Squire Headley for his confirmation. The squire, still appearing somewhat confused, nodded, got to his feet.

"I can tell him now? Is that what you mean?" the squire asked, pointing to Sherlock. "I can tell him that the man your lordship captured never said a word about Sherlock here having anything to do with this Forfeit Man business?"

"What?" The question came from three people: Merry, Walter, and Henry Sherlock.

Jack merely smiled, feeling the last of his tension slowly leaving his body, even as exhaustion began to claim him.

"That's right, my dears," Kipp said, his grin wicked. "Our esteemed squire traveled here with me, still intent on believing in Jack's guilt. If Sherlock hadn't confessed to murder? If he'd somehow convinced the dear squire that he had come here intent on proving that Jack was the Forfeit Man, only to be nearly killed by him? Ah—one can only wonder what would have happened then, can't one?"

"Brothers. Who would have thought? Who would have known? Well, that's it then, isn't it, Clancy? 'The wheel is come full circle.' We probably should be packing, don't you think? We can leave now with happy hearts."

"Yes," Clancy said slowly, watching as Jack, leaning heavily against Merry, slowly walked from the room. "I suppose so. I only wish we could say good-bye . . ."

"You do know how lucky you are only to be wounded, don't you?"

Merry watched Jack as she asked the question, watched his slow smile even as he tried not to wince while she tied the ends of the sling together behind his head.

"But you love me," he said, easing back against the pillows she'd piled against the headboard.

"Yes, I love you," Merry told him. "But that doesn't

mean I don't want to throttle you. Why didn't you tell me what you knew? About your father, about Sherlock—about all of it?"

"Because I wasn't really sure?" he responded, grinning. "Or don't you want to know that I was just talking, just saying whatever came into my head, all the while hoping Sherlock would betray himself in front of Squire Headley—who still, I think, believes I was the Forfeit Man."

"Well, you were."

He sat forward slightly, just enough to reach her as she sat on the bed beside him, lightly kiss her on the tip of her nose. "Yes, sweetheart, but we'll keep that our own small secret, won't we?"

"I suppose," she said, easing back onto the pillows with him. "Just as we'll let Walter and Aloysius believe that the chandelier just happened to come down when it did because it was going to fall down sooner or later anyway." She closed her eyes, shivered. "How could you have done anything so reckless? One minute you didn't believe in Cluny and Clancy, and the next you literally put your life into their hands. If that chandelier hadn't come crashing down when it did—"

"But it did. I believe in you, Merry, and if you said they were in the room, then they were in the room. Besides, I smelled the camphor—or at least I convinced myself that I did. And now it's all over, and I'm going to go to sleep. As you said, sweetheart, I'm a wounded man. You should probably treat me very kindly for the next few days, a week at the very least."

"All right," she said, snuggling against him, her heart full of love for him, yet still feeling faintly frightened, knowing how close she had come to losing him. "I'll be very nice to you for a few days. *Then* I'll kill you."

"That's my Merry," Jack said, smiling at her. And then he

sat up straight, his eyes wide. "My God, Merry, I don't believe it. Merry? Do you smell it, too? Smell the camphor?"

She lifted her head, smiled. "Yes. Yes, I do. They're here. Cluny and Clancy are here. I think they've come to say good-bye." She sat up in the bed, looking around the room, knowing she couldn't see the two ghosts, but unable to stop herself from searching for them. "Thank you, my dearest most wonderful friends," she said as she blinked back tears. "Thank you for all of the years, for all the loving care—and for saving us this one last time. We both thank you, we thank you so very much."

"She said that well, didn't she, gentlemen?" Jack said, kissing Merry's hand. "I know what you'd say in return, if you could talk to us. 'Good night, good night! parting is such sweet sorrow.' And so I'll say good night, and God-speed, gentlemen." He sighed deeply, then eased back against the pillows once more. "I always thought I had no real father, Merry. But I did. I had four of them. Aloysius, Walter, and these two magnificent gentlemen. Do you really think Cluny and Clancy are going to leave us now?"

She nodded, snuggling close to him. "I could be wrong, Jack, but I believe they've stayed to see us happy, to finish the job they started so many years ago. Now it's time for them to rest."

"They deserve it. They deserve everything good in this world, and in the next. I love you, Merry," Jack told her, aiming a kiss at her cheek even as his eyes began to close.

"I know, Jack. I've always known," she told him quietly, smoothing his hair back from his forehead. "Now go to sleep, darling." It was about time, she thought as his eyes shut, considering the fact that she'd laced his tea with laudanum so that he could rest, put the unsettling findings of this long day behind him.

"Did you hear all of that, Clancy?" Cluny said, as the two

ghosts hovered at the end of the bed, dressed in their best costumes, looking fit and ready to travel. "We're magnificent gentlemen." He pulled a huge handkerchief from his pocket and blew his nose. "And my little Merry. So wise, so loving. I'll miss her so."

Clancy sniffled a time or two himself, taking in his last sight of Jack, of the boy he remembered, of the man he'd become. "We did our job well, Cluny. That's all we could hope to do."

"Where do you suppose we'll go now? I always thought we might get to Heaven, but who can be sure?"

Clancy looked at the two young people lying in the bed. Jack was already asleep, poor injured boy, and Merry was fighting to keep her eyes open as she snuggled close beside him. "I don't know, Cluny. Maybe we just find some sort of peace. That could be boring, don't you think?"

Just as Clancy had said the words, there was a slight sound behind them, and both ghosts turned around, to see that the wall had opened up, to let in a view of the night sky.

"Clancy?"

Clancy took Cluny's hand, feeling a need to walk toward that night, that darkness that slowly faded as, in the distance, objects began to take shape.

"Do you see it, Cluny?" he asked, excitement growing inside him. "A stage. A glorious stage. And an audience—do you see them? They're all sitting there, waiting. And . . . and that's our wagon. Look at it, Cluny—all shiny and new, better than new. *Cluny and Clancy, Traveling Shakespearean Players*. Ah, isn't it grand!"

Cluny felt himself floating, Clancy gliding along with him. They were outside Coltrane House now, floating higher, ever higher. "I see it, old friend. I see our wagon—and Portia! Lord bless us, Clancy—it's Portia!"

"We're going home, Cluny," Clancy said quietly. He

turned his head, looked down at Coltrane House, took one long, last look at the two sleeping figures who had traveled their own long journeys, only to come home to each other at last. "We're all home now."

More
Kasey Michaels!

Please turn this page
for a
bonus excerpt
from

Someone to Love

coming in
April 2001
from Warner Books.

The two nattily dressed gentlemen entered Hyde Park through Park Lane, curly-brimmed beavers jauntily tipped on their heads, canes lazily swinging at their sides, their air of sophisticated boredom half-feigned, half—all too real.

One dark and handsome. One fair and more than handsome; almost pretty. Both of them titled, both of them wealthy, popular, self-assured.

Blessedly unattached.

They stopped, posed, sniffed the air like any buck hoping to pick up a scent. Exchanged meaningful glances. Touched assessing fingers to their cravats, shot their cuffs. Proceeded on their way with consciously relaxed saunters, and yet with alert, watchful eyes.

Part predator. Part prey.

Hyde Park had once been a hunting ground, full of deer and boar and wild bulls. Over the centuries, many duels were fought beneath the trees as the morning mist gave way to a watery sun. There had once been fortifications there, military camps dotting the thick grass.

Footpads had once owned the Park, until Charles II enclosed the entire area with high walls and William III had the happy idea of lining the *route du roi* with over three hundred lanterns hanging in the trees.

Now the Park presented a place of peace, of exquisite landscaping, of bridle paths, carriageways, and quiet walks, the air perfumed with the scent of thousands of flowers. The sun-kissed waters of the large, ornamental lake named Serpentine had been the creation of Queen Caroline, who had ordered the damming of the Westbourne so that she and her family could relax aboard either of the two yachts that had once bobbed on its surface.

Yes, Hyde Park was a lovely, tranquil place.

But, as the two men well knew, it remained very much as it had begun . . . a hunting ground.

"Oh, do cast your gaze over there, Kipp," the dark-haired gentleman prodded, nodding to their left. "Not that I need direct you, for I'm convinced we can both sniff out the desperation from here."

Kipp Rutland did as his friend bade him, lazily cocking his head in time to see a rented hack all but running away with its driver, the always hapless and definitely pocket-pinched Sir Alvin Clarke. The man dressed as best he could, which meant that his collar and cuffs were probably on their second turning in order to disguise their fraying edges. Obviously a cow-handed driver, he hung on to the reins for dear life as he tried, quite unsuccessfully, to capture the attention of a young debutante and her protective mama.

"You know, Kipp, young Clarke has as much chance of winning a first at Newmarket with that nag as he does of snagging Miss Oliver in his threadbare matrimonial net," Brady James, Earl of Singleton declared, not without some small trace of pity. "Thank the good Lord I've sworn off marriage, or else that could be me making a cake of myself." He shuddered, elegantly.

"If your comment is meant as some sly, back-handed sympathy directed toward me, Brady," Kipp, who was also the Viscount Willoughby, said as they continued along the pathway, "I will accept it gladly, and with both hands. Now, do you see any prospects for your dear friend?"

Brady's grin was wicked. "Me? You expect *me* to pick your bride?"

Kipp tipped his hat as an open carriage chock-full of giggling ladies drove past. "Why not, Brady? I've always admired your taste. Except for that satin waistcoat you had stuck to yourself the other night. I really believe you should have rethought that choice before appearing in public."

"Silk, not satin, and my valet is over the moon with his new gift. Teach me to listen to my tailor's suggestions when I'm half in my cups. But shall we return to your suggestion that I am to select the future Viscountess Willoughby? Just long enough for me to decline the honor, you understand."

Kipp smiled. "And you call yourself my friend? I'm hurt, Brady, cut to the quick. Oh, very well, if you'd rather not. Will you at least bless me with your opinion as we peruse the available ladies?"

"And how shall I peruse the ladies, I ask you? Invite them, oh, so politely, to please throw back their heads and open their mouths, so's that I might inspect their teeth? No, I think not. Besides, I want you to tell me again why you believe it so necessary to bracket yourself this Season."

Kipp's smile faded. He'd already given his friend Brady some silly reason for wishing to marry, something about tiring of bedding women, then having to get up, get dressed, and toddle off home again.

But at least part of the truth was that Kipp had promised his mother, on her deathbed, that he would marry before he turned thirty, and secure the title before he reached the ripe old age of thirty-five.

He'd turned thirty some six months past, and his promise to his mother had been haunting him ever since. He didn't personally care if the Rutland name died out, if the Willoughby title went to some deliriously grateful distant cousin in Surrey. After all, he wouldn't be there to watch, now would he?

No. He'd be sitting on a cloud, beside his mother, abjectly begging her forgiveness as she delicately wept into her wings.

So he would marry to keep his promise to his

dead mother. That truly was one reason behind his just-begun foray into the marriage mart.

But it wasn't the only reason, probably not the main reason.

"I told you, Brady, I need an heir," Kipp said now, watching as three more open carriages passed by, each with its gaggle of debutantes trying to do their best to appear haughty, and only succeeding in looking as desperate as Sir Alvin had. "I happened to get a peek at my Surrey cousin," he continued, fibbing easily, "and I must tell you, my friend, I shudder to think of that bovine man sitting in my chair, slopping up my wine. Or feeding it to his hogs as a special treat, which seems more likely."

"All right, lie to me," the earl said affably. "I can accept that. But are you sure you wish to enter into matrimony with anyone I would choose? Because there's this little red-haired dancer in Covent Garden—"

"Upstanding, Brad," Kipp said, laughing. "My wife must be upstanding. Not perpetually horizontal. Horizontal I can and do find on my own, thank you."

"Upstanding. Upright. Passably pretty? I should think you'd want at least passably pretty. And not too deep in the pocket, or too full of her family's consequence, Kipp, or else she'll have a will of her own, and God knows you don't want that in a wife. An orphan. Yes, an upstanding, well-bred, passably pretty orphan. With good teeth, for the sake of the children, you understand. Nothing worse than a peer with teeth like a donkey."

Kipp smiled his appreciation. "Ah, Brady, I knew I could count on you. Now, shall we begin?"

To read more, look for *Someone to Love*
by Kasey Michaels.

Don't Miss These Unforgettable Romances from Kasey Michaels

Indiscreet
   (0-446-60-582-4, $6.50 USA) ($8.50 Can.)

Escapade
   (0-446-60-683-9, $6.50 USA) ($8.50 Can.)

Come Near Me
   (0-446-60-583-2, $6.50 USA) ($8.99 Can.)

1122a

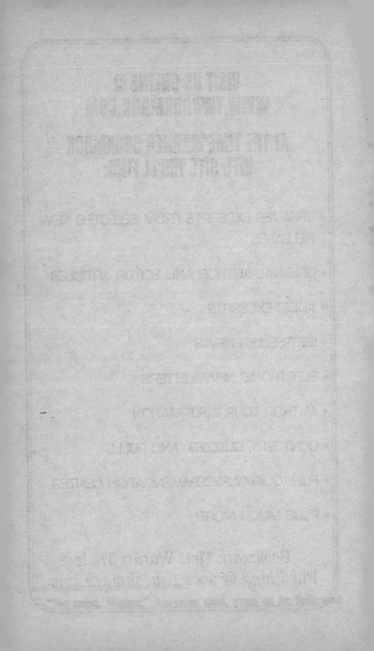